The Pursuit of Quality

Beaumont Publishing House

*"We are what we repeatedly do.
Excellence, then is not an act,
but a habit."*

– **Aristotle**

The Pursuit of Quality

How Organisations in the United Kingdom Are Attaining Excellence Through Quality Certification & Total Quality Management Systems

BRETT WHITFORD
&
REBECCA BIRD

BEAUMONT PUBLISHING HOUSE

THE PURSUIT
OF
QUALITY

First Published in 1996
by
Beaumont Publishing House (UK) Ltd.
C/O- Prentice Hall Europe
Campus 400, Maylands Avenue
Hemel Hempstead, Hertfordshire HP2 7EZ
Tel: 01442 881900
Fax: 01442 257115

ISBN 0 13 264621 8.

The Pursuit of Quality

Library of Congress Cataloguing-in-Publication Data
available from the publisher.

British Library Cataloguing in Publication Data

A catalogue record for this book is available from
the British Library.

The Pursuit of Quality

ISBN 0 13 264621 8.

1 2 3 4 5 00 99 98 97 96

Typeset in Adobe Garamond by Beaumont Publishing House
Cover Design by Chameleon Designs
Film Preparation by Goodfellow & Egan, Cambridge
Printed and bound in Great Britain by The British Printing Company Ltd

THIS BOOK WAS PROUDLY PRODUCED IN GREAT BRITAIN

For those who choose to
take the never ending
Quality Journey,
and for everyone
who believed in this book.
Thank you for your trust and support.

Foreword

Sir Denys Henderson
President of the British Quality Foundation
Chairman of The Rank Organisation

CONTINUOUS improvement in the competitive position of UK industry is an absolutely critical national survival issue. If, in the eyes of the world, we are seen to be slipping behind we will all of us feel the inevitable consequences of a weak currency and the adverse interest rate movements on our businesses, our employees and our livelihoods. And while there is a common concern about pressing social issues such as unemployment and the state of our health services, whether we like it or not none of the things we want as a society is possible unless we are competitive as a nation.

Without doubt, Great Britain has improved its competitive position in recent years and the UK should be well placed to win a larger share of world business. The best of British is the best in the world and UK based companies such as Rank Xerox and ICL have dominated the European Quality Award since its inception in 1992. Many of our small and medium sized companies do a splendid job, too.

As the companies featured in this book have shown there is a strong commitment to excellence being displayed in a variety of UK industries. I am proud to read that the UK companies featured, many of whom are members of the British Quality Foundation, have benefited greatly from their use of the Business Excellence Model. But even the best can always do better and the goal posts of competition are moving constantly.

There is no room for complacency. Sadly, there is too much evidence to suggest that behind the brilliance of our world class performers is a comet's tail of under-performing companies too many of which are not as good as they think they are. While 70 per cent of UK companies think they perform at world class levels, only 2.3 per cent actually do so, according to an IBM/London Business School study.

Although businesses are generally much more aware of customer needs than they were, complacency about competitors is a dangerous ailment, and I would include ignoring the competition from Europe in this category. Too many medium sized businesses see the factory down the road, not Europe, as their main competitor. Although we have been EU members for many years, the UK perhaps looks more to the US than other countries as a source of ideas and markets. The reason is partly one of historical or political ties, partly language and partly because the dollar has been more important for sterling than most European currencies.

However, I believe that the UK's biggest companies – those figuring in the FT SE 100 index – generally are well aware of international competition. They know that to succeed in Europe they must exceed the best efforts of leading European competitors. Nowadays our labour costs are low and productivity is up. Sustained quality improvement is the last part of the equation. I hope this book drives home the Quality message and encourages other organizations to embrace the Business Excellence Model.

It was the establishment of the UK Award that led to the formation of the British Quality Foundation. I was asked by Peter Lilley, then Secretary of State for Trade and Industry, to lead a team to create the framework for a UK equivalent of the European Quality Award and the USA's Malcolm Baldrige National Quality Award. At that time there was nobody to 'own' the award, so the British Quality Foundation was created to provide membership services and training, and also to run the award. I became its first president and chairman.

The Award is now entering its third year. The success of inaugural winners, TNT and Rover, in promoting Quality and excellence is being emulated by the 1995 UK Quality Award winner – High Performance Technology (a discrete business unit of ICL). This success has confirmed the Award's emergence as the premier UK business prize. The number of entrants has been encouraging and we were delighted with the response when we opened up the award to the public sector in 1995; which provided two of the four short-listed organizations.

People are always curious about how many companies enter the award, but that is to miss the point. Nor is it really about winning, although that is the final icing on the cake for the successful companies and the winners are vigorously promoted as role models during their 'reign'. The real benefit comes from completing the entry process – from making a systematic assessment of the business for the submission document through to the assessor reports which all entrants receive.

More importantly for the competitiveness of the nation, the Award encourages and endorses the use being made of the Business Excellence Model by thousands of companies to help them identify major areas for improvement in their performance. The business excellence model is what it was designed to be – an ideal umbrella under which all improvement efforts fit so well, and a universal benchmark against which companies can measure not only their current performance but also their rate of improvement.

Of course, not everyone is ready to enter for the Award. We encourage all organisations to use self assessment against the Business Excellence Model and to assist this process the Foundation has introduced two software based self assessment tools. ASSESS RapidScore is a quick and easy process based on a questionnaire. ASSESS ValidScore is a more rigorous process involving external validation by the Foundation which also carries recognition for achievement of various levels of score.

Like continuous improvement, the pursuit of an ever improving performance is something that needs to be worked on at all times. If this country is to afford better standards of living and look to real lasting prosperity, we need to aspire to be 'winners' and acknowledge with pride outstanding results.

Acknowledgements

The Pursuit Of Quality has been an exciting and extremely satisfying project. The book has been a mammoth task which has taken over twelve months from conception to final production and has required the assistance of many highly skilled professionals.

I would like to thank Marnie for her support and encouragement. Rebecca Bird – Thank you for all your dedication and involvement from the conception of this project throughout the execution. Your excellent efforts researching, writing and helping to manage various parts of the operation have ensured its success.

Special thanks to Pat Evans, President of Prentice Hall Australia, who I greatly admire and respect. At Prentice Hall in the UK, thanks to John Yates, who is not only a brilliant editor but has become a great friend. Thanks also to Stuart Macfarlane – Production Director, Laura Miller, John Atkinson – proof reader and everyone at Prentice Hall.

Special thanks to Alan Jones, managing director of TNT Express whose enthusiastic support encouraged others to work with us. The book would not have been possible with out the support of all the companies and Alan's help was vital. Thanks also to his P.A. – Diane Grogan.

From The British Quality Foundation, I would like express my gratitude to Sir Denys Henderson for his foreword and Chris Carrington who kindly advised me when I first arrived in the UK from Australia.

I wish to express my appreciation to Barry Holland from SGS Yarsley who has been vital to the project in many ways. I also thank Lloyd's Register Quality Assurance.

Thank you to Peter Humphries and Michelle Clark from Securicor who invited me to the 1995 UK Quality Award Dinner. Michelle Clark has been a constant source of inspiration and someone I could always discuss the latest issues in Quality with. John Welch and Barry Gardener have also been able to enlighten me when I have needed "local knowledge."

I was very impressed with the Rover 600's (pictured) which Rover kindly supplied for our use during this lengthy project. Thank you Des Haydon and Glen Fairchild for making my work so much easier. I travelled all over the UK meeting with companies for the book and the comfort of the car meant I always arrived relaxed.

I would like to thank a number of personal associates whose advice and guidance is always available to my organisation. These include Brett Davies our corporate Lawyer at Brett Davies Lawyers, Bill Crerie, Dr Doron Samuell, James MacAuley Jason Drage, Alistair Tomlinson, David Parker, Morris Levitzke, Peter Johnson, David Franklin and Luke Drakeford. And my new friends and advisors in the UK: Rory Driscoll, Brian Woodham, Paul Chesworth from British Aerospace, Chris Worsick from Rockwells, Donnelle Maxwell, Victoria Davidson, Caroline Robertson (our lawyer), Jo Fell, Geoff O'Connell from the Adam Smith Institute, Stephen Hartley, CEO of Moss Brothers, and Kate Calvert –all of whose friendship and business advice I value highly. I would also like to thank the Western Australian Agent-General in London, Bill Hassell. His work in Europe has been very valuable to our state and he and his family welcomed me to London with considerable hospitality and good advice.

Thank you to Andy, Pat, Sue, and everyone at Chameleon Design who worked hard on the cover and showed the exceptional flair that they are renowned for.

To David Steer and the expert team from BPC Consumer Books – thank you for the tremendous effort and extremely high Quality printing.

The film preparation was done at Goodfellow & Egan of Cambridge by Gordan Theobald, thank you.

Thanks also to the people at Clocktower computers who were very helpful when my Mac crashed.

Various contributors have added their expertise to ***The Pursuit Of Quality***. These distinguished contributors include Barry A. Holland, Ross Dunn, Bryan Geraghty, Terry Twine, Graham Salisbury, Hayden Magill, Anwar Osman, The British Quality Foundation and Investors In People. Many thanks for your high quality contributions.

John and Matthew Kelly from European Quality have been tremendous. They manage a very impressive publishing operation and contributed three stories, as well as considerable advice and good wishes. I look forward to working with them on future projects. Julian, one of their journalists, was also very helpful.

A special section has been devoted to the recognition of the various research journalists who contributed to the books success. Thank you, Mark, James, Marjorie and paticularly Samantha Bush for her assistance and interest in all aspects of the book's production. Phillipa Webb also contributed to a story. Thanks also to the many photographers who aworked on the book including Geoff Fisher, Mary-Jane and Ken Bray.

Rebecca would also like to give special thanks to: Camilla Chomley, Anthony Price, Mat and Marie Hagen, and Alison Carthew for all their encouragement; Melanie Avery who was always there; Simone Wheeler for her technical advice; Stephanie Hately for her creative contribution; and Wellington, Tish and Robbie for supporting this venture from afar. But above all to three people whose unquestioning faith in me I can never repay, Helen, Richard and Sarah Bird, my thanks. Of course, to Brett, the person who made it all possible, love your work!

The book would not have been possible without the consent and support of the various companies who are featured within ***The Pursuit Of Quality***. I am very grateful to the people who liaised with our team thank you for your patience and commitment to helping us produce high quality and accurate chapters on your respective companies.

Thank you to everyone who became involved with The Pursuit of Quality whether in a large or small capacity - your contribution is greatly appreciated.

Brett Whitford and Rebecca Bird

CONTENTS

Re-inventing Quality

Brett Whitford

"'WE did TQM last year; it went well and everyone seemed to enjoy it.' The satisfied speaker was CEO of a large multinational. But when asked about the continuation of the process he looked puzzled. 'Do you have any rework in the organisation? Does your finance department send out credit notes? Do you have excess inventory? Are you making warranty payments? Do you have delays in delivery? Do you have inventory shortages?' The answer to all these questions was 'yes.' A little later, and more thoughtfully, he said: 'We haven't done TQM, have we?'"

Michael Hutton from Phillip Crosby Associates related this story in the excellent *European Quality* magazine. Sadly the 'speaker' could have been any number of managers who like to think they have 'been there – done that' with 'Quality'.

During my research for this book I have spoken with hundreds of managers and Quality consultants and regrettably, I have to echo the sentiments of Sir Denys in the foreword to this book when he cites the IBM/London Business School study which finds 70 per cent of UK companies thinking they perform at world class levels when in reality only 2.3 per cent of them are actually doing so.

My best illustration of a lack of understanding of Quality came from the managing director of a large UK business who queried my title: *The Pursuit of Quality* – "Why write a book on Quality? You need to call it something else; Quality was two years ago, we've done that – customer service and re-engineering as well. You have to come up with a new buzz word or nobody will be interested!" I smiled, thinking perhaps this was an example of the famous British irony that I'd heard so much about, then it became clear the guy was serious. Was he advocating management by trendy slogan? This is Great Britain not the USA. Perhaps he had attended one management seminar too many whilst seeking 'the quick fix'. Consequently, we were unable to find room for his story in the book!

I have set out to re-invent people's perception of Quality using the example set by of some of the best large, medium and small companies in the United Kingdom.

To those who understand the holistic nature of Quality as a concept, it requires no re-invention but for those who are jaded and confused by a word which has been casually over used by countless marketing departments for decades, some explanation is required.

First of all, I have a few personal ideas on what Quality is not:

Quality isn't the corporate piracy so popular in the 1980s. Everyone is tired of hearing how millions have been made and lost by shuffling paper and acquiring companies with assets ripe to be stripped. Who is at fault? In a perfect world, it is only companies which don't have Quality operations and are not achieving results that become fodder for corporate raiders. Do we blame the paper entrepreneurs, the stock brokers – the opportunists; or do we blame the mediocre managers who allow their companies to be recognised as under performing and in need of a shake up?

Quality isn't the work of lazy managers with their overzealous accountants who are able to temporarily improve the bottom line results of their companies through wholesale sackings, the removal of benefits, slashing wages and research budgets, and squeezing the last penny of profit from their suppliers. Sure you will always find firms in dire need of this type of medicine and during the world-wide recession almost every company in the UK regardless of size had to impose a cost cutting regime of some description. The question is how did these firms get so unfit and flabby that 'gutting' them was the only solution?

There are also the unsatisfactory management types who allow their companies to fall in to disrepair through neglect. They are what I call the 'bureaucrats' (with no offence to hard-working public servants). These less than enterprising 'Sir Humphrey Appleby's' have mastered the art of comfortable inaction. This sometimes takes years of breeding but eventually they see themselves as stewards who want to preserve the status quo at all costs. Invariably the outside world changes and they are destroyed often along with the businesses under their control.

Fortunately, there is another type of manager, the 'Quality' manager. I don't simply mean the conscientious folk who monitor a company's ISO 9000 certification (though this function is important) but all 'Re-Inventing Quality Managers' from the managing director committed to building an excellent company to the enlightened supervisors who see themselves as team leaders and coaches to their sections. Basically all people who seek innovative new approaches to old problems and are constantly asking 'can we do this better?'

For the final word on 'What Quality isn't', it is important to understand that with unlimited time and resources it is possible to make an excellent product. How often have we heard about the 'heroic efforts' some companies make to keep their customers satisfied? Whilst applauding these efforts towards customer service, the sad fact is that heroic efforts and over engineered products are not Quality. Quality is streamlined, simplified, cost effective processes that don't allow non-conformance. Quality starts in the design of products and services and the way they are built or delivered.

Quality is simply defined by 1994 UK Quality Award winner TNT Express as 'Right First Time – Every Time' and Rolls-Royce with 'Strive for Perfection'. Both companies believe the way to achieve their goals is through continuous improvement. Quality is seen as a broad umbrella for all improvement initiatives – among them empowerment, teambuilding and process re-engineering.

I feel the UK/European Quality Award model for business excellence has been a vital component of the Re-Inventing Quality revolution. As has the overdue realisation that the ISO 9000 standard has to be married to the concepts of Total Quality Management and be installed in a way designed to facilitate rather than discourage continuous improvement.

As this book clearly proves, many of the management techniques developed and pioneered in the United States and Japan can work in the UK and Europe but these methods and ideas have to be modified to suit local cultures.

I am often asked what I have found makes organisations successful. In many ways, the answers I have to give seem (even to me) like motherhood statements, (set targets, form cross-functional work teams, train, trust, empower, celebrate success etc.) which allow the listener to respond: "What's so special about that?" or "We're already doing those things?" It isn't the answer which is wrong but the question! You shouldn't ask "what?" but "How?". Example: "How do you set targets?; How do you form teams?; How do you recognise success in your organisation?".

Despite the above disclaimer, I do have a few 'What to do's which I believe stand out as vital for Re-Inventing Quality in your organisation, but I will add again, all that counts is how you implement these tools and your long term commitment to change and improvement.

I make no apologies for including many well known ideas, which, despite their popularity still aren't being implemented with enough thought. I have not included some of the all too obvious suggestions such as 'listen to your customers' and 'invest in the latest plant and equipment'. The following suggestions are in no particular order but in many cases rely on each other for success:

- Don't let inertia take control of your agenda – conditions will never be perfect to Re-Invent Quality in your organisation – start now!
- Be prepared to adapt new ideas, don't dismiss them – there is no value in slavishly copying others or trying to impose systems you feel are fundamentally wrong for your business but don't discount the possibility of modifying them, even if they come from other industries or management functions.
- Don't expect too much too soon – but look for and celebrate early successes – don't be shy when recognising excellence.
- Keep your goals positive – focus on improving service and revenues **as well** as cutting costs.
- Pro-actively use the UK/European Quality Award model for Organisational Excellence and self-assessment.
- Set accountable targets for improvement but make those targets match your strategic goals – an emphasis on quarterly profits and shipments may stifle stated aims for long term improvement.
- Measure and be attentive – simply paying attention to what people are doing motivates them – what gets measured gets done.
- Make ISO 9000 certification a relevant tool not just a rubber stamp to pacify customer demands.
- Train people in a practical manner emphasising how Quality tools can actually be applied to their day-to-day role in your organisation.
- Trust your people – anticipate responsible behaviour.
- Realise that your workforce lead complex lives – they raise families, drive cars, manage their households and relationships. In essence they are multi-skilled and competent. They can probably contribute more than you are currently asking of them.
- Create an environment where your people aren't afraid to try

something new – and fail – make it easier to ask for forgiveness than permission.

- Teams DO work.
- Include industrial relations, remuneration, performance and Health & Safety issues in your Re-Invention of Quality.
- Understand and map your processes carefully – realise that small, incremental process improvements often need to be bolsted by radical breakthrough change.
- Don't be scared to invest in Quality – savings due to improvements almost always far outweigh the costs of getting started.
- Continually seek fresh ways to maintain momentum and enthusiasm for change and improvement.
- Think of the whole world as your competition not just 'the factory down the road'.
- Remember personalities count – obviously commitment must be seen to come from the top but you cannot allow the message to be filtered – middle managers and supervisors need to be just as enthusiastic.
- Practice what you preach – if you are selling economies and downsizing don't dine off fine china in the boardroom as half the workforce is 'made redundant'.
- Benchmark – learn from successful organisations. Ask yourself, 'am I as informed of the latest best practices as I should be?'

As for the "How", you will find in the 'case-study' chapters ample real-life, practical and achievable examples that have worked and are still working in the UK.

The leaders in this book are unrecognised heroes, not the sport champions, actors and rock stars the media usually promote as role models. They have built their companies and public sector organisations into Quality operations. These hard working people are devoted to the steady pursuit of excellence, and have maintained momentum and enthusiasm for change and improvement in even the most difficult circumstances.

They are customer service champions who believe that Quality is an ongoing challenge with constantly shifting goal posts and raising expectations.

Business people everywhere need to listen to them, especially those in the United Kingdom, as the achievements outlined in this book **have** happened in **your** environment.

If you are a manager reading this book or even a student – the people featured in this book are your new mentors, you should study them, understand and follow their example.

PART ONE

Contemporary Quality Management Issues

I

The British Quality Foundation UK Quality Award

The British Quality Foundation

"EVERY British company must measure up to the best, if we are to succeed against hungry competitors in increasingly open world markets. The British Quality Foundation has raised the flag of excellence with the UK Quality Award. Rover and TNT Express have met the tests of profitability, performance, quality and value for money. Tonight's award gives other companies – not least small but growing businesses – clear examples to emulate.

"We now have the fastest growth of all major economies in Europe. There are huge opportunities for British business – provided we stay competitive.

"The UK Quality Award has put the spotlight this year on two outstanding companies. I am delighted that next year public sector bodies will be able to compete as well. Britain's success depends on excellence in the public and private sectors alike. I look forward to seeing many more winners of the UK Quality Award in future years." – **The Prime Minister, The RT. Hon. John Major MP**, speaking at the first UK Quality Award presentation on 30 November 1994.

The mission of the British Quality Foundation is 'To enhance the performance and effectiveness of all types of organisation within the United Kingdom through the promotion of Total Quality Management.'

The objectives of the British Quality Foundation are to:

- Identify and publicise outstanding role model organisations practising Total Quality Management through the operation of the prestigious UK Quality Award.
- Act as the UK's authoritative voice on issues of quality, both domestically and internationally.

- Play a pivotal role in the future development of quality management in the UK by giving coherence to and creating consensus among those groups interested in quality.

The Foundation is a company limited by guarantee, incorporated in November 1992. Membership activities of the Foundation are funded by some 1,200 member organisations. These range from the large multinationals to sole traders. Members also come from the public and voluntary sectors.

Total Quality Management practices are promoted by the Foundation through the use of Self Assessment against the model used for the UK and European Quality Awards. This model and the use of Self Assessment are explained later in this chapter. Members of the Foundation are able to participate in Special Interest Groups to learn from each other, to form networks and to exchange ideas on best practice. They also benefit from the bi-monthly magazine, *UK Quality*, discounts on courses, conferences, seminars, publications and other activities of the Foundation. By these means the Foundation aims to assist organisations wanting to improve the performance of their operation and thereby to raise competitiveness within the UK.

In addition the Foundation manages The UK Quality Award. This award aims to identify examples of organisational excellence to be role models to improve the quality and performance of UK organisations. The first Award was presented by the Prime Minister to Rover Group and TNT Express on 30th November 1994.

The UK Quality Award is sponsored by private, public and voluntary sector organisations becoming Founder and Key Members of the Foundation, together with some initial pump priming money from the Department of Trade and Industry.

The importance which leading UK organisations and the government attach to quality and the work of the Foundation is best reflected by the active involvement of the Board, The Executive Committee, government and most importantly our membership.

Membership

Membership of the British Quality Foundation is not only a statement of commitment to quality as a management philosophy but it is also, in a very real sense, a declaration of intent that your organisation has ambitions of excellence. It means more than just paying lip service. It means participation in quality. Indeed it is tantamount to issuing a quality policy to your employees, and offering them an opportunity to excel through learning.

The sharing of experience amongst members and the identification of examples of 'best practice' through the UK Quality Award are the tip the iceberg. There is no comparable organisation in the UK which can offer members these tried and tested paths to excellence. Already, over 1,200 organisations actively participate in the Foundation and stand ready to share their experiences with others on the journey of improvement.

There are three types of membership: Founder, Key, and regular. The membership include many examples of organisations which are pioneering business excellence and actively seeking to continuously improve.

Self Assessment

Self Assessment is an internal comprehensive, systematic and regular review of an organisation's activities and results against the UK/European Model for Total Quality Management (organisational excellence). It can be used by all types and sizes of organisations to assess current performance and identify opportunities for improvement. The process allows the organisation to discern clearly its strengths, areas in which improvements can be made and culminates in planned improvement actions which are then monitored for progress. It also gives a basis for comparison, both internally and externally, and shows the progress which has been made.

The approach provides a basis for continuous improvement which will lead ultimately to competitive advantage and organisational excellence.

To apply for the Award you will have undertaken at least one Self Assessment of your business activities. This is likely to be of significant value in its own right and an excellent opportunity to collect useful data and enthuse staff.

The benefits of Self Assessment

"I am so convinced by the approach that I required every ICL organisation to use the Self Assessment methodology to drive continuous improvement" Peter Bonfield, former CEO of ICL.

The primary benefits offered by the Self Assessment process are:

- A rigorous and structured approach to business improvement.
- An assessment based on facts and not individual perception.
- A means to achieve consistency of direction and consensus on what needs to be done.

Additional benefits of Self Assessment are:

- A way to educate people in the organisation on how to apply meaningfully the principles of Total Quality Management.
- A means to create enthusiasm amongst the people within the organisation and give fresh impetus to their pursuit of business excellence.
- A means of measuring progress over time.
- A means to benchmark both internally and against other organisations across the UK and the rest of Europe, including Quality Award winners.

To summarise, the Self Assessment process offers your organisation an opportunity to learn. To learn about your organisation's strengths and areas for improvement. To learn about what Total Quality means when applied to your organisation. To learn about how far down the Quality road your organisation has travelled, how much further your organisation has to travel and how it compares with others.

The exercise will undoubtedly highlight those areas on which to focus to improve your business results.

The UK/EUROPEAN Model For Total Quality Management

This is the model against which organisations apply Self Assessment. The advantage is its completeness as a means for organising a Self Assessment. Since others are using the same model you can learn from their experiences and you will be able to benchmark your organisation against theirs. This means you will be able to compare your organisation, or a part of your organisation, against others. The aim being to learn from best practice and thereby improve the organisational excellence and performance of your own organisation.

Total Quality encompasses all the ways in which an organisation

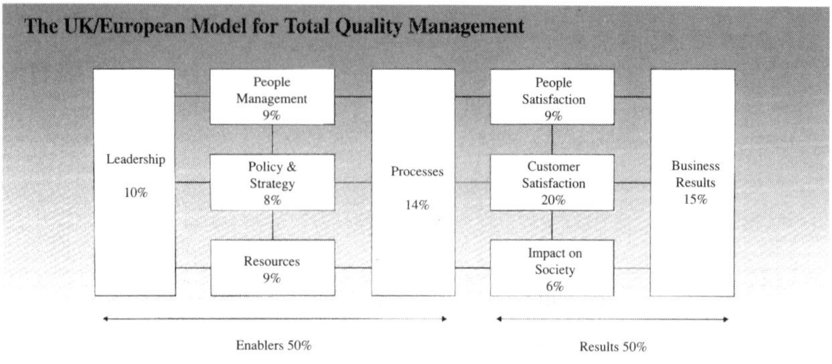

meets the needs and expectations of its customers, its people, its stakeholders and the community in which it operates, enabling a drive towards excellence and competitive advantage.

The nine elements have been identified as the key components of organisational excellence. These have been verified by extensive research across Europe. It is interesting to note that when organisations are asked to describe an example of excellence, even on the most superficial level, they normally identify aspects of the nine criteria used in the model.

These nine criteria are used to assess an organisation's progress towards excellence. We use **Enablers** and **Results** to group the criteria.

The **Enablers** criteria are concerned with ***how*** results are being achieved. The **Results** criteria are concerned with ***what*** the organisation has achieved and is achieving.

Any organisation can benefit from using the model for Self Assessment. The approach will VARY with the time and resources made available and with different degrees of sophistication.

Those entering the Award will be using the model to score their performance. Details on ways to apply the model are given in *The Guide To Self Assessment* which also goes into more detail on the systems used for scoring. For this introduction it suffices to say that ENABLERS and RESULTS are equally valued at 50% of the total score. Applicant organisations will be at the stage of wanting to benchmark themselves against others.

Others may want to take a quick look at their business or service today. Some may want to plan for future expansion using the model as a basis for a business or service plan that goes beyond putting some numbers down to actively considering the processes to ensure success. If this is your first introduction to the model why not try discussing these nine elements in selected areas of your organisation and consider the feedback.

Enablers

Leadership explores the activities and the behaviour of all managers in driving the organisation towards Total Quality and their effort in striving for continuous improvement.

Policy and Strategy examines how the organisation's planning activities, its aims and objectives reflect the drive for continuous improvement.

People Management examines how the organisation releases the full potential of its people, for example employees, to improve its business or service continuously.

Resources examines how the organisation's finance, information, materials, suppliers and other resources are effectively managed.

Processes examines how all the value-adding activities within the organisation are managed and monitored to ensure the continuous improvement of the business results.

Results

Organisations use a number of key parameters to measure performance. For each of these, excellence is assessed relative to the organisation's business/service environment and circumstances. This is based on information which sets out your organisation's actual performance against its own targets and, wherever possible, this is set against the performance of competitors or the performance of the best organisations relevant to your business.

Evidence is required of the extent to which these cover the range of your organisation's activities and of the relative importance of the parameters presented.

Customer Satisfaction evaluates what the organisation is achieving in relation to the satisfaction of its customers with respect to products, services and customer relationships.

People Satisfaction evaluates what the employees feel about the organisation.

Impact on Society evaluates the perception of the organisation amongst the community at large.

Business Results assess what the organisation is achieving in relation to its planned performance.

The UK Quality Award

The 1994 UK Quality Awards were won by TNT Express and Rover Group. These two companies would be the first to declare that they have further to go on the journey towards business excellence but they have demonstrated outstanding performance in all aspects of their operations. They have achieved a high level of attainment in satisfying the 'expectations of their shareholders, customers, employees and other stakeholders. This performance has been achieved as a result of their commitment to Total Quality Management and the application of their Quality improvement programmes through Self Assessment.

All Award applicants are required to submit a detailed assessment against the criteria shown in the UK/European Model for Total Quality Management. The submission is then evaluated according to the weightings of each of the nine elements.

Each application is considered in detail by a team of trained assessors and all entrants receive a detailed report on their submissions. Short-listed organisations are site-visited by the assessors in order to verify the evidence presented in their original submission and clarify any other issues identified by the assessors. Decisions on Award winners are made by a distinguished panel of independent jurors.

All entrants benefit – not just the winners. Everyone receives a comprehensive feedback report based on expert evaluation, identifying strengths and areas for improvement. Moreover, many organisations find that the biggest benefit of all is that the process of preparing an entry in itself causes improvement. Award winners do, of course, receive considerable publicity and much prestige.

Who is Eligible

The UK Quality Award is open to both the private, public and voluntary sectors, provided the organisation can meet all the application requirements and has a substantial business or service presence in the UK. There are four categories:

- Businesses, including subsidiaries, with 251 or more employees
- Businesses with 250 or fewer employees
- Organisations within the public and voluntary sector with 251 or more employees
- Organisations within the public and voluntary sector with 250 or less employees

There will be no distinction in the status of Award winners between the categories, and no overall annual winner. Entrants in each category will be judged in exactly the same way against the assessment model which will form the basis for the Award. It is unlikely that the total number of Awards will be high as the objective is to recognise exceptional and outstanding levels of achievement.

Following the successful work undertaken in the private sector in 1994 a special effort was made in 1995 to drive the use of the model into the public sector. This activity is seen as a leading initiative in the Public and Voluntary sectors within Europe.

Small organisations will receive increasing attention. Considerable work is under way to identify their specific needs and to assess how the Self Assessment process can be made easier and less demanding on resources.

There is considerable status attached to winning the UK Quality Award, independently administered by the British Quality Foundation and supported by the Department of Trade and Industry. The high profile promotion of Award winners will clearly establish them as being among the most successful organisations in the United Kingdom and recognition of the winners' achievements enables them to promote themselves as organisations of established Excellence.

In the year following presentation of the Award(s), winners are able to share their experiences at conferences and seminars organised by the Foundation, which offers a platform for the promotion of their status as leaders in their particular fields.

In addition to enjoying the intrinsic benefits gained through a Quality Management programme, winners of the UK Quality Award can also expect to benefit from the emergence of new customers, new business opportunities and improved customer perceptions of goods and services delivered.

British Quality Foundation

PROMOTING TOTAL QUALITY IN THE UK

II

ISO 9000 and the Small Business

Barry A. Holland
Registered Lead Assessor and Marketing Manager
SGS Yarsley International Certification Services Limited

MUCH has been written and said about BS 5750, or ISO 9000 as it is now called following rationalisation of the terminology. Some of the comment has been complimentary, some not. It has been hailed by 'big business' as a useful tool, which in practice has often had a profound and beneficial effect on the business elements it embraces.

On the other hand it has been slated by many small businesses, being described as a waste of time, effort, money and resources. Criticism has abounded and a multiplicity of viewpoints and opinions have been well aired.

In spite of the apparent deep seated aversion by small firms to the standard, this chapter in *The Pursuit of Quality* examines the criticisms levelled at ISO 9000 and makes constructive suggestions as to how it can be turned to the advantage of small businesses and why it should not be dismissed out of hand.

Whether we like it or not, the practice of Quality Assurance is here to stay and because the measure of a company's commitment to QA is demonstrated by certification to an ISO 9000 series standard, that too is here to stay.

At this point it is appropriate to define the term 'small business'.

The Department of Enterprise (Dti) Definition

The Dti uses the term 'small firm' in its report entitled Small Firms in Britain 1994. The report says there is no 'official' definition of what constitutes a small firm. However, it goes on to quote from the Bolton Report of 1971 which states: a small firm is an independent business, managed in a personalised way by its owners or part owners, and with a small market share.

At the end of 1991, the most recent year for which statistics are available, there were an estimated 2,697,000 firms in the United Kingdom. Of these some 96% employed less than 20 people, just over 91% employed less than 10 and 99% had under 100 employees. Whichever way you look at it, there are a vast number of people who rely on 'the small firm' for their livelihood. In fact, in the UK, nearly 50% of all those in employment worked for companies with less than 100 staff, while in the European Community as a whole, the figure was nearly 57%.

Moreover, the growth in the number of firms over the period from 1979 to 1991 was astonishing. No less than a 60 percent increase took place and of that increase the majority was made up of small firms. The growth of self employment during the same period was 70%.

So it can be seen that the 'backbone' of the UK economy at least is made up of small firms, well over 2.5 million of them.

The growing tide of ISO 9000

At the time of writing, about 100,000 ISO 9000 certificates have been issued in more than 90 countries around the world. It is fast becoming the standard for international trade. Today, certificates are being gained at the rate of 15,000 every year. Companies having ISO 9000 range from one man businesses to multinationals with thousands of employees.

Before embarking on the road to certification or, on the other hand, before dismissing it, the small firm should ask itself, 'what's in it for us?'

It is generally accepted that going for certification involves effort, commitment and expense. So, is it worthwhile? International businesses of all sizes have proved and are continuing to prove that it is.

The benefits enjoyed by those firms which have achieved ISO 9000 depend on the commitment and diligence with which they have carried out the requirements of the standard. Those companies which procure certification in the hope that it will transform their mediocre performance merely by having it will be disappointed.

The benefits which can come from having ISO 9000

No matter what the size of company though, the fundamental benefits are the same and can be listed simply:

Reduced waste
Less re-working

Improved efficiency
Increased productivity
Enhanced profitability
Improved staff morale
Compliance with purchaser's requirements
Work takes place in a controlled environment
Improved market image
Attracts investment
Provides a competitive edge
Increases opportunities to tender
Esprit de corps
Lower insurance premiums

It is the author's belief that small firms abhor unnecessary paperwork and bureaucracy. In fact the three most quoted reasons for not using ISO 9000 are: too much paperwork, too much time and too costly.

Paperwork

Let us look at the other side of the argument by taking three examples.

- If you operate your business with too little documentation, you may run the risk of losing control of such vital activities as regular and effective credit control, with obvious and damaging results.
- If you fail to document safety procedures or list the hazardous materials used in your business, you run the risk of falling foul of the law, again with serious results.
- If you do not keep working drawings up-to-date and modifications listed and recorded, your product will not be to specification.

The trouble and time taken to put right those things which go wrong due to lack of proper documented control is time wasted. Indeed experience shows it takes a great deal longer to rectify problems retrospectively than it does to get it right in the first place.

The very act of committing to paper your activities and procedures helps to keep your business under control. ISO 9000 requirements for documentation are straightforward common sense so why not use them and show you do so through your certificate?

Too Much Time

Yes, it takes time to prepare documentation, to write a quality manual; it takes time to involve staff in this task; it takes time to decide what should be included and how it should be worded.

But how much more time does it take to sort out a complaint from a customer because you did not have control over what was going on? How much is a lost customer worth to you?

How much time does it take to pursue late payers, late because your staff have not sent out statements at the right time or chased up overdue debtors with letters?

You do it already? Yes of course you do but is the procedure consistent every month? Does it ever go wrong because someone is on holiday or ill? If you write down your procedures and, more important, see they are practised, upsets caused by illness, absenteeism, the sudden departure of key staff and a host of other occurrences, are minimised or even eliminated.

Too Costly

Yes, it will cost money to install an ISO 9000 Quality Management System but what if your largest customer requires that all its suppliers should be certificated? You have no control over that decision, however well you think you know them. How much is your largest customer worth to you? When it becomes obligatory to have ISO 9000 because a contract depends upon it, it is too late to start thinking about it.

Help for the small business

Many small firms are under the misapprehension that going for ISO 9000 will cost a fortune, but nothing could be further from the truth. The fact of the matter is that there are several independent certification bodies, one of which, SGS Yarsley International Certification Services, one of the largest and longest established in the business, offers a small business option (SBO) providing an attractive, inexpensive and really practical route to ISO 9000 certification.

A number of general procedures embodied in the standard are frequently not appropriate for small firms, so the SBO cuts these out.

SBO is not, however, the answer for all small firms since there are one or two provisos. First, the firm must have less than 25 employees. Second, certification is confined to ISO 9002, which covers production, installation and servicing but not for design development or final inspection and test.

By streamlining the certification process and making it more appropriate to the needs of small businesses, costs can be fixed at a level which even the smallest business can afford.

A simplified ISO 9000

SGS Yarsley ICS is not alone in the effort to make ISO 9000 more user friendly for the small firm.

The Institute of Quality Assurance has published a Small Business Guide based on a report issued by a joint working group from the National Accreditation Council for Certification Bodies (NACCB) - now known as United Kingdom Accreditation Service (UKAS) - and the Association of British Certification Bodies (ABCB).

Dr Bernard Juby of the Federation of Small Businesses, whose preface introduces the report, says: 'The result [of the working group's investigation] is this Guide which is a refreshing spotlight, highlighting what needs to be considered when the whole question of ISO 9000 series and its relevance to small businesses arises.'

In addition to qualifying and defining the 'Standard' itself and what constitutes a 'small firm', the Guide includes chapters on Quality Options for Purchasers, The application of ISO 9000 to small businesses, and the use of consultants. Part 2 of the Guide, 'An Introduction to the application of the ISO 9000 series of standards in Small Firms, is especially helpful as it lists each clause from the standard, puts it into plain English and explains what it means.

The Guide does, in fact, seem to represent the first real step forward in making ISO 9000 more applicable and manageable for the small firm and, as such, is essential reading for all small firms, even those which 'definitely will not adopt ISO 9000'. The advice and explanations contained in it are clear, concise and helpful. Details of where to get a copy are given at the end of this chapter.

The bottom line

The benefits listed earlier are just as applicable to a small firm implementing the simplified ISO 9000 as to a larger company. But the benefits are only enjoyed through compliance with and judicious implementation of the requirements of the standard.

They are not automatic, so certification does not do anything other than state that your company has put in place a Quality management system.

But one of the most important things to remember is that the effort involved in preparing for certification will have helped to focus your attention on the parts of your business which may have dragged you down, perhaps without you even being aware of it.

So what about pay-back in real terms?

An objective assessment of whether you should go for ISO 9000 or not should include an estimate of the effect on the bottom line of cumulative inefficiencies in the business. Taken individually these may not seem to be important, but taken as a whole the detrimental effect may be more serious than realised.

The very act of examining the Small Business Option Self Assessment Pack for example, and reading the Small Business Guide will help to focus attention on these apparently unimportant areas and may well serve to make the decision to go for it easy to take.

Weigh up the cost of gaining certification against the cost of losing a contract due to lack of a management system which gives you confidence that all sectors of your business, however small it may be, are as efficient as they can be.

Increased efficiency brings with it the ability to compete more effectively.

ISO 9000 should be regarded as the visible sign that your company is doing its utmost to give of its best to its customers.

Useful contacts:

Department of Enterprise, General Enquiries: 0171 215 5000
For your nearest Business Link: 01742 597507
For your nearest Training & Enterprise Council: 01742 594776
Small Business Guide, 'Quality Systems in the Small Firm' (ISBN 0-906810-48-5) is available from: The Institute of Quality Assurance, PO Box 712, 61 Southwark Street, London, SE1 1SB. 0171 401 7227
SGS Yarsley International Certification Services: 01342 410088

Barry A. Holland
Registered Lead Assessor and Marketing Manager
SGS Yarsley International Certification Services Limited

III

The Strategic Importance of Standards and Quality Assurance

Bryan Geraghty
Director and General Manager of Standards
British Standards Institution

THE industrial competitiveness of the United Kingdom is in danger if the strategic importance of Standards and Quality Assurance are not fully understood. In the early 1980s, 90% of the work in the BSI Standards programme was in relation to National Standards. By 1996 the situation has changed radically. In 1996, 93% of our work items relate to European and international work. This shows the shift in thinking about Standards. Following the Uruguay round of the GATT talks and the creation of the World Trade Organisation, Standards, and particularly international standards have grown in importance.

This recognition generated one of the most powerful US trade delegations assembled to visit Europe. In November 1994, a meeting took place between senior US industrialists and the EU at Seville. At that meeting, US chief executives spoke on behalf of the US in a plea to become involved with Standards making in Europe, to create bi-lateral standards to facilitate trade between the two regions.

Subsequent lobbying by BSI and its sister bodies in Europe has secured an extremely important deal with the US. It is now agreed policy (signed by President Clinton and EU President Jacques Santer at the Madrid summit) that the US will co-operate closely in the international Standard setting process drawing on international bodies to achieve the greatest possible use of international standards. What this effectively means is that international standards will form the basis of world trade, and will be used to break down trade barriers.

BSI plays a leading role in European and international standardisation. We are founder members of all the major Standards bodies, and are playing an increasingly influential role in their development.

But we are still concerned that the UK's commitment to Standards remains at this level. Providing the committee members to make the Standards, while crucial to our continuing role, is not enough. To ensure that business gets the standards it needs these committee members need strategic guidance from their own boardrooms.

Standards are technical documents, but in my experience they can and do help UK companies compete in a world-wide market. It is this potential which, by their absence from such debates as occurred in Seville, UK boardrooms are either ignoring or taking for granted. Perhaps though, it is the speed at which the importance of standards is changing that is taking our senior executives by surprise. More and more standards are being produced by the day, and they are no longer purely national.

An excellent example of how BSI is involved in the process of standardisation, and its strategic importance can be seen through our experience with ISO 9000 management systems. BSI Quality Assurance's main activity is to assess the management systems of companies world-wide. British Standard (BS) EN ISO 9000 is the national standard for quality management systems which was first published in 1979 under the title BS 57S0. Since its publication, it has become perhaps the most widely known of all Standards.

The standard itself is quite general and provides a number of requirements which an organisation should follow to ensure the quality of their products or service. These cover such areas as management responsibility, purchasing, process control and corrective action in the event of something going wrong. Quality has a number of different meanings but BS EN ISO 9000 asks the question 'is the service provided or the product designed and constructed to satisfy the customer needs?'

BS EN ISO 9000 can help eliminate the likelihood of expensive errors by detailing the procedures and work instructions covering every phase of operation. The standard spells out what these work instructions should include and emphasises the control of special processes. When defects do occur, prompt and effective action is essential. Segregating defective products is not enough, the cause must be found and the problem rectified.

The popularity of BS EN ISO 9000 world-wide has continued to grow over the last year and the UK continues to produce more quality companies than anyone else in the world leading the way in quality registrations (currently 46.2% of the international total). According to a survey by the international oil company Mobil, *The Mobil Survey*, the results of which were recently released by ISO, at least 95,000 ISO 9000 certificates had been issued in 86 countries up to the end of June last year. This represents an increase of 24,932 certificates from the 1994 total. Growth is highest on a numerical basis in Britain, with 7,284 new certificates since the previous survey. There are currently 44,000 companies registered in this country.

Companies that have been registered to the standard now have an international trading advantage. Because it, and registration to it by BSI, are now recognised in so many of the world's countries, the costly practice of UK companies having to submit themselves to numerous audits by prospective business partners has all but disappeared for ISO 9000 registered firms. The Registered Firm logo on a company's letterhead is enough to reassure many of the world's most prestigious firms that an organisation is run along the right lines and has made a commitment (both financial and in business culture) to producing its products or services to the same standard time and again. BSI's clients that export have pointed to increased business on the back of their registration.

Using BS EN ISO 9000 can bring real economies in its wake: economies in production because your systems are controlled from start to finish, economies in resources and in time spent on planning or modifying designs of products or services. It provides manufacturers with a complete record of every stage of production, which is invaluable for product or process improvement and demonstrates a level of due diligence in relation to any product liability claim.

In an ideal world, every product and service standard will be harmonised at international level. While at present this may be a personal Utopia, I firmly believe it to be the case. It is up to British industry to make Standards a part of boardroom strategy and to realise their importance in the world markets of the next century.

We already have an excellent record – demonstrated by the growth in registrations to ISO 9000 (a British Standard originally) and the relatively new environmental management standards which are being adopted all over the world. We must stay ahead of the game. The danger is that the ISO 9000 model will be replicated around the world – and this time it will be a foreign partner that steals a march on the rest of the world, leaving UK industry in the shade.

IV

ISO 9000 Certification: The Key to Sustainable Competitive Advantage

Anwar Osman
Lloyd's Register Quality Assurance

EVIDENCE of effective Quality Assurance is becoming an increasingly important marketing and sales tool for many organisations. For those involved in export operations, it has almost become mandatory for most markets. There are real cost advantages for customers to receive some form of assurance of the Quality of the products and services they are purchasing. A Quality Management System, combined with an internationally recognised third-party certification, can provide that assurance.

This chapter discusses the effects that ISO 9000 has had on international trade, the benefits of installing a Quality Management System to the ISO 9000 series standards and finally the advantages that have been achieved by gaining ISO 9000 certification.

Introduction

If organisations are to compete effectively either in domestic or overseas markets the Quality Assurance function must become more significant within the strategic development and planning of individual enterprises. As national and international communications become more comprehensive and efficient and the world effectively gets smaller, purchasers have access to a much wider range of products, services and suppliers. Quality Assurance has become a tool increasingly used by marketeers to differentiate between competing products.

A focus on customers can result in satisfied customers, a wider and better product range, fewer customer complaints and a greater volume of business. A focus on internal operations and processes can lead to fewer mistakes and conflicts, improved Quality, reduced cycle times and costs and delivery of the product or service faster and on time. These results are typical rewards of implementing a comprehensive Quality Management System (QMS).

Organisations then have a need to demonstrate this QMS in an objective and timely manner. ISO 9000 certification can provide that objective evidence.

Cost Considerations

International surveys of manufacturing costs indicate that manufacturers spend about 60% of manufacturing costs on purchased items or raw materials, 15% on labour and 25% on overheads. To achieve a 5% reduction in costs requires a 33% reduction in labour, 20% in overheads or only 8.3% in materials.

Hence many purchasers are addressing their suppliers' Quality assurance programs in an effort to reduce the costs of purchased items. Companies are using ISO 9000 as an objective measure of their suppliers' Quality Assurance capabilities.

Global Trends

Quality Assurance has gained massive popularity over the last few years. Over 60 countries have adopted ISO 9000 as their national Quality System Standard and more copies of ISO 9000 have been sold than of all other ISO standards ever produced. Internationally there are at present 20,000 ISO 9000 approved companies in the United Kingdom with a potential market of 85,000 companies. In the US there are 2,000 approved with a potential market of 500,000 companies. Originally restricted to the manufacturing industry, it is more recently being adopted on a far wider scale in almost every business sector. It is a means of demonstrating an ability to be consistent and giving the customer what was specified.

Customers could, of course, carry out a Quality Assurance evaluation of their suppliers, and in many cases this still happens. Some organisations are subject to frequent assessments by various customers (i.e. second party assessments). If all customers could accept a common standard of Quality Assurance then significant economies result. So when the European Community came together with its single market and common Quality Assurance requirements, it became a major driving force. The European Community has global significance in Quality because it placed new market pressures on all producers worldwide who wished to trade with

European companies, or even to compete with European companies in other markets.

The European Community 1992 plan rests on the use of the ISO produced standards as the requirement documents for third-party certification schemes for product (CE mark) and Quality System registration.

Under such certification schemes a company arranges to be audited by a single accredited independent (third party) certification organisation. If the company's Quality System documentation and implementation are found to meet the requirements of the applicable ISO 9000 series standard the certification body grants approval and lists the company in its register of approved companies.

Purchasing organisations can then accept such certification as evidence that the company's Quality System meets the applicable ISO 9000 series requirements.

The European Community are not the only group to realise the benefits of such certification scheme. The same processes are happening in Australia, Canada, America and Asia, particularly for government purchases.

In markets where third-party certification has become widespread, Quality Assurance can still be a competitive weapon. It provides a barrier to new entrants to the particular market and provides an opportunity for the approved companies to operate more efficiently. To achieve further benefits, the process must be taken further to mutually advantageous partnership arrangements between suppliers and customers and the internal customer/supplier relationships within organisations. These arrangements then form the base for a Total Quality Management (TQM) program.

The LRQA Survey

In 1992, Lloyd's Register Quality Assurance Ltd (LRQA) commissioned an independent market research organisation, Research International, to carry out a study into the reasons why organisations obtain Quality Management System certification. The study investigated the impact certification has on their business, both internally and externally and the future of ISO 9000 in a changing marketplace.

The study was based on interviews with 400 Quality Managers and Senior Managers, from a cross-section of LRQA's customer base. To ensure a balanced view, a wide range of companies of different size and industry type were targeted.

The results of the survey are summarised below:

a) Benefits of Installing a Quality Management System

One of the study's most significant findings (refer to Figure 1) revealed that the internal benefits of operating a Quality Management System are greater than its external benefits. Moreover, companies found that the actual results exceeded their initial expectations. 86% of managers concurred that better management control resulted from having a Quality Management System, while 73% said that the system will enable them to deliver a better service to customers and ensure consistency of systems company-wide. Productivity gains and increased efficiency were also reported by 69%, while staff motivation and cost reductions also emerged as important internal benefits.

b) Benefits of Certification

Most of the benefits associated with obtaining certification are external, with results largely in line with the reasons for initially seeking approval.

– ISO 9000's major advantage lies in its ability to open doors to previously closed market segments. Figure 2: shows 67% of managers said the standard had enabled them to stay in business by bidding for tenders from which they would otherwise be excluded.

– For 63%, certification was cited as a valuable marketing tool.

– 49% believed certification had enabled them to maintain or expand their marketshare.

Internal benefits were also perceived as a result of obtaining third party certification. 67% of managers said approval was essential for

Figure 1 Benefits from Installing a QMS

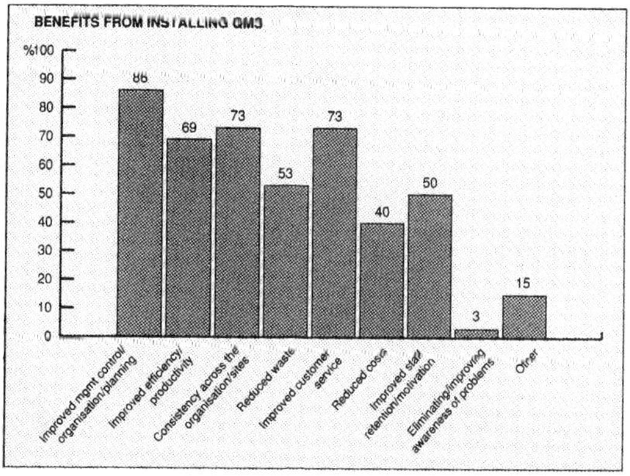

addressing and maintaining Quality Management Systems. 42% said certification had reduced the need for customer audits.

Figure 2 Benefits from Achieving Certification

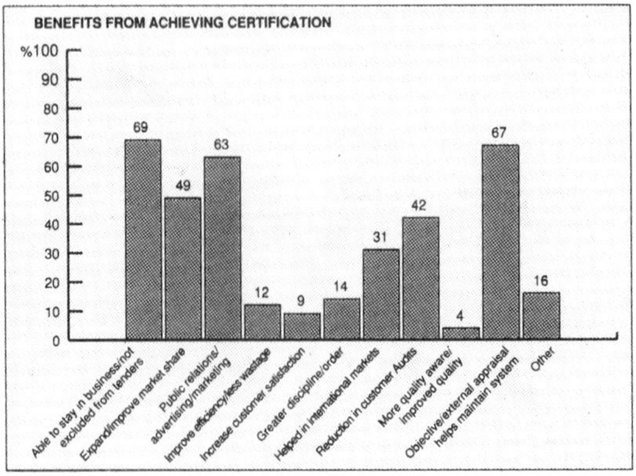

c) ISO 9000: A Long-Term Investment

The benefits of ISO 9000 are seen to increase in line with the duration of approval. This indicates that certification should be viewed as a long-term investment.

From an internal viewpoint, it takes time for organisations to fully reap the benefits of a QMS and to make the system work to their best advantage. External factors, such as an increase in market share, can also take time to develop. Figure 3 below shows how these gains accumulate over five years.

Figure 3 ISO 9000 Benefits Increase over 5 Years

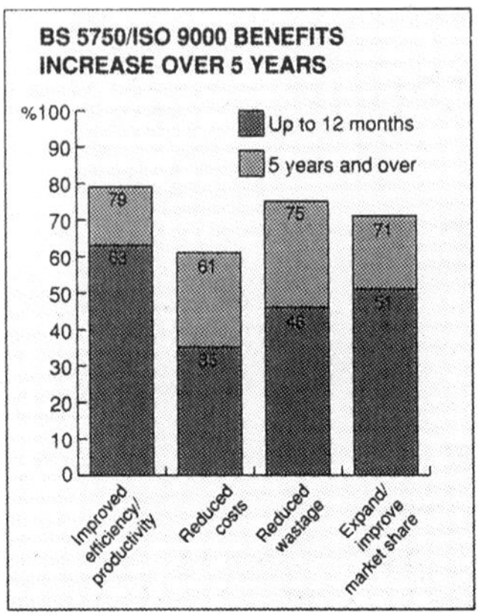

d) Reasons for Seeking Certification

External market pressure was the principal driving force behind the majority of decisions to obtain certification. The most important factor being the increased ability to tender for work from which they would otherwise be excluded. This was cited as a reason by 81% of the managers surveyed.

The need to increase or maintain marketshare was the second most important ranking factor, given by 78% of respondents. Other priorities included better anticipation of customer needs and enhanced marketing efforts.

The benefits associated with internal improvements were given a less important priority as a reason for seeking certification. Nonetheless 70% said they had sought approval in order to achieve greater efficiency and productivity within their organisation.

e) Have Benefits Met, Exceeded or Fallen Short of Expectations

From Figure 4 below, 89% of companies reported the benefits associated with Quality Management Systems and Certification met or exceeded their original expectations. Instances of benefits falling short of expectations were relatively few.

A higher percentage of respondents believed their Quality Management Systems had met or exceeded expectations, with the response to satisfaction with certification coming shortly behind.

Figure 4 Whether ISO 9000 has met/exceeded/fallen below expectations

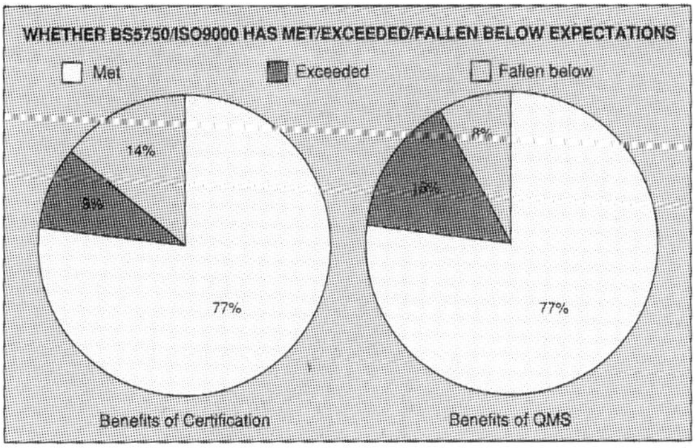

f) Market Sector Analysis

The survey was conducted among companies of different size and industry type. A breakdown of the analysis is given below:-

Small Business

By small business we refer exclusively to those companies employing 25 personnel or less. Of all sectors and type of organisation, small businesses were most strongly influenced by external market pressures. Approval was viewed by 88% as a means of staying in business as it made them eligible to bid for tenders. Three quarters of respondents also cited the need to maintain or increase marketshare.

In line with other segments, small business felt the most benefit from ISO 9000 certification internally, despite originally giving it a low priority.

83% said the standard had improved management control and 70% reported improvements in customer service.

Although under the greatest pressure to gain certification, 64% of small businesses said ISO 9000 improved their ability to tender for work. 48% increased their marketshare.

Food Sector

Reactions to ISO 9000 in the food sector was markedly different to other areas.

Internal factors, particularly the need to improve efficiency and productivity, were seen by 82% of companies as the major incentive for seeking certification. By contrast only 45% saw the need to enter new tender lists. This confirms that food companies rely on the strength of their brands to market products and view internal efficiency as the key to improved performance.

Food companies experienced major internal benefits in line with their expectations. 90% reported improved management control, 76% said third-party certification helped them to maintain integrity in their QMS and 48% cited cost reductions.

Over two-thirds (67%) said it had enabled them to ensure consistent systems across their whole organisation which was an important factor in an industry where takeovers and mergers are commonplace.

Mechanical Engineering

Like small business, the mechanical engineering sector was strongly influenced by external pressures when seeking certification. 87% and 83% respectively reported that the need to tender for new business and maintain or increase their marketshare were determining factors.

For 77% of companies, the main benefit of certification came from increased ability to bid for new tenders. 32% believed it gave them a head start in the international marketplace.

The principal internal benefit for mechanical engineers was the increase in management control, as cited by 86% of companies. Reduction in costs were also identified by 40%.

Electronics

In the electronics sector, companies found that the benefits of certification reflected their original expectations. 76% said that ISO 9000 approval meant new tender bids were available to them and 52% reported an increase in marketshare.

68% of companies considered that certification had boosted their marketing efforts.

From an internal viewpoint, 80% believed they were now better equipped to control their business activities and 78% have succeeded in increasing efficiency and productivity.

Service Companies

Maintaining and increasing marketshare and the need to be considered for new tenders ranked as the major incentives for gaining approval by 84% of companies. 79% were driven by the need to increase their marketshare and 76% by the need to improve their service to customers.

Of all the sectors sampled, service companies gave marketing benefits the highest priority (70%). Actual marketing benefits were achieved by 64% of companies in this sector.89% of companies reported an improvement in management control while 81% achieved consistency in systems company-wide. 69% commented that third-party certification held them to maintain their QMS.

g) A Comparative Survey

Many of the findings of the LRQA study are supported by research by the UK Department of Trade and Industry (DTI) in 1991. Then, the DTI found that QMS certification brings operational efficiency to 89% of companies and increased export sales to 26%, 67% gained marketing advantage, 44% of organisations reported increase in profit after two years, and an average investment payback of less than two years. It was also found that a QMS is beneficial to small companies.

Conclusion

ISO 9000 certification is not an option but rather a reality for companies who wish to retain and sustain their competitiveness in today's highly competitive world markets.

Quality Assurance in all operations of a company is the seed from which profits grow. A focus on company operations through Quality Assurance will lead to lower operating costs and improved customer service. This is supported by the finding of the LRQA survey which identified internal as well as external benefits from implementing Quality Management Systems and gaining ISO 9000 certification.

References
'Setting Standards for Better Business" – Lloyd's Register Quality Assurance Ltd, 1993

Anwar Osman B.E.(Mech.), M.Phys, MIE Aust., C.P. Eng. IQA (Lead Assessor), MQSA, Lead Assessor, LRQA Ltd.
Anwar has managed Quality Systems in manufacturing and service industries for over 11 years. He has also been responsible for setting up Total Quality Management programs and associated training.

V

Without Trust In The Modern Business World You May Soon Have Nothing Left

Ross Dunn
Personnel Director, Blue Circle Cement

YES, of course we know how important it is. We have heard that it is the single most important aspect of modern day business. We know it is essential to our survival. Well, do we really believe that? Do we believe it is even half or a quarter as important as stated. Then what are we doing about it? How much time are we spending on it? (25%, 50% or 75%?). What processes have we changed and what are we doing differently since say three or six months ago? What is our plan to ensure we improve this most important aspect of our business?

If you can give positive detailed answers to the above then turn to a different article - you do not need to read this one. If you can not answer all the above; perhaps have never deeply considered some of the points then read on. I can not promise you all the answers but I do hope and expect to highlight directions and actions that need to be taken to develop trust.

Why is it so difficult? Many will say that it is our past history, confrontational management and confrontational unions. However, these are symptoms and results of mistrust.

I believe the answer as to why it is so difficult is best explained with the following example.

Let us consider a syndicate looking at means of improving. say, market shares. They brainstorm the problem with the following results.

ACTIONS THAT WILL IMPROVE MARKET SHARE

1. **Lower price**
2. **Improve the product**
3. **Increase effectiveness of sales force**

4. **Provide free delivery**
5. **Offer better technical backups**
6. **Buy downstream companies presently not supplying**
7. **Buy out competition**
8. **Increase product range**
9. **Enter into long-term deals with customers**

The list is by no means complete. However it is likely that any one of the points listed, if properly actioned would lead to an improvement in market share (maybe not profit or better business but improved market share never-the-less).

If we consider a similar syndicate looking at the subject of Improving Trust in the Workplace. Their brainstorm chart would be something like this:

IMPROVING TRUST IN THE WORKPLACE

1. **Open door policy**
2. **Provide detailed, relevant information**
3. **Must be 2-way process**
4. **Must have respect**
5. **Openness**
6. **Total honesty**
7. **Needs time to develop**
8. **Need to know one another**
9. **Provide regular relevant feedback**

Whereas with the market-share list, action on any one topic would likely bring improvements. The trust list is different. I would suggest that unless there is action on all the topics trust will not improve. Consider providing information. I have heard people say that the only time business information is supplied to the workforce is to soften them up for pay negotiations or "sob stories" before announcements on restructuring or redundancy. That is - providing information can lead directly to distrust. Honesty and openness must be sustained over significant time to have an effect: must be two-way: must have feedback and be with those whom you know and respect.

Reverse any one of the above to dishonesty, no feedback, no information, no respect etc. and you do not simply have a lack of trust or a lowering of trust but total MISTRUST. So the reason why trust is so hard to achieve is that it requires consistent action on all fronts at the same time.

And that's the challenge. Let us consider the topics listed in the brainstorm one-by-one.

1. Open Door Policy

We all know what it means. The boss is approachable, not secretive and willing to give up his time to people passing his door who want a chat about the business or perhaps something else. However do not believe leaving a door open achieves the above.

I know of a manager whose office is the last one up a dead-end corridor. There is absolutely no passing traffic - and that's why his office was located there - but he says he has an open door policy.

It used to be (still is?) common for a secretary's office to be placed before the manager's so that the secretary could deter unwanted visitors. One should therefore consider the location of the manager's office with great care. It's much more important than many people think, believe or understand.

The internal layout of the office is also important. The manager sitting in a throne-like chair, behind a great mahogany desk with his back to windows through which the sun streams into the visitor's eyes while he sits on a stool 2 feet below the manager is not conducive to free discussion. Although the foregoing is an exaggeration (well hopefully it is an exaggeration) the desk in any office is a psycological barrier. If there is room in the office for an area where people can sit, as equals, and discuss issues e.g. a separate, round table with standard chairs then give it a try. And remember there is a balance to be struck between a manager having an office sufficient to satisfy the needs of customers and external visitors yet not being so lavish that the rest of the business feels resentment.

Once the location and the general geography have been sorted out then comes the attitude. The hesitant visitor who gingerly crosses the threshold into the manager's office to be met with "What do you want?" "Can it not wait" or even a resentful sigh will probably not return. A positive, encouraging, friendly attitude supported by the necessary information or feedback are all essential. The resulting dialogue will go a long way to building the foundations of trust.

The open door policy also covers, in my mind, the function of managers being seen and approachable in the workplace. I do not believe this needs to be a daily duty but something that helps people get to know each other – helps them TRUST each other. It should be carried out as appropriate for your business.

I have heard of a director who believed he should go around a different part of the works each day and, on occasion, come in during the night to see the "lads" on the shop floor. The only message he left behind was that he did not trust the workforce and supervisors. He probably didn't! Be careful of the message you leave behind. Remember most people will start by expecting you to be untrustworthy and will bend everything you do to fit their perceptions.

2. Provide Detailed, Relevant Business Information

If you want someone to be trustworthy - you must first trust them. One easy way to show trust is to provide people with relevant information that affects their part of the business. Get away from this secretive "need to know" business. That's usually managers protecting their own station - "Information is Power". Ask the workforce what they "want to know". If they "want to know" then they have a "need to know". Providing the information shows trust and respect, this can be a huge step forward. If information is secret or of the highest commercial sensitivity this can be explained and in the new culture that is developing will be accepted. Providing people with costs of operations, costs of repairs and company profitability also allows them to see their effect on the business – an essential aspect of feedback.

3. Must Be a Two-Way Process

To work, trust must be mutual. I once met a man who had recently taken over a business. He told me that for the last 6 months he had done everything he knew to get the workforce to trust him but felt he had had no success. I asked him if he trusted his workforce and he said "You must be joking. They'd steal anything that's not bolted down". I don't think he had too far to look to find his problem. Finding it is one thing – sorting it out is quite another.

The answer is to deal with all the issues at the same time. Providing people with information and showing trust in them is a great step. It's much easier to trust someone who trusts you. However the path to trusting someone is not always gentle and regular. It usually requires an act of faith on behalf of management – a step change. The time must be right, the general barriers showing signs of coming down and then the time comes to release the reins. Your intuition will tell you when it's right, "Gut feel" is important - so long as you are not just listening to the problems of the past - so long as you are willing to change – so long as you will stick by your resolution to succeed and not revert to control and punish when the first sign of problems occur. And problems will occur – it's part of the process but the balance will be hugely in your favour – with time.

With properly balanced and structured information being given the two-way process can now be completed by listening. Listening to feedback: listening to constructive ideas: listening to complaints: listening to whackey ideas <u>and then taking action.</u> If people know they will be listened to: know they will get an explanation or know action will take place every time then they will open up with their comments because they trust those they're talking to to respond properly.

4. Must Have Respect

This seems so obvious that it hardly warrants any embellishment. However if trust has to be mutual – so does respect. Inequality of opportunity, artificial barriers of status, unreasonable differences in pay and conditions, attitudes of superiority all adversely affect respect. This is why many companies have removed the preferential parking spaces for directors, introduced a single canteen where everyone can eat together and simple aspects such as common overalls. I worked in an operation where the workforce used to wear blue overalls and the managers wore white overalls. This presumably was to show that managers did not actually carry out mundane, manual tasks – i.e. they didn't get dirty. The anomaly was the operation was in a chalk quarry. Can you imagine the safety implications of white overalls in a chalk quarry!? Overalls are supposed to be worn for safety not camouflage. Thankfully everyone now wears high-visibility orange overalls.

To ensure respect people must be competent. Whatever the level of competence required now and in the future a training plan for each individual is essential. This training plan, ideally for about a rolling 3 year period, should be focused on meeting the Company's strategic objectives, meeting the individual's team objectives and meeting the needs of the individual. Greater skills and greater abilities are part of the foundations of greater involvement which in turn leads to greater success and therefore respect.

Training the workforce also gives them a feeling of security in themselves and the company and that greatly helps TRUST.

5. Openess

A common management saying is "We want to be open and involve others but not until we get our own house in order". They don't want to expose to others the fact that they are not absolutely clear where they are, what they want and how they're going to achieve it. Once they are absolutely sure about such things they then want to be open and involve others - Sorry! Too Late! - and they've probably missed some basic, important issues.

Another piece of mendacity is when people are told such things as "this idea was put before the Board of Directors (or any senior decision makers you like to think of who have unanimously sanctioned it). However, before implementation we want everyone to buy-in to the proposal and thus give it full support".

How many people are willing to make the career termination statement of "the idea's rubbish" Well - No. That's not the way you are supposed to respond if the idea's wrong. You're meant to say the idea's good in principle and then spend the next few weeks gently exposing the errors and omissions. But how many people are close enough to these Senior Executives to be able to spend this necessary time influencing and persuading them? Precious few.

The alternatives are either to say you agree or you disagree or best of all, not to be put in that position in the first place.

If the Board, or anyone else for that matter, want to be open - they must be open at an early stage in the discussions. Sure, they may not like everything they hear; they may lose the power to control but let's at least be honest - either they control or are open to persuasion. They must not pretend to be both.

It is essential that openness is not abused. Incorrect use of information to meet selfish ends will inevitably lead to greater control of information and close down openness.

6. Total Honesty

I once stated while giving a paper at a conference that to achieve real TRUST there was a need for me to be Scrupulously Honest. Afterwards I was talking to a writer who wrote case-studies for a Total Quality Magazine who said to me "You didn't really mean that - did you?" Well I don't know who she had been working with previously or what sort of industries they worked in but I've always worked with a workforce who could see a lie coming from miles away and then remembered it for ever.

But it's much worse than that. After four months in my latest job I had some open sessions with the whole workforce in groups of about a dozen. Identifying barriers to improvement was the general subject. However the general comments were "I remember 15 years ago when a manager said..." Or "I remember 12 years ago when a manager did" I would say "hold on a minute. I've only just arrived. I can't answer all the problems of the past. I want to take us into the future". This was met with comments like "management said they were going to do this 21 years ago and it's still not done, etc. etc." So the lies and errors in the past live on today. Also your actions today will be remembered for years to come.

Scrupulous Honesty is not "I'll tell you everything all of the time". There are, of course, areas of confidentiality and areas of sensitivity that should not be in an open forum. You therefore need to say so and explain why. Just be open and honest with the rest. However, let me put forward a word of caution. Management's job is to continuously look for improvements. If we consider one sensitive area of reducing workforce levels; manning levels have been under the microscope for many years. Management look at restructuring, reorganising, spending capital to automate, etc. etc. I guess that for every actual round of redundancies undertaken ten other possibilities have been considered and rejected. However the workforce only hears of the one that is going to reduce jobs. If tomorrow you decide to be open and say to the employees "There's this tiny germ of an idea that could have implications on numbers employed but I want you to look at it. See if there is anything in it or whether it should be rejected".

All your workforce will hear that communication as "there are going to be further redundancies". Why? Because that's the only way they've been talked to before.

A step change into Total Honesty can have very confusing consequences. The whole process of TRUST needs time.

7. **Needs Time To Develop**

Nobody trusts someone else immediately. It's made easier if the new person comes with good credentials, if there are mutual friends in existence and if you've heard good stories about them.

Many companies are coming from a position of confrontation, mistrust and a history of regularly changing senior managers. When I was at University I was taught there was a management input versus time curve that went as follows:

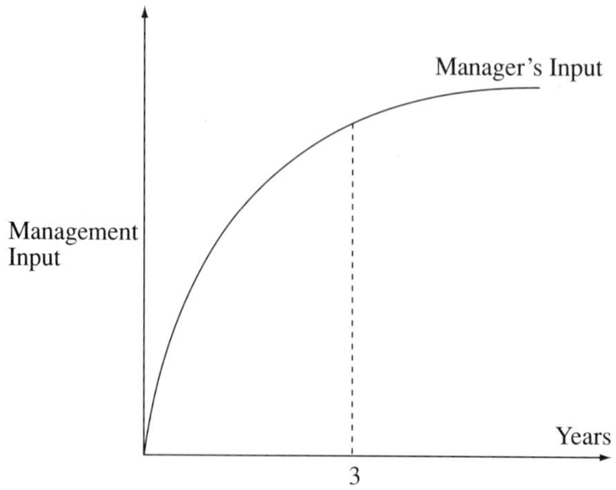

This is great for the manager's experience and knowledge: great for his C.V. - but what about workforce participation? If we superimpose a hypothetical Trust Versus Time curve on the first graph we have:

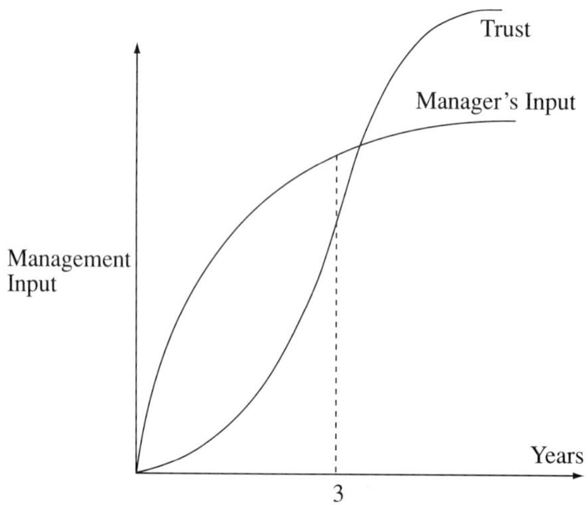

Better to balance the input of the new manager with the trust of the workforce. This allows the whole team to develop; to get everyone involved and to achieve the quickest highest levels of continuous improvement.

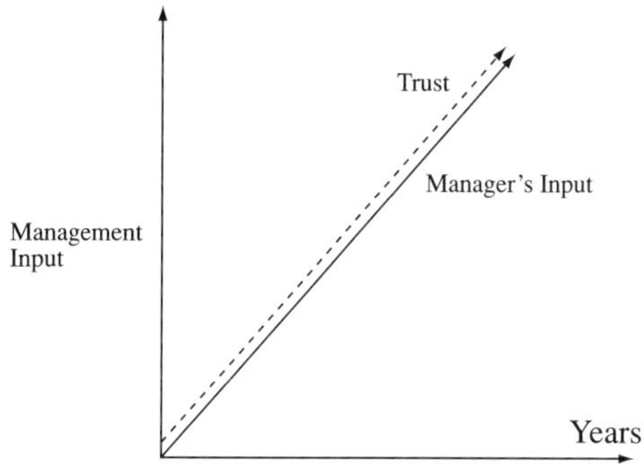

Time brings with it one other essential factor in the business environment – the ability to make a mistake without destroying all that has gone before. If big mistakes are made early on in the TRUST journey then it's one pace forward and twenty paces back. In the early days it's like a game of snakes and ladders with no ladders and hoards of reptiles. However once the necessary standards have been met and maintained for the necessary length of time everyone arrives at the point where a mistake can be forgiven. By then the culture is so open there will be early cries of "Why did you do that", "Didn't you realise" and all that will be required is a "Sorry, I screwed up. It won't happen again".

8. Need To Know Each Other

The previous section said much about knowing each other. It takes time – but why not give it a helping hand. If a workforce doesn't want to socialise with each other outside work there's probably a problem.

Pride in one's job and work tends to lead to close relationships between workmates. Shifts or craftsmen will often spend time together but why not the whole workforce. Works Dances, Bar-B-Qs, golf outings, welfare outings, skittles evenings: if they're not already happening then get someone to arrange them. Involve the whole family.

Other possibilities include arranging evening classes on business premises: French, Spanish, Cookery, Car Maintenance, First-Aid etc. etc. Every business has its experts who can assist or bring in specialists. Run a crèche for the kids and serve some light refreshments. Make it fun. Get people involved. Don't give up at the first hurdle. Get to know each other.

9. Provide Regular Relevant Feedback

Much has already been said about providing necessary business information and that this information is a basic source of feedback: of being open and involving people in Strategy and Vision formulation. But there's more.

We're developing a culture where everyone feels a part of the business - owns the business. They therefore want feedback on everything. Who is on Improvement Teams; how are they getting on: how do we compare with our competitors on a full range of issues; what external recognition is there of our successes etc. Posters briefings, exhibitions, newsletters. flashing electronic notice boards can all be used to provide feedback depending on how quickly it needs to be communicated.

Remember to close the loop on feedback, i.e. ask whether the feedback met the expectations of those receiving it. Get Feedback on Feedback. Yes it's never ending.

Where To Go From Here

Let's go back to the beginning. If you believe trust is important you must have an improvement plan. The plan must cover all points previously mentioned and others that may be specific to your situation. So take all the sections and change something in each to improve. Tell people what you are doing and why. Get feedback, listen to what's being said and develop the next stage.

TRUST is not just a prize worth winning - it's one you **must** win, Without TRUST in the modern business world you may soon have nothing left.

VI

Investing In People For Quality

Investors In People

WITH any investment these days, every business wants to see payback. In an ideal world, high returns over the short term are what is wanted. This is probably why the National Lottery is so popular: but as we know, few get the payback they dream of. Investing in people emphatically does give payback on a UK national investment of around £20 billion a year in training and development. Crucially, investing in people underpins Quality in everything a business makes or does. The Investors in People standard is now an integral part of the drive for improving Quality. It achieves this by releasing the full value of business improvement initiatives. This fact has already been recognised by the employers of around a quarter of the UK workforce who are already involved with Investors in People.

Business today is driven by all kinds of pressures. Profits have to be maintained and increased. New business has to be won. Competitors have to be kept pace with and challenged. New legislation imposes demands while costs need to be held in check. New and better technology marches on apace and customers demand improved Quality and better service and so on. The business gurus would have their audiences believe from their theories that there are infallible ways to meet these pressures.

There probably are some – but which ones to back? There is one proven theory to help employers to achieve Quality and to get where they want to be. The common denominator, proved time and time again, is people doing the job.

Two recent government White Papers on the theme of competitiveness have pointed clearly to the need for a highly motivated and well qualified workforce. They called for employers who see the importance of developing the skills of their employees, employees who take their own development seriously and young people who are well prepared for the world of work. Research in major surveys over the past ten years has consistently found that only a handful of employers dissent in any way from this accepted wisdom. These are facts of business life in the rapidly changing and increasingly competitive business climate of the late 1990s.

People – what they can do and are motivated to do – are the key resource in helping every business do what it needs or plans to do. Whether it's meeting quality standards, confidently meeting the competition, increasing outputs, controlling costs or making the most of new plant and equipment, people are the prime area for investment. A business can have the best business plan ever, the very latest world class equipment, the prime selling position and the most loyal customers. But if the staff and their skills don't keep pace with the speed at which things change these days, all of its competitive advantage will be lost.

What is meant by investing in people? Don't employers do it already? What about their training spend? Don't organisations go to great lengths to hire the best available? Perhaps they do. But there is a clear need to keep this investment paying back and making it improve continuously. To meet this type of long recognised national need, government, the CBI, the TUC and the UK's leading business and training bodies got together in 1990 to develop the national Standard for effective investment in people. Now called Investors in People, the Standard is delivering continuous improvement to the employers of that part of the UK's workforce who have so far become involved. It is based on years of best business practice in managing people – what the UK's most successful organisations have been doing for years.

Investors in People works simply and effectively. It adds teeth to Quality initiatives in every type of business. It doesn't necessarily mean extra training spend or inordinate commitment of time. In many cases, precious resources are redirected more effectively and efficiency gains are made. For the unconverted, it is essential for top level consideration as a matter of urgency. In summary the process goes like this:

- understanding the Investors in People Standard and it's implications for the organisation, its business plans and any current or planned quality drives and initiatives;

- involving managers and employee representatives in the decision to take the next steps, and gaining their support and commitment to move ahead;
- diagnosing the gaps between what is done now and what the Standard requires. This might not give the results expected......but at least a clear message on the differences in perceptions and practice to tackle for a successful outcome;
- working from the gaps revealed, drawing up an action plan of what needs to be done to meet the Standard;
- making the informed commitment to meeting the Standard and communicating this to all staff;
- assigning project management responsibility and resources (cash, time, facilities);
- for all of the people, planning and taking necessary training and development action to meet the Standard;
- bringing together the evidence that the Standard has been met for assessment purposes;
- formal assessment and feedback by an independent, licensed assessor;
- if you've got it right, recognition as an Investor in People decided by a business-led expert panel;
- the publicity which is rightfully the successful organisation's for the achievement in meeting the Standard;
- a lasting culture of continuous improvement and development throughout all levels of the organisation.

How will Investors in People mesh with Quality initiatives which might already be under way? The answer – based on the experience of the many who have done it – is "extremely well". The only regrets expressed by those with this hands-on experience were in organisations which had not introduced Investors in People at the same time as the Quality initiative. There was an admitted tendency to want to tackle initiatives sequentially. This was done in the mistaken belief that the organisation could cope with only so much change at any point in time. But sooner or later there had dawned the realisation that the people at all levels in the organisation were driving and delivering the change and were, therefore, the vital key to everything embodied by it. So whether anyone is embarking on becoming world class, meeting Quality or environmental standards, or customer care programmes, or Total Quality, the point is simple: the people will help to make it – or break it. Inescapably, they are the single factor which makes the significant difference.

The Investors in People Standard focuses on four key principles:

- **Making a public commitment from the top to develop all employees to achieve business objectives.** The Standard calls for every employer to have a written, but flexible plan setting out business goals and targets. The plan considers how staff will contribute to achieving the plan. In particular, it also specifies how the development needs of staff will be assessed and met. This ensures that the business strategy and plans are kept up to date, goals are communicated and clear, and that all of the people know their part in achieving those goals. The management of the organisation are responsible for communicating to all employees this vision of where the organisation is going and the necessary contribution of the employees to it's success. Employee representative bodies, where they exist, are expected to be involved in this process.
- **Regularly reviewing the training and development needs of all employees.** This means that resources for training and developing staff are clearly identified in the business plan. Managers are expected to ensure that everyone in the business has a regular stocktake of training and development needs which matches their necessary contribution to achieving the business objectives. Where they apply, these needs should be related to recognised standards of competence and formal vocational qualifications (such as National and Scottish Vocational Qualifications).
- **Taking action to train and develop people on recruitment and throughout their employment.** This means that necessary training and development is on the agenda for everyone all of the time. This is definitely not about training for its own sake. Action will, of course, be focused on the training needs of new recruits. But equally important is that there will be evidence of ways of developing and improving the skills of all existing employees. Employees themselves should be encouraged to contribute to the process of identifying and meeting their own job related development needs. Thereby, a constructive joint approach between employers and their employees is made possible and the concept – and reality – of commitment to lifelong learning comes about.
- **Evaluating the investment in training and development to assess achievement and improve future effectiveness.** This ensures that mechanisms are in place to see that performance is improving as intended

and bottom line payback is being achieved. No one invests to lose. The investment in, and use made of the skills learned, together with the competence of the staff at all levels should be reviewed against the business goals and targets. An important part of these principles is that appraisal systems should work effectively at all levels. This review of the effectiveness of training and development must be made at top level and lead to a renewal of commitment and setting of targets.

Putting these four principles into practice and weaving them into everything else which is going on in the organisation isn't as daunting as it might sound. Investors in People was designed for business people by business people who were anxious to ensure that it was not a bureaucratic chore – even worse – a glorious job creating paperchase. Much of what is needed to convince an assessor to make a positive recommendation to the formal recognition panel will be generated in the normal course of any well run business. Underpinning the four principles are 24 key points of best practice called assessment indicators. It is against these indicators that the assessment takes place. The assessment process is conducted on a mix of narrative "storyboard" evidence of the journey to meet the Standard, a review of key documents to support specific indicators, and interviews with a sample of staff drawn from all levels of the organisation. At the end of the assessment, a recognition panel consisting of senior business people will consider the assessor's report and decide if the Standard has been fully met. The decision of the panel is conveyed to the organisation concerned and valuable feedback is given.

Key to the whole process of meeting the standard– often called the "journey" – is the active commitment and involvement of senior managers. Investors in People isn't something to be delegated and conveniently forgotten about. Depending on the size and organisation of the business, the project manager will need – and expect – regular support from the top level (e.g. Chief Executive, Managing Director, Proprietor). A successful journey depends upon good communications and management commitment which is demonstrated by regular involvement throughout. The length of the journey will depend, quite simply, on how much there is to do to meet the action plan and how quickly any changes in systems and attitudes can be effected. Most organisations complete the journey to assessment in somewhere between six and eighteen months – with an overall average of thirteen months.

So, why do this at all? What are the benefits? Recent research supports the clear business case for Investors in People. Organisations which had met the Standard reported stronger overall performance in terms of profitability during the period 1992–1995 than those which had not. These organisations also reported greater productivity increases and export sales volumes. Throughout the human resource management area, the recognised organisations could point to improvements in a number of key measures of employee capability. Changes to management of the workforce were being implemented at a greater rate than in organisations which were not recognised.

Case studies of Investors in People organisations clearly demonstrate an impressive range of benefits such as improved earnings, productivity and profitability; enhanced Quality with reduced costs and wastage; customer satisfaction and competitive advantage; improved motivation, skills and flexibility; and public recognition. This isn't promotional hype, it is fact. The proof is in the performance of some of the growing band of Investors in People. Land Rover, ICL, IDV, Boots the Chemists, Unipart, Birds Eye, Walls, Kwik Fit, the Woolwich Building Society and Hotpoint are some of the household names who are proud to have met the Standard. Throughout the UK, organisations in all sectors of the economy, employing from as few as three people to over 50,000 have benefited. Their stories are available from those delivering the Standard. All will agree that Investors in People fitted their strategies and objectives and even the best will admit that they learned something along the way. Whatever benefits a business may achieve through undertaking the Investors in People journey, don't all come at the end of the process. Almost 2,000 organisations have successfully completed the journey – many started to experience hard benefits from the time of undertaking the initial diagnosis to identify the gaps in practices.

Apart from the benefits to the business, employees in Investors in People organisations experience the positive changes which underpin the overall enhancement in personnel performance. Employees report benefits such as better communications – sometimes with long service personnel finally discovering what the organisation is all about. Teams work and pull together better and analyse their output more critically. There are better career development prospects for those who wish to progress within the organisation. Opportunities for flexibility, variety and job interest increase. The rate of achievement of recognised competence based vocational qualifications improves. More people who thought they had finished with learning returned to it with renewed vigour and without fear and prejudice. And overall motivation, morale, the sense of involvement, responsibility and commitment to the job were tangibly improved.

Being recognised as an Investor in People gives the successful organisation the right to use the logo or "badge" on premises and on stationery, company literature and recruitment advertising. This sends a powerful signal to employees, potential recruits, customers, suppliers, sub-contractors and stakeholders. The logo is becoming increasingly recognised as a national hallmark of Quality which speaks volumes about the user's commitment to standards of excellence.

The overall management, Quality assurance and development of the Investors in People Standard is the responsibility of Investors in People UK. This business-led company reflects a wide range of employer, employee and sectoral interests. Investors in People UK based in London, works in partnership with the delivery and assessment organisations throughout the country. A prime concern of the company is to achieve acceptance of the Standard as the international Standard at the forefront of human resource management practice.

Throughout England and Wales, the Training and Enterprise Councils will willingly give advice about taking the first steps towards becoming an Investor in People. Equally, they will give support and advice about completing the journey successfully and keeping momentum going afterwards. In Scotland, this same function is performed by the local enterprise companies. And, in Northern Ireland, The Training and Employment Agency deal with all matters relating to Investors in People. This national network of over one hundred organisations, together with over 300 Industry Training Organisations in the UK are able to help any employing organisation with advice tailored to particular needs.

Assessment is a rigorous, Quality assured process as befits a national Standard. The work is carried out by approved assessors working for Investors in People UK, Investors in People Scotland, the Training and Employment Agency and the Training and Enterprise Councils of England and Wales. The size and complexity of an organisation is a factor in which options will be open to an organisation being assessed.

To end where this chapter started, investing in people for improving Quality certainly isn't a lottery. The clear sense of the business case makes it a surefire winner. Organisations striving to improve quality need to place their stakes by taking the first essential step on the journey now – their competitors certainly are.

Full details of Investors in People are available from Training and Enterprise Councils, Local Enterprise Companies, the Training Agency or Industry Training Organisations. In case of difficulty contact Investors in People UK on 0171 467 1900.

VII

Managing Variation – An Integrated Approach To Process Management

Terry Twine & Graham Salisbury
Xyratex

VARIATION permeates the world. It is the lifeblood of Darwin's Theory of Evolution. Life would be very mundane without the variation within it which makes everyone and everything different. However it is this very same variation within processes which creates quality problems. A world with no variation would lead to processes with constant outputs, in manufacturing terms either all defective or all good. It is the use of statistics to manage and control variation which provides the basis for a management by fact environment within a business. This is best summarised by the following:

"If you remove the source of variability from any process you make it more predictable and therefore more controllable....

.... You can use this to eliminate waste and decay - the key is to improve process capability"

– Myron Tribus – Germ Theory of Management

It is the impact of variation which has tied together the world's of statistics and Quality throughout their respective evolutions. In the same way that Quality thinking has developed from inspecting process outputs to the TQM philosophy of looking at all aspects of a process, the statistical techniques which are used have progressed from sampling plans to methods aiding process control, evaluation and design. The understanding that there is a substantial advantage to designing in quality rather than inspecting it in has been paramount in shaping the application of statistical techniques. This is best summed up by the application of the law of levers shown below, which also includes Quality and statistical tools aligned with the different main themes.

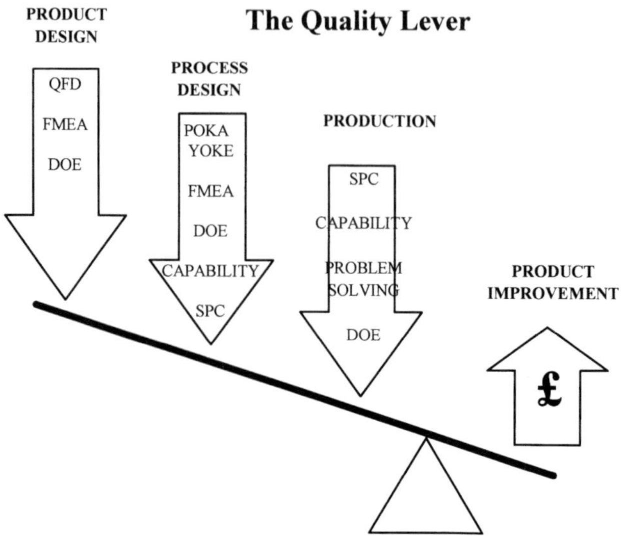

Our belief is that there are a number of guiding principles with respect to quantitative techniques which should be used as a framework for a business excellence culture. The following list, which is by no means all encompassing provides examples with respect to the statistical techniques associated with a TQM philosophy:

1) Customer requirements translated into product and process controls using QFD and FMEA.
2) All measurement processes to be qualified using gauge and attribute R&R studies.
3) Process control (SPC) built into processes from day one.
4) Capability of all key product and process parameters assessed by Cpk analysis.
5) Product and process qualification plans to include design of experiment methods (DOE) to assess product and process robustness.
6) Process changes assessed for effectiveness using designed tests for confidence and significance.
7) Problem solving – start the clock when problem raised implement parallel path methodology.

Each of these themes is developed further in the remainder of this article.

1) Quality Function Deployment and Failure Mode Effects Analysis

The start point for a rational Quality approach must be the understanding of those elements of a product or service which are required by the customer. The next step is then for the supplier business to use it s knowledge to design and develop products and processes which totally satisfy those customer requirements. Quality Function Deployment (QFD), is a method which enables the translation of customer needs (WHAT) into product design, process design, and associated control systems (HOW). The links between these features are developed through a succession of matrices. At the top level is a matrix which explores the relationship between the customer requirements and the design features which are believed will result in the customer needs set being realised. The method brings out the relative importance of each design feature and its link with each of the customer requirements. As a by-product it establishes whether the design features provide a sufficient set of actions to cover the customer requirements, and also whether any of the planned design features are redundant in that they have no link to any expressed customer need! More detailed examination at the lower levels of the matrix structure show which features of a process are important in that they link with a key design feature. At a still lower level of examination, the particular process control

Failure Modes			Analysis			Priority
Failure Mode	Effect	Cause	Occurence	Severity	Detectability	Risk
F1			1	4	10	40
F2			4	1	3	12
F3			8	10	2	160
F4			1	2	4	8
F5			8	2	2	32
F6			6	8	4	192

Customer Requirements (WHAT)	Design Features / Actions (HOW)						
	D1	D2	D3	D4	D5	D6	D7
C1	3			9			9
C2		3			1		
C3	5	1		9			5
C4			9				
C5			1			3	3
C6	9		3	5	3		
C7				5			3
C8	1				5	1	
Relative Importance	18	4	13	28	9	4	20

method may be documented. The basic matrix structure used in a QFD can be augmented with other information if needed. Typically this can include a competitive assessment against the customer requirements set and cost or technical difficulty.

Failure Mode Effects Analysis(FMEA), is a method which can be applied to examine either a product or process for the ways in which it could potentially fail, normally by looking at each characteristic of a product or each stage in a process. It then seeks to establish the effect of each mode of failure. The method is a true problem prevention approach in that it attempts to identify potential problem areas, thereby giving opportunity for early correction. Its application potential is exceptionally wide since its basic structure is sufficiently general to be applied to products, services or systems. The criteria against which each potential failure mode must be assessed are:

a) Criticality or magnitude of impact (rated on a scale 1 to 10)
b) Likelihood of occurring (rated on a scale of 1 to 10)
c) Possibility of detection (rated on a scale of 1 to 10)

These ratings are then combined (typically multiplied) to give a rating for each potential failure mode. Examination of this analysis enables an understanding of those failure modes which must be eliminated from the design, or a safety system installed to minimise their impact. This provides a powerful proactive tool for prioritising the work which must be carried out to assure a product or process rather than reacting to failure as it occurs.

2) Measurement System Analysis

In the same way that variation invades all processes, so it is unfortunately a feature of the measurement process itself. If we are going to make important decisions on the goodness of a product or process, we had better make sure that the variation present in the measurement process itself is understood. This is achieved through running a gauge R&R study on samples of product which span the specification on the features to be tested. The study is structured so that the key elements of repeatability and reproducibility are evaluated. Repeatability measures the variation when the same article is measured by the same person/equipment combination. Reproducibility measures the variation when different people and/or different examples of the same measurement equipment are used. The overall measurement system variation is obtained as a combination of these two measures. The total variation of the measurement system is contrasted against the overall specification for a feature and quoted as a percentage. A rule of thumb figure is that a good measurement system will consume no more than 10 per cent of the feature specification range. Values much in excess of this indicate that quality improvement may need to start with the measurement system itself!

The above approach is generally applicable. If the objective is to assess a measurement system which utilises subjective assessment, i.e. physical sample comparisons, comparisons against a picture, some of the detail of the above needs changing. If our experience holds true generally, subjective features assessment is often a 'poor relation' in measurement system analysis, but it does contribute significantly to overall measurement uncertainty. It must be covered.

3) Statistical Process Control

Statistical Process Control (SPC) is an approach which seeks to assess whether measurements made on a process can demonstrate that the process itself is stable, or 'In Control'. The hypothesis upon which SPC is based is that controlling the process which creates a product enables the product itself to be controlled proactively. To control a process requires recognition that all processes exhibit variation, but the purpose of SPC is to distinguish between that variation which is in effect random, and that variation which is non-random. Random variation is a manifestation of the process itself, caused by very small but non-identifiable changes in the elements which make up a process. A process showing only random variation is said to be demonstrating a 'common cause system', and is 'stable' or 'In Control'. Conversely, a process which is demonstrating a non-random pattern is said to be unstable or 'out of control' where 'special causes' are said to be operating. This is just another way of saying that something out of the ordinary has occurred; the effect is sufficiently large that it cannot be labelled as a random event. The trick now is to identify the cause and eliminate it from the process.

The purpose of SPC is to categorise each process as above and provide the clues to enable a meaningful improvement activity to commence. The charts below show examples of random and non-random patterns and the imposition of SPC control lines which enable the judgement of which is which to be made. This can be of tremendous benefit, since SPC gives a process owner some positive criteria for judging process behaviour, thereby avoiding the errors, false trails, over-control and cost which can arise if left to personal or subjective assessment. SPC is a key feature of a strategy to firstly measure variation and then systematically reduce it.

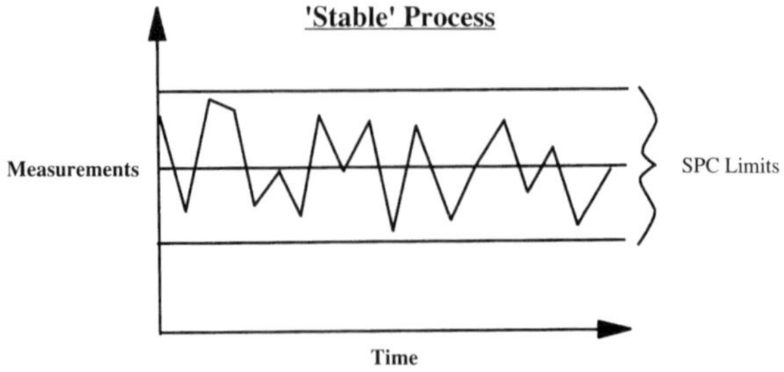

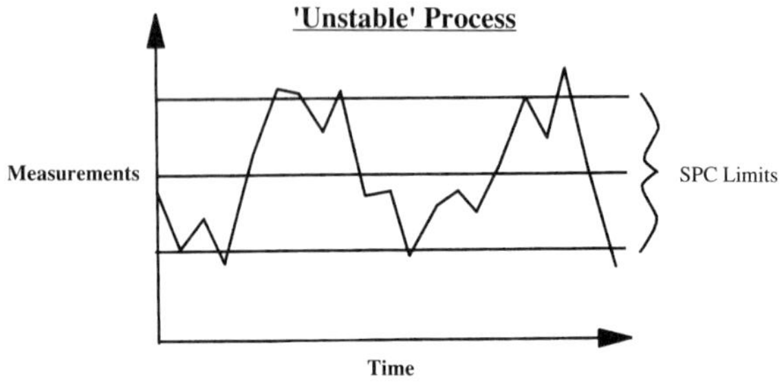

4) Capability Analysis

One of the key requirements of any process must be its ability to deliver a good performance on each of its key characteristics, which matches or exceeds the requirements of the customer. The aim should be that the output of a process is closely distributed around the target performance, rather than just meeting specifications. The method used to combine deviation from the target, process variation and the specification width, is called capability analysis. Firstly, the variation present in the process is established by measuring several samples of its output on the key characteristics. An index of goodness is computed which is a ratio of the variation present in the output of a process, and the specification requirement or tolerance. The main index of goodness Cpk, is typically required to be in excess of 1.33, but this figure is dependent on the characteristic and the sector of business involved. To give some indication of the meaning behind this number, a process with a Cpk of 1.33 will, if the process variation can be represented by a Normal Distribution, be delivering a defect level of around 3 parts per million. To enable a meaningful capability statement to be made, it is essential that the process has firstly been assessed as being 'stable', through SPC. Processes which do not achieve the required Cpk value need examining to establish those features of the process which cause the excessive variation in the measurements.

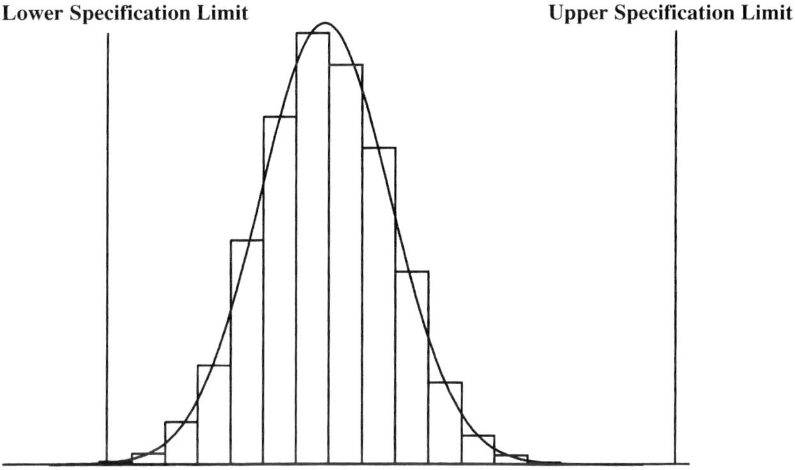

5) Design of Experiments

The title gives the impression that these ideas are surely the province of the scientist, since they above all others are involved in experimentation. That would be a big mistake!

The methods under the general heading of 'Design of Experiments' (DOE), are potentially applicable to areas of a business as diverse as from engineering to marketing, and from manufacturing to personnel. Currently the main applications of DOE tend to be in the fields of engineering and manufacturing, both as a design tool and as a method for solving process problems.

The basic aim of DOE is to seek to understand which of several features of a design or process are important in delivering the performance required on the key characteristics. It is also a very efficient way of gaining important knowledge about a process. The basic approach taken is to quite deliberately change the features of the design or process so that each feature is assessed at least at a 'low' level and 'high' level. The key here though, is that unlike the scientific method which changes one thing at a time and keeps everything else constant, in DOE many features are changed within the same experiment. A typical experiment may result in 8 or 16 separate 'trials' being performed, where each trial has a different configuration of 'high' and 'low' levels of the design or process features. The end result of such an approach is to give a measure of how each feature impacts both the mean and the variation of the key characteristics, as well as an understanding of interaction effects between features. The result is an understanding of which features are important, which 'level' setting for each feature is 'optimum', and some very useful information which enables cost efficient settings to be made on each feature. The approach also gives knowledge on design and process robustness, since it gives information on the sensitivity of the key characteristic to the features in the experiment. To gain a similar level of knowledge from traditional methods using the change one factor at a time approach would require a much greater amount of experimentation. Hence it has been shown that DOE methods are a very cost effective way of gaining knowledge and solving problems which are multi-faceted.

Experimental Matrix

	Temp	Pressure	Time	Day	Tool
1	-	-	-	-	-
2	-	-	+	+	-
3	-	+	-	+	+
4	-	+	+	-	+
5	+	-	-	+	+
6	+	-	+	-	+
7	+	+	-	-	-
8	+	+	+	+	-

Mean Response Plot

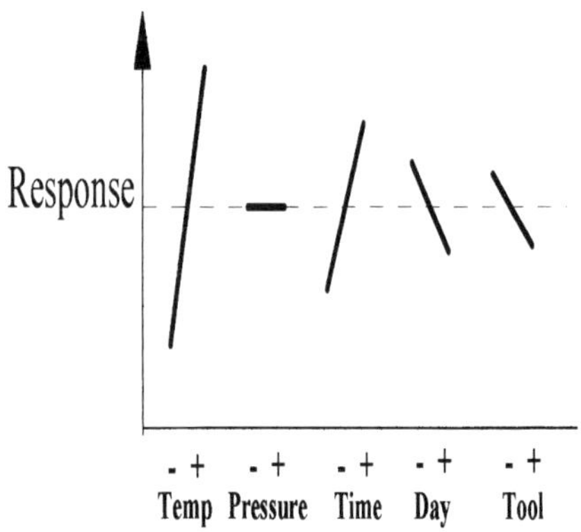

6) Change Management

It is very rare for a process to remain unchanged for its life. Change is the order of the day for modern processes, due to the need to continually seek better approaches which result in lower cost or more efficient methods. Changes to a process can take many forms such as; a new vendor for a part, a new approach to advertising, a different software package or a new application form to name just a few. However, whatever the nature of the change, some approach is necessary to establish whether the changed process is still capable of delivering , or improving on, the performance of its predecessor. Change management enables this to be judged by calling for a specific examination of both the 'old' process and the 'new' process performances, so that a true assessment can be made. The key features of this are the 'significant difference' which the examination is to pick up and the confidence required for the hypothesis, i.e. I need to be 95 per cent confident that my process performance will not deteriorate by more than 2 per cent. This then enables the required sample size to be determined for both processes.

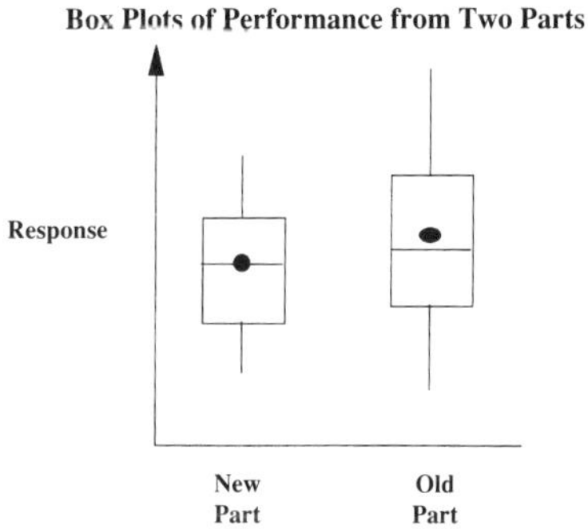

7) **Problem Management**

In spite of all the best attempts by a business to prevent problems from occurring on the product of its processes, business reality is that problems will occur. What becomes key is the ability of the business to solve the problem, and quickly, since depending on the product and market place, time lost here can mean significant customer dissatisfaction and lost money. Much energy is typically expended in seeking the 'crucial' answer to the problem, and a high profile 'hypothesis' of the cause of the problem will be examined and judged for it's association with the problem. Hopefully this 'hypothesis' proves to be the cause of the problem, and in many cases it is true that the knowledge contained in a business does result in the problem being solved in this way. However, there are many situations where the original 'hypothesis' proves not to be the cause of the problem. It is very tempting to embark on another exploration of the next 'hypothesis' to evaluate. If that proves to be unsuccessful, a third hypothesis is explored and so on. The problem with this approach is that in the meantime, time is marching on and that means money. A more efficient way of approaching this is to allow the exploration of the first hypothesis, but if this is unsuccessful, further examination is made based on joining all other hypotheses together into one examination or experiment, in a DOE study. The end result of this approach is a more effective problem management activity, since the end result will be problems solved more quickly.

Conclusions/Summary:

We have discussed a number of statistical quality techniques which we believe provide a solid basis for a fact based approach to managing the product or process lifecycle. This has led to the development of the framework for a business excellence culture shown on the first page. It can be seen that each technique compliments the others to provide a framework for improving decision making. We believe that the understanding and management of variation through quantitative techniques can only lead to improved services and products.

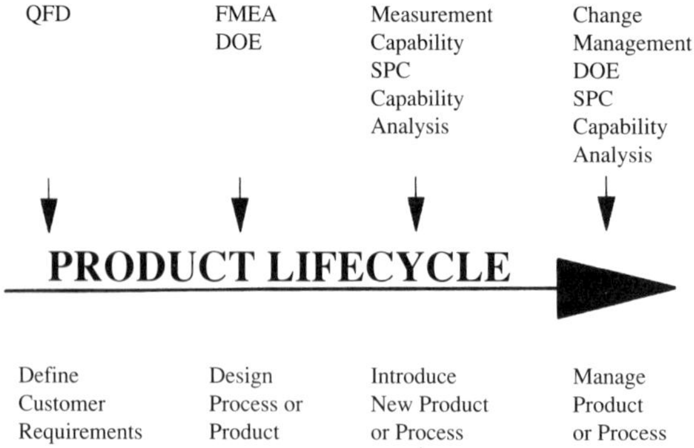

To finish we will leave you with a set of questions to ask of your products and processes:

- Which of your processes have statistical methods built into their design and operation?
- Are you using QFD to cascade customer requirements into your subsequent process activity?
- Have you implemented methods such as FMEA which allow the potential failure points in a process to be understood at process development?

- Have you performed a measurement analysis to quantify variation in the measurement system?
- Have you implemented SPC on your output measures to establish process stability?
- Do you know the capability of your process and can you express it as a Cpk value?
- Do you use DOE methods to help to understand and manage the critical levers in the process?
- Do you assess the impact of change through confidence and significance methods?
- Are the full complement of tools understood and used by staff involved in process improvement?

Terry Twine is the advisory statistician for Xyratex, a £280 million revenue UK owned company, specialising in the manufacturing of computor disk drives, storage systems, test systems for disk drives, communication controllers and sells Information Technology consultancy. His role is one of researching best statistical and quality practices and developing a consulting, education and implementation strategy to ensure that 'best of breed' practices are embedded into the fabric of the business. The widening definition of 'quality' as being synonomous with 'business excellence' has widened the field of application to include business support processes ie. marketing, finance, personnel etc. Terry's previous experience has been 16 years in the car manufacturing industry, again implementing statistical practices into supply and manufacturing processes. Terry is a Fellow of the Royal Statistical Society.

Graham Salisbury BSc, MSc(Eng) works in the Quality & Customer Services department at Xyratex. In 1992, Graham completed his MSc(Eng) at Liverpool University whilst working with Convatec Ltd developing a method for process optimisation. He was awarded a distinction for this work and the GEC prize for the year's most outstanding student. Following this he joined Portsmouth University to work with IBM(Havant) on a collaborative research project looking at raising the effective utilisation of statistical techniques. He is currently preparing his doctoral thesis based upon this work. Since 1994, Graham has worked full time at Xyratex supporting the application of statistical techniques throughout the company, whilst working to embed the techniques into the companies business processes. Graham is also a Fellow of the Royal Statistical Society

VIII

Using Consultants to Manage Change

Hayden J Magill
I.A.S. Management Services

WHAT we must understand first of all is that change is the natural order of things; not to change goes against nature. Change for all of us on a daily basis is a way of life – as individuals, employees, companies, countries and the planet itself, i.e. environmental damage, growing older, learning. If we look now at the title of the chapter – what are the keywords within it? I identify three:
1. CONSULTANTS 2. MANAGE 3. CHANGE:

1. CONSULTANTS

Now a consultant, for the main part, is an expert and as some have said, "an expert is a man who has made all the mistakes which can be made in a very narrow field". But as we all know, mistakes are the opportunities of life that you learn from and base changes and improvements upon.

2. MANAGE

In the dictionary this is defined as, "organise, regulate, be in charge of a business, a person's career, succeed and achieving", which is exactly what we want if we're going to introduce change.

3. CHANGE

Change then, is defined as the act or instance of making or becoming different – alteration or modification. In the case of a company this can be seen as the vision of where the company wishes to be, from the position which it is currently in. So the change to be brought about is the change in its current circumstances to the one of its vision.

Bringing about change of any type in a small, medium or large business can be a complex and difficult task. With the change process, political behaviour between staff frequently becomes more intense and the grapevine is usually very much alive and blooming. Within the change process, policies, procedures, work instructions, and organisational structure usually need to be altered. Staff are presented with the fact that the old ways, which include their familiar jobs, tasks, roles and procedures are no longer applicable. In many cases, people are familiar with their role within a company based on their job title and description. Whether the quality manager, sales manager, bought-ledger clerk, process operator, or floor-sweeper each person will play a role which fits their particular job title and they work within that framework because they understand where their position fits within the organisation. As a result of this people frequently do not maximise their full potential either as an individual or as a member of a team. So, when the change process is under way individuals and teams need to be motivated to continue to perform despite possible turbulence resulting from change.

The process of effectively implementing change has long been a topic that directors and managers have pondered how best to achieve. One of the best ways is to employ a consultant – an outside expert who has done this type of work before, not necessarily within your sector, but who understands the principles and the problems you may encounter during the implementation of your company vision, i.e. the change process of moving from your current position to where you want to be.

One of the major advantages of using an external expert, who may over time become a part-time member of your management team, is that they are not established within your organisation in any particular role. Take the quality manager, for example. Staff members have dealt with him on an ongoing basis and they think they know everything that is written in 'that particular book'. This is where the consultant can be a positive addition to the company because he is perceived as an outside agency, providing a fresh perspective to your company. If he has the right experience he will be able to quickly sum up your current situation and identify potential barriers to the change process.

As a consultant, I have found that most change programmes don't work because the theory they are based on is fundamentally flawed. The most common belief in change programmes is that the place to begin the process is with the knowledge and attitudes of individuals within the company. If you change those attitudes through training, changing roles, redefining duties and responsibilities, or improving communications this leads to changes in the individual behaviour of people within the organisation. These changes repeated by the different people within the company will result in organisational change. Once the people are re-invented through changes in their behaviour, changes within the organisation will surely follow. Well guess what? It normally doesn't – this 'bottom' or 'middle-up' approach fails because the framework within which the people are working doesn't change to coincide with these re-inventions of their role, and consequently the change situation fails as well. In fact, individual behaviour within an organisation is fundamentally shaped by the roles that people play in it – as I said to you earlier; job titles, etc. create boundaries which people tend to work within. The most effective way to change the behaviour of people within the organisation is to put people into a new organisational framework which in fact imposes new roles, responsibilities and relationships with others on them. In other words, they must react to this situation and in a sense it forces new attitudes and behaviours on everyone within the company.

Why then use a consultant? We believe there are many times when engaging outside help will be the right approach.

- Engaging a consultant is a good way of drawing on a larger pool of expertise and bringing a high level of specialist skill to bear on the specific change problem without adding significantly to payroll costs.
- The consultant's fresh pair of eyes and independent view of your current status and your vision, may be what you need.
- Working with your senior management team or a steering committee, a consultant can help to spread the message and make people understand some of the change issues that are going to occur. Obviously, selection of people on this team is a critical issue as they need to be motivated to be able to respond to change and be champions within their own department or section.
- The skills and knowledge within your company may not be extensive enough to deal with the total change issue – especially when working with new technology so a consultant's help could be vital to successfully introducing change.
- You and your staff may be so busy running the company that you do not have the necessary understanding or time to analyse the change problem in detail and plan a solution.

Consultants are most effective when they come into your organisation as a facilitator and provide 'on the job' training. It is fine for the consultant to actually analyse a problem at any particular time but it is even more useful if, he can show and teach someone else within the organisation that same skill. This reduces dependency on the consultant and increases the long term benefit to the organisation.

There are many ways of finding suitable consultants – such as *Yellow Pages* and various brokerage schemes but one of the best ways is personal recommendation or reference from another company. You can also find advertisements in trade journals and your trade association may be able to mention particular names and addresses. Other sources of information could be your local Chamber of Commerce, TEC or Business Link.

How then do you go about choosing the right consultancy? Today, one of the minimum requirements of any consultancy practice is that it be accredited to the International Quality Standard ISO 9001: 1994. Another qualification that a practice should have is the Investor in People award because it shows that its staff are being continually developed to meet the practice and client needs. In many ways, choosing a consultant is similar to the process you should be going through when you recruit any senior member of staff. The first step is to determine what you want them to do by defining your requirements.

- Write out the problem that exists within the company and any reasons why you cannot deal with it yourself in-house.
- What role do you want the consultant to play? A counsellor, mentor, expert adviser, project manager, facilitator or trainer, because these different roles will influence the consultant's approach.
- What does the company consider to be a successful outcome of this change project?
- Define a clear statement of your objectives which may be to increase profits, reduce cost of Quality figures, improve communications, etc. Try to devise a sensible list and then put some specific targets against the items on the list.

A good consultant will help the client perceive, understand and act upon change issues in their organisation. It is unfortunate that many managers often do not know what is wrong with their organisation and need the consultant's help to diagnose where problems exist. The approach should identify what needs to be improved. This can be done by using a Quality planning approach to investigate company activity which represents good business practice and that which does not. At this stage the consultant should work with staff members so they can learn to identify the problems and be actively involved in creating suitable solutions. The consultant should not try to enforce a teacher-pupil relationship but rather build an effective coaching relationship on which they can work jointly to come up with a synergistic solution. Major changes generated could be:

- Improved communication and teamwork.
- Roles and functions of people within the organisation made more effective.
- Group problem solving and decision making.
- Leadership responsibility and authority.
- Inter-group/team cooperation and friendly competition.
- Organisational roles of interaction developed.

A good consultant has the tools and the ability to focus on the specific problem – to define it, to understand what needs to be done and know who else to involve in the problem's solution. To be successful the consultant has to build peoples' commitment and involvement in the change process by gaining acceptance for the steps involved in achieving and implementing the company's agreed vision. As the project continues the original vision and objectives may be subject to change because of information brought to light during the process or the development of process and organisational improvements. This can be a positive process where the initial vision is enhanced through team input thus earning a wider basis of acceptance within the organisation.

With this overall approach to change we are trying to 'unfreeze' people's attitudes and behaviour, 'unfreeze' the structure of the company – making it fluid. Once it is decided by all what the new duties and roles will be and what the changes involve, we then want to 're-freeze' it. What is fundamentally important is that there should be flexibility within this new vision, so that change and continuous improvement are integral to striving, surviving and improving in today's market place. The consultant's role is to gather facts and help create conditions within the company to allow staff to make informed decisions to which they are committed.

Continuous feedback is vital to the change process. Assumptions and conclusions need to be tested to prevent the consultant and company acting upon information which is invalid or out of date. Another factor which may jeopardise the change process is if a company's focus is too narrow, concentrating on only one or two issues such as communication, teamwork or training. The problem is that even if you make improvements in some of these areas they will not necessarily have a major impact on the company. A company can issue a mission or a vision statement about where it is going or about teamwork but it doesn't necessarily mean that staff will know how to form teams, how they function or how to improve communication and co-ordination in the company – they need someone to show them. Again, another role for the consultant.

A company may reorganise its corporate structure but if it doesn't provide its people with the necessary understanding and skills, the new structure won't work. Similarly, training programmes - particularly ones that are 'en vogue' today - such as those based around NVQ qualifications, clearly target competence but rarely do they change the co-ordination within a company. I have found that training of staff can lead to increased frustration when they return to their old roles within the company and find that their new skills are going to be unused. Employees then end up seeing training as a waste of time which can undermine whatever commitment exists to the change programme.

Summing up then on this issue, it is important that these activities are co-ordinated in the correct context and a suitable training plan is devised for your company's needs. The primary target for change should be behaviour; attitudes and ideas are really secondary. Individual knowledge, attitudes and beliefs are shaped within the company by recurring patterns of interaction. When using consultants to manage change, we must follow some sort of a sequence of steps because activities such as training commenced at the wrong time can be counter-productive.

When using a consultant to assist you in the management of change, it is important that you know they will not necessarily report what you want to hear but present uncomfortable facts about your current status - so don't 'shoot the messenger'. It is important to realise that the consultant will bring his own values to the task so you should define these values early in the process. You want him there to help you manage the change process, not decide how he wants to see your company run. So, how should conflicts between the consultant and the company be handled? Before agreeing a project with a consultant, it is important to ask how they will approach your particular situation so you can gauge how compatible they are with your organisation. Most consultants bring a 'toolbox' of change techniques with them but be careful that you are not paying for something that you don't really need. Be wary of consultants who attempt to force a solution upon you because they prefer a particular approach. For instance, a consultant who is committed to an appraisal or maintenance system may find it hard to avoid recommending the installation of such a system. If the change involves computer hardware or software, the consultant may tend to favour a particular software package or hardware company which may ultimately not be suited to your needs.

As we all know with change, or with anything in life, there is usually more than one way of achieving a particular result and the route by which the vision is reached should be clearly be stated in terms of management choices. The consultant should examine how to introduce each approach and indicate the implications of choosing a particular approach so that agreement can be reached between the parties.

The consultant needs to justify each recommendation and should recommend changes based on evidence which can be evaluated by the management team. In the final analysis it is fundamental to the successful introduction of any change process aided by a consultant that the company selects and controls the system adopted – not the other way around. This approach should then deliver positive benefits to the company in terms of effectiveness, self-esteem and morale throughout the change situation.

Hayden J. Magill is a consultant with I.A.S Management Services, one of the leading specialists in the field of Management Consultancy working with many clients in the service and manufacturing sectors. He is a qualified Lead Assessor of Quality Management Systems (Lloyds QA) and a Field Officer for BSI Quality Assurance covering service, textile and manufacturing disciplines. I.A.S gained ISO9000 registration and TEC Assured status in 1993/4.

PART TWO

The Companies

left to right: Neil Crossthwaite (Managing Director – TNT Logistics), Bill Hanley (Deputy Managing Director – TNT Express UK Ltd), Alan Jones (Managing Director – TNT Express UK Ltd), Steve Doig (Group Marketing Director), Tom Bell (Managing Director – TNT Express Delivery Services UK Ltd), David Hanley (Personnel Director – TNT Express UK Ltd), John Howe (Divisional Director – TNT Newsfast)

1

The Right Attitude – First Time, Every Time

— TNT Express (UK) Limited —

IN the express parcels industry where you are only as good as your last delivery the key service quality factor from a customer's point of view is on-time delivery. On-time delivery is a particularly harsh measure as it takes no account of cause or culpability of non-conformance. However punctual performance is a realistic expectation because at the end of the day all the customer wants to know is that his or her parcel will be safely delivered on time.

A simple enough request from an individual customer but when translated to the impressive volumes TNT deals with each week you realise the magnitude of the logistics 'miracle' created by the TNT team. TNT processes two million parcels each week and has more than one hundred thousand active customer accounts. Over seventy thousand telephone calls are made and received every week. The volumes are even more astonishing when put in the context of the no-screening telephone policy of the company which allows callers, both internally and externally, to directly reach the person with whom they want to speak.

TNT has clearly met the challenge of an extremely demanding market place and has received numerous customer endorsements which include the following testimonials:

"Our first business together came through the movement of urgent parts for customers' vehicles that were immobilised. Today that service continues with the best and most inclusive customer service level on offer nationwide of any UK operator... We value the TNT contract for its partnership, its commitment to the values of Customer Comes First, the dedication of all the staff, the constant high service levels, the desire to continually improve, and not least the high spirit, team work and regular smile that puts us all at the very leading edge of logistics" – Volkswagen Group United Kingdom Limited.

"Your proactive approach to the constantly changing needs of our business has been and continues to be second to none with innovative solutions in terms of operating systems, fleet management and environmental considerations." – Lever industrial.

"... you have continuously demonstrated a pro-active approach and throughout our relationship your people have proposed numerous innovations which have helped us reduce our distribution costs. Your staff are always enthusiastic and the TNT make-it-happen mentality helps me sell more newspapers." – Rupert Murdoch, The News Corporation Limited.

TNT has become the carrier of first choice and one of the nation's premier companies. As you delve further into the organisation you soon realise that every single member of staff, regardless of position, shares the same vision and that certain indefinable pizzazz which seems innate in people driving towards a common goal.

Alan Jones, Managing Director of TNT UK says "the company is a specialist in time-sensitive distribution handling an enormous range of products which include almost everything from urgent spare parts, live news, computers and clothing to food and drink. Our market share continues to grow and we have more than trebled our business in the last five years. We have built an outstanding reputation for reliability and have an extensive list of blue chip clients drawn from every sector of the British business community."

Bill Hanley, Deputy Managing Director and Chief Operating Officer attributes the success of the company to an outstanding service ethic. "Our quality service is delivered by a team of more than eight thousand employees who share a passion for getting the job done right first time, every time. It's all about people working together in a climate which fosters success and achievement of best in class performance."

Not surprisingly the TNT Quality programme is about teamwork and requires the whole-hearted commitment and enthusiasm of everyone in the company.

"We have always worked within the limits of our core business which is to provide time-sensitive door-to-door delivery services and supply chain solutions. Our innovations have come from creating new ideas in transport and then harnessing the dynamism and enthusiasm of our people to turn the imagination into reality", according to Alan Jones.

Bill Hanley says "We believe in quality. Our customers demand continuous improvement from us and we know quality is a winning formula for success."

The company knows that quality cannot be divorced from the day-to-day running of the business. Quality must be part and parcel of the millions of transactions which TNT UK performs each week. A focus on customer satisfaction, continuous improvement and visible recognition of individual and team performances is a winning formula.

TNT is a dynamic international organisation with a history of prolific growth in the UK. The TNT Group started as a one-man business in 1946 when Ken Thomas began transport operations with just one truck in Australia. The UK operation was conceived in 1978 when TNT purchased Inter County Express an extremely successful express parcels company employing five hundred staff. In the period to 1996 revenue and profits have increased seventyfold purely through organic growth.

TNT UK has three principal trading divisions – each of which is distinct in terms of the services provided and the nature of the customer relationships. Despite the differences extremely high standards of customer care permeate all the divisions of the company.

The largest division is the express industry market leader, TNT Express Delivery Services which offers a unique range of on demand nationwide door-to-door same-day and overnight delivery services.

TNT Logistics provides specialist exclusive use warehousing and distribution solutions for an extensive portfolio of blue chip companies. The TNT Logistics client list is as diverse as the TNT Express Delivery Services customers are numerous and includes Rover, Lever Industrial, BT, Ford, British Gas, Cow & Gate Nutricia, Volkswagen Audi Group, Victoria Wine, Shell and Rank Xerox.

TNT Newsfast is the leading carrier of national newspapers and magazines. Contracts are held by TNT Newsfast to carry more than one thousand magazine titles which is over 50 per cent of the consumer magazine market. The company also transports more than half of all national newspapers published in the United Kingdom including *The Times, Financial Times, Daily Telegraph, Sun* and *Sport.* In total TNT Newsfast carries almost twenty thousand tonnes a week of newspapers and magazines and consistently achieves a virtually perfect on-time delivery performance.

This company will go to any lengths to ensure on-time delivery. With the precision of air traffic control at any international airport the TNT depot at Atherstone processes at least 150 trailers every night. Each trailer is moved at least four times within the confines of the yard making an impressive six hundred trailer movements in the hours of darkness at this vital nerve centre of the TNT operation.

"Our people have the 'must-get-through' attitude and are empowered to make decisions on the spot. For example my first job each morning is to call Stan Clarke, Depot Manager at the Atherstone Hub to see what has occurred during the critical overnight sort. One night Stan had chartered a Boeing 707 aircraft to provide additional capacity to Northern Ireland because the ferries had gone on strike" recounts Tom Bell Managing Director TNT Express Delivery Services.

"The key is to give employees the responsibility and authority to deal with any situation because if we promise something to a customer we have to deliver – we are selling peace of mind" says Tom Bell.

According to Alan Jones "The real quality managers in our business are all of our people. Each and everyone of our employees is totally responsible for quality. And that approach has made us the market leader in our specialist field of time sensitive delivery."

John Howe, Divisional Director of TNT Newsfast reinforces the importance of being able to react to a situation in a timely manner without procedural constraints: "When we were preparing to obtain BS5750 certification we tightened up our systems and further streamlined our activities. You can't spend ten minutes filling out a form because you want to do something – it has to happen there and then. But five years on the daily measurement processes serve as a valuable monitor of our activity. The very fact that we have BS5750 and the systems supporting our accreditation in place means that we are more efficient. We are for example able to account for actions taken in stressful situations the details of which could easily be forgotten. Our relentless pursuit of improvement in turn makes us more cost effective."

Employees are encouraged to put forward improvement ideas each of which is acknowledged individually and discussed directly with management. One of the most innovative improvements enacted was the appropriately named 'Gizmo' system devised by Peter May and his colleagues in the TNT Northern Region. Peter and his team created the concepts and developed the software in-house for the invention. The Gizmo system has produced significant commercial benefits for both customers and the company by automating parcel check weighing and routing procedures.

After being trialled at pilot depots, Gizmo is now used throughout the TNT Express Delivery Services network to consolidate what were once several distinct manual processes of weighing parcels, checking actual against declared weights, routeing to delivery depots and labelling parcels for onward transmission. This get-it-right-first-time combination of dedicated equipment and customised software has streamlined parcel handling and reduced the incidence of error.

Celebration, recognition and reward are key words at TNT and not without reason – TNT is the 1995 European Quality Award Prize Winner; the 1994 winner of the UK Quality Award; the first express parcels and logistics company to be recognised as an Investor in People; and the 1994 winner of the Northern Ireland Quality Award.

"Every piece of paper which passes across the desk of the Managing Director and which shows good performance by any individual in the company is sent to that individual with a hand-written note of thanks and recognition. When TNT won the European Quality Award Prize and the UK Quality Award, letters of congratulation were sent to each and every employee", says Bill Hanley who is responsible for over ten thousand staff throughout Europe.

The foundation for TNT's most recent successes include the winning of ten Motor Transport Awards in the ten years up to 1995 – a record-breaking performance in the industry. One of these Awards is the coveted Haulier of the Year prize won by TNT UK in 1988 after the company pioneered the distribution of national newspapers by road from Wapping. In 1990 TNT UK became the first transport company to secure the British Standard 5750 Part 1 Quality assurance certification. TNT UK was also the only transport company to win awards in the Department of Employment National Training Award competitions in 1992, 1993 and 1995.

The company's emphasis on self improvement for its young employees has resulted in TNT being one of the ten founder members of

The Duke of Edinburgh's Award Charter for Business. The Duke of Edinburgh's Award helps develop drive, initiative, commitment and self confidence in young people. The Award Scheme also builds skills in team working, leadership, problem-solving and decision-making. Alan Jones explains: "We show real care and support for our young employees. We want them to grow and stay with the company. The Duke of Edinburgh's Award is a rewarding way to help equip our young people to face the challenges of modern business life.

In 1996 TNT UK consists of two hundred profit accountable units which include depots, sites, major logistics contracts, territories, divisions and regions. Each unit is headed by a profit accountable manager who encourages his or her team to provide the highest quality of service and in so doing exceed previous best performance.

The individual commitment required to achieve improvement goals is created by continuous interaction and dialogue between all levels of the organisation. For example, TNT conducts annual company management conferences actively involving all management staff including all junior executives. The delegates represent nearly 20 per cent of the company's employees. The theme of every conference is in some way associated with Total Quality and customer service. The main topic at the latest conference in January 1996 was the positive impact of quality on customer retention. All delegates contributed to the task of identifying the critical processes which influence customer loyalty to help define future improvement activities.

TNT views its customer care programmes which are reinforced by an 'Expressing Excellence' training initiative, as key to the company's success. The key objectives of the Expressing Excellence programme are to:

- exceed customer expectations;
- create a clear customer care policy soundly based on customer research;
- successfully communicate and implement new customer care initiatives;
- measure and improve service quality and customer satisfaction

Tom Bell defines customer care in TNT Express Delivery Services as: "Everything we say and everything we do to enable each of us to meet and exceed our customers' expectations." The principles of internal and external customer care activities within TNT include:

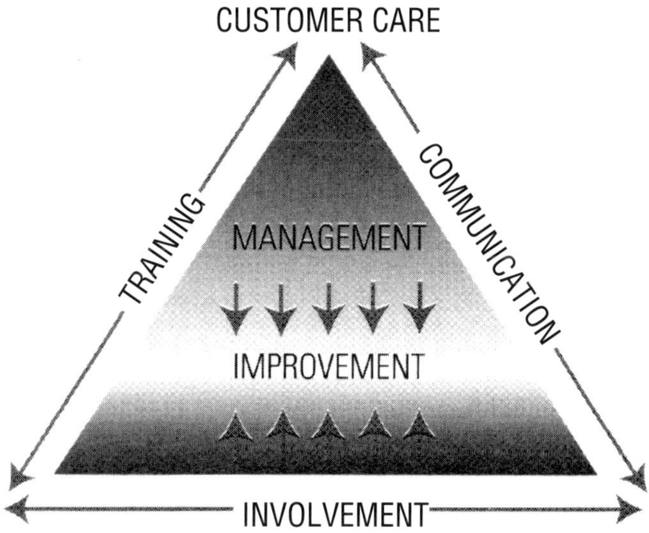

The Philosophy:	Prevention not detection thus avoiding faults in the first place.
The Approach:	Management led as illustrated in Figure 1.
Who:	Everyone in TNT is responsible for Customer Care
The Measure:	By putting more effort into prevention the time and money which is wasted through failure will be reduced and can be made available to meet customer expectations. Waste is anything which adds cost but does not add value.
The Standard:	Right first time and every time

The Expressing Excellence Customer Care training programme focuses on job specific training and has been extended to involve the entire workforce after initial introduction within the company by TNT Express Delivery Services.

Commitment to customer care is discussed at Expressing Excellence training meetings which are held at every company location. The aim of these training events is to continuously improve performance by identifying and correcting gaps between actual performance and the policy commitments. TNT has deliberately avoided Quality jargon because it

TNT Express

Our Commitment to Customer Care.

- We will answer your incoming telephone calls promptly, courteously and within six rings.
- When calling you will always be able to speak directly with the TNT person you ask for, irrespective of seniority and without having to state your name, your company or the reason for your call.
- A team of one field sales person and one telephone sales person dedicated to a defined postcode area will be made personally responsible for the day to day handling of your account. This enables us to establish a sound business relationship and provide you with unparalleled levels of sales and after sales service.
- As a TNT Express customer, you will be contacted on a regular basis at least once every six weeks to ensure that we maintain a close liaison and provide excellence in customer care.
- Should we ever fail to collect your consignment as agreed, we will ensure delivery is made meeting your original criteria wherever possible, at no extra cost to you.
- We pledge to check your collected consignments against their consignment documentation and to verify the number of items, their weights, destination, selected service and postcode. We will then ensure that all your parcels are accurately routed and delivered on time.
- In the unlikely event that we mis-direct one of your parcels, we guarantee to deliver the item direct within the shortest possible time at no extra cost to you.
- We will provide instant access confirmation of delivery information 24 hours a day, 365 days a year via our automatic telephone response system - TNT Tracker. Personal confirmation of delivery is available immediately on request the next working day.
- TNT Express invoicing will always be clear and easily understood. Any query you may have regarding invoicing or accounts will be quickly and efficiently resolved. All enquiries will be responded to immediately.
- Our reputation for safe and secure handling enables us to offer Free Transit Liability cover of up to £15,000 per consignment with confidence, providing extra peace of mind for you.
- In the unlikely event that you have to make a claim, we guarantee that a written response will be forwarded to you within 24 hours and if necessary, a full investigation will be undertaken to resolve any claim.
- We will communicate with you regularly to ensure that you are fully informed of our developments and to seek your opinion on the service we provide, our people and our standards.
- All TNT employees are our ambassadors and they are trained to be efficient, helpful and courteous at all times. Despite the rarity of complaints, we guarantee that should you ever complain about the behaviour, attitude or road manner of any TNT person, the issue will be taken up and we will reply to you within 24 hours.

CUSTOMER CARE AWARD WINNER

Tom Bell,
Managing Director, TNT Express Delivery Services.

believes this creates a barrier which prevents the seamless integration of quality and continuous improvement into day-to-day operations.

The culture of the organisation is one of active involvement at all levels and while formal meetings are established to discuss Quality issues management can be approached at any time to discuss improvement ideas. Each employee is responsible for the quality of his or her own performance and also for improving the quality of his or her work.

TNT continuously improves by encouraging competition. Teams try to beat their own previous best results and attempt to out-perform other teams within the company. Performance is charted on highly visible display boards and awards are presented to the best achievers.

Bonus schemes provide recognition and reward for consistent achievement of above target performances. "We think that people winning and striving to beat their previous best is important. The key test in this company is whether each employee feels as though he or she is being stretched to beat their previous best performance" explains David Hanley, Personnel Director.

Benchmarking concentrates employees' attention on the value of the 'get it right first time' principle and reduces costs by avoiding the need for corrective action.

Not only are employees included in the education process but customers are involved through the TNT 'Commitment to Customer Care' document (Figure 2) which is discussed in all sales presentations. Customers know what to expect when they use a TNT service in all areas of customer contact from answering telephone calls to defining how the company will react in the event of service failure.

The nature, but not the quality of customer relationships varies greatly between TNT Logistics and TNT Express Delivery Services. While the latter offers a largely uniform range of services to many thousands of relatively small customers TNT Logistics has a more tailored relationship with a core of thirty-five major clients.

The TNT Logistics business retention rate is something of a benchmark in the industry with over forty contract renewals recorded in the last five years and no customer losses.

TNT Logistics forms a partnership which is characteristically pro-active and tailored to the individual needs of the customer. Working partnerships not only solve logistics and distribution problems but lead to

TNT Logistics taking responsibility for many different aspects of the client's supply chain. Working alongside the client in partnership allows TNT to develop and implement innovative ways to respond to the changing nature of the business. Figure 3 'The Vision' for TNT and BT in partnership provides an example of a supplier partnership.

"It is not the packaging or the presentation that wins us business. We will go the extra mile and demonstrate a desire to win the business. If a

'THE VISION'

TNT AND BT
IN PARTNERSHIP

The 'Vision' empowers our people to work together with commitment and in a spirit of co-operation to ensure its success.

TNT and BT will create and operate a quality business relationship which harnesses the synergy of our Mission Statements, Values, Guilding Principles and Cultures to provide a model for achieving our respective Worldwide Objectives.

Commitment to quality practices within the relationship will deliver measureable benefits in the operation of our business and increased profit for both parties.

The relationship will be both evolutionary and innovative; it will lead to the exploration of further business opportunities and joint activities for the benefit of our customers, employees and shareholders.

Ross Cribb
Deputy Chairman
TNT Limited

Jerry Stockbridge
Regional Director, Asia/Pacific,
British Telecommunications plc
for and on behalf of
Mike Bett
Vice Chairman
British Telecommunications plc

Dated this 3rd day of July 1991

TNT The Worldwide Transportation Group

BT

prospective client makes a comment about any aspect of our performance we will spend hours addressing the problem until it is resolved to the customer's satisfaction", explains Neil Crossthwaite, Managing Director, TNT Logistics.

TNT and Cow & Gate have been logistics partners since 1986. The strength of the relationship can be gauged from the comments of the former General Manager of the Cow & Gate Nutricia Contract, Mr Mike Pryce: "The best compliment anyone could pay me was to say that I work for Cow & Gate rather than TNT – because that means that they couldn't see the join." TNT Logistics trucks typically display the client's livery and TNT staff wear the client's uniforms. In many instances TNT Logistics staff will provide the main interface with the client's customers.

TNT Logistics provides 'exclusive use' warehousing and distribution for Cow & Gate from a purpose-built central warehouse at Warndon, Worcestershire and outbase locations at Stirling, Wigan and Stanwell; By 1991 TNT operated a 20-strong double-shifted vehicle fleet and employed 83 dedicated personnel on behalf of Cow & Gate in the UK.

However, in early 1992 Cow & Gate advised TNT Logistics of an impending change in its market strategy which would involve a shift in manufacturing to higher value, lower volume products. Over a short period of time Cow & Gate indicated that the product volumes being put through the Warndon based distribution system were likely to be significantly reduced resulting in excess distribution and warehousing capacity.

TNT Logistics focused particular attention on ways of reducing distribution costs for Cow & Gate while at the same time preserving the flexibility and service levels which the existing 'exclusive use' fleet then provided.

At that time, TNT Logistics was also conducting discussions with Lada Cars which was looking for an efficient, cost effective system to handle the distribution of aftermarket parts to its 180 UK dealerships.

Demonstrating a willingness to develop new and imaginative solutions TNT Logistics came up with the idea of integrating the Cow & Gate and Lada distribution operations to provide a cost-efficient service for both companies. Instead of reducing the number of Cow & Gate vehicles TNT Logistics suggested maintaining that fleet but using the spare capacity resulting from the former's reduced traffic volumes to carry products for other companies.

The solution involved the delivery of goods on behalf of Cow & Gate, GE Lighting, SKF and Lada contracts using a shared user fleet of vehicles based in TNT's Glasgow, Wigan, Warndon and Stanwell depots.

By adopting the shared-user solution, Cow & Gate reduced its distribution costs by around one-third on a volume throughput reduced by around 25 per cent.

In turn Lada was able to secure nationwide distribution of components to all dealerships whilst achieving a cost reduction of approximately 33 per cent.

The other members of the 'Logistics Club' jointly developed by TNT and its customers have derived similar benefits from the shared-user concept. The success of providing an integrated TNT Logistics shared user network means that many customers who previously had to rely on a dedicated distribution service, can now receive all the benefits offered by a major logistics organisation, but through a more cost effective solution.

Customer relationships distinguish TNT Logistics from its competitors, as Neil Crossthwaite describes: "Whether we win the business or not we revisit every aspect of the sales process with the prospective client. We want to understand their perception of the first time they picked up the phone to TNT and what they thought of each person they met. We need to know what they thought of our presentation and proposal documents. Our focus is continuous improvement so we have to learn what the customer feels about the TNT operational solution and the price we put forward."

The success of the debriefing process in the business development environment has prompted TNT Logistics to apply the process to existing clients. "Relationships with our clients are supported by extensive reporting mechanisms which monitor service levels, costs and health and safety issues. We cannot become complacent. There is no substitute for regular separate face to face client debriefs to help us continuously satisfy the needs of our customers in a changing environment", says Neil Crossthwaite.

"Total quality management is the enabler which has allowed us to respond to rapidly changing market conditions. We have continuously upgraded our services and value for money propositions by removing wasteful processes" says Bill Hanley.

"On-going self assessment against the British and European Quality Foundation business excellence model is helping us identify and correct gaps in our performance. The work involved in entering the UK Quality Award, the Northern Ireland Quality Award and the European Quality Award competitions has stimulated numerous improvements in our business", according to Alan Jones.

"To succeed we have to be better than the rest. Our aim is to widen the differential between what we do and what others do. We have to continuously develop unique business propositions as others copy our innovations", explains Steve Doig, Group Marketing Director.

TNT is an impressive organisation which has successfully maintained the positive attributes of a small company culture based on mutual respect for colleagues and customers. Youth permeates the company and the majority of employees have grown with the business. Alan Jones explains the key to success: "Our biggest strength is our home grown timber. We look for practical people with enthusiasm, commitment and the determination to succeed – people who will perform outstandingly well for our customers."

"Each member of staff is as important as the next person. Everyone is on first-name terms and we are all prepared to roll up our sleeves and get on with the job. Transport is an exciting and demanding industry. And our people enjoy the job and deliver the goods", says Steve Lay, Managing Director, TNT Newfast.

Bill Hanley sums up by saying "TNT is a success story because of our commitment to customer service and that commitment only comes about through people."

"People in our organisation know that if they work hard and produce good results they will be promoted. We passionately believe in the principle of promoting from within and now have eight thousand excellent people to choose from which is an enormous pool of talent."

"We are a young company with lots of youngsters who want progressive careers; they have joined us because they see we are a good outfit."

Alan Jones concludes "Our people have the know-how and we all have the commitment to give the customer the best level of service. We are totally focused on helping the customer and upon further improving our performance."

Body mount to chassis
Land Rover
Solihull

Chassis build up
Land Rover
Solihull

2

Conquering The Automotive Industry

— Rover Group —

COMMITMENT; Open minded teamwork; No second best; Quality image; Utmost honesty; Effective communication; and Respect – these are the most basic tools of Rover's conquest for Quality. CONQUER is not imposed by management but is one of an arsenal of Quality principles developed and used by the people building Rover vehicles.

Despite its recent investment in plant and equipment, the asset Rover most values is its workforce. The new vehicle and production facility at Land Rover Solihull has provided the opportunity to develop the principles of openness, empowerment, improvement and personal development now enshrined in Rover's way of operating.

The first people to work in the new Land Rover facility in Solihull were team leaders. They were trained to carry out all the assembly operations and it was by obtaining this wide degree of knowledge and flexibility that they enhanced the leadership qualities required to lead their own teams when associates were recruited for the main build programmes.

It was these employees who developed the framework of the new culture and working practices, CONQUER, that are accepted by all who work at the new Range Rover plant Figure 1. All members of the team brainstormed to produce a set of values which they believed they should work by as described by Steve Morgan, Technical Support Manager – Assembly, "We said to the people who were going to build the car what sort of atmosphere would you like to build a car in and they came up with CONQUER. It is a live document and when new people join they are encouraged to question it and introduce new things. These principles are

RANGE ROVER
TEAM VALUES
CONQUER

COMMITMENT

No Skulking
Don't stand back and let others do it.
Give full involvement/participation.
Gain involvement from ALL.

Loyalty
Respect for team & individuals.
Respect for leadership.
Pride in the product.
Pride in the team.
Maintain confidentiality.

Punctuality
Always be on time.
Finish on time.
Utilise time fully.
Achieve targets on time.

Support/Backing
Give help when needed/asked.
Unselfishness.
No demarcation.

Lead by Example
Be a role model.
Don't ask others to do what you are not prepared to do yourself.

Flexibility
Be versatile and willing to accept change.
Turn your hand to anything when needed if competant.

Personal Aspirations
Look to improve yourself, personal development.

ONE TEAM OPEN MINDED

Helping
Be prepared to give and receive help.

Teamwork
Support and strive for a common goal.
Have time for others.

No Barriers
Be approachable.
Share knowledge.

Consider Others Opinions
Don't always think that you have the right answer.
Admit when you are wrong.

Consider Every Alternative
Be prepared to share and copy the best practices.

Be Outward Looking
Always have a positive approach.
Be prepared to look and find better ways of doing things.

NO SECOND BEST

Challenging/Questioning
Be willing to give and accept challenges.
Don't stand back when you know it's wrong.

Good Enough Won't Do
No compromises for quality.

Measuring
Knowing where you are and where you need to be.

Do A Quality Job
Practice what you preach.

Set The Standard
Knowing what is acceptable.

Improve The Standard
Suggestions.
Benchmarking.

Continuous Improvement
Looking to improve whats been achieved.
Keeping up with the times.
Don't stand still.

QUALITY IMAGE

Open Door
Be approachable.
Have time for others.
Be willing to help.

Personal Appearance
Wear clean approved workwear.

Workplace Appearance
Keep area clean.
Keep parts identified.
Keep parts in their correct places.
T.P.M.
Keep amenity areas clean.

Professional Approach
Be Supportive.
Know what, when, how and why.

Quality Vehicle
Working to process and improving where necessary.
Identify issues.
R.F.T. build.

Safety Conscious
Always wear safety footwear and safety equipment.
Safety comes first in ALL that we do.

Non Threatening
Be approachable, friendly and welcoming.
Share your knowledge.

UTMOST HONESTY

Be Truthful.
Don't lie, say what is right.
If you don't know say so.

Admit When You Are Wrong
Hold your hand up.
Be accountable for your actions.

Reliability
Have confidence and faith.

Consistency
Treat everyone the same.

Morals
Don't be influenced, stick to your morals.

EFFECTIVE COMMUNICATION

Question & Challenge
Who, what, why, where, when and how.

Inputs
Use brainstorming and cause and effect techniques.

Listening
Give others the opportunity to have an input.

Involvement
At meetings.
Answering questionnaires.
Using skills.

Clarity
Be precise and understandable, both verbally and in writing.
Use visual aids where necessary.

RESPECT

Recognition
Give praise where due.
Give rewards where possible.

Freedom
Trusted to work on ones own initiative.
Give people space to operate.

Sense of Humour
Allow time for humour.
Being able to enjoy work.

LAND ROVER

constantly open to question and improvement. Everybody's number one priority is Quality, honesty, communication and respect. This is what we all practise and preach here."

All Rover's associates are encouraged to get involved with everything from process improvement to work within the community. The people who operate the plants were involved in the design and development phases. For instance, the signage within the Solihull site was developed as a result of discussion group activity initiated by a small group of employees. Prior to the introduction of the new zoning, navigating around the site was described as chaotic. The members of the discussion group collected data internally and from lorry drivers visiting the site to investigate the type of problems that were experienced in finding locations on a site of Solihull's size. The new zoning initiative established various zones and provided more detailed signage and directions. The group was awarded the 1993 UK Michelin award in recognition of their contribution to workplace improvement.

Discussion Groups or Quality Circles were established in 1988 and by the time of their sixth anniversary in July 1994 there were over 200 groups representing a direct involvement on a regular basis by 10 per cent of the workforce at Solihull.

Discussion Groups are formed by individuals who want to make a change. They meet during non-working hours to discuss local issues. People on the shop floor talk with a sense of pride about improvements they have suggested and implemented through discussion group activity. These improvements not only contribute to the efficiency of the plant, but also to the feeling of teamwork. Claire Dobson from Land Rover assembly explains her involvement in discussion group improvements, "Traditionally we stored batteries in the battery cupboard facing one direction. However, we were finding it difficult to push the necessary buttons to charge the batteries which could result in batteries being removed uncharged. The benefit of the changes we introduced is that we are guaranteed that each battery will always be charged which makes it easier for us and allows us to do our job better for the customer."

The suggestion scheme is another method used at Rover to provide an outlet for associate participation. Participation rates are running at about 300 per cent a year at Land Rover, with every employee submitting an average of three ideas every year. This is compared to a European average of only 14 per cent annual participation.

Each week suggestions are received from the fact holders, the people doing the job who naturally have the specialist information required to improve that job, as to how processes can be improved. "The best suggestion we have had this week involves the use of a modified bolt in the vehicle. The particular worker was fed up with how long it took to fasten a particular bolt so he took the initiative and found a shorter bolt that did the same job. It may sound trivial but when eight bolts are used per vehicle, during the course of the year it represents a saving of thousands of pounds", explains Mr Morgan. Every employee making a suggestion which results in a saving receives 20 per cent of that saving, however, the majority of employees do not contribute for the financial rewards alone.

Rover Group employs 38 thousand people which has increased after a period of significant slimming down during the early 1990s. In 1992 numbers declined to 32 thousand through voluntary redundancy. Rover is now recruiting again and has recorded a huge shift in the proportion of direct and indirect labour, choosing to engage growing numbers of people who design, manufacture and sell the vehicles rather than support people.

There is increasing pride in the company at all levels. The last internal survey indicated that 92 per cent of respondent employees agreed with the statement 'I am proud to work for Rover'. Employee commitment to CONQUER, discussion groups and suggestion schemes all serve as illustrations of this.

While Rover may have been responsive to global automotive needs it has not always shown the same responsiveness to its employees. The first Attitude Survey of people within Rover in 1986 indicated that despite attempts to change work practices employees perceived a problem with management behavioural style. "People understood the importance of Quality to a very high degree; they wanted to do a Quality job to a very passionate degree according to the responses; but in one way or another they said that the behavioural pattern of the management team in terms of setting priorities, defining processes, methods, and facilities for working prevented them doing the Quality job they wanted to do", explains Alan Curtis, Managing Director of Product Supply, Rover Group.

The segregation between management and the workforce which used to exist within Rover no longer exists. "Both sides have met in the middle. Management now accepts that the workforce are not going to leave their brains at the gatepost, because they have something to contribute. The workforce realise that they are stakeholders in the business and the real enemy is coming from motor vehicle manufacturers in the Far East. Everybody accepts that nobody has passed a law saying the Rover Group has to survive. If we pull together we can do something about it and we can bring about change", explains Simon Maris, Public Relations Manager, Land Rover.

As important as it is for every employee to contribute to continuous improvement, it is vital for management to put in place mechanisms which allow it to listen and respond to employee perceptions and suggestions. A method Rover has adopted is known as a 'Bomb Burst'.

'Bomb Burst' is used to execute the contact and testing of opinions between the Quality Council and and other Senior Management teams and the workforce. The mechanism initially involved individual members of the Quality Council (executive members of the Rover Group Board) scattering to speak to employees guided by a question sheet containing five broad subject areas which related to people's understanding of their own process; what their key measurements were; trends in these measures; involvement in improvement activity; and suggestions made. The final question asked was 'When do you think Rover is going to become a world class company?' This was used to open up the conversation and allow senior managers or board members to provide coaching. The 'Bomb Burst' process has since developed to an open discussion which is focused on allowing the respondent to present the information and ask the questions on his/her agenda.

"We originally used 'Bomb Burst' to test the environment and provide feedback. That didn't allow people to ask questions. Because of this we have now torn up the questionnaire and while we have a number of things we want to test, the primary purpose of 'Bomb Burst' is to go and say what is it that you want to ask us", Alan Curtis explains.

Not only have relationships between management and the workforce matured, but this trend has encompassed external relationships between suppliers to Rover and the workforce. Direct interface between the people assembling the vehicles exists with their peers in supply companies. "The people who know best about building vehicles are the ones who do it day in and day out. So you have to give those people the authority to get the job done. For instance, in the past if there was a problem with a component the operator would notify his or her boss, who in turn would transfer it higher through several layers of the hierarchy to a director who would then talk to the directors of the supplier and the message would filter all the way down the company to provide a solution. The cost of this was high in terms of time, money and message distortion. Today many people on the shop floor know their opposite number in the supply company and they not only have the opportunity but the duty to contact the supply company directly when there is a problem," explains Simon Maris.

Alan Curtis is frequently called to give presentations about Rover's transformation into a UK Quality Award winner. He often starts his presentation with a message he believes is particularly valuable about Rover's experience. The message is simple: whatever Rover has done or achieved, it has done so with the same facilities and the same people that it had in a rather different previous environment. Ten years ago Rover did not have the benefit of a corporate parent, the huge insight or a ready made philosophy delivered to the company for implementation. Rover has demonstrated in the very traditional circumstances of a British engineering company that it is possible to make radical change in behaviour and workforce because the organisation wants to do it.

"You can start in a small way, just the way you are, with the same people and make progress. You don't need to know the whole picture and you don't need to see every step of the way before you start. If you wait for that you will never start. Our experience is you must get on the 'staircase', if you want to do something. It may or may not work as you intended, but you can practice on it. It's important to have a period of understanding and consolidation of a level of improvement and then find a new step whatever it is, a new piece of training, a new piece of understanding, or a new piece of technology."

The danger point of each step occurs when a plateau is reached and the goals as defined by the organisation are not being achieved. At these times the leadership of the senior management team is crucial in order to keep everybody climbing the staircase by providing clarity of journey, priority and leadership.

"This is a forever journey and in those circumstances you need the leadership of the senior management team that says we're not always going to be right or perfect but we are generally going to keep on heading in the right direction. We'll expect to find plateaus and periods of relatively low improvement but we will use these. We're using the fact that we have a sense of frustration about what we do next to generate the next breakthrough. This is an important senior management team characteristic."

Rover's TQ Journey has taken it through four stages with the initial assistance of PA Consultants. In retrospect, stage one involved the creation of Quality awareness where a few champions were aware of what needed to be done and started the activity; stage two, Quality promotion involved team work activity with everybody trying to do things better; stage three, Quality management focused improvement activity; and stage four, Quality Empowerment where everybody is engaged in planned and/or voluntary self-sustaining improvement activity completely aligned to the main goals of the business and understanding their role. Rover is attempting to involve continuously higher proportions of its people in this activity as witnessed in the best Japanese companies.

A major influence has been the long and fruitful relationship Rover has shared with Honda, which is well documented. The union which formally started as purely a contractual arrangement in 1979 was jolted into a more collaborative relationship in the early 1980s when Rover received the results of a European-wide manufacturers survey which suggested that it did not have far to slide downward. Rover had lost market share steadily during the 1970s with the arrival of Japanese manufacturers to the UK market and in some of its overseas markets due to similar competitive pressures. This gave the company the incentive to start learning.

However, learning was not enough. When a contingent from Rover visited Honda's greenfield site in Ohio to observe Japanese best practice in a western context it believed it could import what they perceived to be the key ingredients: the introduction of a more involved recruitment process to ensure the selection of the right people; initial and ongoing provision of relevant training; encouragement of the workforce to contribute to the improvement of the business; and improved and more frequent communication within the organisation.

Although Rover tried to emulate Honda's system it realised that it had only scratched the surface. It was this realisation that signalled a change in Rover's philosophy towards Total Quality Management and created a more holistic alignment with Honda's Quality and management practices.

"With the introduction of Total Quality there was an understanding that you had to think in terms of a major change in the management system. You had to buy the whole package", explains Des Haydon, Total Quality Improvement Manager. Mr Haydon fell into the role of TQI manager after participating in basic TQ training and introducing TQ into the international sales companies, in his role as overseas sales director.

Initially, Rover's less directive style of management resulted in a loss of rigour and discipline. In an attempt to create an environment which encouraged innovation the business management structure became more customer focused and process orientated. "This released potential for innovation. However the disadvantage in the first 18 months was that we had a period where people were reinventing things which existed in an acceptable state within the organisation. But people don't destroy what they have had a hand in creating so in a sense we continually try and create an environment where people seek out best practice and apply it to achieve the desired state", explains Mr Haydon.

Prior to 1984 Rover was totally inspection driven which resulted in a culture where inspectors were perceived to be the only people responsible for Quality. To combat this Rover appointed a Quality director at board level in 1986 making Quality a company-level function for the first time. One of Rover's key priorities is the involvement of people in everything the organisation strives to accomplish. This was evident from even the start of the TQI awareness programme. "We trained a small number of senior people, with the help of PA initially and with one more round of help from them we then trained all our own internal facilitators to cascade the programme internally. We had obvious ownership internally, rather than having somebody come in showing us how to do it", remembers Mr Curtis.

With Rover's emphasis on continual learning and company wide involvement it views corporate learning as one of the processes that Rover has identified as an important future consideration, particularly because it needs to transfer this process to multiple sites. Mr Curtis's major challenge is to answer, "What are the ways to improve the effectiveness of people's learning and make people willing to give the learning and make people willing to accept the learning? I think companies that can succeed to a high degree with that will have an enormous competitive advantage so we are putting a lot of effort into it."

Some of the mechanisms used by Rover to encourage corporate

learning include one-day corporate learning events which are held as a matter of routine eight or so times each year. People from each site compile best practice displays and provide a team of people to discuss these. There is little formal presentation time allocated as the emphasis is on individuals visiting all the information displays and talking to people and then meeting in work groups to discuss how they can apply what they have seen to their own work practices. Although it is unusual to develop a complete solution on the day it starts a process building improved practice. Rover is currently tackling the critical question of how to increase the number of events from six to six thousand each year.

The 'Rover Learning Business' (RLB) is a small company-level group created to look at the mechanisms of motivating people to actively seek learning as opposed to just being trained. It is attempting to make people recognise that a job isn't complete until it has been improved and this improvement has been communicated to others.

"I think we are unique in establishing such a distinct learning business within the Rover business with its own board and executive committee. We are still learning about it. The corporate leaning work will ultimately go to the learning business for implementation", discusses Mr Curtis who is a member of the RLB Board. An example of Rover's commitment includes the Employee Development Centres on all sites which offer over 150 in-house courses ranging from French to Finance. These courses are available to all employees.

Rover is moving into a new era, with the formulation of its Quality Strategy 2000, the second of its five-year strategic plans, due to commence in 1996. Rover is now aiming to become a 'class act' in the automotive industry, although few would deny that it already deserves this recognition.

1994 was an eventful and profitable year for Rover with the announcement of the sale of the company to BMW in January and concluding in December with the winning of the UK Quality Award.

During 1994 Rover Group's world-wide sales rose by 11 per cent to 475,500 vehicles from 448, 000 in 1993, an impressive accomplishment considering this growth was set against a background where other major motor manufacturers were suffering recessionary setbacks.

Overseas sales also experienced a dramatic increase of 22 per cent to 219,300 vehicles from the 1993 figure of 180,300. The 1994 export sales accounted for 46 per cent of the Rover Group's total sales cementing its position as the UK's biggest car exporter.

"The 'class act' is intended to imply confidence, a view of what world class is, and a desire to be there. What it can't imply is any sense of complacency or arrogance", emphasises Mr Haydon.

The development of the next five year Quality Strategy is based on a process intended to involve all the stakeholders and fact holders throughout Rover so that when it reaches maturity people will feel a sense of ownership. The process will cascade throughout the organisation starting with executive commitment which will provide clarity of top-level objectives. Significant players within each process will then provide input at the appropriate level.

The Quality Strategy is based broadly around nine company processes: new product introduction; manufacture; logistics; maintenance; sales and service; corporate learning; management of people; product improvement; and business planning. For each of these processes over a five year period a vision is defined which is usually a general description which relates to world class. (Refer to Figure 2). "This implies that we have to find out what world class is. We then produce a series of events and milestones which we have to hit if we are going to have any chance of achieving a world-class vision. This forms the basis for improvement planning throughout

THE QUALITY STRATEGY

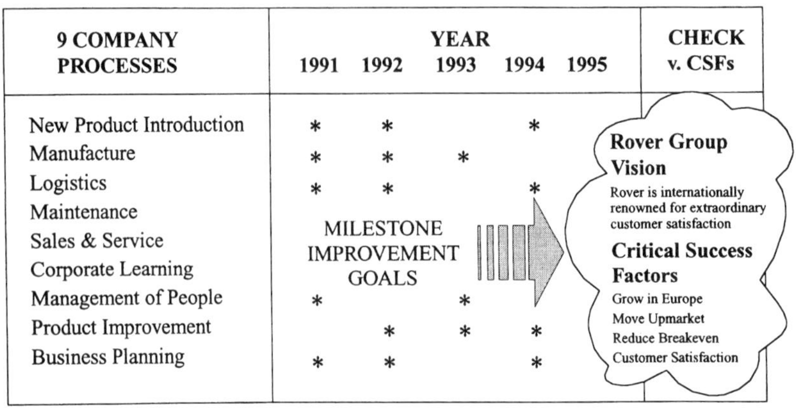

the company. Each business unit has its own Quality strategy which ties into the company objective", explains Mr Haydon.

Mr Curtis, who was Rover's first Quality Director and involved from the inception of its TQM process, cautions organisations thinking of pursuing Total Quality that one, it will be a rocky journey and two, that there has to be strong leadership which is created by forming a Quality Council and binding the leadership of Quality into regular management meetings so that it becomes the normal practice. The third dimension is to make a start. "I find that a lot of our suppliers are paralysed by analysis, paralysed by wanting to know what the whole journey is, how much it is going to cost, and how much time it is going to take. While they are busy analysing they do nothing. I cannot say that often enough as I see so much inertia. Somewhere there has to be a catalyst, but very quickly after there has to be senior team ownership."

Tony Wildman
Total Quality Manager
Texas Instruments Europe

3

Establishing Excellence Throughout Europe

— Texas Instruments Europe —

WHEN Texas Instruments Europe won the 1995 European Quality Award with one of the best scores ever recorded, the company was happy to celebrate but unwilling to become complacent. Texas Instruments Europe (TI Europe) first adopted the European Foundation for Quality Management (EFQM) Model for Business Excellence in 1993 to help the business focus on continuous improvement, people involvement and customer satisfaction. These values haven't gone out of fashion as John Scarisbrick, the President of TI Europe pointed out after winning the Award:

"In certain respects we might have been better off not winning it because the challenge would still be there. But the real challenge is continuous improvement. Business Excellence through total quality today is so fundamental to our business that it has become a way of life. We cannot conceive of doing business without it. EFQM has allowed us to focus all our efforts in a single, common direction, and TI Europe's success today, after only two years of using the EFQM Model, is impressive proof of the importance of Business Excellence for every company."

TI Europe is part of the global operations of Texas Instruments which has its headquarters in Dallas, Texas. Texas Instruments has been a forerunner in innovative technologies. The integrated circuit was invented by the company in 1958, revolutionising the communications and computer industry by allowing the development of more sophisticated electronics systems. By 1996, the company's products and services included: semiconductors, defence electronic systems, software productivity tools, printers, notebook computers and consumer electronics products, custom engineering and manufacturing services, electrical controls and metallurgical materials. The total revenue from patents in 1994 was in excess of $US520 million, and with 55,000 employees worldwide, the parent company recorded a net revenue of $US10.3 billion.

TI Europe was first established in the UK in 1956, becoming the first US-based company to manufacture semiconductors in Europe. By 1996, TI Europe was operating in 16 countries, with manufacturing operations in five countries. The company has revenues in excess of $US 1.6 billion and 5,000 employees in the region. TI Europe is a streamlined organisation with business centres strategically placed to serve the whole continent, and local marketing and sales organisations that ensure strong technical support locally for their customers.

TI Europe's impressive business results haven't come without effort. The world-wide recession of the 1980s affected the business and for three years TI Europe's net revenue growth and profitability were flat. Market share was declining at the same time as high inflation was causing costs to rise.

Discussions were held and a strategy was developed to reinvent the business. To make the required improvements, TI Europe had to radically alter its structures and processes. In 1993, the EFQM Model, with its pan-European approach, was considered the tool to make these changes happen.

TI Europe chose the EFQM model because the company believes it to be the most stringent in the world. TI Europe felt the model went further than the US Malcolm Balbridge model because the EFQM puts equal emphasis on enablers and business results. The benefits of the EFQM model included self-assessment and the focused, external feedback received from European Quality Award assessments.

The 1993 decision to adopt the EFQM model wasn't the first time Texas Instruments had considered Quality. In the early 1980s the United States began to develop a Total Quality Culture based on the work of Crosby, Juran, Demming and the early philosophies of Total Quality Management. In Europe, the concept was implemented through site-based Total Quality promotion centres, extensive training, and a substantial investment of managers' time in Quality steering teams. There was success with this initiative and many operations won local Quality awards. Despite these results, the Total Quality Culture programme also had some shortcomings, including a varied commitment from the different European sites and the need to regularly 'kick start' the programme to maintain enthusiasm.

Alternatively, the EFQM model was considered a European framework, able to rejuvenate the company's previous Quality efforts and bring them all together to focus in the same and in the right direction.

The 30 different organisations within TI Europe were at different stages of maturity as far as Total Quality was concerned. The sponsorship and endorsement of the collective management team was crucial for the EFQM model to succeed. A meeting was held to outline the 'case for action'. To explain the benefits of the plan, TI Europe organised a series of speakers to address the meeting. Speakers from excellent organisations, such as previous European Quality Award winner, Rank Xerox and Texas Instruments own Balbridge Award winning organisation from the US (The TI Defense Systems Group won the award in 1992) convinced the TI Europe managers of the merits of the EFQM approach. Despite cultural differences – on June 18th 1993 – all TI Europe Business and support function managers signed a declaration of commitment to the EFQM model and to using the internal and external EFQM processes in the pursuit of Business Excellence. This declaration, later called 'L'Accord de Paris', symbolised their willingness to dedicate the time and resources necessary to support this commitment.

With the signing of the document a 'common language' was established for TI Europe. A comprehensive communications package was launched to create awareness and understanding and to gain the acceptance and active participation of the organisation at all levels. TI Europe's managers led the process by holding initial EFQM information sessions with their people, communicating the case for action and the plan. In just two months the package was designed, created, and translated into six languages. It was then shipped to the 30 different organisations and over 6,000 people across TI Europe.

To drive the process forward 30 managers were trained by the EFQM as 'facilitators'. Each of the managers was chosen by their business or support group and were issued with a comprehensive set of common tools to conduct the self assessment. Armed with a full understanding of the EFQM criteria, these facilitators could guide their respective organisations through the self-assessment process.

In September 1993, over 30 different organisations underwent their first self-assessment. The self-assessments were largely conducted by the management teams of each organisation, often with a cross-section of employees, and guided by the organisation's EFQM facilitator. Strengths and areas for improvement were listed for each category and scored against the EFQM model. To support the self-assessment process, TI Europe produced a 75 page scorebook on the criteria, which ensured that a common format and approach was used throughout Europe. The scorebook itself divides each EFQM criterion into its constituent elements and provides statements of Business Excellence for each one. In all, over 150 managers across TI Europe devoted at least two full days to this self assessment, bringing the total investment of management time to over 450 days.

In some organisations, focus groups reviewed the self-assessment, resulting in changes to its content or emphasis. Importantly, employees were later involved in the implementation of improvement actions as team members or individual contributors.

Mr Tony Wildman is the Total Quality Manager for TI Europe. He believes the self-assessment has proved to be extremely valuable. Mr Wildman says at first, national characteristics and preconceived attitudes affected the internal self-assessments:

"We know there are mature organisations who score themselves harshly to gain an understanding of their gaps (or areas for improvement) to excellence. There were other organisations who scored themselves higher than their reflected progress. Some countries, tended to emphasise product quality aspects in their scoring rather than the whole process and criteria of the EFQM model. Others may have been tempted to inflate their score so as not to be at the bottom of some imaginary league table. Our solution was to say that only particular organisations had ownership of those scores because they would go into a secure data base, and were not going to be used to generate a league table to 'beef' up the lower scores. A bad score is not a low score, it is one that does not reflect the true status of an organisation. It's not necessary to bring all the scores in line, but to prioritise what needs attention. So the idea is not to be pre-occupied with trying to collect each organisation's score."

The assessment process helped determine where gaps lay in the different organisations within TI Europe, and where improvements were needed. The company understood the importance of each element and correlated their performance in terms of excellence gaps. The goals were specific, measurable and achievable, above all they were followed by performance actions.

To benefit fully from external assessment TI Europe applied for the European Quality Award in 1994. The independent review was able to be used as a source of feedback and evaluation of the company's progress.

There was a high correlation between the internal self assessments and EFQM assessor scores which was re-assuring for TI Europe. The assessment scores reflected areas which needed to be addressed, such as focusing on collective management; commitment to driving and inspiring take up of Total Quality; more management by processes; and a better link between high-level objectives and the contributions of individuals and teams. To achieve breakthrough improvements in particular areas, it was necessary to fully utilise policy deployment. The main elements of policy deployment involve:

- definition of objectives based on given higher-level objectives;
- understanding the current situation, reflection on history, business environment and customer care;
- definition of measurable tracking indices;
- setting of goals for those indices; and
- definition of tactics to reach the set of goals.

The critical aspect of deploying strategies to tactics in this way is the process of negotiation and alignment at different organisational levels, and is systematic because higher-level objectives drive the next lower-level tactics.

Action plans were put in place to close excellence gaps and the key strengths were fed into the application process for the European Quality Award. Each organisation defined its 'vital few' excellence gaps, and the same was done for TI Europe as a whole. The key strengths or 'best practices' that emerge from the self-assessment process are shared across Europe and with Texas Instruments world-wide. In this way the application process has been a catalyst to accelerate learning, and enforce deployment of key actions for improvement.

To close the process loop, the key priorities and areas for improvement are fed into TI Europe's annual Policy Deployment and individual performance appraisal (Development and Performance Management) processes, ensuring consistent alignment of action plans right through the organisation. This is a continuous improvement process, so when the cycle has been completed it is time to begin again, with a new self-assessment to check our progress and measure our improvement.

The tremendous efforts of TI Europe were recognised when in 1994, it was recognised in the top five companies to be assessed. This excellent result was obviously bettered in 1995 when TI Europe were announced the winner of the European Quality Award.

TI Europe has aligned the EFQM model with Texas Instruments own world-wide TI-Business Excellence Standard, known as TI-BEST. The TI-BEST process is used to drive business excellence and has four steps: defining business excellence for your business, performing an assessment, identifying opportunities for improvement and putting an improvement plan in place. The process provides a unifying structure for the quality processes used throughout the world. Texas Instruments in the US applies the Malcolm Balbridge criteria and TI Singapore applies the Singapore National Quality Award criteria.

Business Excellence at TI Europe is based around three key elements: customer focus, continuous improvement and people involvement.

Tony Wildman details the customer focus:

"Customer satisfaction is our primary objective. Total Customer Satisfaction is vital to our success, and we are customer driven in everything we do.

"We gather customer inputs through a broad range of customer contacts, including top level management visits, marketing and sales calls, close liaisons on new designs, product applications and manufacturing, customer service and quality management. Annual Customer Satisfaction surveys measure Customer Satisfaction levels and highlight areas requiring particular attention.

"Information gathered from our customers is the driving element for our business policy and strategy definition, and customer requirements are integrated into the Policy Deployment process. Our business processes start and end with the customer, and produce customer-desired outputs. Our internal measures, such as on-time delivery, cycle-time and product yield, are all driven by customer feedback on their principle care-abouts."

For example, TI Europe responded to customer encouragement and obtained ISO 9000 certification for all of its European manufacturing sites. Suggestions in the 1994 survey prompted TI Europe to create a

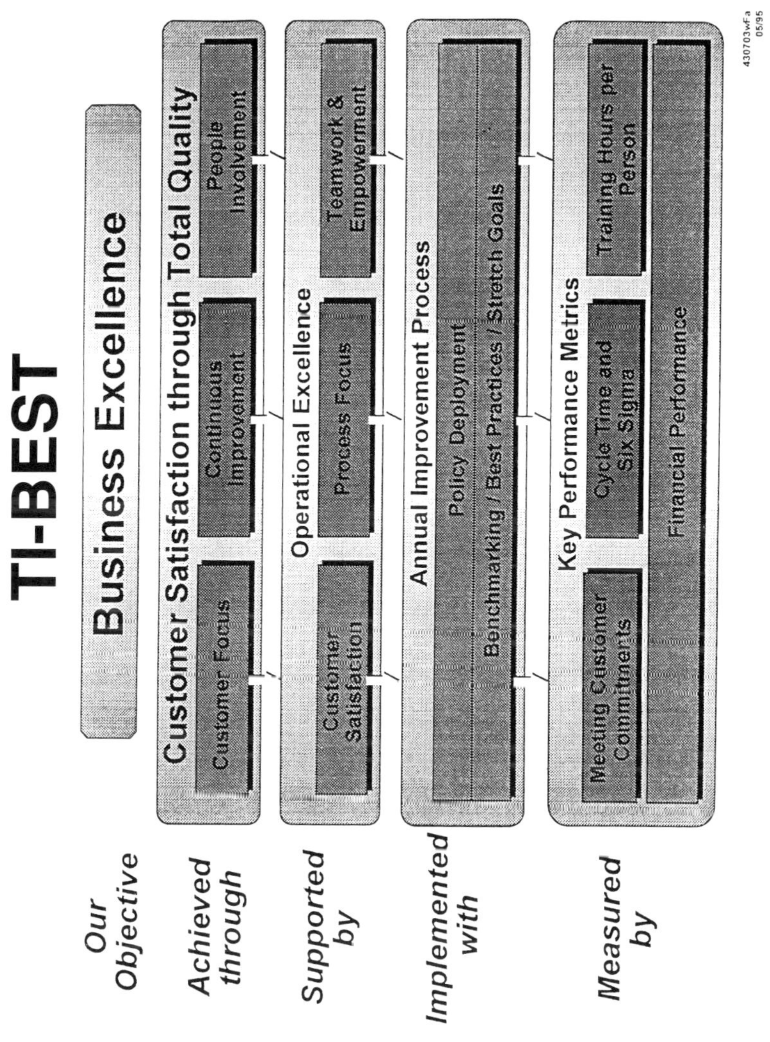
TI-BEST
Our Objective
Business Excellence
Achieved through
Customer Satisfaction through Total Quality
Customer Focus
Continuous Improvement
People Involvement
Supported by
Operational Excellence
Customer Satisfaction
Process Focus
Teamwork & Empowerment
Implemented with
Annual Improvement Process
Policy Deployment
Benchmarking / Best Practices / Stretch Goals
Measured by
Key Performance Metrics
Meeting Customer Commitments
Cycle Time and Six Sigma
Training Hours per Person
Financial Performance
430703wFa
05/95

European Product Information Centre (EPIC) located in Paris. EPIC is comprised of ten multi-lingual engineering experts who handle enquiries relating to TI Europe's semiconductor market. The establishment of EPIC has achieved increased responsiveness, better product information, faster and earlier availability of better samples, and a more active TI European presence with the customer.

Texas Instrument's corporate and business executives act as customer champions, meeting the customer's management, obtaining direct feedback on current and future requirements, reviewing performance and setting targets for improvement. Partnership programmes also enable the company to get the feedback it needs to develop the new products and technologies required by TI Europe's customers. TI's semiconductor organisation works in special partnership with four of Europe's leading telecommunications manufacturers, designing new and improved components for their current and future product requirements.

The second core philosophy for TI Europe is continuous improvement:

"For Texas Instruments it means we must continually strive to be the best. It involves extensive performance measurement and assessment, and setting the highest goals and targets for every aspect of doing business: from customer satisfaction to product quality, from people satisfaction to cycle-time, from business results to excellent corporate citizenship.

"For every TI employee, everyday, continuous improvement means constantly endeavouring to improve their contribution, whether it be through individual contribution or team work, to better meet the needs of their internal and external customers", says Mr Wildman.

The annual continuous improvement process based on the EFQM criteria and outlined earlier in the chapter is facilitated and coordinated by a dedicated European Quality Team. The Team's mission includes enabling the development of Business Excellence by providing support towards the identification, sharing and promotion of best practices.

Selected best practices, from each organisation's identification of strengths as part of their self assessment, are entered into TI's world-wide best practice database. A network of best practice facilitators help organisations load their data and connect groups with an excellence gap to those with a best practice.

People Involvement is included as Texas Instruments recognises that its employees are the basis for the company's success and its most important investment.

"People – motivated, rewarded and developed to their full potential – allow the company to satisfy its customers and generate the revenue stream which makes it profitable. In this 'Golden Circle' of people, customers and results, this profitability in turn allows the company to invest yet more in its people, ever building on their development and satisfaction.

"Teamwork, in which we're a benchmark company, is a fundamental concept of people involvement and empowerment. Today, almost every single TI employee in Europe is a member of at least one team, and these teams range from Quality Steering Teams to Quality Improvement Teams, from Voluntary Effectiveness Teams to fully empowered, Self-directed Work Teams.

"Employees at all levels of the organisation are encouraged to participate in these teams to achieve objectives such as improving processes, cutting costs and reducing cycle time. Cross-Functional Teams are appointed by management and incorporate employees from different levels of the organisation. Each team is responsible for improving an entire process through involvement to ensure a satisfactory end result, with the benefits essentially being passed on to the customer. The Freising wafer fabrication plant set up a team to reduce cycle-time for new products. Targets were set and the cycle-time was reduced from 117 days in the first quarter of 1992 to 63 days in the fourth quarter of 1993, and a further improvement to 49 days in the fourth quarter of 1994.

"Voluntary Effectiveness Teams consist of groups of employees who work on processes which they identify as needing improvement – the problems often have not been detected by management. The teams provide the framework for employees to improve processes in their area. Recognition is built into the process to promote teamwork. These teams give our people the opportunity to contribute, and receive more opportunities to enhance their skills through training", says Tony Wildman.

A considerable amount is invested in training every year, with a goal of a minimum 40 hours training per person per year. The training is designed to give employees the knowledge and competencies they need and to ensure they are developed to their full potential.

The Development and Performance Management process, through

discussion and peer assessment, helps create individually tailored training plans for each employee. Training is matched to strategic business plans and priorities and aligned with specific business objectives through the Policy Deployment process. A European Leadership Development Centre exists to create focused development plans for future leaders and high-potential employees throughout the organisation.

For over 30 years, Texas Instruments has conducted an annual employee survey to measure the satisfaction of its people. In 1993, TI Europe began benchmarking its major sites with other leading companies. The company was independently considered best in class in many areas and the majority of employees regard TI Europe as "a good company to work for".

The success of people involvement at TI Europe has been based on frequent and open communication between employees, supervisors and management at all levels. An environment which nurtures dialogue, shared knowledge, candour and trust has been created and maintained.

In the final analysis it is results that count and the improvements in TI Europe's business results have been impressive.

"There's been a huge turnaround in TI Europe's profitability. We've had a string of record quarters, we've gained market share with our semiconductors for the first time in many years and our latest Customer Satisfaction Survey indicates significant improvement there too",says Mr Wildman.

After achieving so much so quickly it is vital for TI Europe, after winning the European Quality Award, to maintain the momentum of their achievements. Tony Wildman says TI Europe are determined to continue with their ongoing self assessment, and will to continue to benchmark themselves with other companies:

"The big challenge now is to take the best practices in the different Texas Instruments organisations and deploy them across TI Europe. I don't have any doubt that our involvement with the EFQM has been a catalyst in our business excellence endeavours. In some ways it is a harder task to achieve this as a pan-European company because of the cultural diversity. However, TI Europe has achieved a significant turnaround in business results, and people satisfaction. The things we've been doing have steered us in the right direction. As a result of using EFQM to strive for Business Excellence, growth and increased prosperity is back on track for Texas Instruments Europe."

4

Packaging A Quality Service

—ServisPak—

"IT'S always the thing that nobody wants, but has to have and nobody wants it until they really need it because it is in the way." This is the cryptic explanation provided by ServisPak's Chairman and Managing Director, Mr Alec Tuckerman when asked to describe the nature of his business.

From a user's perspective transit packaging is a totally unglamorous business. It takes up valuable storage space if it is delivered before it is needed and costs money and reputations if it is not there when required. However, it is a link in the chain of delivery of product to market which is vital. Without the brown cardboard box, millions of pounds worth of development and investment can be left sitting in the warehouse.

"Because people down the line in companies don't actually know what the cost of a box is, it's just another item they often don't think about until it's too late. So we are often catching up time for inefficiencies, but that's our business", comments Mr Tuckerman.

ServisPak's major strength is that they have found a gap in the market and filled it. They are ducking and weaving around the industry's less flexible giants to provide their customers with a more responsive, just in time service.

"The company was primarily set up to supply corrugated cases on a just in time basis to people who were looking for the type of service the major players in the industry were unable to provide in terms of off the shelf products, not just for standard cases that may be designed to a particular size and strength, but even tailor made products. We would be prepared to hold a certain range of products which could be shipped immediately. The major case makers would normally impose a lead time of up to two to three

left to right: Alec Tuckerman (Chairman and Managing Director)
John Breeden (Commercial Director)
ServisPak

weeks which wasn't something the customer was always willing to accept", explains Commercial Director, John Breeden.

ServisPak is committed to the pledge it makes to each and every customer to provide a service which is second to none. As part of this obligation it is equally committed to upholding its L.R.Q.A registration to ISO 9002 and BS 5750.

ServisPak's sales material informs current and potential clients of this commitment: "All staff are aware of the responsibility for following the Quality system. The Managing Director has overall responsibility for Quality Assurance. Everybody in the company is committed to Quality and all the procedures we have developed are followed and improved in the light of experience."

ServisPak which currently operates out of three distribution centres located at Wallingford in Oxfordshire, Lichfield in Staffordshire and Enfield in Middlesex has come a long way from the days when it recorded its first £1000 of sales at Finchley in 1972. Since this time it has steadily grown to its current position which saw it yield sales of £5.9 million in the 1994/1995 financial year. Company sales have grown by 94 per cent in the past three years to April 1995. Forecasted sales for the current financial year are £8.5 million.

The company's continual growth can be attributed to the expansion of the ServisPak philosophy which it has encapsulated in one simple sentence – 'We deliver the service so you can deliver the goods'. Expansion in this context was achieved by increasing ServisPak's sphere of influence into the Midlands and also London through its Lichfield and Enfield operations. Each operation perpetuates this philosophy further by ensuring that growth continues without compromising excellence in service.

The company has grown from more humble beginnings. Mr Tuckerman and a partner started selling boxes which were either second hand or defective mill runs from larger companies. The early sales operation was based in a flat in London while the boxes were stored in a barn in Cambridgeshire. But this was only the start. "People being creatures of habit wanted standard sizes again and again. So from second hand and recycled boxes the company moved to a stock range of plain boxes which we started selling new. Through personal contacts I started to offer a company called Airfix personalised stock holding which was fantastic for them as we stored their boxes and they called them off when they needed them. The type of services offered by ServisPak started there", reminisces Mr Tuckerman.

ServisPak's current range of services covers everything from design and sample making right through manufacturing to stock holding of customised material as well as holding a large range of standard items for one off or urgent requirements.

Stock is held for a range of 'stock sized' corrugated products and other packaging materials such as polythene foam, tapes, bubble wrap, pallet containers and assorted wrappings, twines and staples, and various postal products. However, 80 per cent of ServisPak throughput is in corrugated cases.

Customer orders are processed efficiently using an integrated computer system between the three distribution centres and delivered within 24 hours from stock by ServisPak's fleet of modern, purpose designed vehicles.

Although relatively small in size, ServisPak's stature in the industry is quite the opposite. It is an influential player in an industry which is dominated by what ServisPak describes as 'the majors' including SCA, The Smurfit Group, David J Smith, ASSI and Amcor. ServisPak employs 45 people at its three operations, the largest of which is the Wallingford distribution centre which employs 30 staff. Nine people are employed at the Lichfield operation and six at Enfield. It is the intention of the company that the Enfield and Lichfield sites should mirror Wallingford, but with a more modern profile.

Malcolm Wotherspoon, the Director who is currently responsible for the Lichfield and Enfield branches, has seen such rapid growth at Lichfield which was only established in May 1993, that he is currently seeking new premises, to satisfactorily service the new business. Malcolm is a long standing member of the team at ServisPak, having joined the company in 1978 as a Sales Representative. He has been a key player in developing many of the company's major accounts and also sharpening the Company's cutting edge in the purchasing area. In the Quality field, appreciating the benefits that the introduction of formalised quality systems has produced, is a keen advocate to see the Company develop its potential even further.

As proof of the company's rapid growth the Lichfield operation which was established in only May 1993 has already outgrown its premises.

The company's growth has accelerated in the three years to 1995. This growth coincides with the engagement of John Breeden as Commercial Director and the introduction of the Quality programme which he has been instrumental in documenting. Mr Breeden came to ServisPak from The Jefferson Smurfit Group which he joined in 1970 as UK Sales Director. With the expansion of the Group, during the period up to 1992, he ran a number of plants in the UK but retained a strong influence on the sales and marketing aspects of the Group's UK interests.

In May 1992, having retired from Smurfits, the friendship Mr Tuckerman and Mr Breeden have enjoyed over many years led to Mr Breeden joining ServisPak, on a part time basis, with emphasis on the commercial aspects of the business.

"Since John has been here the company has taken on a new dimension, including the Quality aspect. We have been able to add a level of professionalism which has earned us respect from others in the Industry", acknowledges Mr Tuckerman.

Prior to preparing for BS 5750 ServisPak was in good shape. However, everybody recognises that the formalisation of procedures required for certification has improved the company.

"A number of companies initially went into ISO 9000 or BS 5750 because they felt that if they didn't, they would be precluded from some potential opportunities, or would even be at risk with some elements of existing business.

"At ServisPak we saw the introduction of a Quality System as being the vehicle to use, to improve systems which in themselves were already sound, even further. Disciplines have also improved and the auditing procedure for instance has made us constantly ask ourselves, can we do it better. The next step from ISO 9002 is 'Managing for Continuous Improvement' which is really what running a business should be about", stresses Mr Breeden.

Like many companies considering Quality certification ServisPak expressed concern that it would introduce an unwelcome degree of bureaucracy to the day-to-day activity of the organisation. One of Mr Tuckerman's fears was that the process would put handcuffs on the company which could be only detrimental as the company is based on flexibility. However, experience has shown that BS 5750 and ISO 9000 have been instrumental in bringing the company back to disciplines and procedures without reducing its flexibility to respond to situations.

Mr Breeden who together with the Quality Assurance Representative has assumed responsibility for the documentation and maintenance of Quality processes asserts that unless one gets involved in BS 5750 or ISO 9000 it is impossible to understand just how much work is involved. "For somebody to do it as part of their day to day routine there is the danger that it will just get shuffled to one side. In retrospect I would try and keep it simpler. We made a lot of hard work in the sense that we have gone into the procedures in more detail than perhaps was required for a company of our size."

"Alec has recognised the benefits but if somebody had said to him before he started that over the next two or three years it was going to cost £25,000, he probably would have said forget it. It's not just the cost, it's also a question of the time it consumes. But having said that I believe we have just about got value for money and particularly if we keep things rolling and move towards the continuous improvement concept", concludes Mr Breeden.

The closeness of the company members facilitates the process of educating staff and administering Quality procedures. All staff are aware of their responsibility for the Quality system.

There is no formal Quality training or even a suggestion scheme in place to serve as vehicles of continuous improvement. The Commercial Director explains the rationale behind this. "Because it is such a close community things happen without having to say lets put some sort of system in place to make it happen. You don't have to drag everybody into the boardroom to talk to them. We are talking all the time. The Managing Director is directly accessible to everybody in the organisation."

The effectiveness of the Quality system is continually evaluated through audits and management reviews.

A visitor to the company soon gains the impression that ServisPak's culture welcomes the opportunity to celebrate success, not only internally but with customers and suppliers. This is a characteristic which generates a remarkable openness and willingness to praise outstanding performances. "When you review the range of major customers and suppliers many have been dealing with Alec in one degree or another for a long period of time.

As a result a very strong loyalty has developed in both directions", explains Mr Breeden.

The intensity of the relationship varies from customer to customer. However, an example of the strength of customer relationships formed by ServisPak is one the company shares with a major international customer.

It is a tremendous accolade that ServisPak successfully developed a relationship and gained the commitment of a European purchasing director who originally couldn't understand why his organisation would consider buying from a merchant instead of one of 'the majors'.

The customer is now buying from ServisPak on a European wide basis. Although this decision only took four months to formalise it was based on 20 years of trust in the people, the products and the service provided by ServisPak as described by Mr Breeden. "It is an account which needs a great deal of nurturing because they have big demands and require a whole range of different products. In terms of the closeness and respect at the levels that we are dealing with I cannot think of too many companies which have the depth of relationships that Alec has with the major customers we supply."

An example of the depth of customer service is illustrated in the response received from a major customer thanking ServisPak for allowing them to meet a Christmas deadline:

"We would like to thank you for your support in expediting the delivery of components during a very challenging time for us. Your efforts have been critical to our ability to ship numerous promotions at Christmas, and will be continued to be needed as we move through the balance of 1994 and into 1995.

"We realise that many of our requests are extraordinary, but be assured they are real and that we do appreciate your efforts. The supplier community is an extension of our own manufacturing operations, and we are applying similar pressures on our own people as part of the supply chain as well."

This kind of relationship is not solely reliant on the loyalty of the client, but also on the loyalty of the staff and the suppliers to ServisPak.

The company recognises that to keep the Quality process on the right track and to pursue continuous improvement it must monitor the effectiveness of the Quality programme with the end user, the customer.

"The policy statement in our Quality manual says in a nutshell that we want to be the best in this sector of the market. We are aiming towards doing what we have said we are going to do and not only aiming towards it but satisfying Lloyd's register and others that we are achieving it", explains Mr Breeden. To this end ServisPak has developed and implemented a customer service monitor.

In total ServisPak has over 700 customers across its three locations. However, at any one time it may be dealing with 250 of those customers. ServisPak's customers differ in size and industry from a small printing company employing a handful of people and whose annual spend is no more than £500 to a major worldwide cosmetic company which spends in excess of half a million pounds per annum on transit packaging with ServisPak.

A random sample of each month's customers is asked to complete a questionnaire ranking ServisPak's performance against the following criteria: speed of answering the phone; sales office and coordinator; ease of placing an order and getting advice; security of mind that what was said would be actioned; delivery period offered; adherence to delivery promise; dispatch and driver's performance; presentation of product; quality of product; sales representative performance; accessibility of management; and commercial aspects. The 12 elements were not scientifically selected but were aspects relevant to the day to day dealings with each customer.

The rating scale is basic: a score of one indicating a very poor performance; five acceptable; and nine excellent.

Analysis of the results is conducted on two levels: by client; and by performance indicator. The analysis of the questionnaire responses is done on an individual client basis to provide a total score indicating the level of service received from ServisPak as perceived by each client.

The scores provided by each of the clients questioned each month are also aggregated by performance criteria to give an average performance indicator for that month and then compared against the previous months' performances in order to analyse any trends and transgressions in performance levels for each performance criteria.

Issues disclosed in the quantitative research together with client comments result in a list of action points which may be general or client specific. The results are not published in a blanket manner throughout the organisation. Instead any issues, whether positive or negative, are addressed directly with the person(s) responsible. Where clarification is required or a particularly bad result is received Mr Tuckerman will return to the client to resolve the situation. It is believed that this sort of vehicle opens the dialogue between customers and ServisPak and gives the customer the confidence that they can discuss any problems that arise freely knowing that ServisPak will be interested in finding a solution.

ServisPak is sitting in an ideal position to take advantage of the increasing tendency of companies to turn towards sole supply in order to simplify transactions and gain the benefits of partnership arrangements. ServisPak's advantage lies in the strength of its relationships with the major suppliers and its experience in logistics.

ServisPak has worked hard to extend loyalties and deepen relationships with suppliers. Ultimately it is striving to create relationships with its suppliers where they are viewed as an extension of ServisPak and ServisPak an extension of their organisation.

ServisPak sits between its customers and its 60 plus suppliers, to put together an ideal packaging smorgasbord using the best suppliers, the most appropriate products obtained at the best market prices and delivers this just in time for its customers' needs.

"This is a benefit to the customer. For example we supply a quarter of a million pounds of business to one customer and use five to seven suppliers to do that. It is such a complicated account and we use our administration knowledge and distribution facility to keep drip feeding the customers all the time. Even if a particular customer was to try and chose the suppliers they probably wouldn't have the knowledge across the whole range of suppliers to cherry pick nor would they have the same purchasing power", says Mr Tuckerman.

"Having a spread of suppliers and obviously knowing the strengths and weaknesses of all the people we are dealing with we can cherry pick. When we receive an inquiry from a customer we know the best place to get a particular product at the best price. Whereas if the customer buys directly from these companies they don't have this knowledge themselves and also do not enjoy the purchasing power that we do", explains Mr Breeden.

In the corrugated case side of the business alone ServisPak has approximately 20 suppliers which includes seven of 'the majors' down to material suppliers which are used on an ad hoc basis as specific needs arise.

With such an array of suppliers it is essential that ServisPak retains control over relationships and quality of supply. The quality of the service received from suppliers is analysed on a week to week to basis with non-conformances highlighted. Because more than half of the suppliers have their own Quality certification they acknowledge that they have the same commitment to ServisPak as it does to its end customers.

Every three months ServisPak sits down with its key suppliers and reviews activity on a weekly basis over that period. The assessment is not as formal as that conducted with customers. However, suppliers are rated in the same way on areas such as competitiveness, delivery on time, consistency of quality, presentation, and availability.

ServisPak has compiled two lists of suppliers. One consists of approved suppliers which have been visited and taken through the required procedures by ServisPak. The other list consists of companies pending approval which includes suppliers ServisPak does not deal with frequently or which have not made sufficient supplies of a particularly high standard.

ServisPak has compiled a third list containing suppliers which have some form of external certification. Suppliers on this third list may be on either the approved or pending approval list.

"Just because they have outside accreditation doesn't necessarily mean that they have satisfied us that they can supply to the standards that we are looking for. On our computer system we can recognise suppliers with external accreditation. Although it has never happened, if one of our customers said we want you to supply our product using an accredited source we would be able to identify it through our system. All our lists have been introduced as part of the Quality system", explains Mr Breeden.

The most visual effect of Quality are the company's distribution centres which have benefited as a result of improved internal procedures and increased Quality requirements from ServisPak's suppliers. "Since we have introduced Quality procedures the warehouse has been a different class. You can't imagine how horrible a corrugated box warehouse may be, bands come lose, containers break. But now I never have to announce when visitors are coming because the warehouse is always tidy and presentable", Mr Tuckerman maintains.

The benefits of ServisPak's attitude to Quality are obvious. Both Alec Tuckerman and John Breeden agree that they are on a winning thing with ServisPak's current direction and Quality emphasis. "We both wish we had started doing this 20 years ago because the Quality management tools are very powerful and they enable a company of unlimited potential to be built."

5

Towards Customer Delight

— Honeywell UK —

DIRECTOR of Quality, Martin Kruger talks of the Quality revolution that has taken place in Honeywell UK over the last seven years. While it was one of the first UK companies in the controls business to achieve certification to BS5750, now known as ISO9000, well ahead of its competition this was just part of the journey towards the company's ultimate goal of creating customer delight.

Throughout the 1980s a number of initiatives were introduced to Honeywell's UK operation in an attempt to respond to the business community's growing interest in the topics of Quality and customer service. Although each initiative had its own special characteristics and usually began with a flourish experience was that they withered within a couple of years.

After several false starts with programmes that were largely imported from other parts of the Honeywell world a final attempt was made in 1988 to infuse Quality into the organisation with the introduction of a Total Quality Management (TQM) programme.

"It began with a recognition that a Quality reputation has to be earned and that in a highly competitive business environment the winners are those who make customer satisfaction the number one priority, not just in theory but in practice. Continuous improvement needs to become a normal part of the way the business is run and not just a 'bolt on'", explains Mr Kruger.

Honeywell was founded in the 1880s in the United States and now has offices and factories in 95 countries. The company began operating in the United Kingdom in 1936 and today provides control products, systems

left to right: Dennis Kennedy (Chairman and Managing Director)
and Martin Kruger (Director of Quality)
Honeywell UK

and services that increase comfort, environmental protection, energy conservation, productivity and safety in homes and buildings, industry and aviation. Of the 2,800 UK employees, some 63 per cent are employed in the sales and service part of the organisation.

Regardless of the business, market or technology sector the company operates in, the discipline of Total Quality Management permeates all activity. The corporate aim is to continue to be recognised as a world-class supplier of top Quality products through delighting customers.

Over the seven years since commencing its TQM process Honeywell UK has continuously improved its revenue, profits, and every other financial indicator. This performance is all the more impressive given the fact that the company managed to sustain impressive business growth in every year in spite of a major recession in the UK during this time.

As acknowledgment of this the UK operation has won the 'Affiliate of the Year' award as the best European performer in Honeywell for four years running. In 1994 the organisation won a special award for long term high level performance and contribution.

"These are the sort of indicators that say to me we must be doing something right because we have come from a position of very much an average performing European organisation within the Honeywell family to a top flight one", explains Mr Kruger.

Behind this success was the company's very clear focus on the customer. It made the jump from associating customer satisfaction with merely product related functions to the level of service offered on a company wide basis. This vision was driven largely by Dennis Kennedy, Honeywell's UK chairman and managing director. He was appointed to this position in January 1990 and with him he brought a very enlightened view of Quality and its role in the organisation. Mr Kennedy has been associated with the introduction of Quality to organisations since 1969, when he worked for a company in which Quality leader Phil Crosby held the position of Vice President.

"Unless every person who deals with the customer shares a common set of values and focuses on satisfaction, or 'delight' in our language you will have upset customers. It is not uncommon to find that a customer who says your products are great may also perceive your service is poor. By service they may well mean that they never get anybody on the end of the telephone when they have an inquiry or they get passed around the entire organisation when they do get through. I can measure our progress in how relatively few calls I get from annoyed customers as compared to three years ago", explains Mr Kennedy. "The key to getting to this stage is the constant iteration of the principle that the customer rules the organisation."

Mr Kennedy regards TQM as the single most important investment made by Honeywell since he joined the company. "It became the lead process into which we folded a lot of other improvement processes because we soon realised that the techniques and the participation of the people were the best vehicles to make the other improvements. We folded in most of our HR initiatives, our training initiatives, our career planning and development initiatives, and our performance appraisal processes as well as our supply team improvement processes. They all came under the umbrella of the TQM process because it is the most motivational set of tools within the company."

Honeywell does not have a corporate Quality department. However, responsibility for the administration of the process and training rests with the director of Quality and a Total Quality administrator. "I'll provide what channels of information I can. I will provide the top level communication support, but I can't do everything for them. If you have customers who are complaining then eventually you have to ensure line business staff deal with that and avoid those complaints in the future", explains Mr Kruger.

Honeywell is moving ever closer towards customer delight as evidenced by the relationship it shares with many of its customers such as BP Chemicals in Hull. Both companies have repositioned themselves for partnership which at the time it was developed represented a radical change in the nature of customer interface for Honeywell.

John Pepper, a project manager for BP Chemicals explains: "Honeywell used to work very much on its own basis. However, it is now working in the spirit of partnership with companies like ours under a memorandum of understanding which governs all the business we do together."

For instance, on one project involving the installation of a distributed control system on a chemical production plant BP estimates that it has saved £75,000 on a £1 million contract which represents a saving of 7 per cent. The financial benefit to Honeywell was estimated at more than £23,000.

"In the past we had a situation where things were almost confrontational and the customer continually checked the work in progress. It has been traditional that the site need dates have always had a large contingency in them to allow for failures. Now we have a more open relationship – the dates have become a reality and all the parties involved understand the level of commitment made by the others. Open book accounting has also been introduced reducing the bureaucracy involved in determining value for money", explains Steve Kelly, Honeywell's engineering manager for its industrial business.

All staff have received Quality training combining a balance of theory and hands on use of tools and techniques in the workplace so they assume ownership of the activity.

For training purposes Honeywell initially selected senior people who were considered 'high fliers'. Just one of the benefits of this was that at a later stage Honeywell could cite involvement in continuous improvement as a factor in assessing people for forward career moves. "That's quite a powerful message. We say that these people are role models, the company appreciates what they have accomplished and gives recognition of their efforts", explains Mr Kruger.

Every member of the board team determines his or her own annual improvement goals and process, explains how he or she is going to achieve these and decides what resources will be required. The top team meets bi-monthly as the Quality Council to monitor the implementation of programmes and plans across the business. Each director is responsible for running a Quality Improvement Team – it is his responsibility to martial his team to do the things they want to do locally. Quality Action Teams are smaller teams which are established to tackle specific issues.

It was vital to ensure that Quality activity was visible throughout the organisation. "If staff are not made aware of what is happening they will assume that nothing is happening. The approach taken has been to take all available opportunities to communicate the facts of the process of TQM", explains Mr Kruger. Facilitators and coordinators are used as local contacts to maintain effective communications. Stories of individual and team achievements are told in in-house publications and management meetings provide updates.

The headlines of Honeywell's Quality newsletter, *Quality News*, herald the on-going success of Honeywell's focus on customer delight and commitment to TQM. One such story involves Honeywell's Bracknell-based Information Centre which is now frequently used as a model example by other organisations.

This central clearing facility sorts 1600 'stray' incoming calls and 1300 items of correspondence each month as well as a myriad of daily customer communications issues, both internal and external.

The Information Centre was central to the activities of a Quality Action Team formed to improve the efficiency and effectiveness in dealing with incoming telephone and written enquiries. As part of its charter the QAT investigated solutions to the problem of ownership of in-coming calls in a move designed to hasten the response time and eliminate risk of customers being misdirected. This was considered a vital factor as 95 per cent of complaints are recorded via the telephone.

So efficient is the service now that a number of organisations use the Information Centre as a role model for their own activity. A major telecommunications company turned to Honeywell for advice in reducing the difficulties experienced by staff and customers in obtaining information about disparate parts of its vast organisation.

Access to the main Honeywell systems enables Information Centre staff to tap into the sales and distribution reports to identify products and sort customer order queries. Input to customer account receivables also identifies orders by invoice number.

"Follow through is a very important aspect of our job – it goes a long way to diffusing any frustration that may have built up. It also underlines the quality of our service and reflects well on Honeywell's drive to delight the customer", comments Ann Judd, Information Officer.

The outcome of the telecommunications company's observations has been the formation of a special team to review their own communications and the establishment of a pilot information centre modelled partly on Honeywell's example.

Honeywell's workforce is one where approximately half of it is based on the road or operates on customer premises. This presented special problems in communicating, training and motivating staff to adopt TQM practices throughout the workforce.

Honeywell acknowledges that when planning the way in which TQM should be introduced it did not give enough initial consideration to this operational characteristic. TQM was essentially portrayed as a team game which was largely inappropriate for an organisation with such a large mobile workforce.

"We do not operate a centralised process. Effectively we ask all the businesses within Honeywell in the UK to plan, develop and implement their own philosophy and approach to improvement because the businesses are dramatically different. For instance, our industrial business involves very large integrated systems and the installation of multi-million pound process control systems. At the other end of the spectrum we are literally selling microswitches in boxes of thousands to washing machine manufacturers," explains Mr Kruger.

A key element of Honeywell's efforts to sustain the use of TQM systems throughout the organisation have been Quality Forums which were designed to encourage 'right first time' working. They underline the belief that prevention-orientated business practice is more cost effective than a 'fix it' one and provide a closed-loop framework for on-going learning and application.

As Mr Kruger explains, "Quality Forums are essentially a series of meetings at which a manager or supervisor sits down with his or her staff using discussion and simple exercises to explore aspects of improvement. They are designed to stimulate debate of Quality issues relevant to individual work groups."

Initially managers worked with facilitators in a process designed to transfer responsibility to them. "Forums have a dual benefit: they encourage managers to become coaches and staff to communicate and focus on day-to-day interactions with internal and external customers and suppliers. Quality Forums create a continuous learning process in that each meeting raises new material alongside review and reinforcement of what has previously been done. This blend is key to new joiners as it enables them to pick up at any point rather than go back to the beginning", explains Mr Kruger.

Forums are about putting Quality into practice at an individual level. A key message promoted at Honeywell is that not all TQM initiatives need to be the result of a group effort. An example of this was the effort of Rob Bentley, a senior sales support engineer within Birmingham's Fluid Controls Group for streamlining stock systems saving £100,000 in the first year. At the time of the stock review it was confirmed that 15 per cent of the inventory, £33,000 worth was sleeping inventory while there were insufficient holdings of the faster moving stock.

In taking ownership of the problem, Rob Bentley set out to reduce the value of the top five items which were valued at £62,000. A year later they were reduced by 63 per cent to £23,000.

"To achieve this I first talked to customers to determine why they had not been ordering certain products in the volumes expected. This in turn prompted a reduction in the number of stock items carried. Obsolete stock items were sold to distributors at reduced prices to clear them and inactive items were broken down into active parts. Demand reports were analysed item by item and future ordering was adjusted accordingly. The goal was an inventory that mirrored our changing market place", explains Mr Bentley. This initiative has resulted in not only cost savings but a more responsive service.

One of the most challenging problems for Honeywell to resolve was how it was going to measure Quality.

"We expected to come out with a system where people would keep records all around the company about Quality costs. This was a total non-starter in our organisation because the most significant element by far in a sales and service group is people's time. How do you measure people's time and how do you get them to do that honestly? The answer is you can't. If you were to measure month by month or quarter by quarter you would not get a worthwhile trend, so we decided cost of Quality wasn't an appropriate measure to us", explains Mr Kruger. "We know our Quality process is working while the organisation is successful in the market place. We are not focusing on removing resources that are currently part of waste, but believe they should be used to do more profitable work for our customers."

While measurement of the notional value of the cost of Quality was important to initiate TQM, Honeywell has subsequently adopted three primary measures of the TQM process.

1. Level of staff participation. The level of participation is a key measure as it is consistent with Honeywell's philosophy that TQM will only succeed through the actions of staff. Part of this was the speed at which staff went through the initial education programme, with the objective of 100% coverage within three years followed by ensuring that all new recruits commence their TQM training within six months of joining.

2. Staff perceptions of TQM benefits to Honeywell in terms of both progress and aspects which require further attention. Honeywell UK conducts an annual staff opinion survey. The divisional results are presented to every group and discussed so that trends and responses are fully understood. Each business then develops its own action plans to address local issues. Corporate issues identified in the survey are addressed at the top level as improvement projects.

The survey provides a benchmark of the views and expectations of all staff with respect to TQM. The Quality Council developed nine key themes which shape the design of the questionnaire and include: measurement processes for encouraging high business performance; communication; customer needs; inter-divisional co-operation; management processes/ style and people.

3. Customer satisfaction. As Quality improvement actions are ultimately aimed at raising marketplace perceptions of Honeywell, the company views the most valuable measure of progress to be customer satisfaction or, in Honeywell's vocabulary, delight.

In support of this stance Honeywell UK has introduced project ACE (Addressing Customer Expectations) which relies on a process of structured face to face in-depth interviews with key customers conducted by Honeywell salespeople to establish the key attributes customers want in a service provider. Salespeople are encouraged to place their emphasis on finding out where each customer wants to be in the long term and work towards this as well as just the immediate sale. Effectively Honeywell is changing its behaviour to match what its customers want, and is using the customer's input to drive this change.

Honeywell has progressively moved towards managing improvement against the European Quality Award Model because it incorporates all stake holder interests. The organisation is looking for progressive improvement against the model.

"I think the model says that Quality is not something we are doing as an extra. It says we are doing things that will give us a viable business into the future because it doesn't differentiate between the effort you put into Quality and the effort you put into running the business. There is a natural flow which says ultimately that this is about business performance and results", explains Mr Kruger.

Every business division within Honeywell conducts assessments against the model. Assessment resources are shared throughout the European organisation and also draw on external assessors who provide a sanity check by not allowing other assessors to make assumptions based on their knowledge of particular Honeywell businesses. At the conclusion of each assessment the relevant director gets a feedback report and a face to face debrief with the assessment team which highlights the strengths of that unit and improvement areas. Directors then lead the improvement activities against the perceived areas for improvement which has resulted in achieving the goal of Honeywell managing by Total Quality.

Honeywell UK does not place primary importance on applying for external awards. The benefit lies in providing the businesses with check points along the Quality journey. Mr Kruger makes the point: "Using the EQA as our basic measurement and management scheme allows us to say where we came from because we are building on our strengths. We're writing down our achievements and the areas for improvement are the point on the horizon we are aiming for. We are moving somewhere which is managed and controlled. Historically Total Quality was a journey into the unknown and you were always feeling your way in the dark wondering if one day you were going to fall over the edge – because that's where the programme fails."

Although the European Quality Award (EQA) is used by Honeywell throughout Europe as its main assessment tool, other parts of the Honeywell world have chosen to use different methods, for instance the Malcolm Baldrige National Quality Award is used in the United States.

Complementary to the EQA the company has developed an internal measure around the world known as the Honeywell Quality Value (HQV).

Unit performance as assessed by the national Quality award schemes is monitored by top management in Honeywell's head office in the USA and year-by-year improved performance is required. Essentially, all around the Honeywell world there is a unified approach to measurement but freedom for local expression of how best to bring about improvement. This is key to enabling sensitivity to the local business culture to be fully worked through. Thus there is now a marked contrast with the prescriptive approach around the Honeywell world in the 1980s which was not successful in the UK environment as highlighted at the very beginning of this chapter.

Assessment feedback is used by units to initiate improvement activity to ensure visible business benefits at subsequent assessments. Top management in Honeywell then acknowledges achievements through award of the Honeywell Quality Value to units which match the world class benchmarks.

Honeywell's basic approach can be summed up through a simple model the company has used to check its TQM activity. It is based on a balance of three components: Determination; Education; and Implementation. Throughout the process there has always been a working combination of these elements.

Determination
- strong leadership from the CEO
- ownership by the directors
- reinforcement through divisional briefings
- long term view of the challenge
- strategy and planning

Education
- rigorous cascade
- careful selection of facilitators
- process for including new recruits
- reinforcement sessions (Quality Forums)
- active management participation

Implementation
- projects introduced at an early stage
- formal system for recording projects progress
- visibility of improvements
- director recognition of improvement teams
- training process linked strongly to action
- TQM made to fit Honeywell organisation (not the reverse).

Impressive customer satisfaction ratings, the profitability of the company, and the enormous increase and effect of the way in which capital is used in the company are all indicators of the success Honeywell has received from its commitment to total Quality and continuous improvement. Mr Kennedy can proudly state that, "We are the leaders in Honeywell's European world and we are one of the few organisations who are better than what we believe to be world class in levels of working capital."

"Anyone running a business has to produce results. The dissatisfaction with TQM is that most people feel that it has no return in the form of business results. If asked to encourage other companies I would tell them to look at the practical results", counsels Mr Kennedy. "There is the financial component and there is the customer element: has your business grown; is your business more profitable; are you getting a good return on all investment, not just TQM investment; have you penetrated new markets; have you grown your existing markets; do you take more from your existing customer base than you did before; have you attracted new customers? In our case I am very satisfied that the company has prospered as a result of TQM as the catalyst. But we've done it here because of the people who work in the company. No company lives this long unless it is a good company and no company can be a good company unless it has good people."

6

A Superior Performance

— The Macro Group —

IT'S a Friday afternoon and the last day of the financial month. On entering The Macro Group's reception area you automatically notice the array of framed documents and certificates on display. As recognition of the Group's superior performance it has been the recipient of many awards presented by a variety of suppliers, customers and industry bodies. The *pièce de résistance* however is the European Distributor of the Year Award presented by Dataquest, part of Dun and Bradstreet.

Meanwhile, the staff members who provide a warm greeting are enthusiastically exploring the recently installed Automatic Call Distribution system. There is nothing particularly out of the ordinary about this scenario, at least for an organisation considered to be a leader in its industry and committed to Quality. But to use a cliché it is the calm before the storm.

Open the doors to the sales area and you are immediately struck by a surge of activity and sense of urgency – phones ringing, people on the move and the electronic display panel flashing messages as the financial month draws to a close and budgets are met. The fast pace requires fast talking and internal acronyms and abbreviations fly ... SPDs, IOFs, GRNs, PSG, ICs ... as sales personnel encourage one another to meet team goals.

For such a fervid environment the product is decidedly unglamorous, unofficially described as 'little black chips with legs attached' or known more formally as semiconductors. Yet the sales team is so enthusiastic and innovative in their approach it wouldn't matter what commodity they were selling.

The Macro Group is Britain's leading, and only ISO9001 certified,

Marianne Culver
Managing Director
Macro Group

Paul Webster
Director of Marketing
Macro Group

Macro use leading edge technology to provide exceptional customer support for some 7,500 active semiconductor customers

franchised distributor of semiconductor components for some of the world's largest manufacturers, servicing the UK, Eire and eastern European markets. The Group, which is primarily a sales and marketing organisation, consists of three trading names Macro, Anzac and Flashpoint. While the core business of each is in essence the same, Flashpoint is differentiated from Macro and Anzac by the markets it serves and the nature of its customer relationships.

Macro and Anzac, which trade under the Macro Group banner, serve a variety of clients and industries such as British Aerospace, Design to Distribution, Siemens, GEC and Fujitsu, as well as a variety of satellite communication, multi-media and automotive companies. These relationships are characteristically long term, some spanning 25 years, and involve high-level customer support and account management through the provision of services such as flexible scheduling, asset management, credit facilities and technical support.

Flashpoint, however, directly services the PC markets and also supports the value added reseller market which tend to be more fickle and opportunistic. Consequently, accounts are typically less established and low maintenance, prompting a business response which is defined by lean inventories, high turnover of product and reduced dependence on technical and customer support programmes.

The Group, founded in 1969, has long been at the forefront of its industry, recording leading levels of service, innovation, stability and profitability. Consistent with the belief that it is essential to provide local service to conform with cultural expectations Macro operates offices in England, Ireland and Scotland. Its 388 strong staff strive to provide fast response, order processing and next day delivery from a warehouse which carries £18 million of stock. In the last three years Macro Group's turnover has increased from £40 million to £80 million. A large proportion of this has been organic growth and the Group is now servicing approximately 15,000 customers and 8,000 trading accounts.

Yet the Group is not complacent in the shadow of its achievements and has recently embarked on an ambitious change process, not for survival but to ensure further growth. "Even though we have had a very successful period, we are still growing and we have to make some strong decisions now while we have the choice rather than when we are inextricably driven. It is an avoidance of crisis management in the future", explains Marianne Culver, Managing Director of The Macro Group.

Marianne joined Macro in 1987 as a sales representative in Middlesex and NW London and from there progressed to an internal position in Inventory Management and Purchasing. The climb from here was swift, progressing to Customer Service Manager of Macro in 1989 and moving to the position of Commercial Manager of Anzac in 1992. While in this post she and the senior management team increased the company's turnover from £7 million to £18 million in two years through, as Marianne describes, "straightforward, durable, pragmatic, logical strategy which primarily involved getting close to suppliers whom we had previously held at arms length encouraging them to give us more product to ship." From a base of solid achievement and following the resignation of Macro Group's previous Managing Director, Marianne was appointed to this position in March 1994.

"We have grown significantly throughout a recessionary period, and we have grown battling against the market perception that you need to be a Pan European or global organisation to succeed. Our attitude is that we can provide world class local service", explains Caroline Dawson, Customer Services Manager, who believes that within the service industries it will become increasingly difficult to distinguish between Quality and Service which is the primary reason the Quality mantle resides with her.

Macro is differentiated from many sales organisations in that everybody sits out on the sales floor, including the Managing Director which is symbolic of the absence of barriers, whether perceived or physical within the organisational structure. "The idea is that everybody is accessible – if you have an idea, a suggestion, or a problem you can go directly to the most appropriate person and while we do have some hierarchical structure it doesn't serve as a political barrier preventing access to people further up the ladder. If the MD is the most appropriate person to talk to then you talk directly to the MD", explains Caroline.

The Group employs people with drive and who are not restrained by perceived limitations, which is consistent with Macro's culture. Similarly the introduction of ISO9001 certification, in October 1993, was not seen as a hindrance to the business in any way. The top-level Quality manual consists of only 11 pages as Caroline explains: "We do not have a Quality department and we are not bound by a rigid Quality manual. We negotiated with BSI during their assessment visit in the same way we would negotiate with a customer to arrive at the most appropriate outcome. The BSI point of view is that providing the appropriate processes are in place and kept up to date then it does not have to be any more onerous on say Field Sales than prior to receiving certification. In fact only two of the 18 clauses are relevant to 80 per cent of the company and they involve contract review and corrective action."

The top-level Quality manual specifies that management reviews chaired by the Quality Director and attended by all managers with operational responsibility for sales and service will occur on an annual basis to ensure:

- That all procedural documentation is up to date and that it continues to meet the business aims and objectives of the Group.
- That the internal audit results are used to ensure that the documented Quality system is fully implemented.
- That the non-conformance statistics. published monthly are used to identify corrective actions.

Each operational group has a series of minimum standards designed to ensure that the Group offers exceptional customer service and remains profitable. Employees are then measured against these standards as part of their performance review process.

Macro's TQM initiative, 'Mission to Improve', of which ISO9001 certification is just one element, was launched with the involvement of the entire organisation to combat negative perceptions and resistance to change. "Because people realised we were doing so well it was difficult to explain to them that we could be doing better", explains Caroline. "When we launched our initiative we invited every employee to the sales floor on the first working day in January and each was greeted by the Group's new mission statement personalised with their name, placed on top of their PC to instil a sense of ownership. This type of activity refreshed our Quality approach but more importantly impressed upon everybody the essential message: remember the day, but remember your significance to it and to providing a Quality service. Although this one day was significant we are constantly looking for ways to improve our processes. This will not only allow us to stay ahead of the competition, but to move further away from them", explains Caroline.

The Group's mission statement was originally drafted by the senior management team with input and guidance from staff, customers and suppliers. It pledges that: "The Macro Group strives to achieve the highest standards on behalf of our customers, suppliers and staff. Our strengths are characterised by our clarity of purpose, quality of leadership, dedicated teamwork, mutual respect and desire for excellence. Our goal is to maximise turnover and minimise cost to achieve optimum profit in our chosen market place." To again indicate that the Group's quality initiative is not a static process the mission statement is under review to see if it still reflects the attitudes of the company members.

Macro's constant drive to improve quality performance is underpinned by a culture of measurement across the whole company with minimum standards set for each operation. "Measurement of Quality processes is a key issue for a service company because unlike a manufacturing company we can't say that we have saved £100,000 from putting a different bolt in a car on a production line. Often the cost has to be quantified in terms of lost opportunities. We will benefit by removing noise (errors) from the business through our IT platform, for example, which will allow us to make our processes more efficient", explains Paul Webster, Director of Marketing. Paul joined Macro in 1991 as a senior manager from a background in the electronics industry and moved to his current position in 1993.

Macro started measuring its performance 18 months prior to the launch of the 'Mission to Improve' initiative and continues to investigate ways of increasing its efficiency. Every material return received or credit raised because of error, which not only inconveniences the customer but adds to business costs, was investigated. Measurement is conducted on a departmental level and frequently on an individual level across nine categories such as invoicing error, short shipments, faulty product, incorrect pricing. Once problem areas were identified the company developed departmental minimum standard service commitments taking input from all staff on what they wanted their service commitment to be as an individual and as a member of a team.

Subsequently the Group has developed Customer Service standards designed to improve the Quality of the services it offers specifically covering:

- Accuracy of order processing
- Accuracy and timeliness of deliveries
- Quality of technical advice
- Staff training

Performance in these areas has been targeted and quantified, with measurement systems put in place to report regularly to the Managing Director on the company's performance. Macro polls users of its services on elements such as: accuracy of delivery; quality of packaging; and effectiveness of the selected carrier. It is then the responsibility of all managers to ensure that the areas of their responsibility comply with all aspects of the Macro Group Quality control system.

Consistent with the Macro Group's mission to constantly strive to achieve the highest standards on behalf of its customers, suppliers and staff was the introduction of Macro's ADVANCE programme.

The objectives of this programme are to:

- Effect tangible, long lasting improvements to costs of trading, Quality issues and service levels;
- Produce comprehensive, objective reviews of each supplier's performance; and
- Statistically measure and factually quantify criteria across all trading areas.

The programme forms the basis of a manufacturer/Macro Group business review conducted at a senior management level. The franchise development manager assumes responsibility for the programmes and co-ordinates and documents the assessments from each department which are reviewed in conjunction with supporting documentation.

The review is broken up into a number of process areas including: the Sales Group; Product Marketing Group; Logistics and Quality; Information Technology and overall performance. Performance is rated using a points system based on specific measurement criteria for each element. In some critical service measurements penalties are given for particularly poor achievement. As an example delivery performance and accuracy are measured where the criteria for on time are: Poor <80%; Average 81%–91%; Good 92%–97%; Excellent >98%. In the event that on time delivery occurs on less than 70% of occasions a one point penalty is incurred. Accuracy is measured in terms of non receipts, short shipments and wrong receipts as a percentage of total shipments.

A prominent philosophy at Macro is that people are key to the company's success. A scheme introduced to emphasise this belief was the Local Hero scheme which rewards and recognises staff on a monthly basis by department for exceptional performance. "When we originated the scheme there was some management debate as to why we should reward people for doing their job. However, the other side of the argument is that in general British industry is not good enough at saying well done to its people", explains Caroline.

One of the significant elements of the Local Hero scheme is the awareness generated of departmental standards. To win the award one of the criteria requires that the candidate is recognised for providing exceptional customer service by an internal customer. Every department has a box for this purpose and individuals can nominate colleagues when they have received exceptional service. The field sales team has extended this scheme by introducing a similar programme to recognise quality service provided by staff to the end customer.

The Macro Group provides a participative environment in which to work encouraging all employees to contribute to improving the business. An example of a staff lead initiative was the development of a procedural document outlining internal best practice for the internal sales team created by people in the division. It contains step by step procedures which are flow charted providing details such as: the skills required in the division, levels of authority, questions to ask at point of enquiry and setting up a contract.

"As a company which continually changes we have had to develop our people so that they understand these changes are not introduced for the sake of change but rather to improve the systems and improve their working environment", explains Paul. "Part of the solution has been to introduce consultative cross-functional teams of employees in recent years to review current activity, look at problems and just explore what could be different."

Improvement is driven forward using discrete cross-functional teams which are established to review particular practices. Caroline provides an illustration of this type of improvement activity: "One of our contract managers consistently managed to deliver his customers' invoiced requirements to them the next day. He dealt with major clients who required the utmost flexibility often requiring the option to alter their orders until 6pm of the day prior to delivery. We could never understand how he managed to incorporate their needs within the tight time frame. The key was that he knew the system better than anybody else so we put him on a brainstorming team to improve the process. His method was simple, he had encouraged his customers to place their orders by supplier because this is how our warehouse is organised, so his invoices were assembled more efficiently. He was actually educating his customers to order within the parameters of his picking list which was of no consequence to them but expedited the process at his end."

The Group has recently undergone substantial re-organisation of its management structure which in turn has impacted on the sales function. As a product of organisational change the number of direct reports to the Managing Director was reduced from 10 to a more manageable four. "This resulted in six people, most of whom still work for the Group, who no longer directly report to the Managing Director. Potentially this can lead to feelings of demotivation and isolation so we have focused on making people feel valued in their new roles", explains Paul. "It's all about discussing the change process with everybody, but especially those most directly affected by it so they understand why things are changing and how these changes will impact on them. We are not going to try and rebuild private pyramids but we will give people direction so they can see what they can achieve and how they will need to develop to realise these goals."

The re-structure was generated by senior and middle management team activity. The Managing Director facilitated the process by selecting teams to give it some structure, establishing the time scale and the reporting procedure. Functional teams reviewed the company's key functions including sales and marketing, logistics, and warehousing.

Macro is in essence a sales operation. Consequently, the restructure had a significant effect on the sales team. "When we were planning the geographical restructure of the sales area we spent a lot of time categorising accounts; defining strategies for selling to different tiers of accounts, quantifying the number of accounts in each geographic area and determining what information we possessed on the database and what we needed to generate", explains Marianne.

The internal sales department is now divided into four geographical teams which sit together on the open-plan sales floor to increase the level of interaction and replace the traditional individual rivalry with a healthier sense of team spirit. "There is now increased ownership, responsibility, personal respect and mutual trust. The message is if you are looking for somebody to rely on, look at your neighbour."

With change and restructuring comes a need for training. At every performance review training and development requirements are determined and highlighted by the HR department. By way of example Marianne explains, "all warehouse personnel are now making use of technological changes and are scanning everything using bar coding. The personnel in the warehouse are some of our longest-serving employees with an average age of 40 so with the introduction of bar coding in 1994 we had to provide a lot of training because many of them had no previous contact with computerised systems."

In support of Macro's training commitment it has compiled a database of every employee, the nature of training they have undertaken and their level of achievement, with certificates signed by the Managing Director presented to those who successfully complete a training course. Every person recruited to the organisation completes an in-house induction course, success in which determines whether the candidate is formally employed by the company.

The Macro Group has invested heavily in its IT capability. All field sales staff are provided with a laptop so that they can process data immediately and to ensure they have access to on-line information. Every employee has a PC operating a windows environment providing access to MIDASS (Macro Integrated Distribution and Sales System), a bespoke sales software system.

The concept of MIDASS is based on providing the customer with a single point of contact who can meet all requirements without keeping the customer on the telephone for longer than necessary and without placing the onus on the customer to remember details from past transactions. In part this is achieved by providing the sales person with as much information as possible about customer accounts and product details. "The sales system is geared so that a customer can make an enquiry, convert an enquiry into an order, reschedule an order, etc. and only needs to speak with one person to satisfy any of these needs", explains Caroline.

MIDASS allows the sales person to open a customer file on receipt of a call using a variety of prompts. A company name is sufficient to open the relevant file which then contains a barrage of information such as personnel responsible for managing the account, details of the last order transacted and enquiries not converted.

Macro's major suppliers are connected to the system via Electronic Data Interchange (EDI) and provide production and lead-time information on a 24-hour basis. "Everything we do is in an effort to remove the irritation factor, because once that is removed we can get on with the business; we have the stock, the price and we can deliver it tomorrow", says Caroline.

"Importantly we are not just servicing our suppliers and external customers, but also our internal customers. That's where the Quality issue is critically important because inter-departmentally we knew we were making it very difficult for ourselves to reach decisions because of the chain of communication and the amount of paper processing it required. We are a substantially different organisation to five years ago. We can now provide a far more rapid response through more on-line information which in part relies on continued investment in IT, but also in defining and refining the internal processes", explains Marianne.

"We are the accredited and preferred distributor with major clients which reflects that we are constantly listening to our customers, our suppliers and our people. It is essential not to forget about your people because they are your ambassadors who drive the business. You cannot run a business without good quality people, developed and nurtured through a commitment to training and through recognition and reward. To achieve this we need to be cash generative and profitable which puts you in a better position to reinvest in your people to make them feel valued. We try and instil confidence in our people and give them every opportunity to express their views which is something the Macro Group has always done and must continue to do."

Mel Gosling
Assistant General Manager, Corporate

left to right: Alan Clarke (Director), Michael Bright (Chief Executive), Robert McCracken (Director), Philip Condon (Director)

7

Time For Quality

—Independent Insurance Company—

INDEPENDENT Insurance was formed in 1987 from the faltering UK branch of American Allstate. However, the expertise and impatience of the new management team rapidly distinguished Independent Insurance as a market leader. The management team, led by Michael Bright, now Chief Executive and Managing Director, initiated significant changes embracing all spheres of the company's activity.

A fundamental philosophy which differentiates Independent Insurance from much of the industry is its practice of underwriting to make a profit rather than for cash flow. In 1987 the company recorded a gross written premium (the closest thing to turnover in the insurance industry) of £36 million and incurred a loss of £1 million. However, the company's commitment to performance improvement and its eagerness for results returned GWP of £46 million and profits of £5 million in its second year. This was only the start of the turnaround and by the end of 1994 GWP was £279 million contributing profits of £23 million. GWP is predicted to be more than £400 million by the end of 1995.

Success has continued to flow from the company's early growth and profit – the stock market float of Independent Insurance in 1993 was oversubscribed; it acquired the ongoing business of Aegon UK, a company larger than itself in terms of income in late 1994; and it was voted Best Overall Insurer for the third year running in 1995 by brokers at the Insurance Industry Awards.

The company operates in the UK general insurance market selling exclusively through brokers. It is committed to remaining a broker only company and has pioneered a select approach choosing to conduct the bulk of its business with less than 200 brokers who are referred to as 'Club Brokers'. This select approach is the cornerstone of the company's strategies.

"The importance of the broker relationship cannot be undervalued and to demonstrate our commitment we conceived and developed the 'Club' concept which provides a package of benefits to our key brokers including exclusive products, training and marketing assistance, IT consultancy, access to senior staff and profit share on the business that they write", explains Mel Gosling, Assistant General Manager Corporate whose role encompasses responsibility for Total Quality Management as well as IT Strategy.

The results Independent Insurance have achieved to date are even more exceptional given that the environment in which it competes has become increasingly competitive since the 1980s. Dramatic changes have required individual companies to adapt or withdraw from the competition. The insurance market is consolidating and will continue to do so as commentators predict further merger activity. The size of the insurance industry has already declined from 150 main players in the UK to no more than 50 which in turn has resulted in a redistribution of income.

The impact of these trends on Independent Insurance has been positive as Mr Bright explains: "There is no longer a common agenda for the insurance industry which started to fragment in the early 1980s both in terms of the nature of supply and its attitude towards commercial and personal consumers. Gone are the days where the consumer had no influence over the product and how it was delivered. Today the consumer is regarded as King and each supplier has developed a different set of objectives to meet their needs. This situation has occurred because of a number of factors, the most significant of which are that the insurance industry no longer supplies a homogeneous range of products; and segmentation has occurred in both the end market and in the nature of distribution channels used to supply the product.

"Adapting and meeting these challenges has enabled us to grow more than tenfold in eight years and achieve a consistent record of profit growth. At the end of the day it is the quality of the product and the service provided to the customer that is crucial. What makes this company stand out from the others is that we believe in the principles of insurance and we don't take short cuts – we underwrite every single risk that we write."

The insurance industry has been hit by technology harder than many other industries in the UK, not so much because the technological impact is different but because it was so far behind industry in general that the 'catch up' speed needed to be greater. For example, most of the business was bought through broking connections up until the late 1980s. This practice has been replaced by telephone based, personalised direct marketing operations, particularly at the retail end of the market such as Personal Lines business.

Telephone operations now account for a third of the market and continue to grow. At the opposite end of the supply spectrum many captive insurance companies have been formed where a particular company develops such a wide spread of risk they can undertake to insure it themselves.

Independent Insurance employs over 1,200 staff in 14 offices around Britain and it writes all main classes of general insurance. "At Independent Insurance, we have always operated a policy of developing products in consultation with our broker colleagues. This means that we can provide the covers demanded in a dynamic and highly competitive market place", explains Mr Bright.

The company's products fall into three main categories: 'Commercial Lines' including professional indemnity, business liability and corporate solutions; 'Specialist Lines' including marine, accident, sickness and travel insurance, contingency and special events coverage; and 'Personal Lines' including home insurance, Homeworkers, motor and schemes and affinity groups.

Despite Independent Insurance's innovative product portfolio it is acutely aware that it cannot rely on that alone as Corporate Manager Kevin Pallett explains: "It is becoming increasingly difficult to compete on product attributes alone within the insurance industry because the number of differentiating factors between one company's offering and another is diminishing. The service you provide to the end customer and brokers therefore becomes one of the key deciding issues. We are actually competing on Quality and our ambition to offer a world class service, not just in our industry but measured against the best in the world, is reflected in our statement of corporate aims."

In the face of numerous potential management distractions choosing the appropriate time to launch the TQM initiative was imperative to ensure that it was accepted and adopted by management and staff alike. The need for TQM was identified in 1990 at a planning conference, however the implementation of new computer systems during 1991 and 1992, and Independent Insurance's stock market activity in 1993 prevented its introduction until 1994.

At the time of TQM's introduction the company had undergone rapid growth and received industry recognition for the quality of its service, however Independent Insurance still regarded TQM as an essential strategic element to ensure continued prosperity as Mr Gosling explains: "We know we are a successful company and we need to continue to be successful. Independent Insurance is no stranger to change because we acknowledge that we can't stand still in an industry which is changing and improving rapidly. It is important that we maintain our reputation as a market leader, by offering world class service and above average return on investments to those who invest in the company, including the 70 per cent of our staff who are shareholders."

At a planning conference in July 1993 a decision was made to implement TQM which was followed by management and staff briefings and the establishment of a top quality team known as the Quality Management Team. The delay in implementing the initial stages of the TQM initiative provided Independent Insurance with the opportunity to conduct extensive research of both its customers and employees as well as to investigate the cost associated with not operating a quality programme. "In quantifying the cost of quality we had two objectives: firstly to establish how much not getting it right first time was costing us and secondly to identify some priority areas in the company. Although we couldn't calculate an overall company figure for the cost of quality, the specific figures we did produce were sufficiently frightening to justify taking action. In some areas we estimated that up to 40 per cent of our expenses were going down the drain", says Mr Gosling.

The Quality improvement structure adopted by Independent Insurance (Figure 1 which is reproduced with the permission of Price Waterhouse) is modelled on the organisational structure and accordingly requires every member of staff to participate in the process. The structure consists of three primary levels: the Quality Management Team; a hierarchy of Quality Improvement Teams; and a number of Quality Action Teams,

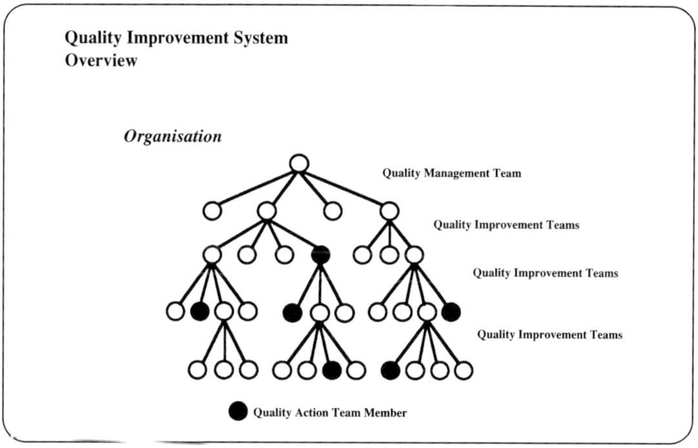

Price Waterhouse © 1993

ad hoc teams which evolve to address specific issues that cross various functions.

The Quality Management Team which consists of the Chief Executive and his direct reports is charged with the overall responsibility for managing the process which involves the following activities:

- Leading the quality improvement effort
- Planning, installing, and managing the system
- Creating the systems and environment for problem solving by others
- Providing a charter and guidelines for Quality Improvement Teams
- Appointing and managing Quality Action Teams

The team meets regularly and each member is responsible for one of the eight core elements of the programme which are:

- Commitment
- Awareness
- Results
- Organisation
- Planning
- Accountability
- Recognition
- Renewal

For instance, Mr Pallett is responsible for the 'renewal' aspect of the Quality programme which involves maintaining the momentum for the programme, and making Quality an integral characteristic of the corporate culture so it ceases to be perceived as a special programme. Mr Pallett maintains that renewal becomes automatic once the other elements are realised. "The role of the QMT is to bring all the managing elements together so that our Quality effort contributes to the bottomline. This means planning and organising our activity carefully so that everyone contributes and understands that Quality really matters."

The key to the successful implementation of Independent Insurance's quality initiative is that it is driven from the top, the chief executive, who is appropriately responsible for the 'commitment' aspect. "Unless all our Senior Managers are totally committed to the programme it will fail. We are committed because we know that our Quality Improvement Programme is contributing directly to growth and profits", explains Mr Bright.

Quality Improvement Teams (QITs) mirror particular departments or groups of people working in the same business area. They are selected by the Quality Management Team which establishes performance targets for the Quality Improvement Programme and defines key areas on which the QITs should focus.

Membership of the QITs consists of a unit supervisor who reports

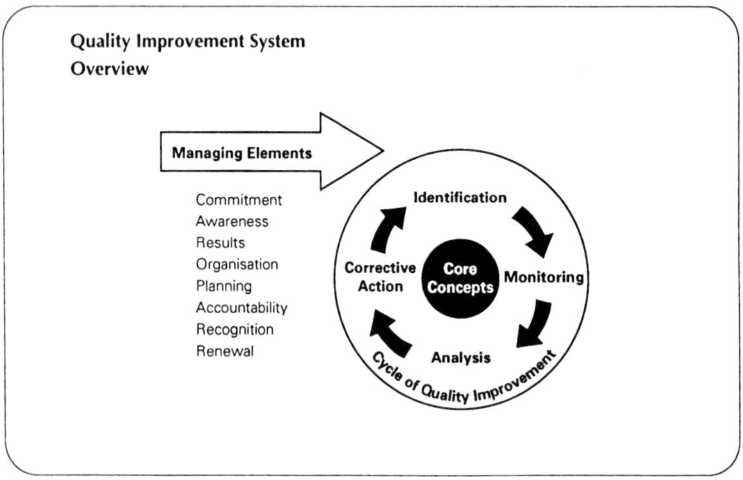

Price Waterhouse © 1993

up through the organisation to the QMT and their direct reports. Teams use the Cycle of Quality Improvement as shown in Figure 2 (reproduced with the permission of Price Waterhouse) to identify and eliminate defects and remove barriers to quality work. A hierarchy of QITs exists to examine local issues through to corporate policy.

Regardless of the level at which a QIT is operating it is expected to focus on issues which improve customer service, reduce costs to the company and/or the time it takes to do certain parts of a job. There are a number of QITs whose members are geographically dispersed. In these situations members need only attend meetings on a monthly basis rather than weekly.

Quality Action Teams (QATs) are formed to address specific company-wide issues and for this reason typically have a cross-functional membership. The lifespan of a QAT is determined by the duration of the problem as they are disbanded once the problem is resolved again adhering to the Cycle of Quality Improvement.

A full time Quality Manager, Anne Harrison was appointed in April 1995. One of her primary responsibilities is to provide a focal point for QITs to help them with problem selection, simple progress monitoring, and provide guidance and coaching to improve the quality of the service they provide.

Initially three QATs were established to tackle the three biggest issues identified in the internal research. These included incomplete and incorrect proposal forms received from brokers; IT issues; and reconciliation of broker accounts where brokers dispute the accuracy of the account.

The QAT set up to investigate and address incorrect/incomplete New Business Personal Lines Proposal Forms consisted of people from different areas of the business including marketing, underwriting, processing and also brokers towards the end of the exercise. Mr Gosling was a member of each QAT to provide continuity between the teams. To put the problem in context, all brokers are required to complete a proposal form for any risk submitted to Independent Insurance. However, typically 70 to 80 per cent of those forms contained incomplete or incorrect information which prevented the company processing the business immediately and therefore required additional time and effort to return to the source to obtain those details. The estimated cost to the company annually of this problem was in excess of half a million pounds. Using the Cycle of Quality Improvement the team arrived at the following recommended corrective actions:

- Redesign of proposal forms
- Assessment of underwriting issues
- Involvement of members of the public at the design stage of new proposal forms
- Further involvement with brokers and personal lines unit staff with form design
- Education of brokers

The corrective action reduced error rates from a previous high of 89 per cent in some instances to less than 30 per cent in 12 months equating to an annual saving of more than £250 thousand in processing costs.

The Cycle of Quality Improvement provides a systematic problem-solving methodology consisting of four elements (identification of quality problems, monitoring, analysis and corrective action to eliminate identified problems) which are repeated until a performance standard of Zero Defects is achieved.

Price Waterhouse commenting on the misconception that inspection plays a role in the quality improvement process suggests: "Inspection does not improve quality – less of the output may contain defects, but costs increase and they tend to become permanent." Price Waterhouse has provided advice to Independent Insurance since the inception of its TQM initiative and the relationship between the two organisations has since then evolved into an on-going partnership.

The theory behind the Quality Improvement Cycle was introduced to Independent Insurance staff in a workshop situation. The stages of the four step Cycle of Quality Improvement as developed and defined by Price Waterhouse include:

- **Identification**

  Recognising the problem through unit self-assessment, customer interviews, existing performance indicators, quality barrier discussions or referrals from other units;

  Defining the nature and extent of the problem, and the effect of the problem using methods such as process flow charting or requirements analysis for input, process, output and customers;

  Logging to record defects and barriers as well as the status of corrective action;

Prioritising the order in which barriers or defects should be addressed using methods such as impact and trend ranking where top priority is assigned to the defect having the highest impact and the least favourable trend; effort analysis where top priority goes to the defect requiring the least effort to solve; benefit analysis which concentrates effort on the defect with the greatest potential saving on resolution; frequency analysis where top priority goes to the defect occurring most frequently; or priority is assigned according to experience and judgement.

- **Monitoring** key defect areas to measure defect levels, track the progress of corrective action, and establish and maintain awareness by gathering and displaying defect frequency and trend data.
- **Analysis of the situation** to find the root causes of defects so they can be eliminated by corrective action. The tools that can be used in this process include brainstorming, cause and effect (fishbone) analysis, Pareto analysis and experimentation.
- **Corrective action** through the elimination of defects at the root cause ensuring that the situation is monitored after corrective action has been taken to ensure that defect reduction objectives are met.

The value of using the Cycle of Quality Improvement is that it makes the teams address all aspects of a problem as Mr Pallett explains: "Taking unacceptable processing times as an example, it is not just about changing the way the computer system works, nor about changing people's attitudes, nor necessarily about changing the whole business process. You need to act on all three so that they interact in a way that provides the ideal solution. So in answer to this problem you would review a number things such as encouraging more from the operator, simplifying the forms or asking whether certain pieces of information are even needed", explains Mr Pallett.

Independent Insurance has already derived significant benefit from introducing TQM to its operation, however it still presents a challenge for the future as Mr Bright explains: "We are unashamedly very results driven and strive to achieve those results within ever tightening deadlines. Just as expediency is part of our culture, we need to infuse Quality thinking into our everyday activity so that it ceases to be a special programme."

left to right: Fiona Walters (Organisational Development Manager – Securicor Custodial Services), Richard Powell (Managing Director – Securicor Custodial Services), Michelle Clark (Divisional Quality Manager – Security Services)

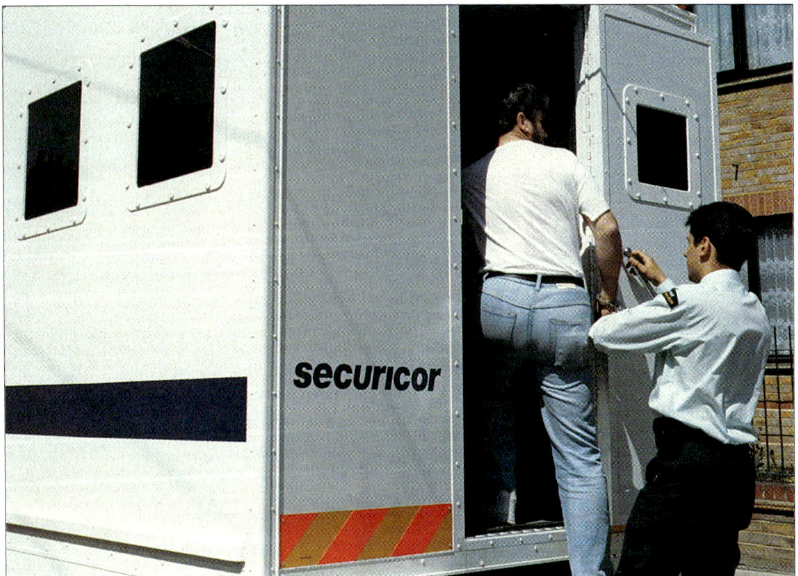

Securicor Custodial Services

8

A Safe Pair of Hands

— Securicor Custodial Services —

IN the UK, the name Securicor is synonymous with security; the word even appears in the Oxford English Dictionary. However, the Securicor Group currently operates internationally in 35 countries providing a comprehensive portfolio of business-to-business services encompassing security, distribution, communications and related activities. Part of the Group's mission is to provide world-class services in a number of well considered market sectors where its capabilities and resources enable it to maintain a prominent market position. More fundamental is its desire to ensure that the Securicor brand remains synonymous with integrity, reliability and security. This theme has been consistent throughout the development of the Group and is maintained across each of its operating divisions.

As Henry McKay, Chief Executive of the Security Services Division, comments: "Our aim is to continually provide customers with Quality services that add value to their businesses. Our business is very people-dependent – in fact, in the UK alone, we employ more than 16,000 people in security related activities. We recognise that, on a daily basis, our reputation for quality of service is very much in the hands of our employees, so recruitment, training and customer care programmes are given the highest priority. This significant investment, combined with a strong emphasis on developing management capability from within the organisation, has supported the company's growth both in the UK and overseas and at the same time allowed us to diversify into related businesses such as Custodial Services."

Securicor began life in 1935 operating with a small group of guards in the West End of London and commenced a tradition of expansion using a 'service on service' approach. Building on its existing expertise, it became involved in the secure transport of cash, which over time gave it the resources and capability to undertake the distribution of valuable goods and then parcels. Over the next three decades the Group grew and diversified through the provision of support services to the starter businesses and the development of complementary services.

Following a period of tremendous growth and success in the 1980s, Securicor divisionalised to group its businesses in a more logical manner and provide a stronger focus in all activities. Since this time, there has been a pronounced devolution of management and control to strategic business units within four key business divisions:

- Security Services, with companies providing secure transportation, processing and redistribution of cash and valuables, guarding, alarms monitoring and response, and custodial services;
- Distribution Services covering parcels, document and freight distribution, both domestic and international, including the provision of integrated logistic solutions;
- Communications including cellular products and service provision, radio systems and Linear Modulation technology, telecommunications equipment and technology, Datatrak vehicle location and data communication, electronic engineering and design;
- Business Services as varied as vehicle fleet services, hotels, recruitment and computer services.

"Although the Securicor Group has a very strong commitment to Quality (highlighted by its commitment to the British Quality Foundation and founder sponsorship of the UK Quality Award), each of the divisions is given the scope to develop independently and focus on its specific needs", explains Michelle Clark, Quality Manager for the Security Services Division. "The Group has deliberately not enforced a directive approach to business improvement, recognising that although they share the same Securicor core values, the diverse range of businesses display very real cultural differences which respond to different methods of business improvement and Quality management. The principles of Total Quality remain the same, of course – it's just the practical application that varies, but there are many common areas where we try to ensure that experience and best practice are shared."

One of the most recent additions to the Securicor stable of companies, and one which represents a natural progression in the Group's development, is Custodial Services. The formation of this company has drawn heavily from the expertise and services across the established Securicor businesses.

Few people or organisations can claim to have willingly entered the prison system – a characteristic which distinguishes Securicor from many of its traditional competitors. Securicor Custodial Services was established in response to the Government's privatisation programme for prisons and prisoner escorting activities. The company has equipped itself to meet the needs of four general areas of activity outsourced by the Home Office: court escorting; the design and management of prisons; immigration; and electronic monitoring of offenders.

The strength of the Group's 'service on service' activities was very evident during Custodial Services' tender preparation for the prestigious £20 million a year Metropolitan District escorting contract. This was the company's first contract, which after careful planning, went live in June 1994. It involves the movement of approximately 200,000 prisoners per year between police stations, prisons and courts and maintaining their safe custody at court.

"The resources for this contract were drawn from many of the Group's specialist divisions. This involvement included the provision of purpose-built security transport vehicles by Bedwas Bodyworks, a Business Services division company; the provision of advanced communication systems by Cellular Services; vehicle tracking and monitoring provided by Datatrak; provision of IT systems by the in-house divisional IT function; sourcing and fitting branches by the divisional Property function; physical monitoring of security at the branch locations by Alarms and Guarding companies, and negotiation for medical and catering supplies by the divisional Purchasing function. Someone once commented that the only thing Securicor didn't provide for this contract was the prisoners!" explains David Winter, Deputy Chief Executive, Security Services Division.

In establishing a presence in the custodial services sector Securicor has overcome a number of obstacles. Law and order is always high on any political party's agenda and therefore any potential outsourcing of public sector work is likely to attract some opposition.

But as Sir Peter Imbert, a non-executive director of Securicor Group and formerly Commissioner of the Metropolitan Police states: "The police are not the right people to transport and look after prisoners. They themselves would wish to be concentrating on what they are appointed to do: patrolling our streets, investigating crimes, preventing crime and generally serving the community. They shouldn't be driving prison vans. That is a waste of enormously valuable resources."

Another of the initial challenges experienced in establishing Custodial Services was defining the nature and requirements of its customers as Richard Powell, Managing Director, Securicor Custodial Services explains: "As a customer the 'government' was difficult to define because it is represented by a number of different agencies. In the case of the prison service it was a relatively easy task because there was a central, dedicated unit established within the Home Office to manage the prisons privatisation process. However, court escorting was more complex because this process had never been run by central government. It was managed by the police who were localised in 43 different constabularies and the prison service which is organised at a local gaol level.

"There were a large number of users including the courts, court staff, legal representatives, prisons, prisoners and of course the Home Office, all of whom had a different view about what they should receive. To simplify the process we identified the key customer as the one who paid for the service, the Home Office, which today provides a dedicated monitor to measure our performance against set criteria.

"There was also a balance to strike in that although the Home Office may believe that the contractor is delivering well against the established performance criteria, those at the operational level may be dissatisfied. I believe that Securicor have addressed this. Indeed a Home Office performance survey conducted during the first year of operation showed that nearly all court staff felt Securicor delivered a service equal to or better than that provided previously. Our everyday operations were rated as satisfactory or very satisfactory by 97 per cent of Court Clerks, Police staff and prison respondents."

Defining value for money presented a problem for both the Home Office and Securicor because central government did not have a comprehensive understanding of what the cost of the court escorting and prison operations had been prior to approaching the private sector.

"When we were invited to tender for the initial contracts we were given very few objective service delivery requirements with which we had to comply, and in the main contractors were invited to suggest appropriate levels of service which were generally accepted by the Home Office",explains David Beaton, Projects Director. "If you imagine the standards as pieces of a jigsaw puzzle, the pieces provided by the government only gave us half the picture. The remaining gaps represented a risk to us as the supplier and to our stakeholders. To eliminate risks we introduced our own standards which in many instances exceeded the targets provided by the government. These were built into our price from the outset of the contract."

Of all the companies competing for custodial service contracts Securicor is the only one which is publicly listed and it is the only organisation which provides services to a diverse range of industries. The Securicor brand has been built on the concept of the 'safe pair of hands' and the risk associated with failure in this sensitive and high-profile arena is potentially damaging to the entire Group. Therefore, the need for exacting internal standards and procedures above those issued by the government is essential to protect the Securicor name.

The potential risk to people and property associated with duties discharged by companies in the Security Services Division is substantial and therefore demands daily adherence to stringent procedures. Along with many other companies within the Group, the Securicor Cash Services, Guarding and Alarms monitoring companies have all obtained ISO accreditation for their branches and offices, and have viewed registration as a good opportunity to reassess and improve current systems and practices. While Custodial Services has yet to approach registration, the company has been committed to Quality principles from its inception. "The nature of Custodial Services's contracts requires that its performance is measured against continuing improvement of standards across key deliverables, hence it was necessary to introduce Quality programmes from the beginning. Our record to date is impressive and based on sound procedures", explains David Winter.

When Securicor first entered the custodial services market, contracts were offered on a cost-plus basis because neither the customer nor the suppliers understood the full magnitude of the service required. However, with improved knowledge of the processes involved, contracts have evolved to become fixed price in nature, providing an element of stability for both the government and the contractor.

Conforming to fixed-price contracts, accompanied by stringent performance standards which are designed to become more rigorous over the duration of the contract, has meant that continuous improvement processes were observed from day one and have become an integral part of the company's culture. While contracts will continue to become more complex and the process more defined, they will remain fixed price and in the main, long term in duration. For instance, the contract to build and manage a prison for 800 inmates at Bridgend, South Wales is fixed over a 25 year period. "If your quality level is your price level at the beginning of a contract you have placed yourself in a very dangerous position because you do not have the flexibility to respond to the market", explains Richard Powell.

In line with the Group belief in the importance of good recruiting and training standards, Custodial Services places a similar value on its people. Seventy-five per cent of Custodial Services's costs are payroll-related, such as salaries, national insurance, etc. so it was decided very early that the business should be focused accordingly as Fiona Walters, Communications and Development Manager, explains: "If 75 per cent of your costs were in an item of technology you would take time to understand that technology and make sure that it was absolutely right. This was the view we took when we established our business. If the risk is in your people then you make sure you have the right people."

The company culture sets standards for behaviour. "In our everyday dealings with each other, prisoners and anyone that we come into contact with, we should be professional and treat people with respect. Valuing colleagues as individuals means that all of the skills and qualities within the team can be combined to achieve the task at hand. Treating prisoners in a non-judgmental way, rather than acting out of fear or prejudice, results in a less confrontational working environment", explains Fiona.

The three working principles which underpin the company mission and culture are 'Tell us', 'Do as you would be done by', and 'Superman/superwoman does not exist'. These are explained below:

Tell us

The company encourages an open-door policy at all times. Employees are actively encouraged to communicate their views and concerns at all times. Good communications management is essential to support operational staff. This is particularly true in a company with a flat management structure and few managers.

Do as you would be done by

Decision making should be devolved to where best information is available. Professional objective assessment is therefore required to ensure appropriate decisions are made. This requires staff to act in a non-judgmental manner when dealing with prisoners and with their colleagues. Recognising that all members of staff have an equal contribution to make, it follows that racism and sexism in any form are not tolerated.

Superman/Superwoman does not exist

Responsibility for problem solving rests with the team. It is implicit in the team approach that too much reliance is not placed upon any one person. The involvement of the whole team encourages all members to participate and take responsibility for problem solving. This approach allows individual strengths to be exploited whilst weaknesses can be compensated for, contributing to the identification and management of operational risk.

The importance Securicor places on interpersonal skills goes beyond merely what is said or done in a given situation, and focuses on the appropriate management by staff of their relationship with prisoners. In addition to the above, the following initiatives were introduced. For instance: The design and colour (Ulster green) of the uniform differentiates it from that of the police and the prison service, which may have been viewed with hostility by prisoners and acted as a barrier to establishing good communications. The absence of rank on uniforms is consistent with the principle that everybody is expected to take equal responsibility regardless of rank. Also name badges indicate each officer's full name, ensuring professional accountability.

"Initially a degree of concern was expressed by custody officers over displaying an officer's full name to a prisoner. However, it does break down barriers – it says 'I don't mind you having my name' and more importantly the prisoner sees that our custody officers don't mind disclosing their name which can open up the communication channels", explains Richard Powell.

Securicor has introduced sophisticated and exacting recruitment policies and training arrangements. Officers need to show they can act impartially and professionally when dealing with prisoners and can exercise tact and discretion in often stressful situations. Therefore, Securicor requires no formal educational qualifications but places great emphasis on personal qualities. Extensive screening and psychometric testing is carried out before a candidate is selected for training. As many as nine out of ten do not reach the required standards.

Fundamental to establishing the company's culture is the strong emphasis placed on initial training. Successful candidates are given a comprehensive eight-week training programme to meet the requirements of the Home Office. The course covers five broad areas: legal framework, prisoner management, security, supervision and control, and first-aid with special emphasis being placed on interpersonal skills.

The training defines and reinforces the company culture, in the context of providing guidance for working together effectively, eliminating fear from the workplace and encouraging the free flow of ideas. Candidates are taught that risk management involves thinking about the implications of their actions before they act, for both themselves and the company.

"Our job is to move prisoners safely and securely. We recognise that we cannot rely solely upon procedures and security equipment and key to our success is the effective management of relationships at the interpersonal level. From a simple 'Good Morning', to negotiating with someone who has barricaded themselves in a cell", explains Fiona Walters.

"Communications are absolutely key. If we stop communicating with staff there is no way they are going to continue communicating with prisoners. By using interpersonal skills as the first line of defence we successfully manage our risk," agrees David Beaton.

In addition to Operational meetings, Team briefings occur regularly to disseminate company wide information and news on aspirations, successes and problems to a workforce which is largely dispersed. Key messages are taken from the senior level and managers at other levels add their own briefing points. This culminates in a formal briefing in each branch and in every court within 72 hours of leaving the Managing Director's office. Each manager responds to the respective team's questions. Questions that they are unable to answer are fed back up the line management chain. This system has provided a formal vehicle for both upward and downward information flow for all levels in the organisation.

A cross-functional communications working party comprising representatives from all business areas was established to define and develop methods of effective communication. Team Briefing and the Company's in-house magazine were developed through this team activity.

Securicor's constant and continuing challenge is to ensure that the Securicor brand remains synonymous with integrity, reliability and security. And, as Roger Wiggs, Group Chief Executive, explains: "No business, whatever it produces, is successful without people. Securicor is no exception. It is the people who make it work, first and foremost."

"I don't think many companies completely understand the depth to which Quality has to run through an organisation on an ongoing basis. For many it has become a marketing tool while others think it is about procedures and systems and forget that it is about people. That's why our approach is so different. We have said systems and procedures are important but without getting the hearts and minds of people behind them they cannot deliver", concludes Richard Powell.

Right to left: John Devaney (Chief Executive), and John Welch (Head of Quality), receiving Eastern's Certificate of Membership of the European Foundation of Quality Management from Ian Raisbeck (Chairman of the EFQM Executive Committee).

Examples of EQUIP stands at Eastern's Teamwork '95 – a forum for recognition and innovation.

9

Switch On To Quality

— Eastern Group —

"YOU have to put some investment into quality up front. We started with the view that it doesn't cost money to satisfy your customers, it costs money to dissatisfy them. What we are doing is beginning to pay off." John Welch, Eastern Group's Head of Quality Development, knows what he is talking about. After working in Quality for excellent organisations, Rank Xerox and ICI, John Welch and his team are facilitating a very successful and enthusiastic Quality culture throughout Eastern.

Like all organisations seeking a Total Quality approach to business, the support of the leadership team is vital. At Eastern, Chief Executive John Devaney, clearly spells out his commitment to Quality:

"What we are talking about is business excellence. That is something every company needs to offer if it's going to be successful in the future, because customer expectations are continually increasing."

He points out that in the electricity industry, every customer will have a choice of supplier by 1998, when deregulation is complete and adds:

"The company that focuses on the customer will succeed above all others. It is really the supplier that best meets the needs of the customer, treats them well and gives them that little bit extra who will be the supplier of choice."

Eastern Electricity is the largest Regional Electricity Company and one of the top energy companies in the UK, with a strong track record of delivering good returns to shareholders and high quality services to customers.

The Group includes Eastern Electricity, the largest supplier and distributor of electricity in the country; Eastern Natural Gas, one of the top six independent gas suppliers; Eastern Contracting, serving the domestic market and tackling major projects; and Eastern Generation, which operates and builds power stations in the UK.

Eastern's way of working is based on four Core Values which were outlined in the Group's 1995 annual report:

- Belief in serving our customers
- Belief in profits and growth
- Belief in our people
- Belief in social and environmental values

"These values underpin our corporate vision which is to provide a quality of service in the energy and network management sectors which will make us the customer's choice."

The development of a formal Total Quality plan at Eastern began in 1992 as a project within the first Management Development Group (MDG). The Management Development Group was a group of 12 "High Fliers" chosen to be developed for future management responsibility. The group selected "Quality" as the subject of its development project. Two members of the team, Richard Harpley and Kay Turner, presented their findings to John Devaney, who agreed that the concept of a "Quality" approach was important for Eastern.

Richard and Kay were released from their duties and set about investigating the best way for Eastern to proceed. Consultants TQM International were chosen to help set the strategy. One of the early recommendations was for a Quality Director to be appointed. So in effect, Richard and Kay had the honour of appointing their own boss, John Welch. This has to be one of the ultimate examples of empowerment in UK industry!

To get started, a series of awareness days were arranged at Eastern's management centre in Essendon, Hertfordshire. Between November 1993 and August 1994, some 120 events, titled "Working for our Customers" were held. John Welch explains:

"Ninty-five per cent of Eastern employees attended these sessions. We developed the course ourselves without using consultants and utilised our senior managers as hosts. We invited people to step forward to become Quality Champions to facilitate the breakout discussion periods. Volunteers came from throughout the group and were trained in how to present the sessions; many of these champions have since taken on a valuable role as a Quality Facilitator. At the same time, Eastern started its Quality education, from the top, via 2-day Managers' Workshops.

John Welch personally ran the early managers' workshops, supported by Kay and Richard. "Running them myself gave me the opportunity to really get to know Eastern and its management; as part of the workshop, we looked at the company's culture - its stories, the rituals, the role models and the power structure, among other things. I was able to gain a whole host of information", said John.

From the beginning, measurement was considered an important part of distinguishing the Quality Process from short-term programmes. Measurement is central to Eastern's strategy and an important component are the company's customer surveys. A representative group of customers are surveyed and the results are used to set ongoing measurable objectives.

The initial customer survey identified eight key problems as perceived by customers, these were called "Big Burner" issues. The senior management team around John Devaney became the Quality Steering group and they were supported by the Quality Development Team under John Welch. Each member of the Quality Steering Group became a sponsor for a "Big Burner" project and was assigned a member of the Quality Development team to act as a facilitator and help the managers co-ordinate their efforts on quality.

John Welch has a word of caution for other companies who may be starting out: "These projects were too big to tackle in the beginning. The projects we undertook were the right ones, but earlier on, we should have broken those large problems into smaller components. It is important to give yourself the chance of early small successes."

The "Big Burner" projects addressed a number of issues including the way customer complaints were handled and improving the billing process. Significant improvements have been made to both these areas and subsequent surveys have indicated an increase in customer satisfaction.

Eastern's major achievements since embarking on its Quality Process in 1993, have come mainly from the following key areas:

Quality Network

As outlined above an extensive Quality Network has been put in place consisting of the Quality Steering Group; the Quality Development Team (around 8 full-time secondees from all parts of Eastern) and the Quality Facilitators Network.

Customer Focused Measures

A key set of Customer Focused Measures has been defined based on the Customer needs and wants established by the Customer Surveys. These measures, many of which are additional to the standards set by the industry regulator, are highlighted at the monthly executive meetings.

In addition to the goals and targets set for the Electricity business, Eastern has more recently developed them for both Gas and Contracting.

The measures for the Electricity business cover:

- Quality of Supply
- Billing Accuracy
- Courteous Service, covering responsiveness to customers
- Service Recovery - how well Eastern responds to customer complaints.

To promote these goals and aims, a substantial communications effort has supported the drive for improvement in each measure, and has been paying off. The awareness of these measures, and the attention given to them, has helped to make significant improvements. For example, the proportion of bills amended subsequent to the original invoice has more than halved during a period of eighteen months. Improvements to complaints measures are mentioned later in this chapter.

Many of the Quality Improvement projects referred to below have been set up to support improvements in these measures. Measurement is a key component of Eastern's Quality strategy - and it's working well.

Communication

A high level of awareness has been generated through the company's "Working for our Customers" days mentioned earlier, and this programme is being considered for follow-up in 1997 to reinforce the message and keep it fresh.

Regular communication is maintained through a variety of high calibre mediums. The Eastern company newspaper *Cable* won the 1995 Company Newspaper of the Year award. The glossy tabloid is very well produced with a mix of corporate information and company personalities

– an obvious "human interest" in employees ensures the paper gets read. The successes of quality teams are often celebrated in the paper's pages.

A quarterly professionally produced video called "Network TV" provides a further way of promoting the quality message. Once again, the quality improvement teams are shown as inspiration for others. A further innovation is the use of On Line Information to outline what improvements teams are working on to allow an exchange of ideas throughout the group and to prevent duplication of effort.

Traditional communications methods are also used such as Team Talks and plenty of staff briefings, so everyone is constantly informed.

John Welch's team has sought strong links with Eastern's Corporate Communications department ensuring the Quality message receives attention and visibility.

Education

To ensure people know what to do with the information they receive, extensive education opportunities are regularly presented to all employees.

By 1995 all senior managers and a large percentage of middle managers had received basic training at Quality Workshops. Training in problem solving skills has been provided extensively and is available to all. This training is making a contribution to a change in management style and culture, as it helps to break down barriers and create a common language. Process improvement training has begun and the techniques are being used widely.

Business Processes

The training in Process Improvement has given valuable support to the implementation of re-designed processes, arising from a major BPR (Business Process Re-engineering) project in 1994/95 affecting mainly the Network Engineering function of the Electricity business.

A major consultancy firm was hired to lead the BPR project, supported by an "in house" consultancy group. Breakthrough improvements were identified as essential to Eastern in order to become a customer-focused organisation, where processes provide customers with their requirements - effectively and efficiently - rather than hierarchical and traditional functions.

Eastern has moved to flatter structures, with many self-directed teams in place to deliver the re-designed processes. These teams are using the Quality techniques of process improvement and problem solving to define the "how to" lower level processes to support the high level "what" processes.

The focus on process improvement has meant that Eastern has been moving towards preventing problems, not just solving them as they arise.

Customer Complaints and Queries

This area has been the focus of a major "Big Burner" quality improvement team. The team made twelve recommendations which are being implemented. Actions are being taken to address key areas of complaints. The results of this initiative are already being felt with a significant reduction in the number of complaints made to the industry regulator, OFFER. Response and resolution times of all complaints made directly to Eastern have tumbled substantially.

Eastern's Quality Improvement Projects (EQUIPs)

For Eastern this has been a very successful area with more than 150 EQUIPs established and many improvements being implemented. This process has to date involved more than 800 people - around 15% of the workforce. Eastern defines Quality as "Continuously meeting agreed customer requirements, at least expense, *by releasing the potential of all people in Eastern Group.*"

The EQUIPs are how Eastern gains the most benefit from their human resources and the people are able to use the EQUIPs to improve their workplace and make their job easier. Significant progress has been made through the EQUIPs, but what are they? How have they been formed?

EQUIPs have been established to tackle Quality issues, using the problem solving processes to get to the root cause of difficulties and come up with practical solutions. More recently, they have been using the Process Improvement Process, where appropriate. John Welch explains:

"We are proud of how we've done this. In some companies, Quality processes fail because they are seen as communication or training exercises and nothing gets done. But with the EQUIPs, we've started the action process at the same time.

The EQUIPs are doing far more than just chatting about problems, they are not "talk shops". They are not an excuse to delay, but an opportunity to take action on a problem that might have been hanging around for some time.

The people in these teams don't just make recommendations, they're already making changes which are helping staff to do their job, cutting out unnecessary work and having an impact on the customer."

The EQUIPs have a common thread by addressing one or more aspects of the four core values that underpin the company's vision, but the major focus is on the "belief in serving our customers".

Anybody in the company can identify an issue to be examined. The process entails a proposal being put forward that an EQUIP be set up to address a particular issue. The proposer, with the help of his/her manager then seeks a "sponsor" for the project. It is important that each of the projects has a sponsor so that he/she can provide guidance as required and help them through any barriers that may arise. For example, if a potential solution is considered too expensive or too late, due to a long term system change, the sponsor may encourage the team to look at alternative ways to address the problem.

Each EQUIP has a sponsor, team leader and facilitator. The facilitator may be a member of the Quality Development Team or any of the 60 part-time facilitators that exist around the company.

A control log is kept of all the EQUIPs that are being worked on and the Quality Development Team updates it every six weeks. The list is available as a document which is sent to all managers and it is available also through the OLI (On Line Information) on the company's computer network.

The following examples have been included to provide a glimpse of EQUIPs in action:

One of the first EQUIPs set up, as indicated earlier, was in the area of customer complaints. The EQUIP was formed with the aim of discovering the root causes of complaints and learning from them to prevent repetition.

Some questions asked initially included: Why do customers complain? When do they do it? What are the similarities? How can they be prevented?

"The aim is simple, but there isn't a quick fix answer", says EQUIP member and regulation adviser Tony Evans.

"Reasons for complaints can vary greatly and as a result many different solutions are called for and constant analysis is required."

One of the actions started by the EQUIP has been the formation of staff-run complaints workshops at Eastern Electricity's Customer Service Centres at Bedford and Rayleigh, which, as the main public face of the company is where many customers' complaints are directed.

"The basic aims of the workshops are to make people more aware of what's gone wrong, get them to talk about and learn from them, and cascade the information down to their colleagues", explains EQUIP member and customer services manager Keith Argent.

This is often achieved through members of the group forming sub-groups with colleagues.

"It's only by pooling all our knowledge and working together that we are going to get rid of recurring complaints", says Rayleigh customer service assistant Debbie Burgess, a member of one of the nine workshops set up so far.

A further result from the EQUIP has been the establishment of a complaints forum led by senior managers, which meets monthly to look at both complaints trends and individual cases, and frequently appoints ad hoc teams to look at specific issues.

"It's not simply a question of finding an answer to an existing problem and saying that's it," says EQUIP member and former regional engineer Steve Cannon, "It's an on going process and there are also cultural issues. My background is engineering and I've noticed in that area a more sympathetic approach is being adopted towards customers. People are also becoming more willing to take responsibility for a problem and resolve it rather than pass the buck."

Another EQUIP has completed a study into "The Cost of Quality". The EQUIP looked at unnecessary spending.

"Some people said we should call the EQUIP "The Cost of Poor Quality", says team member Ian Mackay, Customer Services Resource manager at Bedford. "We looked at the cost of not getting it right."

The team's main task was to pinpoint the areas of major spending in the electricity business and estimate the savings that could be made through quality improvements.

They found that cost savings of more than 20% could be made in repairing and maintaining overhead lines, while metering was costing 12% more than it should and expenditure on sub-station maintenance could be cut by 18% - all with a positive impact on customers! Many of these issues have been addressed in the Business Process Re-Engineering Project. Once the team's job was done, new sub-EQUIPs were set up to delve further into the root causes.

With over 150 EQUIPs, almost every area is covered. There are EQUIPs which have: improved ID cards to thwart bogus callers; reduced jargon; improved billing methods; made it easier for staff and customers to understand tariff information; and redesigned the bill to make it more understandable and user-friendly.

The work of the EQUIPs is detailed regularly in *Cable* which includes colour team photos and stories recognising their success, and more recently in a new publication called *Quality Matters.*

A forum for recognition and motivation was organised with a huge event entitled "Teamwork '95". The day saw 30 EQUIPs and 11 Eastern Company stands demonstrating their achievements; some of the stands highlighted related topics such as safety. The teams went to considerable effort to give very professional presentations. John Welch proudly outlines the day:

"We held Teamwork '95 on November 9th, World Quality Day, to show our people that what we are achieving is part of a bigger picture. The small team organising the day worked together for four months and the end result was incredible. They totally transformed an aircraft hangar at the Imperial War Museum at Duxford, Cambridgeshire - the display had the professionalism of a top exhibition."

The event was a great success for Eastern with 1,400 people attending throughout the course of the day. It was so successful that Teamwork '96 is already being planned, with all employees invited to an even bigger and better event.

Teamwork '95 also had a stand promoting environmental issues. Eastern had just been awarded BS7750 the Environmental Standard. As one of Eastern's core values, the environment is given a high priority.

Eastern's Environmental Management System (EMS) started with a commitment to an environmental policy. After audits and reviews, the system was established by designating responsibilities, preparing registers of the main environmental effects and relevant legislation, setting targets and establishing a management programme and procedures to meet them. The requirement to set continual improvement targets and monitor progress is a fundamental component of EMS as specified in BS7750.

John Hill, Eastern Group's Environment Business manager believes changing staff attitudes has been one of the biggest factors in Eastern's success to date.

"We will continue to increase awareness through effective communication, training and initiatives which encourage staff to take ownership of the issues. Everyone at Eastern needs to understand why they must take action to reduce the environmental effects of their work."

Like most companies following the Quality path, Eastern has experienced some barriers to maintaining momentum including the old chestnut – "Been there, done that – Quality was yesterday" but the enthusiasm of the people who have got involved and the results of improvement projects has overcome most resistance. In addition, John Devaney and his senior management team have continued to show their commitment to the Quality process.

To ensure a continued effort, Eastern has become a member of both the British Quality Foundation and the European Foundation for Quality Management. The next phase of Eastern's "Switch-On to Quality" will include a full self assessment based on the UK Quality Award Business Excellence model in 1996 – they have started with a partial assessment in 1995.

John Welch says Eastern have no immediate plans to apply for a UK Quality Award, but with falling numbers of complaints to OFFER, improvements in performance against published guaranteed and overall standards and in other Customer Focused standards, Eastern would have to be a contender in the future.

John Devaney concludes by expressing the effect the Quality Process has had on Eastern's people thus far (but recognising that there is still a lot more to do):

"The significant majority of people who have participated in EQUIPs and other improvement projects talk of the benefits they have enjoyed, such as meeting people from other areas of Eastern and gaining new skills and techniques. Perhaps most important has been the chance to be involved in "making a difference" and being recognised for that contribution. We know from our customer surveys and focus groups that customers are noticing the difference."

Mike Jackson
Chief Executive
Birmingham Midshires

Tony McGarahan
Head of Corporate Relations
Birmingham Midshires

10

"We'll Exceed Your Expectations"

— Birmingham Midshires Building Society —

BIRMINGHAM Midshires' origins can be traced as far back as 1849. Since then it has undergone over 50 mergers and become one of the UK's fastest growing building societies. By the close of 1995 Birmingham Midshires was the country's 10th largest building society, employing some 2,200 staff and operating a 120 strong branch network across 25 counties in England and Wales.

In terms of profitability Birmingham Midshires has made significant advances since 1989/90 when the annual report on the performance of the top 20 building societies from city stockbrokers placed it last. By the end of 1995 it was ranked seventh.

The 1980s was the period in which the Society expanded most dramatically with asset levels increasing from £150 million at the start of the decade to £3 billion by its conclusion. However, in retrospect Birmingham Midshires acknowledges that growth is not always synonymous with improvement, prosperity and success. The factors which contributed to the Society's accelerated growth eventually contributed to corporate ill health. Birmingham Midshires, plagued by a lack of strategic direction, management 'indigestion', and ineffective risk analysis and provision for bad debts struggled to cope with a deepening recession.

Massive acquisitive growth, in part facilitated by the 1986 Building Societies Act which liberalised financial services and allowed societies to expand into real estate and insurance broking, as well as the general merger activity of the 1980s tempted many in the industry, including Birmingham Midshires, to diversify into areas outside their core function.

Distracted by the momentum of its immediate growth and seemingly abundant opportunities, Birmingham Midshires failed to devise a new strategy to take it into the next decade. However, the Society capitalised on the lessons learned during this period and has developed the right vision and leadership, an empowered workforce and a business-wide desire to prove they are "First Choice" to ensure the longevity of the growth achieved in the 1990s.

In 1990 the Society appointed a new chief executive, Mike Jackson, and together with a fresh management team created a new vision for Birmingham Midshires. Mr Jackson was formerly a Senior Vice-President at Bank of America. While Mr Jackson was the chief architect of the Society's change of course in the early 1990s the implementation was and continues to be very much a team effort. Birmingham Midshires describes its vision as: "To be First Choice for our customers, our people and our business partners, growing profitably for the benefit of members by being extraordinarily: *Friendly*; *Informed*; *Responsive*; *Service orientated*; and *Trustworthy* and, in doing so, exceed their expectations." These five corporate values were identified after discussions with its people and provide the platform from which all business activities are driven. The Society's track record to date is impressive with approximately 16 per cent of its customers agreeing that the Society regularly exceeds their expectations and an overall satisfaction rating of over 97 per cent.

Birmingham Midshires' commitment to quality is reflected in its membership of the British Quality Foundation, European Foundation for Quality Management and Investors In People accreditation but more significantly it is evidenced by the way it interacts with all its stakeholders.

Birmingham Midshires recognises that quality is not an expense – it is a culture, a way of thinking and ultimately an investment in its own future. Quality is not something that can be easily instilled into a company. It requires excellent customer service, commitment to the product and people who care about what they do.

This attention to detail is obvious as soon as you enter the Society's corporate centre at the Pendeford Business Park in Wolverhampton. The £30 million head office, opened in August 1995, is home to over 1,000 people who were previously located in six geographically dispersed buildings that presented a significant obstacle to effective internal communication and prevented enhanced, technology-led customer service.

The new centre was designed to facilitate the flow of information throughout the Society, encouraging discussion between people on both work-related matters and on a social level, each of which contributes to a spirit of team building.

The open-plan cross-shaped building, which was designed in consultation with the Society's core stakeholders (internal and external), is state of the art incorporating provisions for future IT system requirements, but more importantly it is inviting to the visitor. The absence of doors and individual offices eliminates many traditional organisational barriers. Without the benefit of an introduction it is unlikely that a visitor could identify the managers because they sit with their teams at identical desks and on identical chairs. There are no departments only teams, each of which focuses on a particular process. It is anticipated that the building will support a 24-hour operation in the future where people will be allocated a work space each time they arrive for work.

Another quality which distinguished the Pendeford complex from a more traditional office setting is the balance struck between the business and social aspects of the work environment. People are encouraged to take leave of their work to watch the news for example on one of the televisions provided in common atrium lounge areas on each floor or browse the showcase of artwork which cover the walls.

Every piece of the one hundred plus piece collection is representative of the First Choice values Birmingham Midshires strives to deliver. Some reflect the sense of community, from which building societies have their origins, while others are intended to inspire those working at the Society. A painting entitled 'Everyone Can Fly' is reflective of this intent providing the message that everyone has the ability to spread their wings and try something new even if it involves an element of risk knowing that if they fail somebody will catch them. "No matter how large we become as a corporation we must always display a local, caring, human, friendly, sincere attitude to all the people with whom we interact", explains Tony McGarahan, leader of the Corporate Relations Team.

The establishment of effective communications within Birmingham Midshires and between the Society and the numerous stakeholder groups with which it interacts became one of the cornerstones of the Society's recovery and the basis of its continued health. Prior to 1990 the Society placed very little emphasis on corporate communications. It neglected many of its key stakeholders including its own people, the community it served, city analysts and the media and even its customers.

To correct this situation Mr McGarahan was recruited in 1991 and introduced a structured communications process, which initially focused on two key stakeholders: the media, to correct their misconceptions and its people, to inform them of the state of play and their future role.

The perceived greed of financial institutions in general has traditionally been a favourite target for the media, which consequently undermines confidence in the sector. The potential for damage was intensified in the 1980s because of Birmingham Midshires' 'lack of desire' to cultivate relationships with business commentators and provide them with accurate information.

"We recognised that the media was a key stakeholder in the business so we decided to make it an ally instead of ignoring it as we had done throughout the 1980s and early 1990s. We forged similar partnerships with other stakeholders. We view partnering as critical to the way we operate so we have identified and clearly defined our stakeholders. This information is reflected on our stakeholders' wheel shown in Figure 1.

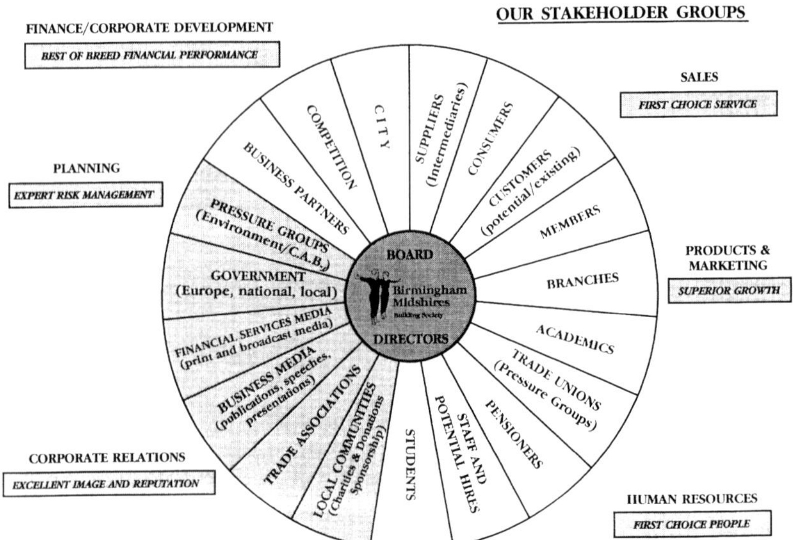

Shaded areas = Corporate Relation's main stakeholders

From the initial focus on staff and media the stakeholders' wheel has expanded to incorporate every group which potentially has an impact on our organisation. We've linked this to our corporate plan so that the model defines which stakeholders impact the various parts of the plan", explains Mr McGarahan.

Birmingham Midshires has also made a communications pledge to every person within the Society that: "We shall create the conditions for high quality, open communications. We each have a right to expect this to happen – and a shared responsibility to ensure it does." The pledge is based on the following ten principles:

- We practise and promote open, honest and timely communication and we listen to the views of the staff when implementing corporate and business plans.
- Regular participative meetings of work-teams are held.
- We are each regularly informed of corporate goals and performance and have an opportunity to attend annual face-to-face meetings with a member of the senior leadership team.
- We are told of Society news and announcements, where possible, before external audiences.
- We each have access to our line managers, who will visit us regularly.
- Society-wide corporate internal and external communication materials are distributed according to standards set and agreed by Corporate Communications.
- All new staff are given Society and departmental induction training to help their understanding of the organisation's goals, their local team environment and its place in the business.
- We are each encouraged, wherever practical and without compromising service quality, to meet people with whom we have regular business contact.
- We each have access to updated organisation charts/telephone directories and key departmental/project contact points.
- We are each entitled to bring lapses in this pledge to our line manager, team leader or Management Team member for resolution.

A number of communication vehicles have been developed by the Corporate Relations Team including a weekly news sheet and monthly magazine, both of which have a business focus in order to disseminate corporate and local team information.

To ensure that corporate messages are delivered consistently throughout the branch network and Pendeford the Society operates a team briefing programme known as 'Team Talk'. A central information pack is produced each month which is delivered to the various teams by Team Talk coordinators who then encourage discussion on each subject, as Mr McGarahan comments: "For example, if costs are too high the 'Team Talk' will focus discussion at local team level on the part they can play in helping the business reduce its costs in the next quarter. If best practice is identified by one of the teams this is then disseminated throughout the organisation. It is our attempt to devolve ownership of communication into the line. Importantly, the Team Talk coordinators are not managers to ensure that the exercise is not seen as a propaganda stunt. Anybody can be nominated for the position and as a result we have a number of junior people who act as facilitators."

The Society is the first to admit that it is not perfect with 3 per cent of customers indicating that they are not satisfied with the service received. But Birmingham Midshires views complaints as an opportunity to communicate with its customers and improve its service.

"Getting people in the front door with good products is pointless if they're going out the back door because of bad service", is a blunt message issued by Mr McGarahan to the Society's workforce. "The name of our game is to do more for our customers than they expect from us." This philosophy is the strap line of Birmingham Midshires' second wave of its service strategy commenced in 1993 which focuses on issues such as customer satisfaction, measuring customer wants and needs and handling complaints. Initiatives which have been introduced since 1993 include a mystery shopper programme; team attitude surveys; a customer retention team which focuses on saving defecting customers; business partner relationship-building; and service level agreements.

While Birmingham Midshires has a dedicated Quality Team every person in the Society is charged with the responsibility of exceeding customer expectations. The Corporate Quality Team exists to take up the cause of the customer and ensure that the organisation responds through: promoting 'exceeding customer expectations'; service recovery; measurement of customer satisfaction; Quality First awards scheme; and Quality Days, training events for Society people.

Communicating with customers has become a priority as Mr

McGarahan explains: "The changes we have made since 1990 have been based on the simple premise of asking the customer what they think of our service and how it needs to be improved. We can't improve a situation until we know what is right or wrong about it so as a result many of the changes to this business, its products and its processes are a direct response to what the customer tells us."

Birmingham Midshires has physically changed processes and policy in response to customer comments. Cross-functional change teams are established to review and implement change in all areas of the business from policy to the revision of service standard. For example, a cross-functional team was involved in resolving problems arising when an obsolete account was replaced by one which provided a higher rate of interest. The change-over between accounts was not expeditious and resulted in a large number of customer complaints.

"In 1992 more than one in ten customer complaints were about low-yielding discontinued accounts. After a carefully managed two-year trade-up campaign these complaints virtually ceased, helping overall satisfaction to reach industry-beating levels. Over the course of the two-year campaign approximately 660,000 savings accounts were transferred from closed obsolete accounts to modern, higher paying alternatives", explains Mr McGarahan.

"It is often tempting to relegate complaints to the back of our 'to do' lists instead of making them the number-one priority ahead of other work. But the reality is, as the statistics indicate, that a dissatisfied customer is likely to take their business elsewhere and tell at least ten others of their experience, while a highly dissatisfied person will tell up to 25 family and friends," cautions Mr Jackson. "We view every complaint as valid because it provides us with an opportunity to create or consolidate a customer's loyalty. Consequently, the resolution of customer problems and complaints is seen as a priority and a valuable use of resources, time and effort."

Mr McGarahan describes two customer problems which were resolved by Birmingham Midshires people in a First Choice manner. While each of the examples is unique, the responses were standard in as much as they were appropriate for the situation in order to exceed customer expectations.

"A customer telephoned the head office late one evening complaining about an incident which occurred in one of the branches. The HR

Director, who took the call, calmed him down and discussed the nature of the problem. The customer's response was that he didn't know what he was going to do, but on returning home he would have a stiff brandy. The Director rang the Area Manager and explained the situation who in turn responded by visiting the customer's home armed with a bottle of brandy, an apology and an invitation to discuss the problem. With the problem resolved we not only retained that customer but gained another, the customer's son visited the branch the following week and opened an investment account."

"A corporate relations team member, Helen Jeavons, received a call from a distressed customer explaining that her branch had let her down. In response to this situation Helen sent the customer flowers and reassured her that the situation would be resolved by the Society. The customer was so impressed with the service that when she heard a talk-back show on the radio discussing the generally poor service provided by banks and building societies she picked up the telephone and told the audience how her building society had helped her. After hearing the story the announcer allowed her to disclose to the 460,000 listeners that it was Birmingham Midshires which had exceeded her expectations. How about that for third-party endorsement and free advertising."

While some may claim that it is not practical to provide every customer with this level of attention Birmingham Midshires would argue that not only did they exceed the customer's expectations in a high-risk situation, but converted them into ambassadors who will recommend the Society to friends, colleagues and family alike, as Mr Jackson explains: "By working individually and in teams to eliminate issues relating to delays, errors and policy and turn disappointment into delight we can increase income, cut costs and improve the reputation and image of the Society. On average, each customer is worth around £50,000 to the Society over ten years – a substantial lost opportunity if we don't live up to expectations. If all those who are currently dissatisfied took their business elsewhere we could lose £135 million to our competition in a decade."

Since 1991 the Society has asked over 700,000 customers their opinion of the Society and invited comments about the level of service they receive. Analysis of the adjectives used by customers in their First Choice questionnaire comments has provided the Society with a picture of what contributes to outstanding service. The Customer Focus Team went

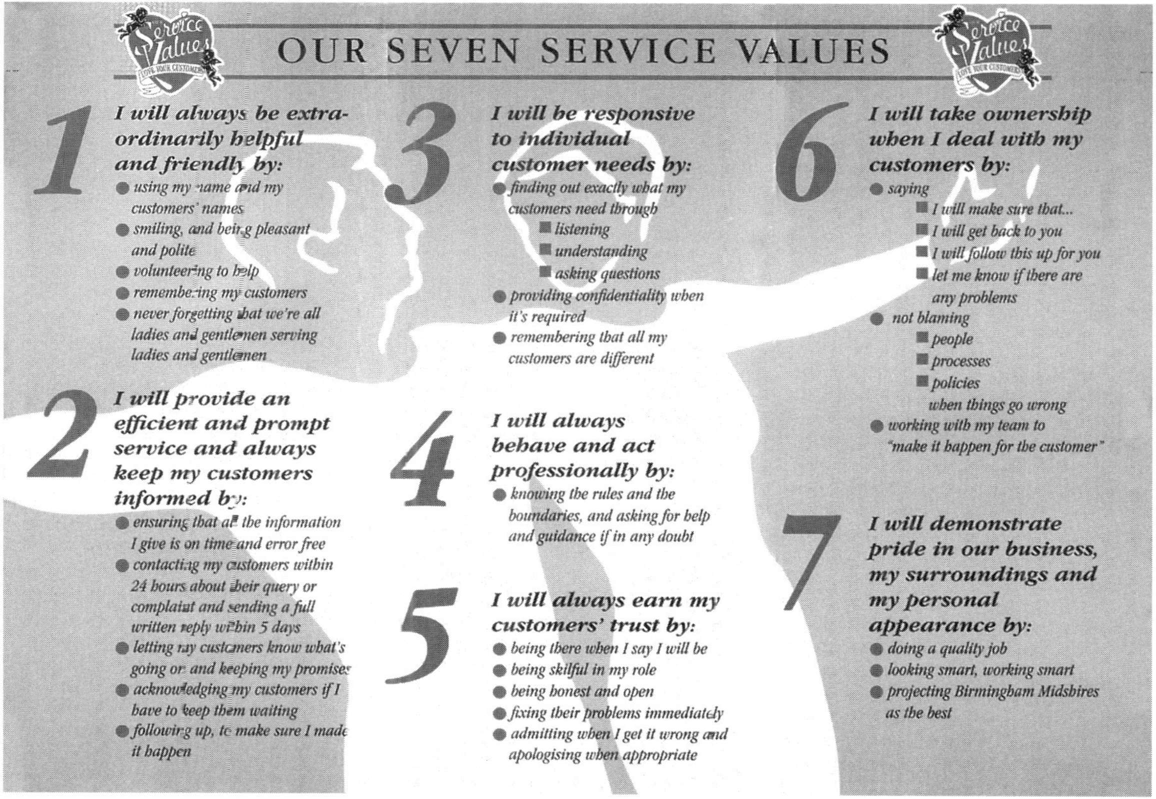

OUR SEVEN SERVICE VALUES

1 I will always be extra-ordinarily helpful and friendly by:

- using my name and my customers' names
- smiling, and being pleasant and polite
- volunteering to help
- remembering my customers
- never forgetting that we're all ladies and gentlemen serving ladies and gentlemen

2 I will provide an efficient and prompt service and always keep my customers informed by:

- ensuring that all the information I give is on time and error free
- contacting my customers within 24 hours about their query or complaint and sending a full written reply within 5 days
- letting my customers know what's going on and keeping my promises
- acknowledging my customers if I have to keep them waiting
- following up, to make sure I made it happen

3 I will be responsive to individual customer needs by:

- finding out exactly what my customers need through
  - listening
  - understanding
  - asking questions
- providing confidentiality when it's required
- remembering that all my customers are different

4 I will always behave and act professionally by:

- knowing the rules and the boundaries, and asking for help and guidance if in any doubt

5 I will always earn my customers' trust by:

- being there when I say I will be
- being skilful in my role
- being honest and open
- fixing their problems immediately
- admitting when I get it wrong and apologising when appropriate

6 I will take ownership when I deal with my customers by:

- saying
  - I will make sure that...
  - I will get back to you
  - I will follow this up for you
  - let me know if there are any problems
- not blaming
  - people
  - processes
  - policies

  when things go wrong
- working with my team to "make it happen for the customer"

7 I will demonstrate pride in our business, my surroundings and my personal appearance by:

- doing a quality job
- looking smart, working smart
- projecting Birmingham Midshires as the best

through the 1994 questionnaire replies to produce a database of 497 adjectives indicating the number of times each occurred.

These were then broken down according to the customer's overall satisfaction level to give a valuable insight into the factors considered important by customers as Mr Jackson explains: "The big find was that the word 'exceptional' frequently appeared in the 'exceeded expectations' category. There is a clear message there – the way to move customers from 'highly satisfied' to 'exceeded expectations' is to offer exceptional service by putting ourselves in their shoes. Words used most frequently by satisfied customers paint a clear picture of what pleases them: 'polite', 'courteous', 'friendly' and 'wonderful'."

This analysis was used to frame "The Customers' Vision" which outlines Birmingham Midshires' commitment to customers. These behaviours are not made up as the Society's analysis of customer comments indicated that the 80 per cent of occasions where expectations were exceeded were as a result of people displaying all or some of the actions listed in The Customers' Vision.

In line with the Society's aim to exceed the expectations of its customers it has revitalised its service values by making them more emotive and ensuring that they are integrated into the business culture, as well as being easy to understand and use.

Independent research revealed that Birmingham Midshires' customer satisfaction levels, which reached a high of 97.1 per cent in 1994, exceeded the average customer satisfaction ratings for the building society industry by 10 per cent and by 35 per cent in the banking industry.

In support of these results Birmingham Midshires was named the UK's number-one service organisation in the 1993 inaugural Customer First Awards sponsored by the *Daily Telegraph* and First Direct, and in 1994 Midlands Service Excellence Business of the Year, by accountants Arthur Andersen and *Management Today magazine.* In December 1994 it won the West Midlands Business of the Year award presented by the CBI, Price Waterhouse and *The Birmingham Post.* Most recently Birmingham Midshires reached the finals of the 1995 *Sunday Times*/Unisys Customer Champion awards.

Celebrating these awards and recognising the efforts of those who contributed to the Society's success is a priority at Birmingham Midshires. The Society has a number of recognition and reward schemes ranging from an executive award, which allows any member of the senior management team to give a cash reward to an individual or a team on the spot for providing outstanding commitment and service, to a simple personal thank you using a postcard: "Caught in the act – Thanks for your help – You did a great job" which can be attached to a piece of work or handed out.

"Having completed a trip to the States last Autumn to look at a number of service issues including reward and recognition, one lesson was that you don't need to spend lots of money – a simple thank you, pat on the back, a smile, body language are often sufficient," comments Mr McGarahan.

However, a more formal element of the Society's recognition structure is the 'Magic Moment Awards' which recognise people who have been caught in the act of exceeding customer expectations. "We are trying to encourage people to automatically exceed expectations all the time. Every month we are going to recognise people who delivered to their internal or external customers Magic Moments by presenting awards to celebrate the achievements of others. Each monthly winner goes forward to the annual jamboree which culminates with the presentation of the Magic Moment of the Year awards, the winner of which will receive a prize such as a trip to the Caribbean. The monthly prize-giving attended by all staff is a massive training exercise, it is not just about rewarding people, but training people to do it in their own daily activity in individual teams", explains Mr McGarahan.

Moving into its new building represents the achievement of one of the primary objectives of Birmingham Midshires in terms of visually positioning the Society as a quality organisation, but it is in the throes of one of its biggest challenges: transforming the business so that all of its products, processes and services are customer focused to the point where a customer can ring in and be provided with one point of contact for all of their transactions.

"There is a real business meaning to all of what we do, it is not a management fad. Our business was on fire – our profits had declined to £6 million by the end of the 1980s but in 1995 we announced profits of £44 million. We were a £3.4 billion business in 1991 but we have enlarged that to £7 billion in a recession. Customer satisfaction has increased from 88 per cent to 97 per cent and over 77 per cent of our people, when asked in our annual MORI attitude survey, said they were proud to work for the Society.

"We have gone from being one of the worst-performing building societies to one of the most progressive and we are now recognised as a world-class service organisation whose focus on dazzling the customer is paying off with loyal and delighted customers and balance sheet growth", concludes Mr McGarahan.

11

Recognising Excellence

—PAC International—

THE 'Inside UK Enterprise' scheme is a project backed by the Department of Trade and Industry, which selects excellent companies and asks them to open their doors and allow other businesses to benefit from their expertise. Each of these companies is making a tremendous contribution to the general improvement of UK Industry. PAC International Ltd is one such company, whose dedication and commitment to excellence is used as a benchmark for the rest the country.

PAC International is a UK market leader in the manufacture of integrated access control systems. The company's products are also exported throughout Continental Europe, Scandinavia, the Far East and the USA. Product design, development, sales and marketing and manufacture are all undertaken at PAC's impressive purpose built factory in Stockport, Greater Manchester. PAC employs approximately 95 people and in 1995 had a turnover of £6.36 million.

In simple terms, access control systems allow you to decide who goes through which doors in your building and at what times. PAC's product range starts with a simple two door controller, Easikey, and moves through to sophisticated multi-site PC based systems. A range of reading technologies can be used on PAC systems including proximity, hands free, infa-red and wiegand. All PAC manufactured products come with a five year guarantee against electronic failure and the PAC proximity card and key carry a lifetime guarantee. PAC's products are sold through a distribution network with no direct sales being made by PAC itself. Sites successfully using PAC systems include hospitals, electricity companies, universities, Police forces,

left to right: Peter Tudor (PAC'sChief Executive), Glyn Ford (M.E.P. Manchester East), David Hopkins (TEC Director and M.D of Audio Design Services)

left to right: Sue Davison (PAC's chair of the S.O.S. committee), Nick Gillingham (picutured with the gold medal he won at the Commonwealth Games for the 200M Breaststroke), Vanda Murray (PAC's Sales and Marketing Director), Nigel Love (S.O.S. Vice Chair – North)

Financial institutions, breweries and many more. 'Blue Chip' clients include: the BBC, British Gas, Motorola, Unilever, Severn Trent Water, local authorities including all the London Boroughs, Chase Manhattan Bank and National Westminster Bank.

The company was founded in 1978 by two entrepreneurial engineers who built a reputation for the company based on the continuous development of new and innovative products. The company experienced tremendous growth and in 1986, PAC was purchased by Expamet International PLC – a group of companies supplying products and services to the security, industrial and building markets worldwide, from manufacturing bases in Europe and the US. In 1994, Expamet recorded a pre-tax profit of £5.8 million on a turnover of £130.4 million. However, during 1995, Expamet decided to exit from the security sector and concentrate on its industrial and building markets and at the end of 1995, PAC was acquired by Blick plc.

Blick is a very successful group who have now completed 10 years of unbroken profit growth since going public in 1986. Blick's group objective is "To design, supply and maintain a complete range of systems to meet individual customer requirements for the management of human resources at their place of work or in the community". Blick's product range includes: time and attendance, radio paging and door entry systems, all of which have a strong synergy with PAC's own product range. In fact, Blick and PAC have been working together on several levels for many years, and PAC could not have found a better partner and parent.

One of the founders remained with PAC as managing director but after PAC's acquisition by Expamet, as is so often the case, the skills required to found and initially develop a hi-tech company are not the same as those required to consolidate and grow the business to the next stage.

The recession of the early 1990s affected PAC in the same way as many other organisations and the company faced a number of problems: decreasing sales, few recent new products, no strategy, poor communication, too many managers, an inflexible production system, and a reliance on a few major customers. The company was slipping dangerously close to not breaking even and the decision was made by the group's management to restructure; this included the appointment of a new managing director. Unfortunately the management hand-over itself took six months which further demoralised staff.

Peter Tudor was appointed chief executive in 1992 and was immediately thrust into a very difficult environment. Despite the problems, he was heartened by a number of positive elements the company had in its favour including: a reliable product, Total Quality foundations, good marketing and image; an impressive facility, some export markets already established, and being part of the successful Expamet Group.

Peter Tudor was well prepared for the challenge he faced at PAC. Having completed his undergraduate degree in 1978 from Oxford, he began working for Schlumberger, an oil equipment and field services company. Schlumberger is a favourite company of Tom Peters and is praised in his book *In Search of Excellence* for the way the company empowers its employees. After eight years with Schlumberger, Peter read for an MBA at Cranfield. On successful completion of his MBA, Peter Tudor joined Expamet and spent four years managing the group's door manufacturing operation in the North East of England, before he was appointed to turn around PAC.

Despite PAC being bureaucratic and overmanaged, Mr Tudor found some excellent managers on his arrival. One of these was Vanda Murray, the Sales and Marketing Director who was keen to grow and improve the business.

As a first step, the overall number of managers was reduced as were the number of hierarchical management layers. The bureaucratic, and some may say remote, management attitude was also removed to create a more informed and open culture.

Together with the revised and reduced management team Peter Tudor put together a three year strategy for 1992 to 1995. The strategy contained four key headings:

Improve operations:

- Reduce manufacturing lead time from 5 weeks to 1 day
- Manage stock more effectively
- Invest in Information systems
- Analyse returns/improve quality

Increase Customer Base

- One customer accounted for 24% of total sales
- Only 16 active UK customers

Increase Technical Support

- Phone support/Training/Testing

Invest In Development

• Engineers/Training/Equipment

To help achieve this strategy a heavy investment in Total Quality Management systems was made. In 1989, Expamet initiated a group-wide approach to quality using consultants, Crosby Associates. The Group management believed all subsidiaries should use the same consultancy to ensure a consistent approach and enable best practices to be shared in the same language across all the companies in the group. A Group-wide steering committee was established to oversee continuous improvement.

It was obvious to PAC's managers that continuing with Crosby Associates was the best way to rejuvenate the quality process. Training was undertaken at Crosby's Richmond training centre with trainers being trained, so they could return to PAC and run workshops for the rest of the company. Peter Tudor believes training is an excellent way to show management commitment and is heavily involved in training. He personally gives induction Quality training to all new staff members. He says: "The person in charge has to show that he is actively working towards Quality, that's the only way you can make Total Quality work. As managing director you have got to be prepared to stand up and say what you want to happen. You can't bring in a boffin in a white coat to give lectures and expect the same results."

Vanda Murray maintains that the choice of consultancy matters less than the training content:

"I do not really think it matters which consultancy you use as long as you find a structure that you think will work for you. We like the basic concepts of Crosby, the philosophy that all work is a process and that there are four absolutes: Definition, System, Performance Standard, and Measurement. You need a framework to stimulate the development of your own Quality structure. I also like the Crosby belief that 'the definition of Quality is conformance to customer requirements'." says Vanda Murray.

A Quality Improvement Team (QIT) was formed to steer the Quality Improvements Process. The QIT was deliberately formed with few members from the management team and an emphasis on having representatives from all departments.

"We have six people on our QIT and the membership changes annually. To maintain momentum, you have got to involve different people. Each member of the QIT is responsible for one or more of 'The 14

Steps' as outlined by Crosby. We're a young company, so our people are keen to be involved. At the end of each yearly cycle we have an Open Day (held in September) and we hold a presentation for the outgoing QIT and announce who the new team will be. We are on our fifth generation QIT in 1996, which means 30 people out of a work force of 95 have had direct exposure to running Total Quality. The proof that the process is succeeding is evident when senior managers are no longer on the QIT – you have to get the managers off the team, otherwise the QIT just becomes another management meeting," explains Peter Tudor.

The '14 Steps' followed by PAC are:

- Management commitment
- Measurement
- Quality Awareness
- Zero Defect Planning
- Zero Defects Day
- Error Cause Removal
- Quality Councils
- Quality Improvement Team
- Cost Of Quality
- Corrective Action
- Education
- Goal Setting
- Recognition
- Do It All Again

Of these measurement is considered one of the most important. Vanda Murray explains:

"Measurement is vital. You need to look at your business and break it down into processes and then break it down again to set goals based on what is important to the business. Individuals can then set measurements for their own areas. In our Sales & Marketing department we measure our customer calls and question the response times: Are we responding to customer enquires within two hours? – if not, why not? What can we do to improve? Is further training required? Our measurements also change, once you get over one hurdle then you go onto the next one."

An early success was achieved in 1992 with the company's certification to the ISO 9002 standard. The certification was important to PAC's clients and helped the company focus on its processes but was considered a stepping stone towards zero defects rather than the total solution.

Two of the first strategic goals set by Peter Tudor were to:

(i). Broaden the Customer Base; and,

(ii). Reduce Cycle Times.

Both the above goals are key components of the company's core strategy. Research proved that an important component of broadening the customer base was reducing the period between orders being placed and products being delivered.

"Until 1992 we had been growing with the companies we initially worked with. About 10 installation companies accounted for nearly 80 per cent of our business, these were large distributors who didn't mind five week lead times. By 1995 that figure has increased to approximately 40 installers. We have been able to spread our risk, because our improved work practices have attracted new clients. After extensive customer research we found out that customers required deliveries anywhere in the country within 24 hours. These companies didn't want to hold stock and normally would only be notified themselves a few days before they would be required on building sites to install the product.

"So our challenge to help us gain these new accounts was to change our manufacturing process. We succeeded and now if a customer places an order before 3:00 pm we can dispatch the product the next day," says Vanda Murray.

Mike Price, PAC's Operations manager was heavily involved in improving the manufacturing process.

"Virtually every product was taking four to five weeks to deliver. Our aim was to improve the lead times to enable next day delivery without increasing our stock levels. This meant working closely with our suppliers and in some cases getting them to add value to their materials and importantly, multi-skilling our workforce," Mike Price said.

PAC began by looking at each product individually. For example to reduce the cycle time of the Easikey range, a product by product analysis of build methods was undertaken. Value analysis of the product was also made to identify areas to reduce cost.

The first round of improvements saw the product build time reduced by 40% from 45 to 27 minutes, a second round saw this time improved to just 21 minutes. Because the company had evolved from a research and development base a number of test and inspection procedures were built into the manufacturing process, by modifying the process many of the tests were able to be eliminated with no reduction in quality standards. Other improvements included:

- The re-organisation of benches.
- Outsourcing more work to suppliers – giving them the responsibility of preparing materials to a higher stage of completion.

- The building process was restructured so sub-assemblies were produced and stocked, these could later be redirected into a number of final product streams and;
- multi-disciplinary training and multi-functional workstations have allowed greater flexibility and responsiveness.

A customised KANBAN system has been put in place with most materials being issued to the point of use. The stock still held in traditional stores is released to the workplace from signals generated by production workers. Supplies are ordered 'Just In Time' from suppliers through an EDI link that ensures next day delivery.

The resultant improvements made by PAC have been very impressive, the question is how were these improvements conceived and implemented? The quality culture and tools developed by the PAC team have made the difference.

Quality Action Groups (QAG) have been established to identify possible improvements to the company's operations. For example the Production QAG looks at ways to improve the manufacturing operations. The team is comprised of manufacturing staff and the members are rotated regularly to maintain enthusiasm. Some very useful improvements have been made by this group. Improvements have been made in various areas but particularly design, which have resulted in easier assembly and a reduction in the number of parts required thus saving time and money.

A Corrective Action Team is also in place to study customer returns to introduce changes which will improve quality. The team has introduced a number of improvements to products since it was established in 1992. For example, field research indicated there was a problem with the vandal resistant reader. The problem was that the design of the reader sometimes allowed a component to be damaged during installation. The solution was to redesign the press tooling. The change involved changing suppliers but as a result of careful design the press tooling was simplified to enable the component to be formed in one operation rather than five. This has helped reduce the cost of the component and the new tooling produces an improved case which is free from tooling marks – another problem identified with the old method.

Staff do not have to be part of a team to suggest improvements – in fact, improvements are encouraged through a number of schemes. One is the Error Cause Removal form which can be filled out by any staff member to outline a 'situation which is making it difficult for me to do my job right first time.'

After the instigator has filled out the form ownership is passed to the 'Stepholder' who is responsible for managing the form and initiating discussions with the relevant managers or directors. Details of actions are filled in on the form and then the instigator signs the form to indicate they are satisfied that their problem has been resolved and the form is then returned to the stepholder to be logged and filed.

Another of these schemes is the "PONCBUSTERS" award. PONC is the term used to describe the Price Of Non-Conformance – the cost of not doing something right the first time. This is one of the key measures used in PAC's Total Quality system. Anyone can put forward a suggestion which improves the company's working environment, process efficiency or saves money. The proposals are reviewed by the manager of that department and the Quality Improvement Team. Gift vouchers are given to the staff that make the best suggestions.

Recognition is a very important part of quality at PAC. Four key Quality recognition tools are used:

Quality 'Q' Card

The Quality 'Q' Card is a small card used for thanking a colleague for their hard work/assistance with day to day tasks.

Quality Recognition Letter

The Quality Recognition Letter is used by other staff members to recognise a PAC employee for their outstanding efforts on a particular project or other aspects of their work, efforts which are over and above their day to day activities. One copy goes into their personnel file and another copy goes to the QIT where it is considered with other nominations for a place on a Quality Recognition Event – a day or evening out.

Quality Recognition form

The Quality recognition form is completed each quarter by the PAC management Team. They nominate at least one member of staff each from any department, who has worked exceptionally hard and who shows an outstanding commitment to Quality. Once these forms have been submitted to the QIT up to six PAC employees will be chosen to go on a Quality recognition event.

Awards

Awards are given annually in the following categories and are voted for by all PAC employees: Quality Person of the Year, Quality Team of the Year, Customer Service Person of the Year, Manufacturing Person of the Year, and Product Development Person of the Year.

Further recognition is provided through PAC's very professionally produced newsletters which include a *QIT Bulletin* and a *Supplier's Quality Link*. The *QIT Bulletin* communicates a variety of information including recognition of employees and PONC goals which have been set and attained. To make the newsletter entertaining a Quality crossword and competitions are sometimes added.

Communication with customers, suppliers and staff is further enhanced with a very successful Open Day event. A theme is developed for the day and previous years have been very successful with over 500 people attending each year.

Perhaps the most powerful way of maintaining enthusiasm and momentum for improvements has been the success of PAC. The company has expanded into export markets and now supplies its products throughout the world. This success has been built on exceptional customer service and a constant re-evaluation of PAC's products and services to ensure they are meeting customers' stated needs. Further evidence of the company's commitment to continuously improving in all areas is the Investor In People Award that PAC attained in 1994.

Peter Tudor concludes with his view of what Quality has achieved:

"We have been working hard at Total Quality Management for the best part of five years. The success of TQM is evident in the way we work at PAC. Everyone is involved and subscribes to the importance of continuous improvement – I like to quote Ford: 'We are in a race with no finishing tape and if we stop we die'. We all realise the importance of measurement. We measure what we do not to assign blame, but to keep our processes under control. Key to this, is understanding the requirements of both internal and external customers. In fact we define quality as 'Conformance to Requirements'.

"We have worked towards having a full partnership arrangement with our clients and suppliers who share our vision of doing things right first time, every time."

12

Customer Driven Quality

—RAC—

AS anyone who has required roadside assistance will testify, the arrival of an RAC patrolman is one of the most welcome sights a stranded motorist can have. The well earned reputation of the RAC as a quality, customer service organisation didn't come from formal Quality programmes or certifications but from almost 100 years experience in delivering an excellent service.

The decision to pursue continuous improvement and implement World Class management techniques has proved that the RAC is a mature organisation, willing to evolve for the benefit of its customers.

In 1897 a group of motoring enthusiasts began the Automobile Club of Great Britain. They declared the organisation to be 'a society for the protection, encouragement and development of automobilism'. To express his interest in motoring, King Edward VII gave his patronage to the club, and in 1907 the society was renamed the Royal Automobile Club.

The early club revolved around social and sporting events for an elite few, but in 1901 the Motor Union was founded as an addition to encourage a wider group of motorists. In the same year the first uniformed patrols, or guides, were seen, while in 1904 the first motoring tours started and the first motoring handbook was published.

Roadside telephone boxes date back to 1912, the same year the RAC's famous 'Get You Home' service was born after a motoring journalist – who had a breakdown – suggested the need for a rescue operation.

Through the decades the RAC has grown to provide a range of motoring services to its customers, including roadside assistance, insurance, legal and touring services.

Dr Fred Lamb
Director of Quality
RAC Motoring Services

The RAC now has approximately six million members and is one of the leading motoring organisations in the world. Since the late 1970s the market has changed considerably. Previously, the RAC and the AA controlled the breakdown service sector. In the early 1980s a number of smaller companies came into the industry and created pressure on the leading firms' market share. This fundamental change in the industry provided the incentive for the organisation to re-evaluate its strategy, with the aim of providing the most effective and efficient range of services for the motorist.

As a result the RAC underwent an ambitious and exciting period of restructuring and growth. Greater emphasis was placed on the RAC's core activity – the rescue services. More than one hundred extra service patrols were put on the road, more than 1,300 and £60 million has been spent on new technology and buildings.

During 1985 it was apparent the RAC's system of call taking was reaching its maximum capacity. Call takers filled out breakdown forms and transferred the information to a radio controller by a conveyer belt, often many attempts were needed before contact could be made with a patrol.

The hunt for a computer system took RAC representatives around the world. An interim system was developed and used to refine and test until extensive training ensured the new CARS (which stands for Computer Aided Rescue Services) system was working well.

The result is that the rescue service has been completely revolutionised by the replacement of time consuming methods of taking and passing on members' information. A network of computerised rescue centres around the country helps locate a stranded motorist and, within seconds, transmit the data to a screen in the cab of a service patrol out on the road.

The investment in this technology gave the RAC the most advanced computerised emergency rescue system of its type in the world. The technological improvement also heralded a period of intense growth with the number of registered members growing from 1 million to around 6 million in just 10 years.

Despite the investment in technology and buildings, the RAC believe that its greatest asset is its employees, whose motto is to be Personally Accountable, Caring and Enterprising.

In 1993, the RAC made the decision to implement a formal Total Quality philosophy. One of the organisation's first steps was to appoint Dr

Fred Lamb as Director of Quality. Dr Lamb had been working as an external consultant for two years but the RAC understood that their commitment to Quality would require a new full-time 'driver'. Dr Lamb was ideally suited for the position with many years experience. The first task was to lay the foundations of the formal, structured approach to Total Quality Management within the executive team.

"We spent most of the first year working closely with the executive to explain what it was we were asking them to get involved with. You cannot launch a mass programme without commitment from your leaders and leaders will only commit when they completely understand what it is they are committing to. We looked at issues like how you would improve process management systems; established the vision, the mission and agreed to future strategies. We had to work hard to convince the executive. Like any responsible management team, they investigated the new strategic proposals vigorously. They understood that if you take Quality seriously you have to look at it as a major strategic direction for the organisation. Quality is not actually a programme, it's not an add on extra, it is a transformation of the way you do things, and therefore it was taken slowly and very seriously", recalls Dr Lamb.

Once executive support was established, a decision was made to gradually bring the message to the RAC as a whole, culminating with a launch event in 1994. A decision was made not to call the new strategic direction a Total Quality Management Programme. For the first year the concept had no official title. Prior to the launch, discussions were held to decide upon a name, Customer Driven Quality was chosen. The customised name gave ownership and originality to the concept – 'driving' is something everyone at the RAC can relate to! As well as the name, a distinctive logo was designed to be used on RAC Quality material and on a badge presented to everyone participating in a registered Quality project. The executive wrote vision and mission statements for the RAC.

The vision for the motoring services part of the organisation is "Outstanding service, delighted customer". The RAC has published a little blue book containing 'Basic Information' to explain Customer Driven Quality, in it the Vision is put in perspective:

"A vision is a statement of our ambition in life, of our intention to achieve something important and inspiring. A vision is not something you put on the wall and forget, it must express a shared enthusiasm for something we all really care about. Our Vision expresses our intention of being the premium supplier. It demands from us behaviour that shows that intention is serious, otherwise it is just a set of high-minded words.

"It needs the support of a Mission statement to clarify what it is that we want to achieve, in more concrete, measurable terms, and it needs a set of Values to define how we will behave while we are fulfilling our Mission."

The Group Mission (what the organisation will actually set out to achieve) is:

- to provide a balanced portfolio of services which enhance the security and the peace of mind of motorists;
- to expand profitably across the business, securing a competitive leadership edge through providing the highest quality and best value for its members, customers, business partners and own people; and
- to champion socially responsible developments in motoring matters, anticipating the needs of all motorists, and providing an independent voice for them.

The different parts of the RAC have their own individual missions, which express their unique contribution to achieving the overall Group Mission.

The RAC has also clear values which articulate the way staff should behave while pursuing the mission. These values express the new culture of the organisation.

The values are summed up in the value statement:

"We value our integrity and our image as a quality organisation, in which every employee demonstrates pride in being part of the RAC, every member and customer is delighted with our service, and every business partner is glad to be associated with us."

The statement of values is not an empty 'motherhood statement' but contains clear directions on what personnel should do to 'live' the values. The statement contains a second part to assist in this process.

"Therefore we will:

- respect and aim to satisfy our members, our customers, our business partners, and our colleagues, as individuals.

- demonstrate a management style which is open and which encourages a spirit of trust and teamwork.

- help everyone to develop his or her individual potential to the full by providing the encouragement, the information, the training, and the tools he or she needs:

– encourage everyone to be personally accountable, caring and enterprising in the pursuit of ever higher levels of quality:

– demonstrate concern and compassion for anyone in trouble by doing our best to help."

It is well known that the culture of an organisation is easily detected by those that come in contact with it. The culture determines how people behave, how they spend their time and the areas they invest their resources. The RAC feels that the above resolutions must be a guide for the organisation's daily behaviour. As a service organisation having a strong set of values and living by them is vital.

Customer Driven Quality is the tool which will achieve these goals. The Quality management system is central to the RAC's business strategy. The organisation sees it as a way to differentiate the RAC from its competitors and to be the premium supplier.

The Customer Driven Quality strategy has four foundation stones:

1. Focus our whole organisation on delighting our customers.
2. Use the full power of our entire team to keep us in front of all our competitors in the eyes of the world.
3. Continuously improve all our business processes, making them simple, free of defects and failure costs, and quick to respond to the changing needs of our customers.
4. Manage by fact, using good, well analysed measurements to control and improve our business.

By clearly detailing their Vision, Group Mission, Values and Quality strategy, the RAC provided its workforce with a solid foundation and a core philosophy. Communication and training became very important, as the way the powerful material and ideas were presented became crucial to the success or failure of the Quality Management System.

To enhance communication systems and allow information to flow upwards throughout the organisation a comprehensive training programme was arranged for all RAC managers, including first line managers. This involved training 350 people. Consultants were contracted to assist in 'training the trainers' with the first courses being run by consultants, the next were delivered jointly, and finally, all courses were conducted internally.

"Everyone with 'people' responsibility went on cross-functional, workshop oriented courses. We used these training sessions to find out what concerns or inhibitors the staff felt would hold the organisation back. The main question was 'Is management going to stick with the change process and Quality philosophy or is it just a fad?'. Normally, in those sorts of training sessions inhibitors usually come out, but we also tried to identify positive things that could move the company in the other direction - that was quite important. The role of the leadership at the time was instrumental for success at that stage, dedication and commitment has to be displayed by management or all the training and communication efforts are wasted", explained Dr Lamb.

Shirley Jones is the Public Relations manager for the RAC and was brought onto the Quality implementation team midway through the implementation to provide a higher standard of communication:

"I would advise other companies going down this route to plan the communications process alongside the education process, right from the start, even six months before you implement anything. You need to have stakes in the ground before you launch the programme and you need to work on when to give it a boost. Budgeting for all of those activities is also important, because Quality doesn't come without a cost, and I think any company embarking on this sort of journey needs to recognise that initial investments are going to be quite high for both training and communication, and they need to work in parallel with one another. Personality and style matters. The people delivering the message should be dynamic and vibrant", says Shirley Jones.

Dr Lamb warns against an *ad hoc* approach to communications:

"Communication of your message needs to be a process. We began by communicating through a series of stand alone projects. We had a launch event, we started a newsletter, we issued the *Blue Book* and we had an awareness course. Early on, we probably looked upon communication as a set of projects which were brought in to support educational requirements and so forth, and that was definitely misguided.

"During our 1996 budget preparation, I made my biggest request, education, and my second biggest request, communication. The third biggest request was for recognition, and the fourth was systems support to support the management system. These are the essential areas - you educate people, you communicate with the people, you recognise and reward the people, and you have to have some mechanism of knowing what's going on for managing and controlling and detecting if there is a health problem with the processes."

During 1994, teams were formed to improve business processes. To help identify processes to be focused on and improved, a suggestions scheme called 'Best Ideas' was instigated. Senior executives undertook a series of site visits, listened to employees and held discussions to identify priorities.

Process Improvement is considered key to the RAC's Quality system. The organisation considers that improvement can only be sustained by constant process change. These leaps are supported by smaller, incremental 'Kaizen', improvements. This combination ensures that the RAC can sustain it's improvement process and exercises the full creativity of the teams to enhance process performance.

A Group Quality Council was established to facilitate the projects and provide feedback to the rest of the organisation. The executive team also receives presentations from groups, requiring junior people, who are participating in team activity to give presentations (often for the first time) to very senior managers. The standards of the presentations are very high and the staff are comfortable using Quality terminology.

In March 1995, two initiatives were launched to recognise the quality efforts of individuals and teams. The Flying Lady Award for Quality is given to teams who demonstrate excellence in Quality project management. The teams present their Quality project to the Quality council for judging. The award is for team effort and seeks to recognise those people who have used Quality techniques to complete a particular task. The Silver Salver recognises individual commitment to Quality enhancements.

While the internal recognition system inspires and motivates staff, the RAC as a whole is seeking to maintain the momentum for continuous Improvement through the European Foundation for Quality Management, Business Excellence Model. The model has the same emphasis as Customer Driven Quality with a focus on People, Processes and Measurement. Although the RAC's objective is not scoring points or winning awards, the organisation is aiming for a world class score in their self assessment.

At the end of 1994, the executive team did a first assessment against the EFQM model and found that progress was being made. If progress continues at a satisfactory rate the RAC may become an entrant for the European Quality Award in the near future.

To further measure how the RAC is progressing with its key strategic improvement objectives a scorecard has been developed.

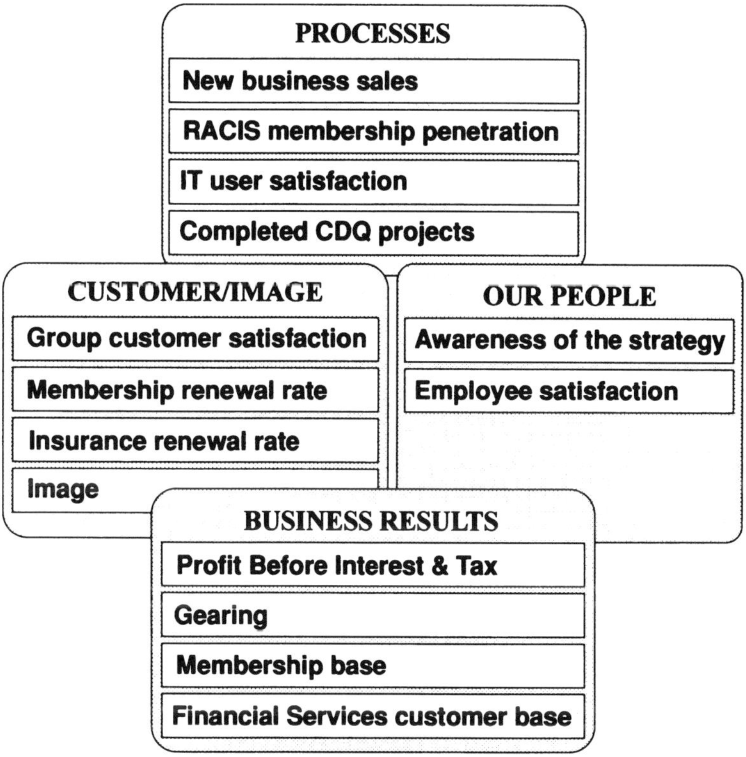

The scorecard is structured like the EFQM model. The RAC believes the scorecard items must be in balance to ensure the long and short term health of the business. The scorecard is further explained in the *Blue Book*:

"To strikingly show this balance, the scorecard is presented each month in the simple format shown above. The various sections are coloured as 'traffic lights' depending on how they stand against plans and targets. Green if the item is OK, amber if it needs to be watched carefully, and red if the item needs action. The full data and targets are of course on the detailed scorecard behind this simple presentation.

"These measurements signal what is really important, and they motivate action. 'What gets measured gets done' is true - and it is important this should be true, since measurements are pointless unless they are used to guide action. Each item on the scorecard has an owner who is responsible for gathering and analysing the data, and ensuring that improvements are in place for all the red items.

"The scorecard holds the set of measurements that is used by the Group Management Committee to close the loop in the Quality Management System back to our vision, to ensure we do indeed deliver outstanding services to delighted customers."

The efforts of the RAC to date have definitely moved the organisation towards achieving that goal. A number of divisions are working towards or have attained ISO 9000 Certification. Dr Fred Lamb sums up the importance of Customer Driven Quality:

"Ultimately, Quality is in the peace of mind of the customer. In a rescue situation our customer is often very stressed and their expectations are quite high. The people who work in our breakdown service have a natural desire to serve and want to perform well. Through our Quality Management System we have been able to harness this attitude and develop it throughout the whole organisation. In the not too distant future, Quality won't be considered a programme or add on, but simply the way we do business."

13

Constructing Quality

— Ardmac Group Ltd —

THE construction industry is one of the most challenging and demanding of all business sectors. Recessions have at times devastated the building market and historically the industry has suffered more than most from downturns in the economic cycle.

R. Baden Hellard described the special difficulties associated with implementing Total Quality Management (TQM) in the construction industry in his article 'Constructing Harmony' (*The TQM Magazine*, Dec 1991). "In construction, there is an essential difference in the application of TQM principles, in that a construction project has a finite life. It has a beginning – with the establishment of the need; it has a middle – the design and development of the solutions to those needs; and an end – the implementation by the contractor of the solution in the physical construction. After which, the project's people structure and the other physical resources which have been employed are broken down and redeployed on other projects under other managers for other organisations."

While quality management systems are entrenched in the manufacturing industry, the construction building sectors have found it more difficult to adapt to quality systems, particularly because of the high level of sub-contractors and suppliers, the frequently itinerant workforce, and the number of one-off jobs.

In a construction project every contributor becomes a customer of the other. In most projects the 'customers' are the client, who originated the project, the architect, the surveyors and engineers, the general contractors and the specialist sub-contractors.

As Mr Hellard points out it is the above challenges which make a

left to right: Siobhan Gordon (Quality Manager), Kevin McAnallen (Managing Director), David Leggett (Group Construction Director) Ardmac Group Ltd

TQM philosophy so vital for success. The team at specialist construction company Ardmac understand the benefits of TQM and have grown their business to become a highly respected leader in their field.

Ardmac began in 1977 as a small entrepreneurial family business involved in the construction industry in Ireland. With a family history in the building industry, it was not surprising the three McAnallen brothers, Kevin, Sean and Brendan became involved in construction. Brendan started the business by participating in small contracts specialising in partitions and ceilings, and Sean and Kevin joined him later.

Working as an internal construction company gave the organisation the ability to identify a number of highly specialised niche markets.

Ardmac are now Interior Construction Specialists with three primary areas of activity. The areas are (i) Commercial Interiors; (ii) Cleanrooms for the Microelectronics Industry and (iii) Sterile Rooms for the Pharmaceutical and Biotechnology Industry. By 1995, Ardmac had offices managing five autonomous regions or profit centres throughout Ireland and the United Kingdom. The Ardmac group employ 150 people and forecast a turnover of £15 million in 1995.

So how did Ardmac survive recessions and prosper in the 1990s to become an industry leader?

Ardmac's managing director Kevin McAnallen believes the company's success has everything to do with implementing Total Quality Management.

Kevin joined the company in 1981. He feels his previous position as managing director in a division of General Electric, ill prepared him for the trials of small business. "I went into the small business environment thinking I could apply the same management values and systems I had previously applied in General Electric. I soon discovered that different skills where required. There is a big difference between managing a company with virtually limitless institutional resources and one where the proprietors are responsible for supplying capital."

The recessions of the mid and late 1980s caused many problems for Ardmac. The growing company had cashflow difficulties and a large commitment was required from the directors to enable the company to survive. Ardmac returned to profitability in 1989. The company was being run in a very entrepreneurial way. In 1989–90 Ardmac's management team realised that the management systems they had in place were inadequate to control the business.

The directors knew the company had potential for growth. They wanted to develop a strategy that created the professional management systems that would enable the company to grow.

Quality systems had been looked at but mainly in the context of achieving ISO 9000 certification. Some clients had expressed an interest in Ardmac's plans regarding certification and many tender lists were specifying ISO 9000 as a minimum requirement. A number of Ardmac employees saw ISO 9000 certification merely as a marketing tool. Kevin did not like the idea of a quality system that was little more than a certificate on the wall and a manual that sat on the shelf and was dusted down once a year during re-certification audits.

"I felt that if we were going to implement a quality system it had to be one that was an important part of how we managed the business", says Kevin. Kevin attended various quality management seminars including one by TQM/Polycon. "I was impressed by their approach, unlike others who were trying to apply a manufacturing quality system to construction, TQM/Polycon put emphasis on the need to develop your management team. We hired them as consultants. Ron Baden Hellard, their chief executive, an architect who had worked for many years as a quality management consultant to the construction industry understood the issues effecting the business. He produced a report based on interviews with twenty of our managers and supervisors. I asked him to include an assessment of our strengths and weaknesses in the report. The final document has been very useful for us," explained Kevin.

Ardmac have adhered closely to the initial 'blueprint' and Kevin still refers to it. Ardmac has spent a considerable amount of money on consultants but Kevin believes the funds spent on the initial report to be the most worthwhile. Kevin warns against an over-reliance on consultants: "I developed the conviction that consultants cannot implement TQM for you. They can make you aware of issues to focus on, read the level of knowledge and inspire a lot of effort, but they cannot implement it."

The TQM strategy began to be implemented in 1992. Attaining certification was still important to Ardmac but it was not the main objective. Although the company could have completed its documentation in twelve months it was felt that the objective should be to develop a Total

Quality organisation, thus developing and training Ardmac's people became the priority.

Consultants were involved in the initial training programmes and helping redesign Ardmac's organisational structure. The new organisational structure was the framework for all other aspects of the company's activities, systems and documentation. It is designed as a 'route map' for communications internally and for identifying contact points for external contacts. In the M.A.P.S. philosophy used by Ardmac, M stands for Marketing – everything concerning getting the order, A stands for Administration – everything to do with seeing the company continues to function and gets paid for it, P is for production, and S stands for Strategic thinking.

Some key professionals were hired for management roles in the new structure. One of the new managers recruited was David Leggett, who became the Group Construction Director (including responsibility for TQM implementation). David was formerlly the managing director of a major construction company and has played a key role in the evolution and development of the company.

The new TQM philosophy was introduced to Ardmac's workforce through a series of meetings where information was shared and the new management concepts were explained. The employees met with management in groups of 25 to 30 people, initially a number of the workforce were cynical about the changes.

Siobhan Gordon, Ardmac's quality manager understood how important it was for everyone to support the implementation of TQM: " Recognition of the need for a quality system was perhaps one of the first obstacles we encountered when introducing TQM to our personnel. Ardmac has always had a good tradition of quality workmanship and know-how at the functional level of construction. We had to help people understand that we needed to have professional management systems as well. The prospect of dealing with possible scepticism or even cynicism was daunting. In some cases 'converting the people' was a slow process but it was essential if we were to reap the potential benefits afforded by embracing a quality system. The success of TQM was dependent on the collaboration of all our colleagues and they were unlikely to change unless they also recognised the need."

'Converting the people' was made easier because Ardmac had won some very prestigious new projects and these projects required a very professional management approach.

"One never really knows if the fact that you are implementing a quality system is instrumental in helping you win prestigious projects, but I believe working on projects for these quality clients helped us develop our quality systems", comments Kevin.

An excellent example of how client feedback was used to improve the business came from work on the Intel Corporation Component Manufacturing Site.

Ardmac/PCI (a joint venture with an American partner, Performance Contracting Inc) was one of 15 contracting companies on the Intel contracting team who completed a £130 million project; the team was lead by Jacobs International. Two months into the contract Kevin McAnallen was involved in an eventful on-site meeting with Fred Hall, one of Intel's managers.

"In 30 seconds I learned more about TQM from Fred Hall than all the people I've ever known. Jacobs were unhappy with our performance and I couldn't understand why because we were on programme and the quality of the work was acceptable. Fred Hall turned to me and said: 'Your results were achieved through heroic effort!' I said I knew exactly what he meant because people had worked all night to get the job done. But he then said: '*You* may have known you were going to achieve the deadline, but *no one* else on this team did, in fact they'd already decided that because of the way you were approaching the project you were not going to make it!'

"Fred's views gave me further awareness of the need for structured management – a proactive approach to controlling the process rather than a reactive approach that achieved the desired results but required a superhuman effort. I think the way we reacted to Fred Hall's comments were very positive. Within a very short period of time we had established a better way of managing projects, but like all pieces of learning it came in an instant."

Stan Corrigan, the Regional Director for the Intel site said at the time: "The concepts of teamwork and the system approach of Ardmac's TQM programme have been central to the substantial progress that has been made on the site since June 1992. Ongoing improvement and recognition of achievement are the major results of the various training programmes that have been carried out."

Ardmac's philosophy of developing Partner Relationships was in large measure the inspiration for developing the joint venture with Performance Contracting Inc (PCI). One of the key benefits derived from the partnership was the concept of 'Zero Accidents' which had been pioneered by PCI and which made them one of the safest contractors in the USA. Kevin McAnallen recognised the parallels in Ardmac's 'TQM' programme and PCI's 'Zero Accidents' programme and commenced a process to integrate the two programmes.

'Zero Accidents' is now a key element of Ardmac's TQM programme, the implication being: "Who's going to volunteer to be the first accident!" Ardmac considers its investment in safety training and awareness small when compared with the value of its workforce.

Training has been vital for Ardmac to achieve the outstanding results detailed above.

"Education and training are the essential pivots upon which our quality system revolves. To enable personnel to progress along the TQM learning curve we have invested in a group-wide training programme involving both in-house trainers and external training bodies", says Siobhan.

Initial training took place in a series of seminars. Siobhan points out that these training seminars were successful because they were voluntary, people were invited to attend.

Contemplating the requirements of BS EN ISO 9002 certification, Siobhan Gordon, said, "It is crucial that whilst developing TQM within our organisation that we strike a balance between the 'people' and 'paperwork' aspects of our quality system. It is possible to place too great an emphasis on establishing detailed documented procedures which can develop into a 'paperwork mountain' leaving personnel confused and disgruntled. Only by placing concentrated effort in developing our people alongside our procedures can we hope to achieve our goals.

"Our Quality Systems Manual is not a method of imposing bureaucratic measures on personnel. Far from it! It is an invaluable 'working tool' which if used consistently as a source of reference helps our people perform their everyday duties in an effective and quality orientated manner."

Kevin adds that "a manual of several hundred pages, full of forms and procedures can be quite off putting to someone from an entrepreneurial background. Some employees were under the impression that they had to know everything about the organisation that was documented in the Procedure Manual. The idea of a Procedure Manual is for an employee to become fully aware of what is required of them – the processes and procedures for their specific areas of responsibility."

An important aspect of Ardmac's quality system is the company's strong belief in a 'teamwork approach' whereby each member of the organisation plays an integral part in the development of TQM.

Siobhan explains, "Participation of personnel can be reflected in our establishment of task forces/workgroups. Key personnel from all levels of the organisation are selected to participate in the task force most relevant to their areas of responsibility. The task forces established are centred around some major functions of the business; Contracts Management/ Commercial/Sales/Purchasing and Personnel as examples. The purpose of each task force is to establish and document quality system procedures in their respective groups and to define a strategy to ensure procedures are effectively implemented at all levels of the organisation. By forming task forces we are able to release the potential of personnel whilst promoting a culture based around the need for participation from a representative section of the organisation."

Task forces or workgroups are often used for specific areas of activity and then are 'wound up'. The groups have considerable freedom in deciding how to implement procedures because they have to 'sell' them to their peers.

Anyone can originate a change. A suggestion for a change of procedure is given to the quality manager who distributes it to other parties involved in that particular procedure and as other comments or suggestions are made they are then passed back to the originator. The whole process usually takes only a few days and people are proud to say they are involved in the way the procedures manual is written and improved.

The management team at Ardmac understand that effective communication within the organisation is vital to involve all employees in the process of implementing TQM. Often in smaller organisations information tends to be circulated to a few key players, and is not distributed in a formal manner. Ardmac developed an internal newsletter titled *Insite*, which informs employees of the company's progress and commitment to Quality.

The newsletter often contains information on TQM topics. In April

1995 a list of Ardmac's 'Ten Commandments' (see Figure 1) to make the continuous improvement process easier was published.

The 'Commandments' according to ARDMAC's Workforce

For the Total Quality Management approach of continuous improvement, "Ten Commandments" have been drawn up as a medium through which the process can be made easier. The thinking behind these "Ten Commandments" is, that in order to carry out a job with maximum effectiveness, employees should receive complete co-operation and assistance from their superiors. If this is not forthcoming under any of these captions, the worker's right is to demand that the commandments be obeyed in full by his or her superior.

1. TELL ME THE TRUTH.
Do not bear false witness against me!
I have no time for euphemisms, which fail to address the situation as it is. Being overly subtle with words solves no problems.

2. EXPLAIN WHAT WE ARE DOING SO I CAN UNDERSTAND.
Thou shalt not leave me in the dark!
Do not expect me to know what is best without giving me the full details in a language I can understand. You are the expert – pass on some of your expertise.

3. TELL ME WHAT YOU EXPECT ME TO DO.
Keep my duties holy! Give me a proper job description. Set me fair and realistic targets. Keep me appraised of deadlines. Don't set me up to fail!

4. PAY ME TO DO IT.
This commandment is, for some reason the most easily recognised among Ardmac Employees and needs no explanation

5. LET ME DO IT.
Be free with your advice and listen to my concerns, but please do not interfere with my earnest endeavour...

6. HELP ME DO IT.
...although, a little push and a few incentives wouldn't go amiss.

7. TELL ME HOW I'M DOING.
Honour my rate of progress chart! Be blunt and honest. I am not a slacker (if I was, I wouldn't ask you to do this). I cannot guess progress if I don't know what to improve.

8. LISTEN TO ME SO THAT YOU UNDERSTAND.
Allow me to put my case forward. I am human, so sympathise with my difficulties. Acknowledge that I can offer new ideas.

9. REWARD ME IF I DO WELL.
Success breeds success! Pat me on the back, promote me, pay me more and remember that my success is your success is the company's success.

10. SACK ME IF I FAIL TO TRY.
I promise to always commit myself. This is the only commandment that looks as if it was written by the boss.

FIGURE 1.

The 10th Commandment which reads: "Sack me if I fail to try" has a note saying it is the only Commandment which looks as if it was written by the 'boss'! Kevin is quite clear about his managerial style: "I think it is necessary, when initiating the TQM process, to be decisive (maybe even autocratic) because initiating by consensus would be virtually impossible, but informing employees is one of the keys for them to become more empowered. It's for others to say that my style has become less autocratic, but a lot more people in the organisation do things I used to do. I think that's a measure of their empowerment."

To ensure the process of continuous improvement is just that – continuous, a regular program of internal audits and self-assessment is in place. Each month the regional directors carry out a self-assessment of how they think their personnel are progressing.

The Regional Monthly Self-Assessment Report is based on assessing four factors to ascertain whether more needs to be done in a certain area. A points system of 1 to 5 is used. The four key areas are: *Understanding* of procedures; *Implementation* to assess how effectively procedures are being implemented; *Action Plan* to gauge what action is required to move the implementation process forward; and *Support Requirements* to assess what support the quality department can provide to ensure full compliance with procedures. The 'gaps' or shortfalls are then analysed and weak areas are improved. Ardmac is familiar with the European Foundation For Quality Management (EFQM) Self-Assessment Model and may soon adopt the EFQM model as a company-wide assessment tool.

Clearly Ardmac has reaped numerous benefits from its approach to quality. The company's impressive list of clients and partners include: Intel, Jacobs International Inc, Courtaulds Engineering, MacAlpines, AMEC, British Aerospace and British Gas.

Many of these clients praise the TQM philosophy at Ardmac. Typical is the Special Merit Award the company received from Intel as part of the Hibernia Operation. By making effective use of their quality system Ardmac completed the project in a manner that resulted in the company recieving this prestigious award. The Special Merit Award recognised Adrmac's achievements towards 'Zero Defects and Quality Workmanship'.

The financial rewards of implementing TQM are evident in Ardmac's increased turnover, which has shown a growth of 40 per cent per annum. The company is also more profitable although profits have to be balanced against a high investment in TQM of between £300,000 to £500,000 which is a sizeable commitment for a company with a £15 million turnover.

Ardmac continues to be excited about the progress made by the implementation of TQM, as Kevin explains:

"You can see something being born that you know would never have been possible in any other way – if you don't have a process and a systematic approach to management you can never learn. In this business you are selling people skills and management. If you want to remain a small business you can have well-meaning individuals who do their own thing. Alternatively, you can have an organisation where people do things in a consistent, predictable way where there is shared knowledge. I have no doubt that both our profitability and our ability to grow, and manage that growth, is totally to do with the implementation of TQM. I expect we will be able to continue growing rapidly, because we've laid the foundations. We're at a point where people are 'fired up' and motivated to keep improving, our team is committed to be the best".

Stephen A Carter
Managing Director
J. Walter Thompson

14

Quality & Creativity

— J. Walter Thompson —

MANY commentators within the advertising industry have questioned what business an advertising agency has introducing ISO certification to its day-to-day operations, let alone the industry – and at what cost?

The advertising industry's main trade journal, *Campaign*, suggested that "there were a myriad of practical objections to imposing a management system that has its roots in the manufacturing industry on an industry that is by definition varied and based on individual flair. As one senior figure had noted, the best results in advertising and media buying often come from breaking the rule book...BS5750 is a pernicious irrelevance for the advertising industry and must be exposed as such before it becomes a millstone around its neck."

This was certainly the attitude expressed by a large proportion of commentators in the advertising industry in 1993 when J. Walter Thompson, Britain's largest advertising agency was the first to receive BS5750 (ISO9001) certification in January of that year.

The article posed the question – why will a BS5750-accredited agency produce work of a higher quality than one that isn't? Mr Doric Bossom, was the JWT Account Director charged with the responsibility of overseeing the certification process and still maintains three years on that clients are not likely to detect the influence of certification in the product or the advertising, rather, in the service they receive from the agency. "There is no suggestion that BS5750 (ISO9000) was, or will ever be, a distinguishing feature in the selection of an advertising agency. At the end of the day agencies are, and will continue to be, selected for their creative, strategic and media skills. However, what it does demonstrate is that creativity and business discipline are not incompatible."

"It is implicit within the standard that a company which runs itself in a disciplined fashion will deliver its clients a better service or product more frequently at a lower cost. In essence BS5750 (ISO9000) is concerned only with the internal disciplines that exist in an organisation, the methods and procedures that the company has for communicating and recording information passing within the company and between it and its clients or suppliers", explains Mr Bossom.

When JWT embarked on the path to BS5750 certification in June 1992 it was breaking new ground as there was no model for a large full-service advertising agency to follow. It continued only after carefully considering the issues involved and satisfying itself that it would not jeopardise the creative capability of the agency.

Once reassured the standard was translated from scratch by Mr Bossom, with the assistance of consultants, into a language and format that was relevant to an advertising agency. JWT successfully distilled the standard into three meaningful points which were applicable throughout the organisation. The essence was that BS5750 (ISO9000) required an organisation to write down: what it needs to do; what has been done; and whether what was done was checked. JWT then applied these principles to its activities. The staff were not directly exposed to the consultants in order to protect them from Quality jargon and a situation which was potentially confusing or intimidating.

"Many of the control processes were already in place, and simply required documentation. JWT has always prided itself on its in-house systems, 90 per cent of which were consistent with the standard's guidelines, prior to certification. The development of an advertisement from client brief to the finished magazine, newspaper or television commercial takes it through a number of departments and has consequently had to be well managed and regulated. It was therefore only necessary to introduce a handful of extra disciplines to fill in the holes and bring the system up to the standard's requirements", says Mr Bossom.

JWT formed an internal project team drawn from Account Management and Traffic. The five members of the team were all trained in quality assessment. However, the development of the necessary procedures involved over 50 people in various departments. In co-operation with department managers over a four month period Mr Bossom penned the procedures according to individual departmental needs and produced 17 individual departmental volumes which collectively form JWT's *Procedures for Quality.* Mr Bossom likens the process to a huge new business pitch which culminated in a four-day presentation to the BSI assessors: "Commitment to certification only took 225 days, which is half the time usually taken by a company of our size. People in advertising agencies characteristically rise to a challenge and you can easily galvanise 450 people in a building to work towards a common aim with amazing energy because nobody wants to let the team down."

The media volume is the largest containing 20 pages while the creative department's volume is deliberately concise consisting of only five pages based on the reality that the 'creatives' need to be freed from the constraints of bureaucracy and administration. "Creatives generally work in teams consisting of a copy writer and art director to create an inspired, original and distinctive idea in response to the client's brief in a given period of time. Our first concern was to protect this engine room because without the creative department we would not be able to move forward", explains Martin Jones, New Business Director for JWT London. In essence, all the creative people need to do to satisfy JWT's Quality procedures is to show a brief for whatever they are working on which is something they have always done.

JWT pursued certification with the knowledge that BS5750 could not legislate how creative work was developed and was careful to build the system around the creative department, not over it. "The purpose is not to improve the efficiency of the creative people, because they perform better when allowed freedom and flexibility. However, you can provide an improved framework within which they operate by providing a better briefing, improved planning and by ensuring that the end result can be tested according to the original intention by providing enough creative managers who are capable of judging the work," explains Mr Bossom.

As primarily a paper-based system, the standard has a more pronounced effect in departments such as traffic, production, account management and finance. Improved inter-departmental communications has consequently been a key benefit derived from BS5750 (ISO9000). For example, when the traffic department briefs the print department they have to do so in writing. If they ask for an estimate then they are obliged to provide them with sufficient information about the kind of publication in which the advertisement is to appear. Alternatively if the print people have to create a mock-up and pass it on to traffic there has to be a way for traffic to check whether print has done its job properly. Accordingly there is a control process for that purpose to ensure that departments are precise about their communications.

Discrete changes to a number of behind-the-scenes aspects of the business resulted in tangible improvements to client service. While Mr Bossom acknowledges that none of the revised activities represents a breakthrough in Quality management they all contribute to the overall efficiency of the agency. BS5750 (ISO9000) ensures that things such as call reports are properly and comprehensively written; client briefs and creative briefs are rigorously reviewed and checked; all work is seen and approved by the relevant people before leaving the agency; estimates are assembled carefully using written specifications in all cases; and any problems or client complaints are properly sorted out.

Savings from the introduction of BS5750 (ISO9000) have accrued from the decrease in the number of errors resulting in write-offs, a situation where the client does not pay for an unacceptable product. JWT estimates that the cost of certification (£40 thousand in the first year for consultancy fees and stationery, and £10 thousand per annum to maintain the system) was recouped within 12 months from merely reducing the number of write-offs.

In the three years since the award of BS5750 JWT's revenue has increased by 24 per cent, billings have grown by 35 per cent, creative profile has broadened and the client base has expanded exponentially – 23 per cent of JWT's clients have been with the agency for over 25 years but 43 per cent have joined the agency since 1993. However, the agency is wary of suggesting the degree of cause and effect between these growth indicators and ISO certification because of the influence of other external factors.

What is attributed directly to BS5750 (ISO9000) is the time saved through a right first time attitude as Mr Stephen Carter, Managing Director of JWT London explains: "Time is the most precious commodity we deal in during the creative process so our view was that the primary benefit of introducing a formal total quality system and rigorous procedures and processes was the prevention of wasted time."

In part the original motivation to attain certification came from clients such as Kodak, Jaguar, Parcelforce, Kraft and Esso which had either wholly or in part certified their organisations and were indicating that they would prefer their suppliers to follow suit as a general commitment to Quality.

JWT's certification was welcomed by the majority of clients as a vehicle to enhance communications and further align the agency with the management philosophies adopted by Quality organisations. Documenting procedures also assisted JWT to educate clients about their role in interacting with agency staff such as the importance of providing considered written briefs and signing estimates promptly.

Certification is seen as a mark of professional excellence. JWT has always prided itself on its professionalism and being a leader in the industry – Quality was therefore consistent with its image. However, because the agency does not view it as a distinguishing feature certification is only used as a marketing tool when particularly relevant to a prospective client.

Prior to and post ISO certification JWT has been a process efficient business. "The benefit lies in being able to spend more time focused externally on clients and prospective clients and on new opportunities and less on maintaining the existing status quo because the existing status quo is more efficiently run. But I don't use it as a reason why a client should appoint us", explains Mr Carter.

JWT is no stranger to measurement, accountability and responsiveness. Many of its practices are at the leading edge of current marketing thinking. It had played a significant role in pioneering and developing new and better ways of measuring effectiveness prior to BS5750 (ISO9000). Advanced market modelling techniques enable JWT to show its clients exactly what they are receiving for their money, in terms such as market share and sales performance. JWT handles more brand leaders than any other advertising agency including Kit Kat, Esso, Dulux and Andrex.

JWT observes a distinctive approach to creative advertising which it has developed and refined over many years into a tool kit or a collection of disciplines and principles which can be applied to any problem, in any market, at any time. These are recorded in four volumes, spanning over 650 pages – *The JWT Media Person's Handbook*; *The JWT Account Manager's Handbook*; *The JWT Guide to Research*; *The JWT Manual of Tools of the Trade for Advertising Planners.*

The most important principle and the nearest thing JWT has to a doctrine carved in stone is the concept of "responses, not messages". In layman's terms, the audience must be involved as active participants in the communication rather than passive receivers of information if advertising is to be successful. "It is the difference between a comedian informing an audience of how funny he is, and telling them a brilliant joke."

Evoking the right response is dependent on knowing your audience which is why JWT has invested considerable time and effort on quantitative research. Armed with this knowledge a creative brief can be written expressing the brand's benefits in terms which are relevant to the audience and most likely to achieve the desired result. This creative output is then measurable against the brief.

JWT is renowned for its stable of memorable advertising campaigns. Throughout its 70 years, JWT has and continues to handle more market leaders across a range of industries than any other agency. Forty one per cent of clients spend up to £1 million while 30 per cent have billings in excess of £5 million. The agency prides itself in being able and committed to providing the same level of service to every client.

The role call of clients is impressive – from Boots to Barclays, De Beers to Esso and Jaguar Cars to Nestlé Rowntree to name but a few. It is also the agency associated with long-running advertising campaigns such as the Oxo family, the Andrex puppy, the Dulux sheepdog, the Mint with the Hole and the Kit Kat Break. And for all those who believe that certification stifles creativity JWT is the winner of numerous IPA Effectiveness Awards both past and present.

In addition to the production of television commercials, press advertisements, radio commercials, poster and cinema commercials JWT has a wide range of additional facilities and resources allowing it to take responsibility for every aspect of brand communication. Available facilities include a print production department, television production department, art studio, information centre and public affairs unit. It is also able to provide its clients with point-of-sale production, packaging design, database marketing and telemarketing services amongst others.

The services that JWT offers have increased in response to the changing nature of client requirements which are moving away from traditional advertising to encompass a broader marketing stance, known by catchphrases such as total communications and integrated marketing.

A significant example of this market change is JWT's work for

Lloyds of London. In 1994 the agency was appointed to oversee Lloyd's brand and communications strategy which involves managing a research project, production of corporate videos and a range of other non-broadcast communications material – in short no advertising. JWT's adoption of these changes is consistent with its view of business success in the future.

"The truly successful companies of the 21st century will be small, flexible and creative. A challenge which is particularly relevant to the advertising industry is the maintenance of fluidity and experimentation within a commercial context. The advertising industry is essentially unpredictable, generative and creative in the genuine sense of the word – where a manufacturer can reproduce the same model and derive efficiency benefits we would go out of business. We need to generate pure creation every single time and the eternal dilemma for agencies which want to grow past a certain critical size, which we do both locally and internationally, is how do you manage order and 'creative chaos'", explains Mr Carter.

JWT introduced BS5750 (ISO9000) to ensure efficiency of process, responsiveness and ultimately client satisfaction through exceptional service. Mr Carter attributes poor customer service standards at least in part to the British culture: "The English certainly and the British generally are not a nation who are given to unashamed displays of emotion which is exactly what customer service is – in our context ensuring that when a client goes into a presentation room in an advertising agency that the cups are clean, the coffee is piping hot, the room is tidy and the presentation is cuttingly excellent. They may receive the last bit but not the other three because it would be a public admittance that you have gone to some effort. There seems to be a natural reserve that specifies that it is more embarrassing to try hard and fail than not to bother. This is a scenario that endlessly replicates itself in the commercial world."

There are still members of the advertising industry who hide behind the veil of chaos, unpredictability and glamour in the knowledge that outsiders continue to romance the stereotype, as security. However, the reality is that agencies will be forced to become, if they are not already, accountable for the effectiveness of both their creative output and their business practices in an increasingly competitive and financially driven industry. "The advertising industry is very volatile. JWT has been in the top three agencies since 1926 based on billings, revenue, people, client base... you don't get to be in that position by standing still and admiring your past", says Mr Carter.

In 1995, JWT was still one of only two British advertising agencies to obtain certification leaving BSI wishing its courtship with the advertising industry would flow as smoothly as one of JWT's campaigns:

I don't see the point of getting certified
I don't see the point of getting
I don't see the point of
I don't see the point
I don't see the
I don't see
I don't
I do

(Adaptation of a campaign designed for De Beers Diamonds – engagement rings – in 1984)

15

Tae Be The Best

— Blue Circle Cement Scotland —

"WHEN deciding to implement Total Quality Management (TQM) an act of faith is required on the part of company's management. Your employees need the opportunity to succeed – you have to trust them in order for them to trust you." This view of how to successfully implement TQM comes from Mr Ross Dunn. Ross is one of the most qualified people in the UK to discuss TQM having been General Manager of Blue Circle Cement Scotland, running the successful Dunbar works and in 1995 joining the executive of Blue Circle Cement to become Personnel Director.

The work of Ross and his team at the Dunbar works, Scotland was recognised when the company won the Quality Scotland Foundation Business Excellence Award and the National Society of Quality Through Teamwork Perkins Award. The business unit also holds an Investor In People Award.

The views of Ross expressed in his no-nonsense Scottish brogue give a clear understanding of how Blue Circle Cement has been transformed into a Quality organisation. The company's use of effective communication to develop an empowered workforce has seen significant improvements in business performance and a high level of customer and employee satisfaction.

Blue Circle Cement is the United Kingdom's largest cement producer. The company supplies half the country's cement requirements from its ten works. Their Dunbar works is the only cement manufacturing process in Scotland.

The way Blue Circle Cement Scotland has approached its implementation of TQM is best summed up in their motto, "Tae be the

Rear left to right: Colin Cooper, Tommy Rice, Bryan McCraw, Stuart Higginbottom
Front left to right: Iain Campbell and Ross Dunn
Blue Circle Cement Scotland

Best". The success of Blue Circle's Scottish management comes not from slavishly copying American or Japanese management philosophy but by studying the latest management techniques and learning from them.

The changes at Blue Circle are not merely cosmetic or understood only by senior management and quality gurus but by the workers themselves.

Stuart Higginbottom is an employee who started working for Blue Circle straight from school, and is in a unique position to comment on the radical changes that have occurred since 1993.

"When I first joined the company you always felt obliged to follow the ways and working methods of the older more experienced employees. The idea of being anti management and the 'them and us' syndrome was viewed as being the norm. Ownership and pride were words never uttered or contemplated. Communication only took place with your direct supervisor. The managers were the men in suits who darted in and out of the offices.

"Those who showed any signs of being keen and enthusiastic went very much unnoticed. Promotion and even recognition prospects were very, very low. Lads who had originally shown enthusiasm fell into the ways of the older men.

"This way of working went a long way towards the fundamental reasons of the workers at the lower levels having this in-bred distrust of management and thus created the hostile relationship between the two groups. However the changes I have witnessed at the factory have been phenomenal. Attitudes have drastically changed by both management and workers. There is team building, consensus decision making, and one-level meetings. People are able to stand up and be heard. All this seems an eternity from my original experiences. This facility to be heard has had a dramatic effect on many of my fellow workers' attitudes. People believing in ownership and trust of fellow workers is now the norm."

The improved atmosphere at Blue Circle is very different to the early 1980s when the cement industry was characterised by high manning levels and relatively low wages. The workers' pay was supplemented by high levels of overtime – a working week in excess of sixty hours was not uncommon. The workforce were paid adverse-conditions money and bonuses during plant shutdown periods.

Tommy Grieve, an AEEU Shop Steward at Blue Circle, explains those difficult times: "The more hours you worked, the dirtier the job and the longer you took, the better you were paid. The structure actually encouraged overtime and breakdowns became more frequent. Strict demarcations were observed, so it was not unusual to have industrial disputes on these and many other matters which constantly disrupted production and further increased the bitterness of the workforce. Every attempt at change was viewed with intense suspicion and was bargained over. When I became a shop steward in 1974, one of the first duties was to be landed with a six-week strike over condition payments. The lesson learned from that experience we should not forget; the damage to the company and the hardship endured by the workforce and their families. The resentment and bitterness lasted for many years afterwards, and it quickly became apparent to all that this was a road to nowhere – but it seemed the only way at that time."

The mid-1980s brought recession. Product demand was in steep decline and there was fierce competition, especially from lower priced foreign imports. Blue Circle Cement was not able to compete internationally.

The problems facing Blue Circle Cement were too severe for the company to correct with one or two minor improvements, radical change was required. Massive investments in plant were made and the latest technology was installed at the Cauldon and Dunbar works. Both senior management and unions agreed that a change in working practices had to be combined with the large capital investment in plant in order to achieve a substantial improvement in productivity.

The shared vision for the future was to have a highly skilled and flexible workforce, working as an integrated team which, together with the new technology, would be able to compete with the best in the world.

The key elements of this new vision included:

- enhanced skills for individuals with a reduction in the number of job grades, leading to greater flexibility
- introduction of a simple pay structure with the elimination of paid overtime and bonuses and increased basic wage levels
- significantly reduced manning levels and a reduction in total labour costs.

Blue Circle Cement, with the assistance of the Advisory, Conciliation and Arbitration Service (ACAS), Work Research Unit (WRU) reviewed the best progressive work practices of competitors and companies from a variety of industries and countries. As an independent body, ACAS was seen to be impartial by management and unions. It therefore had credibility with the unions which would have been difficult to achieve using other sources of assistance. Groups comprising of managers and shop-floor personnel went on visits to selected companies. These visits were useful in formulating the new policies and also proving that the new practices had already been successful elsewhere.

The new ideas and work processes were developed into an employment package named the "Integrated Working and Stable Income Plan". The package was originally linked with the investment programmes at the Cauldon and Dunbar sites. The package was so successful at these sites that it was implemented throughout the company's other cement works.

Achieving acceptance of the package throughout all levels of the company was a task that required a high level of communication, flexibility and understanding from both the unions and management.

The "Integrated Working and Stable Income Plan" was not just about changing work practices and pay structures but perhaps more importantly it meant changing the attitude and culture of the organisation.

The negotiations to implement "Integrated Working" took over two years and involved a two-tiered approach. There were negotiations at the Senior Group Management level with national trade union officials on broad principle and discussions of substance and detail at works level with local managers and shop stewards.

Eventually an agreement was reached that contained four key improvements:

(i). The Stable Income Plan was implemented. The Plan contained a monthly salary based on an annual hours contract. Under the contract, employees are paid for an annual total of 2,250 hours. This is made up by 2,028 hours worked in a seven-shift system and a bank of 222 flexi-hours per year for overtime, this is paid at double time. The benefits of the annual hours contract have been considerable. The company now has stable labour costs and the workforce have a stable monthly income paid by direct credit transfer, fluctuating workloads are covered and employees are encouraged to work effectively and productively rather than prolonging jobs to increase their earnings with overtime payments.

(ii). Fourteen job categories were reduced to three. Narrowly defined individual job descriptions were replaced by broader teamwork orientated, multi-skilling. This was vital to improve flexibility and reduce demarcation. A large investment was made in skills training and employees were required to learn new skills, including first-line maintenance. For example, an engineering Craftsman (mechanical) would learn the skill of electrical isolation to qualify for the skills classification allowance. Manpower was reduced as employees could be deployed in a variety of capacities in the works.

(iii). A new 7 x 3 continuous shift system replaced a four shift system that limited staffing flexibility and could not accommodate further reductions in the basic working week of 39 hours. The advantages of the seven shift system included: all workers becoming flexible and able to share work, the need for day workers was reduced, shift groups took on more responsibility and old divisions between shift and day workers were minimised.

(iv). An extensive training programme to improve management and teamworking skills was put in place. The training was designed to change the old hierarchical culture and promote flexibility and mutual respect. The training aimed to end demarcation disputes, encourage co-operation and develop team leaders.

The new work system and pay structure was a major step forward for Blue Circle Cement but it was really only the beginning of the company's journey to become a world-class organisation.

Ross Dunn arrived in Scotland in 1993 and in April it was decided that the company was ready to develop a Total Quality culture.

Total Quality had been attempted twice before and each time expectations were raised with little or no change; some of the workers described these attempts as "more total chaos, than total quality".

The new initiative was greeted with predictable scepticism as Ross readily admits, "Suspicion there definitely was but you could also feel enthusiasm, hidden by 30 years of controlling, autocratic management. There was a latent potential waiting to erupt, the trick was to allow this to happen in a controlled manner."

Initial training was aimed at senior management, supervisors and trade union representatives since it was felt their support was vital. These groups felt the approach was right and the shop stewards and first-line supervisors requested the opportunity to brief the rest of the workforce.

From the beginning the aim was to invite the entire workforce to attend a two-day introduction to Total Quality. This was different to the first attempts in two important ways. Firstly, everyone was being **invited** rather than forced by senior management to attend the training and secondly, **everyone** was to be trained and **everyone** was to receive the **same** training.

The whole workforce agreed to the training which consisted of team building, interpersonal skills, communications, management style and everyone being given a Myres Briggs personality test. During the training the principles of Total Quality were taught and everyone was asked to identify the barriers to change.

At the initial training sessions it was suggested that a Total Quality Steering Group should be formed made up from a cross-section of the workforce – management, marketing, process, craft and unions all represented. Iain Campbell was Accounting Controller at the Dunbar Works and was invited to attend the first Steering Group meeting, he was surprised to be asked to become Total Quality Steering Group Chairman.

The purpose of the steering group was to oversee the implementation and progress of the Total Quality programme; to receive presentations from improvement teams; to produce a vision statement and most importantly – **make it happen!**

OOR VISION

Wi'honesty commitment trust and pride a'body workin' side by side

S*afety first – enviroment too*
C*ustomer satisfaction*
O*perate profitably*
T*eamworking through consensus*
L*ook for continuous improvement*
A*ll for one and one for all*
N*atural choice*
D*etermined: –*

Tae Be The Best

Iain Campbell stated:

"Everything which appears in the vision statement came from the whole workforce via brainstorming sessions. After the initial training, teams began to form. To ensure the meetings were well structured and focused, the team leaders who emerged were given more training including problem solving and presentation skills. To further support the teams and the whole initiative, a cross-section of the workforce was invited to be trained as facilitators. So we then had in place classic improvement teams, cross-functional groups, facilitators and a Steering Group. These supplemented the existing teams of Work's Teams and Business Unit Managers and changed the traditional hierarchical structure. This is our Total Quality structure.

"We employ 210 people all of whom have bought into Total Quality and accept our safety initiative. By April 1995, 80 per cent of our workforce have involved themselves directly in Improvement Teams, this has resulted in an average of 40 teams in place at any one time. We have teams to look at multi million pound costs like power and fuel and we have teams to plant roses at the Works' entrance. The most significant difference I've found with this approach to Total Quality compared to previous efforts, is that this time, we talk to each other, we help each other and we trust each other."

Ross Dunn believes the exceptional results outlined above have been achieved because the workforce has been empowered through trust and effective communication.

"Empowerment is a system designed to enable everyone who has a good idea for improvement to carry it through – either by themselves or as part of a team. It is not something you can bolt onto an existing process. It is part of a larger structure which must have a supporting culture as its foundation. The barriers described earlier had to be removed from our organisation and the foundations Iain outlined had to be in place", said Ross.

An empowerment process was developed by the Total Quality Steering Group (**see flow diagram Figure 1**). "Our flow diagrams are probably the most powerful tools in our Total Quality bag. The Empowerment Flow Process provides two alternatives at each stage of the development of a 'new good idea'. First, if the idea can be accomplished at that particular stage, then the instruction is 'DO IT'. Secondly, if further

EMPOWERMENT FLOW DIAGRAM

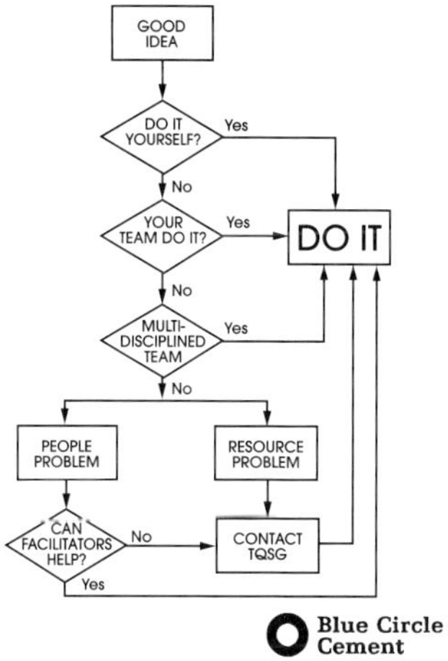

support is required, then the flow process directs the person towards positive completion at every stage. If an individual cannot accomplish his good idea he will get support from basic teams, multi-disciplined teams, facilitators or the Steering Group – who will all help to solve the 'people and resource' problems which may be holding the good idea back. Since the Steering Group makes decisions by consensus, there is no way anyone in the business can be prevented from acting on a good idea. This process gives our people as much power as they want to take from it. We have a workforce that is sound, loyal, mature, well trained in all aspects of the job and responds with extraordinary energy and enthusiasm to being treated as such. The process allows everyone to participate to their highest levels which offers the ability to achieve the highest possible results", explained Ross.

Trust is a vital component of empowerment. Ross Dunn believes without trust empowerment will fail: "Many companies pay lip service to such words as trust, openness and cooperation but actually conduct the management of the company with closed minds behind closed doors. People are encouraged to come up with ideas only to be ignored or denied the means of implementing them, empowerment merely to come up with suggestions is not empowerment. Both of these practices work against mutual trust. Managers must trust the workforce with all types of information pertinent to their business, for example, information on sales, costs and profits must be freely given. The workforce also needs detailed feedback and because they are trusted the workers will find it much easier to trust their managers."

The trust and encouragement of initiative at Blue Circle has brought many examples of improvements both for the workforce and for the bottom line. A new shower block has been approved; plant has been upgraded and ownership groups are responsible for the new equipment;

COMMUNICATIONS FLOW DIAGRAM

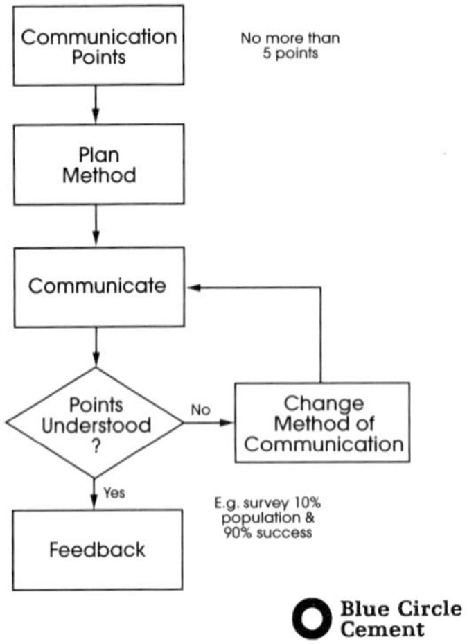

Safety has been improved; running times have been increased and costs cut."

Increasing the amount of information provided to the workforce was identified early as a necessary part of Total Quality, but the way it was communicated was also very important. Communication involved six monthly briefs, fact sheets, monthly newsletters, weekly briefs, graphs etc. A communications flow diagram (**see flow diagram figure 2**) was produced to ensure the vast amount of information was providing a consistent message. The resulting communications were more structured; used no more than five main points (preferably fewer); and feedback surveys were used to ensure the message was understood. If the message was not understood then the method or style would be examined and the communication repeated until it was successful.

Clear and constant communication is also vital to maintain the momentum to continuously improve. Change is difficult for all organisations and individuals but it is the only way businesses can improve. Ross Dunn points out that the people you have driving change make the difference, the contributions of everyone are important but having people like Iain Campbell on the Steering Group make the process easier.

Experience has also taught Ross Dunn that "The longer you leave anything the way it is, the more likely you will lose momentum for change. Even though it is difficult and you consider what you are doing to be successful, you have to change your systems and processes before they stop being successful – you have to keep the initiative."

A final word from Ross Dunn? He says: " Blue Circle Cement Scotland has now become a true quality organisation and we feel we are justifiably proud of our total business performance, customer satisfaction and the recognition we have achieved."

16

Anglia Puts Its Stamp On Improvement

—Royal Mail Anglia—

THE book trade has Frankfurt; the toy industry favours Harrogate; the fashion business the chic catwalks of Paris. All are variations on the annual fair, a place where practitioners gather to show off their own new ideas and get a close up look at everyone else's. In its quest for the corporate grail "to be recognised as the best organisation in the world distributing text and packages" the Royal Mail descends on Milton Keynes once a year for its Teamwork day. There the pick of team improvement projects from similar events in the organisation's 19 business units go on display in a shop window for ideas and inspiration.

It is, though, not the kind of show where exhibitors walk away with a rosette. "The big prize is recognition of that team's improvement project", says Keith Harrison, director, quality at Royal Mail Anglia, one of nine Royal Mail operating divisions and short-listed in this year's UK Quality Award public service sector.

In the four years since Royal Mail Anglia was formed as an operating division of the UK's public postal service, it has collected a formidable portfolio of tools and techniques to take forward improvement and staff involvement.

Royal Mail Anglia is one of nine regionally based operating divisions formed by Royal Mail when it was restructured in 1992. Royal Mail Anglia's boundaries run north to south from Spilsby to Tilbury, east to west from Great Yarmouth to Buckingham. Its 17,000 employees deal with 13 million letters a day, serving a population of 7.3 million from 11 main sorting offices including its headquarters in Chelmsford, Essex. Annual turnover is more than £420 million; in its latest financial year Royal Mail

Keith Harrison
Director, Quality
Royal Mail Anglia

Anglia's 'contribution' – the difference between costs and income generated – to Royal Mail profits was about 14% of turnover. Its handling of intra-division letters – those posted and delivered within its area – is best among Royal Mail's operating divisions at 95.5% of first-class mail processed within publicised targets. It is an Investor in People company.

Within the Anglia operation the hothouse for Quality improvement at local level is its 'bright ideas process'. This is designed to bring on the germ of an individual idea into a fully flowering project. Initially, staff suggestions, whether written or verbal, are responded to by their manager. If after discussion with its originator an idea looks worth pursuing it can be implemented locally or forwarded to someone in the company who can.

Promising local ideas are passed to a 'Quality Guidance Group', more than 200 of which have been set up in all local areas to steer the co-ordination and prioritisation of improvement ideas and activities. Participation in quality guidance groups is voluntary but local managers make facilities, rooms and release time available as needed so groups can meet at least monthly. About one-third of the workforce of 17,000 is involved in the groups and related action. The proportion of employees taking part in continuous improvement activity beyond their day-to-day duties has approximately doubled in each of the past three years and is targeted to hit 50% in the current financial year.

An idea that passes the Quality Guidance Group's sifting is returned to the initiator to start a Quality improvement project. At this stage the idea enters the Royal Mail's 12-step Quality Improvement Process (QIP) at one of three points which "put the customer identity into it", Mr Harrison says. Ironically, it was a lack of local detail in Anglia's generic measures of customer attitudes that prompted a recently completed QIP project at the Sheringham delivery office. Its awareness that divisional data left gaps in its knowledge of what local customers thought of its performance led the office to generate and distribute its own questionnaire to sharpen the picture.

This pursuit of the customer view and the integration of customer considerations at the inception of improvement projects goes back to the beginnings of Quality development within Royal Mail. In 1988, two years after its formation in an internal shake-up of the Post Office, the chairman, Sir Bryan Nicholson and his executives committed the organisation to a new way of working which they dubbed 'Customer First'.

By the time Royal Mail in turn re-formed itself four years later, around nine operational divisions, of which Royal Mail Anglia is one, much of the cultural change and executive training associated with the Customer First shift had been completed. However, training in Anglia's first year of separate operation was channelled into rolling out Customer First awareness and re-skilling to front-line staff. Customer First is now largely invisible in the corporate geology as succeeding programmes have moved to the forefront of the business plan, but it forms the bedrock on which later developments have rested.

Among the most significant of these programmes has been the sustained effort to promote ownership of the improvement process by line management. This has hastened the integration of Customer First by making sure the total quality message is not positioned specifically under the Customer First banner.

A key to the spread of ownership has been the role played by the Royal Mail Anglia quality support team. The team's brief is to introduce concepts into the organisation, ensure a certain level of understanding has been reached and then fade supportively into the background as line managers assume leadership of the practice. The size of the team – six people – guards against the danger of it becoming a separate fiefdom perceived as having responsibility for Quality. "It was seen as a separate functional team at the start", says Mr Harrison, "but now the organisation is more mature, there are few issues and it is seen to be moving as a team." It has not, he stresses, been a "painless" transition and in addition to sponsoring "natural champions" part of its role has involved educating cynics. "We don't have a policy of compulsory redundancy so you can't just get rid of the cynics", Mr Harrison says. "You have to find other ways to manage the issue."

Finding and supporting natural champions who willingly run with the quality ball is a common text-book solution, but each organisation has to find its own way to translate the theory into practice. During the later stages of the Customer First roll-out, Anglia's quality team progressively trained up local "presenters" who then cascaded the training down and were put in place to support local managers. "They were our natural champions", Mr Harrison says.

Leadership by role model is a strong theme of Anglia's Quality development and was recognised as such by the UK Quality Award assessors. In the same way that the Royal Mail business mission underpins Anglia's improvement strategies, so its 'Leadership Charter' guides the Quality leadership drive. The four elements of the charter encompass 'vision', 'commitment', 'management approach' and 'communication'. Earlier this year Anglia completed the main phase of its Leadership for Results programme, a training cascade to deploy the charter among managers. "The main elements [of the programme] concentrated on the cultural change required in turning managers into team leaders", Mr Harrison says. The series of three-day Leadership for Results workshops involved groups of managers of mixed seniority and specialism. Each of the 150 workshops was led by a senior manager immediately below board level and had an executive committee member committed to one session.

Included in the programme was an understanding of the 'effective leadership feedback' (ELF) process by which managers are regularly appraised by their team. Every six months they have to respond to a 30-point questionnaire about their leadership style which is completed by their team. Any agreed actions are incorporated into the manager's personal improvement plan.

Although this aspect of leadership review remains confidential between manager and team there are 'soft issue' measures around the programme which can gauge its effects. "They show an improving trend since the programme was in place", Mr Harrison says.

Assessment and review

On the level of unit and business performance, Anglia is adapting the Royal Mail assessment and review programme to monitor progress towards its Total Quality goals. Both the 'business excellence review' and the 'unit excellence review' are based on the UK/European business excellence model that underpins the UK Quality Award – though the terminology has been simplified at unit level to help its deployment. But while, for example, the 'policy and strategy' element of the model has been re-christened 'planning', the model itself has not been altered.

"The words have been simplified by front-line teams so it is understandable to them", Mr Harrison says. "The objective is to get them involved in business-oriented activity."

The unit review involves a self-assessment against the business excellence model and Anglia was chosen as a pilot division within Royal Mail to test the process. Trials this spring among an initial batch of ten units made use of the system of trained supporters that characterises Anglia's Quality deployment. One unit, Norwich Distribution, has since gone on to the optional stage of accreditation within the division, which like the Quality Award process involves an assessment by a team from outside the unit. The process will be rolled out to Anglia's remaining 240 main units over the next two years.

By then the division itself will be ready to undergo its third business excellence review – a once-every-two-years assessment carried out by a team from other Royal Mail business units. Its findings have a big influence on business planning activity and the latest review, carried out this June, has yielded a "comprehensive feedback report highlighting strengths and opportunities", Mr Harrison says.

The broad view given by using the business excellence model makes it a valued implement in Anglia's toolbox. "The model is an excellent framework for linking elements together into a broader picture", Mr Harrison says. With the benefit of hindsight Mr Harrison believes the roll-out of Customer First would have been different if the business excellence model had been available at the time. Training would have concentrated more on practicalities than around the concepts and the organisation would have been more cognisant of the leadership issues at the front of the model.

"We went into Customer First purely on a cascade basis and the middle-tier of management was cascading and training areas they didn't really understand", he says. "It's only through seeing the behavioural and cultural changes within the business that they've started to understand why we were saying what we were saying in 1988. The business excellence model particularly has provided an excellent framework where they can link lots of the activities they thought were disparate to show exactly where the business is trying to get to in terms of business results. It enables us to link business objectives to the running of the business. You couldn't do that at the beginning."

Reproduced with kind permission from *UK Quality,* Nov 1995, UK Quality Award edition.

17

"Pride In Our Work"

— Stalbridge Linen Services —

"FOR many years I could not understand why we were so unique. Our philosophy was so simple that it was beyond me why others found it difficult to achieve. We used to go and collect from customers and what we received, we returned. We washed the work clean, finished it well, packaged it properly and returned it on time. When it went wrong we were quick to make amends. From early on there was a commitment to Quality. Because others found it so difficult, we gave our customers the best service and in doing so we were able to charge realistic prices.

"Pride in our work is essential and all team leaders, supervisors and staff must accept full responsibility for Quality in their respective areas. The growth in size of this company has placed the burden onto our team leaders to ensure that controls and discipline are in force and that they train and motivate the staff to excel and ensure that this philosophy is adhered to.

"Our goal is to improve year on year in a manner that will mutually satisfy our customers and stakeholders."

– Stalbridge Linen Services Vision for Quality.

David Coulter founder and managing director of Stalbridge Linen Services makes success sound so simple and straightforward.

Laundry is a very demanding industry being both labour and capital intensive. David founded Stalbridge Linen Services in 1975 in East London with no capital and little business experience. In 1981 Stalbridge Linen Services moved to Shaftesbury in Dorset, this site has consistently grown and by 1995 covered 30,000 square feet, employing over 200 people

David Coulter
Managing Director
Stalbridge Linen Services

For Quality the finished product still relies on the human touch in spite of technological advances.

undertaking an annual turnover in excess of £6 million. Their impressive building houses hundreds of thousands of pounds of the world's latest and best laundry technology.

How did Stalbridge Linen Services become the leading laundry and linen hire service to the hospitality and catering industry? According to David it is a matter of common sense, "I've read management books by people like Peter Drucker and what they are doing is stating the obvious. You talk to the customer, find out what they want and provide it. If something goes wrong you find out why and sort it out straight away."

He had previously worked as a laundry production manager and understood the production side of the laundry business but needed to learn how to market and run a company. David began by reading a book on telephone selling and letter writing, he made a list of four prospective clients and called them, three out of the four said 'yes' and a company was born.

David used a combination of innovation and hard work to get started. His first clients were wine bars and pubs in the East End of London. The work involved collecting, washing and pressing tea towels and bar mats. His first "laundry" was the laundrettes around the East End and all the linen was hand ironed. Within a year David was able to arrange a small bank loan and move to premises in Milborne Port, Dorset, a 600 square foot industrial unit he fitted out with two dilapidated 25 lb industrial washing machines and an old linen press.

The initiative shown by David and his early partners to begin the operation also grew it. "Every time I went past a pub or wine bar on our collection and delivery routes I would then call them and offer our services, later we became involved with a small restaurant who recommended us to another restaurant which was part of The Mecca Group. The Mecca Group restaurants became a large part of our business and we expanded from bar mats to all types of restaurant linen" says David.

David never missed an opportunity to sell Stalbridge Linen Services, during a meeting with his bank manager he learned that the Chairman's internal catering facilities had some special tablemats and serviettes which were very difficult to process. David contacted the owner at the laundry in Shaftesbury for some technical advice, by the end of the phone call David had made him an offer for the Shaftesbury factory. This acquisition heralded a period of high growth into the 'Square Mile' district of London.

Servicing corporate dining rooms became a niche market which grew rapidly and many prestigious firms became regular satisfied clients. Stalbridge Linen Services gained a reputation for reliability delivering through snow storms and even providing an undisrupted daily service to News International during the Wapping industrial dispute.

The company later expanded from laundering customers' own linen to hiring linen and garments, and then also designing uniforms for the catering and hospitality industries. The rapid growth meant that David, who confesses to starting out with little management training, was responsible for a huge laundry operation with 18 radio controlled vans making 500 business calls a day to a demanding, blue chip client base spread as far afield as York, Swansea, Plymouth and London.

Being at least 100 miles from their main markets makes Stalbridge Linen Services place extra emphasis on 'getting it right first time'. "Our aim is 100 per cent reliability of service, our clients' demands will be met, the distance is an advantage because it means we have to be so much better than our competition. We even have an emergency service that delivers to Central London within two hours", says David. "This is the kind of thing that differentiates Stalbridge from other laundry companies."

In is usual for linen and garment hire companies to have contracts with their customers. David's view is that contracts tend to be barriers to exit for customers when the linen hire company is giving a poor service. Stalbridge Linen Services do not have any contracts, they stand or fall by their service, David feels that business is a partnership and the lack of written contracts implies a trust on both sides.

The trust has been repaid by some of the United Kingdom's most respected catering operations including Harvey Nichols, Aramark Catering Services, The Waterside Inn at Bray, Catering & Allied and Summit Catering Services. The majority of Stalbridge Linen Services' new business comes from referrals and recommendations from satisfied customers.

As well as servicing the linen needs of caterers who manage permanent sites, Stalbridge Linen Services also meets the challenge of providing linen and staff uniforms at a number of prestigious annual events. The company provides services at the Chelsea Flower Show, The Wimbledon Tennis Championships, Royal Ascot and the Henley Regatta. Letheby & Christopher provide catering services at many of the same events and appreciate Stalbridge Linen Services' attention to detail. Purchasing Manager for Letheby & Christopher, David Little comments, "We chose Stalbridge because apart from the first class product that they offer, we recognised a like minded, Quality driven company reflecting many of the initiatives that Letheby & Christopher have set out to adopt, ISO 9002 and the Investors in People Standard for example."

Sometimes customer service isn't just about servicing existing requirements but exceeding their expectations with ideas for products that the client may not have considered. Stalbridge Linen Services lived up to their reputation for innovation by introducing coloured jackets for chefs to enable clients to bring their corporate colours into the kitchen. In 1994 a £180,000 ironing line was purchased. David Coulter believes it is the largest automatic feeding/folding tablecloth ironer in the world, combining a high quality finish, with minimum maintenance and low energy consumption.

It is this type of constant focus on innovation and change that keeps Stalbridge Linen Services ahead of the competition. David seeks out challenging clients and markets, he believes these demanding clients help drive the company forward.

In the first 13 years of the company's existence it grew at an average of over 50% per annum. David recalls: "Slowly the small management team that had grown the company were breaking up, and by 1989 I was the only executive with any real management experience."

David recognised that his entrepreneurial style of management, whilst vital to establish and grow the business, would need to be complimented by people with experience and knowledge. This was not a difficult decision to make but it is not clearly understood what a critical and traumatic period any company faces when it is entering into a change from an entrepreneurial to professionally managed era.

"I had a number of very fine, young, very committed, developing people but with very little management experience, just at a time when there was a need to have more competent management leading the company. There were times when I don't know how we managed to get the job done. I was personally working 15–17 hours a day, and it was a heroic effort by everyone concerned. There was a real buzz throughout the company but our young inexperienced people were relying on firefighting decision making, rather than foresight and planning.

"A customer once said, I was an autocrat trying to be a democrat but people in larger companies don't understand that while 'big business' has many specialists who may be experts in a couple of disciplines, the smaller businesses, the one man operations, have the real business people who have to deal with everything. Making the transition is difficult but I had to learn to delegate, to get the best out of our people."

David did have difficulties selecting the right people for these senior positions and teaching them the unique culture at Stalbridge Linen Services. He also feels that he had trouble 'letting go' of the many tasks he would routinely carry out and with delegating decisions. It was difficult for the new managers because they didn't understand the business as well as the founder and may have felt it was easier to leave the decisions to David.

"They had a lot of knowledge and experience but they didn't understand the culture of the company, you can't always transpose a business plan from one company to another.

By 1994 we had a situation where the new external managers at senior level were found to be lacking, while the young, inexperienced people from the late 1980s had gained a lot of knowledge and experience. In the meantime, a programme of re-engineering and training was established. The training was to focus on personal development, communication and multi-skilling but first existing management structures were questioned.

David knew that conventional hierarchical management structures would not be suitable to achieve the company's goals and created a new flatter structure. Sitting in a traffic jam one day helped David realise the crux of the problem. The slower vehicles at the head of the queue were preventing the faster ones from getting to their destination a little quicker. This flash of inspiration encouraged David to return to the company and fire the existing management, requiring them to re-apply for their jobs. Most of the managers were re-employed but in different areas. Alan Mulholland, Stalbridge Linen Services' Operations Leader described the change, "We went from one day having defined managers running each department to the next day being in teams with empowered team leaders."

Empowerment is aimed at giving a sense of control, a feeling of ownership. However, care was taken as many individuals prefer to be instructed and directed. David feels "If a company says they've re-engineered and none of their senior management have been redeployed or sacked then it hasn't been done properly."

Stalbridge has always been very time-based, daily dead-line after dead-line has to be achieved. Everything needs to be collected, processed and delivered in 24 hours. The success of Stalbridge proves that you can have both a demanding and enjoyable working environment. There is no better motivation than knowing that the managing director would roll his sleeves up and perform any task in the company to maintain customer satisfaction.

It is made clear to all employees that they are expected to be enthusiastic and dedicated to work with a commitment to satisfying the customer. David likes to involve the staff in not only what is happening to the company, but also in sharing some of the benefits of the success of the company, by introducing things like profit related pay, and shares within the company. This, linked with job security, has meant that labour turnover is very low.

David has a firm commitment to "push decision making as low as possible". The change in the management structure was only successful because of a very high emphasis on training. The staff couldn't be expected to succeed after the radical changes without new skills, Stalbridge Linen Services invested heavily in a variety of training courses for it's employees. The company has its own in house trainers who are complemented by external consultants, college classes and multi-skilling.

Multi-skilling is an area where the increased training has really benefited the business. Tish Ricketts, the Evening Team Leader explained: "Multi-skilling has been very positive. We are all able to do each others jobs, if someone is not at work then someone else can take over and the section will still run effectively. Supervisors are moved around as well to build an awareness of each others responsibilities. A balance has to be drawn for the need to change and a requirement of people for stability."

David offers a word of caution for companies considering training programmes: "Our company culture places a high emphasis on training but you have to look at the benefits of the type of training, companies can spend a lot of money on training without getting good value. When we started everyone was going on virtually the same courses, and not necessarily the ones they could use. We had to become more focused on what we were trying to achieve and the relevance of our training improved."

Stalbridge Linen Services' commitment to training made them the first Commercial Laundry to gain the prestigious Investors in People

Award in 1994. The Award recognised Stalbridge Linen Services' real investment in all its staff through training and development and the company's corresponding improved business performance.

On receiving the Award David Coulter said: "It is important to all the Stalbridge employees, many of whom are shareholders, that we succeed and there is a strong determination from within the company that our success is built on the foundations of training, personal development and communication so that all our colleagues in positions of responsibility will have the leadership qualities to bring Stalbridge forward."

Quality Management System

Customer inquiries and a keen interest in remaining an industry leader led Stalbridge Linen Services to consider gaining ISO 9002 certification. David could see that increasingly companies and potential customers were using ISO 9002 as an objective measure of their supplier's quality systems and procedures. The implementation of the Quality Management System however was an example of the problems created by new managers and outside consultants not clearly understanding the business. They wrote systems for the quality procedures manual but when we were audited, what we were doing didn't match what was written down. It wasn't our systems that were wrong but the way they were documented.

"I knew we were a Quality company so my Personal Assistant, Gillian Hudson, and I decided to go through the manual and revise it. This time we made sure the senior managers asked the people actually performing the processes to write their own procedures for the job. At first it was hard to convince the senior managers to let their staff do it but the revised manual truly reflected our Quality systems and we were awarded the ISO 9002 standard by BSI in 1993.

"The ISO certification has been a strong foundation for us to build on, but you must continue to improve and keep revising your procedures. You must always be looking to make things easier, simpler, more efficient and productive", explains David. "When you are listening to what the customer says, you have to draw a line between what the customer actually needs and what they actually want. It can often be customer demands that create more systems, creating more activities, more costs and thus higher charges."

Stalbridge Linen Services understand that ISO 9002 doesn't guarantee customer satisfaction but it is a system of quality procedures led by people that are audited to ensure consistency within the work place. Therefore a customer focus is vital, the company had to be careful not to become too introspective. A theme has been developed, with the motto 'Together We Achieve More'. "We have to achieve our targets with customers, colleagues, suppliers and shareholders, ensuring we move forward together in harmony", says David.

Stalbridge Linen Services also provides a safe working environment. As in every other part of the business Stalbridge has worked towards excellence. The company's approach to safety was recognised in 1995 by a British Safety Standards Award for the highest level of achievement in safety. The Award is given to companies which can prove a safety record which is 20 per cent better than the national average for their industry calculated by lost time through injury or ill health.

The future should hold even greater commercial success for Stalbridge Linen Services. In 1995 the company was acquired by Johnson Group Cleaners Plc the largest dry cleaner in the UK and the US, and one of the leaders in the UK apparel rental market. The two businesses complement each other because both Stalbridge Linen Services and Johnson Group Cleaners Plc service customers in the food and catering industry. Both genuinely believe the customer is king, as shown by the comments of Richard Zerny, Johnson's Chief Executive, at the opening of Stalbridge's new 10,000 sq feet extension: "Let us never forget that the future will always depend upon having 'delighted' the customers."

David Coulter believes that the relationship with Johnson has provided Stalbridge with a further competitive edge. The acquisition has enabled Stalbridge to utilised Johnson's well-sited national plans and will help provide an even better service to customers in the Midlands and North.

The improved management systems have meant that David can now delegate more and take a strategic view, planning future growth and profits. "Four people running 100 metres each in a relay is more efficient than one person doing it by themselves. The company is now like a jazz band – a team of talented individuals playing together, one player can go off for a break but the music will keep playing."

David's role is to ensure his self motivated team fully appreciate and communicate the vision and aims of the company. David states "Where necessary I can encourage and drive action and change, and in doing so allow others to experience and share our success.

"There has been no magic formula for our success. We have positive determined leaders. We have developed a great workforce with a degree of skill but we always believe we can do even better. I am rarely satisfied, more often than not I am more demanding than many of our customers. I feel more comfortable with criticism than praise because at least I can improve on the former but not on the latter."

18

A First-Class Operation

— Hogg Robinson Business Travel International —

WHAT do you do? You're a very busy senior executive in a Blue Chip company and time with your family is precious. You're at the airport, about to jump on a plane and you find out your son's girlfriend is travelling on a different passport and needs a visa before she is admitted into the United States. Worse still, you and your family are flying to Aspen for Christmas using your hard-earned 'Airmiles' points to provide the tickets. The same ones that have restrictions on changing flights and don't allow cancellations...

What do you do? You are in the Middle East, in a country where it is customary to seal a business deal with cash. Your company has entrusted you with US$35,000, you pack it in your briefcase and it is stolen almost as soon as you arrive. Unless you present this chunk of money, the deal is off. You ring the money transfer companies and they can't help you raise such a sum in the time you require. You need the money within 24 hours...

Both the above 'horror stories' are true and normally the outcome would be a battle with bureaucracy and major unpleasantness. In both these cases (and numerous others), the experience and customer service ethic of Hogg Robinson Business Travel International (HRBTI) stepped between their customers and potential misery.

In the first case, nothing could be done prior to departure to get the visa at the airport. So Hogg Robinson BTI's people sent the main party off to the USA; picked up the son and his girlfriend by car and took them straight to the American Embassy. Using their contacts at the embassy, Hogg Robinson BTI had the visa issued immediately. The couple overnighted in London and Hogg Robinson BTI picked them up the next

David Radcliffe
Managing Director
Hogg Robinson BTI

Norman Bewley
Client Services Director
Hogg Robinson BTI

Kevin Ruffles
Total Quality Director
Delivering the key note speech at a Hogg Robinson Quality Initiative Conference in July 1994

morning, meanwhile Hogg Robinson BTI's airport staff had smoothed the way to put them on the next flight – even though they were on 'Airmile' tickets which aren't allowed to be changed. They lost just 24 hours of the family holiday.

The second problem appears even more daunting as the transaction couldn't be done in time, even via a bank. Working with their travel industry connections, Hogg Robinson BTI delivered to the businessman, within 24 hours, another briefcase containing US$35,000. The creativity of Hogg Robinson BTI's people found the solution. By placing the required funds with a large hotel chain, Hogg Robinson BTI was able to get the local hotel to release and deliver the cash. The contract was completed successfully.

The above examples show 'Quality' in action. Further proof of what an empowered, customer focused workforce can do. Hogg Robinson BTI has a reputation for excellent service, a reputation that has been independently endorsed by consumer association reports and industry recognition such as the 1995 Business Travel World Award for being the Best Business Travel Agent (multiple sites).

Formed in 1945, when a single branch office was established to service its parent insurance company, Hogg Robinson BTI Business Travel grew steadily in size and stature to its present position. Just 50 years later, the company works with over 6,000 corporate clients who benefit from Hogg Robinson BTI's purchasing power and the multitude of services offered through its national network of 37 Business Travel Centres and by way of nearly 100 implant offices (travel management operations based on customer's premises). Hogg Robinson BTI has more of these on-site locations than any other travel management company. Hogg Robinson BTI employs 1,558 people.

The company is part of Hogg Robinson BTI plc, which has divisions specialising in financial services and transport as well as travel. The company is the only major multiple business travel agency that is British owned.

In 1990, Hogg Robinson BTI became a founder shareholder and managing partner of Business Travel International (BTI), the largest organisation of its type in the world, with annual sales in excess of US$20 billion.

In 1995, through strong organic sales growth and sensible cost controls, Hogg Robinson BTI increased annual profits by 54 per cent to a record £7.06 million profit on a turnover of £42.6 million.

Almost 40 per cent of the FT-SE Top 100 companies are clients, along with many other household names from around the world.

The impressive results of 1995 began to be put in place five years previously, when the company wasn't achieving to its full potential. Hogg Robinson BTI had been the market leader in the UK for a long time and management may have become a little complacent. Also, client buying patterns in the travel industry began to change, with customers seeking a consolidated global buying approach. Subsequently, Hogg Robinson BTI began to lose business.

It became obvious to the Group's chairman at the time, that the company's good name alone would not be enough to guarantee future prosperity. This view became a catalyst for change and a new managing director, David Radcliffe was appointed in 1991.

David Radcliffe put together a 'new team', and built a team spirit based on the resolve to stop the downward slide and turn the company around.

Central to this goal was the aim of repositioning Hogg Robinson BTI from a commission based agency to a fee-billing business travel management company. This meant creating a structure which enabled consistent high-quality service to be replicated throughout the company. National or International clients had to be given the same service whether they dealt with a London branch or one in Glasgow or Manchester.

To facilitate this process and to reinforce Hogg Robinson BTI's commitment to Total Quality, Kevin Ruffles was appointed Director of Quality in the new team. Kevin Ruffles was previously the Divisional Director for the South of England and had a reputation for detail and a strong belief in formalising systems throughout the group.

Kevin's appointment at Hogg Robinson BTI was a first for the industry as no other company had a Quality Director on the board. Rather than establishing a large Quality department, Kevin appointed one other person and agreed with David Radcliffe that the whole company was his quality resource. This way everyone became responsible for quality and no-one could say: "It's not my job, go ask the quality department."

In early 1992, the decision was made to pursue ISO 9000 certification and to develop the standard into a platform for superior customer service, in a way that applied to Hogg Robinson BTI's business.

As the standard is largely manufacturing based the first six months were a steep learning curve for Kevin Ruffles and his assistant Colin Purser. The time was spent on training courses and talking with some of Hogg Robinson BTI's 'Best Practice' customers who had been through the process.

Once the foundation was set, the focus became 'how do we get this message out to our people?'

It was decided to start with pilot sites strategically picked so all parts of the country were recognised and involved. Glasgow, Manchester and London Bridge business travel centres were the three big centres chosen. Six implant operations were also selected bringing the total number of pilot sites to nine, these sites had a combined staff of 180 people. They were Nissan, Hewlett Packard, Glaxo, Esso, Coopers & Lybrand and Kodak. It was no coincidence that these were among the companies who shared their quality advice freely with Hogg Robinson BTI and are each renowned for their own commitment to excellence.

"Once we interpreted the standard and how to apply it to our business, we spent four months working with our people – without even starting to write a procedure.

"To actually get our people to work on ISO 9000 was easy, they were very enthusiastic. We explained to them that they had an opportunity to change our organisation. They thought: 'I've got a chance to make a name for myself here and I can look back in time and say that we were one of the pilot sites for this new management philosophy', so there was a bit of kudos attached to the process.

"We called for volunteers to champion ISO 9000 and began working with them. The difficult part was to get their line managers to buy in – middle managers – who weren't on the site but were responsible in profit & loss terms for these employees. Some of these people viewed ISO 9000 as no more than a selling tool and believed that a company with a good pedigree like ours didn't need it, but we slowly and surely worked with them. As soon as we had the whole company moving in one direction, a spotlight was thrown on the people that were clearly not going to change and those who said 'I've always done it this way and I'm not going to change'. You have to give these people the opportunity to change but at the end of the day if they don't change, you've got to change them", recalled Kevin Ruffles.

Procedures were written to cover areas such as; arranging airport meetings and assistance; customer satisfaction feedback; in fact every area that affected the customer. Procedures were written in flow-chart format to aid understanding.

The first successful certification took nine months, making Hogg Robinson BTI the first multiple site travel agency to receive ISO 9000. Within four years the whole company was registered and benefits were beginning to be felt throughout the organisation. Business Development Manager Stewart Harvey, explains:

"The initial impact of ISO 9000 was additional work and burden. The procedures are sensible enough but the paper work can eclipse the primary role of giving customers a good service if the procedures are too bureaucratic. The aim of our procedures is to give our customers a better service and improve the efficiency of the company.

"After our period of transition there is comfort in adopting the type of procedures which lead to an increase in both confidence and a willingness to contribute more ideas and improvements to our systems. This was true of the pilot sites and remains true elsewhere. We need constantly to challenge what we do and how we do it. If we seek to deliver a service that will be perceived and described as excellent, we need constructive criticism, involvement and teamwork."

SGS Yarsley was chosen as the certifying body that audits Hogg Robinson BTI. SGS demonstrated an understanding of the travel industry with previous certifications including divisions of Qantas, British Airways and Hotels. Barry Holland from SGS Yarsley believes "Quality Assurance is crucial in the travel industry because business travellers and holiday makers alike need the confidence that their requirements are being fulfilled.

"The comprehensive nature of Hogg Robinson BTI's service meant the resulting assessment was a complicated task and Hogg Robinson BTI is to be congratulated on its impressive level of understanding and control throughout the certification process."

Clients of Hogg Robinson BTI have expressed support for the company's quality initiative. Typical are the comments from David Roberts, national purchasing manager of Coopers & Lybrand, who said:

"Quality of performance is difficult to measure, because everybody's perception of quality is different.

"The introduction of ISO 9000 standards into Hogg Robinson BTI's implant has given us as a client a recognised way of measuring its performance and service. It has resulted in a much sharper operation and ensured that any problems can be quickly identified and resolved."

Clients such as British Telecom have spelt out that the company's commitment to Total Quality Management was one of the factors that influenced its decision to move its account to Hogg Robinson BTI.

Company-wide certification was just the first step in building a Quality culture throughout the company.

"The certifications were not the end of our efforts to improve standards but the beginning. ISO 9000 has provided us with the framework to further develop the business.

"People often say, 'did you start with TQM first or did you first go for the ISO 9000 quality standard?' I felt it was best to put the standard discipline in place first, and then build on that foundation. As we improved, it gave us a framework which allowed us to make universal improvements to the business and not slip back to the old way of doing things. In our case the business was so decentralised it was necessary to have a standard procedure first. If you go to M&S or McDonalds you know what to expect before you go in, with us it was very much the personality of the manager that determined the service in each office which meant it was virtually impossible to be consistent and to share best practice."

The emphasis turned towards continuous improvement with a series of workshops introducing Total Quality Management firstly to Divisional and Area managers and later for all employees. These were followed by a series of one-day workshops entitled 'Leading Teams to Quality', which focused on the key management skills of building teams and leadership. The workshops were run by the Hogg Robinson BTI in-house training team with an emphasis on ideas suggested by clients who had already conducted similar sessions. One of the simple exercises designed to prove the value of teamwork involved individuals trying to remember all the Kings and Queens of England since 1539, then forming groups and repeating the exercise. The results always improve considerably.

The workshops were designed to create a high level of understanding of the principles of TQM and to facilitate views and ideas to improve the business. The 'Golden Rule' at these Quality seminars was to have a director attending each one and answering questions for at least an hour. This was a huge commitment from the directors as by 1995, 110 workshops had been run for employees throughout the company. These sessions were vital to prove management commitment but it was crucial that the ideas, suggestions and criticisms from people attending the workshops were followed up. When staff felt action was being taken based on their input, they became very enthusiastic.

A system of 'Quality Circles' was implemented to work on many of the suggestions that came from the workshops. The aim of Hogg Robinson BTI's 'Quality Circles' is to obtain as many views and opinions as possible on a particular subject and make recommendations to management.

The first of many Quality Circles to be formed was named 'Project Honey' and examined how Hogg Robinson BTI rewards and motivates its workforce.

The group initially felt money was the most important element in the reward process, whether it was overtime, an increase in salary or bonuses. However, after looking closely at the factors influencing the motivation of employees, it was felt that the need to be recognised for work performance and achievements were stronger motivators than pure financial reward alone.

From this point the group started to consider other ways of recognising and rewarding staff achievement. The group gathered ideas from colleagues and clients and chose some key topics to be discussed in detail:

- Long-term service awards.
- Managers guidelines – To implement a more uniform approach by managers when rewarding, motivating, appraising, and developing staff.
- Recognition and rewards.
- Grade/salary structure.
- Individual/team recognition.
- Suggestion scheme.

Once the proposals were completed and costed in minute detail, 'Project Honey' was presented to the board. The proposal has been implemented with favourable results.

Other projects have been established to reduce waste, cut costs and increase efficiency. Incentives such as profit-related pay have been introduced to promote these improvements, now the bottom line result has a direct effect on how people are paid.

Everyone in the company is able to form a Quality Circle and are invited to participate via the high-quality *Focus* company magazine published monthly by Hogg Robinson BTI. The magazine has regular columns from the various functions including quality and a 'Talkback' page with a 'no holds barred' approach to issues. Personnel can voice opinions, ask questions and contribute to Quality Circles and management issues. The magazine is also used as a vehicle to provide recognition to staff and maintain motivation for improvement and change.

To further stay in touch, managing director David Radcliffe invites 12 people, chosen at random each month, to join him for lunch. The confidentiality behind the luncheon's door is like a doctor's surgery and people are encouraged to speak freely about any topic they wish to raise. Initially there was some suspicion but as staff began to see changes based on their comments and the lack of retribution for speaking their mind, they were very supportive. The key point being 'management actually listened and took me seriously'.

Plans for the future at Hogg Robinson BTI include a company-wide re-engineering project known as Genesis. The process will entail a total re-evaluation of the company's entire business processes; a focus on culture change and management practice; and continuous improvement. Its aim is to make Hogg Robinson BTI managers more efficient, more effective, better informed and more in control – in short – 'better managers in a better company'.

Because of the changes made by the 'new team' and the focus on quality, Hogg Robinson BTI has a new self-image and is growing and prospering. The company is innovative, flexible and different. Management understands that everyone has ideas to contribute and these are encouraged. Most of all Hogg Robinson BTI delivers, each part of the company contributes and team spirit is considered the 'final, crucial reason' why they are different.

Kevin Ruffles advises other managers not to become too obsessed with buzz words, believing that 'Quality' is basically common sense that encompasses all areas of a company.

"Quality encapsulates the whole philosophy, the other buzz words are just elements of it. I think as more and more people start to understand the totality of the task, they will realise, it's not a gimmick or a technique but a tool which gives you the ability to move an organisation successfully through change.

"There is a growing demand from clients who say if you haven't got the ISO certification and you haven't got Total Quality programmes, then we are not going to deal with you, we are going to deal with someone who has. We are also seeing clients who are keen to look not at one-year contracts but long-term partnerships and they are not going to commit to you unless you are forward thinking. If you are not creative and if you aren't introducing quality across all areas, you won't get the business. Our clients' enthusiasm for excellence has seen them play an important role in the quality systems and techniques we are putting in place and Hogg Robinson BTI is a better company as a result."

19

A Bold Venture

—NSK Bearings Europe—

IMAGINE you could start afresh – bulldoze your factory, rewrite your workplace agreements and start again with nothing but a 'greenfield'. How would you do it? If you wanted to build a world class manufacturing plant that would grow and thrive, you would follow the example set by NSK Bearings.

Operation Bold Venture was the name given by NSK's Japanese parent Company, Nippon Seiko, to the founding of NSK Bearings, Peterlee Co. Durham in 1976. It was the first Japanese manufacturing investment in the North of England. Nippon Seiko was seeking a manufacturing base to increase the company's market share in Europe. The Peterlee site was chosen because it was a new town in the heart of a region with a great engineering tradition. The town provided NSK with the land, facilities and the people to build a successful operation.

Nippon Seiko (NSK Ltd) is the second largest bearing manufacturer in the world, employing 17,000 people worldwide with assets of over $US4 billion. NSK Ltd have 23 plants globally, including operations in Brazil, Japan, South Korea, Switzerland, Germany, United States and the United Kingdom (UK).

The NSK operations now include four plants at Peterlee. These incorporate a joint-venture plant with AKS.

When the NSK Bearing plant started production in 1976 the company employed only 79 people, now in 1996 it employs over 700. In Japan its principal activities include manufacturing ball and roller bearings, automotive components, steering equipment, and fall screw and linear guides. Bearings manufactured by NSK are used in appliances such as

Eddie Jones
Training Manager
NSK Bearings

Richard Coitino
Deputy Managing Director
NSK Bearings

NSK Bearings' Assembly Lines

washing machines and video recorders, motor cars, and the aerospace industry; 80 per cent of Peterlee production is exported to Europe.

NSK's principal customers include the Rover Group, Nissan Manufacturing UK, General Motors, Hotpoint, TRW Group, Toyota, Robert Bosch, Meco, Huwood, BSL, and Rolls-Royce Aerospace. Many of the blue chip organisations that have chosen to work with NSK have endorsed the company's commitment to excellence with quality awards, partnerships and 'Vendor Rating' approvals.

NSK has received ISO 9000 registration for all its manufacturing sites, been accredited with *Investors in People*, and has won three National Training Awards.

To achieve the impressive results outlined above the company has followed a strategy of marrying the most advanced manufacturing facilities with the best work practices. Quality is the standard upon which the entire organisation was founded.

Historically, many managers consider building a Quality culture based on continuous improvement only when their business is in trouble or serious decline. The managers of these firms hope that a Quality approach to managing will save their company. There are many examples of this being the case, with companies being 'turned around' and prospering. NSK's Japanese owners took the opportunity to build a Quality UK operation from day one.

Light engineering, such as bearing manufacture, was new to the Peterlee area, which was situated in a region which had a tradition of strong unionism in heavy engineering industries such as coal mining and ship building. In 1976 a number of major industrial disputes were causing problems for UK industry. NSK was able to avoid many potential difficulties by putting in place a Single Union Agreement.

The agreement was negotiated with the Amalgamated Engineering and Electrical Union (AEEU) which has over 95 per cent of eligible employees in membership.

The new agreement allowed for flexibility, mobility and career progression. True flexibility meant no demarcations or constraints on working practices. The agreement included flexibility and mobility clauses to allow for multi-skilling. The mobility clause permits the maximum utilisation of labour and thus minimises redundancy. 'Management has the right to reasonably assign, having due regard to the employee's capabilities, any employee to any job to maintain production schedules.' The flexibility clause gives management the right to temporarily assign employees, without extra pay, to a higher or lower labour grade. Career progression through grades was established to further advance skills through training.

NSK Training Manager Edward Jones says that the agreement also made Total Quality a requirement from the first day of production. But the local workforce took some time to realise that this type of agreement would benefit them. Mr Jones explained the situation:

"NSK has a firm but fair managerial style which clearly specifies standards to achieve the minimum base of behaviour required on site. The company has audits to ensure high standards are maintained in a variety of areas, for example the cleanliness of the workplace. In the early days it perhaps didn't go down too well because at one point NSK had a high employee turnover, of about 18 per cent. This was probably because people didn't know what to expect. Throughout the 1980s employee turnover decreased and in 1995 the company had a turnover of less than 2 per cent."

Those who adapted to the accountable style of management and remained with the company were glad they did. In the early 1980s a serious recession struck and the market demand for many products was seriously reduced. The company took the typically Japanese approach of not retrenching employees. The company had invested resources into training and believed it was important to maintain a stable work environment for their employees. The rationale was if they made their most important resource, namely people, redundant the company would have to train employees when conditions stabilised. Mr Jones continues:

"NSK's approach to the recessions stood it in good stead for the future, because unlike most companies who were laying people off, NSK used that period to incorporate intense training to aid in the development of employees. In the recession of the early 1990s, this philosophy was again followed with holiday shutdowns extended from two weeks to three weeks to boost cost savings. NSK came out of the recession relatively unscathed, returning to growth very rapidly."

Furthermore, in 1987 NSK expanded their original factory and the company was producing 6.5 million bearings a month, with 80 per cent of its gross being exported across Europe. In 1988 and 1989 the company built two additional plants at Peterlee – a forging plant, and a precision steel ball plant, which more than doubled its workforce to 800 people. In 1990 the steering components plant was also built at Peterlee. The rapid expansion meant NSK had to work hard to ensure that the culture being developed continued to suit the company's vision of excellence.

Training and development were seen as vital to build the sort of culture NSK wanted. Also, in the late 1980s the company realised other organisations were approaching equivalent standards of quality which was up until then NSK's competitive advantage. NSK realised its future competitive edge would have to come from its employees, and training would be a critical factor in achieving continuous improvement. Training for teamwork and in the use of Quality Circles began as early as 1982.

"In the '70s and '80s teamwork was an alien concept to workers in the region. One of NSK's section leaders was sent to Japan to study Quality Circles at the parent company with a plan to implement a similar programme in the UK.

"When the section leader returned from Japan it was quite apparent, in discussions with the management team, that it would be impossible to tell employees to 'just go and form Quality Circles', because people weren't used to working together and being interdependent. Although the workplace is structured in cells, the workers are autonomous because of the type of technology involved. Instead, we introduced what we called the 4As activities. Our 4As concept is very similar to a Japanese system known as 5Ss but we wanted to customise the approach to suit our UK workforce. The 4As stands for Arrangement, Accessibility, Area, and Affirmation. Arrangement covers the structure of a process, Accessibility focused on the efficient layout of materials or tools employees used in their daily work, Area covers the cleanliness and order of the workplace, and Affirmation closes the loop to incorporate feedback and a result", outlined Mr Jones.

The company invited and facilitated employees to work together in groups of twos and threes using the 4As to focus on improving their own work environment and conditions. Small budgets were made available to assess how to reduce oil on the shopfloor and noise in the factory. Training was operating in conjunction with group activity to 'cascade' throughout the organisation. The company had a high level of participation with 106 voluntary teams registered from a workforce of 350. Since 1987, over 100 NSK employees have been trained in Japan.

The teams were formed voluntarily and ideas for issues to examine and improve came from the employees themselves. The teams would receive training as they worked on a problem. Problem-solving techniques such as the 'Seven Basic Tools' (brainstorming, etc.), were taught and immediately able to be applied.

To maintain the momentum for improvement and to focus the workforce on specific priorities, a 'Group Activity Programme' was introduced to direct improvement activity. Ideas could come from the shop-floor, or management could advise an individual to form a team to undertake a certain task. The teams are cross-functional and given every assistance to find solutions or improvements.

The managers select areas to examine from a programme of Total Management Planning (termed locally as TMC). Total Management Planning involves Department managers making an 18 month analysis of each department including a review of current capabilities, problems and concerns, countermeasures available, investment, effectively looking at the whole department's processes. Priorities are identified and these become the source of projects for Group Activity Teams.

The training and the culture at NSK has ensured a lot of informal or Kaizan improvements are made. This activity is a natural part of working at NSK and is often unrecognised, for example a worker will simply go ahead and make an adjustment to a conveyer which will reduce down time. The management knew a lot of Kaizan improvements were being made and wanted to quantify them. A Small Improvement Groups system was put in place. The systems allows small groups or individuals to register improvements they make and enables these improvements to be quantified. In six months the company had implemented 150 improvements. The success of these Groups has been recognised externally with The Assembly Department Small Group Activity Team winning the Northern 'Q' Factor Award for Quality Improvements Through Teamwork in 1993.

To make these improvements the employees at NSK have made use of their Quality Circle training. A number of these tools have been successfully utilised. Cause and Effect Diagrams have proved useful for solving problems.

Problem solving notice boards are placed in the workplace to enable employees to break down and analyse problems by identifying the facts as they see them. If an employee identifies a problem on the shop-floor, they write it down on a coloured sticker. Other group members can then see what problems or shortfalls exist and if they have an idea, they can stick a different coloured piece of paper on the board with an answer or suggestion. In this way expertise can be passed across different shifts.

Mr Jones says this can be an extremely powerful tool that allows progress to be traced, the board can also be used as a focus for team meetings. But he warns against complacency:

"It is necessary to constantly monitor the progress of the problem featured on the notice board because sometimes the board can stand there like a brick wall and begin to be ignored, but if there's something happening on it the attention stays with the notice board. As soon as you leave it for a week nobody notices it."

The new or changed processes are then monitored to ensure that efficiency is increased or cycle time reduced. All effected employees are asked for their thoughts on the changes.

Employee accountability has always been encouraged at NSK, responsibility for quality is effectively put in the hands of the operators. The employees have input into policy formation which is an important part of ensuring quality products emerge from the factory floor. Operators are trained on how to produce and confirm their own quality; independent checks are built into the production processes; fail safe checking systems are confirmed every two hours; when a problem is detected then the problem products are clearly defined and 100 per cent inspected; and operators are informed of what is required of them by clear written instructions.

The essence of NSK's process management is a collection of shopfloor management principles which manage continuous improvement. The core value states that a problem is not solved until the root cause is identified and action is taken to prevent the re-occurrence.

"An operator is responsible for the quality of everything that goes into the machine and everything that comes out of it. He has the authority to turn his machine off if there is a problem, even though this drastic action will disrupt the whole process line. We have different means of identifying defects - x is low risk and is usually a scratch on the bearing, a z+ is a quality defect which would cause severe problems for the customer if it managed to get through the production line. If we get a z+ everything in that area stops and all products going through the line are pulled back. The area manager would be called out, and there would be an immediate meeting on the shopfloor. There would be a thorough investigation to find out what happened, how, and why, and importantly how the bearing managed to get through the process. The production line would not start again until the root cause is solved. Wherever possible the company has a series of fail-safe checks to minimise the potential for human error. By doing this the operators become the custodians of the process, 80 per cent of their role is quality assurance rather than just pressing buttons", details Mr Jones.

Training has focused on developing and building the company's skills base as well as teaching Total Quality principles. The workforce is multi-skilled so training must be tailored to meet NSK's objectives. Considerable investment has been made by the company to train its own instructors. Japanese trainers initially came to the UK to teach but they have now been able to be redeployed as local instructors became qualified.

A combination of skills and 'people' management training ensures that by the time an operator has moved through the technical grades to the role of supervisor, he has the necessary skills to be a leader in a team environment, which essentially makes employees better supervisors. Supervisors learn to respect operators.

Effective supervision is vital to maintain continuous improvement. NSK's rapid expansion placed a lot of pressure on the organisation, especially its supervisors who have been recognised for the vital role they play in areas such as communication and they are trained and remunerated accordingly.

NSK employee Mr Chris Dudgeon is an example of someone who has been promoted through the levels of the organisation by participating in NSK's various training opportunities; a clear example of *Investors in People. Investors in People* is a national quality standard that encourages employers to see staff development as the key to business success. Mr Dudgeon progressed from grade five (new) operator to senior engineer, gaining ONC, HNC and degree qualifications along the way. Mr Dudgeon, who didn't achieve at school, completed 13 years of study, and is himself a National Training Award winner. He comments on the company's attitude to staff development and training:

"The aim is to get everyone working together, sharing ideas and opinions so that as working practices change, they seem to do so naturally. The senior managers genuinely listen to all ideas and many of them get accepted. If they don't, we are told why. In the same way, training is seen as something that benefits everyone. Cost is still an issue, but not if you need the training to do your job and are willing to pass the expertise on to others. Enthusiasm is what we all seem to gain – for the job, for the company and for achieving something that's worthwhile."

One of the most difficult aspects of continuous improvement is sustaining the enthusiasm for change. Whilst training is an important part of maintaining an ongoing commitment, other ideas must be found to stimulate the process.

In 1994 the company reviewed its strategic focus to home in on six areas to meet the demands of its *Challenge 1994* programme. NSK is focusing on customer satisfaction, business management leadership, people management, supplier performance, process improvement and environmental and society issues. The company understands it is necessary to achieve the lowest cost base for product manufacture, with consistent high levels of quality and service.

"Quality was our competitive advantage through the '80s, but competitive pricing is the factor which is going to be a necessity. In the future, Quality in delivery is a must, and if companies haven't got those attributes will not survive in business. Approaching the year 2000 NSK will have to be even more globally competitive and there will be additional pressure to stay a world-class company if we're going to continue to compete in international markets. We recognise that we now have to make another step of change to maintain continuous improvement in order to deliver lower priced products. The company is carrying out a complete environment survey of community attitudes, suppliers, customers and of course employees to glean a total picture of our operation. A new step change programme termed 'Beyond Product Quality' (BPQ) is now in action.

"Every three months we benchmark with the rest of the NSK operations throughout the world. We are the best plant outside Japan, but we want to be globally competitive. We still have to compete for funding to build factories and extend our operations, and keep building our capability in the marketplace.

"We've started using the European Foundation for Quality Management (EFQM) model for reflection and measurement, and we try to measure ourselves in a stern way", says Mr Jones.

By using the EFQM model the company is planning ahead to ensure continuous improvement is an ongoing feature of the company. Mr Jones believes a long-term view is required by companies seeking to become global market leaders:

"You cannot compete if you don't change, and you can't implement a Total Quality Management programme and instil a cultural change in three years. NSK has had 30 years experience in Total Quality – we plan our progress in such a way that what we're doing today is preparing us to continue delivering returns in four or six years time. It reflects the essence of 'Beyond Product Quality' – Everything we do we do in a Quality Way!"

20

Strive For Perfection

—Vickers plc—

VICKERS plc is an excellent example of a successful, and growing company. In 1995, sales increased by 57% to £1,443.8 million and group profit before tax was £75 million, compared with £44.8 million for the corresponding period in 1994 – a growth of 67%. With such tremendous results it is obvious the company can provide some lessons for the rest of British Industry. The Vickers Group is a member of the British Quality Foundation and subscribes to Quality philosophies in its operating divisions. The main divisions include Defence Systems, Propulsion Technology, Medical and Automotive.

Defence Systems

The Defence Systems Division had an order book in 1994 of £1.5 billion. The division builds the Challenger 2 Main Battle Tank for the British Army and the Royal Army of Oman. It is one of the engines of growth for the company as a whole (and has acquired other defence businesses in recent years).

Propulsion Technology

In 1993 the company formed the Propulsion Technology Division by grouping together the aerospace and marine engineering businesses. The new operation has been very effective and the individual companies in the group have become leaner and fitter. The division has a turnover of around £200 million. The marine propulsion business has been particularly successful, both through acquisitions and because of the outstanding activities of its water jet propulsion company KaMeWa.

Medical

The Medical division has the world's strongest neonatal intensive

Left:
The 1996 Rolls-Royce Silver Spur

Right:
The 1996 Bentley Brooklands

Left:
Johnny Herbert driving a Sauber Ford which is powered by a Cosworth V10 3.0 litre F1 Engine – 1996

Right:
Engineers examine a Ford Scorpio engine at Cosworth Engineering

care business and is performing well in difficult markets. In recent years the division has taken a number of initiatives to improve operating efficiency including reducing its distribution costs in Europe.

Automotive

This division consists primarily of Rolls-Royce Motor Cars and Cosworth – famous for advanced engine technology. These companies are the ones I have chosen to focus on for this book. As two companies with very different cultures, their stories offer inspiration and practical advice for business people seeking to be the best.

Rolls-Royce Motor Cars

"Strive for perfection in everything you do. Take the best that exists and make it better. When it does not exist, design it. Accept nothing nearly right or good enough."

When Henry Royce announced his philosophy for Rolls-Royce Motor Cars, he wasn't hailed as a 'Quality Guru' – although his words could easily be those of Deming or Crosby – he simply created a marque of motor cars with a name that has become synonymous with one word, Quality.

The Rolls-Royce philosophy is reflected in the company's vision: "To build the finest motor cars in the world".

In a market where the aspirations, requirements and of course expectations of its customers are enormous the company stands alone. In many respects Rolls-Royce and Bentley can be seen as having no direct competition but it is vital that the company maintains its mystique and the high standards that have seen its cars recognised internationally as the most magnificent ever built.

Despite manufacturing one of the most sought-after products in the civilised world, even Rolls-Royce felt the effects of the world-wide recession of the late 1980s – early 1990s. Bernard Preston, Rolls-Royce's Director of Quality, remembers the abrupt turnaround which began at the end of 1990, which was ironically the best year in the company's history:

"Come 1991 sales in most markets severely declined. It really was a worldwide recession. Every market that we were selling into was affected – the United States, Australia, Japan, UK, Europe – every market was the same, it was quite extraordinary."

The success of the mid to late 1980s wasn't wasted at Rolls-Royce: a number of improvements were put in place including the establishment of an MRP II production planning and control system which eliminated the shortage-driven manufacturing process; there was investment in a new paint shop, which in 1990 was the most up-to-date paint plant in Europe; a world class IT infrastructure was established; and the Bentley marque was further developed together with a number of feature-driven model changes for both Rolls-Royce and Bentley to keep pace with other luxury products.

Despite these achievements Rolls-Royce's management felt that a number of opportunities were missed during the period leading up to the late 1980s. Among these missed opportunities were: purchasing new plant for the machine shop instead of focusing on the vehicle assembly process; a lack of investment in manufacturing engineering which led to a weaker process capability; and not addressing industrial relations issues.

The directors responsible for Manufacturing and Personnel, Peter Hall and Charles Matthews were determined to tackle these issues and they led a determined change process.

Between 1990 and 1993 Rolls-Royce had to face a significant downturn in sales volume and the total workforce was reduced from 5,000 people to about 2,300 people. Such upheaval gave the company the impetus to change Rolls-Royce's culture of "no change".

Bernard Preston explains:

"Our task was to build a framework that supported rather than inhibited change. We had to stop change being seen as an 'event' and make it continuous through an improvement process. We were helped and influenced by Gemini Consulting Group during this period and they had a really good look at the business, over an 18-month period. We had to realise that now we were a smaller company, we needed to be leaner and more creative in order to maintain our profitability. So we changed the way we approached the business. We restructured. Some of our overseas offices were closed but we revitalised our corporate environment by addressing new markets and new revenue possibilities whilst simultaneously working hard at our existing business."

The company was structured into an organisation that relied on multi-functional project teams to manage engineering projects, this was a dramatic departure from the hierarchical engineering department previously in place. The move towards project teams removed the old philosophy of jobs for life with no position being guaranteed for longer than the life of the project.

Ten manufacturing zones were created. These are business units actually making the cars and are complemented by ten selling regions. A central resources department manages the business but is decentralised with finance people being involved in other business units.

Alongside the new organisational structure, industrial relations were also tackled. In 1990 all national agreements were terminated and the company withdrew from the Engineering Employers Federation, this allowed Rolls-Royce to re-negotiate its labour agreements. The number of union representatives on the site was reduced and a new Greenfield Site Flexibility agreement was established which was designed to be the equivalent of a single union agreement. This new agreement signed in 1991 was given the title 'The Green Book' and contained a paragraph vital to facilitating real changes in work practices.

'To support this approach it is agreed that all the unions party to this Agreement will end any restrictions to the demarcations based on union spheres of influence. Full flexibility and mobility of employees will be needed to ensure full use of resources and to support the team approach. Accordingly, employees will undertake any work which is within their capabilities, irrespective of grade or specialism anywhere within the Crewe site or off-site as required by the Company and undertake any training necessary to achieve this.'

As Bernard Preston recalls, the agreement took some selling to the workforce:

"That was the watershed paragraph and at first people didn't like it, but if you talk to them now, they will tell you it's the best thing for themselves and the business.

"We asked the question throughout their training – you seem to disagree with this multi-skilled teamworking approach and yet you are doing it at home. So, what's the difference?

"What the Green Book was about was the elimination of demarcation, the introduction of teamworking, skill-broadening, customer focus, empowerment, training, Health & Safety and the environment. We wove Health & Safety into the teamworking approach: it shouldn't be considered something that is done on the side by the medical centre – we said 'it's your responsibility within the team for safety' and safety has improved. But the key feature of the Green Book was the introduction of a Teamworking culture with working team leaders with a manufacturing zone comprising of 10 teams as noted earlier."

Teams also became the vehicle through which both major and minor improvement activities were undertaken and Natural Work Teams, or NWT, entered the Rolls-Royce vocabulary.

"A Natural Work Team is a group of people who come together to work on a specific short-term project. A project team is a team that is brought together and might develop a whole new car, or a whole new manufacturing strategy. These teams tend to be longer term.

"We use NWTs for almost everything we do. We will bring a cross-functional group of people together to get all the skills in you need, create a vision and objectives for the team activity, set out some deliverables and go for it. There is a lot of empowerment. But teams are not formed for the sake of it and our requirement is that the team has got to add some value to the business", says Bernard Preston.

In 1992 outsourcing commenced as the company had to lower its cost base and felt that it could source high-quality components more competitively than manufacturing them. In 1994 a project-based pay review and profit related pay system was established. An appraisal process for the shop floor was introduced and an opinion survey was completed for the first time in 1995.

Mr Preston continues:

"Also around the time of the 'Green Book' agreement, we had to take some radical decisions in our approach to Quality. We no longer have an inspection department. We don't have a Quality Assurance department. These may seem like bold moves but we said to ourselves – how can we introduce teamwork and say to the teams that you've got accountability for the work you do, when we've still got an inspection department – you can't do it: the two don't fit. So we had to make that bold decision and take away those functions, with the Quality specialist being drafted into the teams. Our results have proved the point, our 'right first time' Quality has improved dramatically."

To facilitate teamwork an extensive training programme was undertaken. Everyone was trained:

"When we started Total Quality we made the judgement that we were going to educate everyone. We were told at that time that you only need to educate those who need to know and they will educate the others but we made the decision that if we were going to do this everyone would need a common language.

"One of the benefits of the education, which we didn't really think about at the time, but which proved to be one of the key motivators for change, was to recognise that the training raised the level of debate in the organisation. It gave us the chance to face up to old attitudes, old assumptions, and some of the in-built negativity, cynicism and scepticism. In the training sessions people were very assertive with their views. We had people from throughout the factory questioning the merits of the new ideas and management's sincerity. When that happened we would bring in one of the Directors and debate the issues. This approach really raised the level of debate. If you don't talk about the issues you can't change your organisation because the negative attitudes may still be held. If you don't challenge these beliefs, then people go away feeling the same. They might look you in the eye and say 'oh yes, I agree' but once they are back in the workplace you find they haven't changed a bit."

To train the workforce Rolls-Royce followed Land Rover's experience by training some Quality leaders – people off the shop floor, people out of the offices – cross-functional people. Altogether about 130 people were trained as trainers who then conducted the training.

The employees were trained and given a 'Tool Box' of continuous improvement techniques which included problem solving, tally sheets, cause & effect analysis and brainstorming. The tools were presented as a process for continuous improvement not as a set of management theories. Multi-skilling and the use of the tools were a real sticking point. Bernard Preston explains how the workforce were converted: "To help them comprehend what we were trying to do, we said to people – 'what do you do at home? Do you do a bit of decorating? Do you do any gardening?' (answer: 'yes'). 'What about your car?' (answer: 'well, I maintain it myself'). 'Obviously, You're multi-skilled at home, – why not bring those skills in to work?' The message struck home."

When you move through the Rolls-Royce factory in Crewe and actually speak with staff working on the cars you get a sense of the enthusiasm and the real benefits of the change process. Phillip Jones is an associate (the title given to all Rolls-Royce staff) who works as a fitter. He confesses that initially he was more cynical of the changes than most.

"My view was I have 29 years experience in a company which is making the best cars in the world anyway – this is just another fad! Obviously, over the last five years we have found out that it isn't. The training and development matrix that we've set up is working. We have become multi-skilled and also have Total Quality training in areas like presentation skills, we are even given business awareness training so we understand why the company makes the decisions it does.

"The major benefit we now have is freedom to make decisions in our own process areas. Years ago we had an engineering support function and it seemed that engineering was set in an ivory tower – you only saw engineering managers when they came down to tell you how to do your job, or the foremen would make decisions for you. The difference today is that you are given a budget – what you think you will need for your project. We are empowered to decide what solutions are best for our section.

"We now meet with our suppliers whether they are internal or external and discuss problems and potential improvements with them. We speak directly with our dealers to ensure they have no problems and we also have owner surveys in which customer comments are fed directly to the people who are working on that section of the car. We can now look directly at what we are doing, if there is a customer complaint it is our responsibility – the problem is no longer somebody else's."

The type of feedback and communication outlined by Phillip Jones is just part of the extensive communications effort undertaken by Rolls-Royce. Other measures include Team briefings, company newsletters, open forums with directors and extensive customer surveys followed up by 'customer champions'.

Mr Preston is proud of the thoroughness of Rolls-Royce's efforts to ensure total customer satisfaction.

"When a customer takes delivery of one of our cars, we conduct market research using a questionnaire. We will contact a customer at regular intervals: after 6 weeks, 9 months, and again at 18 months. In the six weeks questionnaire we ask 'would you like to be involved in more research with Rolls-Royce?' If a customer ticks the 'yes' box then they might receive a phone call from an independent researcher who goes through a pro forma and spends about 40 minutes with the customer on the phone – asking all types of questions. For example, if a customer responds with, 'well, I'm not very happy with the quality of the seats', then the researcher seeks further details – 'well what aren't you very happy with?'

And this information is fed back to the team who made those seats. Through our customer quality tracking we have a record of all the things that people have said– everything. Sometimes we record an interview with the customer's knowledge and at promotional events, take videos. For example, if you went to one of our driving events, we would say 'would you mind spending a few minutes going through a questionnaire with us?' If the answer is 'no', we then ask: 'would you mind us videoing this, so we can show people back at the factory?' and if we get the answer 'no', then we record that interview."

The information is widely disseminated, it is given to the project teams, manufacturing, and to the Customer Relations Executive in case there's a problem. If a customer says 'I am very unhappy with this car', then within 24 hours anywhere in the world he will get a phone call from the local Customer Relations Executive. The information also goes to 20 trained Customer Champions around the factory in Crewe. The role of the Customer Champions is to provide information to employees who want to know more about customer feedback.

"There is a Customer Champion no more than 50 yards at the most, from where our associates work. The Champions are trained to read the data from our customers – a lot of data – so if you are working anywhere in the factory, it doesn't matter where you are, if you want more information there is somebody that will give it to you. And not only do they have that information, they also hold the tapes that we've recorded, so if someone is really interested the Customer Champion can say 'here's the tape, pop it on in your car on your way home and listen to it', the same goes for the videos."

"One of the key goals we've written this year is for the Customer Champion to tally sheet the number of enquiries they get and then, using local promotional activity, encourage 10 per cent more each month. Customer Champions will have that as a goal to deliver as part of the Key Goals process. This is our unique way of bringing our customer to the plant, and making our people aware of their needs."

The company's 'Key Goals' and 'Windows Planning' systems are the processes which translate and interpret the company's operating plan and strategies into things which associates do. Mr Preston explains how these management processes are used for continuous improvement:

"Our mission is 'To build the finest motorcars in the world and last year we set out our strategic aims and we communicated those strategies to everybody in the organisation in the 'Key Goals' brochure. We have an integrated strategic approach, with strategies embracing marketing, product, manufacturing, logistics and people all combining to deliver success for the future.

"We use the 'Key Goals' approach and we set key goals for each year which cover the whole business.

"In this way our management process consists of a mission and strategies supporting that mission. The individual elements of the strategies and operational goals are published in what we call a 'Key Goals' brochure and in more detail through the 'window planning process' which clearly spells out quarterly targets for improvement to the man on the job."

The brochure describes the guiding principles by which the company operates and then details the key goals for each successive year. The accountability and responsibility for each goal is attributed to named individuals and it is their job to deliver either the key goal, or their part in it, successfully.

The Window Planning process is even more specific. To attain key goals a number of plans with set targets for that 'Window' or quarter are identified. For example, a plan may be to reduce the number of non-conformance parts to 30 per week by the end of Window three. The Key Performance Indicator (KPI) or measure would show that in window two the number of non-conformance parts was 44 per week. At the end of Window three the KPI would show if the team was successful. Such precise targeting of improvements encourages people to become more creative and really think about what can be done to improve the result.

Rolls-Royce has achieved its tremendous results by unlocking the potential of its people. The company has striven 'to develop a culture where enterprise and personal accountability are of prime importance and are encouraged accordingly'.

Rolls-Royce Motor Cars Limited has improved both its trading position and its efficiency through creating an environment where the quality of the manufacturing processes match the consistent and exceptional quality of the Bentley and Rolls-Royce cars it delivers.

Bernard Preston concludes with his view of the future:

"I believe very firmly in this process of change and I know there are more things we can do. If other British companies took this approach and firmly believed in it, then it would enhance the UK's competitiveness against its competitors around the world. I've absolutely no doubt about that at all. It can be difficult, but you have to start. You have to take the first step and keep on going. There are so many opportunities for everyone, no matter what their position or industry."

Cosworth

"Although there have been many rewarding events in my motor racing career, I am delighted to recall how many victories and milestones have been achieved with cars powered by Cosworth or Ford-Cosworth engines. It has long been a pleasure for me to work with the team at Cosworth, whose engines always seem to have plenty of race-winning power, lots of torque – and great reliability. I'm convinced that they must now be the world's most successful designer, builder and operator of racing engines, and I certainly am proud to have been associated with them." The measure of quality has always been customer satisfaction and customers don't get more demanding than Formula 1 ace, Mario Andretti. His thoughts appeared in the foreword to Graham Robson's award-winning book *Cosworth: The Search For Power* (Patrick Stephens Ltd, 1995) and echo the sentiments of numerous other successful drivers who have relied on Cosworth to give them the winning edge.

Racing is the image always associated with Cosworth but the 1990s have seen some consolidation of the other specialist work Cosworth has been involved in over the years. The company has been part of the successful Vickers group since and has extended its commitment to the manufacture of 'road car' engines and the Cosworth casting of selected engine components.

The special culture that has been developed at Cosworth through heroic efforts on the race track is the envy of many other organisations seeking to build a close knit team environment. In many ways the culture at Cosworth hasn't come from textbooks or management training courses but from a powerful spirit of innovation and the will to win that came from the company's founders. When Keith Duckworth and Mike Costin met as young men at Lotus, Mike was head mechanic on the Lotus race team and Keith was an engineer. By combining their names the new company Cosworth Engineering Ltd was formed with the aim of providing a general engineering service for motor racing. Mike unfortunately was tied to Lotus contractually for three years, so Keith took responsibility for building the company through the start up phase and held the majority of Cosworth shares. The first year of trading for the company was 1959. In just 37 years the company has become legendary with a brand name that stands for excellence in engines.

In 1996 the firm employed over 1,200 people in the UK and USA and had considerable racing success. Michael Schumacher driving a Benetton-Ford with a Cosworth designed and built Ford Zetec-R engine won the 1994 Formula 1 Driver's World Championship. In Formula 3000, Cosworth engines were used by the winner of the European Championship for four successive years, while in the North American Indycar series, Ford Cosworth XB engines scored four more race victories in their third year of competition. In addition, Ford-Cosworth engined cars again recorded numerous rallying successes. In many ways the competitiveness of the racing industry drives Cosworth employees to achieve greatness but it has also caused some challenges for the company.

In the Racing Business Unit there is a race every fortnight so it is easy for the division to measure its success. This is very different from the other three business units casting, manufacturing and road car engines, which may have manufacturing contracts that last for five years. The challenge for Cosworth was summed up by an employee during a consultant's survey of company attitudes. The employee described Cosworth as 'islands of excellence with too few bridges'.

The survey conducted by Cricket consultants is part of the Cosworth Total Quality initiative called 'Winning Together'. The brand values of the Cosworth name have been identified as Drive, Endurance, Daring, Insight and being 'First'. It is important that any Quality programmes do not inhibit these values.

Many companies seek to create corporate cultures similar to Cosworth's through Total Quality Management and Re-engineering but Cosworth has to be careful that process improvement doesn't stifle its business units. This is unlikely as it is impossible to apply regular procedures or ISO 9000 to Racing where the ingredients for success include innovation and a 'can do' approach. Heroic all night efforts are often the norm during the racing season.

Scott Brownlee, Cosworth's Public Affairs manager, believes an important part of the process is showing the relevance of change to the highly talented group of engineers working at Cosworth.

"From the company survey we can now say 'this is what we are'. To move forward we are going to tailor our goals specially for each business unit. This process will take time as the organisation isn't used to thinking along these lines.

"A lot of enthusiasm for change comes directly from Charles Matthews, Managing Director and Chris Woodwark, his predecessor as Chief Executive and now Chairman of Cosworth. When Chris Woodwark joined the company, we were profitable but not growing, Chris and the management team developed an aggressive growth strategy – the first the company had seen."

Cosworth now has a vision which takes the company further than simply producing the world's best racing engines. It now has the strategic goal of 'Winning wherever it competes'. That means in all of its four business units.

The operating philosophy of growth is consistent with the 'plc' status of the Vickers Group but the prestigious racing ancestry of the company has not been forgotten by the new management team. Engineers are still given room to function and the authority to make decisions. The retirement of the company's founders was a turning point for the firm but Chris Woodwark believes they felt the time was right for change:

"The heritage and ethos they instilled in Cosworth is still part of the company and it is being developed and built on. The nice thing is that they understood change was necessary when they retired in the late 1980s and they still take an active interest in the success of Cosworth."

The Worcester-based Cosworth Castings business developed a process which has become known as an innovative and perfect example of organic growth through diversification. In 1995, £25 million was invested in a new facility to meet the growing demands of the automotive industry for high quality precision castings for aluminium cylinder heads and blocks. Work has been carried out for Ford's American operations, Jaguar, General Motors and Mercury Marine as well as 'Top Secret' prototype work for unspecified clients.

The Road Car Engine business unit has grown considerably, with work being carried out not only for Ford (a long-time and well-known partner) but also Mercedes-Benz, General Motors and Korean manufacturers. An operation has been established in the United States and this is seen as a growth market for Cosworth.

With so much work being carried out for rival companies the Cosworth code of ethics has put a 'Chinese Wall' between different teams to ensure security of individual clients. The amount of diverse development keeps the company on the leading edge of engine technology and all clients benefit from Cosworth's varied experience.

Cosworth is a broadly based company with a bright future, like Rolls-Royce the company has a strong brand name that carries its own peculiar mystique. It is fitting that Cosworth Chairman Chris Woodwark was appointed Chief Executive of Rolls-Royce in 1995 after a distinguished management career in the automotive industry. While the two companies have no formal links the lessons learnt by each firm will be passed on to the other.

Mr Woodwark concludes with his vision for the company: "My vision for Cosworth's future is that our team will remain at the forefront of engineering excellence, around the globe, and continue to succeed across all its racing and business activities."

21

Making IT Happen

—P&P—

"OUR commitment to Quality processes and procedures has been central to our success in the 1990s. We have substantially changed our approach to the information technology (IT) market during the last fours year and this refocusing of our business has been strongly supported by an outstanding quality ethic which has been adopted by everyone at P&P". In his role as Group Managing Director of P&P, David Southworth has embraced the Quality concept, using it as a powerful tool of change. This commitment has helped establish P&P as one of the leading providers of IT products and services.

This success has been recognised by an impressive range of awards. P&P has been presented with Awards for Excellence for its training and technical services by *Computing Magazine,* whilst its subsidiary QA Training, has been similarly recognised on three separate occasions. In addition, the Group's commitment to Quality and specialist capabilities are reflected in the array of accreditations it holds from the world's largest computer manufacturers.

P&P is a leading IT company with offices throughout the UK and in Europe. The stockmarket listed Group has a broad portfolio of customers including many Financial Times 500 companies, public sector organisations and computer businesses.

The company supplies computer hardware, software and communication products from manufacturers such as IBM, Digital, Compaq, Microsoft, Novell, Hewlett-Packard and Toshiba. But its supply is not restricted to solely sales, it also offers flexible rental and finance packages for periods ranging from a single day to a number of years.

David Southworth
Group Managing Director
P&P plc

But perhaps one of the most distinguishing features of P&P is the wide range of IT services which it offers, including consultancy, networking, training and technical support.

The commitment to provide such an impressive range of products and services explains why the performance of P&P continues to be outstanding. In 1995, the Group's profit before taxation increased by 57 per cent: from £8.0 million to £12.6 million. In the same year turnover increased by 30 per cent to £342 million.

However, P&P has not always enjoyed such success. Founded in 1980, the Group began life as a wholesaler of personal computer products. By the end of the decade it had begun to supply some computer services but product distribution remained its core business.

Traditionally, the IT industry had boasted high margins, but by the late 1980s these margins had been significantly reduced. Consequently the "middle man" was being squeezed and, as a distributor, P&P was greatly affected. To compound the problem, the Group was experiencing declining customer satisfaction.

As Mr Southworth explains, "The market was polarising. On the one hand, customers were looking for a broad range of products to be supplied quickly at the lowest possible cost. On the other, they were looking for companies who could provide advice about, implement and support entire computer systems. In short, the market was demanding specialists not generalists and P&P was in danger of becoming the latter."

"In 1991 we were under severe pressure, so we embarked on a programme to fundamentally change the way P&P was represented in the marketplace. Such a major change was bound to take a number of years and we needed the support and commitment of our employees from day one. We committed to a regular communication programme and sought to involve staff at all levels in the change process. In other words, we mapped out the future for P&P and invited them to join our voyage."

Thus in the period from the beginning of 1991 to the end of 1995, the Group underwent a major reorganisation, withdrawing from the high volume, low margin distribution sector and reorganising into lines of business, each of which focuses on a specific area of information technology.

Today, P&P has lines of business which specialise in consultancy, training, technical services, desktop products, communications and mid-range solutions, amongst others.

To establish these business areas the Group had to introduce new skills through acquisition and organic growth. The employee mix has changed with the addition of trainers, consultants, networking specialists and technical experts who have helped grow the total workforce to over 1,300 people. Furthermore, since 1990 P&P has acquired a number of companies from within the UK and Europe to add complementary skills which reinforce its position in the market.

This process of change was assisted by a Group-wide Quality programme which resulted in ISO certification for P&P. The quest for ISO9001 Quality Assurance was started by P&P's Technical Services business which recognised that large corporate clients were beginning to deal only with certified companies. Initial success for this business was soon followed by other areas within P&P and accreditation is now maintained across the key product and service areas of the Group.

But P&P maintains that quality is about more than simply acquiring the ISO badge. John Crawshaw, Logistics & Quality director at P&P comments: "ISO9001 is just one part of the quality picture at P&P. Quality systems, service levels, employee involvement and customer satisfaction are equally important parts of the quality mix.

"The ISO 9001 certificate is one thing, but there have to be benefits from modifying our processes, it is not change for its own sake but for the sake of improving overall efficiency. There has to be a return for the company and the customer. So, giving the customer what they really want and benefiting as a result is what it is all about and that requires much more than a certificate on a wall."

Customer satisfaction has been a guiding force for P&P. Since the early nineties the Group has encouraged employees at all levels to develop close links with customers. This approach has enabled opportunities across P&P to be identified, and allows the company to determine which products and services will best benefit individual customers.

"What differentiates P&P in the market is that we have very broad capabilities yet provide these in a specialised way. If a customer wants computer-based training they deal with our training business, when they need complex networks they work with our technical services business", explains Mr Southworth.

P&P is also one of the leading suppliers of integrated solutions which draw on skills and resources selected from across the Group. Mr

Southworth highlights the importance of Quality processes and systems when providing such services: "P&P customers have the flexibility to buy from the individual lines of business or to choose solutions which P&P delivers drawing on skills and resources selected from across the Group. The latter will typically involve multiple lines of business with each working closely with the others to deliver a seamless solution to the client. Our Quality systems and service level programmes integrate the individual parts to ensure success at every stage."

The provision of specialist services has succeeded in setting P&P apart and it is now one of the top ten support companies in the UK. Although the company has provided IT services since 1988, it is the increased emphasis of the 1990s which has led to considerable expansion. Today, over 60 per cent of the total workforce is dedicated to delivering a comprehensive range of consultancy, implementation and support services.

"We are not a run of the mill supplier, we work in specialist areas and provide powerful systems as well as desktop products. And, thanks to our service capabilities we can support, as well as supply, entire IT infrastructures. In fact, many companies outsource their IT requirements to us which is why we base a lot of people on customer sites", Mr Southworth says.

An example of such a situation is the work P&P is doing with Land Rover Vehicles, part of the Rover Group. Land Rover wanted to increase productivity at the desktop throughout the company, but also sought to save money in the process.

In October 1995 Land Rover Vehicles launched a Productive PC Procurement Programme – a new way of deploying PCs within their organization. The aims of the programme were to increase productivity at the desktop throughout Land Rover Vehicles while saving the company money in the process – challenging objectives for both the company and its chosen supplier. To partner them in this Quality programme they clearly needed a company which itself has high Quality standards – so they chose P&P.

The main element of the programme was to replace all existing desktop and laptop personal computers within Land Rover with standard systems using the latest technology which is specified to last the life of the unit. This increases user productivity while eliminating the need for non-value added support activity such as technical specifications, upgrades, problem diagnosis and correction and so on. The new systems were to be leased rather than bought.

P&P's role in the process is to provide a fully managed service for the entire process from specification, through order administration to installation at the desktop. The user's system is replaced with a brand new, fully operational PC of substantially higher specification which is pre-configured with all the necessary software and networking connectivity.

To achieve this P&P uses an advanced procurement process which it has tried and tested in the market place and is documented to comply with the model which the British Institutional Standards Organisation has recognised as best practice. The process is implemented by a dedicated team of people including management, engineers and schedulers. The team is supported by a management information system developed by P&P which is known as IMPAQS - Integrated Management Process Assured Quality System. The system mirrors electronically the order to install process.

By the end of 1996, some 600 PCs will have been replaced as part of the programme, which will then start over again. Another of Land Rover's objectives is to continue to replace their PCs within two to three years, eliminating the need for out-of-warranty repairs.

The management of Land Rover Vehicles is delighted with the success of the programme to date, with cash savings of £300,000 projected over the first two years. Also each year 10,000 hours of support activity has been eliminated and some 95,000 man hours potential released back to the business. In effect the programme has enabled over £1.5 million per annum of low value IT activity to be refocused onto core business processes.

The quality of P&P's contribution is recognised as fundamental to the success of the programme. Peter Yorke, Information Centre Manager and sponsor of the programme comments, "the quality of the service provided by P&P has more than matched our expectations.

"All targets in Phase 1 have been exceeded with 90 per cent of users describing themselves as happy or very happy with the service provided by P&P. Only one user was not satisfied. The user was in fact one of the pilot installations and helped identify a short-fall in one of the processes. This was quickly remedied, proof indeed of the value of a pilot. Much more typical were the comments from users such as 'Exceptionally fast installation', 'Efficient and friendly service' and 'Good standard of professionalism'."

Though the programme is a replacement programme, it has been adapted to support the installation of new equipment. Using the infrastructure that has been established this can be done to aggressive service levels. Requests for additional PCs can be met very speedily, often on the same day if necessary. Other value-added spin-offs include an ongoing software audit, recorded on IMPAQS, to ensure legality, with all software media and licences held centrally within the IT department. A training programme is also taking place to maximise the business benefits of the programme – again such activity is recorded on the IMPAQS system.

The programme is already acknowledged within Land Rover as a success and plans are under way to replicate it in another area within Rover Group. The Productive PC Procurement Programme is undoubtedly a tribute to the quality of both Land Rover Vehicles and their chosen partners, P&P.

P&P embraces training as another important avenue for differentiation. Operating one of the leading end user application training organizations, it has the capacity and resources to educate up to 100,000 delegates each year. P&P's training arm is well recognised for its involvement in major projects, tailor-made training programs and for providing application training courses from 14 locations throughout Britain. The acquisition of QA - a company primarily concerned with technical training and consultancy - in 1994, has added to the strength of P&P's position in this area.

Meeting customer needs through efficiency and reliability has also been of primary concern for P&P. Of particular importance is the concept of zero defects, which the company has been working on since 1994. At this point, the company estimated that 98 per cent of what it did was within the Quality system's guidelines. However, the Group was looking to improve things further and to eradicate errors.

In order to achieve this, all procedures are constantly re-evaluated as they are performed. If a problem is detected, the company looks to find the cause. When the cause is identified, special attention is paid to prevent the situation recurring.

The process of implementing a zero defects policy began with the logistics and warehouse functions.

"In such a competitive industry even the smallest error can mean the difference between success and failure. We aim to provide the highest levels of service in the industry and have continually re-evaluated what those levels should be. As a result, our logistics and warehousing service levels are now incredibly high", says John Crawshaw.

He adds, "the improvements in service have been self fulfilling as the workforce has striven to improve their performance with every new success."

Indeed, the warehouse has proved that it can come very close to achieving zero defects. In the last six months of 1995, only two out of 460,000 products were unable to be picked, packed and dispatched on the same day. P&P believes that this level of efficiency is due to the fact that everyone in the warehouse takes a special pride in their work to reach a stage where the team takes personal responsibility for any mistakes that occur.

Effective communication is essential if zero defects are to be achieved. P&P holds regular communication sessions for individual teams and every three months a presentation focusing on Group strategy is given by the directors to each member of staff. The aim is to help everyone understand the importance of their role within the overall picture.

The Group also utilises electronic communication methods to keep everyone up to date. The entire workforce has access to e-mail systems which provide a fast and efficient method of communicating across all locations in the UK and Europe. The P&P computer network is also being used to support the Quality systems, as John Crawshaw explains:

"Our Quality and procedure manuals are being transferred to an on-line system based on Lotus Notes. This will mean that anyone who needs to look up procedures will have the latest version at their finger tips. We will no longer have large folders which have to be constantly updated, taking-up space and absorbing administrative time. We will reduce the paper flow, save time, save money and have access to a real-time Quality Management System."

The move to a computerised system is just one example of the innovative way in which P&P manages its Quality programmes. By adopting a flexible approach, P&P can quickly adapt its systems in line with organisational developments, such as the addition of new business areas.

When the Group acquired the Scottish company Computers for Business, it was clear that many of P&P's ISO procedures were appropriate to the new subsidiary. Computers for Business has subsequently adopted the tried and tested Quality system of its parent. In so doing it has reduced the approval timescale and established a system which is compatable with that of P&P – ensuring that the two companies are able to work closely together.

P&P appears to be guaranteed a healthy future in the IT industry. With its commitment to meeting customer requirements and to supplying the latest technology, it is more than likely that P&P will play a leading role in the industry's future. And in doing so, it will continue to set itself apart from its competitors through Quality and differentiation.

"Differentiation and Quality are two key words for us, because ultimately it all comes down to the customer. We are very much focused on the customer, we do what the customer wants, we develop our organisation in the way the customer wants and we deliver Quality, we differentiate on Quality and we base all our operations on providing high Quality service to customers. That's what it's really all about", explains Mr Southworth in a final summary of P&P's successful philosophy.

Alan Hulcoop examines a model roof designed by one of the CI teams to demonstrate Redland's dry fixing process.

Mike Penny holds local CI reviews at every month's Executive meeting, which take place at a different works each month.

22

Building A Team Culture

—Redland Roof Tiles—

IT has been said many times that Quality is about people. Anyone who understands what it takes to instil a Quality culture into an organisation will tell you that you have to get your people involved. What is said less often is that the calibre of people driving and managing the continuous improvement process is equally important. The commitment of Redland Roof Tiles Managing Director, Mike Penny and Alan Hulcoop, Divisional Quality Manager to the philosophies and practices of Total Quality Management (TQM) has contributed much to the continuing success of their company. Without leadership and enthusiasm, Quality initiatives are doomed to fail.

Redland Roof Tiles began in 1919 as the Redhill Tile Company based in Reigate, Surrey. The company expanded rapidly after the Second World War and became a public company in 1955. By 1992 its parent company, now known as Redland Plc was one of the world's leading producers of construction materials, with factories in almost every west European country as well as Australasia, the Far East, Africa and the USA. Redland Roof Tiles activities are essentially based in the UK with 862 employees in 15 locations with a turnover in excess of £80 million.

Redland Roof Tiles produces high-quality roof tiles in concrete, clay and slate, and in 1991 it was awarded the Queen's Award for Technology for its reconstituted slate called Cambrian. The company is a leading supplier of pitched roofing materials in the UK, with approximately 36 per cent of the country's market. The strategy of the company is to have the best products, the best quality of service and to deliver more customer value for money than any competitor.

To achieve this strategy, Redland Roof Tiles listens to its customers, and uses extensive Customer Perception Surveys which compare the company with competitors and the industry norm. The results are statistically weighted, and show as a percentage how much better (or worse) Redland Roof Tiles is compared to the rest of the industry.

The surveys help Redland Roof Tiles focus on areas to improve. In general, customers saw Redland as being no worse than their competitors. As Redland's aim is 'to be number one', the company felt it had to be seen as considerably better. Quality was considered as a way to achieve that goal.

The building industry has been slow to recognise the benefits of quality systems; Redland Roof Tiles has been one of the industry's pioneers. Beginning in 1982, Redland Roof Tiles sought and obtained British Standard Kitemark licences for its relevant products. Restructuring in 1989, as a result of the U.K. building recession, brought into being a dedicated Quality Assurance department. The department was established to assist the company to take advantage of its product and service quality in lean markets and prepare for greater competitiveness through all aspects of quality in the future.

Over the next four years Redland Roof Tiles concentrated on obtaining BS 5750, part 2 (ISO 9002) registration for its operations. Alan Hulcoop believes that the Kitemark and ISO 9002 registrations give the company's products and processes a firm quality foundation. The focus initially was very much on production. To bring internal sales and collection depot staff into the system, further registrations were sought and obtained, but to build awareness of quality throughout the company something more was required:

"To make quality relevant to every department we needed to establish it as a strategic business issue with continuous improvement rather than just meeting standards. We still valued our registrations as they are the backbone of our systems but we began to look for a quality model that linked people with their processes so we could measure and continuously improve our results", explained Mr Hulcoop.

In 1993 Redland Roof Tiles looked carefully at the Crosby model which is based around the 'cost of quality' and 'zero defects'. At the time the Crosby model was considered too difficult to implement because the culture at Redland wasn't ready to cope with the concepts. The company has started looking at the model again in 1995 as the workforce now understand that '100% right first time' means 100% not 99.9% and that zero defects is not only a target to aim for but possible to achieve. Also, Redland Roof Tiles is becoming increasingly interested in accurately measuring the cost implications of TQM improvements.

Another model considered was the American Baldridge Award. Monier, a 100% owned US subsidiary of Redland was having a lot of success with Baldridge, particularly in getting their people involved. Redland Roof Tiles eventually decided to use the European Foundation for Quality Management (EFQM) model because it focused on business excellence through leadership and people management with a customer focus. Mike Penny saw that the model could be used to ensure every department within the division was empowered and committed to the quality policy.

Redland Roof Tiles now had to get the model into everyday, company-wide use. This required a re-evaluation of the role of the Quality Assurance department, in particular the Quality Managers.

"We used to have our Quality Managers patrolling the factories and checking products on the shop floor. Employees used to think that because the Quality Manager walked past their area without making any comments they must have been up to standard. The Quality Managers were seen by employees as Quality controllers and inspectors, which stopped employees from owning the responsibility of quality. That is why we made a deliberate decision to reduce the number of Quality Managers and modify the role of the remaining ones, at the same time we delegated responsibility for quality to the shop floor. We moved the Quality Managers from production into a role interfacing via stock control with sales and thus started the spread of Quality to other departments. Five quality managers now cover the whole of the country and focus on a wide variety of issues from production to spending time with our customers", said Mr Hulcoop.

A 'cascade' system was used to explain how to use the EFQM model, beginning with senior management and progressing to 'Quality Champions' from the shop-floor. In March 1993, Mr Hulcoop presented Total Quality and the EFQM Model to the executive and senior managers. While unequivocal support was demonstrated from the executive, the senior managers initially thought measuring each department against the EFQM model would be too difficult and time consuming for them personally.

"I could see how relevant the EFQM model was to our business, because I had been on several training courses. The senior managers couldn't, because the model was being presented to them for the first time. I had difficulties getting the senior managers to commit their time, so we asked them to select a middle manager from their area to serve as a Functional Chairman. Staff who had an interest in TQM were chosen and trained in the use of the EFQM model. This took the onus off the senior managers and allowed them devote themselves to managing. The senior managers were happy to be trained by their Functional Chairman at a later date", explained Mr Hulcoop.

The functional chairmen took ownership of the EFQM model and began self assessment of their departments. The Functional Chairmen even modified the scoring system to make it simpler. Mr Hulcoop was happy for them to do this but retained the percentage based system for company wide assessment.

After their initial training, the first task of the Functional Chairmen was to brief all staff in their departments on the Continuous Improvement initiative. The company chose to call the initiative Continuous Improvement rather than Total Quality because Quality had connotations that it was solely a production issue and not relevant to all areas of the operation. It was important also for people to understand that ISO 9000 wasn't being abandoned because of the move towards a Total Quality approach. ISO 9000 certification would still support the processes.

Alan Hulcoop found the main difficulty for the Functional Chairmen, as they made their presentations throughout the company, was the attitude that Total Quality Management was a short-term programme and the belief that "If I keep my head down it will be all over in two years and I'll escape unscathed." This attitude formed because a number of short-term campaigns such as *Being the Best, Redland Really Tries* and *Putting the resource where it does the most good* had already been implemented. These programmes were designed to last 18 months to 2 years. Whilst they were effective, these campaigns didn't have an ongoing Continuous Improvement philosophy. The message that Continuous Improvement is an ongoing way to manage the business began to be understood but it required education and the perceived commitment of the executive and senior management.

Within five months of the EFQM model's launch all Redland Roof Tiles Departments were looking at how they worked and how they could improve using the models guidelines. Continuous Improvement (CI) teams were established in each department to look at various issues and to identify and solve problems.

To ensure the CI team meetings ran smoothly and constructively, thirty-one champions or facilitators were selected from the shop floor. Unlike the Functional Chairmen, the champions were not trained in self-assessment but instead learnt how to manage meetings and team dynamics.

The simplified scoring system developed by the Functional Chairmen was used to monitor the team's progress. The system uses a simple one to ten. When a project begins it is scored as one and when it is completed it is given a ten. The scores for each team are averaged and if a low average of those scores emerges too many new projects are being introduced to that team and not enough are being worked on, and if a high score emerges then the team is completing projects, but not introducing enough new ones to its activities.

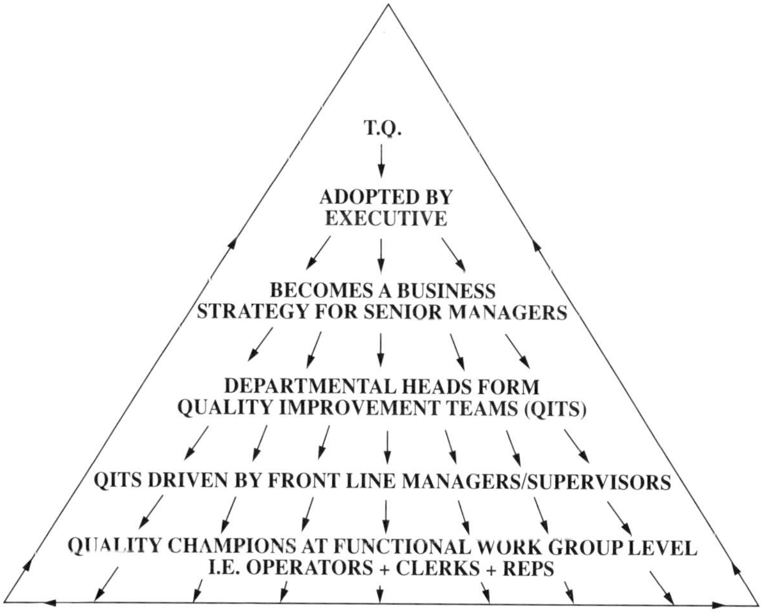

As Divisional Quality Manager, Mr Hulcoop received a large amount of information from the CI teams. To maintain momentum it was vital that the teams received swift feedback:

"The CI teams were meeting on a monthly basis and the champions sent the minutes of the meetings to myself to read with the understanding I would provide feedback, but because I was so busy the minutes were sitting in a file and the CI teams were in danger of losing enthusiasm. You have to recognise these things as you go along, and you have to react to them. This resulted in the organisation setting up a National Steering Committee (NSC) to help collate information and audit CI team activity against the EFQM model. Part of the audit is used as feedback and guidance for teams and part to establish the best performing teams for the company's annual Quality Award. The Award is a recognition scheme to promote enthusiasm and not part of CI results. Suppliers also receive a Quality Award if they have made significant improvements to their products and services to Redland Roof Tiles."

The NSC was made up of representatives throughout the organisation, including employees on night shift who can be isolated from the process because of a lack of communication.

"Our Managing Director, Mr Mike Penny, went down to the works one night and asked how continuous improvement was going. The production operator of the concrete mixer asked what continuous improvement was! It was then we realised the message was getting filtered at some stage in the process, so we deliberately used our night-shift production operator on the NSC", said Mr Hulcoop.

Through the NSC the company has emphasised that Continuous Improvement is not another management tool, but rather a process for employees to become involved in. The whole idea of having the CI teams was to increase employee involvement because essentially it is the front line managers, supervisors and Champions who have the closest contact with customers. Targets are set to deliver improvements to customers, such as invoice to credit ratios and telephone response times. Once targets for improvements have been identified, the NSC reviews and audits the teams three times a year to ensure results are delivered. As a result of CI team activity Redland Roof Tiles has started to build up a picture of its strengths and areas for improvement. Mr Hulcoop says some teams have remained unchanged for two years, whereas other teams change all the time to maintain their effectiveness. He continues that one particular team hadn't met for six months and nobody from the shop floor said anything, but once the team leader had been replaced teamwork began again.

Plant Manager for Redland Roof Tiles, Stirling Works in Scotland, Mr Alfie Leggett, encourages other companies to become involved in the process of continuous improvement. Mr Leggett, previously a store person, is enthusiastic about the results achieved by CI teams. Efficiency improvements on the Stirling Tile Plant has saved a minimum of £39,000 per annum. He explains:

"Initially CI teams were met with caution and suspicion from employees. The most commonly expressed concerns were things like: would management support the teams; would CI teams be a short-term focus; and would money be made available to make it happen. From July to December 1993, 24 improvements were made to processes and the plant. Since then an operating budget has been made available to the teams to purchase items which employees think can make additional improvements to the plant. We feel this is a signal from management, giving further encouragement to the teams to act on their own initiative. Being involved in CI team activity has been gratifying for all concerned, working on your own initiave, seeing a sense of team spirit and building it. The gulf between management and the workforce has certainly been bridged by better communication. If anybody has any doubts about the merits of CI teams I would say that the reservations they may have were undoubtedly felt by us. However, we have learnt that everyone has something to offer. The real expert is the person who has been doing the job for years. In the past there has been talent which has been overlooked, but now we have the opportunity to use our experience and take advantage of it."

There are numerous examples of successful CI teams. The CI team at the company's Bedworth Works significantly reduced yard turn-around time to achieve Just-In-Time (JIT) delivery. Prior to establishing a CI team Bedworth were only turning around 78 per cent of the customers' vehicles within the customers' desired 45 minutes. Building industry customers required a Just-In-Time service, ofter they would phone in their orders while their trucks were on their way to the Redland yards.

"What was happening was the load manifests were taking too long to prepare. The driver would arrive and would have to wait for the load manifest to be printed off and the load made up. What the CI team started to do was to anticipate loads for regular customers. Small loads are now made up because we know we usually sell a certain tile in a particular quantity. Employees can now look on the computer screen to assess whether a regular customers' load should be made up. Flexibility in the ordering system was also implemented to allow for a customer to pick up additional tiles while their truck was still in the yard. There is quite a lot of speculation in the process, and there could be extra work involved if employees got the load manifest wrong, but things have improved. What employees are actually doing is using their knowledge more intelligently. The team also approached the Sales department to give them advance warnings of any orders to further narrow down the needs of the customer. The teams have achieved 100 per cent success in turning around every truck within 45 minutes for many consecutive months."

Other examples include: Internal Sales reduced invoicing errors, thus having to raise fewer credits; South Cerney CI Team found a way to recycle waste mortar saving up to £22,000 per annum; and Service Department CI teams have reduced complaints against them saving up to £148,000 p.a.

With such impressive results it is important to maintain the momentum for change. By focusing on their people Redland Roof Tiles believe even more improvement can be made. The company has invested heavily in training and safety. Two staff have been appointed full time to develop appraisal systems, training programmes and new CI training modules. Employees are trained while they are working on real improvement projects, so they can see the value of their new skills immediately. The training is part of Redland Roof Tiles, Investors In People programme.

Motivation is maintained through communication. The company produces a monthly newsletter called *The Circular. The Circular* is used to introduce or reinforce concepts of TQM and Continuous Improvement. The tone is friendly and informal with cartoons and anecdotes.

Once every year Redland Roof Tiles carries out a company-wide CI survey through its Executive and makes an analysis of the whole company against the EFQM model. Every other year Redland forwards a report to the EFQM in the form of an application for a European Quality Award (EQA). Feedback from the EFQM is used to draw up an action plan via the NSC to add impetus to the Continuous Improvement programme. In the first application submitted to the EFQM, the Foundation judged Redland Roof Tiles to be well on the way to becoming a Total Quality company.

Adding to the tools available to the teams also maintains enthusiasm for change. In 1995 team members were taught how to use process mapping to analyse procedures. Use of process mapping has lead to Multi-Functional Teams being formed from people involved in each process, including those from other departments – another innovation.

Redland Roof Tiles have been rewarded by their commitment to Continuous Improvement. The company readily admits it has some way to go to achieve its stated goal of business excellence but the real improvements that have been made to date have benefited the company's customers and employees. To conclude Alan Hulcoop expresses his thoughts on Redland's Total Quality approach: "TQM is very much a people issue – it's about people taking an interest in each other. I can't say our cultural change is complete yet, but employees are interested and team participation is increasing. It's quite revealing when you sit down and talk to the guys on the shop floor about some of the improvements they could make because often they're simple things, but it's the sum total of those improvements which make the workplace a better place to be and give our customers a better product."

left to right: Steve Roe (Quality Manager),
Professor Barry Popplewell (Non-Executive Director) and
John Crathorne (Managing Director)
Stoves plc

23

Continuous Improvement For Growth & Development

— Stoves plc —

STOVES plc, Britain's only significant independent cooker manufacturer, can proudly boast the capability to launch products at a rate of one or more a day together with the production responsiveness and flexibility to build any one of their range of 1000 different models on demand for delivery within two and 10 days.

In fact Stoves' flexibility is greater than any other European cooker factory allowing it to produce short runs of a particular product when required and to switch manufacture to another product range exceptionally quickly and efficiently. "We are aiming to become the very best in our chosen market sectors. To become a world class company producing world class products you need a Quality programme, but to that you need to combine other elements. For us those elements are innovation and investment in flexible manufacturing processes to allow us to reduce our cycle times while improving Quality", explains Stoves' Managing Director and Chief Executive, John Crathorne, formerly chief of Thorn EMI's major domestic appliance division. Mr Crathorne has spent 35 years in engineering and the domestic appliance industry and was awarded the MBE for his services to the domestic appliance industry in 1995.

Stoves' commitment to Quality was recognised when it won one of the first North West Quality Awards, the Brian Redhead Award for the company which had done the most to enhance the reputation of the North West presented by the BBC in November 1995.

At the core of Stoves' philosophy is continuous improvement as Mr Crathorne explains: "Growth is not an accident. It requires you to be very precise in terms of the markets you target and the channels of distribution you engage – you have to offer the right combination of brand, price and features to the appropriate cluster of customers to gain an advantage. So Quality for us is not something that stands outside the business, rather it is an integral part of the way we think. I walk around every day and see thousands of opportunities for us to keep getting better and it impresses me that things change and improve on almost a weekly basis."

Within Stoves the belief is held that mass production, with its demotivating lack of individual involvement, results in poor Quality. Instead this system has been replaced by small production teams which work on a cellular basis, taking full responsibility for different stages of production and focused on continuous improvement. In this way Stoves aims to build in Quality throughout the production process replacing dependency on inspection of the finished product.

Stoves employs 720 people at its Prescot site, 79 per cent of whom work in manufacturing. The company manufactures a range of gas and electric freestanding cookers and built-in ovens and hobs which are sold under the brand names Stoves, Stoves Newhome and Valor. It also manufactures built-in ovens for other manufacturers and retailers' own brands and designs and produces leisure cookers and power showers.

While still the dominant sector, the freestanding cooker market is gradually declining while the market for built-in ovens, which is currently dominated by imports, is expanding to fill the gap.

Today's market for domestic cookers is mature and highly competitive with approximately 98 per cent of all households possessing a domestic cooker. Therefore, it is not only crucial to incorporate Quality into every stage of design and manufacturing but to back this up with Quality service. "Distribution has moved from the traditional gas showroom to a variety of outlets placing increasing importance on the selection of distributors who as partners will enhance your reputation jointly in the market place. In response to market changes we have also generated our own committed field support activity", explains Mr Crathorne.

In support of this commitment Stoves provides support on all of its products relevant to electrical and mechanical breakdown, upheld by a team of 37 service engineers which is earmarked to increase to 50 by the close of 1995 to guarantee a comprehensive UK-wide after sales service.

Stoves as it exists today was created in 1989 when a management team led by Mr Crathorne and Sean O'Connor, Stoves' Non-executive

Chairman purchased Yale and Valor's loss-making cooker business at Prescot, Merseyside in a management buy-in. Since the acquisition Stoves has recorded outstanding growth. All financial indicators have improved despite a decline in the cooker market of approximately 25 per cent by value between 1988 and 1994. An operating profit of £3.4 million on a turnover of £48.6 million was announced for the year ending 31May 1995 which reflect increases on the previous year of 63 per cent and 17 per cent respectively.

Part of Stoves successful transformation is attributed to the effective utilisation of on-going market research which drives both its marketing strategy and its product development programme which has allowed it to develop its brand portfolio and significantly expand its product range.

"Thorough market research is essential in order to identify precise consumer needs. Manufacturers, retailers and installers must clearly understand what their customers want and tailor their products and services accordingly. From our own research, we know that the features, pricing, retail distribution, efficient installation and swift service back-up have to be absolutely right", explains Guy Weaver, Marketing Director. Cooker market trends are continually monitored to allow Stoves to provide its customers with the products they want to buy in domestic markets and increasingly in export markets.

However, the company's immediate strategy for the future is to continue its investment in improving manufacturing processes to increase flexibility and product Quality, while reducing costs. "A small player in a global market has to continually respond faster with unique products than the competition so that when a customer wants a new product we can launch it in a matter of days, not weeks or months. We are moving closer to our ultimate goal of mass customisation where we can involve the customer in the process of designing the precise item they want in their kitchen," says Mr Crathorne.

Since the management buy-in Stoves has invested approximately £10.2 million in plant and equipment to enhance the flexibility and capacity of the manufacturing process. An example of this investment is Stoves' hydroform plant which forms steel using water pressure enabling the company to produce the necessary oven cavity sizes from a steel coil. Compared with conventional techniques used by the majority of cooker manufacturers, the process is quicker, machinery can be changed much more rapidly to produce different cavity sizes and the process uses up to 20 per cent less material.

Stoves uses computers extensively throughout the design process, in commercial and financial areas, customer service support, planning and even within manufacturing processes. Mr Crathorne stresses, however, that they are not utilised to drive the factory. "The factory is essentially operating on the philosophy if you haven't sold it, don't make it. Just in time manufacturing methods have reduced our stock levels to a two day maximum, particularly of finished goods, resulting in significant cash flow benefits. Our stock turn has increased from four times to 18", explains Mr Crathorne.

Reinforcement of product Quality in the factory, for example, has been achieved through the development of automatic testing facilities which ensure that each appliance is tested in accordance with the specified procedures. This information is captured on a central computer which then issues a bar code for each appliance passed.

"This process has been developed with a sizeable contribution from the people interfacing with that part of the business. In turn it will lead directly into the next generation of interface between field service engineers and headquarters. Scanning the bar code on the product will automatically give the service engineer a picture of what the product was like when it left the factory and assist him to locate a fault," explains Barry Popplewell. Prof Popplewell is a Non-executive Director at Stoves and has acted as a part-time consultant to the company on business excellence and Quality initiatives since 1989. He was formerly group Quality director for Philips Scientific, part of Philips Electronics and is regarded to be one of the UK's leading Quality practitioners having published a number of top selling Quality management texts.

In early 1992 Stoves commenced manufacturing built-in ovens and hobs based on modular design and cellular production techniques to increase manufacturing flexibility. Modular design enables a large number of products to be produced from a number of interchangeable components or modules which in turn allows the company to decide at a late stage in the production cycle what the final products and brands are going to be because components can be dedicated to particular models towards the completion of the production cycle. Cellular production, which involves a number of people working around a central work station, has improved the efficiency and Quality of the manufacturing process. In November 1994, the company began to manufacture freestanding cookers based on a similar modular design.

The assembly of finished cookers is undertaken by cells of up to nine people. Stoves currently operates approximately 30 of these cells. Each team is a mini production line with its members working in a U-shaped formation around a central work station. This helps to facilitate communication, which in turn improves efficiency, Quality standards and morale amongst team members. The teams are also responsible for prioritising daily production and communicating with suppliers, who are sourced world wide.

Since 1989, Stoves has reduced the number of direct material suppliers with which it deals from 170 to approximately 80 and has actively managed its business to reduce its holding of stocks of raw materials. This has entailed the development of close relationships with chosen suppliers, some of whom are the sole suppliers of particular raw materials and components to the company. A growing number of these suppliers now operate under the company's Kan Ban system, in which they are an integral part of the manufacturing process and are responsible for maintaining component supplies at the company's site, frequently delivering on a daily basis direct to the cells they are supporting.

Stoves has an advanced supplier development programme because it views supplier relationships as one of its key strategic activities. It hosts an annual supplier conference where representatives of all supplier groups make presentations to the group about their annual performance and in turn Stoves provides details of its benchmarking findings of suppliers in areas such as Quality, reliability, design changes and cost benefits. "Where there is a major mismatch between the design, Quality, reliability or price the supplier will be given time to work with us to identify ways in which they can close the gap to ensure that both parties prosper. We have asked them to pick up the pace of change themselves and I think they will be surprised at what they can achieve in a year's time", says Mr Crathorne.

Examples of efficiency improvements conceived in the factory are numerous. Stephen Roe, Quality Assurance Manager provides one such example involving the review of packing procedures for consignments of hobs to caravan manufacturers. The original practice required each hob shipped to be fitted with polystyrene ends and placed in a cardboard box at a cost of £2 per unit. Once received the manufacturer would unwrap the components and store them until they were required. Stoves, which employs Kan Ban systems within its factory, wanted to supply its own customers in a similar fashion. Following a factory tour with a customer which manufactured caravans Stoves decided to replace its existing packing procedures with a system which uses purpose made, re-useable racks into which 16 hobs can be placed. The hobs are transported in the racks preventing contact and damage and allow the manufacturer to remove the hobs on an as needs basis, returning the rack for restocking.

The system allows the customer to eliminate panics from the production process by receiving supplies of components ahead of production. The primary cost savings to Stoves resulted from eliminating the need to supply packaging which also had a positive environmental impact, and through decreasing administration costs because the company no longer had to process individual order forms and invoices. The changes resulted not only in savings for Stoves but also to the customer because they no longer had to dispose of excessive amounts of packaging and damage to the hobs was reduced.

New product development is undertaken by the company's engineering department, currently employing 33 people. Their work encompasses industrial design, production engineering and component and product development. To date the company has registered or applied for registration of 38 patents which relate to both products and manufacturing processes.

Stoves which operates its own training school invests half a million pounds per annum on the training needs of its employees. For instance, all engineering recruits receive three months training and work experience in R&D, customer service, and in the factory which improves internal communication and permeates an understanding of the inter-relationship between departments. This level of training is even more exceptional when you consider that every one of Stoves' engineers has already qualified and practised as a service engineer before joining the company.

Stoves pays great attention to fostering an environment which encourages innovation. Part of its success can be attributed to the mix of extraordinary talent and camaraderie within the workforce, but also to fostering an environment which encourages the person doing the job to improve the job by extending the boundaries.

Across the whole range of Stoves' activity from the factory layout to the customer service operation is an inbuilt flexibility which allows change to be embraced swiftly. "The factor that differentiates us from many companies is that we will not postpone change just because we haven't perfected the new process to a 99.9 per cent level. By that stage you are so exhausted perfecting and implementing the change you don't revisit the process for five years by which time it is usually at least four years out of date. Most organisations find this approach alien, however we are committed to continuous improvement as opposed to a search for an illusionary 'first time' perfection", explains Prof Popplewell.

"We are not prescriptive about how things are done, instead we tell people not to get too used to the way things exist at any particular point in time because it is inevitable that they will change at some stage. We do not pay too much attention to job titles, for example, because this gives us a degree of flexibility in the way we change boundaries. One of the strengths of this company, because we are in a growth situation, is that change is not equated with job losses. In fact we have been able to create jobs as well as achieve tremendous operational improvements."

Although the company actively removes barriers to growth and change it endorses Quality audits or 'ZAP' audits. These ZAP audits are conducted for the benefit of managers and workers in every area of the business and identify weaknesses which the individual groups are then responsible for resolving. Each manager makes a presentation to the management group and discusses what is occurring in their group and the progress made in various programmes. This is an interactive process which gives all areas of management an appreciation of how their activity affects the other parts of the organisation.

ZAP, Stoves' Company -Wide Quality Improvement programme, helps ensure that the needs of every customer, internal or external are met. "ZAP doesn't mean anything – it means what ever you want it to mean", explains Prof Popplewell. "To me ZAP is what we do to our competitors every day. ZAP to the people in the factory may mean you improve a particular product or process. The main intention is that it distinguishes between the past and the future."

The company wide policy aims to ensure that quality and reliability occupy the highest position in operating priorities. It is supported by the following objectives:

- To establish and maintain an environment which encourages all our employees to pursue constant improvements in the Quality and reliability of our products and services, thereby enabling us to "be the best"
- To implement a way of working that enables employees at all levels to identify, analyse and resolve problems.
- To do things "right first time" and thereby eliminate waste.

Measurement of Quality indicators and ensuring that they are visible are core concepts of ZAP. "Quality indicators are displayed throughout the workplace and team briefings are held around them on a monthly basis. The factory operates on a 'pull' system – we only make what we have already sold – people know what we have achieved and what we need to achieve. Quality is very much a tangible subject at Stoves and the end result is that the company is continuing to move forward", explains Prof Popplewell.

A Times Two Improvement programme was initiated when Stoves was presented with the reality that it was going to double in size and had to decide how it was going to accommodate that growth. It had two choices: to double the workforce or to halve the number of process transactions and problems. The latter option was selected and the company embarked on a programme whereby managers of each section in their own way identified the key processes in their area, investigated measures to reflect the processes and then halved the required number of transactions. The outcome was a company wide map of 88 Quality indicators representing the key process activities.

As Mr Crathorne emphasises: "No one in the company is either so senior, so junior or so specialised that they cannot become involved in improving the company's overall performance. It is based on the simple principle that there is always a way to do things better."

24

A Shared Vision of Excellence

— Bio Products Laboratory —

BIO Products Laboratory is part of a growing number of public sector organisations which must continuously improve on standards with greater cost efficiency.

BPL's major products are derived from plasma, a rich source of protein. The fresh frozen plasma received by the organisation contains the protein fractions which are necessary for the correct clotting of blood. These blood products, such as Factor viii, are prepared at Elstree in a form which can easily be used by Haemophliliacs at home as well as in Hospital. This treatment, first produced in bulk at BPL, has improved the quality of life for Haemophiliacs in the UK. BPL also produces Human Albumins and Immunoglobulins, the latter are widely used by the medical services in the prevention of tetanus, chicken pox and hepatitis for example.

BPL is part of the National Health Service and furthermore falls under the umbrella of the National Blood Authority (NBA). T he NBA is a Special Health Authority and was formed out of the Central Blood Laboratories Authority in 1993. The NBA is also responsible for the operation of the collection of blood and plasma through the Transfusion Centres. Pressure from a market economy has increased the rate of change within the NHS and BPL operates in an increasingly more competitive market place.

BPL's Total Quality Facilitator, Bill Moir, explains; "We have major competitors in Northern Europe and North America. Our customers display brand loyalty to our product because our raw material is given to us by blood donors. Our product is highly regarded because of the way it is collected and tested. The NBA ensure those procedures are undertaken

Bill Moir
Total Quality Facilitator
Bio Broducts Laboratory

in the safest of all possible conditions. We supply a very high quality product, but our competitors seek to compete on price and hospitals are under pressure because of the increasing amount of restriction on their finances, and are tending to focus more on price."

Government protectionism has been replaced by the concepts of customer service, marketing and competitive pricing. Previously the products from BPL were simply distributed throughout hospitals, whereas now they have to be sold. From the sale of their products to Health Authorities and hospitals, the turnover each month for BPL exceeds £4 million.

Although BPL is part of the NHS, the organisation originated from the Institute of Preventive Medicine which was set up by Bacteriologist Joseph Lister in the latter years of the 1800s. Joseph Lister, amidst opposition from the anti vaccination league, received patronage from Lord Iveaugh, a friend of the Prince of Wales, and was able to find a suitable place to establish his Institute both in London and in Elstree at Queensberry Lodge. The Lodge was part of a 32 acre horse breeding and hackney carriage training farm, which Lister bought for £8,000 in 1902. Eight scientists lived in bachelor accommodation in the central house, which was built in 1851.

In 1954 as the scientific possibility of producing human albumin solutions and bovine factor viii was becoming apparent, the Biochemistry Department broke away from the Institute and formed the Blood Products Unit, which is now known as Bio Products Laboratory .

As a major supplier of smallpox vaccine, the Lister Institute went into liquidation in 1978, because of the reduced requirement for the vaccine, and the site was bought by the National Health Service. BPL is therefore situated on the site that was originally part of the Lister Institute.

A new Chief Executive, Richard Walker, was appointed to BPL in 1992. With a proven business background from ICI Mr Walker brought to BPL a knowledge of the pressures and commitment needed in business, and experience of implementing Total Quality Management (TQM). Mr Moir says prior to Mr Walker joining the organisation, BPL existed in an environment where meeting product standards was deemed sacred, but the attitude which essentially prevailed was that the standard would do rather than striving for continuous improvement.

"When Richard Walker joined I think he was surprised we had

survived in our previous environment. BPL had some big questions to ask itself with more competitors in the field of plasma derivatives. We had to know where we were going to be placed in the market in 10 years time, and have a corporate plan to help us get there."

An additional commitment was needed to introduce business concepts to the public sector. Because of tight budgetary constraints and the emotive nature of health care, the portfolio of health has often been a difficult ministry to reform. With increased competitiveness in blood products, BPL, under the NBA, has been criticised for selling its products on international markets, with the insinuation that the organisation was not meeting national requirements. The accusations were made worse by the fact the organisation receives its plasma from Blood Donors. BPL only sells its products on international markets if it has totally fulfilled the requirements of the NHS. This naive view makes good copy for the press, but little practical sense. In fact a more efficient use of blood products world-wide means a better UK service. However, these arguments only make it more difficult for a public sector organisation to excel in a competitive environment.

In implementing TQM it was essential for BPL to maintain its culture of traditional health care. BPL has always had a commitment and understanding of the life saving benefits of its products. Its senior staff turnover has been traditionally low, and the organisation has been recognised for its quality research and the effectiveness of its products. BPL adhere to the standards set by the Medicines Control Agency (MCA) which ensures procedures and standards for quality control. BPL employs 500 people. Its workforce is comprised of highly qualified employees, one-third of whom are graduates, and a large proportion of scientists. In addition, the organisation is an equal opportunity employer with a large proportion of women in production areas.

In 1993 BPL approached Consultant Gib Hancock at Herts Quality Consultants to help the organisation implement TQM. Mr Hancock explains how he perceived the organisation when he did an initial survey, in which 12 per cent of BPL's employees were surveyed.

"What struck me was the people in the organisation had a tremendous feeling of 'public good'. They actually liked helping people to lead better lives and they were really motivated by that. A lot of people had been there for a long time, so there was a good community feeling about the place."

The initial step towards implementing TQM was to get a new consensus on what sort of an organisation BPL wanted to be. After much consultation this was formulated as a vision statement. The vision statement was derived from a wider need to ensure BPL was cost efficient, and that the organisation had the appropriate people to help implement TQM, and essentially ensure its success.

BPL's vision statement describes the organisation as the leading UK supplier of high quality plasma products in a changing environment.

This vision statement attempted to incorporate the trade strengths of one organisation while encapsulating the wider implications of the competitive make.

It states that BPL will continue to be a leader by understanding and meeting customer needs; developing new products and technologies; investing in the skills of their people; and working together for continual improvement in all their activities. To achieve the vision it is necessary to incorporate values in the organisation to focus on customers, employees, teamwork, ethics, quality, health and safety and a commitment to minimalise environmental waste. After the vision statement was written each department formulated a mission statement which had key departmental success factors to achieve their mission. Their mission statement essentially incorporates the contribution the Department will make towards developing the organisation's vision. Again extensive consultation covered concerns and ownership of all the people directly involved.

At the same time extensive training began. Initially 100 managers were taken off site for a management development seminar which was based on the principles of the teachings of Deming. Mr Hancock explains that while the organisation was up to standard in quality control, it had invested few resources into managerial development.

Because BPL only recognised career development as progression into management, many scientists moved into the position of managers. That has been the career path for many scientists at BPL.

"BPL had some superb scientists who eventually moved into managerial roles, with little help or training. The organisation now develops managerial skills and awareness through training, but some people take longer to get the TQM message than others. There are still people on a day to day basis who are influenced by the old paradigm thinking. They haven't altogether taken TQM on board, but as momentum is gained by people thinking and behaving in a new way, those who initially found it difficult to change get swept up in the change itself."

Mr Hancock explains it is essential for managers to implement changes for the benefit of the whole organisation, and not just the success of their own particular department, which was reminiscent of the old culture at BPL. This is especially significant in the allocation of budgets. Mr Hancock explains the preferred cultural change needed in the organisation: "We're trying to get away from the attitude that everyone meets their budget at the expense of the organisation. With TQM you have to look at the benefits of the whole organisation, so if one department has a surplus in budgets they could allocate it to another department who has a shortfall. The attitude that single departments operate autonomously has to be overcome to optimise the whole system."

After additional managerial seminars, six mangers were taken away for a week to be trained as instructors. Mr Hancock explains:

"The idea was to transfer specialist skills into their organisation. The six managers did presentations, and we developed an appropriate instructors guide for them to pass on the basic TQM concepts and skills into BPL. I provided them with support materials, and they had manuals and overheads to help them in their training courses."

The six instructors conducted two types of courses for the remainder of the workforce. A short course was aimed at giving an employee the general tools and techniques of TQM, and was primarily chosen by production operators and some of the office staff. A longer course focused more on conceptual thinking and the philosophy of TQM, such as brainstorming, process flow charts, deployment flow charts, and statistics process control. Mr Moir says employees could choose which course they went on.

"We were really quite excited about the course because we hadn't done much in-house training before. We thoroughly enjoyed it because every week we saw different groups of people. It was great to see my colleagues, who were new to teaching, improve and develop their techniques, and to see how they incorporated personal anecdotes into the training.

People started to get excited, and submit improvement ideas. At the end of the courses we asked employees to use the tools and techniques of TQM. We asked people who submitted ideas to talk to their respective managers and form Quality Improvements Teams to work on improving processes. It seemed, to some members of staff, that in the past their managers hadn't listened to them when they had suggested improvements."

In the public sector, the area of health has been notorious for generating waste because of the sheer spending power generated from massive budgets. It is essential for BPL to strive to reduce waste. Several beneficial outcomes have eventuated from the formation of Quality Improvements Teams. A department within the organisation was throwing away perfectly good boxes when re-packaging samples when the boxes were surplus to requirement. One of the Production Operatives in the department who sounded the alarm had known this had been happening for a long time, and couldn't understand why the boxes were being thrown away. As a result of this improvement BPL saved £40,000 by reducing waste.

Another improvement was made in the departments which ensure product quality standards. Mr Moir explains:

"The Materials Management section orders chemicals from our suppliers. They are delivered to the warehouse who allocate the chemicals to the Quality Standards section, who supply Chemistry section with samples. Chemistry then supply the results back to Quality Standards who supply Materials Management with materials for processing. All three departments rely on each other and operate within a chain. What was happening was Materials Management was ordering chemicals in bulk, so for two days every month chemicals were flooding into the organisation, and there was a problem with storage. Because of this the Chemistry department also had too many batches of chemicals sent down to them. Few of the managers realised this was happening, until one manager decided it would be a good idea to agree a release date for chemicals. The department selected people who worked on the problem. We talked about who the internal supplier and customer was, and where the ownership of the process was. When people started talking about the problem they gained a better understanding of the processes involved. We now 'drip feed' chemicals into the three departments."

Mr Moir says that particular team also realised the importance of approaching the external supplier when something was unsatisfactory. The perception which initially arose from the team was that because BPL were a relatively small manufacturer they would not be viewed as being important to the external suppliers: "We learnt a lot from this exercise . You cannot be of the mindset that because you're a small customer nobody's going to be bothered. The fact is there are lots of organisations out there who are implementing TQM so there is a need for a better understanding of the relationship between customers and suppliers."

According to Mr Moir it is important to keep Quality Improvement Team meetings short and to the point. The meetings, he says, are best kept to 45 minutes maximum: "If the meetings are relatively entertaining and people are doing something they find useful, and have influence over, they feel more powerful in an organisation, because they are suddenly part of its decision-making process. It's going to be marvellous for people because empowerment is what a lot of people have wanted for a long time. People live complicated lives. They buy houses and motor cars, send their children to schools, have complex relationships, go on holidays and do the weekly shopping. We employ them to put bottles in a package, but that's no indication of who they are."

A genuine interest in the well-being of employees contributes to the cultural change at BPL, which includes assessing stress levels in the organisation. Stress management seminars offer techniques for employees to adopt in their work environment. A health care consultant, Janet Williams, conducted the initial seminars in groups of 16 to help collect data from 64 people within the organisation to assess what factors contributed to stress. The three hour seminar involved a questionnaire, and offered techniques to help reduce stress, including breathing exercises and relaxation. After the seminar Ms Williams was available for individual consultations.

"It's a matter of assessing what makes people's lives sadder than they need to be. We need to examine our staff's real concerns. They are not only concerned about wages, other issues such as adequate local bus services may by more important."

BPL is a public-sector organisation which does not measure its results in terms of profits, but because the organisation has demonstrated greater cost efficiency and a commitment to continuous improvement it has a reduced the perceived need for privatisation. Mr Moir says Central Government has been brutally efficient in setting targets in the public sector: "Some of those targets are not achievable, but BPL can certainly meet its targets because we produce therapeutic and diagnostic blood products in a manufacturing environment."

According to Mr Hancock, managing change in an organisation is a slow process. He offers his definition of TQM with the phrase "Total Quality is a State of Being."

"When there is a shared sense of purpose and guiding values, when behaviour is not influenced by fear, when action is based on meaningful data and sound prediction, when suppliers and customers accept that they are interdependent upon each other, and when the hearts, the minds and the expertise of all the people are engaged in a continual search for better ways of doing things then Total Quality becomes a search for excellence and the potential for improvement is boundless. "

As Bill Moir states; "You need to know where you're starting from and where you're going to. It's hard to relate that to essential change in the organisation in order to achieve the vision statement. It is paramount to identify what needs to be done and the process changes which need to be made in order to develop the vision and become the Organisation whose future would be secure and to which everybody would be proud to belong. That's what BPL are doing with their Total Quality Process'."

Albert Hickman
Manufacturing Manager
Thorn Lighting – Spennymoor

25

"Best North East Factory"

— Thorn Lighting —

IN 1993, Thorn Lighting's Spennymoor plant won Management Today's Best Factory Award in two categories – Household Products and Best North East Factory. The same year the company won numerous other awards including Barclays Company of the Year award. As part of the 'Inside UK Enterprise' programme the factory is one of the most visited model sites in the UK. Yet, just ten years previously the plant was in decline and suffering from the traditional ills all British industry seemed to be facing after decades of malaise.

The radical change and improvements the Spennymoor plant has undergone are a clear example of what can be achieved when workers and management understand that the problems facing them are caused by competition from the international market place and not each other.

Thorn Lighting is one of the world's premier lighting manufacturers. The company specialises in the professional light fittings and control gear market. It has operations in 28 countries, eight with manufacturing facilities. Thorn Lighting employs over 4,000 people around the world and serves more than 100 global markets. Following its buy out from Thorn EMI plc in September 1993 in a £162 million deal, the company is now Europe's largest independent light fittings company.

The factory at Spennymoor, County Durham, employs 1,100 people to design and manufacture lighting equipment. The main product is fluorescent lighting for shops, factories – in fact most types of commercial and domestic premises.

A visit to Thorn's design and test centre illustrates the vital difference lighting can make to any setting. The facility has rooms specially equipped to allow customers to assess various lighting options

In retail environments, such as supermarkets, lighting is considered a vital marketing tool, poor lighting is well known as a major turn-off for shoppers. In factories studies have shown that lighting contributes to productivity, simply changing your lighting could see a major improvement in output.

Thorn's facility gives lighting designers the opportunity to test their ideas but some designers prefer to fit out actual stores to ensure the set-up is just right. This degree of precision often means Thorn Lighting is called on to customise items and produce products to order. Despite the huge range of products in Thorn's range, 50 per cent of the factory's output is made to order. Speed and flexibility have become vital as these products generally need to be produced to the tight deadlines common to the building and interior design industry.

The design facility has been moved from Enfield (hundreds of miles away) to a new technology centre (about 100 yards from the production area) which is fibre-optically linked to the fabrication area. Previously production problems related to design were unable to be dealt with immediately, this created a bottle neck while designers found the time to travel to Spennymoor.

The new technology centre has been built in place of what was a finished goods warehouse. The warehouse was no longer required as the improvement process eliminated the need for £4 million worth of inventory.

As well as the design centre, the Spennymoor plant houses a wide range of process technologies which contribute to the assembly and manufacture of lighting systems. These processes include electronics assembly, plastic injection moulding and sheet metal fabrication.

Thorn has been making light fittings at Spennymoor since 1951. 'Pop pack fittings, transistorised gear and high volume control gear were transferred from other sites to Spennymoor between 1979 and 1985. The transfer created a consolidated manufacturing base with a higher volume and lower overhead costs.

However, in 1988 it became evident that in spite of the new investment in high volume production plant and equipment the company was falling behind as a world class manufacturer.

Albert Hickman, Thorn Lighting's Manufacturing Manager explains:

"Our manufacturing director and the senior management team recognised the need for change. They were facing a decline in turnover both in the UK and our export business, which reflected a lack of confidence from customers and regrettably its own sales force. This resulted in several satellite factories around the County being closed and wholesale redundancies throughout the company.

"We identified the main causes of our problems as a combination of ineffective management /leadership, an inflexible workforce, a traditional payment by results remuneration scheme and outdated manufacturing technology. The payment by results scheme created hundreds of different wage levels. Some workers worked harder than others and were paid less.

"It was an environment of 'I'm alright Jack' with no focus on factory performance or customer service. Poor communications between the management and workforce resulted in a lack of trust and an 'us and them' mentality – there was no ownership by the people of their company."

Further problems were created by the wide spread of unions represented on the site. Although not militant, the various unions created enertia and hindered change. Demarcation and poor training inhibited the cross-functional use of labour making the workforce inflexible. Absenteeism was high with an average of 14 per cent of workers not at work on any particular day.

The manufacturing process itself was outdated making the cost of manufacturing too high. Old machinery and traditional methods were used. The process was fragmented and didn't allow the full variety of products to be produced. Component supply from a large supplier base (over 450 different suppliers) was poor. Work-in-progress and the stocks of finished goods were high and the wrong types of products were being produced. The main problem with the manufacturing process was that products were produced in a large batch, large volume basis. The warehouses were being filled with products that weren't being sold. This unresponsiveness to customer needs resulted in bad service.

A strategic approach was needed to halt the slide and equip the company for survival in the 1990s. Management recognised that the competitive edge would come from the company's people, having realised that with each pair of hands they received a free brain. To maximise this resource the employees needed to own both the company and the change process. The issue of ownership became the key. The challenge became to

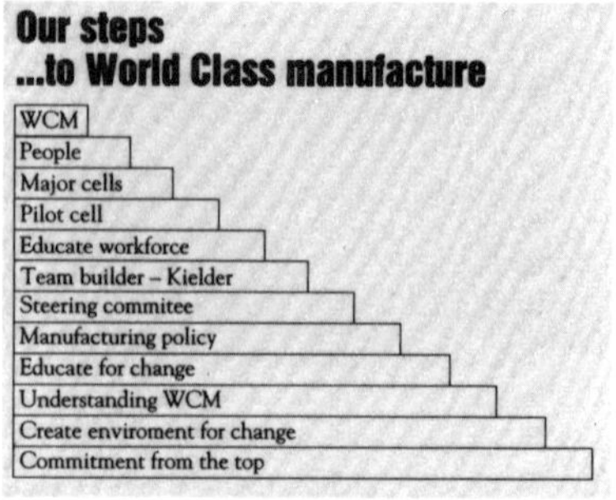

help the 1,100 people to understand the direction that Thorn needed to go and to change 40 years of attitudes and traditions.

The 'Route to World Class Manufacturing' begun by Thorn Lighting in 1988 is represented by the company as a series of steps (see **figure 1**). These steps are a lesson for any organisation seeking to emulate Thorn's admirable performance. It is important to recognise that these steps were not taken individually but were concurrent activities.

1. Commitment From The Top

It was vitally important for everyone to see and more importantly to feel that there was a long term philosophy of continuous improvement. It was equally important that everyone was committed to change. Albert Hickman reinforces the importance of this step:

"Commitment from the top is vital, because if you haven't got that you can pack up and go home, you'll fail. It's the people at the top that create the vision, provide the resource and the support to succeed. We've been fortunate in Thorn Lighting for many years, we have had that commitment from the top. The commitment has to be genuine and sincere and everybody in the plant must believe it is a long term philosophy and not just the flavour of the month. You can't get 1,100 people into a room and say we are rubbish tonight and we're going to be world class tomorrow – that just doesn't work."

2. Create The Environment For Change

Management Structure

The existing multi-tiered management structure inhibited communication. Three layers of management were eliminated – a reduction from seven levels to four and the status of the first line supervisor was elevated. This helped push ownership of the manufacturing process further down the organisation as well as improving the speed of communications and decision making.

Team Briefing

The Industrial Society was used to train Managers and Supervisors in 'Team Briefing'. The plant stops for half an hour each month and everyone is briefed on the company's performance and other aspects of the business. The brief is cascaded down from the managing director. The most confidential information such as profit forecasts is shared with the workforce and this level of trust has been rewarded. The 'Team Briefing' has become a two way process with input on issues being fed back to management.

New Productivity Scheme

The acceptance, after months of negotiation and initial refusal, of a new productivity scheme paved the way for flexible working and ended restrictive demarcation practices. The new productivity scheme was voted on by the work force and the first ballot went against the new proposals. Management, working with the Shop stewards addressed the workers again and this time majority support was obtained.

The new scheme encouraged a focus on total factory performance and customer service, rather than individual rewards. In 1992 the scheme was totally removed and replaced with a guaranteed wage – people are now motivated for the right reasons – productivity and customer service performance has greatly improved.

Skilled/Semi-skilled – Flexibility

The removal of the incentive and job evaluation schemes paved the way for flexible working and ended restrictive demarcation practices. For example, an agreement was reached under which mechanical tradesmen receive extra training and a pay increase in return for being available to do any mechanical job in the factory, a similar agreement exists for electrical tradesmen.

Removal of Inspection Function

Over sixty inspectors were employed in production areas checking to see if what the operator produced was correct – a non-value added activity. They were all removed and integrated with production teams where everyone became responsible for the quality of their products. There was an immediate increase in productivity and a reduction in quality costs.

Open Honest relationship with Trade Unions

The number of union representatives were reduced, now nine shop stewards represent the entire workforce.

Regular communication and discussions with both Senior Trade

Union representatives and local shop stewards were held, involving them in the change process and utilizing their 'powers of persuasion' to the full.

3. Understanding World Class Manufacturing

Management attended seminars held by Coopers & Lybrand and US manufacturing guru, Richard Schonberger. Visits were made to World Class Manufacturing companies including Black & Decker, IBM, ICL and Nissan. These visits were undertaken in order to understand fully the implications behind the concept and as a learning process.

Schonberberger's World Class Manufacturing methodology was adopted as the best approach for the plant. "In contrast to some of the alternatives that we looked at, what we liked about Schonberger's strategy was his hard, techniques-based approach," stated Albert Hickman.

Schonberger said "bring your machines and equipment together for families of products into a manufacturing cell and put into them highly motivated teams of people who are trained in World Class manufacturing principles (Just-in-Time, Total Productivity Maintenance, Statistical Process control, Kanban etc.) – give it to them and let them run the business." He also believes that management should: "Keep it simple. Simple is cheap; simple is flexible; simple is visible and simple is reliable."

In addition the following objectives were developed:

(i). Cost reduction through effective inventory control, scrap reduction, work efficiency and total preventative maintenance.

(ii). Better delivery performance through good planning and control and reduced lead/set up times.

(iii). Greater customer satisfaction through Total Quality Control achieved via right-first-time and zero defects procedure.

4. Educate for change

Senior Management recognised that their enthusiasm and commitment alone would not be sufficient to push the changes through. They needed to share the vision.

The support of other key individuals – production managers, key engineers and senior union officials was seen as vital. These people were sent to presentations by Schonberger and visits to Black & Decker, IBM, ICL and Nissan.

They became the 'disciples' of the new concept and played a key role in selling it to the rest of the workforce.

5. Manufacturing Policy

Central to the success of the changes has been the manufacturing policy which provides a clear description of the principles and policies adopted.

Senior managers went off-site, facilitated by a consultant called David Francis to translate their vision into a policy.

As well as developing a company mission statement, every activity of the company was covered in this policy document. Management commitment and ownership was achieved as each section is championed by a senior manager. It was given to the workforce – a cross-section of employees went off-site, analysed the contents and identified things that they felt should be included or excluded. Their proposals were presented to the senior management team back on site, Changes were implemented and a final document completed. Manufacturing Director Terry Smith regards the policy document as the 'bible':

"The Manufacturing Policy Document is now in its sixth edition, our managers are responsible for continually driving the policies. The document also serves as an educational resource which enables management to communicate and share our vision throughout the plant."

The document addresses all aspects of the changes and reinforces the company's commitment to its employees. It is presented in an easy to read format and given to every employee so they are aware and feel part of the changing environment.

MISSION STATEMENT

Our mission is to be a World Class Supplier of Lighting Solutions.

By involving all employees in the process of continuous improvement, we will exceed our internal and external customers expectations, providing quality products and service at a competitive price, ensuring the profitable long term growth of the Company.

(Quality definition 'Conformance to requirements')

6. **Steering Committee**

To plan and manage proactively all aspects of the change process, a committee of Senior Managers was appointed. It encourages employee involvement and ownership by establishing cross-functional and cross grade task forces – which include union representation, to examine specific change issues.

One such team, headed by a 'disciple' (production Manager) was given the responsibility of designing and implementing the initial 'pilot cell', (Schonberger said "start with a success") which was to provide the foundation for the focused factory concept of stand alone cells where product families were manufactured in their entirety.

The teams submitted reports and presented their findings to the steering committee for approval. The reports recommended the management structure, plant layout, space requirements and manning levels etc. Once approval has been given the task force is then empowered to implement the recommendations and establish the cell.

7. **Team Building – Kielder**

An essential ingredient of cellular manufacturing is the ability of individuals to work together in a flexible team environment. To help develop this new attitude and to break down any feelings of resistance, team building training for all employees was conducted on a voluntary basis over a number of weekends at a management training centre in Kielder Forest, Northumbria.

Teams drawn from across the hierarchy and functions worked together to solve a variety of tasks in a challenging off-site setting. The purpose was to demonstrate the advantages of real team work through outdoor activities such as building a raft. The exercises proved that everyone, no matter what their position, could contribute to the successful outcome of a task. In addition, it gave senior managers an opportunity in an informal setting to explain where the company was going and what the employees' role was going to be. The adoption of new manufacturing techniques was the only way to ensure the company's long term survival.

Initial workforce reluctance to attend was overcome when union representatives volunteered to go first and returned full of enthusiasm and commitment to the training.

Team building training is widely perceived as playing an important role in changing attitudes – to date over 950 of the 1,100 employees have attended with each weekend of 25 people costing approximately £4000 – a powerful sign of management's commitment to change.

8. Educate Workforce

In addition to team building the workforce was equipped with the skills and knowledge to carry out their new roles. They were educated in the benefits of, and received skills training in World Class Manufacturing techniques. Schonberger videos were shown and training given in JIT, preventative maintenance (TPM), statistical process control (SPC) and the concept of continuous improvement and problem solving methods.

The senior management believed that the more employees were educated, the more receptive and responsive to change they would be.

9. Pilot Cell

In April 1988 the cellular manufacturing concept was initially piloted for the Discharge Gear products. Responsibility for its operation, including Quality, was devolved down to the cell manager and his team, drawn from the initial task group. Realistic objectives – in terms of reduced changeover/set up times, scrap and work in progress (WIP) – were established and achieved: changeover times were down by 83 per cent and WIP by 99 per cent. The pilot cell, positioned in a prominent location, not only tested the concept but acted as a highly visible symbol of the benefits of the cell philosophy. Its advantages in terms of both improved working environment and efficiency was clearly visible to the whole workforce and the initiative was widely accepted.

10. Major Cells

As a result of the pilot's success, major cells were launched across the plant. As with the Discharge Gear cell, each was constructed with full employee involvement and is based around a family of products. All involve flexible work practices with theQuality inspection function removed and an emphasis on waste elimination and responsiveness to market demand.

11. Continuous Improvement ...Thro' People

The new manufacturing strategy based on World Class Manufacturing principles brought with it many changes, but none greater than that of the change in attitude of the whole workforce. More than £2 million has been invested in training at Spennymoor. This was recognised in 1992 by the presentation of a National Training Award by His Royal Highness, the Prince of Wales.

Through a four year education and training programme, including internal plant tours, everyone appreciates where the company is going and the role they are expected to play in its success. The company is committed to training with £1 million spent on training in the last financial year.

The eleven steps outlined above were just the foundations for continuous improvement at Thorn Lighting Spennymoor.

The next stage has seen a focus on changing the culture. The initiative builds on World Class Manufacturing to create a Total Quality Management environment which is known as World Class Excellence.

The initiative allows teams from every function in the company to integrate fully and to focus resources and efforts towards total satisfaction for both internal and external customers.

Continuous Improvement facilitators have been trained to support these groups and make them more effective. Their role is to provide training guidance, help and to free up any obstructions.

A Right First Time – Every Time principle has been adopted and is becoming a way of life that will eliminate waste in the organisation, reduce the cost of manufacture, improve quality and delivery and increase profitability. Albert Hickman explains:

"Every single person in Thorn Lighting has a contribution to make. It is staggering that the industry standard for the cost of quality – that is getting it wrong – is between 20 and 30 per cent of turnover, which in our manufacturing area alone amounts to £25 million. We have a lot of potential profit at our finger tips."

A drive to reduce material costs has also been undertaken. Terry Smith, an advocate of cost control, points out that material costs comprise between 50 and 80 per cent of a typical products' cost and don't involve any expense to reduce.

Terry Smith's philosophy is to identify an item's cost and then challenge the need for that particular type of component. He has established Value Analysis teams which have been highly trained in cost reduction and value engineering techniques. The teams, comprised of design and production engineers, are focused on a certain area and to maintain a sense of urgency are disbanded after six months. Terry Smith believes that the six Value Analysis teams that he has in operation at any one time save the plant £1 million a year.

A supplier reduction and development programme has also been established to form partnerships with suppliers. The original supplier base of 580 has been reduced to 260 and 50 per cent of the plant's £44 million material purchases are single sourced.

Momentum is maintained by monitoring and measuring performance using benchmark techniques and also from the continued commitment of the senior management.

Albert Hickman proudly concludes:

"We have transformed the Spennymoor factory into one of the most modern Light Fittings and Gear factories in Europe. The factory is clean and attractively presented – a good environment to work in.

The achievement we are most proud of, however, is the change of attitude that has taken place with our employees.

Gone are the restrictive practices that have dogged British Industry for so many years. We now have people and equipment that are totally responsive to change.

The results speak for themselves: production changeovers now take only minutes, whereas previously they took hours – perhaps even days. This means we can economically produce short-runs, have shorter lead times and generally be more receptive to our customers' needs in the 1990s and beyond."

The Employment Service

26

Working For Change

— The Employment Service —

"FOR the Employment Service to make the changes we had to make, a new management style was needed throughout the organisation. We needed to give everyone a clear understanding of what their roles and responsibilities were and become more output orientated.

"I wanted an environment that would encourage innovation, allow flexibility, promote responsibility and help people feel accountable. Together we had to create a culture which promoted candour and fostered new ideas." – Mr Mike Fogden, Chief Executive of the Employment Service.

The Employment Service is a semi-autonomous Government Executive Agency and was part of the Employment Department Group. As Chief Executive, Mr Fogden is now responsible to the Secretary of State for Education and Employment.

The Employment Service has a network of 1,100 local offices located throughout England, Scotland and Wales. To manage these branches, England has seven regional offices, and Scotland and Wales each have their own office. The service employs approximately 40,000 people. In 1993/94, the Employment Service's operational budget was in excess of £1,390 million and £8,000 million pounds in benefit payments were made on behalf of the Department of Social Security.

The scale of the Employment Service is immense. In 1994/95 the organisation found work for over 1.25 million people; handled over 2.55 million vacancies; and made around 60 million individual benefits payments.

The concept of the 'Executive Agency' was put in place in the late 1980s. The initiative was intended to introduce new operational freedoms to some of the major bodies responsible for delivering government policy. It was expected that significant improvements in the quality and efficiency of service delivery could be achieved by removing traditional constraints and by giving agencies greater flexibility to develop practices and processes customised to their own specific needs.

Under this plan the Employment Service has been granted significantly greater management and operational freedoms than other parts of the Employment department. These freedoms apply in areas such as the employment of staff, obtaining and accounting for resources, and developing operational practices and systems.

Under the agency arrangements, the chief executive negotiates an Annual Performance Agreement with the Secretary of State, which establishes the formal targets by which the service's performance will be evaluated. Within this framework, the service then produces an operational plan detailing the steps and activities that will be undertaken to deliver the performance targets. The services against the targets are set out in its publicly available annual report.

The performance management structure is then replicated at key levels in the organisation. The directors of the regional offices agree and monitor similar performance targets, operational plans and resource allocation with the manager responsible for running each district in the region. The district managers then agree and monitor similar measures with each local office in their own districts.

The establishment of agency status for the Employment Service, and the attendant granting of greater operational freedom, has both driven and enabled much of the change that has occurred in the service in the 1990s. Alongside this core shift in the service's status, however, various other aspects of the Employment Service's structures and activities have continued to develop, in response both to developments in government policy and to more general changes in the external environment.

Some examples of these changes include:

- Rising unemployment in the early 1990s and increased needs of unemployed people required the Employment Service to develop and extend the range of employment programmes. The Employment Service has introduced a 'Jobseeker's Charter', which sets out the nature and the standards of service which clients can expect to receive.

- In the 1980s benefit payments and job placement work were divided between two separate offices – the Unemployment Benefit Office and the Jobcentre. The integration of these two functions (despite their separate cultures) has produced improvements in both quality and efficiency by creating a single integrated local office network.
- Changes have been made to the selection criteria. The Employment Service has moved away from the traditional Civil Service reliance on educational qualifications to a competence-based selection process.
- A new remuneration structure has been developed with the introduction of performance-related pay and grading arrangements throughout the organisation.
- Major improvements have been made to the Service's information technology systems. In one of the biggest civilian computer projects in Europe, the old unemployment benefit system was updated. A new Labour Market System was designed by users and is currently being introduced.
- A programme of market testing has begun, starting with support functions. The programme includes market testing the provision of Jobclubs and of services such as assessment and counselling for people with disabilities. The prospect of market testing has been an additional motivation towards exploiting the potential quality and efficiency benefits which come from the greater flexibility of agency status.

To take the Employment Service forward a package of 'ES Essentials' which includes critical success factors has been developed. These values and characteristics were identified through a series of meetings and workshops held by senior management. These sessions resulted in some broad views about the new organisation, particularly in areas such as empowerment, open communications, quality, and respect and fair treatment of employees.

This work was useful in helping the senior team to clarify its thinking about how the organisation should develop.

Aim

The aim of the Employment Service is to promote a competitive, efficient and flexible labour market by helping into work unemployed people, especially those who are disadvantaged, and to pay benefits and allowances to those who are entitled to them.

Objectives

The objectives of the Employment Service are:

- to offer unemployed people, particularly the longer-term unemployed and others at a disadvantage in the labour market, help and advice in finding work or appropriate training;

- to advise unemployed people claiming benefits or allowances on their entitlements, obligations, and responsibilities and to help and to pay those who are eligible promptly and accurately;
- to offer people with disabilities particular help and advice in finding and retaining work or appropriate training and to help and encourage employers to make work or training opportunities available to them;
- to identify, investigate and where appropriate take action to prosecute those suspected of benefit fraud or of colluding in it;
- to provide services to all its clients in accordance with the standards and expectations set out in the Jobseeker's Charter;
- to manage the delivery of all its programmes and services efficiently, effectively and economically, and within the resources available.

The Employment Service has also outlined the 'outputs by which we are judged' these are:

Annual Performance Agreement

Meet APA targets which reflect client needs and government priorities.

Living Within Our Means

At every level in the Employment Service, use the resources committed to us properly and effectively.

Value For Money

Quality and continuous improvement at every level to deliver the same for less or more for the same.

The way to achieve the desired outcomes is made possible by a number of critical success factors:

- People – A capable, well trained, committed and flexible workforce.
- Products and Services – Responsive to labour market and client needs;
- Resources – To secure and manage the resources required to deliver its aims and objectives;
- Infrastructure – Complete integration and timely delivery of business led systems;
- Management and Organisational Structure – An open and honest managerial approach built on delegation so that decisions are taken at the most effective point providing clear lines of responsibility and

An environment which celebrates success and learns from mistakes, encourages teamwork and treats people with decency and fairness.

- External relationships – Ensure the Employment Service has a positive and productive relationship with all customers and stakeholders. The agency seeks to maintain the confidence of ministers and effective working relationships with TECs, etc.

Simply developing a statement of values and aims is not sufficient to build ownership. The organisation began to take active steps to translate these values into reality for employees in their every-day work.

Mr Fogden sees internal and external surveys as an important step:"I had set out my own understanding of where I wanted to lead the organisation. I told my colleagues that we now had a clear picture of what was expected of the Employment Service (ES) and what we wanted of people working in the organisation.

"If I had to pick one key piece of infrastructure that has paid the most dividends in terms of providing a touchstone in seeking to manage change and to develop a new culture, it was our decision in 1988 to establish the annual Employment Service Staff Attitude Survey. The survey is carried out each November. We have asked around 20 per cent of Employment Service people, covering all our functions and geographical spread, a series of questions to elicit their view of the organisation, its development and management and their job. We have retained a common series of questions so that we now have a reliable time series to begin to plot shifts over time. We can also compare ourselves to other organisations running comparable surveys. The Employment Service questionnaires cover issues under five broad headings:

(i). Job Satisfaction.
(ii). Organisational image (which includes views on the management of change).
(iii). Communications.
(iv). Development and training.
(v). Personnel issues.

"Generally the shifts in the views of people within the ES have been positive in direction, certainly in terms of the factors within our control. The organisation does, however, accept that it needs to continue to learn from experience."

In parallel, the agency also runs a National Customer Satisfaction

Survey which provides valuable data on what the people using the service think and which aspects are of most concern to them. The survey is carried out each year by an independent organisation. Mr Fogden believes that in a changing environment, these surveys have been an invaluable insight into the reactions of the people who are both carrying through the changes and whom the changes are affecting.

"The Employment Service vision was used as the basis for a series of 'capability' workshops where managers assessed the ES position and its capability to move towards and eventually reach the vision – essentially bridging the gap between where we were and where we wanted to be.

"We also made the decision to bring in outside consultants to work with us on the analysis and design of our change programme. The key criterion was that the consultants should be able to work with us in identifying areas for change and implementing them.

"The findings from the capability workshops were distilled into nine change requirements, we identified principles which the ES change programme should satisfy. These principles were based on output from the capability workshops, interviews and further development work. Change activities should:

- Be flexible enough to adapt to different labour markets and different political administrations.
- Relate directly to the changes required.
- Be coherent and co-ordinated.
- Be integrated with existing and developing activities.
- Be practicable and affordable.
- Be manageable, measurable and in prioritised steps.
- Be undertaken to reflect the new vision and values.
- Demonstrate senior management's commitment to change.

"The change requirements and the design principles were developed into a programme for action. It was vital that the change programme should not be just a head office 'bolt on'. Thus the 'Agency Development Programme' was devised, consisting of six 'workstreams', each consisting of a particular block of work. This issue of accountability for the programme was tackled by assigning each of the six workstreams to an individual member of the Executive Board.

"The six workstreams were: Roles and Accountabilities; External

Relationships; Organisational Performance/Developing support arrangements; Developing the Culture; Developing Managers; and Individual Performance.

"The workstreams were thus identified separately but we intended them to integrate closely with one another and provide a coherent approach to meeting the ES change requirements. The sixth workstream – Individual Performance – was envisaged as having the potential to draw the other workstreams together at the level of the individual", says Mr Fogden.

Centrally, a Change Management Unit was established to support the board and to facilitate improvements. The Change Management Unit is a small group of people who work with managers throughout the Employment Service to help them develop a more innovative approach to achieving business objectives.

This interchangeable team works within the organisation and focuses on the way it is progressing towards the goals set out in 'ES Essentials'.

Barbara Wiles from the Change Management Unit outlined her thoughts on the unit's role:

"Although culture is one word for this process of development, our practical approach to the job tells us that it is really about 'the way we do things around here'.

"We work with managers and their people to help them move towards the desired culture in a way that suits them best and fits in with their time scales. Our goal, like everyone's in the Employment Service, is to help achieve improved business performance."

The Change Management Unit works with all levels (District; Regional; and national) and all grades. Staff from the unit may operate as a catalyst or guest speaker at workshops; or to organise and facilitate events in response to general requests. Individuals can also use the Unit as consultants for particular problems around the management of change.

"We have expertise in running special business management workshops with our colleagues from the National Training Centre, developing networks, using the latest business tools for measuring individual and organisational behaviour, offering advice on developing and evaluating questionnaires, spreading good practice and information on a range of management, organisational and cultural topics. We have skills in video production and believe it to be a useful tool. We also have a wide range of contacts both within and outside the ES so if we can't give our people an answer it won't take us long to find out!" Says Ms Wiles.

Mr Fogden believes that the Change Management Unit has been very successful as a resource to support the regions and areas in their change initiatives.

To further develop an Employment Service culture in which creative work practices and ideas for maximising value for money and delivering business objectives are encouraged, recognised and promoted throughout ES, a series of actions have been undertaken.

Improvements were identified through a series of Local Office Manager workshops, where managers drawn from each of the regions were invited to explore the concept of creativity and innovation and what made it effective. The group was encouraged to share examples of good practice and the results which impacted favourably on performance. 'Creative Business' events were held throughout the areas to replicate the process.

One problem that was encountered at these events was the perception of managers that they had little control or influence over day-to-day operation and that it was important to involve the area management team. This type of problem is not unique to the Employment Service but it is likely to be more significant in the public sector than private, particularly where the organisation is responsible for the disbursement of public money. The role and circumstances of Public Sector organisations limit those organisations' freedom to act, no matter how much the managers want to empower people. In order to tackle this perceived problem the ES Change management Unit facilitated workshops for complete area management teams. An 'Organisational Culture Inventory' was used to assess the culture of the team and work up ways around any problems in performance.

A database of innovative action was established and managers were asked to assemble examples of innovative practice in their regions and directorates. The concept was taken to inter-regional events to broaden the base of involvement.

Good examples were established as pilots in which local managers were encouraged and supported both by their manager and by the change manager. Two major initiatives have been successful – 'Pet Hates' and 'Simplified Circulars'. The Pet Hates initiative was designed to encourage people in local offices to challenge existing bits of bureaucracy which appeared to add no value to the Agency's work and find alternative and/or improved ways of operating the process or get rid of it entirely. One important aspect of this initiative was the emphasis on local people involved in making any local initiative succeed or fail. The Simplified Circular initiative was prompted by demands from the original Innovative managers group to be allowed to determine locally how any given head office instruction was implemented.

To maintain momentum for change and improvement the process is repeated and lessons have been learnt by ES as a whole. Positive recognition and support from senior management is given to the managers and staff undertaking the initiatives and videos have been produced to address the issues and encourage people to relate the ES vision to their day-to-day work.

There have been a variety of activities and approaches adopted by individual regions. These include various Total Quality methodologies, employee and management development techniques and development designed to meet external standards such as ISO 9000 and Investors in People.

For example, the management of the West Midland region have been successful through their use of Total Quality philosophies. The decision to introducc a Total Quality approach in thc West Midlands reflected a range of factors, in addition to the fundamental, organisation-wide changes that were occurring as a result of the move towards agency status, was the fact that the West Midlands had been traditionally seen as one of the service's least successful performers, consistently failing to deliver the standards of performance required by national targets.

Various attempts had been made to improve performance, including a regular and highly intensive process of performance management which involved the regional director investigating highly detailed figures produced by local offices with the aim of identifying problems or inaccuracies which could then be corrected. In retrospect, this process can be seen as part of the problem – encouraging a culture that was more concerned with covering up problems rather that resolving them. Success was measured in terms of the Manager's ability to come through the review process unscathed.

In the face of these problems, the region's former director, Martin

Raff, believed that the changes throughout the Employment Service offered an opportunity to radically alter the operation.

Martin Raff was a relatively long-serving member of the ES, who was accustomed to the traditional ways of thinking in the Civil Service, with a style and approach that was top down, bureaucratic and centralist.

Despite this background, Martin Raff, supported by a team of full-time quality facilitators in the region, rapidly became a strong advocate of Total Quality. Because he was respected for his more traditional role and skills in the service, his advocacy of the new approaches rapidly began to win many converts in the region.

Before 1989, Mr Raff's knowledge of Total Quality was virtually non-existent; it was in 1989 that he visited the Nissan Factory in County Durham. Having heard of the steps taken by Nissan to improve performance, Mr Raff was curious to see if any of the techniques could be applied in a service environment. The visit demonstrated that employees could work together in ways which were very different. Martin Raff comments on the visit:

"There were enthusiastic teams, empowered to improve their performance and using statistical analysis to do so. Although Nissan operates in a very different environment from us there was no reason why many of the techniques could not be directly translated in to a service environment. We could use Nissan's techniques to unlock a significant reservoir of individual talent and commitment."

Thus enlightened, Mr Raff looked at various models such as Deeming, Crosby and Juran, eventually settling on Deeming's methods to introduce the programme. Training for senior and junior staff members began over the next 18 months and skills such as brainstorming, flowcharting, fishbone diagrams, data collection, Pareto analysis and the production of quality charts for measurement were taught.

Initially, middle managers were not focused upon but it soon became apparent that this layer of management required special care as they felt they were "being pulled in a dozen different directions" as a result of the changes. Later the region drew on the work of Juran and sought to move away from merely achieving smaller incremental changes towards 'breakthrough' (radical and sustained) performance improvements.

Each step the West Midlands Employment Service has taken has highlighted for them how much they still need to do and helped them along to the next phase. The region has since moved on to large-scale organisational alignment and plans to look at overall management and operational processes.

As a result of the initiatives described above, the West Midlands region has made substantial improvements in its operational performance and undergone a discernible change in culture.

The example of West Midlands is just one of many improvements the Employment Service has undergone. The regular surveys have shown considerable improvements since 1989.

The Employment Service has recently introduced a new change project to refresh earlier programmes and to help people cope with further major changes which will refocus the core business and reduce costs.

Mr Fogden concludes with his views for the future: "We have made some comparisons with outside organisations and the results have been encouraging, in fact, many of our results are reassuring but there are no grounds for complacency.

"We have relaunched our suggestion scheme (called Thinking Aloud) and we really want to maximise the networking and informal exchange of ideas to share all achievements across the organisation and sustain progress in the face of continuing external change.

"The Employment Service has earned a good reputation in responding to new opportunities, we must now be ready to meet fresh challenges."

Trevor Walton
Quality Manager
Davy International

27

Building on a Quality Foundation

—Davy International – Stockton—

THE development of the Quality culture at Davy International's Stockton operation has closely mirrored the evolution of Quality principles in the UK. It has progressed from a system driven by inspection through Quality control and Quality assurance procedures to the ultimate infusion of Total Quality Management throughout the entire organisation.

Davy International Stockton was established in 1873 and today employs approximately580 people at its offices in Stockton-on-Tees in the North East of England. From here it provides a comprehensive range of project services from consultancy to design, procurement and sub-contract manufacturing, to construction and commissioning which it has engaged for the successful implementation of numerous projects from Australia to Zimbabwe.

The Davy Group, a member of the Trafalgar House group of companies, employs 4,000 people in operating centres around the world including Sheffield, Poole and Stockton in the United Kingdom; South Africa; Clecim in France; Cosim in Spain; Pittsburgh and San Franciso in the United States; Canada; and Chile.

Davy International Stockton has effectively managed Quality issues throughout its history by constantly emphasising the importance of 'getting it right the first time'. Its mature systems and procedures were developed over many years to satisfy customers from the iron and steel sector, the energy sector, and the nuclear industry in particular. For many years Davy Engineers had been required to adhere to a whole range of standards including nuclear standards and as a result had been exposed to rigorous quality system requirements. When the industry requirement emerged for third party accreditation to ISO9001 Davy International Stockton was in a ready position to simply adjust its existing procedures.

There is nothing new about Quality Assurance standards in the engineering profession as illustrated in Figure 1 detailing the history of Quality assurance in the United Kingdom. In the 1970s and 1980s Davy

THE HISTORY OF QUALITY ASSURANCE IN THE U.K.

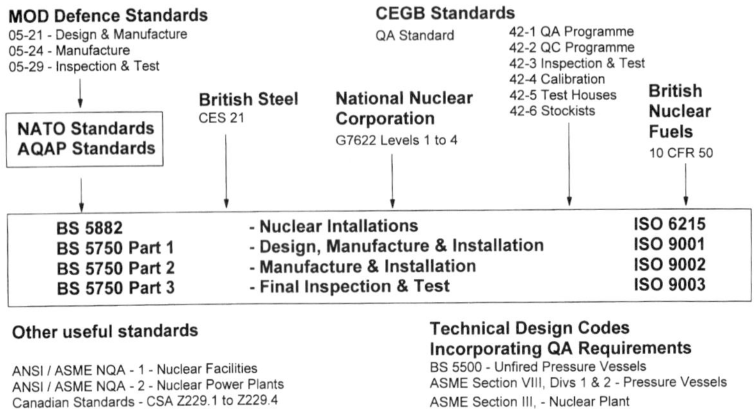

International Stockton adhered to a wide range of client national standards which were applied to projects according to contract requirements, industry and plant location. The requirement for strict adherence to the various standards resulted in the rapid growth of client second party pre-contract assessment and post contract audits which were both repetitive and time consuming. The standards of self assessment also varied from very thorough assessments by clients involved in the nuclear industry to cursory visits from assessors from other industries.

As a result of the time consuming nature and duplicationarising from the variety of standards contractors were obliged to conform with the development and adoption of the British Standard 5750 (ISO9000) and the advent of third party assessment was welcomed by Davy International Stockton. It was perceived by major contractors as a means of providing more consistent application of Quality System requirements on both multi-national and domestic projects while reducing the level of client assessments.

While this is a positive scenario Davy recognises that success is dependent on rigorous application of the standard by organisations and the integrity of independent third party assessment bodies and their registered assessors.

Trevor Walton, Quality Manager for Davy International – Stockton believes that: "One of the prime benefits of the ISO9000 system in the UK is the reduction of audits we have to carry out on suppliers, but probably more important is the reduced number of audits being conducted by our own clients."

The Stockton operating centre specialises in blast furnace technology including design and rebuilding and is the world leader in this field. This activity is the primary focus of the Iron and Steel Business Division, however, the company consists of three business divisions each of which has it own sales/proposals, process design and plant layout sections. The three divisions are:

- Iron and steel
- Energy and environment including wide ranging technologies for nuclear power, energy, water/sewage treatment, incineration, and site remediation
- Minerals and non-ferrous engaged primarily in minerals and metals extraction and processing worldwide

The Iron and Steel business division is presently the largest accounting for between 50 and 60 per cent of the work on the Stockton site, while the Non-ferrous business division is the smallest absorbing 15 per cent of the workload. In recent years the area of greatest growth has been that of the Energy and Environmental division which is attributed in the main to the growth of the nuclear industry, water/sewage treatment and its off-spins although there is now a rundown in nuclear work.

Detailed design is carried out by a central engineering division which covers a wide range of engineering disciplines: civils design, structures design, mechanical plant design, pressure vessels design, fluid services design such as piping and hydraulics, electrical design and instrument design. The construction site management and quality services are also provided from the engineering division which employs over 200 people. Other separate functions include purchasing, personnel and administration which are illustrated in Figure 2.

The unique structure of Davy International Stockton encompassing

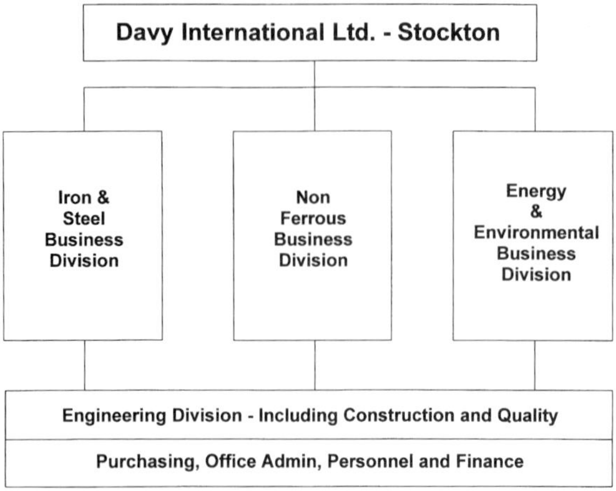

the three business areas has allowed it to weather industry fluctuations better than other Davy operating centres and some other engineering firms.

"It is a credit to the vision of the board of directors at Stockton that one of our strengths and assets is our diversity of activity. Other operating centres which focused primarily on iron and steel have gone through bad times. However, Stockton has consistently contributed profit to the group because while the iron and steel industry has been quiet, the nuclear business was growing so we were able to keep our bases loaded and keep our 580 people occupied", explains Mr Walton. Stockton has been among the top profit makers for the Davy Group every year since 1986.

Mr Walton has a background in heavy engineering, but has worked in Quality Assurance for over 18 years with a long involvement in the UK Nuclear Power Programme. He is also a Registered lead Assessor and a fellow of the Institute of Quality Assurance.

The operating procedures adopted by Davy International Stockton have existed for many years and have been progressively reviewed and updated to reflect changes in the company and in the standards. Today the three tier system includes:

Tier 1 The Quality Manual which is structured around ISO9001 and defines company policy towards meeting ISO9001 and other Quality systems and standards still in existence such as BS5882 and ANSI standards for nuclear facilities; the American Standard for Mechanical Engineering (ASME); and defence standards AQAP and NATO. This document also incorporates Davy Stockton's Quality policy statement and environmental policy statement.

Tier 2 The second tier covers three areas of documentation: company operating procedures; safety procedures including European Union legislation; and personnel, finance and administration procedures. The company operating procedures address sales and proposals; contract receipt; contract control; engineering design; purchasing and supplier Quality; and construction sites.

The above procedures were largely in place in the late 1970s but were updated to ensure consistency with BS5750 Part 1 and ISO9001 requirements.

Tier 3 Departmental Work Instructions provides detailed procedures defining how tier 2 requirements would be met at the micro level through department manuals and project specific instructions which are withdrawn after completion of the respective programmes.

It was against this background that the company was assessed against the requirements of BS5750 Part 1:1987 and achieved approval in 1988 through Lloyds Register Quality Assurance with little difficulty.

Mr Greenwood, Stockton's Engineering Director explains the advantage ISO certification provides to an engineering workforce which requires maximum flexibility in its day to day activity.

"We have a large group of engineers who may work on a nuclear project one month and on a water treatment facility the next. When working in the nuclear industry for example the checking procedures are extremely stringent and require the engineer to do an alternative calculation to check not only the answer but the logic – you may have the right answer but the wrong sum. However, there is not always the necessity or the benefit in enforcing these procedures on an engineer designing a conventional water filtration system. This presents the problem of how to get engineers working on nuclear projects one month and water treatment the next to consciously engineer down."

"We have successfully achieved this in the way we have structured our procedures. We have sufficient flexibility to allow managers and designers to choose the right approach for specific situations and there is an emphasis on the designer or manager to make the right choice for the particular piece of equipment and plant at that time. All ISO and the procedures do is allocate that responsibility to him or her in a clear fashion.

It is however important that the approach is agreed at the beginning of the contract and that the normal monitoring procedures are applied."

In 1990 BS5750 Part 1 approval was extended to worldwide construction site activity. Attaining this proved to be more difficult because of the differing nature of individual construction sites.

Each site is usually unique in terms of site facilities, services and provision of hardware, software, office administration services, and the team of site manager, key staff and mix of suppliers and subcontractors. In many instances site managers may be resistant to change preferring their own tried and tested methods. Equally lessons learnt by management and staff on sites often goes undocumented and is forgotten when a new site is established with different management and personnel.

Davy International Stockton's management system for site activities has ensured that procedures have been developed to address the above issues and particular attention has been given to site set-up, planning and education and training of site staff.

Two of Davy's primary criticisms of ISO9000 are that the specification of ISO9000 does not guarantee a perfect product and that clients and purchasers often go for the cheapest price tenders without due consideration of ISO9000 compliances.

In the first instance Mr Walton contends: "Some purchasers believe that by specifying ISO9000 and Third Party assessment they are fulfilling their responsibility to ensure a product is fit for purpose. This is a popular misconception. ISO9000 can ensure that the supplier has the right systems in place to be capable of producing a perfect product. If a product is incorrectly or poorly designed, specified or manufactured mistakes can still be made. We take the view that it removes some of the risk rather than providing a guarantee of a satisfactory product. However, when things go wrong ISO provides the mechanism to correct the error and prevent it from happening again."

The second complaint is often echoed by suppliers who have introduced ISO9000 and lost work to a competitor whom has not introduced the requirements on the basis of a lower cost bid. However, on this count Mr Walton maintains that: "Price has always been and will always be a prime consideration for clients and purchasers when choosing a supplier. ISO9000 should not be viewed as a licence to increase prices but can be used as a sales tool to improve clients' or purchasers' confidence in the supplier's ability to supply Quality products. Previously demonstrated capability and satisfactory past performance are an acceptable justification for using a particular supplier. Therefore clients and purchasers with records of satisfactory supply may legitimately choose a supplier on that basis whether that supplier holds ISO9000 approval or not."

Davy has progressed from ISO certification to TQM as the driving force of its Quality culture. "ISO certification helps you achieve certain things but it doesn't necessarily help you become a world class company. Clients are starting to expect more. Once they would ask if you had ISO, now they are asking if you run a TQM programme. We now accept that ISO is no longer a distinguishing feature when bidding for projects, although you are expected to have it as part of your system. We believe that the way ahead is to move into TQM activities in addition to ISO9000", explains Mr Walton.

The company is focused on improvement and to this end Davy International Stockton has put into operation a programme for implementing Total Quality Management which covers all the company's activities.

The TQM initiative commenced in September 1991 when a steering committee was formed and Trevor Walton was appointed as TQM manager. The steering committee chaired by Dr Barry Phillipo, Managing Director was established to promote and control the launch of TQM at Stockton.

The committee ensures that the annual programme of TQM activities is implemented and that an infrastructure is maintained to effectively action ideas submitted by individuals. It also monitors the activities of the formal improvement teams set up to investigate company wide areas for improvement.

The TQM programme is based on a foundation of strategic five year planning embodying company goals and policies; ISO9000 Certification; a common understanding of Quality aims; and systems auditing. The pinnacle of achievement is continuous improvement, the key principle of TQM. The message communicated within Davy is that continual improvement will only occur if every person critically reviews every aspect of his or her work effort and seeks to improve upon it as a continual process.

Other TQM principles adopted at Stockton include:

1. **Prevention – not Detection.** Investment in the prevention of

failures is seen as the most effective way of protecting customers by ensuring they do not receive defective goods and sub-standard services. In doing so it reduces costs incurred by waste, errors, re-work and checking.

2. **Changing Style**. All activities require clear objectives, visible performance measurements and continuous improvement in efficiency and effectiveness. Davy is developing a culture where everyone is encouraged to be supportive of colleagues and to work together as an effective team with all departmental barriers eliminated. TQM gives staff in different functions a common language for improvement.

3. **Involvement of Everyone**. An integral part of Davy's culture is that every individual must take responsibility for the quality of his or her own work and create continual pressure for constant improvement.

4. **Right First Time**. This is based on the reality that it is costly to compromise on Quality and is therefore vital if the company is to maximise its performance.

These principles are encapsulated in Figure 3 which illustrates the essential steps in achieving TQM as defined and used by Davy:

The essential steps in achieving TQM

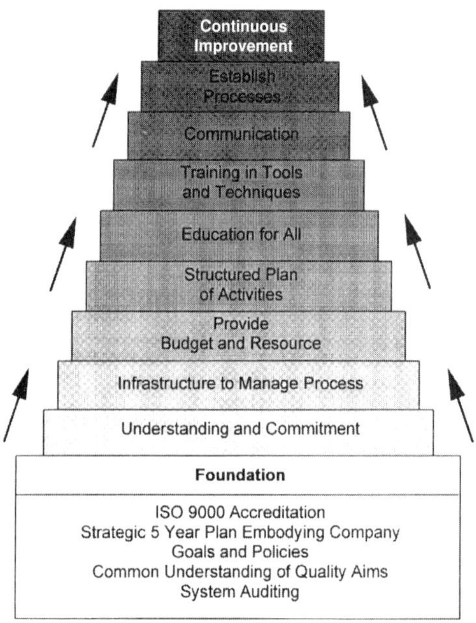

TQM was launched in January 1992, starting with an information and training seminar for all directors and senior managers. Each manager was responsible for transferring that information to his or her department in a series of one-hour briefs, supported by a member of the steering committee.

Initially two Quality Improvement Teams were established to address company wide improvements to support the departmental improvements identified and pursued throughout the company. This later increased to six teams.

An early and motivating success was recorded by a small group from the Civils and Structures Department which identified and implemented three improvements in their department within six months. The largest involved a review of the blast furnace tower design with the Iron and Steel Plant Department at a cost of 90 man-hours. The team identified savings of £100 thousand through updating the design philosophy and reducing the amount of steelwork in the towers which are on average 35 metres high and dominate the skyline on any steel plant.

A dilemma resulting from this improvement was how the organisation should quantify the resultant saving and future savings from TQM improvements. "Do you count it every time you build a new furnace as a saving that came out of a TQM initiative or every time you win a contract because it has reduced your bid by that amount", questions Mr Walton. "What we have chosen to do is count this improvement saving once and although some may argue that it is underselling the benefit derived from TQM it is consistent with our culture which largely views exaggeration and overselling as negative."

One of the original company wide Quality Improvement Teams established to review the archive systems used by Davy facilitated the disposal or recycling of 6,354 bags of records, amounting to 50.14 tonnes of paperwork which was no longer needed. Initially the team reviewed and clearly defined those records which the company needed to retain long term. Other elements reviewed included improving the location, storage and access to archives by moving them on-site and providing adequate resources.

Additional space was created in departments by transferring relevant documents to archives and converting hard copy archives to microfilm. An information database and central filing system were then established to record all archived material. The total revision of the archive process from planning to finalised implementation took 14 months and involved at various stages a seven person team and the long term cooperation of all departments.

"I think there is a high awareness of what can be achieved through TQM in this organisation because we have a number of Japanese organisations in our geographical area such as Nissan. We can learn a lot from their business and Quality practices and to this end we have tried to increase the level of interaction between these companies and us. I invite local companies to Davy to give presentations to our staff which is part of our policy to learn from their experience. The biggest influence from these companies has been through their effect on local suppliers because their Quality concepts and ideas are specified to their suppliers which in turm affects the way they operate. There is a high level of Quality awareness in this area which benefits local industry in general", says Mr Walton.

Davy has a large number of suppliers because it sources all its hardware externally. Although it has a close relationship with its regular suppliers it does go out to competitive tender and depending on the contract will specify ISO certification as an essential criterion especially in the nuclear work. In the Iron and Steel business area for instance it will request this information and use suppliers on the basis that they have ISO certification or have a long recorded history of satisfactory past performance. New suppliers are visited and assessed.

The next step in the supplier relationship is to establish measures of performance through collaboration with supplier groups to review both the methods used by Davy to specify equipment and also the processes and performance of individual suppliers. "We plan to bring suppliers to the site and sit down with them in an effort to investigate more efficient ways of working together for our mutual benefit. It is really moving into a partnering arrangement with key suppliers and we are anticipating through this we will gain enough confidence in one another to reduce the level of inspection without compromising the Quality of the product", explains Mr Walton.

Davy 's customer care programme is viewed as one of the successes of the TQM programme. As part of this programme a technical liaison was initially established with a major customer. The objective of this technical liaison is to promote discussions on subjects of mutual interest, provide resolutions to technical problems, promote technological developments and ensure world best practice is achieved within steelmaking to enable both Davy and the client to attain cost and technological advantages.

The Liaison Committee meets regularly. Through a series of formal meetings improvement exercises are identified and executed by teams consisting of members from both organisations. Mr Greenwood explains: "One of the primary difficulties we experience with clients is identifying who the true customer is. Is it the person paying for the equipment or the person using the equipment on a day to day basis? The former view a project as successful if it is completed within budget whereas the people using the equipment may have experienced problems but because there was no direct liaison between us and the users they were never identified. It's a question of getting to the right people who are the engineers and operators using the equipment.

"I believe that collaboration, joint ventures and partnering is something that will increase in British business and in the next few years we will see a large growth in the number of projects that are handled on a partnership basis with the client in an even closer relationship than we have already. The advantage for the contractor is that sales costs are reduced because you service the client according to an established agreement and from the client's point of view they have a team which knows the operation so there is no learning curve making the operation more effective and efficient. It is a win/win situation which is what business is all about."

Quality Representitives
left to right: Steve Phillips, Clive Davison (Quality Manager), Peter Calland, Ann West, Bob Gilham, Richard Foulger (Chief Environmental Health Officer), Mary Milne, Dean Powell, Fiona Beddoes, Steve Glass
London Borough of Bromley

28

Quality For Local Government

London Borough of Bromley
— Enviromental Health & Trading Standards —

A CHARTER Mark is the sign of excellence for the public sector organisations such as Government services, water and electricity companies, schools, hospitals and police, in fact any public service that deals directly with members of the public can enter. The Charter Mark is also given to exceptional local council services but only a maximum of 100 are awarded annually by the Prime Minister. One such Charter Mark holder is The London Borough of Bromley, Environmental Health & Trading Standards who were awarded one in 1993.

To win, Bromley's Environmental Standards Health & Trading Services division had to show that it was:

- Setting and achieving acceptable service standards.
- Providing clear and easily obtainable information about their services and performance.
- Consulting with their customers and providing them with choices about the services Bromley provides and how they are delivered.
- Being courteous and helpful to their customers.
- Quickly putting things right when they go wrong.
- Ensuring their services represent good value for money.
- Ensuring customer satisfaction.
- Showing that they have improved their performance over the past two years.
- Having in hand plans to make further improvements at no cost totheir customers.

All the above achievements contributed to the Charter Mark Award.

The Environmental Health & Trading Standards of Bromley Council did not stop improving upon receipt of the Charter Mark (which is assessed after three years and can be taken away) but searched for ways to improve further.

The London Borough of Bromley is the largest of the London boroughs with an area of 59 square miles and a population of 295,000. The North of the borough borders onto inner London and is mainly suburban with a small amount of light industry whereas to the South the borders meet with the Counties of Kent and Surrey and include much open space and farmland.

The Environmental Health & Trading Standards Division, as the name suggests, provides the council's Environmental Health & Trading Standards services which, since 1992, have been fully integrated in order to make the most effective use of available resources.

In 1990 Members of the Council agreed on a set of principles which are reflected in the main aims of the Division:

- To promote and protect the public health of the people who live in, work in and visit Bromley;
- To ensure fair standards of trading;
- To enhance the Quality of the environment and
- To provide our services at a cost and Quality acceptable to our customers.

The division has also outlined a series of priorities:

- To provide a high Quality service which responds to the requirements of our customers.
- To investigate complaints of public nuisance.
- To investigate consumer complaints.
- To ensure the maintenance of proper standards of environmental health and trading standards.
- To monitor the local environment and identify risks to health.
- To work closely with the Health Authority and other organisations in the promotion of good health.
- To ensure that our service is readily available to all people living and working in Bromley.

The clarity of the aims and priorities of the Division stems from a general drive in the 1980s to make local government more accountable. Richard Foulger is the Chief Enviromental Health Officer in Bromley. He is responsible for the Environmental Health & Trading Standards Services and outlines the factors affecting local government services.

"There were a lot of issues being considered, like the privatisation of services, compulsory competitive tendering, government reports, the audit commission on performance of a whole range of services but particularly Environmental Health & Trading Standards. Questions were being asked – can you provide better value for money? Can you improve the Quality?

"Then there were the general issues of diminishing resources. Central government grant levels were lower and there were limits on local authorities as to how much they could raise locally. There were more regulations in quite a few areas; there were more duties imposed on local authorities with no extra resources. Demands from the public and all sorts of users increased. Local authorities were under quite a bit of pressure to continually improve and provide better value.

"All these changes meant that everyone had to take a close look at what they were doing and how it was being done: Were we doing it in the most efficient way and making the best use of our resources? I think traditionally in many areas of local government we had done what we thought it appropriate to do and to a certain extent we had hidden behind what we had considered to be our statutory responsibilities, therefore we had to perform tasks in exactly the way we always had.

"The 1980s saw a very significant change in the traditional approach. We were moving towards more consultation with our customers and users and were trying to find out what their expectations and needs were from local government. We were trying to rewrite the agenda, if you like, for the way in which we provided services in the future. That was the starting point. I think it is also true to say that our customers, especially in a place like Bromley, are fairly well aware of what the local authority should be doing and increasingly, through government pressure, pressure from the audit commission and pressure from the media, are more inclined to express their dissatisfaction with the services than they were previously and through that put greater demands on local government.

"When I was appointed to the chief officer post here in 1990, the first significant task was to critically analyse what it was we were doing, why we were doing it and how we were doing it. The process involved the managers within the organisation; we took them away and said, "Let's have a really good look at what we are doing, why we are doing it and try to prioritise and try to develop a vision of where we think we want to be in two or three years time, bearing in mind all of these pressures and the fact that we wanted to become more customer focused in what we were doing."

The pressure on local government also came in the form of market testing, some services had to be market tested by law. The Environmental Health & Trading Standards Services has never been subject to compulsory testing but the council asked all services to carry out feasibility studies into what the possibilities were for market testing. Mr Foulger described the initial thoughts on market testing:

"The mere request in itself brings quite a lot of uncertainty with it, because the managers then started saying, 'Right, we've done some work on clearly identifying what we think we ought to be doing and consulting our customers. If we find ourselves in a position where we have got to be competitive – what other things do we have to start thinking about in terms of getting ourselves into shape?' It was quite an intensive period of taking a close look at what it was costing us to do what we do. Did we know what it was costing us? The answer was no. So we did a lot of work on trying to identify unit costs of providing the various types of services."

Environmental Services has a wide range of customers including councillors, restaurant owners, residents and people running business, in fact all the 300 000 people in Bromley are potential customers. The vision outlined earlier was developed to meet these complex needs.

"I think the important thing is that we have a consistent policy that is acceptable to the customer. It is simple but I think Vision Statements should be easy to understand. Quite often organisations think, "Oh, it is implicit – we all know why we come to work". But people did not realise why they came to work really. Now they do.

"The danger can be, because it is fairly simple, you just pin it up on the wall and then do nothing more about it. We were not prepared to stop at that. The first thing we did was to reorganise ourselves in a such a way that we became customer focused", explained Mr Foulger.

The next step was driven by the council accepting that it needed to consult more with the public and needed to be more explicit about what standards of service delivery the public could expect. This was a central

WHAT YOU CAN EXPECT	WHAT WE WILL DO	WHAT YOU CAN DO
A fair & impartial approach to investigating complaints of noise nuisance. 	• Acknowledge all requests for service. • Offer advice on any actions possible. • Approach the person complained about in an attempt to find a solution. • Consider legal action against persistent offenders who ignore requests to be considerate. • Offer advice on alternative action if we are unable to help.	• Explain the problem to the person making the noise and try to come to a compromise, if you can. • Keep a record of all conversations/letters. • Gather all relevant details of the noise problem. Keep a written record of dates/times of any disturbances.
A service which is accessible, prompt & efficient. 	• Respond within 3 working days. • Visit on the same day for noise complaints needing an urgent response e.g. burglar alarms. • Provide an out of hours service 7 days a week for serious noise nuisances which happen outside normal working hours e.g. parties, burglar alarms.	• As soon as you are aware of a noise problem that you want our help with, let us know. • Accept that investigating a noise nuisance takes time. • Let us know in advance of events that are likely to be serious noise problems.
Courteous, professional & well trained staff. 	• Give you the name and contact number of the person dealing with your complaint. • Try to make sure that that person is available to take calls between 9 - 10am and 4 - 5pm, weekdays. • Provide an answer-phone service when staff are not available to answer a call because they are out making visits. • Keep your details confidential. • Tell you what is happening. • Assess noise disturbance to decide whether action can be taken.	• Tell us of any change in circumstances. • Accept that sometimes we may be unable to resolve the problem. • Seek our advice about noise and how to control it. • Give us your name and address. Unfortunately anonymous complaints cannot be investigated.
That every effort will be made to prevent or control the noise. 	• Try to find a practical and reasonable solution to every noise problem. • Make up to 3 visits to assess whether a noise nuisance exists. • Visit at the time the noise normally occurs, including visits outside office hours. • Use noise monitoring/recording equipment where necessary and offer advice on specialist noise problems e.g. sound insulation, aircraft noise.	• Think about your neighbours. • Be prepared to accept a compromise. • Keep all noise to a reasonable level, especially the volume of televisions, radios, & stereos. • Tell neighbours in advance if you hold a party or need to carry out noisy building works etc. • Use noisy equipment, such as lawnmowers and washing machines, at reasonable hours. • Train your dog not to bark excessively. • Make sure that burglar alarms are fitted with a 20 minute cut-off device and 2 key-holders are registered with the local Police.
A cost effective service which provides value for money. 	• Ask you what you think of our service. • Set, monitor and regularly review the standards of our service.	• Tell us what you think about the service. • Let us know if you are unhappy with the outcome or if you think we are not meeting our published standards.

government initiative as well, examples include Health Department's patient's charter and the British Rail charter.

A range of methods are employed to involve customers and encourage feedback including customer surveys – written and telephone, market research by consultants, talking to voluntary youth groups, setting up customer panels, using focus groups, getting local organisations involved and even plans for utilising the Internet.

The consultation with the community was used to establish a series of Quality standards or promises. Pamphlets outlining the service are published and widely distributed. The pamphlets outline what the customer can expect, what the council will do and what the customer can do to facilitate a more efficient service(see sample pamphlet). These commitments are an important part of the customer focus at Bromley.

As well as getting customers involved, the Environmental Health & Trading Standard's staff and managers had to be enthusiastic advocates of the new way of working. To gain the commitment of the managers a series of 'Away Days' were arranged.

The managers were taken on residential training and teambuilding courses which helped encourage the managers to think along the same lines. An open atmosphere gave everyone the opportunity to speak freely and people didn't feel threatened as discussions focused on improving processes not blaming individuals for problem areas. Richard Foulger expressed his commitment to Quality and expected the same from the other managers. This commitment is vital as shown in Table 1, which outlines why 80 per cent of Quality initiatives fail.

WHY DO UP TO 80% OF QUALITY INITIATIVES FAIL?

- **Lack of commitment from managers**
- **Unclear vision and leadership**
- **Inappropriate/outdated structures**
- **Long standing team/individual problems**
- **Poor time allocation**
- **Lack of enthusiasm/low moral**
- **Insufficent expertise**
- **Lack of training**
- **Poor planning**

To ensure success at Bromley, Richard Foulger believes it was vital to get everyone in the organisation involved and help them understand that they have a role to play in making certain everything is delivered as expected to the end user. Staff know they are either providing a service directly to the user or serving someone who is. This attitude has developed a culture in which excellent service is recognised as a mission for everyone in the organisation.

"The most important step you will take is deciding how you will gain the commitment of the staff and establish a culture in which the staff recognise the organisational approach as their own and not one being imposed by management. In other words, the people involved in the delivery of the service are those who need to be involved in the development of your Quality systems. Additionally they need to be empowered to alter and amend the systems within an agreed structure, in the interests of improving the Quality of service delivery", advises Mr Foulger.

The application for the Charter Mark Award in 1993 was used as a vehicle for cultural change. Staff from all levels were involved in the application process. Preparation for the Charter Mark and the success in winning the Award were not seen as an end but merely a step on the path of continuous improvement. However, winning the Award, Environmental Health & Trading Standards did not want to stand still but move forward. The next step was to appoint Clive Davison as Quality Manager. Mr Davison is a environmental health officer with substantial Quality assurance skills. He was the person nominated to help guide Bromley to the next stage – the use of formal Quality systems such as ISO 9000 to ensure consistent Quality standards. The appointment of a Quality Manager to drive cultural change was another indication of management commitment and reinforced links between staff and senior management. Mr Davison provides expertise and support throughout the organisation.

The approach Bromley have taken has been to fully involve staff from the outset and to ensure that effective means of communication have been maintained between staff and management. Communication channels have included: staff newsletters, staff exhibitions, team meetings, an annual staff meeting, individual appraisals, 'sounding board' meetings between staff representatives and management, and Quality training.

The process began with the training of ten staff, each representing a specific work area, in Quality assurance techniques. These people weren't the managers of their areas but volunteers from all levels of the operation who had an interest in the Quality approach.

The team returned to the department as an enthusiastic and informed group. They were given the role of Quality Representatives and are responsible for taking forward the Quality management process in terms of:

(i). Gaining support and involvement from colleagues in their work teams;

(ii). Reviewing, amending and monitoring procedures relating to service delivery;

(iii). Undertaking the auditing process to ensure the effective execution of the Quality systems.

The Quality representatives have played an important role. in a variety ways. For instance they decided, after looking at how other organisations had documented their procedures, that they didn't want to describe the divisions, various tasks as a written screed comprised of precise instructions but preferred to use flowcharts instead. To keep the instructions as concise as possible a notes page is often included. The flowcharted procedures manual has proved much easier to use on site as staff can go straight to the section they want clarified. (See Figure 1.)

The Quality Manager has direct access to the Divisional Management Team (DMT) and acts on behalf of the Quality representitves. Quality is on the agenda for every meeting of the Divisional Management Team, with the DMT receiving monthly reports on progress which include issues arising from the Quality representatives' team needing decisions from the DMT. It is incumbent on the DMT to respond quickly in order not to impede progress and to give a clear message to the staff about the commitment of management.

Training Programmes continued with all staff and managers undergoing training with an emphasis on Quality. Managers received further training in change management and Total Quality.

To overcome initial scepticism concerning the value of Quality management techniques a number of training sessions focused on reviewing and improving actual processes rather than only relying on theory. Mr Davison explains:

"We recognised that there was resistance. The Quality reps recognised that it is quite natural, when things are changing, for there to be a bit of

QUALITY MANUAL	8: DOG WARDEN SERVICE LOST DOG REGISTER ADMIN PROCEDURE	SECTION	CONTRACTS & INVESTIGATIONS		
		STAGE	LOST DOG REGISTER - ADMIN		
		REF	QM 12 - 8 CILDR	ISSUED BY	
		REV	A.2	DATE	20/7/95
		SHEET	3	OF	3

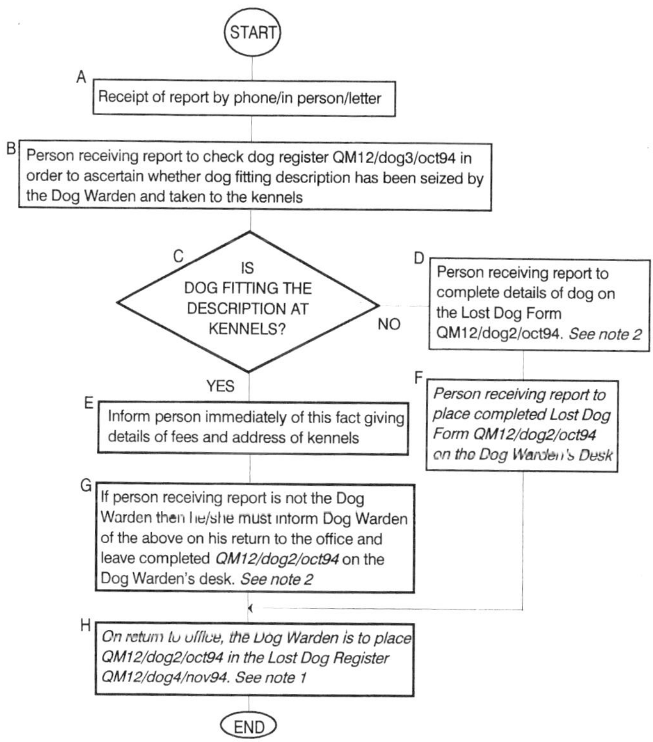

BROMLEY ENVIRONMENTAL SERVICES DIVISION

denial and resistance and it was our job – the manager's job and the Quality rep's job – to recognise this and get people to start exploring how Quality could be of benefit and how the system could make the job easier and give people more confidence in the work they do. We were aware of the management theories but also focused on practical things in order to overcome resistance to change.

"There are still a few people around who are cynical but you get that in any organisation. There are not nearly as many as there might have been had we not been going through these processes with a constant consideration for the importance of involving people. Nobody in any team can say that they have not had the opportunity to make a contribution."

It was the Quality representatives who sought formal certification to ISO 9000, as Richard Foulger explains:

"My view was, that we would not make application for an ISO 9000 if we felt that formal certification would add to the sort of bureaucracy that was not helpful to us. I have continued with that philosophy. The view of the Quality reps was: 'We've put all this work in and followed the structure. We think it would be rather nice to apply for ISO 9000, to at least see if all the work we've done would enable us to get the accreditation.' So, we are in the process of seeking a third party audit and formal assessment."

The quest for ISO 9000 has been a motivating force to keep the improvement process going. Enthusiasm has been maintained through a range of initiatives including ISO 9000, the Charter Mark and Investors In People. The department is also a member of the British Quality Foundation which has specific criteria for local government.

A number of cross-functional Improvement teams have been established and have contributed many cross-divisional changes that have resulted in greater efficiency and customer service. There are plans to implement cross-departmental teams throughout the council.

Some of these improvements include:

- An out of hours work pack. Suggested by a Quality representative, the pack has not cost anything to put together but contains essential items to deal with out of hours emergencies.
- Check lists have been created to aid inspections.
- Computer and communications equipment have been upgraded. This has ensured data is accurately entered and service requests are monitored and acted upon.

- A Training & Competency matrix has been developed to identify professional/technical training needs.
- Service delivery to both blind and deaf users has been improved through action taken by staff under the Quality initiative. Staff identified and arranged appropriate training themselves.
- Power has been devolved to staff. For example money back guarantees to customers dissatisfied with service Quality.
- Best practices are shared ensuring a consistent service.
- A contingency plan has been put in place for the reactive teams to ensure response times are met in times of peak demand.

The above improvements are just a few of many that have contributed to the success of the Environmental Services and Trading Standards Department. Richard Foulger feels the work of his department can be used by other local authorities to improve their service.

"Most managers in local government are so consumed by day to day problems that the thought of embarking on such a process is too daunting to contemplate. This is a real difficulty, as managers today have little time or don't feel justified in taking the time for reviewing procedures and creating a vision for the future.

"The further we go down the Quality path, the more I am convinced that it is the right way to approach many of the problems facing us in government today.

"For my department the long hot summer of 1995 will be remembered as much for the soaring number of requests as the soaring temperatures. We had enormous difficulty coping with the volumes and struggled to satisfy our response times. However, I believe the situation would have been far worse had it not been for the attitude of staff which arose from the development of a culture of continuous improvement in service delivery.

"It is all about our people, the most important factor in achieving your goals is getting the support of the people you work with. If they do not feel they are all partners in the Quality system it is unlikely to succeed."

left to right: Barry Hopewell (Vice-President, Operations)
and Tom Hinchliffe (Managing Director)
ICL High Performance Technology

29

Planning For Excellence

—ICL High Performance Technology—

UK Quality Award Winner (1995) ICL High Performance Technology demonstrates a tenacious approach to business planning which has seen the company totally transform the reputation of its products and services. The achievement is greater in that this has taken place not only in adverse economic conditions, but also in a declining market-place.

ICL High Performance Technology (HPT) was originally a research and development unit of multinational computer company ICL, acquired by Fujitsu in 1990. It became the mainframe computer development division in the 1980s, and an autonomous business unit in January 1992. Its main business today is producing corporate computer systems, principally for the financial services, local and central government, public utilities and retail markets. Its best known product is the Series 39, a powerful mainframe which uses ICL's Open VME operating system.

HPT has about 25% of the UK large computer systems market and a worldwide installed base of over 1,800 systems, typically sold to Information Technology or Data Centre departments of large companies via ICL sales units.

1994 turnover was more than £100 million, based on inter-company transfer prices. HPT employs over 1,000 people at its site in West Gorton, Manchester.

In 1995 HPT became a division of the ICL High Performance Systems group which includes direct sales operations.

Over recent years ICL High Performance Technology (HPT) has used Total Quality tools and techniques to make massive improvements to both products and customer satisfaction while making a fundamental change from a cost centre with research and development responsibilities to a profitable autonomous business unit. Substantial cultural and organisational change was needed, but now HPT faces its biggest challenge to date: how to survive, thrive, innovate and change in a declining mainframe computer market.

Over the past 20 years, rapid technological change has resulted in personal computers with more power than most mainframes of the previous era at a fraction of the price. Large system prices have fallen much faster than volumes have increased. HPT therefore needs to build on its new product streams to supplement revenues from mainframes. While new products, notably GOLDRUSH parallel database server, and DAIS distributed application integrator have already achieved technical acclaim, HPT now needs to turn engineering success into business results – and concurrently develop new products. Improved time to market is also paramount: "Our approach to Quality involves combining engineering excellence with business excellence", explains Tom Hinchliffe, Managing Director.

The Quality challenge of the 1980s was conformance: variable hardware and software quality were key causes of customer dissatisfaction. HPT realised early that consistency of hardware and software quality was critical to survival, and the company successfully tackled these problems. A measure of the successful transformation has been the achievement of three Queen's Awards for Technology and being voted "Mainframe of the Year" in two consecutive years, by readers of Computing Magazine.

The Quality challenge today is to engender and sustain total commitment to excellence at every level of the business. HPT's achievement in winning the UK Quality Award is testimony to its commitment to consistent self-assessment and long term business planning.

The Business Excellence Model

Parent company ICL has a well-earned reputation as a leader in Total Quality Management techniques. Design to Distribution Ltd, an autonomous division of the computer giant, won the 1994 European Quality Award, and the ICL corporate quality strategy is firmly based around the UK/European Quality Award model. Total Quality has been a constant theme of HPT's activities since the early 1980s. Tom Hinchliffe chairs a Quality Steering Group of senior managers that has overseen the drive for continuous improvement since 1986. In 1994 the steering group evolved into a business excellence team with a dedicated programme manager. HPT adopted the European Foundation for Quality Management (EFQM) self-assessment award criteria as the core of the company's Business Excellence programme. "The primary aim of the project was improving the business", explains Barry Hopewell, Vice-President, Operations. "So we labelled the exercise as a business excellence activity, rather than a Quality initiative."

"The Business Excellence Model is an ideal tool for measuring performance when facing the challenges posed by the need to innovate and add value in a declining market sector" says Divisional Quality Manager David Freeth, a member of the ICL Quality Council. HPT uses the business model as a tool for assessing the need for improvement across all areas of its operations, and have appointed a dedicated Business Excellence Programme Manager, Brian Hart, to monitor performance. A senior manager is allocated to each of the nine elements of the model, with Tom Hinchliffe setting the pace in the leadership category. A wide range of communication methods are used to re-inforce the improvement message, including electronic mail, newsletters, wall posters and workshops. Team leaders hold monthly team meetings with their people and senior managers brief all staff several times per year in sessions which include questions and discussions. The effectiveness of communications is monitored by an employee opinion survey which is carried out, reviewed and refined each year.

"We extensively involved people by spreading the concept of self-assessment throughout the organisation. Many managers have taken the methodology on board and use it as a tool for improvement within their own units", Barry Hopewell says. Consistency is assured by conforming to a set of divisional policies and standards formulated by David Freeth and unit quality managers. HPT has implemented a formal recognition process to reward teams and individuals based on the following criteria:

- role model behaviour leading to quality improvement
- exceeding expectations
- putting the customer first
- best practice
- meeting promises and commitments
- elimination of waste.

Recognition takes the form of local, bronze, silver and gold awards. Informal means of recognition such as 'thank-you' cards are used widely. HPT staff are active in developing and delivering courses and presentations on Quality issues and regularly entertain visitors from other UK corporations who wish to learn from their TQM experience.

Strategy and business planning

HPT has a five-year business plan, reviewed annually, containing four key strategies:

- achieving business excellence
- supplying products and services to existing customers
- developing new streams and new channels
- changinging resources, skills, and culture to achieve the significant transition needed.

Twice-yearly organisation and management reviews are held to ensure that necessary actions are taken to develop and achieve the plan. Critical factors have been identified and targets specified. The "Strong Business Competence" factor, for example, has a target for an assessed score against the business model.

The strategic plan is communicated to everyone in HPT in twice-yearly business briefings presented by Tom Hinchliffe. Mindful that its history as a development centre might be a potential source of conflict between development and business planning priorities, Tom Hinchliffe also chairs a "reconciliation" review three or four times a year, designed to ensure that both areas of the business are given equal priority.

HPT benchmarks its strategic and business planning approach against other companies and compares process performance with other companies and with other ICL divisions. Non-management "think tanks" have been formed to explore technical, marketing and capability issues using information gathered in benchmarking exercises. Output is processed by a senior management workshop which results in follow-up action teams feeding recommendations into the strategic plan.

Changing from a development division to an autonomous business unit coupled with the fast-moving nature of the information technology (IT) industry has led to substantial reviews of the company's vision and mission over the last three years.

As part of ICL, HPT has always had a strategic planning process but Barry Hopewell says that "using the business excellence model has given us a systematic way of looking at ourselves as a business to help the transition from a development centre to a business unit". HPT's vision is now "to be the most trusted supplier of Enterprise computing capability in our chosen markets", and its mission is "to provide a family of products for mission-critical Data Centre computing".

While new business streams are well under way, the company is well aware of its responsibilities towards its existing customer base. "We work with customers to understand how our products can help them gain business advantage", says David Freeth. "New product development is a two-way process. We need to listen to customers and also educate them as to the opportunities presented by our innovations. For example, parallel servers enable customers to work simultaneously on large databases – manipulating, sorting, extracting, etc. – without slowing down the main system. This can yield enormous productivity benefits, but customers need to experience the technology to understand its potential. This presents strategic challenges for our sales and marketing teams, and involves everyone in the organisation. Meeting customers gives the team invaluable opportunities for two-way feedback. I am now much better able to appreciate the sort of things that concern customers and the business effect that apparently minor product changes can have", commented Barrie Williams after a visit to HPT customer, Leeds and Holbeck Building Society.

Customers themselves are enthusiastic contributors to the process: "I am always happy to assist in formulating policy and developing strategy" commented a spokesman from Congleton Borough Council.

Process management

HPT was one of the first ICL divisions to achieve ISO 9001 certification in 1989. The implementation and documentation of processes has been driven by the requirements of that standard. Development and support processes have been supplemented by business management and trading processes. HPT's top-level process model was redesigned to reflect the flow through the value chain and provide a framework for the systematic improvement of critical processes.

To coincide with the use of self-assessment against the business excellence model, a Process Working Party was set up to identify best practice. This has produced HPT's 'Good Process Guide' which includes guidelines for the creation, introduction and continuous improvement of key processes and emphasises the need to define and agree success criteria (measurements and targets).

Since 1986 the company has trained everyone in the understanding of process management and improvement and has emphasised how each employee fits into a supplier-process-customer chain. HPT defines critical processes as those which are key to achieving business results and the critical success factors defined as part of the strategic plan. These are reviewed either annually as part of the Quality System Review or through specific process reviews.

Improving customer satisfaction

Measured against mainframe competitors in a 1987 customer survey, ICL failed to achieve a single first place in fifteen categories of customer satisfaction. By 1994, a comparative survey placed HPT either first or second in half of the 32 attributes used to assess the company against DEC, IBM and Hewlett-Packard. HPT's key focus is total end user customer satisfaction. An important recent development has been the refinement and extension of the process from satisfaction with product and service quality to total business performance.

HPT aims to delight its customers in each key area of the business, and uses gap analysis to measure its progress. For the less than delighted customers, HPT benchmarks its complaint handling procedures to ensure that it identifies and uses best practice to solve problems and learn from mistakes.

Dramatic software Quality improvements are partly the result of products maturing, but most significantly because of improved problem-solving processes. A dedicated corrective action team has reduced the number of incidents where a problem was not resolved the first time from almost 200 per week in 1989 to 20 per week today.

Business results

Since HPT products are mainly sold through other ICL organisations, revenue is expressed in terms of inter-company transfer prices. While profits and revenues show a decline between 1992 and 1994 owing to the contraction of the mainframe market, 1994 profit figures were more than twice the budgeted figure. Inventory levels, debt control percentage clearance rates and costs generally either show improvements or, where the nature of the market and industry denies any improvement, performance well ahead of budget.

In non-financial indicators HPT has also fared well, with software delivered quality, hardware delivered quality and hardware and operating system reliability all showing significant improvement. The Quality system itself has also improved. A BSI external audit in the last quarter of 1994 raised a mere two non-conformances even though this was the first audit against the revised standard (BS EN ISO 9001: 1994) an astonishingly low figure for an organisation of this size.

The number of site visits needed by an engineer is a good indicator of product reliability. Although typical customer configurations have almost doubled over five years, the number of site visits has been maintained or in many cases, reduced.

On time delivery is an important Quality differentiator. Since 1993, HPT has achieved more than 98% of all deliveries to committed lead time against a 100% target.

The various improvements achieved show through in sales performance with 15 competitive new business gains won in 1993-4. Notable new customers include Provincial Insurance, Gwynedd Health Authority, Panathon in Greece and Vodaphone in Germany, amongst others.

Repeat business is the lifeblood of any company, and a direct indicator of the success of Quality policy. HPT Customers like The Inland Revenue, British Gas and the Department of Health and Social Security have affirmed their commitment to maintain and upgrade their systems. The number of users of ICL's Open VME operating system environment continues to grow.

Planning for success

The success of HPT's self-assessment programme can be attributed to a number of specific factors, but the most obvious lesson is that a rigorous and painstaking approach to recognising and solving problems will yield results, no matter how great the challenge. Tom Hinchliffe explains: "HPT have focused on their customers and their people – the vital ingredients. Continued strong performance in the mainframe business has enabled HPT to continue to make a major contribution to ICL's profits despite difficulties elsewhere in the industry since the early 1990s."

It is no mean feat to change from a research and development centre with marginal direct profit and loss accountability to a fully functioning business unit. By adopting the business excellence model, HPT has not only made this transformation, it has taken the opportunity to restyle itself as a leader in business excellence. HPT's targets will test the model to the full. The company plans to almost double its revenue per employee over the next three years, with over half of revenues generated from new product streams.

The goals are ambitious, but the odds favour an organisation which not only has HPT's technical reputation and resources, but also the ability to improve from the poor customer service reputation of the 1980s to the point where companies like General Motors number among the visitors keen to learn about their TQM implementation. Above all, it has people and pride on its side.

Reproduced with kind permission from *UK Quality,* Nov 1995, UK Quality Award edition.

30

Building Mutually Valuable Relationships

— Trinity Motors of Hinckley —

TRINITY Motors is one of the Rover Group's top performing dealerships in the UK, not only in terms of the number of vehicles sold (in relation to market size) but also because of the high standards projected by its facilities and staff resulting in exceptional customer service.

Trinity Motors which operates franchises for Rover, Land Rover, LDV Commercials, Citroën and Unipart together with Texaco and BP Forecourts is based at Wharf Farm in Hinckley. It was founded by Chairman, Robert Woodward over 30 years ago and although it has experienced substantial growth since the second half of the 1980s it continues to strive to retain its friendly family atmosphere, providing personal and committed services on a local basis at both its Hinckley headquarters and at its sister operation in Nuneaton. Both locations offer a full range of sales, service and parts facilities with forecourts at Hinckley and two other local sites. In fact Trinity Motors is the leading parts wholesaler and retailer in the Midlands region.

Since 1982 the company's turnover has grown from £3 million to over £30 million (in 1995) while employee numbers have increased from 30 to over 200 people in the same period. Throughout this growth the company has remained private and independent despite predatory interest from major groups.

To its customers and prospective customers it makes the pledge that: "Above all we want to get to know you and listen to all your requirements and needs and then work out with you how to best satisfy them. This way we become friends and build mutually valuable relationships." Trinity Motors' attention to detail, such as delivering each vehicle to its new owner

left to right: Terry Brown (Quality and Service Development Director), John King (Managing Director), Tracey Potter (Personnel and Training Manager)
Trinity Motors of Hinckley

with a full tank of petrol, adds pleasure to the handover experience and nurtures enduring relationships.

The relationship does not end when the vehicle is transferred to the new owner. All customers are contacted after taking delivery of their vehicle to ensure that any problems or queries are resolved. The department of first contact will then facilitate the introduction of the customer to other parts of the dealership. For instance, sales staff will always introduce new customers to the service staff so that customers feel known and valued.

One of the company's most fundamental aims is to ensure customer satisfaction and to this end it conducts on-going measurement of customer satisfaction levels and seeks to identify areas in which improvements can be made. To facilitate this process Trinity Motors developed and implemented its Quality Assurance system which defines policies and Quality procedures in accordance with BS5750 Part 2 which it obtained in 1995. Trinity Motors remains the only motor dealer in its marketing area to have achieved the award across its diverse areas of activity.

This reinforces Trinity Motors' position as a 'Quality company with properly developed and documented policies and procedures and working practices across the whole of the company which are rigorously audited, checked, monitored and recorded by both internal and external auditors in an on-going way", explains John King who joined Trinity in 1987 as Managing Director from Rover Group.

Trinity Motors' Quality policy defines that the company will offer the highest level of customer satisfaction to all its customers and ensure a commitment to getting it right first time, every time.

The four critical foundations upon which Trinity Motors' success in winning, satisfying and retaining its strong customer base are:

- Universally acknowledged and 'sought after' **Product** offerings;
- Highly trained professional and committed **People** providing the customer service;
- Thoroughly considered and proven **Processes** by which it conducts and manages the business; and
- Comprehensive and outstanding **Premises** fully equipped for the task at hand.

The automotive industry has undergone dramatic changes both in terms of product Quality and attitudes to customer relationships over the last 10 years as Mr King explains: "I think there has been a change in mentality – up to seven or eight years ago the Quality of vehicles was less reliable and consequently there was almost a siege mentality in dealerships where sales and particularly service people were defensive. However, Rover Group now has an excellent image and because of its reputation as a prestige vehicle manufacturer, expectations are high in terms of both service received and vehicle Quality. This recognition motivated Rover to initiate a dealer programme which emphasised the importance of providing customer satisfaction."

In the early stages of this programme there was an emphasis on the physical appearance of the dealerships. However, over time this perception was adjusted placing greater significance on customer involvement and signalling a transition to a Total Quality philosophy. A catalyst behind this change was the recognition of and response to customer perceptions obtained through customer research which has remained a cornerstone of Trinity Motors' customer approach.

From Rover's initial introduction to Total Quality, Trinity Motors commenced its own programme with a view to achieving BS5750 certification, not as an end in itself but rather as a means of providing consistency of operation to the organisation.

"We took the view that we had a premium product, and our premises were first class so we had to develop the processes which is where the involvement of our people came in", explains Tracey Potter, Personnel and Training Manager.

Trinity Motors' 215 members of staff participated in the process and were involved from the onset through an introductory two day training course using the company's in-house training facilities where the steps to certification were outlined and the tools of TQM such as the four Ps (Product, Premises, People and Processes), brainstorming, cause and effect analysis, and flowcharting were introduced.

To generate the initial excitement for the programme Trinity Motors provided training to inter-departmental groups which were intentionally mixed to encourage interaction and understanding between departments. Traditionally, automotive dealerships tend to be highly departmentalised into areas such as sales, service, parts, and administration which often resulted in a culture where the person cleaning the car, putting away the parts or the accountant didn't relate to the customer at the customer service reception.

"Through the initial training followed by the formation of Quality Action Teams we encourage mixed groups of employees to permeate an understanding of each department's role, needs and constraints and the ultimate effect this inter-relationship had on customer satisfaction throughout the company. By providing training at the onset and facilitating mixed groups, any cynics of the process were soon converted by encouraging them to play a more participative role, such as taking ownership of work groups and resolving different problems using the TQM tools. It was quite alarming because by using cause and analysis methods many people soon realised that the root cause of many of Trinity's problems were human factors and to a lesser extent processes", explains Mrs Potter who together with Terry Brown, Quality and Service Development Director facilitated the training, process development and documentation necessary for ISO certification.

The workforce was involved in defining procedures and processes. Work Groups commenced by brainstorming ideas from which the procedures were drafted using a flowchart concept to introduce each procedure which was then supported by a full written description.

"We started off with this method which worked well for general procedures in areas such as accounts and administration, however, when we came to the service elements we experienced some difficulty in reaching consensus. In order to move the process forward we decided to implement the procedures as they were and then improve them where necessary," explains Mrs Potter.

Trinity engaged a university student to assist with the documentation for BS5750 rather than going down the more expensive route of engaging consultants. This had a dual benefit – to the company financially and to the student, valuable experience. When developing its procedures Trinity took into consideration what the Standard required, what the dealership wanted and also elements of consumer research. Once the procedures had been prepared all employees were given another day of training to introduce them to the documentation, examples of live procedures, the amendment process, and internal Quality auditing.

"At the end of the day our procedures manual provides the best training device in the world. It provides all parts of the organisation with a consistent approach which enhances our corporate identity. The only exception is when a specific franchise dictates that it requires a particular activity performed in a specific way", explains Mr King.

The path to certification took nine months, using RAC as the accrediting body. "We decided to use RAC because we had just become a registered RAC body shop for accident and repair work. We took into account people's perceptions and decided on assessors who also had direct experience in the automotive industry thus providing a particularly relevant auditing service", says Mrs Potter.

All Trinity Motors' procedures are held in a central system, which is based around M-Power software developed by Hadleigh Marshall, but uses templates developed and modified by Trinity Motors to meet its exact requirements. The system is used for tracking, amending and administering the Quality manual, procedures and documentation and operates using Microsoft Word allowing information to be readily retrieved and read. However, only the Quality Administrator is able to access the system through a release process to make changes to the procedures which is necessary to preserve the security aspect.

Where concerns exist as to the effectiveness or appropriateness of a particular procedure the person reporting the divergence completes a Quality Concern Report detailing the problem and then passes this to the line manager who details the appropriate corrective action. The person then authorised to implement the changes is responsible for listing all the people who will be affected by those changes on the back of the Quality Concern Document and cascading the reissued procedure to these people who sign off against it. Changes are then put directly into the system.

For instance, access to the VOM (Vehicle Ordering Module) terminal was occasionally restricted due to the office being locked at certain times and the key unavailable. This resulted in delays for processing and amending vehicle orders thus causing delivery delays. By completing a Quality concern report the problem was officially raised and brought to the attention of the relevant parties instead of staff members either ignoring or tolerating a sub standard situation. The corrective action in this instance involved the programming of the Land Rover office's equipment to run VOM.

"In principle, handing over a vehicle to its new owner may seem a simple function, however when you map out the process from preparation of the vehicle to delivery to the customer there is huge scope for mistakes which may then diminish the customer's enjoyment of the handover. Of course this then has an impact on their propensity to conduct repeat business with us", explains Mr King.

Prior to handing over a new or used vehicle to the purchaser each vehicle is taken through a Quality Check Report where the tester assumes the reactions and attitudes of the customer to how Trinity Motors has presented the car. Only when each of the criteria which include the completion of cleaning/valet; operation of door locks, windows, mirrors, wipers and washers; mechanical components; and paint and bodywork for example is checked to the satisfaction of the tester is the vehicle classified as being acceptable to go to a customer.

Trinity Motors actively pursues a policy of delivering continuous improvement in all areas, the focus of which is building better relationships both internally and with customers. "At the end of the day we are selling relationships, not cars or parts. We try to get people to join the Trinity Club, customers, salespeople and employees alike", says Mr King.

Culturally the company has evolved so that everybody within the organisation is available and accessible to meet and talk to customers at any time. The cornerstone to Trinity Motors' Quality progression has been customer involvement through research together with rigorous internal measurement. While the concept of involving the customer originated from its relationship with Rover, Trinity has undertaken its own customer research, the most fundamental of which has been the use of Customer Clinics.

Customer Clinics for each franchise consist of between eight and ten randomly selected customers and are conducted at the dealership by Rover and Land Rover personnel. The group is video recorded for later reference and results are also compiled in a report by Rover and Land Rover using anecdotal quotes and general examples gleaned from the informal yet structured discussion.

"Focus groups are useful for filling in the gaps which often arise from quantitative research because statistics never give you the whole story, the hows and whys. Customer responses are put into perspective through the use of clinics because they take into account elements such as previous relationships with the dealership", explains Mr King.

Problems or mistakes identified then serve as a guide to required improvement areas. The manner in which Trinity Motors then corrects any errors is the key to minimising damage to customer satisfaction. For example a recent focus group report presented the following scenario:

"There was an instance of a customer paying slightly too much for the car they purchased as a result of an error in the salesperson's calculation. The customer contacted the dealer when he got home, who immediately accepted the situation. A cheque for the amount overpaid was delivered to the customer the next morning, thus leaving the customer happy. The situation may, in itself, be unique but it demonstrates clearly how effective the actions of acknowledging the error, accepting responsibility and rectifying the situation quickly can be and how the impact on the customer's satisfaction is minimised."

As a measure of its internal efficiency Trinity also undergoes regular Mystery Shopper surveys and quantitative research such as on-going customer satisfaction reports which are compiled on a quarterly basis and collect the views of a large selection of Sales and Service customers on every aspect of their contact with the Dealership and its services.

One means of ascertaining the level of service provided to prospective clients is via Mystery Shopper questionnaires administered over the telephone by Land Rover which review all elements of customer contact from the number of times the phone rings before being answered and the initial greeting through to the follow up offered and actually made by the salesperson.

Although from a sales point of view the ultimate test is whether the hypothetical customer would purchase a car from the dealership, there are any number of elements during the contact which can be improved upon to ensure that the customer not only makes the purchase but appreciates the process because of its efficiency and the provision of full information. Elements investigated include:

At the end of the conversation, which of the following did the staff member say or do?

Thanked you for calling...+1
Good-bye (or similar)...+1
Confirm the action to be taken, sum up the conversation...+3
Encouraged you to call if you had any further queries...+2
Offered to call you with further information...+2
Asked/made sure you knew where the dealership was located...+2

Gave opening/closing hours…+2
(Maximum of 7 points awarded)

Which of the following information did the staff member ascertain during the course of the conversation? (By asking questions or in general conversation, with or without prompting)

Whether you had test driven the enquiry vehicle…+4
What other vehicles you have looked at, are considering…+3
When you were thinking of buying…+4
Type of driving you do/vehicle usage…+3
Details about your current vehicle…+4
Why you had called this particular dealership…+2
None of the above…+0
(Maximum of 20 points awarded)

The scoring system is primarily based on the premise that customers will not always ask for what they want and therefore sales staff must be proactive in discussions rather than purely reactive. Not only does it allow the dealership to gauge its responsiveness to customer requirements but it also provides it with learning points from which individuals can improve the level of service provided.

As an on-going process Rover systematically canvases Trinity's customers with a questionnaire probing all areas of the dealer/customer relationship and contact. Each quarter Trinity receives not only individual results for the dealership but also a comparison against a dealer average.

Rover also provides customer satisfaction ratings comparing dealers against regional and national averages for sales customers, aftersales customers and overall customer satisfaction to provide a satisfaction index on a quarterly basis.

Results are discussed at team meetings which are conducted on a regular basis at various levels throughout the company such as directors meetings, managers meetings, department meetings and team briefings making customer service and Quality issues prominent on everybody's agenda.

Rover with its own rigorous Quality commitment provides dealerships with sales and CSI league tables for individual zones detailing their position compared to other dealerships and the area average on a monthly basis and year to date. This encourages dealers not to become complacent with past results as they analyse their own performance in relation to other dealers and general market activity.

Adherence to Quality practices in the repairs division is reinforced through Trinity's Quality Performance Qualification programme which was introduced in June 1995 to audit individual performance ratings in terms of: Quality which is ascertained from customer feedback, number of repeat visits required to fix the problem, customer complaints reports, and Quality tester assessments; attitude; and housekeeping and cleanliness. It is tied to a bonus qualification scheme which is applicable to all Rover and Land Rover technicians, as well as accident repair, paint and bodyshop technicians.

QUALITY PERFORMANCE QUALIFICATION

GRADE	-	A	B	C	D
DESCRIPTION	-	'Excellent'/ 'Outstanding' 'Very Pleased'	'Good Without Delight' - Possibly Odd minor Problem	'Inconsistent'/ 'Some Real Dissatisfaction'	'General Dissatisfaction '
POINTS	-	(5 POINTS)	(4 POINTS)	(3 POINTS)	(NIL POINTS)
1 **QUALITY**					
• Customer Feedback :		☐	☐	☐	☐
• Repeat Visits/CCR's :		☐	☐	☐	☐
• Quality Tester Assessment :		☐	☐	☐	☐
2 **ATTITUDE**					
• Timekeeping/Motivation/ Teamwork :		☐	☐	☐	☐
• Customer Care and Workmanship :		☐	☐	☐	☐
• Training Skills and Personal Development :		☐	☐	☐	☐
3 **HOUSEKEEPING AND CLEANLINESS**					
• Personal and Workplace Appearance :		☐	☐	☐	☐
• Working Practices and Disciplines :		☐	☐	☐	☐
• **GRAND TOTAL POINTS :**		☐ +	☐ +	☐ +	☐
				GRAND TOTAL POINTS =	☐

SCORE	:	**36-40**	:	**110% HOURLY RATE FOR BONUS EARNINGS**
	:	**33-35**	:	**100% HOURLY RATE FOR BONUS EARNINGS**
	:	**31-32**	:	**90% HOURLY RATE FOR BONUS EARNINGS**
	:	**below 30**	:	**50% HOURLY RATE FOR BONUS EARNINGS**

While it serves as a device to allocate bonuses it provides a constructive guide for employees to improve their performance. Assessments are conducted by workshop managers who rate their staff on a four point scale as illustrated in Figure 1. Ratings are then discussed with the worker and improvement areas pointed out and addressed. The programme which is in its pilot stage was developed with the support of a cross-section of technicians.

Workshop technicians are traditionally paid a bonus calculated on the number of hours sold compared to the number of hours worked to determine their efficiency. For instance, if a technician sells 110 hours and works 100 hours then he (she) is considered to be 110 per cent efficient which generates bonus earnings. However, rather than just pay the bonus Trinity proposes to filter it through individual qualifications determined by the new Quality Performance Qualification programme.

Many of Trinity's technicians also participate in the Accredited Technician Programme (ATP), a scheme developed for all Rover technicians. Technicians are registered at the training school by their National Insurance Number and any training that they undertake is recorded on a database with points allocated for the number of days and complexity of training they undertake. "If they achieve 600 points they become an accredited Rover technician, with 800 points they become an advanced Rover technician and with 1200 points they become a Rover Master technician of which there are only 28 throughout the UK and we have three here at Trinity", explains Mrs Potter. Trinity's line managers select the course candidates based on individual potential, interest and existing skill base determined through an appraisal process. Similar schemes exist for Land Rover technicians and sales personnel.

Trinity Motors with its attention to customer satisfaction is committed to continually monitoring and improving its service levels and facilities. However, despite the sophistication and frequency of its research mechanisms the most rewarding feedback is unprompted from customers recognising a job well done: "I should like you to know that the whole experience was a pleasure. We were treated fairly, openly and with a great deal of courtesy and professionalism. Within a short space of time we were led through the range of vehicles with a care and understanding which was almost beyond belief." This response is typical, but only one of many.

left to right: Steve Chamberlain (Managing Director), Bill Lally (Sales Director), Ann Clarke (Design Director), Mike Gardner (Financial Director)
Claremont Business Environments

Marks & Spencer Financial Services – Training Department
Chester Business Park

31

Quality By Design

—Claremont Business Environments—

CLAREMONT Business Environments, as the name suggests, designs creative office environments – the influence of which on both staff morale and efficiency cannot be understated. Endorsements from Claremont's clients describing: "long term partnerships"; "unlimited amounts of energy and drive"; "excellence in Customer Service"; "a determination to exceed customer expectations"; and "teamwork from all levels of staff" all indicate a commitment to Quality.

In consulting to many of the UK's most prominent organisations such as Littlewoods, Barclays Bank, Boots, British Nuclear Fuels, Department of Social Security, Grant Thornton, Hewlett Packard, and TNT Express (UK) Limited Claremont also exposes many of the myths of modern management. These are highlighted in Claremont's quarterly newsletter, *Workplace,* published for clients and prospective clients . Many of the points made are fundamental not only to office design but also to the management of a progressive, Quality-driven organisation which is possibly why Quality is so ingrained in Claremont's day-to-day activity.

For example, myth one of 'performance, power and proximity' assumes that one's title and place on the organisational chart should determine the location, size and furnishings of one's office. Claremont, however, suggests that: "The present reality supports the existence of multiple layers of responsibility within every level of an organisation, which runs counter to the separatism of the classic hierarchy. As an example, it is a short-sighted salesperson who doesn't understand his (her) company's accounting system; an uninformed designer who doesn't listen to the marketing department which is not in contact with the customers; and as ineffective as a human resources director who isn't acquainted with the company's products and services. Corporate pyramids are flattening because companies have learned that they work better when people share, rather than withhold information and stay in close contact with the public." The point as it relates to office design is that the office plan should be integral to the business, and not a grid laid over an organisational chart.

Among the many similarities which can be drawn between office design and management practice is that to be effective, an office plan has to recognise the potential of the people in the office and not simply pay attention to the lowest common denominator, the job description.

This disposes with the myth that people performing the same function should be grouped together. The benefit of a mixed discipline work environment is illustrated: "Imagine an incredibly effective salesperson. She (he) may have learned a technique from a customer service representative, who in turn admires the skill of the courteous office receptionist, who in turn models herself after the professionalism of the director of research, who respects the ability of the office librarian, who readily acknowledges that most information is not written down and therefore makes a point of talking every day to the mailperson who is in touch with the entire organisation."

Claremont has a team of designers and technicians who, assisted by in-house Computer Aided Design, can direct every aspect of office refurbishment, furniture installation, and interior alterations. Claremont is a dealer for, and shares a close relationship with the Steelcase Strafor Group, the world's leading designer and manufacturer of office furniture. It also offers an extensive product and service portfolio itself including Fabritect, Claremont's specialist furniture care and maintenance division; and the recently added specialist presentation and training environments division, Viewpoint which provides complete audio visual solutions.

The company was established 17 years ago, with both Ann Malone, Quality Manager and Peter Lomax, Quality Co-ordinator forming part of the original seven member team, albeit in different capacities. The 100 plus people company as it exists today grew from a core business of selling computer supplies, with furniture as only a sideline. However, the business developed as technological advances made computer equipment more compact and organisations identified the need to integrate this new technology into an office environment. As Peter Lomax explains: "When we were initially involved in the computer supply business computers were housed in a room of their own and offices were dotted around this central point. However, the advent of smaller computers during the 1980s which could be stored in a cupboard or on a desk top presented us with a new set of challenges – all of a sudden we were asked to design offices for people instead of machines. It was at this point that our relationship with Steelcase originated."

It comes as no surprise that a company which is in the business of providing office environments to facilitate effective communication and Quality work practices has adopted the highest of standards for its own operations. The checklist of questions Claremont, a member of the British Quality Foundation, encourages prospective clients to ask themselves to determine the effectiveness of their current office environment could be mistaken for part of an internal audit or management review. They include:

- How does your office review and reward people's performance?
- Does your office motivate people to work effectively?
- Does your office provide enough interaction between people? Workers and management? Different depart ments? Between the company and the public?
- How many workers does your office support? What kind of tasks do they perform?
- Is work team-orientated? If so, does your office physically support teams getting together to meet and work together?
- Are managers or executives easily accessible (open-door management)?

Given the industry in which Claremont competes they are their own best advertisement. Ideally an office should reflect the personality of the group or company, adapting to change as circumstances shift and situations vary. Claremont's own open plan office has been created from an old warehouse and is spacious, bright and colourful, befitting a theme of fun and celebration, but also efficiency that pervades the company. The company practises what it preaches with managers sitting in the open plan environment next to the rest of the workforce and admits to socialising very well as a company.

Claremont obtained certification to BS5750 Part 1 in 1992 and has recently been successfully reassessed for ISO9001 to cover its design capability. Although Claremont is one of only a few companies in the industry to have gained certification, its Quality story did not start with the desire to obtain certification for marketing purposes or to meet tender requirements, but rather as a progression of its internal customer care initiatives and general customer focus. Ann Inman, Group Marketing Manager was instrumental in introducing Customer Care and initially assessing the value of BS5750 certification to the company. "Customers and prospective customers can draw confidence from the fact that customer service is the core value around which all our other services revolve. ISO9001 merely reinforces this belief", comments Ann Malone.

Peter Lomax supports this view: "The ISO certification is only a milestone on the way to Total Quality. In itself it means nothing - apart from indicating that the company can document things properly. The benefit is realised only when people understand why you have achieved it – that Quality procedures assist the company achieve its profit goals and improve customer perceptions. It's a feeling of Quality rather than just a set of documents which you work to and are occasionally assessed against."

"We embraced Quality around the same time as the industry was in recession. In hindsight it was the best time to start because it made everybody concentrate on those issues which were important and subsequently helped the company develop and strengthen when many companies were struggling to survive", explains Peter Lomax. "We needed the procedures to ensure that departments from sales to design through to installation reacted to each other appropriately in order to eliminate mistakes."

The company is currently readdressing the Quality issue in a bid to refresh and reawaken Quality commitment, partly through involving new staff who weren't exposed to the original campaign.

Everybody is involved in the process which is largely based around group discussion between the various departments to glean what people understand about Quality, what changes they would make to the procedures, and how their day to day jobs could be improved not only within departments but on a company wide basis enveloping inter-departmental relationships.

"When we achieved BS5750 certification we made a conscious decision to take it a step further and provide the customer with more than he (she) would ever expect. This rejuvenation of Quality in the company is intended to make it nature rather than just a series of rules and regulations", explains Ann Malone.

When initially preparing for certification Ann Malone, with her understanding of the various functions and personalities at play in the organisation, wrote the procedures in consultation with the departments to expedite the process. The key requirements were to make the procedures simple, concise and easy to understand. Documentation was refined so that it remained at a workable minimum, with examples of a single form satisfying multiple functions being commonplace.

"At the time of compiling the procedures the company only consisted of 100 people which is still small enough to take a personal approach. Even now, because the Quality system is such an integral part of the way we do business you just naturally fall into it", explains Ann Malone. New recruits to the company are introduced to those procedures which are immediately relevant to their role and progressively learn the others as they interact with other departments.

Like any successful Quality initiative, Claremont's was supported by the Managing Director, Steve Chamberlain, however he was not the sole leader, as Ann Malone explains: "It has to be led from the top but not in isolation. It comes from three angles – the top, the sides from the customers and other departments within the company and from the bottom, the individuals in the workplace."

To capture the imagination of the workforce Claremont proposes to introduce a suggestion campaign which is not designed around a box on the wall but rather a suggestion week.

"Once a customer, always a customer" is the approach taken by Claremont with every client dealing and to this end it strives to achieve continually higher Customer Service standards. One method it has engaged since 1992 to measure its success in this area is the use of customer service surveys. Feedback is sent to the directors and everybody involved with a specific project via the return of survey results and a covering letter summarising the company's performance. The current survey monitors the provision of services to customers after they have had their new office environment installed and seeks to identify ways of improving on the standard it has set. The current questionnaire requests that customers score the company's performance on a scale of one to 10, indicating bad to good service. The format probes the following areas:

- Sales Performance: product knowledge; understanding customer needs; response to telephone calls; sales presentation; presentation of quote; and overall management of the project by the salesperson involved.
- Design Performance: response tothe brief; clarity of plans; standard of presentation work; adherence to deadlines; importance of design input in winning the business.
- Installation Performance: on-time delivery; management on-site; tidiness on completion; behaviour and appearance of installation team; installation completed-on-time; response to requests for variances to agreed layout; final installation appearance.
- Dealership Performance: telephonists response to your phone calls; response to any message left; response of other staff; treatment on arrival at Claremont; paperwork associated with project.

In all sections clients are encouraged to make comments and provide improvement ideas for both products and services. In line with Claremont's push to revitalise their Quality processes the customer service questionnaire is currently undergoing revision to make it a more proactive instrument in determining customer expectations prior to their experience with Claremont and then to gauge how these expectations were met. "Through this revised process we will collect information which will allow us to benefit other customers through our knowledge of market expectations which we will then meet and exceed as opposed to defining and working to what we think the client may reasonably expect", explains Ann Malone.

Claremont encourages anybody who has contact with the company to write down suggestions, problems or complaints they may have. Described as an 'unofficial suggestion scheme' it is not intended as a witch hunt but rather an indication of how the company, departments or individuals are performing. Any comments are returned to the relevant individual or department and addressed accordingly.

For example client feedback indicated that after installation, if a problem did occur Claremont's response times to resolve the problems did not consistently meet client expectations. In order to correct this situation

Claremont in conjunction with Furniture Management Services, its sister company, dedicated a service vehicle and a furniture fitter to the job of visiting clients in response to installation problems. However, they have gone one step further and now take the initiative to call on clients on a regular basis after installation to resolve any problems that may exist prior to the client initiating contact.

"At the end of the day we want to achieve a level of service and professionalism so that our clients will have absolutely nothing to gain from going elsewhere", explains Ann Malone. This is a view reinforced by Mr Chamberlain: "One thing we must never forget is that customers are 'apparently' spoilt for choice – this means that modern businesses must use weapons which exceed the traditional process of outlining the features and benefits of a product at a fair price. Customers are now looking much more at the value added by the supplying business partner – the knowledge provided, the skills delivered, the ongoing service – through all these value added chains must run one thought processs – consistent Quality – then the customer may never feel the need to choose and will remain a firm business partner providing ongoing revenue to fund the never ending Quality improvement process".

Claremont is taking client relationships to a new level which is consistent with its policy of supplying a solution not just a piece of equipment. Unilever, a multinational detergent, food and personal products manufacturer decided at the beginning of the 1990s that many of the buildings at one of its major research centres, at Port Sunlight near Chester, needed either refurbishment or a total rebuild. The requirement was for the Centre's appearance to reflect the company's international reputation for excellence - and to convey "a world-class environment for world-class research".

Claremont won the tender contract to furnish the new, purpose built centre and compiled a team of specialists who commenced the project by conducting an exhaustive analysis of the available space and the day-to-day requirements of the new 450 strong workforce. From this research Claremont designed and installed interior furnishing which provided the ideal environment for team-oriented working, subsequently acclaimed as a major innovation in the design and layout of a laboratory and office environment.

This initial introduction led to a stronger partnership between

Unilever and Claremont. As a result of the first phase Unilever identified the need to appraise the effectiveness of its existing West laboratory adjacent to the new building at Port Sunlight. A project team from Unilever was charged with the job of providing a facility which not only projected a professional image to visitors but also provided staff with a pleasing work environment. The strength of Claremont's reputation resulted in the secondment of a Claremont designer, Nick Dodds to the Unilever team for the duration of the three month project which conducted a detailed appraisal of every aspect of visual image and effectiveness from overall laboratory layout to visitor handling.

As part of this research visits were made to the sites of companies with world class reputations and interviews were conducted with representatives from 50 top companies such as Marks & Spencer, Royal Mail and British Gas. The project resulted in a series of short term and long term recommendations which are hallmarked for implementation.

The project highlights Claremont's ability to produce effective solutions within existing office environments in order to increase efficiency and help reduce costs. "It is a remarkable project for Claremont. In the office environments industry, most companies are asked to respond. In the case of Unilever Research, we exposed the need – and worked in partnership with them to help achieve their goals", explains Nick Dodds.

And just in case you were in any doubt over the value of coffee rooms, drinking fountains and lunchrooms, Claremont provides the following advice and indeed practices what it preaches: "Good conversation breeds good ideas, and spontaneous conversation breeds the best ideas of all. It's really not necessary to worry about the square feet allotted to the lunchroom when what matters is a frame of mind that encourages interchange. If such energy exists on a personal level, then surely a company can only benefit by channelling and challenging that energy to business needs." This philosophy is indeed key to the way Claremont operates and is encapsulated in everything it strives to achieve.

32

High Flying Leadership

— European Air Catering Services —

"IF you can change you will not necessarily be better, but if you have to be better you are obliged to change. People are scared of change. Sometimes our people might feel we change for the sake of it, which could be true, because resistance to change is enormous and resistance can only be overcome by people expecting constant change.

"I intend that we will continue to change, not just for the sake of it but actually because we need to change. We need to change because of our customer, we need to change because of our competitors, and all the time the change process in industry just goes faster and faster and if we don't maintain our enthusiasm for change, we can be sure that competitors will." Per Sköld, Managing Director of European Air Catering Services holds strong views on the need for modern industry to be prepared for constant change and improvement.

With a PhD in Psychology and many years experience as a successful management consultant, Per Sköld has the first-hand knowledge to support his views. The excellent results being achieved by European Air Catering services under his leadership make him doubly qualified to comment on the need for change and continuous improvement.

European Air Catering Services (EACS) was established on 1 February 1982 primarily to serve one customer, British Airways. EACS is contracted to cater for all BA European and domestic services.

Within EACS there are 15 departments which are divided into Support and Operations. All of these departments combined have in excess of 900 staff who produce up to 30,000 meals a day. This caters for 185 flights every 24 hours. Shifts prepare meals round the clock.

left to right: Chris Purkess (Quality Co-ordinator)
and Per Sköld (Managing Director)
European Air Catering Services

EACS is managed by Gate Gourmet International. Being the world's second largest airline caterer, Gate Gourmet operates 69 flight kitchens in 22 countries and employes 14,000 people. In total they produce on average 100 million meals per year.

EACS are obviously in the catering business but the job also entails a large logistics operation, as Chris Purkess, EACS's Head of Quality Processes explains:

"We cater for eight different aircraft, each with different requirements. The product itself isn't finalised until four hours prior to departure. To add to these problems or rather 'challenges' an aircraft may have to be changed at very short notice. Bearing in mind each aircraft has different equipment and stowage requirements, these changes have to be made quickly, efficiently and without compromising the very high standards our customer and ourselves hold.

"In addition there are five menu cycles which change every seven days each Thursday. It can be safely said that this is everybody's least favourite day."

Passengers have become much more discerning and to serve their needs, EACS provides over 20 different types of special meals ranging from gluten free meals through to kosher meals and meals for children. Of course the company also ensures that strict food safety and hygiene measures are maintained throughout the operation.

"In some quarters you still hear that airline meals are 'plasticy'. This reputation arose from the very early days long before we came on the scene and when there was probably some validity to it. Today however nothing could be further from the truth – certainly not with the meals we produce! Our customer, British Airways commits substantial resources to ensuring menus are developed that reflect their own high standards as an airline. As their catering contractor we work in partnership with them through the efforts of our Executive Chef Mick Cowdrey and his assistant Charlie Olsen who attend workshops with both BA and suppliers ensuring that the latest culinary concepts are developed on a continuing basis.

"Another thing that most people unconnected with the industry don't realise is that it isn't just food we provide. We are also responsible for providing duty free and cabin sales goods to flights. This consists of such things as liquor goods, beers, soft drinks, cigarettes, watches and perfumes. Additionally we also provide other ancillary items such as hot towels, head sets, first aid boxes, games packs for kids and other items which make the passenger's journey more comfortable and enjoyable", says Chris Purkess. Chris has specialised in Quality Management for the last three years. He has held a number of management positions in both operations and training and previously spent ten years with the British Army. Chris is a qualified Lead Assessor and TQM Facilitator with in depth training in Self Assessment against the TQM business excellence model developed by the European Foundation for Quality Management.

EACS's policy for Quality has been directly linked to its business aims as outlined within the company's vision and mission statements:

MISSION

EACS is dedicated to providing error free
meals and related services to strengthen
our customers' competitive edge and be the
quality caterer of the market.

Our targets are 100%:

- on time performance
- according to customer specification
- food safety
- always at a competitive price

VISION

We will be the partner to British
Airways and their customers,
achieved by quality people,
developed through a professional,
caring leadership, with a
commitment to innovation.

The above statements were established back in 1991 by the senior management team and many feedback sessions were given to all levels of staff in order that a full understanding was obtained.

This was by no means EACS's introduction to Quality management, which happened in 1989 when Per Sköld attended a seminar given by the well known Quality guru, Phillip Crosby. Although not necessarily understanding or agreeing with everything that was said, Per was nevertheless motivated towards developing the quality culture of the company.

The company decided to call the approach TQP (Total Quality

Performance). The word 'Performance' replaced the word 'Management' to ensure the initiative was seen as affecting the whole company and not just relating to the upper echelons of the business.

In the beginning many quality initiatives were implemented but not all were successful. Chris Purkess feels that much of the initial drive was superficial with lots of posters and gimmicky things like 'Quality' T shirts and drinks mats.

"There were also many good ideas that through our eagerness and enthusiasm were not completely thought through and therefore not totally successful. For instance, one idea was to have a 'quality street' whereby each department would have a designated space within one of the corridors where they would each place pictures, text, graphs etc. to show what they were doing to improve quality within their own areas. Initially this generated enthusiasm amongst the supervisors and staff and was seen to be worthwhile. Ultimately however, the momentum dropped and the initiative fizzled out. Another idea was the 100% club which involved representatives from each department meeting monthly to discuss inter departmental issues with the objective of jointly reaching agreement on improvement measures. Unfortunately, the process wasn't properly facilitated and in practice all that developed was conflict and arguments which tended to remain unresolved.

"One initiative that was implemented in 1990 and which has been very successful was the introduction of Supervisors seminars. These were held offsite and involved all Managers and Supervisors getting together in an environment which promoted open and honest discussion on various issues without fear of retribution. Although it was met with some initial scepticism it soon took hold and has undoubtedly been a key factor in the development of a culture in which Supervisors see themselves as part of management. Like many other labour intensive industries a large percentage of our supervisors have been promoted into their current positions and so it has been a long hard process. These seminars incidentally have long since been referred to as 'Management Seminars' which although only a change of name, it is indicative of the strides we have taken", explained Chris Purkess.

All of the early initiatives even if not totally successful contributed to the overall development of a culture in which Total Quality became the way people and processes were managed. Previously 'Quality ' was only considered important for the end product.

In February 1992 EACS moved location from an old building where the operation consisted mainly of manual handling, to a multi million pound purpose built, highly technological building. This was a massive change with all the associated problems. However, it was important that the paying passenger was given the same high level of service without disruption. To all intents and purposes this was achieved, even during the settling in period where the company had to overcome many day to day problems.

Later in 1992 after a lull in quality activities (due to the move), consultants were employed to give in depth training to five selected managers who would consequently facilitate a cascade of training throughout the organisation.

The training was based around the following model:

- The external customer
- The managers role in delivering quality
- A disciplined approach to quality improvement
- Continuous improvement

To achieve the above, four key training modules were established:

(i). Organising for Quality
(ii). Problem solving
(iii). Interpersonal skills
(iv). Teamwork

The training has been ongoing and all levels of management have now been trained. Improvements are currently being made to the training to include a more 'user friendly' version for non-management staff.

The vast majority of EACS's workforce are of Asian origin, many of whom have over the last few years developed into management positions. One of the most popular people in the building is Mr Nirbai Singh Gill, who joined the company 13 years ago as a General Hand in the 'Wash Up' area. He is now Head of Department for Despatch and Internal Services and is vital to the smooth running of the unit.

In 1993, EACS decided to implement a Quality Management System based on the ISO 9002 Quality Standard.

In order to gain a deeper understanding of the process and to learn from any mistakes made, initial implementation was to be made at a separate bonded stores unit known as Unit One. Cherree Bristow, the Quality Co-ordinator based at Unit One was made available to assist in taking the project forward. Cherree's main function prior to working on ISO 9000 was investigating and answering customer complaints and checking bars to ensure they had been packed correctly. Chris Purkess who led the implementation of ISO 9000 explained that the system was viewed as a means not an end:

"Although achieving registration to ISO 9002 standard was the ultimate goal, I nevertheless wanted to implement a system which was flexible to change, contributed to our goal of continuous improvement and did not require excessive resources in order to maintain it.

After a great deal of effort and with the support of all the management and staff at Unit One, our goals were met and in September 1994 registration was achieved at the first attempt."

As testimony of the company's success many tangible benefits can be identified. Some of these were:

- Reduction in customer complaints from 43 to 4 per month
- Reduction in supervisor shifts from 5 to 3 per day
- Reduction in sickness from 7.5% to 2%
- Reduction in holding stock from 7 days to 3 days
- Cost per unit saving of 7.1%
- Increase of over 5% in volume of bars packed per staff member
- Consistent high performance since product change in May '94.....(variance in efficiency 3.4% as opposed to 12.6% variance over same period '93)
- Additional contract to supply bars to BA domestic lounges
- Contract of agreement renewed for a further two year period

Building on our success we obviously wanted to continue the good work in our core unit. We set our goals as follows:

- To establish best practices in all aspects of the operation
- To establish control in order that identified best practices are carried out consistently
- To develop a programme of continuous improvement through an ongoing schedule of internal audits with corrective and preventive measures clearly established

and lastly...

- To achieve registration to ISO 9002

"I have deliberately left ISO registration as the last aim as my fear is that by focusing primarily on the minutiae of the standard, a system is introduced which does not meet the fundamental needs of the business and can in fact slowly strangle it through overbureaucracy. Having said that, the ISO standard is an excellent framework but must be kept in proportion with the needs of the business", continued Chris Purkess.

In addition to using the ISO framework as part of the company's continuous improvement programme, EACS have a number of key initiatives, especially important are; Internal Benchmarking and Operational Staff Training.

The Internal Benchmarking programme is managed by the parent company Gate Gourmet and is world-wide.

Units throughout the organisation are assessed by an independent audit team using a questionnaire to identify best practices and areas for improvement. Identified best practices are then communicated throughout all units in order that where necessary they can learn from and benefit accordingly. Areas that have been identified for improvement are then built into the business strategy of the unit involved. To date 45 catering units have been audited including EACS which was rated amoung the top three.

The Operational Staff Training programme is a training programme developed for all employees in the unit on an operational level. It consists of a large number of short work based training modules which cover all the work positions and tasks within the unit and are known as FMTs – Five Minute Training. The targets of the programme are:

- To cover the total requirement of competence
- To ensure that nobody does a job in which they have not been trained.

"I have structured our quality system so that as each area completes its procedures documentation, FMTs are written and a training plan formulated relating to the processes identified as opposed to the individual functions. This ensures that our management style is process and not functional oriented", says Chris Purkess.

A schedule of audits is then carried out on each area with the emphasis on evaluating the effectiveness of the procedures and implementing improvement practices. This moves away from the traditional ISO 'compliance' audit and therefore retains flexibility and is conducive to

AIRLINE CATERING	FIVE MINUTES TRAINING (FMT)

Module no: ST/SM/20	Job Holder: STOREMAN	Department: STORES	Updated by: T GARWOOD
Description: HOW TO USE A TEMPERATURE PROBE			Issue Date: July 1995
			Issue No: 001

Aims & Results:

The fundamental aims of this training session are:

To learn the correct method of using a temperature probe

After the training you will be able to do the following task:

Correctly use the temperature probe, carry out temperature checks

The Quality improvement achieved through this FMT is:

A reduction in the risk of bacterial contamination through careful temperature monitoring

Location: Stores Office/Training Room	Planned follow-up: Hygiene Officer to review after one month	Pre-reading/video: N/A

Training:

Description:

Ref:

Before you take the temperature of any product:

Wash your hands.

Put on disposable plastic gloves.

Take the Thermometer with attached probe.

Wipe the probe with a temperature probe wipe. This will sanitise the probe.

Turn the thermometer "on".

Take a food sample.

Insert the probe into the food sample. If the food is vacuum packed place the probe between two samples.

Wait for the reading on the thermometer to stabilize. This will take approximately 30 seconds.

When the reading stops the thermometer will give you the temperature of the product.

Remove the probe from the food.

Dispose of sample if the probe has entered the food.

Turn the thermometer "off".

Wipe the probe with a temperature probe wipe.

Remove gloves and dispose.

Wash your hands.

Enter the temperature onto the Purchase Order/Temp Control sheet.

IMPORTANT

You must change your gloves and wash your hands for every product, even if received in the same delivery or the temperature checks are taken at the same time.

continuous improvement. It also enables the corporate benchmarking programme to be integrated fully without overlapping with our own quality programme.

The Internal Benchmarking team that audited EACS identified a number of best practices. Including two that had a massive impact on EACS's overall quality programme:

1. Approval of and agreements made with suppliers.
2. Customer service.

Food Safety is of paramount importance and as such suppliers need to be approved to ensure they can conform not only to the very strict UK legislation but also to standards laid down by EACS, their customer and by the Airline Catering Code of Good Catering Practice guidelines (which is even stricter!).

Suppliers are categorised into risks: High, Medium, Low which is based upon:

1. Product type
2. Volumes
3. Past history (if known).

The risk category determines how often the supplier is audited. Audits are conducted by EACS's Hygiene Officer, Pat Clark, against a set of criteria laid down by the company's customer, British Airways.

From the audit a report is derived with several possible conclusions:

1. Fully approved
2. Approved with minor non-conformances
3. Conditional approval for certain products (major non-conformances on other production lines)
4. Unacceptable to supply any product type.

Recommendations with time limits are identified within the report. If a company wishes to continue to supply EACS, Pat Clark will conduct a follow up visit at the end of a set time period.

When a supplier is fully approved it will not be visited until the scheduled time for the next audit or unless any problems in relation to food safety occur.

There is a committee called the Supplier Technical Audit Committee (STAC) which sits every quarter. This is made up from technical and purchasing personnel from British Airways, EACS and Alpha Flight Services who are the catering contractor for British Airways out of Gatwick.

The aim of the committee is to share resources and information between the three companies. It constantly reviews its mission and policy statements in view of any new food safety legislation and requirements. This ensures that catering units have a safe product entering the production unit. There is more and more emphasis being placed on this issue because catering units are now tending to move towards becoming assembly plants rather than production units with more completed products coming in through the supply warehouse. There are obviously bottom line benefits for moving this way, however, completed products which require no further manipulation need to be monitored more carefully as they represent the highest risk.

EACS deals with a core of main suppliers, all of whom have undertaken a Service Level Agreement covering various areas such as menu change details, product description, out of hours contact, order processing, delivery details, etc. In addition, there is a standard format specification document which each supplier has to complete together with a photograph of the product they are supplying. This is a very detailed specification outlining a number of key areas to ensure that both quality and consistency of product is achieved. These specs are held at the EACS Inbound Stores dock and form part of the company's receiving procedures.

A strict monitoring of supplier performance is carried out and any problems and particularly trends are discussed and evaluated at a monthly procurement meeting held with British Airways and attended by the EACS Customer Service and Purchasing Manager Brian Lyons. This is not to say dialogue isn't carried out with the suppliers themselves. There is also an ongoing process of direct dialogue carried out by Brian Lyons who also ensures that a performance review meeting is undertaken with core suppliers on a regular basis.

Satisfying and exceeding customer requirements is accepted amongst leading organisations as fundamental not only in respect of quality but in driving the business forward in general. EACS are no exception to this and take great efforts to meet these ends. Chris Purkess explains how EACS ensures the customer is king:

"We have in place a customer service function which includes four Customer Representatives available on a 24 hour, 7 day a week basis. These reps have a number of responsibilities, not least to maintain positive customer relations and act as an active link between the customer and our internal departments.

"They liaise with the customer on a daily basis and are proactive in developing new ideas and ensuring any new instructions are understood and implemented by all relevant departments. They also ensure that any complaints received are investigated and responded to within 48 hours (even though we only have one customer, in reality we feel accountable to everyone who receives our meals). If any trends are identified the relevant departments are informed who then work to put in place preventive measures so as to ensure that as far as possible problem areas are not repeated. The reps also ensure that compliments are also communicated."

An agreed standard has been set by British Airways in which EACS is judged on a cumulative basis over a one year period.

This is known as the Performance Bond and measurements are made on a monthly basis against set targets on key areas such as; Food Safety, Customer Complaints, On Time Performance and Wastage.

EACS have designed their mission statement to reflect these priorities and the ultimate target is 100 per cent in each area.

If successful, EACS receives recognition of this from their customer in the form of a certificate and of course continued goodwill!

The company's results over recent years reflect British Airways satisfaction. Recently this was further demonstrated with the signing of a further five year contract. Chris Purkess plans even better results:

"In the future, EACS will be developing and exploiting its strengths for maximum effect. Training, management development and customer service are all high profile areas. In addition to this, extra emphasis is now being placed on developing our key business processes.

"Being honest with ourselves and looking critically at how we do things and then systematically prioritising and addressing key issues is fundamental in our strategy for continuous improvement."

Per Sköld concludes with some advice for other 'leaders':

"Getting a culture change like the one we have had over the past six years, requires a spark to set it off. Then it becomes a question of people believing in the core philosophy and spreading this belief throughout the organisation. For this you need 'Champions', dedicated people who believe it is right and are prepared to see it implemented.

"Any successful Quality programme has to be led from the very top

– not even one step below, otherwise it will fail. People have to see you believe what you are saying, they aren't fools and insincerity shines through immediately.

"I have never quantified targets or said that we are using Total Quality to raise profits or increase efficiency. I believe that, in time, Total Quality will be the only way we can compete. Without this approach we won't be able to attract and recruit good staff or even train our people better than the competition.

"The outcome of Quality for us, has been to, rectify our errors, become more efficient and out perform our competitors – I don't need a calculator to tell me this makes us more profitable."

33

Achieving The Mark Of High Quality Service

—Willis Corroon—

WILLIS Corroon is recognised as a leading supplier of high quality risk management, insurance broking and financial planning services. One of the principal business segments within which the Group operates is that of UK retail which involves the provision of these services to industrial and commercial undertakings and to private individuals throughout the UK and Ireland and worldwide for multinational clients.

The company's origins can be traced as far back as the 1820s to a private firm, Henry Willis and Co which became Willis Faber & Dumas Ltd after a series of mergers during the 1800s. The company went public in the 1970s and merged with another large UK insurance broking group, Stewart Wrightson in 1987 and finally with an American broker, Corroon & Black in 1990 to form the present group, Willis Corroon Group plc.

Willis Corroon Limited (WCL) is the Group's principal corporate entity within the UK retail sector, employing 2,000 people and delivering its services through seven regional companies and several specialist companies in 24 offices, dealing directly with its clients. The company was recognised in 1995, for the fourth successive year, as the UK's largest direct insurance broker, based on the aggregate turnover of its clients. However, WCL is an industry leader not only in terms of its size, but also in its drive to incorporate Quality into every aspect of its activities.

The Willis Corroon Group's commitment to Quality is not limited to WCL and the Group is a member of the British Quality Foundation, the European Foundation for Quality Management and the British Deming Association. In the USA Willis Corroon is a founder member of the

Charles Lucas
Quality Manager
Willis Corroon

Quality Insurance Congress, created in 1993 by members of the insurance industry to promote key Quality principles in the conduct of business.

WCL reinforced the commitment of the Group to Quality by obtaining registration to ISO 9001 (then BS 5750 Part 1) in the early 1990s. Other parts of the Group, including its offices specialising in captive insurance company management and several of its specialist risk management operations achieved registration at the same time. The Group's arm specialising in group pension scheme administration is registered by Investors in People.

The first direct experience of ISO 9000 (BS 5750) for WCL occurred at its Maidstone office, when the possibility arose of being precluded from doing business with a prospective corporate client due to the absence of ISO 9000 (BS 5750) registration. This incident was significant enough to generate further consideration and debate within the office and WCL as a whole about the benefits the ISO 9000 (BS 5750) registration could offer.

The Maidstone office chose to pursue registration, which it received in 1992, making it the first insurance broker to apply for and receive registration. However, WCL's major competitors were quick to recognise the advantages to be gained from registration.

The Maidstone registration became the catalyst for a company wide approach to the subject. Despite the growing competitive necessity of registration, the primary perceived benefit was the use of registration as a vehicle to refine procedures and consolidate activity between the company's diverse and semi-autonomous offices.

By 1994 each of the WCL's offices around the United Kingdom and Ireland had successfully undergone assessment by BSI Quality Assurance, allowing the company to establish common service standards and procedures which ensure consistent quality throughout the organisation.

Key to undertaking this Quality initiative was the establishment of the National Quality Steering Group (NQSG) to oversee the registration process in all WCL's offices and the subsequent maintenance requirements of registration. The NQSG consists of nine senior members of staff from different regions and parts of the company. The representatives were appointed by the WCL Board based on their overall knowledge of all aspects of the working of the company. It is chaired by the Director of the company responsible for Quality – currently the Deputy Chief Executive.

The Group engaged the advice of inhouse consultants from a subsidiary of the Group which provided BS 5750 advice as part of its service. On the advice of the consultants BSI Quality Assurance was selected to carry out assessment and registration.

The consultants were responsible for briefing each office's senior management on the requirements for achieving ISO registration, which were conducted in the latter part of 1992. "We decided to seek registration for each individual office as opposed to WCL as a single entity because of the diverse nature of our organisation both in terms of geography and activity. However, to ensure consistency of approach, we decided to compile a single Quality Manual for WCL and also a National Quality Procedures document, which defines how WCL expects key elements of the business to be handled, irrespective of the location or specialism of a specific office. This provides consistency because all local procedures are based on the national procedures. The local offices were required to produce local quality procedures based on the national format to describe their processes in detail", explains Charles Lucas, Quality Manager.

The national procedures were drafted by NQSG members following consultation with colleagues and submitted to each part of the organisation for their comments on both style and content. "We started off by including too much detail in the procedures, which resulted in a cumbersome document that was prohibitive to use. We gradually refined it through company-wide discussions to produce short, sharp procedures which are user friendly", explains Mr Lucas. A consultant was assigned to each office to provide guidance in the preparation of local procedures in accordance with the Standard.

"We initially found the Standard difficult to interpret in relation to insurance broking because of its manufacturing bias. In many respects we were breaking new ground because we were pioneers in pursuing registration in the insurance industry, if not the service industry. We put our own interpretations on the Standard and consulted BSI Quality Assurance to ensure that we were operating within acceptable parameters, which in many instances prompted long discussions. For example, although we generate financial documentation we don't believe that we use statistical techniques in the sense referred to in the Standard. Whilst we contend that we are not a statistically orientated organisation in the sense that we use standard deviation and other such mathematical devices we feel that we need to keep this matter under review. While many of the clauses seemed at first sight, to have little relevance to our situation, we were still required to document each in a way that demonstrated that we were aware of the clause and had taken its provisions into account", explains Mr Lucas who assumed the role of Quality Manager in January 1994. Prior to this appointment Mr Lucas spent over 20 years in broking and handling client business as well as a further five years as an administration director in one of WCL's regional operations.

Another element of the Standard, which at first glance, did not appear relevant to an insurance broking company is that of calibration of equipment. However, on consideration of its activity which includes the use of risk management specialists and risk control surveyors it became obvious that WCL needed to conform with the requirements of the Standard and verify the calibration of equipment such as flow meters for testing sprinkler systems and sound meters for measuring noise in industrial environments in order to ensure the validity of results.

After the national and local procedures were completed the consultants conducted a pre-assessment audit to determine whether the organisation was ready for the BSI's scrutiny. The BSI assessments followed and registrations were completed for the entire organisation by July 1994.

WCL pursued registration to ISO 9001 which includes the design component because the company offers services and products which are customised and consequently require an element of design. As Mr Lucas explains, "We are looking to distinguish ourselves as leading insurance brokers in that we do not in all cases just buy insurance policies 'off the shelf' but we design insurance programmes and in some cases policy wordings tailored to our clients' needs after reviewing their situation. Our services will often also include the design of risk management programmes."

The design of an insurance and risk management programme typically occurs in a new business situation and involves a series of initial meetings with a prospective customer to gain an understanding of their business and review their existing arrangements. From this information a programme is designed to meet their insurance and in many cases risk management needs. ISO 9001 requires that procedures are put in place to control: the planning phase; design inputs to ensure that the requirements are understood from the onset; design output to ensure that the final design meets the original requirements; design verification to test the design on completion; and design changes.

Recording the design procedures presented a degree of difficulty because as Mr Lucas describes: "WCL is an entrepreneurial company and the people who do the design work do so almost intuitively. In the past we had not formally recorded the processes in sufficient detail to satisfy the Standard. However, compliance with the ISO 9001 Standard has now made us more deliberate in our design process so that we adhere to the requirements of recording, reviewing, verifying and validating our activity."

Initially the decision to pursue ISO 9001 (BS 5750 Part 1) required extensive discussion to convince the BSI of WCL's design process. At the time the BSI had only limited experience with the insurance industry. The necessity to register WCL's design capability required the BSI to modify its standard assessment procedures on some occasions. For instance, although design is involved in a significant proportion of WCL's cases, it is not universally required, so it became necessary for WCL to guide the BSI in the selection of suitable cases for review in place of the common practice of randomly selecting files.

"We are now more disciplined in evidencing that we have carried out checks. Our procedures have been sharpened up and we have become more methodical in our approach," explains Mr Lucas.

Although WCL recognises that ISO 9000 registration forms are only part of an on-going Quality programme, the introduction of soundly based and efficient procedures has resulted in a reduction of waste and time-consuming re-working.

For example, there is greater appreciation and use of information generated by the complaints procedures. "The Quality system required these procedures to be organised more clearly so that the people responsible for the individual offices were better able to review and act on complaints, which now provides the manager with a more accurate picture of this aspect.

"The process of obtaining ISO registration brought to the fore many individuals who had not previously been prominent in their offices. However, having had this task given to them, they seized it and blossomed, resulting in improved career development opportunities", explains Mr Lucas.

Another area of improvement within WCL is the company's

internal auditing capability. WCL adopted a dual level auditing programme which reviews operations at a national level and local office level. Local audits tend to be less formal than their national counterparts and are conducted by members of staff from within individual offices. Typically, there are six or so trained auditors in every office.

As part of the national audit programme senior managers visit offices for which they have no direct responsibility to conduct an audit on behalf of the NQSG, which is responsible for monitoring the national Quality programme. The national audit team consists of 25 senior people drawn from around the organisation. "It assists the company because auditors visit different parts of the organisation and in doing so identify best practice, which they can then transfer to their own and other parts of the organisation. This kind of management review has also proved to be valuable because it imposes a sense of discipline on managers who may otherwise become distracted from adhering to procedures by other key activities such as obtaining new business or servicing clients", explains Mr Lucas.

"Having achieved ISO 9001 we are now looking at how we should take Total Quality Management forward. The difficulty is that ISO placed a strain on the company and we couldn't face another major initiative at this time. We realise we cannot stand still and we are now looking at a more gradual approach perhaps using the European Quality Award Model for self assessment as well as reviewing to what extent we should involve other parts of the Group", explains Mr Lucas.

Many of Willis Corroon's Worldwide offices and associates are in the process of achieving ISO 9000 registration, which has been achieved recently in Germany and Belgium. "Others have made varying degrees of progress and due to our success in the UK we conducted a seminar for the European offices early in 1995. Whilst we were able to provide advice and assistance, offices need to do it for themselves, because in the final analysis it has to be their system", explains Mr Lucas who offers the following advice to those thinking about ISO registration: "It is important to resolve why you are trying to achieve ISO registration. Decide whether the organisation will benefit from formal registration such as ISO 9000 or whether it should just be looking at Quality generally. Many companies in some industries applied for ISO 9000 because they felt pressured to do so by their customers. However, while it does provide a very good framework for developing Quality it is not an end in itself. There are other ways of achieving Quality using programmes such as the EFQM model or Investors in People rather than automatically seeking ISO 9000 registration

"Willis Corroon Limited has certainly benefited considerably from achieving ISO 9001 registration and it would now be difficult to see the company operating as efficiently without it. The company is now ready to examine additional ways of developing its approach to Quality."

34

Service As An Exact Science

—Severn Trent Water—

SEVERN Trent plc is one of the world's largest privately owned water services positioned amongst the 100 largest listed companies in the UK. Its main activities include: water supply services; waste water services; waste management services; water technology services; and design of customer service software systems.

Severn Trent Water's contribution to the group is substantial – its 1994/95 turnover was £847 million providing profit before tax of £308 million. Employing 6,200 people in 15 operating districts this company is both diverse and dispersed. Severn Trent Water prides itself as being a leading provider of water supply and waste water services in the UK serving eight million people in an area stretching from the Bristol Channel to the Humber Estuary in the north.

However, Severn Trent Water, like many of Britain's privatised utilities, is forced to combat public confusion between truth and perception encouraged by unfair generalisations made by the media. Perhaps this environment has given Severn Trent Water added incentive to excel because the reality is that it is a low cost, high quality supplier.

European drinking water standards are the highest in the world and Severn Trent Water is amongst the best in Europe. Only the United Kingdom and Switzerland attain levels of 99 per cent compliance, and since 1993 Severn Trent Water has achieved a record performance of 99.8 per cent. Despite being one of the most profitable water service companies in the UK, Severn Trent Water has the second lowest average charges of the ten water authorities privatised in 1989.

Brian Duckworth
Managing Director
Severn Trent Water

Terry Kitson
Head of Planning &
Performance
Severn Trent Water

The average monthly number of written complaints received by the company has dropped by two-thirds since the end of 1991. Severn Trent Water's efforts to improve customer service and its efforts to transform itself from a traditional public utility into an efficient service company was recognised by the award of the Government's Charter Mark in 1992. The infusion of Quality into every corner of the organisation and a strong emphasis on teamwork have been the main vehicles for its success to date and survival in the future.

Dr Terry Kitson, Head of Planning and Performance describes the competitive and social pressures Severn Trent Water faces and the role Quality will play in binding the organisation together: "The rate of change and the increasing pressures that we face are unlikely to diminish and we need to prepare all staff for the times that lie ahead. Of particular importance are the threat to our customer base and the fact that acquisitions, takeovers and mergers are now a real fact of life as we have seen with attempts to acquire other utilities and speculation that there may be only five or six at the turn of the century. But the people who will hold the high ground at the end of the day are those who are delivering genuine customer service."

"We have determined that we will differentiate ourselves from others in our sector through customer service and asset management. Subsequently there has been the need to position our staff for continual downsizing. In order to hold people together and give them a common sense of purpose in these turbulent times we are seeking to change corporate culture which is always difficult. We are doing this through a programme that we call Working for Quality."

Dr Kitson who has a PhD in water resources commenced his career in 1972 joining one of England's 128 water undertakings which became part of Severn Trent Water in 1974, making him one of the company's long serving employees. In his role as Head of Planning and Performance Dr Kitson has wide ranging responsibilities including the Total Quality Programme, process re-engineering, financial and operational auditing, performance review, strategic analysis and the production of the company's five year Master Plan enveloping Quality as 'business as usual'.

The company divided its Working for Quality (WfQ) programme into four phases which involved initial evaluation to determine whether to pursue a Total Quality Management programme. The decision to pursue this programme was made in April 1993 launching the next stage which involved pilot studies using a group of approximately 20 people.

In stage three a presentation package was produced and launched in September 1993 in an awareness cascade including all staff led by Directors and then Senior Managers. By mid February 1994 most of the 6,500 employees had participated in an awareness session. In turn these sessions promoted the voluntary involvement of one-third of staff in team improvement activities which the company views as "a quite remarkable demonstration of personal and corporate commitment".

The last stage in the Severn Trent Water's Quality chronology is the challenge it faces today – "Creating an environment of total commitment where Working for Quality becomes a part of everyday working life and is not something that only occurs in formal groups".

Severn Trent Water has received many accolades saluting its success in not only Quality circles but within industry in general. In 1994 the 'Most Admired Companies' survey showed that the company had moved ahead tremendously from its position in 1992: it was perceived as the second best water services company from a field of 10; sixth utility from a field of 36; and 65th company from a total of 260.

It was also the recipient of the 1994 Perkins Award which is presented to the organisation which can demonstrate the best progress in its continuous improvement programme during that year. Through verbal and written presentations the company was examined on all elements of its Quality programme including: Commitment to Quality improvements; Quality education and training; Quality measurement; Quality commitment and recognition; and future plans for continuous Quality improvements.

Severn Trent Water firmly regards the award as recognition of the "efforts put in by people throughout the organisation to make Working for Quality our new way of life". Recognition through awards is seen as a means of illustrating the company's progress to the few internal and external sceptics who still remain.

Severn Trent's vision statement focuses on the importance of teamwork in helping achieve company objectives: "Our purpose is to be a world leader in the water business founded on a strong home water utility base. We will foster a style of management based on personal responsibility and trust through a team of enthusiastic, innovative and well trained people always maintaining ethical and professional standards, and focusing on care for our customers, our colleagues, our shareholders and our environment."

Similarly the company's Total Quality programme contains something for all its stakeholders. "You can almost match our four objectives with the different interest groups we serve: the shareholder is looking for cost reductions or income generation from this programme; the customer is looking for a rising level of service with lower costs or improved efficiency so long as this efficiency is paid back to them; employee satisfaction is important to us as we are only as good as the enthusiasm and ability of our workforce; and the environment, everybody who lives and works in the Midlands is our customer and although they may not pay us directly for it we are conscious of the community and environmental care. To balance all these needs is a difficult act to pull. We have to balance the short term wishes of shareholders with the long term interests of protecting our assets, the health of the nation and the environment – all of which is played out in the public domain."

Severn Trent Water is committed to achieving higher customer satisfaction and higher employee satisfaction, together with higher levels of efficiency while maintaining its excellence in regulatory compliance. In order to achieve this the company chose to release the energy and inventiveness of its staff to continually find new ways of improving Quality and eliminating waste through a culture founded on WfQ.

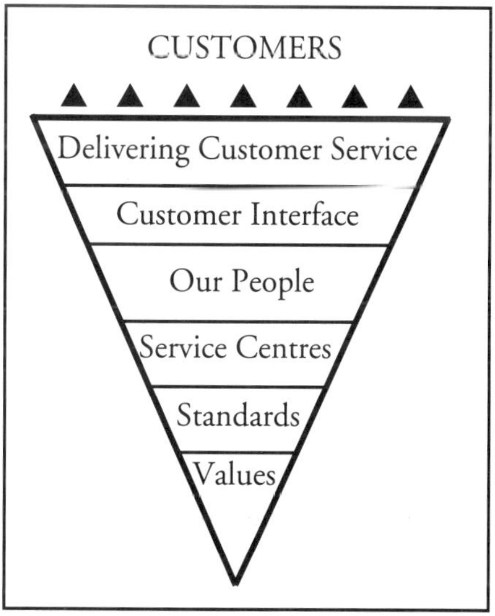

The programme is based on six principles. All staff are aware of them and encouraged to meet them in their day to day work are as follows:

1. Customer First – The external dimension

- knowing the expectations of the external customer
- listening to the voice of the external customer

- translating their words into Severn Trent Water language
- building their views into the way the company conducts business

2. **Constancy of Purpose – The leadership dimension**

- inspiring a shared mission
- holding onto long term aims
- demonstrating enthusiasm
- leading the improvement process
- acting as a role model
- coaching not judging

3. **Focused Involvement – The people dimension**

- involvement through open effective teamwork
- cross-functional teamwork
- empowerment
- training as a necessity

4. **Act on Facts – The knowledge dimension**

- disciplined approach to improvement and problem solving
- analyse for root causes
- informative data and correct interpretation
- understanding the impact of variability
- measuring and targeting improvement at all levels

5. **Process Emphasis – The systems dimension**

- satisfying internal customers
- treating external suppliers as partners
- mapping, controlling, improving all processes
- cross-functional improvement teams
- measuring process effectiveness

6. **Continuous Improvement – The learning dimension**

- treating mistakes and errors as opportunities
- challenging the status quo
- seeking out best practices (benchmarking).

All staff members are offered a wide variety of training courses ranging from technical and equipment usage to personal training skills and job knowledge training courses. Specific courses covering team building and teamwork have been designed for any member of staff who is either joining or forming a new team or where it is felt that a refresher course is required.

Each of Severn Trent Water's 24 Quality Facilitators were provided with 14 days of in-depth training over a three month period. They now have the necessary skills, tools and techniques to deliver awareness and process review team training; facilitate process review and improvement activity; and help change the culture.

As part of Severn Trent Water's customer first emphasis it has evaluated the training needs of its contractors, as representatives of the company. One of the major initiatives arising from this was the introduction of the Sewercare programme, which is a code of practice emphasising the role of Customer Care within Sewerage Construction works. In addition to the completion of work, the Customer Care programme ensures that work is carried out with respect and consideration for the needs of customers and that those affected in the community know what is happening, why, how and when.

As a company that welcomes motivational awards, Severn Trent Water also places importance on recognising the Quality service it receives from contractors and suppliers. The company presents an annual award to the Contractor of the Year recognising good customer service and Quality of workmanship, and supplier awards. To qualify for a supplier award the applicant must supply Severn Trent Water with distribution materials totalling a quarter of a million pounds or more, none of which are defective. It also recognises service aspects such as accuracy of invoicing and the responsiveness of the sales department.

The company has also launched its own internal Quality Award for Project Teams based on formal judging criteria such as the provision of clear benefits; use of clear methodology; good team work; clear use of tools and techniques; standardisation and review; involvement of others; documentation; and Quality of presentation.

The key to WfQ is firmly entrenched in teamwork as described in Severn Trent Water's Working for Quality Staff Handbook: "We are used to thinking that it's individuals who make the difference. Some expert has a great idea, everybody else goes through the motions, and that's how you become successful. Working for Quality says no. Working for Quality says that the key to success is people working together. That means teamwork."

Severn Trent Water has established various project teams involved with Company Quality Improvement Projects (CQIP) usually identified and owned by a Director, Local Quality Improvement Projects(LQIP), and Weighty Quality Improvement Projects (WQIP). All encourage the use of cross-functional representation including craft and industrial staff and involvement from all levels of the organisation. "What we are now attempting to do is develop a departmental focus, so instead of Total Quality being something teams do off line, it becomes what all our teams do all the time. Each department team will have its own purpose statement supported by objectives", says Dr Kitson.

LQIPs have a local impact and are chosen by objective criteria such as: high level of customer dissatisfaction; high level of employee dissatisfaction; high level cost to the company; causing lost income; or causing failure of regulatory or other standards. The problem, activity or process selected for analysis must be within the responsibility of a local manager who becomes the project owner. The last band of improvement projects, WQIPs, have a direct company wide impact and must be agreed and owned by the Senior Manger responsible for the area under review.

One team's work on a Quality Improvement Project has been nationally recognised, recently being nominated as a finalist of the 1995 Michelin Award. The Goscote Works Performance Team was established to investigate the performance of the Goscote Sewage Works over a five year period from 1986 to 1994 with particular regard to operating practices, plant, and sewage composition.

Over a six month period the team succeeded in finding a solution to reduce the threat of equipment failure at the plant. The steps in the problem solving process were: define the problem; analyse for root causes; generate solutions; plan and implement solution trials; measure the results; and standardise the solution.

This project highlighted the importance of involving the right expert people for the project at hand, good team leading and facilitation of the process, and also data gathering.

Initially concern was expressed in parts of the organisation at the lack of coordination and resulting overlap of activity: "Whilst Working for Quality is proving a useful tool/process, how much is it costing the company overall – where are the paybacks? Why are Districts and other Departments tackling the same or similar issues? There appears to be a distinct lack of coordination in this area. As the company approaches the next five year period, we must surely examine the real effectiveness of Working for Quality", was one employee's concern.

In response to this concern, Brian Duckworth, Managing Director of Severn Trent Water explains that some duplication is regarded as a small price for creating greater awareness and commitment in the process: "The intention was to get people involved and not be overly constrained by groups. If some duplication occurs then so be it initially. It is important to give people the opportunity to express themselves, to put forward their thoughts. However, some element of control is desirable; projects shouldn't go on for ever."

All Quality Improvement Projects must conform to certain requirements: be facilitated; be registered on the Quality Improvement Projects database; have a project plan; have a Steering Group; use the appropriate tools and techniques; document the process and the results; report progress; and share results and experiences with other districts and functional departments.

Severn Trent Water's Customer Service Strategy serves as an example of how WfQ has permeated the organisation and assisted in the revision of work practices. The company's Customer First emphasis was reinforced in 1993 with the re-structuring of the Customer Service Departments and appointment of a Customer Service Director with responsibility for all staff whose prime role was either direct customer contact or support for frontline staff. It involved areas as diverse as treatment and distribution of drinking water, sewage treatment and the sending of bills to customers.

The revision of the strategy commenced with the formation of a working party and a workshop for 30 frontline Customer Service Staff who were charged with the task of providing data to enable the managers to assemble the strategy.

Various topics were discussed using tools, techniques and methods of analysis from the WfQ programme. Items covered included customer expectations, measurement of customer service and improving customer perceptions. "The results from the initial workshop were refined and consolidated to provide a report which developed the company's thinking and attitudes as to the type of company it wanted to be. This in turn led to a segmented approach in which we separately identified customers' core product needs, individual service needs and the demands of society in the community", explains Dr Kitson.

The strategy was drawn up by over 100 staff from all disciplines working together to analyse Severn Trent Water's current approach to customer service and the improvements required to ensure that the company was organised to deal efficiently with all customer enquiries or complaints. "Our basic objective was to meet agreed customer expectations at least cost with maximum employee satisfaction. We also recognised however that there was considerable opportunity to exceed customer expectations in respect of individual contact with them."

Six cross-functional teams were established to analyse individual aspects of customer service – ethos, physical interface, staff, standards, technology and support. The involvement of all staff at all levels encouraged wide ranging ideas covering all aspects of the company and ensured ownership of the resulting recommendations. The whole process took approximately 10 months to complete and culminated in a conference attended by over 300 staff representing all levels and departments within the company who were then encouraged to cascade the details to their colleagues.

Together with long term strategic initiatives Severn Trent Water introduced four key customer service standards which included that all visitors to the company's offices will be seen by the appropriate staff member within five minutes of their arrival; all customer letters are to be answered within five working days 75 per cent of the time and within 10 working days 100 per cent of the time; customer telephone calls are to be answered within an average of 15 seconds and a maximum of 30 seconds; and whenever a customer meeting is scheduled the company will agree to come either in the morning or the afternoon and will keep the appointment.

Severn Trent Water is still in the process of determining where it should lie on the standardisation spectrum. "As a company we can't be totally standardised, but we need to sit somewhere along the spectrum because we need to provide some sort of framework. Our policy is that whenever we interface with a customer a standardised response must be given in terms of waiting times, forms used and so on. However, in respect to how people achieve this standard response they are given scope to use different methods."

Communication within the organisation is viewed as a constant challenge. Information is currently disseminated through a number of channels including newsletters, information boards, employee conferences, lunchtime briefings, but most importantly through direct personal briefings.

The company conducts monthly Team Meetings to disseminate company news to all staff via their line managers. However, the emphasis is on providing local items of interest and discussion of these topics is encouraged. Managers then feed comments back to the directors for consideration and resolution where required.

Every Severn Trent Water Director observes an annual programme for visiting district offices and departments within the Head Office. The object of each of these visits is to hear employee views, answer their questions and establish how the WfQ programme is progressing in each area.

The benefits ledger introduced in 1994 serves as a communication device produced bi-annually to track project progress. All teams register the projects they are addressing, initially identifying potential benefits, then again after some modification and finally when the project has been completed.

EXAMPLE FROM THE BENEFITS LEDGER

Situation before Improvement	Consequence	Potential Benefits	Benefit Area	Pounds where appropriate
Due to the poor performance of the works (especially the presence of scum/mousse on the final separating tanks) the works has considerable resources focused upon it in an effort to resolve the problem.	Significant investigatory costs have been involved during the period April 92 – May 93: COD Monitoring (£2,500) Lab costs (£2,200) Extra Analytical Costs (£33,000) Chemical dosing trials (£6,700) Process development costs (£14,500) Tankering exercise (£15,000)	The elimination of further and future investigatory costs.	S	74,900

In conjunction with the introduction of the WfQ programme Severn Trent Water ensured that relevant measures were also introduced or modified simultaneously to take account of the new way of working. Dr Kitson firmly believes, "If you can't measure it – you can't manage it and consequently we are constantly reviewing our methods of measuring and ensuring that the information gathered is both analysed and fed back into the process to ensure continual improvement." Good measures are viewed as those which measure process performance; relate to customer requirements; are owned by those doing the work; can be a source of pride; are easily understood by everyone; and are consistent and well presented.

"We recognised the need to produce a WfQ measurement hierarchy which breaks the measurement process down into key activities which indicate: progress made in establishing the underlying principles; the progress made towards the WfQ plan; direct WfQ results and high level Company progress", says Dr Kitson.

The key measures are individually owned and sponsored by the Directors who receive updated information throughout the year to ensure constant monitoring and the relevant action is taken. These measures are closely aligned to the requirements of the four major stakeholders outlined in the company's objectives, namely customers, employees, society, and shareholders. Each key area is broken down into sub-measures. For instance customer measures include drinking water Quality, value for money, response time to enquiries, number of complaints received, and customer opinion of Severn Water. These are obtained via customer tracking research and are communicated to all staff through monthly team meetings.

Relevant employee measures include: staff turnover, welfare, absenteeism, purpose, performance review and development, and competence. Teamwork is highlighted when reviewing performance and staff are assessed against criteria such as their willingness to share knowledge, time and experience with team members; listening to and considering the views of other team members; and effort channelled into team performance rather than individual goals.

The contribution made by staff is recognised and rewarded based on the following values: teamwork; integrity; openness; care; respect; drive; and competence. Severn Trent Water has introduced a profit related pay scheme, STEPS (Severn Trent Enhanced Pay Scheme) which offers increased take home pay to all participating employees by reducing the amount of tax they pay. "This allows employees to share in the benefits from the growth in profits from the Group's business activities and encourages a feeling of company teamwork where everybody gains from increased effort and commitment", explains Dr Kitson.

Staff opinions and attitudes are obtained through an annual staff survey, QUEST which includes a section on WfQ and quarterly WfQ tracking surveys. The results indicate that the adoption of the WfQ programme has been encouragingly rapid throughout the company - 98 per cent of respondents were aware of the WfQ approach; 89 per cent understood and approved of WfQ; and 79 per cent believed management was fully committed to WfQ. These results serve as a motivating factor and every employee received a personal copy outlining the programme's success.

Another key indicator of the success of the programme is the rate of voluntary formation of Quality Improvement Teams which tend to be cross-functional. "Severn Trent Water made the conscious decision not to inject the entire organisation to a shallow depth preferring to allow the process to free wheel to see whether champions emerged and they did. In the period from September 1993 to April 1994 the number of teams grew from zero to 125. By April 1995 over 2000 employees were involved in 240 teams working on WfQ issues pursuing 570 improvements which equates to a potential benefit of £10 million. To date over £1 million worth of benefits have been realised," enthuses Dr Kitson. Improvement teams are classified by benefit area, savings, increase in income, improving customer service, or improving customer satisfaction.

Dr Kitson genuinely believes that a good Quality program can turn a company around and make all the difference. "It is a differentiator and a motivator. People basically want to feel that they are doing a good job and that they are valued. I believe the six Quality principles do a lot to hold people together and it makes them feel that they are contributing to an impressive company, which is important."

left to right: Richard Watson (Managing Director),
Teresa Vaughan (QA Manager), Peter Turnock (Sales Director),
Emma Barham (Technical Administrator)
Bentley Chemicals Ltd

35

Moulding A Quality Company

— Bentley Chemicals —

BENTLY Chemicals is an example of a smaller size company competing to supply what could be described as a galaxy of multi-million pound industries and to succeed it has had to advance as quickly as the industries it supplies. So, it should come as no surprise that this distributor of silicone, resin and adhesive products was the first in its field to achieve ISO 9002:1994 and did so within 11 months of commencing the programme.

Silicone products are used across a broad range of applications from coating electrical connections to the manufacture of moulds for ceramic figurines. It is used in an even more exhaustive list of industries:

- Aerospace
  sealing and bonding
- Defence
  moulding, protection, bonding and encapsulation
- Automotive
  gaskets, gearbox, transmissions and sumps
- Transport
  sealing, encapsulation, lubrication and gaskets
- Architectural Moulding
  moulds, masters and coating systems
- Prototype Moulding
  moulds, high definition precision casting grades
- Ceramic Printing
- Silicone Pad Printing
  casework moulds

- Telecommunications
  encapsulation, sealing and bonding
- Appliances
  encapsulation of electrical components.

Bentley Chemicals' products are also used in the construction of sets and special effects for sci-fi television and film production through to components in the electronics, automotive and aerospace industries. The aerospace industry alone is valued as an £8 million market.

It provides the lesson that a small company can achieve Quality registration and achieve it quickly without sacrificing day-to-day efficiency and the high level of personalised customer service on which small companies often pride themselves.

Bentley Chemicals employs four full-time staff and has a turnover of approximately £1.3 million. It is mainly concerned with the sale and distribution of silicone based products as a UK distributor for Rhône-Poulenc, which has been described as the French equivalent of ICI. Although this product range accounts for the bulk of its sales, it also promotes resins, special-effect products, casting systems adhesives and very high-temperature resistant sealants from the USA.

While Rhône-Poulenc has its own depot in the UK, Bentley Chemicals holds stocks in its own warehouse in Kidderminster and sells and distributes the products to a customer base of nearly 700 organisations throughout the UK. Rhône-Poulenc has received accreditation to ISO 9001.

Bentley Chemicals was established in 1978 and has spent most of its life concentrating on supplying the craft and giftware industry because its products are ideal for making moulds. Although this market still accounts for 50 per cent of its sales, it now supplies a complete cross-section of industry.

Bentley Chemicals operates in a technologically advanced field which is constantly finding new applications for existing products and adding new products to the existing range. The product showcase continues to expand with their suppliers engaged in a continuous programme of Research and Development. The company receives technical back-up from its suppliers and of course is vigilant for technical developments in the industries it supplies.

"The advantage that we have with our products is that there are constantly new applications and once you have solved a technical problem for a company, they are invariably a customer for a long time. It's a question of constantly looking for new applications and accepting the fact the markets you have been strong in the past will eventually offer lower margins as competition increases as time goes on", explains Richard Watson, Managing Director.

The way that Bentley Chemicals has been able to achieve its current level of growth and maintain its lead in the industry has been through creative selling and coming up with ideas to solve its customers' problems. The company has strengthened its position in its existing markets by increasing its product range. Apart from selling silicone in its various forms, the company also trades in polyesters, polyurethanes and epoxies as well as a whole range of adhesives and speciality products. The number of product references held in stock has increased from 20 in 1989 to a level of at least 700 products in 1995. The largest sales remain in RTV silicone rubber, in the form of either two-part consisting of a base and catalyst or one-part which cures once it is exposed to moisture in the atmosphere. There are only four fully integrated suppliers in the world for these silicone products.

"One of the major points about the company is that we look at the total application of products and their inter-relationship. Most distributors in this country either distribute resin, rubber, or fillers, but they don't distribute the complete system. We now offer a very complete system. We can develop products that suit the customer's application. We are finding that more and more companies want a sole source and they want somebody who can come in and talk about it all", says Peter Turnock, Sales Director.

Bentley Chemicals has not always experienced the same level of growth that it has today. By 1989 the company had run into some difficulties with a turnover of £296,000 and a dangerous reliance on one customer for 80 per cent of its sales. However, in March 1989 it was purchased by the current Managing Director, Richard Watson, who revived it by developing the electronics and engineering markets.

At this point in time Bentley Chemicals had no formal Quality systems and no Quality manual. It was not looking for a TQM approach and had no estimate of the cost of poor quality.

The conclusion of the Department of Trade and Industry's (DTI) Enterprise Councillor in his business review of Bentley Chemicals during its application for funding towards BS 5750 certification in March 1993 provides a concise description of the company at this time. "This is a small, fifteen-year-old company that has had substantial problems, but is being vigorously turned around by its new owner. It is essentially a selling and distribution business lifting itself up by the boot laces, and on the face of it doing so very successfully. In the process it finds itself dealing with some very large organisations who will require their supplier to possess BS 5750 and without this the company will be denied access to important markets. In the circumstances a Quality initiative is appropriate and recommended."

And so, Bentley Chemicals embarked on the Quality journey. A journey which has been instrumental in the current and on-going success of the business.

Bentley received a grant that covered two-thirds of the initial expense of the accreditation process from the DTI. However, Mr Watson explains his philosophy on the cost of Quality – "We don't have a big company attitude where we sit down and work out a budget for projects. We didn't actually have a budget as such for Quality registration, but we knew roughly how much the net cost was going to be. It was difficult to put a figure on it, but the net cost to us was £3,000. In total that equates to £9,000 including the funding. However, you need to compare this cost to the overall picture of the company and what it can provide so long as the system is continually reviewed, updated and implemented."

The engagement of a Quality consultant was a major but essential cost. However, if the time dedicated by all the employees who participated in the review and documentation process was factored into the total cost, it is estimated that the original figure would double.

Small companies often perceive that it is more expensive for them to embark on a Quality certification programme than a larger organisation. Bentley Chemicals' Quality consultant, Michael Palmer, the Principal of MAP Quality Management Services, suggests that this should not be the case. "The cost of certification has in fact decreased over recent years. The real costs associated with the programme are those required to improve the current system, document the system and implement an ongoing improvement process which all contributes to the efficiency of the organisation and its subsequent success. Therefore it is not true that the relative cost is high for small organisations, nor is it true that it is more viable for large organisations. It should not matter whether the organisation has four or four thousand employees, the operating system needs defining anyway to provide the basis for improving business."

Striving for Quality assurance certification is valuable for the on-going health of the company. It is not a one-shot quick fix. "I would have no hesitation in recommending other small Companies pursue Quality certification, but that they do so with their eyes open and not expect magical overnight changes. An immense effort is required by everybody and in a small company each individual's input will be more significant than in a large organisation. While it wakes up small companies as to how and why they are doing things, you need a dedicated person to oversee the complete process. At the initial stage, implementation can seem very time consuming because of the documentation required. However, it must be realised that the initial stage is purely that and it does pass, after which the benefits can start to be realised", Mrs Teresa Vaughan, Quality Assurance Manager warns.

Both Bentley Chemicals and their Quality consultant echo the same message that commitment is the key to success. During the initial implementation phase, the company was, as it remains to date, in a growth situation so it had to grapple with keeping increasing numbers of customers satisfied and also writing and implementing the system. While it helps if there is one person dedicated to the task of documentation, it is still necessary for everybody to find the time for Quality.

During the documentation phase, companies need to recognise two key factors. The first is the necessity of introducing effective time management if it doesn't already exist in the organisation. This ensures that the company's emphasis remains firstly on the customers' requirements. Secondly, documentation should be approached with the knowledge that it will prompt the question, 'Can things be done more efficiently or effectively?' Where the answer is yes, the company must create the time to alter the system.

The selection of the consultant is important because as Mrs Vaughan points out, not every consultant will have the right 'fit' for the company. "In early discussions with consultants some had the big company attitude and a jobs-for-the-boys type outlook. We were not regarded as a big company and appeared to us that they didn't hold us in very high esteem. If you are not given the support, you don't have a great deal of incentive, and the project could be deemed a failure before it starts."

Initially the company was working towards BS 5750 Part 2. However, a month prior to the official assessment date, the company decided that it would be of benefit to aim for ISO 9002:1994. Subsequently, all the documentation was revised and updated to incorporate the changes within the standard.

The motivation to go for Quality registration initially came from a couple of customers and the potential of winning accounts in the aerospace industry which insisted that suppliers be ISO certified. However, the original motives were further reaching than just obliging customer requirements. "From a personal point of view, the company had grown so much in such a short space of time, it was becoming impossible for me to control and required systems to be put in place. Once we had introduced ISO 9000, it was satisfying from everybody's point of view that a total system was in place and that there were actually good reasons for it. If everybody adhered to the system then they know, and I know, that the job is being done and that the customer is getting what they want. This ultimately gives me peace of mind in knowing that the business is being run ensuring total customer satisfaction", explains Mr Watson.

Mr Palmer views it as vital that any organisation considering Quality certifications asks themselves the question. 'What are we going to get out of it?' "You may receive accolades from your customers, but the essence of it is that you are getting a better company. At the core of the standard is the principle of corrective and preventive action which is a philosophy any business can use. I say that it is of immense value for an organisation to go through this process as a means of developing progressive business practices regardless of whether or not they decide to pay for the certification at the end of the day."

Over a year after receiving formal ISO 9002:1994 certification from their assessor Det Norske Veritas, Bentley Chemicals Quality Consultant still provides surveillance audits and advice. "Quality certification is not a finite process. There should be no end and the company must be able to confirm that it does some good and this should be primarily through the continuous improvement process that it promotes", say Mr Palmer.

During the original assessment visit, Bentley Chemicals received nine minor non-compliances, however, the company looks at the raising of a non-conformance as a positive action because it indicates that people are vigilant and recognising deviations from the Quality Procedures. All

Corrective Action Reports (CARs) are analysed and preventive action implemented to avoid repetitive and cost errors.

As part of the Quality programme, the company holds monthly Quality review meetings where CARs are discussed. All staff attend the meetings and report the problems they have experienced in that month. These meetings are for the benefit of everybody and are there to discuss all Quality issues and any problems being encountered. They also offer the opportunity to highlight and discuss any changes which could be made to the benefit of the system and ultimately that of the employees.

With around 700 products ranging from small 50gm tubes to 200kg drums, packaging and transportation methods are as important as the Quality of the actual product. CARs identified that one of the greatest problem areas was in the area of transportation of the product to the customer. The number of problems experienced with late deliveries or product being lost, smashed or spilt was unacceptably high at 19 cases per month. Prior to formally recording the number of non-conformances and disseminating this information throughout the company, the situation reached the point where goods were being personally delivered by individual staff members to ensure on-time delivery, although the extent of the problem was still undetected.

As the carrier only compensates a percentage of the actual damage or loss, Bentley Chemicals relied on its insurance company to cover the rest of the claim. However, money and time was wasted and at the end of the day the customer placed the blame with Bentley Chemicals. By measuring the incidence of non-conformances, the need for corrective action was identified and the carrier changed. This changed the philosophy of the company – the cost of Quality could be measured. Once the area had been identified, it was easier for people to recognise other areas where improvements could reduce the cost of quality.

Bentley Chemicals' supplier base is small compared to the number of customers. The company currently has some 23 suppliers and with the exception of four, all are either registered to ISO or in the process of receiving registration.

The bulk of Bentley Chemicals' Quality system is internal and so the impact on the mobile sales force is minimal.

"Everybody within the company is supportive of the Quality System because they know it is there for each individual's benefit. They know how it helps ensure the company runs proficiently thereby minimising mistakes and ultimately preventing the need for repetitive, time-consuming and annoying corrective action. Everybody knows their position within the company and also within their particular working areas. Individuals know where they have been, where they are going and how they are going to get there because it is all fully documented", explains Mrs Vaughan, and this is important. All aspects of the business can be traced to establish the current position of a customer order or to investigate customer or supplier history for a period up to three years.

The organisation is essentially a service and sales operation where the other functions within the business exist to support the sales and customer service team. Administration, records, purchasing, financial controls, stock controls are largely handled on computer.

The new business enquiry rate is extremely high with the customer conversion from the enquiries reaching 78 per cent. This is attributed to all personnel, their telemarketing training and the rapid response rate provided by the company. In the majority of cases, Bentley Chemicals will provide a same-day response. Bentley chemicals opened 190 new accounts in the 12 month period to March 1995 which is an increase of 155 per cent over the last two years.

The old adage that 'It is the business that you refuse which is the business that makes you money', has prevailed in Bently Chemicals' situation, as Mr Watson explains, "The advantage of the products we have is that it is not the norm for a customer to chop and change supplier. When you eventually win an account you should expect, particularly with the right backup and the right service to have that customer for a very long time. If he (she) is the type of customer who is going to keep chopping and changing suppliers, on price for instance, then we are not particularly interested."

The film and television industry is a large market for Bentley Chemicals. Sky One reported the launch of a sci-fi series, Space Precinct as having the most dazzling special effects on TV with a budget of £25 million and 200 technicians who created monsters, aliens and outer space sets. A key ingredient to this were the various materials supplied by Bentley Chemicals.

Mr Turnock believes that the Quality programme helps more on the industrial side than on the special effects side, although it is all relevant. "It all helps because you can say to customers you are going to get a guaranteed Quality product that is manufactured under the control of ISO 9000. Our Quality systems mean we can guarantee a material. This is actually very important in the case of Room Temperature Vulcanising silicone going onto the face of an automated manikin because the maker wants a ten-year guarantee on the life of movements. They tested our product with over 100,000 facial movements to ensure that after 10 years it was still going to be functional. If it doesn't stand up to the strain they've got to make the whole model again which involves heavy expenditure."

Mrs Vaughan summarises the effect Quality has had on Bentley Chemicals and the cultural changes it has evoked. "It is apparent, especially in a smaller business such as this, that the Quality system makes everybody important. Instead of being another cog in the wheel with a name, the persons title is used and they see it in print. Each person can see they do have a critical role within the organisation. There is no difference between Directors, Managers or Administrators. If any one individual is missing then a complete segment of the Quality system is missing. Everybody is part of a chain. No one individual is more important than anybody else as everybody is required to make the system work."

It is obvious that everybody within the company still gets a buzz from having achieved certification and witnessing the contribution it has made to Bentley Chemicals' continuing growth into more advanced and profitable industries.

*left to right: Howard Whitesmith (Group Managing Director),
Brian Parsons (Quality Assurance Manager), Terry Nicklin (Marketing Manager)
Domino Printing Sciences*

36

Quality In A High-Tech Environment

—Domino Printing Sciences PLC—

LIKENING the company's development to chapters in a book, Howard Whitesmith, Group Managing Director of Domino Printing Sciences plc divides the company's history into three distinct stages: the first is characterised by Domino's infancy in an emerging market; the second tells of the trials and tribulations of a fun-packed but chaotic childhood; and the third and most definitive to date chronicles the company's progress into adulthood.

The over riding theme which emerges during this progression is that Domino is a survivor and it was the commitment to Quality principles at a defining time in the company's development that has elevated Domino to a position of market dominance. In 1995 the company recorded a turnover of approximately £100 million which is more than double the figure of five years ago.

The story begins in 1971 when Graeme Minto, the company's founder was researching multijet printing at Cambridge Consultants. In 1978 he left to form Domino, with a licence to manufacture and market ink jet printers. The principle behind ink jet technology was discovered in 1746, but it wasn't until the late 1970s that it became possible to make it a commercial reality with the advent of modern electronics. With his entrepreneurial outlook and engineering bias, Graham Minto had developed the right product at the right time for what was to become an enormous market and the company skyrocketed to overnight success.

It is undeniable that the catalyst to Domino's accelerated growth was the 1980s EEC directive requiring the marking of all perishable goods with a 'sell by' date together with the introduction of other legislative regulations such as the lot numbering of pharmaceutical products.

However, from this point the market rapidly expanded to meet the needs of a myriad of industries including medical, agriculture, electronics, metals, cosmetics/toiletries, ceramics, automotive, chemicals, and construction. As a market leader in the application of ink jet systems and other printing technologies Domino services a comprehensive range of industries, including those listed above, throughout the world.

Domino now has subsidiary companies in the Netherlands, Germany, Spain, France and the United States and a distributor network in another 65 countries. One of the benefits this structure provides is that Domino can provide timely service support worldwide.

The business can be broadly divided into two areas: the coding and marking division which represents approximately 65 per cent of business and commercial printing servicing customers in the commercial world of printing who require systems which provide variable data marking, addressing and numbering allowing a publisher to target its audience for advertising purposes as one example. These systems involve not only printing technology but advanced software capability.

Domino became Domino Printing Sciences plc in 1985 when it was floated on the Stock Exchange, an initiative which was 43 times over subscribed. Mr Whitesmith joined the company in 1986 to an organisation which he describes as: "Lots of fun, full of activity, and very successful, but totally disorganised. The product was the best that it could be, but we were in no position to take advantage of many of the available opportunities because we were too busy trying to meet customer demand and shipping the product out the door."

At this stage in the company's development the threat of becoming another one of the many local high technology 'Cambridge Phenomenon' companies which later failed was very real. Mr Whitesmith believed the only remedy was to become a more professional and outward looking company through the infusion of Quality principles.

Cambridge's commercial centre has been built on scientific innovation and technology development influenced by the presence of the university and the sense of progress that it embodies. However, reviewing the vast array of high technology companies established in the Cambridge area during the 1980s Domino is certainly the most successful and one of the very few that has survived and maintained its independence. Today,

Domino services 15 per cent of the Japanese market which is a sizeable endorsement of the company's product and service Quality.

Mr Whitesmith engaged Brian Parsons, a colleague from Philips where they had both been exposed to the rigorous implementation of Quality practices and processes, as Quality Assurance Manager. Together they established a Company Wide Quality Improvement programme which made a substantial contribution to the longevity of the company. Mr Parsons now acts as the Group's Quality conscience, although he is based at the UK operation.

One of Mr Parsons's first remits was to prepare the company for BS5750 (ISO9000). Initial discussions with distributors, subsidiaries and customers about delivery performance revealed that many believed Domino was an 'arrogant' organisation. "We attached a Quality feedback form to every machine shipped inviting the customer to comment on his/her experience with Domino – was the equipment delivered on time, was it damaged, was all the documentation correct, did the machine work? From this we immediately identified the areas of the organisation which needed to improve", explains Mr Parsons.

The structure and style of the organisation was informal with each staff member undertaking several jobs and working long hours in a bid to grow the company. At this stage the company consisted of approximately 150 people who were geographically scattered with various departments housed in different buildings contributing to inefficiencies in the communication processes. It was not until 1989 that the UK company moved to its current 100,000 sq ft headquarters in Bar Hill bringing the entire operation under the same roof for the first time.

Domino's own design of continuous ink jet technology uses a highly versatile drop deflection technique. This technique involves electrically charged droplets which are deflected as a matrix to form characters on a surface to be printed. Ink is pumped through a small nozzle, about the diameter of a human hair and vibrated to form a jet of equal sized droplets. Domino printers form 64,000 or 128,000 drops every second all of which can be given an individually selected electrical charge. The droplets then pass through a constant electrostatic field and charged drops are deflected sideways. It is this deflection in line across a moving surface that creates the dot matrix from which characters are formed.

It is with the same precision that the company approaches its

Quality commitment and in 1991 Domino became the first industrial ink jet company to receive BS5750 Part 1 (ISO9001) certification.

At Domino, Quality is not an add on - every element of the business is enveloped by the philosophy. Consistent with this approach, Domino introduced Company-Wide Quality Improvement (CWQI), instead of the more traditional TQM programme, with the simple message that Company-Wide means everyone: "Everyone in the company, from the Chief Executive down, has an important role to play. No one in the company is either so senior, so junior or so specialised that they cannot become involved in improving the company's overall performance."

In the context of CWQI Domino defines Quality as giving the customer what he/she wants, every time, on time and at the right cost. In short customer satisfaction – each and every time.

CWQI awareness training was delivered throughout the organisation including subsidiaries in Europe and the USA, as well as to suppliers and distributors. The CWQI programme was launched in October 1987 and during the first six months over 500 people attended the one-day awareness training sessions. Since then regular sessions have boosted the total to over 1800. The education process started with Graham Minto, who prior to this contact had never viewed Quality as something to which he could contribute, and has been extended to every employee who joins the Domino Group in the form of a one day induction to Total Quality.

Domino views the manager's role a special one – because Quality improvement cannot be delegated to specialists, managers are called on to first grasp the principles and techniques of CWQI, practise them, explain them to the people for whom they are responsible and then most importantly convey their own commitment. The ongoing process is maintained through recognition of effort and the encouragement of success.

As Quality permeated the organisation and people accepted that Quality meant conforming to standards they started to ask where the formal requirements for their jobs were recorded. It was against this background that the new Quality manual and procedures were written to formalise the company's activities and in turn this led the company down the ISO certification path.

After the original euphoria of gaining ISO certification and introducing everybody to CWQI had subsided, Domino provided its programme with a boost by introducing a MAD (Make A Difference) campaign. On a Monday morning people returned to their workplace to find it infested with footprints. From this novel introduction staff were left questioning what the footprints represented which started them thinking laterally and by the end of the first week they were encouraged to provide MAD ideas. The participation rate was exceptional. The 330 people on site at the time generated over 3000 ideas – an average of eight ideas per person and a 99.9 per cent participation rate. Suggestions are now a routine part of everybody's role and have resulted in substantial accumulative savings.

A typical example of a MAD saving, originating from the dispatch department, involved the removal of redundant practices. As a matter of course Domino included a standard English operating manual with every consignment destined for the Japanese market. However, as soon as the consignment was received the manuals were removed and disposed of because the English version was of no practical use. By removing this practice Domino saved £10,000.

Domino's principal activity is the design and assembly of its products, therefore the Quality of the finished item is reliant on the Quality of the suppliers providing the various components. Domino chooses to deal with suppliers who have attained ISO certification and conducts a thorough review of its current customers and track record as Mr Whitesmith explains: "We want to build relationships with other Quality companies because in the long run even if you pay a little more you know that you are going to save money."

As a result of CWQI Domino rationalised its supplier base from 250 to 120 key suppliers, preferring to give specific vendors the entire supply contract for a particular product. "One of the big successes has been the involvement of a number of our vendors in the development of our products. For instance, a vendor supplying steel fabrication provided us with a member of his staff at his expense for a month to finalise the development of a cabinet. The benefits of this interaction are that the vendor feels a sense of ownership in the process, problems can be resolved in the design stage and the process is subsequently more cost effective", explains Mr Parsons.

"Components are supplied on a just-in-time basis where key suppliers have expanded their range to meet 100 per cent of our requirements and in return we have given them all our business in a particular area. We operate kanban systems and in many instances the suppliers deliver directly to the shop floor. One supplier expanded his range to meet our requirements and now comes once a week with a vehicle that carries all his stock. He goes to the line side bins, determines what we require, replenishes the stock and once a month bills us for all the items. This relationship is based on trust. Why do you need an invoice for 100 washers when at the end of the period if you have made X machines you know you must have used Y washers?"

Domino makes a conscious effort to learn from supplier relationships because of the superior knowledge they possess of their components and application. A typical situation is the manufacture of circuit boards, where Domino traditionally sourced all the components and then subcontracted the manufacturing process to an external operation. In a bid to improve the efficiency of the process Domino now delegates the responsibility for sourcing the components to the subcontractor which saves time, effort and space on the shop floor allowing Domino to concentrate on specialist fabrication and assembly.

As in the game of Dominos the Quality process require sonly one component to fail and the impact can be felt around the entire organisation if systems aren't in place to provide the necessary damage control to stop a chain reaction. Mr Whitesmith describes such an incident.

"In 1995 Domino announced its four yearly results amidst the biggest crisis the organisation had ever experienced in terms of product Quality. The company had developed new technology around a print head improvement which had been field trialled following all the stages we thought were appropriate. We launched it to positive industry response and sold 1500 before receiving feedback from the field that problems were occurring with 40 per cent of these machines. We stopped shipment and didn't resume for three months until the problem was resolved. It was a difficult decision because sales had increased momentum, training had been provided, and there were many examples of the product being outstanding in meeting customer requirements. The problem originated at a component supplier who had changed his process from hand crafting the initial batch to main production of inconsistent Quality and we didn't pick it up in time."

While the cost of this deviation adversely affected the bottom line Domino was not prepared to risk the long-term reputation of the company by continuing to ship a product of which a proportion was sub-standard. Although the past reputation of the company was strong enough to retain customers the challenge ahead of Domino is now to rebuild customer confidence, making its commitment to Quality all the more vital.

Domino has learnt from this sobering experience, and while it has not affected supplier relationships it has improved the process governing the introduction of new technology. Domino now keeps extended checks beyond the trial of new technology and has introduced another milestone to the checking process so that once all the stages are signed off a main production signoff is conducted.

Domino has introduced a product alert system based on a simple traffic light system using red, amber and green paper. It was traditionally used for putting mainstream products on hold if the test department found something wrong, although anybody can raise a product alert if they suspect a problem. It was not introduced as a Quality initiative, but rather to improve communication between business teams around the world. "For example, if a problem arises a red product alert is raised and people know that the product is on hold and are advised of a corrective action plan and time frame for the resolution of the problem. An amber alert signals that the product is ready for release which then occurs on the green alert. Filling out a report and issuing a red alert forces people to formally recognise the existence of a problem and the need for corrective action. These sort of things provide a structure which constantly reinforces the Quality message", explains Mr Parsons.

Domino's Quality Policy states that:

We must ensure that our present and future customers are always satisfied with the products and services which we provide.

Every Domino customer must find that:

- They can communicate with us
- We listen and respond to their needs
- We are reliable and do what we say we will do
- We deliver the right products on time, every time
- We are aiming for zero defects in all our products, services, information and advice.

The aim of Domino's Zero Defect Policy is not restricted to products alone, but also applies to those tasks carried out by all employees. Zero Defect Quality demands that each of us is right first time in every task we undertake. Total customer satisfaction will only be achieved when we conduct our internal daily operations as if we were each others customers.

Our collective task is to increase customer satisfaction throughout our whole organisation and into the external markets for our products and services.

Individuals are given a check list to gauge their own personal contribution to CWQI based on four questions:

- Have I identified my customers?
- Do I know how they judge my Quality?
- Am I measuring my Quality levels?
- Am I improving my Quality?

Mr Whitesmith prefers to make an impact on the Quality programme by walking around the company. He provides direction and conveys the message that if a situation is not ideal remedy it instead of putting up with it. An example originating in the dispatch department brings to life his effect on the workforce. "A copy of the order form is placed on top of every machine to be shipped which serves as a final check to ensure that all ancillary items are included with the machine. While I was walking around I noticed that the copy quality was illegible. Instead of ignoring the situation I encouraged the people in the department to determine if the documentation was required, and if so was it useful in its current state. The key message here is that they shouldn't accept that level of quality from an internal supplier. The logistics team is now investigating the whole process and has identified that 56 different individual transactions are taken to process an incoming order through to a dispatch document. That equates to 56 opportunities for error. The target is now 15 transactions." The morale of the story is that, "You can chair committees and stand on platforms delivering words of wisdom but unless you lead with your feet nobody is going to take you seriously."

The vast array of visible performance indicators throughout Domino from the international sales offices to the assembly plant gives an indication of the importance the company places in measurement. The provision and communication of Quality indicators at both a departmental and personal level is central to CWQI illustrating to every member of the company how well they are meeting their customers' requirements.

"Only by measurement can we find out how we are performing. Displaying results does not make them worse, but NOT displaying them makes them useless. Unless we display our results neither we nor our customers will be aware of how we are performing, what we need to improve and how much we are improving", Mr Parsons explains. "We have a measure in the factory called the Time of Quality which measures the level of defects in terms of how long it will take to rectify particular problems which is then quantified in monetary terms. This provides us with the amount of money wasted on a weekly basis in rectification and rework which provides tremendous potential for improvement."

A performance declaration at the door of the assembly unit serves as an example of one of the variety of charted performance indicators providing a reminder of the daily state of play:

This period is…working days long
We are planning to ship…machines
To date we have shipped…machines
There are…working days left
So the average is…machines a day
Does this meet the factory plan?…
Is there a factory backlog?…
What is the factory backlog?…
Our prediction for tomorrow is?…

Domino is in the business of providing complete coding solutions. It can provide or design the process, equipment, and ink to label almost any product from the most delicate of flowers to critical applications such as labelling the parts used in the European Fighter Aircraft. However, the company is ever conscious of both the need for continual innovation and the identification of emerging markets if it is to retain its status as a world leader. It proactively seeks new technologies and applications and has broadened its sphere of activity to pursue the development of non-ink technology such as laser technology through its own R&D, joint ventures and acquisition.

The dilemma of how to manage Quality in a high technology company without stifling the innovation and creativity required in the new product development process has been overcome by re-directing the traditional technology driven approach and embracing a customer focus through the use of the Kano model and Quality Function Deployment (QFD) model.

As Terry Nicklin, Marketing Manager explains: "Quality is all about capturing the voice of the customer. It involves asking the customer what they want and then providing just that. The problem we have with the development of our product is that often the customer hasn't thought in detail about the specific product attributes they need or want."

Innovation at Domino is driven by cross-functional teams including representatives from manufacturing, marketing, engineering and service departments which ensures that from a core base of technology the product derived is fit for purpose thereby meeting the criteria that the marketing department indicates the customers are demanding.

Market research and customer satisfaction surveys are used to develop an understanding of the 'business drivers' which guide customers' product preferences. Customers are asked directly and indirectly what they would like to see incorporated into future new products. Small meetings of users in 'focus groups' have been used for this purpose.

In addition, consideration is given to the 'basic' factors – those unspoken factors – like safety – which customers take for granted – but which have to be taken into account in design. Another category of unspoken requirements is the 'attractiveness' (sometimes called 'delight') factors which are those things which customers cannot yet imagine so cannot specify, but which if provided would cause satisfaction. The approach is called the Kano model after its inventor.

The House of Quality or Quality Function Deployment (QFD) model as illustrated in Figure 1 was introduced by Domino in 1994 and has become the standard means of facilitating product development. It allows a company to identify what is important to the customer and to deploy the appropriate resources through good design. The end chart becomes a template, providing a common language by which all members of the multi-disciplinary team communicate. It forces the marketing people to be clear about what the customer requires and on the other hand forces the technical people to develop features which are important to customers instead of innovating for technology's sake. It also provides a mechanism for discussing and ranking issues and allows changes to be accommodated early in the process when it is relatively inexpensive to do so.

"I like to describe this business as having three axies: a technology axis, a marketing axis and a distribution axis which sit in a three-dimensional model. In the last five years we have doubled the size of our cube and will hopefully achieve similar growth over the next five years by watching distribution, being driven by the market and developing very responsive technology", concludes Mr Whitesmith. This achievement will be maintained because CWQI is in the hearts and minds of everyone at Domino.

Build a better mouse trap and the world will beat a path to your door.

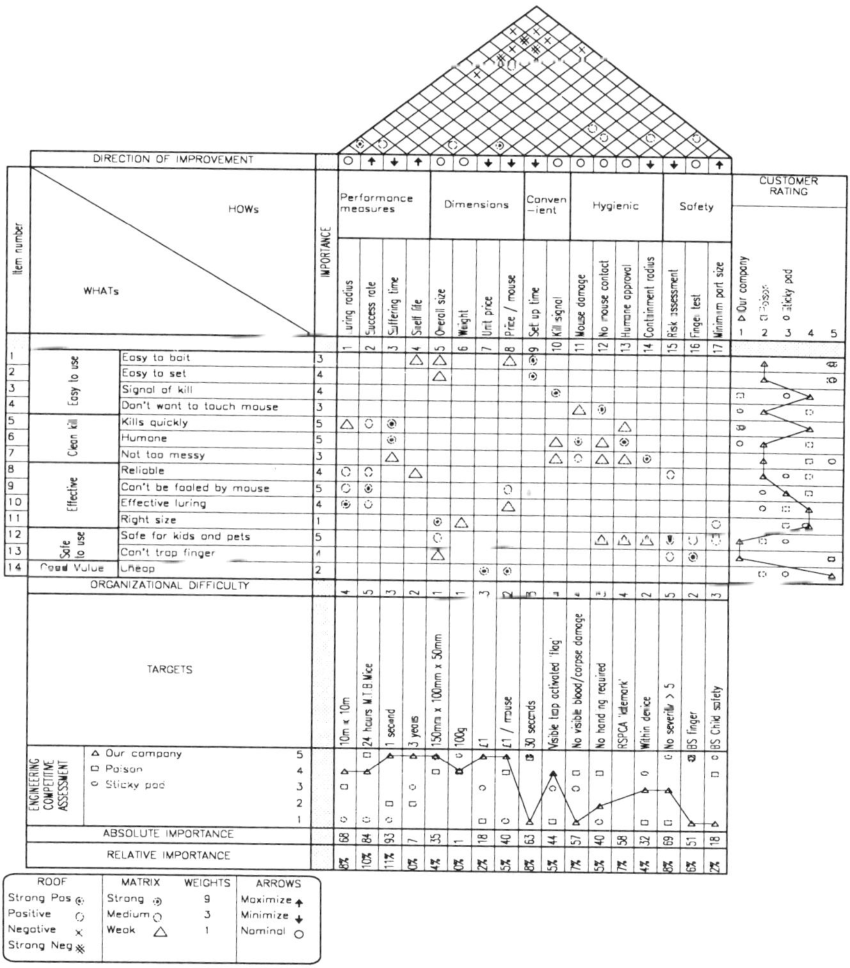

© ASI Quality Systems 1996

Richard Hegarty (third from the left) and some of the Partners of Hegarty & Co Solicitors

37

A Quality Law Firm

—Hegarty & Co—

"WHETHER we are dealing with a private client or a large commercial organisation the underlying principle to our work is Quality. From the first contact to the final correspondence we aim to get things right first time."
– The Partners, Hegarty & Co 1995

It is no coincidence that Hegarty & Co not only becamethe first firm of solicitors in Peterborough to achieve ISO 9000 but also was accredited in only nine months. Rather it is a combination of two important factors. Firstly, Richard Hegarty and the growing team of partners had been building a commitment to developing systems and procedures since 1974 as an internal goal before they had even considered the 'Quality Standard'. Secondly, the practice has an enthusiasm for the principles of Quality which gave it the impetus to manoeuvre through the minefield of adapting and translating what is essentially a manufacturing standard to make it relevant to the legal profession.

Richard Hegarty established the firm in 1974 on the day he qualified with help from his father, a retired executive legal clerk. Although he had previously run a branch office, this was a positive, bold move to learn from the mistakes he had witnessed in other practices. As Richard says, "I'd seen the errors that others had made whilst working for two firms during my articles. If you went into an old style firm, there was minimal communication. This practice has always set out to be heavily administered with an emphasis on control."

Due to investment from the Peterborough Development

Corporation, the recessions of the 1980s did not affect the area. As the town prospered and house prices rose, Hegarty & Co expanded, taking on the first partner, Tim Thompson, in 1976. In the early 1980s, the expansion had reached a point where it was necessary to 'run an administration and retain control'. As Richard Hegarty says, "The firm became too big to say to two or three people 'do this, and this is how we're going to do it'. You have to then start communicating down effectively." It was this realisation that formed the basis of a standardisation of policy that evolved into the ISO 9000 accreditation.

The Hegarty & Co handbook which embodies these procedures began from humble foundations.

"It started as a collection of memos on green paper which all the staff knew they must keep together as a reference. We were definitely trying to get everybody pulling in the same direction. We had to tell them the policy and standardise." This system had obvious limitations with the need to constantly update and avoid contradictions. By 1983, it had become too unwieldy and was collated into a handbook issued to each member of staff. This gradually evolved into a comprehensive set of procedures and standards which were annually updated with feedback and input from the staff. Richard Hegarty highlights the necessity for employee involvement in this continuous improvement, "In all things you have to carry the staff with you, the more you involve them, the more they are going to say, 'I had something to do with that and it is applicable to me' ."

The success of the Hegarty model is validated by its syndication under licence to all members of CONQUEST, a legal group of which Hegarty & Co is a member. CONQUEST bought the rights to the handbook for its members as it was becoming increasingly important for them to have a comprehensive guide to procedures. The Legal Aid Board had started granting franchises to those practices which met strict Quality and procedure standards, a prerequisite of which is a handbook. Richard Hegarty in his role as one of the seventy-five regionally elected Law Society Council members was also involved in a working party which formulated a 'template handbook' for use by the society's members.

Hegarty & Co considered accreditation the next logical step because their clients were beginning to demand it. As Richard says, "We were acting for clients who were accredited and they routinely asked for it from their suppliers. If you were a supplier of nuts and bolts they would ask you for it, so why not their lawyers? "

How did Hegarty & Co adapt the manufacturing based standard into a format relevant to the legal profession ?

The partners began by applying for a DTI grant and appointing a consultant to guide them through the process. As Richard Hegarty continues, "We used a consultant who had been involved with a law firm before which is why we chose him. It was difficult coming to terms with the terminology, understanding the way it was written and applying it to the legal side. One particular example was understanding and applying 'Purchasing Data'. For the legal profession this is not only the control and standardisation of stationery and forms but also the less tangible areas such as Land Searches and Expert Opinions. In the case of Expert Opinions, there is a need to check that not only the expert got it right and that it agrees with instructions but also that it is indicated on the document that it has been checked."

Hegarty & Co were also keen to ensure that the translation of the Quality terminology was made as accessible to all members of the team, "That process is ongoing, every time we make an amendment to the Quality Manual we ask ourselves if we can improve on the language to make it more user friendly."

The partners realised that it was important to ensure that the Handbook and the Quality Manual remained separate entities. The Handbook retained its status as an easy-to-use reference book issued to all members of the firm. The Quality Manual required some minor alterations and additions to the procedures. For example, a list of subcontractors was set up and a document retrieval slip designed. The slip was used whenever a document was taken out of a file to keep an up-to-date record of its location. As this had not previously been done it was questioned as being unnecessary and bureaucratic. As Richard points out, "The idea of taking out an important document and not keeping a record is ludicrous but it was not something we had done before."

During accreditation to ISO 9000, the partners were eager to expand the boundaries and embody their own 'quality of procedure and quality of output' in symbiosis. Richard Hegarty believes it is important to monitor the actual quality of the legal work otherwise, as he explains, there is little to stop, 'ISO 9000 being all about giving bad advice efficiently'.

With this in mind, Hegarty & Co included their own 'Quality Audit' in the procedure manual and as a part of the Quality process. Richard Hegarty explains how the partners achieved a standardisation of legal work: "What we've done for a number of years, every two months, is to take ten files at random from each fee-earner. In an effort to improve the actual quality of the legal service, we check them in detail to make sure they are being dealt with correctly. The person checking the files fills out a comprehensive 'Quality Audit Form' which comments on how the file is being managed. This includes comments on whether the client is receiving replies straight away and whether the letters are being set out properly."

SGS Yarsley was chosen to audit the Quality systems not only because it had experience certifying other law firms but also because it was accredited to a national body. Chris Trott who ran the audit for Yarsley was a lawyer, which the partners believed would give him an understanding of the environment. Hegarty & Co was in the enviable position of attaining the accreditation within nine months without a pre-audit and with only minor non-conformities. This was due to an effective training programme that set out to explain the standard to all the employees. The partners made the need for the 'people to own the process' their top priority. The induction process now includes an introduction to ISO 9000 and there are continuous training updates. The most important factor is that the employees were already used to having all the procedures set out in their handbook. As Richard Hegarty explains, "Chris Trott went around and talked to everybody and if the member of staff didn't know the answer they could say 'To be honest I don't know but I know the answer is in the Handbook'."

Richard Hegarty and Martin Bloom, the partners mainly involved in the project, dedicated many hours of valuable time to achieving the accreditation and Richard admits that this was costly. This was in addition to the consultant and auditing costs. The question of how worthwhile the final result is and how it counter-balances the outlay is often raised by other lawyers. Richard has a positive affirmation to these questions, "Some firms don't have the resources we have to throw at Quality systems so they are very anxious about the initial costs. I think it has paid for itself time and time again. We have expanded as a firm and we are the only firm in Peterborough not to have laid anyone off during the recession. I put that down to the systems we have got that help us to attract work." The quality of the client that the practice is attracting is also improving. Hegarty & Co realises that they are often in competition with larger firms for clients and feel that the standard gives them an edge. The tenders that they have put forward for Local Council work would not have been acceptable before since the Councils routinely demand Quality standards from all their suppliers.

Hegarty & Co regards the benefits not only in terms of marketing but also in cost reduction terms. At a time when clients feel more empowered to complain, it is vital to have procedures that deal effectively with any problems and minimise any negative effects. When a new client is taken on, they are fully briefed on the ways that they can complain to another fee-earner, not the one dealing primarily with their account. The partners see it as a way to ensure the quality of the legal work in an environment which needs to retain an important sense of autonomy. Richard Hegarty outlines this: "Years ago it was said in the firm that it is a grouping of twenty individual solicitors and they are all doing their own thing in their own way. In standardising, you could be seen to be forcing people to do it your way but if you involve them in designing the process then hopefully they will agree that it is their way not just yours."

Hegarty & Co also complies with the Practice Management Standard which is partly based on the ISO 9000 and has committed to the Investors in People programme. Richard Hegarty, in his role as a Council member was involved in the Law Society working party which formulated this Standard to apply strictly to lawyers. It includes sections on finance, balance sheets, management structure and case management. Hegarty & Co needed to comply with Practice Management Standards to obtain all nine of the Legal Aid Franchises that it holds. The influence of the Practice Management Standards will increase when they are brought under a form of auditing which is planned by the Law Society. Richard believes this is important because "Lawyers certainly in the past have not been good at practice management. I think, also importantly, attitudes are changing. As lawyers go through Law School, they are taught a lot more about practice management and business."

In the legal profession as in many others, the standards are becoming more Quality focused because the clients are demanding it. Hegarty & Co viewed the next step forward for the practice to be an involvement with the Investors in People programme. Mark Dodds, marketing manager, was primarily involved in this decision. He felt that ISO 9000 did not focus on the training of staff and that there was still a skills gap. All the members of staff had worked hard at making the Quality Standards a success and in the light of this found their own roles to be lacking. Mark describes how he believes there is a need to concentrate on the individual: "I think before the focus was very much on keeping the specialists up to date technically. Sometimes the people involved felt that they were tools to be used rather than part of the business. This initiative makes it more relevant, why we have management structures and why we have cash flows. It is making sure that the staff realise we are working towards the same goal. For example, if anyone needs help with communication skills to deal with, say, an angry client, we try to supply it. If they don't feel comfortable in these situations then it is not going to help us or the client." By committing to the Investors In People programme, Hegarty & Co have achieved a greater sense of staff identity and involvement. This obviously required changes in attitudes at the top level of the firm as well. The partners now openly communicate the business plan and the staff benefit from a profit-related pay scheme.

There was a strong feeling that the firm did not want to rush the Investors In People programme. The goal of the programme was not simply to obtain a logo to put on the firm's letterhead, but to allow the staff to profit as much as possible from the process through maxium involvement. As Mark Dodds explains, "It should be an ongoing process, people can see the difference between where we were last year and where we are now. This is how ideas and communication develop."

The future for the legal profession is one of ever increasing demands from clients. This is demonstrated by large commercial clients favouring practices which are nationally accredited. Richard Hegarty and his partners are already involved in this future. They understand the increasing need to compete for clients and how much more cognisant those clients of what legal work involves. As he explains: "Twenty years ago you would never tell a client how long you spent working on their brief, nor explain how much it was going to cost before you did the work. Things have changed and the legal profession must adapt to that. There are still sections of the profession that live in a different decade, they won't exist for much longer."

Hegarty & Co has extensively invested in IT, to improve the speed and accuracy of communication and increase efficiency. There is a computer on every desk, so all external communication can be standardised. The firm realises that this is vital to further expansion, not only in the United Kingdom but also in the areas of European Law that their clients are beginning to demand. Through the DTI initiative and Government commitment, Richard Hegarty believes that the country has progressed far in Quality Standards. It is these which allow it to compete on a world stage.

There are many tangible achievements from the firms' involvement in Quality. This is evident in the continuing expansion of the firm and its on-going enthusiasm for improvement. Hegarty & Co is a pioneer that has both a belief and an investment in the future which will guarantee dividends. As Richard Hegarty maintains, "Although there is an element of marketing in ISO 9000, we didn't go into it just to say we've got it. We did it because we perceived benefits. It would be wrong for any firm to go gain Quality Accreditation simply for marketing purposes. I really don't think it would work because all you are getting out of it in the end is a press release to say you've got it. There wouldn't be the enthusiasm from within the firm to allow it to continue. What you've got is not the end of the matter, it is an ongoing commitment."

Ken Sinfield
Group Divisional Director
Sun Alliance Europe

38

Turnaround Strategy – People & Processes

— National Vulcan Engineering Insurance Group —

AT the core of National Vulcan is engineering expertise and excellence. Today National Vulcan is the nation's leader in engineering insurance, and inspection across an array of industries and disciplines including boiler and pressure plant, electrical and mechanical plant, computers, and construction projects. National Vulcan operates a range of complementary businesses, including design and distribution of valves, boiler repair, general business insurance, plant and computer security systems which are synergistic.

The inception of the engineering insurance industry and indeed National Vulcan came during the industrial revolution in the UK and the advent of the cotton industry in Lancashire. Industry became dependent on high pressure boilers, which at the time were frequently defective and consequently volatile. The damage to property and the loss of human life was devastating on the all too frequent occasions when boilers exploded.

Motivated by these catastrophes a group of business people created and enforced standards for the design and manufacture of boilers. Legislation which followed created the need for inspection activity and from that insurance activity flourished, thus giving rise in 1859 to what was later to become National Vulcan and a key moment in British industrial health and safety history.

From this beginning National Vulcan's business has diversified into other lines of insurance both in the UK and abroad. By 1991 when Mr Ken Sinfield, now Group Divisional Director of Sun Alliance Europe, joined National Vulcan as its Managing Director, the company had a turnover of approximately £70 million and interests in 65 countries. However, in the years prior to this the company had become complacent in the presence of what appeared on paper to be significant and sustainable success within what it assumed would always be a captive market. It had relied almost solely on its reputation for technical excellence for many years without significant change or effort.

Staff expected (and got) jobs for life, and were very inward looking working within an organisation defined by 55 different job grades. A contributing factor which was fundamental to National Vulcan's staidness was the predisposition of people to remain with the company for life, as Mr Sinfield explains: "Most people had worked their way up through the organisation and had no concept of what it was like to work in a modern environment.

"We had an approach which said if you can bring each job down to its lowest common denominator you can then give each person a tiny part of a task, grade them accordingly, and pay them the least amount of money. As a result people didn't understand how their role affected the big picture, nor did they acknowledge that the world in which the company operated was changing rapidly", explains Mr Sinfield.

One business journal (*Marketing Business*, June 1994) summed up the severity of National Vulcan's change of fortune: "National Vulcan Engineering Insurance Group is a classic example of a company driven to business process re-engineering by a crisis. A massive downturn in its fortunes, from a profit of £6.1 million in 1990 to a £6.3 million loss in 1991, showed that the company was seriously out of step with the needs of its markets." It became essential to develop an effective turnaround strategy.

One of Mr Sinfield's first remits on joining National Vulcan, after reviewing the situation was to take the top management team away from its daily responsibilities in order to discuss the difficulties the company was experiencing and reformulate the corporate strategy. This was approached with the clear goal to return the company to profit and win back the confidence of its customers. National Vulcan's objective was to dominate its market place through being the highest quality, lowest cost operator in the UK engineering insurance sector. "We decided that we had to induce radical change concentrating on three key processes in the business, initially with the assistance of consultants", says Mr Sinfield. These three key processes were:

- **Insurance Administration** - issuing insurance policies on plant and machinery.
- **Handling of Data** - maintenance of an extensive database to manage

the inspection of insured plant.

- **Plant Inspections and Reporting System** - scheduling of the activities of National Vulcan's 500 home-based engineers.

For each of the three key processes project leaders were asked to re-examine the core processes and report on how National Vulcan currently handled them within a working day. Activities which previously took months to complete were to be completed within the working day.

The business was broken down into small customer orientated units, each of which had to produce a business plan as Mr Sinfield explains: "We engaged ourselves in very detailed planning. We had an overall company plan which was supported by a plan for each profit centre and then every individual in the company compiled what we called a "My Plan" which identified what they needed to achieve as an individual and how this contributed to their department. This was then linked to their training and development requirements and planning." Prior to re-engineering the company job succession was accommodated on the basis of 'filling dead men's shoes'. However, the company has now introduced people from outside the organisation to fill top level roles in a bid to transform the culture while promotions are now based on ability and are made quickly and radically, throughout the company.

The establishment of 'outrageous targets' required people to operate within tight deadlines which made it necessary to educate people to think laterally. A 24 hour target was set for issuing policies, despatching inspection reports and updating the plant database. The second key criteria was that only one person should be involved in processing customer transactions, regardless of where in the company they arrived.

"We said that if a project is going to take longer than six months it shouldn't happen. Where some projects took three months to complete, staff were told that whatever they did had to be completed within a working day. The very saying of it and the ruthlessness with which we guarded that ideal, meant that people were forced to think laterally", says Mr Sinfield.

Teams focused on parts of the processes where individuals could add value. The rest was either cut or automated. The administration system was chosen as the area for most experimentation. National Vulcan can now boast that its administration system take 24 hours to issue a policy rather than three months, the plant database is no longer months out of date and end-user complaints have significantly reduced.

With the exception of one excursion into computerisation in the

1980s the systems employed by the company were basically paper based. One glimpse into the nature of work conducted by National Vulcan provides ample evidence of the inefficiencies this fuelled.

National Vulcan employs over 400 engineers who inspect plant and machinery such as boilers and cranes at the client's site to ensure they comply with various legislative requirements. National Vulcan insures about 1.5 million items, and because it inspects most of them more than once a year, it processes about 2.5 million records annually.

After the engineers had made their inspections, they would type up their reports using one of the 400 different forms available and make several carbon copies. Once completed the reports were mailed in batches twice a week to Manchester. There they piled up awaiting the attention of an acceptance engineer, whose job it was to check the field engineers' reports. Once they had reached the top of the pile, the reports needed only a few minutes checking. Each acceptance engineer was struggling with a back log extending up to six months. To add to the customer's frustration, if the acceptance engineer had any queries, the report had to be mailed back to the engineer and the cycle began again. The insurance business was no more efficient. Issuing a new policy involved 43 steps, 10 different departments and 20 pairs of hands.

"Only when we had defined what was required of the three key processes and determined how they should function did we look at how they should be computerised", says Mr Sinfield. The first exposure National Vulcan had with automating its systems was not a complete success, however with the benefit of hindsight it provided a valuable lesson for the future in terms of how best to develop a workable system. The first data base was set up in the 1980s to assist engineers log the numerous components they inspected on each plant visit, as well as to schedule subsequent inspections. No computer skills existed within the company at the time so National Vulcan engaged a large 'specialist' organisation to develop the system. But developed in the absence of engineering insurance expertise the system was cumbersome, difficult to operate and did not do what it was commissioned to achieve.

Although National Vulcan's previous experience of IT developments did not favour further commitment to change and investment, joint business/IT teams were established to facilitate rapid delivery of the new system. Using development tools which made it relatively easy to simulate what would be delivered, users were able to see whether or not a system met their needs.

"The only way to build a system is in small building blocks using teams which are led by business people. I'm convinced our approach to IT is a major reason for our success. Even when you have rationalised the process, if you can't deliver that in a service sense then you're dead," comments Mr Sinfield. "The fundamentals are in place and we have taken a modular approach so we can add to the processes all the time. The core system on the insurance side for example is on version 30 because it has developed through incremental steps."

In sum, among the key lessons learnt from National Vulcan's first and arguably the company's most dramatic period of change were:

- Strong leadership and active participation of the chief executive is essential;
- Rigorous targets are required in order to achieve tight deadlines through challenging people and encouraging lateral thinking;
- *Supportive* IT structures and systems should be developed only after the key processes are defined and refined;
- The change process needs to be led by those with the greatest expertise and enthusiasm rather than superiority.

"From the onset of the program we have been honest with people telling them everything we possibly can and involving the union in the process. Every month, every manager has to stand up in front of their people and pass on the messages we think at the highest level they should hear in addition anything they think at a departmental level staff should know. The idea behind this cascade approach was that problems are also fed back up the mechanism. I spoke directly with staff at open forums to disclose financial and management information and they were given the opportunity to ask anything they wanted", says Mr Sinfield.

National Vulcan, with the crisis of the early 1990s behind it, has in the 12 months to January 1996 continued to make progress in two significant areas: National Vulcan's "Strategy 2001" and shifting attitudes from "task management to the leadership of people".

A Vision For The Future

"Strategy 2001" was established to ensure that National Vulcan achieved the right balance between short term policy and more far-reaching challenges which the market will present as the company moves towards the next century. Unlike the urgent re-engineering effort of its core processes which was driven from the top, 'Project 2001' provides greater opportunity for staff involvement.

The steering group for 'Project 2001' consisted of an eight-strong executive team plus four full time and three part time business people representing different areas of the business and two independent consultants. The group's main task was to set goals and mastermind the overall planning of the change process. Key to the new strategy is the conviction that it should reflect the interests of the four main groups of stakeholders: customers, staff, shareholders and business partners, especially brokers.

National Vulcan operates in a niche market. Its vision is to be leader in the field of Engineering Risk Management by 2001. The problem the company confronted was how to achieve this. In answer, 'Project 2001' was conceived to develop the blue print plan for how National Vulcan could achieve its 2001 objective: "To be the world leader in engineering risk management, by profit, service and technical excellence."

"Project 2001" took five of the brightest young managers away from their day to day activity and allocated them several areas to investigate and reform, concentrating on the central theme of risk management as Mr Sinfield explains, "We defined ourselves as a risk management company rather than an inspection or insurance company. We want to be the best risk management company in the world in our field. To accomplish this we had to define the qualities required by a company of this kind which then determine aspects such as the projects we should implement, the sort of people we employ, where we should do business, what lines of business we should pursue and who our clients should be."

The project team spent nine months talking to customers, business partners and staff. They then formed sector based focus groups to brainstorm future issues. Staff were encouraged to take part in "People Focus Groups" which addressed issues such as communication; health, safety and welfare; and reward and recognition. "The results were both encouraging and inspiring", says John Bynre, Core Team Member during the project. "The way staff approached these issues was both professional and realistic and many of their recommendations have now been adopted into the long term plan. A bigger benefit, however, was the feeling of ownership and involvement this gave to the participants. We suddenly found everyone was a 2001 champion."

The next stage was to communicate the plan. "Experience showed the only effective method of communication was face to face. Although clearly time consuming it was essential and the team spent much of their time communicating clearly to all areas of the company. The way forward was to take every member of staff away for a day to both communicate the vision and gain feedback and views", says Mike Seddon, Head of TQM. The *event* was held in a Manchester Centre hotel over three days, with one third of staff attending each day. As National Vulcan staff are based in all parts of the country this was a major logistical exercise. The outcome was hundreds of constructive ideas and opinions which have helped to shape the future activities of the company.

The company is now in the process of implementing the strategic plan born out of 'Project 2001'.

From Task Manager To A Leader Of People

"National Vulcan is a company built on know how. Its products and services are built around the expertise of its engineers and underwriters. For decades managers of the company were selected from within the ranks because they were good at their job. This may have been as an engineer, underwriter or salesman, but rarely as a leader of people", explains Mr Seddon.

To support the re-engineering process there was a need for a cultural change. The roles of staff needed to change as dramatically as the systems in which they operated. Empowerment, the breakdown of hierarchical structures and encouragement of innovation required a very different management style.

A programme was designed with the mission statement: "From task manager to leader of people" which 150 of the company's senior and middle management attended over the first twelve month period. The programme was developed in-house by Alan Horan, Management Developer and Mr Seddon and was very much focused on the change of style required for the future management of the company. The programme is now mandatory for newly appointed leaders.

The programme was built around a week long residential event with the emphasis placed on participation. Business simulations and activities created around the themes of planning and communication were at the core of the program but in every situation the debrief revolved around people issues. "For instance, evenings started with a business simulation, with debate and discussion on the day's topics carrying on in the bar, late into the night. One light hearted measure of success was in the weekly pub quiz! National Vulcan has a winning reputation, having failed only once to win in the first twelve appearances," enthuses Mr Seddon.

Belbin's Team Roles were used as an aid to understanding preferred roles and as an explanation of differences in behaviour observed during the activities. This facilitated discussion on interpersonal relationships particularly within a teamworking environment.

W. Edward Demming's, "The Experiment with Red Beads" linked process and people in a dramatic and powerful way. Demming used the experiment to explain "variation" within a process but National Vulcan took that a step further and explored the role of people working within the process. This approach opened up discussion on appraisal and motivation.

By selecting delegates from all areas of the company and by mixing youth with experience each event created a sense of team spirit amongst those attending. One of the many successes of the programme was the breakdown of barriers between staff working in different areas of the company, as Mr Seddon explains, "There is now greater understanding and support for what individuals are doing in their respective parts of the workplace. The programme was also designed to identify individual development needs which have been incorporated into personal development plans."

National Vulcan's position of market dominance continues to be enhanced by the effects of its extensive re-engineering and the implementation of new systems. Profits are on the rise and it was voted the Best Engineering Insurer for the fourth year in succession in 1995. Despite the apparent speed with which National Vulcan returned to corporate well-being Mr Sinfield cautions that cultures cannot be changed quickly or readily.

"It is a five to seven year process at best. We are five years down the track and it will take another five years until we see the reforms we have commenced take full effect because culture just seeps through an organisation and until those old attitudes have really been buried they will continue to haunt the organisation, although on an increasingly less significant basis. Strategy 2001 is our final attempt to totally transform the company", concludes Mr Sinfield.

39

Passion & Obsession

—ICI Paints Europe—

PASSION & Obsession are exciting, even exotic words. They are not concepts that spring to mind when thinking about paint. In fact, most people probably think the only pastime duller than watching paint dry is manufacturing it.

Not so, according to Chris Donovan, from ICI Paints Customer Service and Quality section:

"To survive and compete in today's turbulent world requires customer and product awareness to be part of our day-to-day culture; the love of change, the customer and our products is essential! We need to change attitudes, put emotion back into our business and to seek new and innovative ways of making improvements.

"Our emphasis is on implementing the 'Passion & Obsession' revolution through a team-based approach. Small, natural work groups are most effective, as people respond and give their best when they work together. There is also no limit to what a person can achieve if completely involved. Opportunities for our people to air their views must be easily achievable and welcomed. Even the smallest ideas are just as important as the big ideas and should be carefully recognised."

The concepts of Passion & Obsession are inspiring the ICI Paints workforce but the strategy is just one of a series of initiatives designed to provide even greater service to their customers.

Part of Imperial Chemical Industries plc, ICI Paints has 15,000 employees worldwide. The company's headquarters is in Slough, (United Kingdom) with 45 manufacturing sites spread throughout 22 countries.

ICI Paints

ICI Paints is a global leader in its three chosen sectors of:

- decorative paint,
- coatings for food and drink cans, and
- refinish paints for vehicles.

For its market-leading decorative operations, ICI Paints is organised regionally for markets in North America, Latin America, Europe and Asia Pacific, while the refinish and packaging coatings businesses are structured globally.

In the specialised market for internal coatings for food and drink cans, the packaging coatings business is a world leader.

An emphasis on customer service, innovative technology and strong branding has given the business a leading position in many countries with familiar brand names such as 'Dulux', 'Glidden', and ICI Autocolor.

The considerable success of the ICI Paints Europe division has been achieved through a disciplined approach to managing the business. Like most companies in the industry, ICI Paints experienced a very difficult trading period throughout the late 1980s. Management was restructured and the new management team began to examine ways to address the significant concerns which were undermining business performance.

At all times a 'Focus on the Customer' was maintained and this vision became the way forward for ICI Paints Europe. In the early 1990s a mission was developed for the business:

"The business mission of ICI Paints Europe is to win and keep customers for its range of superior quality surface coating systems."

The mission also contained specific targets:

"With customer service as the core value, the business will grow towards a return on net assets approaching 35 per cent by 1993."

To support the mission a number of key business objectives were identified to focus on:

- Customer Service and Quality
- Maximising return on net assets
- Safety, health and the environment.

The leadership team understood that to achieve these goals the employees would have to be involved and developed to enable them to make a contribution.

To begin, the key business objectives were cascaded through the organisation so everyone knew the role they would play in the company's improvement process. The workforce learnt that customer service is about "making sure every interaction we have with a customer is positive" and that Manufacturing Excellence means continuously improving processes.

It was not difficult for staff to understand that improvement was required. For example in February 1991, the probability of a customer contacting an ICI site to place an order by telephone and the call being answered within four rings, with the order delivered on time, in full and picked correctly was only 55 per cent.

Alan Thompson, ICI Paints head of market research conducts an annual customer survey. His work has found that the important areas for customer service and Quality were:

1. Availability/Delivery
2. Pricing
3. Product Range
4. Product/Colour Quality
5. Sales Support
6. Advertising/Promotion
7. Container/Package Quality

The survey results were used as the basis for a set of measures to monitor customer satisfaction. The key measurement was On Time In Full (OTIF) delivery of orders but other areas to measure included:

- Raw Material Supply
- Invoice Adjustments
- Product Quality and Packaging
- Telephone answering
- Recipe Accuracy
- Customer Complaints
- Sale Call Frequency
- Manufacturing Right First Time
- Credit Response Time

Everyone in the company was educated in what On Time In Full actually meant. A booklet clearly outlining the criteria, implementation and expected results of the scheme was produced. According to the booklet OTIF is the measure of how well ICI ensures that their customers receive "the product they specify (Assembly Accuracy) in the quantity they order (In Full) and on the date they request (On Time)".

"OTIF % = % Assembly Accuracy x % In Full x % On Time"

Everyone is encouraged to share accountability for the whole process. Responsibility for maintaining the required standards are devolved to the workforce who are then accountable for achieving the targets set.

The three elements of OTIF are measured by:

- Assembly Accuracy – Performing checks on a random sample of no less than 1:15 to ensure the item is selected as specified and 'fit for the purpose' in an undamaged container correctly labelled, clean and without leakages.
- In-Full – comparing the actual delivery items with those specified on the original order. The result must be 100 per cent or 'In-Full' fails.
- On-Time – monitoring the actual delivery date to the customer's initial order request date. An important distinction made by ICI is that 'On-Time' is not an agreed-by-negotiation date. The delivery has to take place on the date originally requested by the customer or 'On-Time' is considered to have failed.

Initially the greatest improvements to the above measures were achieved by focusing on five key areas:

Forecasting Accuracy

It was vital for Sales and Marketing to be able to forecast accurately to enable Supply, Production and Distribution to plan effectively.

Raw Materials OTIF

This is a measure of the response from the Purchasing and Supply departments to requests from Production for raw materials and containers. It is applied in exactly the same way as ICI assesses OTIF to their external customers. Accurate forecasting has enabled supply to have the right raw materials and containers ready for Production.

Manufacture to Plan

Production manufactures to the agreed plan. Accurate forecasting and the appropriate raw materials and containers being on hand has enabled the company to do this. Manufacture to plan is the measure of how many batches on the plan were completed.

Service Level Monitoring

To ensure ICI makes and distributes products that customers want, this measure reports every order item failure against the site responsible for its production. This is a key measurement of performance and every failure here is reported in great detail.

Accountability

Everyone in the organisation share in the accountability for improving OTIF, so everyone works to identify in detail the areas the company can continue to improve and is involved in setting targets and strategic plans to achieve them.

The On Time In Full scheme has been supported by a variety of other services including: regular sales representative calls, full technical support, prompt promotion material and merchandising, efficient administration, easier placement of orders, and improved provision of information.

Another measure which ICI Paints encourages its people to consider is the company's Return on Net Assets (RONA). Staff have been given training in the subject and understand the issues involved including the 'cash to cash cycle'. Information on factors concerning ICI Paints profitability is regularly published in the company's internal magazine. Such open and frank discussion of trading conditions gives the workforce a sense of trust and inspires them to work together to continually seek ways of improving the RONA.

To support On Time In Full, an MRP II system was established with the aim of providing the crucial 'predictability of manufacture' factor. Process technology and methods improvement has increased the 'right first time' average for batches of paint from 20 per cent to over 70 per cent, which as Operations General Manager David Harrison says is close to the world's best for the industry:

"Historically the paint industry has adopted a 'master chef' type approach as the materials and processes were not particularly predictable. The skill was in quickly adjusting an incorrect batch to meet the required specifications. That was the tradition; the discipline our business now works with calls for robust product specifications, and the use of materials which have clear characteristics and consistency. We now insist that our suppliers supply a consistent product so our batches don't vary and we measure and control our manufacturing processes very tightly. That has helped us improve from 20 per cent to 70 per cent right first time and most of the remaining 30 per cent is final-stage colour refinement. So we have been very pleased with our results. A further benefit has been our ability to produce smaller batch sizes which in turn has reduced inventory levels, and waste."

ICI Paints next area of focus was logistics robustness. The company used consultants Oliver Wight to help them maximise the benefits of their MRP II system. Oliver Wight has developed a checklist of 35 questions which help managers become more competitive. By answering the questions, a manager can grade his company's MRP II system into one of four categories: A, B, C, or D. ICI Paints Europe is a 'Class A' manufacturer.

A 'Class A' rating means that the company's Planning and Control Processes are "effectively used company-wide; generating significant improvements in customer service, productivity, inventory, and costs" and that "continuous improvement has become a way of life for employees, suppliers, and customers; improved quality, reduced costs, and increased velocity are contributing to a competitive advantage."

The checklist examines the effectiveness of MRP II in the organisation and other topics including: Just-In-Time, distribution resource planning, business planning, manufacturing strategy, continuous improvement, and sales and operations planning. David Harrison feels the checklist has been very useful in focusing and improving the organisation.

To achieve Class A status David believes team involvement is vital. To facilitate team involvement Investors In People has been selected as a standard to attain. The standard is considered useful by ICI Paints because the company has responded well to the discipline of outside accreditations such as ISO 9000. Investors In People was evaluated as useful and is well on the way to being awarded.

At the Slough manufacturing plant, most of the workforce has undergone teamworking events which focus on problem solving and work-place improvement issues.

The General Manager of Business Development, Kitty Hulme is an energetic Canadian who has led the Passion & Obsession team. Kitty also has responsibility for advertising and public relations. In some respects her job is made more difficult by the fact that ICI Paints is already a world-class operation. Maintaining motivation for further improvement can be difficult but her enthusiasm and commitment inspires the Product Improvement Teams and the Customer Prosperity Teams. The Product Improvement Teams draw people from market research and marketing as well as technical and national account salespeople. The Customer Prosperity Teams are led by account managers who deal with retail outlets such as Texas Homebase and B & Q. These teams look at issues from the customers' perspective and examine service opportunities to help the retailers sell more products and how ICI Paints can serve them better.

"Rather than just having marketing people working on these issues we bring in every element of the business. This way we make sure the right people are focused on the product and product quality. The team environment has created a mindset where everyone leaves their status and position at the door and thinks creatively about the product and related issues.

"Years ago when I first began in business there was a lot of emphasis by individuals on their personal knowledge and expertise in certain areas, their attitude was knowledge is power. In our team culture that attitude doesn't exist – the more general information the team understands about other disciplines, the better the results that team achieves. The team culture is so ingrained that even employees who aren't part of a particular team feel able to pass on relevant ideas freely. We have reached the stage where we really understand our customers' businesses and have the attitude that when they prosper so do we."

Kitty believes in seeking out best practice not only in ICI or the paint industry in the UK but across a broad group of industries internationally:

"You can have all the right intentions but miss out on important developments. It is a fast-changing world and we constantly review our processes to decide what we should continue with and what should be changed. As a company we can't afford to look only at what is happening within ICI or the United Kingdom but need to examine the progress being made in North America or Australia. We keep up with advances in other industries as well, such as, the latest Just-In-Time techniques being implemented in the clothing industry. ICI Paints is very good at learning from our international operations and our customers. Importantly, we are equipped to share our information on best practice throughout the company worldwide, this certainly contributes to our market leadership."

An example of ICI Paints commitment to 'making things easier for our [their] customers' through constant re-evaluation of procedures comes from ICI Autocolor. The company has developed a special customer service programme to which everyone is accountable and against which everyone is measured.

The involvement and enthusiasm of every member of the organisation is encouraged as the division's managers understand this is the only way to succeed.

The first step towards providing a better service was asking ICI Autocolor's customers how happy they were with the service. For many companies that's the easy bit, actually acting on the feedback and recommendations takes more effort.

A number of solutions were developed in key areas of customer concern:

- Simpler paperwork to save time
- Better management of orders
- Faster, easier ordering methods.

The most important thing from the customer's point of view was how quickly orders were fulfilled and delivered. Customers not surprisingly were very negative about 'out of stock' items.

ICI Autocolor completely revamped their computer system so they were able to monitor stock levels more closely and take remedial action should the rare instance of an out of stock item arise. The warehousing operation was also completely redeveloped to capitalise on the latest storage and distribution techniques to ensure on-time delivery.

A Customer Service Co-ordinator was assigned to individual customers to manage orders and smooth out any difficulties, this gave customers a direct contact point and provided them with any assistance they needed.

Paperwork was also listed as an area of concern. ICI Autocolor redesigned its paperwork to make it clearer and easier to cross check. Delivery notes were redesigned for 'at a glance' reading and given a number which matches the corresponding invoice.

Ordering has been made easier through 24-hour-a-day fax ordering and the ability to order via the telephone directly through the customers' personal Customer Co-ordinator. An Electronic Data Interchange (EDI) system has also been arranged with corresponding benefits for customers

These improvements have made business easier for ICI Autocolor's clients. The company philosophy of: "By developing and encouraging shared accountability at our end, we aim to help things run more efficiently at yours" has been put in practice to benefit its customers. The sentiment is reiterated by Steve Canham, Chief Executive of ICI Autocolor:

"The real secret of success is to make your customers more profitable by working with your company than anyone else in the industry."

ICI Autocolor is just one of many examples of how ICI Paints' teamwork, creativity and attention to detail has maintained its place as a world-class company. Other areas of improvement include the environment and Health & Safety.

In conclusion, the activities outlined in ICI Paints 'Passion & Obsession' Activity Kit provide an excellent example of the way momentum for continuous improvement is maintained. They range from simple commonsense ("If you see a damaged, dirty or faulty product in a store – buy it!") to encouraging strategic thinking and awareness of opposition brands and ICI Paints position in the marketplace.

The final activity card tells staff it is now up to them and asks the questions: "What practical ideas do you and your team have to improve our business?" and "What can you and your team DO to move us to becoming more passionate about our customers and obsessed by our products?".

The advice which follows could apply to any business and is an example of the type of thinking required to be among the world's best:

"Remember – small is beautiful, so why not take the initiative to suggest and implement improvements that will form the building blocks of the bigger mountain – the kind of ideas that you can get into action almost straight away. There is no such thing as an insignificant improvement – even modest changes in working practices, ideas to benefit our customers and end-users, will accumulate into a much more impressive figure!

"Brainstorm your ideas using the checklist below as a guide:

- No idea is too small to start with.
- Do something soon.
- It is easier to ask forgiveness than permission.
- Ask yourself 'Does this add value for our customers?' and 'Is there anything I can do faster?'
- Measure SOFT and HARD customer feedback ... and share it quickly with those who can effect improvement.
- Think each Monday, 'Is there anything we can do 1% better for our customers this week?'
- If in doubt – TRY IT!"

40

Service & Convenience

—Color Steels—

"OUR product has a lot of potential and all of us in the plant are committed to Total Quality – we've seen the benefits in a short space of time in terms of the changes we have made under the umbrella of Total Quality Management. We are committed to change through Quality processes."

The philosophy of Color Steels is on-going commitment to change. This pursuit of Quality has not only resulted in tremendous market growth, but also ground-breaking Quality Management practices.

Color Steels, based in South Wales, is a leading service centre for precoated steels in the UK and one of two subsidiaries of Precoat International. In 1995, Precoat International was successfully floated on the Official List of the London Stock Exchange.

Color Steels currently stocks over 500 different types of precoated steel. A variety of processes may be carried out at any one time. These processes include slitting, decoiling, blanking, notching and piercing. The advantages of precoated steel compared to post-painting are reduced costs, enhanced quality, convenience and the avoidance of environmental hazards.

Throughout 1995, Color Steels continued to make good progress. Sales increased by 34 per cent to £31.6 million. Undoubtedly, the biggest contributor to this growth was the development of new applications for the company's product, particularly in the lighting, white goods, brown goods and office furniture sectors.

The service centre concentrates on the purchasing of bulk quantities of precoated coil on long lead times from the manufacturers and providing end users with processed, fully inspected material in various shapes and

The Training Game
Color Steels Ltd

Lyn Williams (seated)
Managing Director
Color Steels Ltd

forms ready for immediate use. Increasingly customers are being supplied on a *just in time* basis. Among its regular customers, Color Steels claims household brand names such as Candy, Creda, Hoover, Hotpoint, Siemens and Thorn Lighting.

Color Steels' commitment to Quality has been well recognised and rewarded. In 1991, the company was invited by the South Wales Electrical Company to compete for their performance, efficiency and productivity award, which was subsequently granted. Later, it competed on behalf of the South Wales Electricity Company and was recognised by NEC in Birmingham for its work. In 1992, the factory was accredited with BS5750 Part 2 approval. In addition, it has received accreditations from many of the companies which it supplies. In 1995, Color Steels was pronounced *Best Overall Supplier* by the Thorn Lighting Group.

Commitment to Quality first manifested itself in the changes that began in the late 1980s and early 1990s. Since 1990, the company has invested approximately £6 million in the restructuring of its manufacturing system. In 1991, Color Steels changed the structure of the operating procedure within the plant, which involved renovating and refurbishing the facility. A large part of the investment was in the installation of new and technologically advanced equipment, the majority of which was supplied from Germany. This resulted in some strategic changes being made in the systems, the facility and the plant.

The emphasis which Color Steels places on the immediate availability of materials for customers requires constant efficiency and reliability. "The market place is looking for *just in time* Quality Assured suppliers. So the role of pro-active distributors like ourselves, has become more vital. We are producing unique products in the main, only about 20 to 25 per cent of the stock that we produce is for general stock applications, and the rest of it is virtually tailor-made in terms of dimensions, colour and so on. In order to assure customers of the quality that they expect, improvement must be an on-going process", explained Mr Lyn Williams, Managing Director of Color Steels.

In monitoring improvements, Color Steels has not stopped with the ISO 9000 certification. "We have found that there is some value in the certification, but it is of limited value. What we value most is accreditation from our suppliers and customers. Taking the Thorn assessment, for example, that was a full two-day affair and they meant everything they said in terms of conformity. If we did not meet their criteria, we would be found wanting on the level of supply.

"We are also working at the moment with the Bristol Quality Centre. The trouble with ISO 9000 is that it is only saying we have a system. The real positive role of Quality must be linked to results and what I like is the new approach which portrays how Quality is really linked to the performance of the business. It means that we are not happy to stop and say, 'OK, we've got a Quality System' – there really needs to more a fundamental linkage with performance. And that is what I believe the Quality Centre is trying to put into place – that to me is the way forward."

Mr Williams maintains that the emphasis of the *just in time* system is on accessibility. "We have over 500 accounts in the company; the average order size from each customer is only about one tonne, so they are looking for relatively small quantities with good availability. What we have in place are various controls in terms of performance management – delivery on time performance, spoilage and an over-all productivity."

Color Steels recognises the importance of maintaining organisational efficiency to ensure that the needs of customers are met. The company relies heavily on Kanban strategic stocks which are specified materials that are stored in bulk until the customer requires their immediate use. Kanban stocks are seen as vital in ensuring delivery on time – usually within two days of ordering – in order to give the customers the level of response necessary for them to continue their own operations without any interruptions.

While Color Steels has looked at alternative systems, Kanbans have been the most efficient means of guaranteeing on-time delivery. "We have looked at EDI and in some ways we found it useful. I can see the benefits of it in a global sense, rather than on the basis of next-day deliveries. And in some fields I can see EDI taking over. But for our business, Kanbans are very much the required system."

In many ways Color Steels acts as a bridge for its customers. It has an intensive process of value adding and materials are produced in accordance with the specific shapes, colours and dimensions that each individual customer requires. Furthermore, through this process the company is continuing to expand in terms of new uses for its product. In some cases, Color Steels is now performing primary processes for its customers. And the standard of this process is assisted by the large amount of expertise within the team as well as the being constant monitoring by inspection. The combination of *value adding* and *just in time* supply has proved to be of great benefit to the many companies which Color Steels supplies.

To maintain continuous efficiency, Color Steels has placed considerable emphasis on keeping pace with technological innovations. An early part of this move was the introduction of a new IT system. This system is multi-lingual and multi-currency and its introduction was designed to provide the business with a much broader platform on which to work.

"IT is very much part of the over-all process because it states: 'here is the new equipment, we have a computerised centre so that the operator will be able to transform an order requirement quickly, relate it to the width of the material and the computer will automatically set the machine to classify the requirement rate'. The level of improvement in this type of venture is enormous. Besides the extra quality of the product we are producing, we have very high benefits in terms of labour utilisation and internal productivity."

The company has also embraced the technology of bar codes which it uses to communicate information and there is considerable scope to further develop this technology. "It will not be too long before we have the same disciplines in place that they have in the supermarket for scanning, for Quality, for invoicing, for payments – in all aspects we are moving in that direction and as far as we are concerned, we will be leading that drive, not following it."

However, improvements have gone beyond simply installing more efficient equipment. Having made some strategic investments, the Chairman of the Board suggested that it was time to change the people's attitudes. But in order to change the people, it was necessary to change the culture.

Color Steels recognised the importance of instituting a programme of Continuous Improvement which would create an environment that was committed to Quality. The first stage of this process took the shape of altering the management team. Following that, some cultural aspects needed to be addressed – it became apparent that what was needed was to give people a voice.

"We realised that it was very important to create an environment where people genuinely feel that their contribution is meaningful. Unless you do this you are wasting your time. Some of the changes made at the plant were also important for people to realise that Quality cannot be faked", Mr Williams explained.

"For example, shortly after I first came to this company we had a major customer visit. The old Works Manager issued eight white coats and when the customer came he could not believe it. He had been there before and so he knew that they were just dressed up for the day.

"You see, you cannot fake it. Ultimately, you must give the people the opportunity to express themselves and to feel that they are meaningful in this particular business."

As a part of the Continuous Improvement philosophy, meetings were arranged for employees to attend. As is often the case, people were initially reluctant to attend, and when they did, it was often with mixed feelings.

Mr Alan Davis is Works Director at Color Steels and one of the people directly responsible for implementing the cultural change. "To begin with, I think people were very suspicious. When people have preconceived notions about the way things are to be done and then someone comes in with a fresh approach, they say: 'Hang on, what's this chap on about?'. But by talking to them and involving them in meetings, we tried to allay their fears at the time. That helped, but obviously it did not help everyone."

Ensuring on-going communication and the provision of information is one of the fundamental aspects of Continuous Improvement for Color Steels. "One of the things that I was keen to do when I got here was to pass down the idea of ownership which we picked up from companies like Thorn. We have moved to the point now where we have two or three operators who sit in our Quality meetings with our customers and suppliers", said Mr Alan Davis.

The use of psychometric tests has also played a major part in the process of improvement. The tests are used to develop team work. Employees are divided into teams and the results of the tests are analysed and then plotted as distribution scores. Training models are then developed to improve the performances of the teams whose results reflect a requirement for further training.

Color Steels has since introduced a revitalised training approach and in doing so, has formed very close links with the local university, technical college and other institutions. These links have resulted in the successful improvement of team work principles, identified potential within the team for further advancement and involved many of the members of the process control team in issues of supervisory management.

As Mr Williams explains, the response to change has considerably altered. "What I notice now, is that occasionally I will have people saying that they are a bit disappointed because someone else is on the last course, while they believe that they should have been – so it has turned itself on its head now."

As part of Continuing Improvement, teams are set up on Quality, productivity, real work and spoilage and those teams change throughout the year. This constant restructuring of teams is designed to ensure that there are always new ideas coming into every aspect of the company.

Much of the production process is monitored in terms of individual responsibility. Recorded beside each specification is the name of the manager, so that there is individual accountability in every aspect of production. In addition, Color Steels keeps lists of the operators being employed in the plant and monitors their individual confidence levels for the various sections. The operators, in turn, receive the results in the form of operating statistics with regard to such issues as delivery on time, items in quarantine and outstanding claims.

As Mr Williams explains, "Ultimately, unless you impart to your work force exactly what's happening, how can you expect them to respond? They have dynamic bonuses where they can enhance their earnings on a weekly, monthly or quarterly basis and they need to know these details."

A unique component of Continuous Improvement at Color Steels is a board game that the company has devised. Manufacturing processes are recreated by the use of a small-scale and simple reproduction of a working environment in the shape of a game – the purpose of which is to illustrate the necessity of Quality on time.

"I wanted to have some sort of practical demonstration, rather than just getting them in and talking to them like a teacher. I thought it would be much better if they could see something happening around a board game", said Mr Williams.

During each game, a team will occupy the various positions around the board. By doing so, each employee is able to better understand the roles of fellow workers. The game is made effective by the introduction of a few random defects. The objective is to identify the defects and prevent them from making it through the production process.

Each game takes approximately one hour to play and orders are introduced on a ten-minute cycle. One member of the team is placed in control of the game – taking on the role of Quality Control Manager. Throughout the game there are three observers in the room, monitoring the progress of the person in the position of control. The results of their efforts are mapped on a scoring chart according to how well they performed in various aspects.

Ultimately, however, this innovative form of Quality training is much more than a game. The 'game' has many serious benefits in terms of demonstrating the importance of Quality on time and in allowing each employee to gain a better over-all understanding of the production process. Moreover, it is further relevant because those employees who score well, may then be sent to Cardiff University for external training.

And as Mr Williams explains: "Those who have returned from the courses have shown a dramatic improvement in terms of their performance on the shop floor. We've identified the potential, given them some formal training and when they come back, they see the job completely differently.

"I think it's important for a lot of operators, if they're undertaking training, to be able to see that they're going to get some sort of benefit from it at the end of the day, not just quality of work, but also externally. I think that it is important to them that they have their certificates."

With a long track record of sales and profit growth and with the ever-increasing range of products available, Color Steels views the future with confidence.

Mr Williams believes that in a business the size of Color Steels there is always the opportunity to express entrepreneurial strengths. This belief is illustrated not only by past success, but also by the significant growth potential that the company has charted. With developments leading towards participation in the automotive industry, the company looks to be leading the drive towards achieving this potential. As it does, it will be with a realisation that it is only with Quality that the acceleration can continue.

"We are a business with enormous potential. We are extremely enthusiastic about our product and the superior level of service we provide. We genuinely believe that we have something special to offer."

41

Planning For Quality

— Southern Water Services —

WHILE Southern Water Services may not perceive that it has progressed a substantial distance down the Quality Assurance path it has maintained a reputation in the water and wastewater industry that is second to none, providing a solid basis from which it can extend ISO9002 certification.

Southern Water Services is the principal subsidiary of the Southern Water Group employing some 2,100 of the Group's 3,500 employees. Other companies in the Group, several of which have already been certified to ISO9001/2, provide a range of complementary functions such as engineering services, environmental services, systems technology, and specialist services and products ranging from vehicle contract hire to bottled mineral water.

Improvements to drinking water, and wastewater treatment and disposal, dictated by European legislation will cost the company a massive £2 billion over the next 10 years. To minimise the cost passed on to the customer through price increases Southern Water Services has embarked on a long term campaign to increase efficiency related savings through the introduction of new technology and improved working practices, of which Quality Assurance is a cornerstone.

"The major reason for implementing quality systems in Southern Water Services is our continuing drive for cost savings whilst achieving ever higher standards. The introduction of Quality systems ensures that the two can be achieved side by side", explains Stuart Derwent, Managing Director.

Southern Water Services provides water and wastewater services to over four million customers in Kent, Sussex, Hampshire and the Isle of

Seated: Stuart Derwent (Managing Director)
Standing: Barry Gardiner (Regional Quality Systems Manager)
Southern Water Services

Wight. Softening the impact of potential price increases and boosting customer appreciation of the planned improvements is a difficult task as Barry Gardiner, Regional Quality Systems Manager explains: "Our problem is that when a customer draws water from the tap it looks perfect. We are now about to invest heavily in improving the quality of the water by removing minute traces of pesticides for instance, but despite these improvements the customer is still going to draw water that looks the same."

The Drinking Water Inspector (DWI) commissioned Professor Stott to report on the methods currently used by the DWI in auditing water companies. Amongst the report's conclusions was that 'an informed public could reasonably expect water companies to operate to standards of inspection and control at least equal to those being commonly operated in private industry, standards which are embraced by ISO9002'.

In this context ISO9002 certification is relevant to a number of Southern Water Services' business units including water supply, distribution, and customer services. Professor Stott's report to the DWI recommended that companies implementing good QA systems can expect the number of major audits conducted by the DWI to decrease in frequency from annually to every four years, a calculated potential saving to Southern Water Services over a four year period of up to £90,000. Therefore, the incentive to pursue certification is substantial.

"The major drivers for implementing ISO9002 within Southern Water Services are to minimise waste and mistakes, thus reducing costs and to assist it meet stringent regulatory requirements which are paramount in reducing any risks associated with water quality", explains Mr Gardiner.

Mr Gardiner commenced working for Southern Water in an operational role in 1974, introducing ISO9002 to Hampshire water supply in 1993. From this position of experience he started to drive Quality forward throughout other parts of the organisation and was appointed to his current position in which he is encouraging the development of a company wide continuous improvement culture. Success in this task is dependent on both process knowledge and leadership. "I am not a Quality professional which is important – as an operational manager I can sell the concepts because of my knowledge and credibility. However, I have a strong support team providing Quality Assurance, ISO and continuous improvement expertise."

Mr Gardiner believes the only three reasons for introducing Quality to an organisation are to: improve quality and control, improve efficiency and to reduce cycle time. "There are no other reasons for doing it, not even for marketing purposes. You have to ask why the customer is asking for ISO certification – he is trying to ensure that he receives conformity of the product or service he requires, which can be determined by requesting the company's non-conformance record."

Southern Water Services has outlined a four year Quality plan describing the course the company will take to achieve Quality improvements and ISO certification. The plan is renewable each year so that progress can be measured and targets revised.

While Southern Water Services can include management by fact and compliance to exacting external audit processes amongst its strengths it admits that it has traditionally controlled Quality at the wrong end of the process supported by a stringent customer complaints policy. Southern Water Services' Guaranteed Standards Scheme dictates how customer complaints are handled. For example it states that all customer complaints must be recorded and investigated and a reply forwarded to the customer within 10 working days of receiving the complaint.

"What we are trying to achieve now is a right first time attitude and building a lot into prevention. In terms of maturity we are superb at answering complaints but we are only just addressing why we are getting the complaints. For instance, at a Hampshire site we found that twice a year we would receive a lot of taste complaints from people. As a result of our Quality initiative we tracked this to a micro algae which came from the first flush of the river after spring. We remedied the problem by using a powder activated carbon which reduced the taste complaints. Progressing from just identifying the problem, we want to be able to predict when it will occur using Statistical Process Control methods so we can prevent any potential reduction in quality", explains Mr Gardiner.

The company's commitment to Quality is highlighted by the policies it has adopted for the provision of drinking water and the treatment of waste water not only to meet its regulatory obligations but also to satisfy customer needs and expectations.

In support of Southern Water Services' goal to become a service industry leader it is committed to:

- **Customers** through the provision of a first class service at a value for money price;
- **Environment** by meeting standards and being aware of how we impact on the local community;
- **Leadership** ensuring that business needs are met through the adoption of the best management practices;
- **Organisation** by ensuring improved operational performance through continuous improvement;
- **Training** of staff and contractors so that they are fully aware and able to meet the company's objectives; and
- **Business Process** through the adoption of performance, efficiency and accountability controls around the guidelines of ISO9000 with certification of key areas to demonstrate effective management.

The process employed to move the company forward embraces four key foundation elements (fully committed leadership, continuous improvement, good base systems and training) to help the organisation move towards the adoption of a continuous improvement culture as illustrated in Figure1.

A Quality Systems Team reporting to the Finance Director, Mr Eric Hutchinson has been formed to facilitate the implementation of the

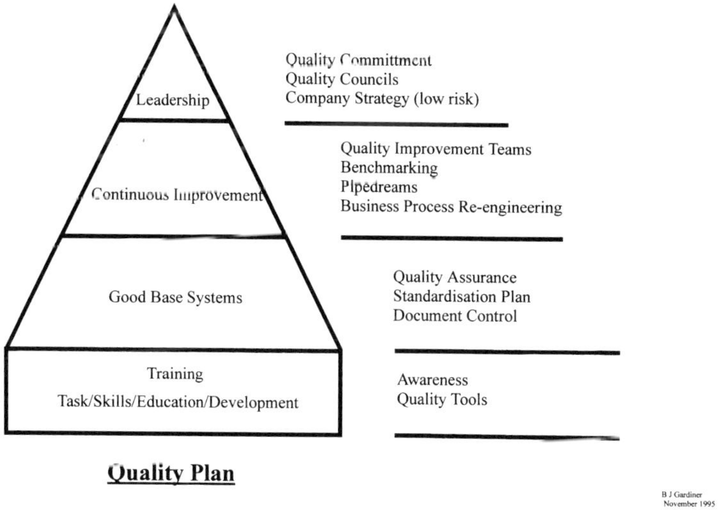

Quality Plan

Quality plan throughout the company. Quality Councils have also been established in a number of Southern Water Services' areas to facilitate the continuous improvement process. Although the Councils have limited executive power they wield significant influence within the company by providing direct communication of the best ideas to make continuous improvement effective across the company culture.

By early 1996 Southern Water Services predicts that it will have attained ISO certification in parts of its water supply business in Kent, Sussex and Hampshire. The programme will then be extended to the remainder of the water supply areas. Extension of ISO certification to Water Distribution and Customer Services will happen over a two year period.

The application of Quality Assurance to wastewater treatment, sewage treatment and sludge disposal, which is the major part of the business accounting for approximately two-thirds of the key business processes, is likely to occur over a longer time frame with operating and maintenance manuals being produced gradually as new plants become operational.

The production of comprehensive operational and maintenance manuals is an important step in preparing for certification. Ideally, Southern Water would prefer to engage its own operational staff to produce the manuals, however as the technical authoring skills required do not currently exist within the company it will outsource the task to a specialist organisation as required. The expertise of operational personnel will be used to provide the information and the specialist will convert this into a format which can be easily read, understood and used.

Standardisation is one of the key elements of the company's drive towards continuous improvement. Southern Water Services' 'Standardisation Plan' initially identified 54 major systems which exist across all functions within the company, although this is not an exhaustive list. As part of a pilot programme a Quality Improvement Team selected 10 systems which could operate in a controlled environment to apply four of the 20 clauses outlined in ISO9002 – management review, document control, verification (audit) and training. The initial 10 have been expanded to 15 and now provide the starting point for the revision of all major company systems as gradually the number of systems that come under document control, for instance, is increased.

The company operates a largely paper based document system currently. It is however, evaluating computerised systems with the intention that only the controlled document will be held electronically, with all paper copies becoming uncontrolled. The company currently uses paper with a special coloured logo for controlled documents so any document which is photocopied and comes out black is identified as being out of date and unsafe.

The identification, specification and costing of the critical company systems is perceived to be key to building a foundation on which further efficiencies can be made. Through continuous improvement Southern Water Services will eliminate or minimise areas which do not service the customer, either directly or indirectly by making those that do more effective.

"We have asked staff to write down what they do and then do what they have writtendown, which is then checked by internal auditors. The auditor of a process is usually an internal customer of that service.

For instance, the internal organisation which is responsible for distributing the water to the end customer will audit its suppliers, the water supply section, which takes the water out of the ground and treats it. We have to entertain a lot of statutory audits from external organisations, so as long as we do not impose too many internal audits they are very effective because they are viewed in a non-threatening light and as an opportunity in improving the job", explains Mr Gardiner.

Southern Water Services is initiating company wide change through the re-organisation of the company from a county basis to a functional basis in order to standardise systems across the company and adopt best practice.

There is an increasing emphasis on the formation of 'service agreements' within the company as its management structures become more functional. Service agreements open the dialogue to enable different groups of people, in a client/customer relationship, to identify the needs and wants of both parties in a formal way, so that the service provider can meet the expectations of their customers and vice versa through improved understanding of the entire process and individual roles. A *How to Set-up a Service Agreement* handbook provides information on areas such as how to undertake a functional analysis, identifying critical success factors, establishing performance measurement, audit and management review.

"For instance we have a contracting company, Pipeworks, which undertakes our infrastructure work and repairs leaks. We negotiated a performance specification with them whereby they committed to repair 80 per cent of all leaks within five days and 100 per cent within 12 days, although most are repaired on the same day. They are then measured against this standard and when they are consistently exceeding the original requirements we will revise the standard to reflect this improved capability", says Mr Gardiner.

Just as important are external supplier relationships which are approached in an innovative fashion as Mr Gardiner describes: "While we don't insist that our suppliers have ISO9000 we have to conform to the European procurement directive which for instance requires us to advertise in European Journals and invite tenders. We compensate by considering the cost of doing an audit of potential suppliers in the cost of their tender to ensure that their management techniques meet our requirements."

Southern Water Services has motivated people to contribute to continuous improvement in a number of ways. It initially operated a number of Quality circles, which have metamorphosed into Quality Improvement Teams extending throughout the company. "I facilitated a Quality Improvement Team made up of supervisors which looked at the number of manhole covers the company purchased. Originally we purchased 78 different kinds from a variety of suppliers. The team rationalised this down to 11 varieties now provided by a sole supplier, saving the company in the region of £150,000 per year. These groups have been successful because they have been encouraged by management", says Mr Gardiner.

The open involvement and 'empowerment' of staff in the Quality improvement process is having the most profound effect on two particular groups of employees – supervisors and middle management. "As part of our review of organisational effectiveness we asked why we employed a group of people to supervise, when theoretically the people they are supervising have all been trained to do their jobs. Consequently we are starting to use these supervisory skills in a different way to provide planning, condition monitoring and review improvement issues. We have provided four years of Supervisory development training which turned them into managers rather than supervisors. However, this process then puts pressure on middle managers so we have recently introduced training for this group on Optimising Quality which explains the relationship between prevention costs, failure costs and quality."

The key message the company promotes is that everybody owns the processes they use and therefore has the responsibility for managing and improving them. As a result management starts to listen and question if they have been stopping people from doing their jobs better. This principle is illustrated by Southern Water Services' suggestion scheme which is more formalised that your standard box on the wall type approach. 'Pipedreams' is based on the premise that healthy ideas need to be shared and ensures that the best ideas are firstly communicated and then developed and applied across all relevant parts of the company. The sophistication of the scheme is rivalled only by that of the ideas received. Everybody has the opportunity to submit their suggestions in writing. In every county based site a Co-ordinator administers the scheme, acknowledging suggestions and undertaking research as necessary. Suggestions are then considered anonymously at monthly Management Team Meetings.

If there is a possibility of a suggestion generating large savings or having particular merit in improving the services provided to customers, it is referred to the Group Assessment Panel consisting of Financial, Technical and Personnel Directors.

Southern Water Services' aim is to relate the awards to the anticipated savings. At the local level, Divisional and Company Management Teams can make awards of up to £500 and the Group Assessment Panel can approve payments of up to £5,000. However, a proviso is made that the amount of an award may be reduced if the individual's job involves direct responsibility for improving service or standards.

A key element in promoting cultural change is training, the majority of which Southern Water has the resources to provide in-house. Lunchtime workshops in major administrative centres have already been used to introduce and promote the concepts outlined in the Quality plan and further training will improve Quality awareness and convey how to use Quality tools and specific techniques. All future development programmes will also include a Quality module.

As Mr Gardiner emphasises: "Why invest all your thinking in 10 per cent of the workforce, why not 100 per cent because they have all the good ideas. We find that when staff have come from outside they ask about our Quality policy. We are now moving forward using a commitment to Quality as our guiding philosophy."

David Ball
President and CEO
Nortel Ltd

Micheal Jones
Director
Quality and Customer Satisfaction
Nortel Ltd

42

In Search of Customer Value

— Nortel Limited —

NORTHERN Telecom may have started as a small manufacturer of telephones in Montreal in 1895, but it is now capitalising on two of the great currents running through the world economy: globalisation and the information revolution.

Nortel, as Northern Telecom is now known in celebration of its centenary, is a leading global provider of communications solutions. With 1995 revenues of $US 10.67 billion, an increase of 20 per cent over 1994 revenues, and 57,000 employees world-wide, it is the world's largest supplier of digital telecommunications systems.

Despite its Northern American origins, 39 per cent of Nortel's revenue is derived from global activity. The corporation, which introduced digital technology to the telecommunications industry in 1976, has more than 110 million digital lines in service or on order in 90 countries including North and South America, the Caribbean, Europe, Middle East, Asia, and the Pacific Rim. Nortel provides products and services to the telecommunications and cable television industries, businesses, universities, governments and other institutions world-wide. The North American operation oversees the global product strategy, however, each region is given the freedom to pursue its own course of development.

NT Europe was restructured in 1994 as part of a global strategy to move the company closer to its customers. The European organisation which encompasses activities in the UK, mainland Europe, the Middle East, Africa and the CIS was divided into two marketing units: Nortel Limited and Nortel Europe.

Nortel Limited supplies and supports markets principally in the UK and Turkey but also across mainland Europe, the Middle East and the CIS. There are 2,500 employees deployed in five customer-facing divisions: Netas in Turkey, BT, CATV, Cable & Wireless and Alternative Operators together with support groups. It contributed 80 per cent of the management earnings gained from Nortel World Trade which overall contributes approximately 38 per cent of the corporation's revenues. This was an outstanding performance for a relatively small number of employees. Michael Jones, Director, Quality and Customer Satisfaction for Nortel Limited, believes these results are directly related to the company's understanding of customer value, and the way it manages customer relationships and empowers its people.

The objective of restructuring the region was to build an organisation that would improve customer satisfaction, reduce duplication and drive profitability, by adhering to the following guiding principles:

- Organising operations around customers;
- Allocating profit and loss responsibility to customer-facing business teams; and
- Aligning closely with the lines of business.

Account teams became stand-alone business units which now provide their customers with a single point of contact for integrated solutions, bringing together products and services from various service providers within Nortel. Close co-operation between the account teams and market support groups ensures a close alignment between customer needs and product strategies.

This commitment is reflected in the company's quality and customer satisfaction policy and is consistent with the corporation's core values which describe the behaviours expected of staff, leaders and managers.

"Nortel has only one standard – excellence. Excellence means providing external and internal customers with innovative products and services that exceed their expectations and are superior to all other suppliers. Excellence through continuous improvement is the responsibility of every employee."

Mr Jones has Europe-wide responsibility for quality and customer satisfaction for Nortel Limited. Before joining Public Switching Europe, a small entrepreneurial company within Nortel in 1991, he spent 17 years at H.J. Heinz in various roles including R&D, production, project management and industrial relations. One of Mr Jones's early accomplishments was assisting the public switching company to obtain ISO 9001 registration in a six-month period as he explains: "We achieved registration using a novel approach rather than presenting everybody with endless bureaucratic, top-down procedures. I recognised that we needed to incite everybody to participate so we gave every individual the responsibility of collating a personal quality file which reinforces the ideal that everybody is responsible not only for quality but also for their own career."

The use of Personal Quality Files (PQFs) was then extended throughout the re-structured company to encourage all staff to take ownership of their career and their role in the customer chain. The PQF contains all the information an individual needs to perform their job.

Nortel Limited is registered to the ISO 9001 standard, which was achieved without writing a single new procedure as Mr Jones explains: "Most businesses are overwhelmed by procedure writing, but we worked with the BSI to register the company against our core process model (as shown in Figure 1. The assessment was based on our processes rather than procedures. Instead of supporting the bureaucracy of documentation we are supporting the key values that flow through the business."

Nortel Ltd. Core Process Model

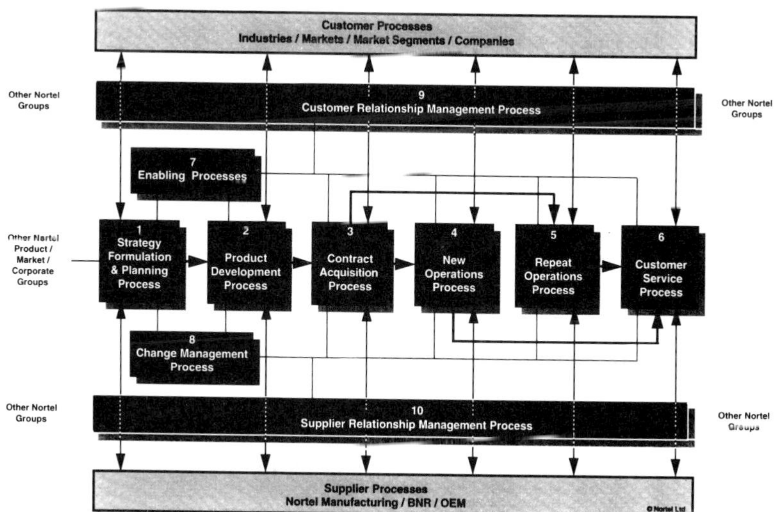

In 1991 Nortel re-launched its TQM programme, Excellence! It adopted a wide-ranging approach which included: benchmarking studies with world-class companies; a complete review of its vision and mission, customer and employee focus, processes, leadership policy, and reward and recognition vehicles; management by fact and analysis; extensive company-wide training of behaviours, quality concepts and analytical tools; and the formation of continuous improvement teams. However, despite apparently doing all the right things the initiative failed to deliver all the anticipated results.

For instance, staff hailed the arrival of teams, which they believed would increase their involvement in the decision making process. Individuals worked enthusiastically in teams for hours, month after month but the teams became less effective as management starved them of attention and as individuals lost faith and ran out of energy.

"We determined that a fundamental part of the problem was that we attempted to motivate people to rally behind the cause (vision, mission and values), while monetary issues such as career and income became a secondary consideration. In hindsight we acknowledge that we, like many other companies which attempt to sell a TQM initiative to their people, delivered the inducement in the wrong order and failed to immediately address employee concerns such as, 'What's in it for me?'," explains Mr Jones.

A number of key lessons were drawn from Nortel Limited's early attempts to introduce TQM which have proved critical to the success of subsequent efforts. These lessons include:

- Use new tools to solve specific problems;
- Provide timely and situation-specific feedback so that it can be used effectively and is not perceived as a threat;
- Provide skills training linked to specific applications so that it is not forgotten or seen as irrelevant;
- Create an empowering environment.

"Fundamental to the success of the re-engineering programme was recognising the culture in which we were operating and working from within that culture rather than challenging it", explains Mr Jones. "As an engineering based company people were accustomed to dealing with highly technical problems so we did not try to introduce quality through simple language and theories. We needed to use the tools that managers were using within their business and apply those to operational problems they were experiencing."

Initially, 'Early Victory Teams' (EVTs) were established to provide, as their name suggests, early success to capture the attention and support of the workforce. A poll of employees was used to identify issues which people believed prevented them from delivering against their objectives. These were then refined using priority analysis to pick the top six issues. The 'Cabinet', Nortel Limited's senior management team, then appointed a team leader for each issue who was considered 'big' in the organisation and respected by their colleagues. In turn they appointed a team which was typically given only six to eight weeks to complete their analysis and implement changes. A diary commitment was scheduled with the MD at the outset to review each team's *achievements*.

The EVTs investigated issues such as direct margin protection and enhancement; portfolio simplification; project cycle time; R&D for margin; pricing policy ; and financing, cash and provisions.

The EVTs which were seeded throughout the organisation were also used to disseminate training. "The key lesson is to deliver training in a situation-specific context so that people are almost unaware that they are receiving new training and education. It is essential to develop and use this new knowledge to resolve problems they have already identified as being fundamental to the operation of the business and to their success. You need to deliver results every day, every week and every month", says Mr Jones.

The results derived from the work of the EVTs were substantial. As an example two teams established to review Margin Protection realised savings in excess of $US1.6 million.

One team identified that a form required to obtain financial approval to bid for business omitted a hardware allowance component. This resulted in the underestimation of final project costs. "We identified that the software tools we were using during the bidding process failed to factor in the cost of racks used to carry cables. Until we established the EVT we were unaware of the magnitude of the problem – 8 per cent of the total bid hardware was being lost on every occasion." The benefit to the company of this discovery and subsequent reform was in the order of $US1.5 million (margin protection).

Ask Mr Jones what distinguishes successful companies from ones which struggle to implement TQM and his reply is deceptively simple: "It is not the model that you use, or the rationale, or the intellectual completeness of what you are doing - it is in the doing and the subsequent learning. This has to be integral to the way the business operates."

Nortel Limited's "Customer First Campaign" focuses on 'doing', but aims to increase the pace of Nortel Limited's achievement by translating incremental improvements into step changes of behaviour supported by seven core enablers. Those seven core enablers or programmes are: knowledge sharing, customer value management, self assessment, process management including change management, customer relationship management, customer satisfaction and employee satisfaction.

Knowledge Sharing

Knowledge sharing requires the creation of an environment where people have access to the appropriate information and share that information openly. Nortel Limited has dedicated a room which is used by the Cabinet to conduct its regular meetings surrounded by essential management information which is constantly monitored, updated and visible in the room.

Similar rooms for knowledge sharing have been replicated by each of the business units throughout the company. Some have chosen to construct rooms while others have created virtual rooms using an electronic environment.

Competitor and market information is captured and analysed regularly so that emerging trends can be investigated. This information is then synthesised into a customer value map which determines where Nortel is placed in terms of price and non-price attributes versus its competition.

Customer Value Management

Figure 2, Nortel's "Value Cycle" illustrates the company's market as defined by the interaction of customer, shareholder, employee and management and competitor interests. The intention behind the map is to ensure that the company continues to provide customer value in order to generate customer loyalty, as Mr Jones explains: "Customer satisfaction is not a complete measure because it does not provide an accurate reflection of customer loyalty. We have survey data which indicates that even when we are delivering 100 per cent customer satisfaction, customers may still use our competitors which indicates that customers perceive that our competitors provide better value. Customers base their purchase decisions on a number of price and non-price elements which they use to compare service providers. Customer value is therefore the key measure."

Each of the relationships represented in the "Value Cycle" has a specific deliverable, an outcome and a corresponding measure. For instance, staff deliver customer value through being responsive to customer needs. The outcome of which is loyalty as indicated by market share.

Business Management Assessment (BMA) - Self Assessment

Nortel's self-assessment model is known as Business Management Assessment (BMA). BMA provides a regular and systematic review of the organisation's activities and results, based on the European Foundation for Quality Management (EFQM) model. The Quality and Customer Satisfaction group is charged with driving BMA implementation and review throughout the company. The Turkish company, Netas, was named in the top five companies in the Eurpean Quality Award in 1995, while the UK operation is preparing its first entry for 1997.

Process Management

The ten processes outlined in Nortel's core process model (Figure 2) are the key elements in the company's customer value adding chain progressing from strategic development to product development, obtaining new business, providing the service (both new and repeat), and then servicing the customer. At each stage the company is conscious of the need to carefully manage its relationship with both customer and supplier.

Each of Nortel's processes identifies a number of outputs which are considered mandatory boundary conditions. These outputs provide alignment to subsequent process steps. Each process may consist of up to three levels. The primary or corporate level defines the boundary conditions for the core process. The secondary or regional level provides further detail and defines the boundary conditions that must be met by the core process. The tertiary or business unit level defines any mandatory local variations that must be addressed.

The Nortel Cabinet is divided into three select committees: Strategy and Marketing Operations; Organisation and Business Re-engineering; and Project and Product Operations each of which assumes responsibility for core processes and core programmes as defined in Figure 3. The role of Cabinet members is to provide direction and momentum which they achieve by: agreeing the vision, targets, objectives and plans; resourcing those plans; reviewing progress; removing roadblocks; communicating

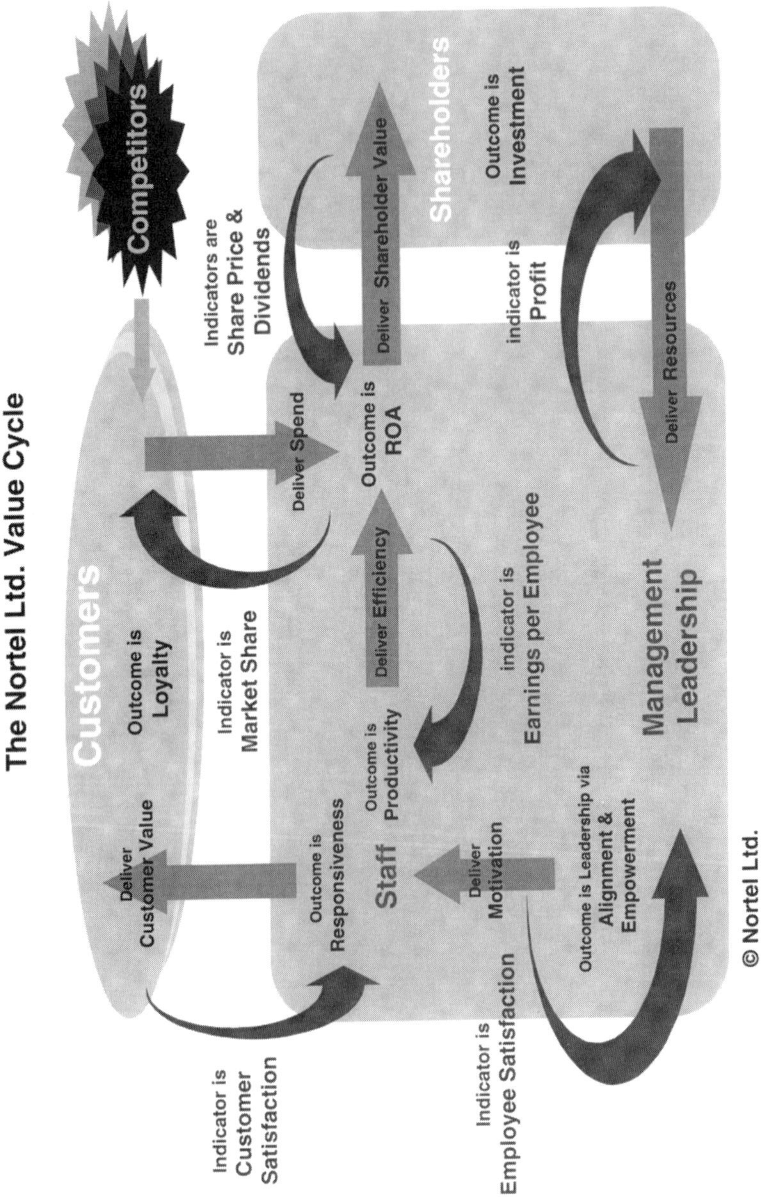
The Nortel Ltd. Value Cycle
Competitors
Customers
Outcome is Loyalty
Indicator is Market Share
Deliver Customer Value
Deliver Spend
Indicators are Share Price & Dividends
Deliver Shareholder Value
Shareholders
Outcome is Investment
indicator is Profit
Deliver Resources
Outcome is ROA
Deliver Efficiency
Outcome is Productivity
indicator is Earnings per Employee
Outcome is Responsiveness
Staff
Deliver Motivation
Outcome is Leadership via Alignment & Empowerment
Management Leadership
Indicator is Customer Satisfaction
Indicator is Employee Satisfaction
© Nortel Ltd.

Figure three

	Model Elements	**Core Processes**	**Core Programmes**
Nortel Cabinet	Leadership Business Results		
Select Committees of Cabinet			
Strategy & Marketing Operations	Policy Strategy Customer Satisfaction	Strategy Formulation & Planning Product Development Contract Acquisition Customer Relationship Management	Customer Value Management Customer Relationship Management Knowledge Sharing Customer Satisfaction
Organisation & Business Re-engineering	People Management Processes People Satisfaction Impact on Society	Enabling Processes Change Management Core Process Model	Self Assessment (BMA) Process management with a Customer Value Focus Employee Satisfaction through Alignment and Empowerment
Project & Product Operations	Resources	New Operations Repeat Operations Customer Services Supplier Relationship Management	

needs and achievements; learning from the lessons; and recognising success.

Customer Relationship Management

In order to coordinate communication between the customer and various layers of the Nortel organisation, as well as provide immediate access to customer information the company has introduced an account management system which revolves around a standard brief for each customer which provides details such as the customer strategy, key decision makers and influencers, customers likes/dislikes, contact plan, and visit reports.

The specific account teams maintain control of this process and have to be consulted prior to any customer contact. Any piece of information is regarded as important so the account teams coordinate feedback retrieved from every customer contact. This ensures that any person making contact with a client can do so with complete knowledge of previous transactions.

Customer Satisfaction

Nortel interviews 1,800 customers annually throughout Europe using an independent research company to conduct face-to-face and telephone interviews. Corporate, regional and local customer value targets are established from which personal objectives are established using a process known as Managing for Achievement. "The customer value transaction is the key to all Nortel's activity – how can we be better than the competition in the eyes of the customer. Everything radiates from this point.

Customer satisfaction is so important that as a business we may exceed our goals for return on assets for example, but unless we achieve the base line for customer satisfaction our total score is reduced to zero", explains Mr Jones.

Employee Satisfaction Through Alignment and Empowerment

Employee satisfaction is measured using an annual survey administered by a third party organisation. The results are cascaded to work groups who use them to prepare action plans. Information on business results, employee satisfaction and customer satisfaction is also delivered to each site on a quarterly basis by the President through a series of meetings known as the 'Nortel Express'.

Nortel Limited has avoided creating a prescriptive environment where employees are dominated by procedures. Instead it fosters an 'expert environment' which provides opportunities for people to be innovative, responsive and assume responsibility for their actions. The company's approach is based on the provision of four key elements, framework, foundation, focus and freedom (shown in Figure 4) as Mr Jones explains: "We tell people to take care of their customers in a way they believe is appropriate. The organisation assists by providing training to make each person an expert in their field and giving them best practice procedures. What we will not do is tell them to turn to page three of a manual and follow a list of instructions."

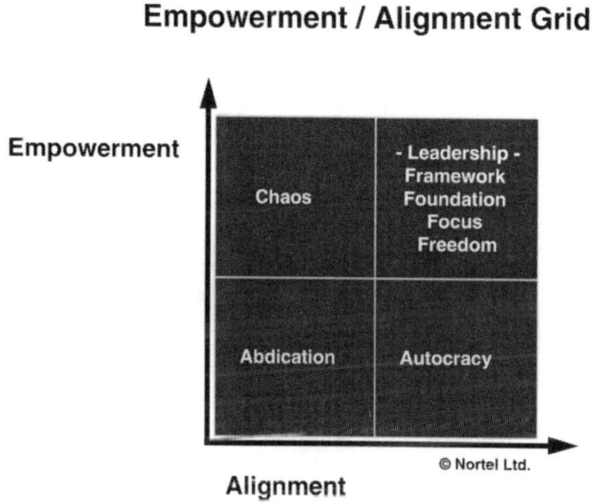

Nortel's experience indicates that an empowering environment, should exist on three levels: organisation, team and individual. The characteristics of each are described below.

- The empowering organisation actively shares information; promotes honest and direct dialogue; takes learning seriously; puts systems and structures into place which are creative; minimises blame for mistakes; makes goals and targets clear; rewards effort and achievement fairly; clearly defines boundaries at all levels; and expects a positive pushing of these boundaries.
- The empowering team shares power and responsibility around; encourages active participation towards clear goals; values diverse contributions; faces disagreement squarely; and provides freedom and boundaries for its members.

- The empowered individual sees that choice exists; takes action to improve things; is prepared to accept risk; learn from their experience and is eager to learn more; their focus is wider than their immediate responsibility; supports other people; and makes life and work intriguing and satisfying.

"I believe in people and the greatness of individuals. If you take a group of individuals, each of whom has a keen sense of their own worth and values, and is prepared to fight for what they believe in you will naturally have a highly effective organisation. Many interventions at an organisational level miss the point entirely – you don't have to impose procedures and rigid systems because if you have the right individuals and provide them with an empowering environment they will create the supportive structures needed to produce an effective and powerful organisation. It's all about fractals", summarises Mr Jones.

43

Striving For Excellence

—MML Field Marketing—

"THE British are yet to develop a passion for providing service excellence. This is a situation I used to accept, but now will not tolerate. I have launched my own personal campaign to introduce Quality to service industries simply by acknowledging and rewarding exceptional service, and refusing to remain silent when I'm given mediocre or bad service", emphasises Paul Narraway, Managing Director of MML Field Marketing Limited. All of MML's staff share the same passion for service Quality and it is against this background that MML has driven Quality into its own culture.

When MML made the decision to pursue ISO 9002 registration it didn't openly embrace the standard, instead it studied and adapted it to create, "Striving For eXcellence" or SFX, the company's own Quality policy. Any internal reference to BS 5750 or ISO 9002 has been replaced by SFX. But was this decision more than an exercise in semantics? Yes, according to Mr Narraway. "BS 5750 smacked of bureaucratic jargon so we conceived SFX which defined why the standard was going to help us as opposed to hinder us. We are striving for excellence in everything we do – excellence in our attitude and excellence in our people which were key to our ability to turn the company around."

To put the introduction of SFX into the context of the company's development, MML had been one of the largest and most successful field marketing companies in the UK until the mid 1980s but over the pursuing years it lost its way in terms of profitability, turnover and employee numbers. This was partly a result of increased competition from other companies vying for field marketing budgets, but also because of internal

left to right: Lisa Hopcraft (Staffing and Quality Director),
Paul Narraway (Managing Director), Areta Breeze (Information Manager)
and Ted Jones
MML Field Marketing

upheavals. "MML had been very successful and almost single-handedly managed by its founder for 20 years. However, when he retired from the business in the mid 1980s there was no natural successor or management structure in place to sustain MML's success. The absence of good management guidance coupled with an over reliance on a small number of clients put the company in a precarious position", says Mr Narraway, who joined the company in December 1992 by which time the preparation for ISO 9002 registration was well under way.

The driving force behind obtaining ISO 9002 registration was Ted Jones, a former Deputy Managing Director of MML. Paul Narraway, who has a background in advertising, sales promotion and sponsorship, was initially sceptical of the introduction of ISO 9002 to MML and wary of restraining what is in essence a creative agency with unnecessary bureaucracy. Mr Jones explains: "One of the initial motivations for pursuing ISO registration was to ensure that MML did not miss opportunities to tender for business from clients such as British Telecom who were implying that at some point in the future they would require suppliers to obtain registration."

The services provided by MML to BT are essentially logistic in nature, for example the provision of a payphone serviceability improvement programme which requires the planning and management of a team providing regular checks of 42,000 payphones across the UK. Over 1,500 field staff were engaged on one project over a 15-month period requiring the highest standards of efficiency both at management level and across the field force.

So with a healthy degree of scepticism ISO 9002 was introduced but in a form which would support initiative. "When I joined MML I found a company that had lost its way somewhat but that I had inherited great people with a few good clients who had started to lose confidence in their ability. SFX became a major part in the drive to revitalise the company", explains Mr Narraway.

The purpose of the SFX system is to ensure that MML provides the best possible standard of service to its clients, through the skills and commitment of staff and the effective and efficient use of material resources. MML's mission "To be the UK's leading field marketing company recognised as the industry benchmark for innovation, delivery, quality of staff and their performance" is ambitious, but attainable through commitment to the principles behind SFX. The four principles upon which SFX is based are:

- The Purpose: Only by striving for excellence in ourselves and everything we do, can we expect to achieve excellence for our clients.
- The People: Just as we are individuals so too are our clients. Through our individual skills and commitment we can identify and fulfil their needs.
- The Practice: We use our resources, both human and material, effectively and efficiently to maximise our quality and to ensure our value.
- The Point: With excellence and commitment we will make profit. With profit we will realise our ambitions and be rewarded for our achievements.

'Field marketing' encompasses a range of functions including merchandising, short-term tactical campaigns, sampling activities, event organising and roadshow programmes, auditing and collecting information through mystery shopper exercises, for example. It is a people industry, as Mr Narraway emphasises when he says that "MML's product is people". The London head office consisting of 23 staff is responsible for account management, and providing information systems, finance and staffing support to coordinate various field teams of up to 1,000 people spread throughout the UK at any one time. MML has over 5,000 people registered on its database from which it primarily draws its field team requirements, although on occasions MML will advertise for specialised people.

MML's commitment to SFX has shown positive returns with a £6 million turnover recorded in 1994, an increase of almost 20 per cent on the previous year. The company was established in 1961 and is a wholly owned subsidiary of Young and Rubicam, servicing clients such as Pedigree Petfoods, Mars, Shell, BT, Sky TV, and Coca-Cola on a regular basis.

Its Quality formula has clearly been effective on many of MML's long-term client relationships such as Pedigree Petfoods, with whom MML has worked since 1978. Initially, MML's role was shelf-filling in multiple grocery outlets. This relationship has evolved and MML now provides and manages a team of 100 plus permanent field staff on Pedigree's behalf, undertaking stock and order functions, store auditing and the development of retail and wholesale trading relationships.

The field people who work on the Pedigree account consider

themselves to work for Pedigree rather than MML. Pedigree has spent a lot of time nurturing this feeling through gestures such as inviting the field staff to social functions and recognising their contribution to Pedigree's business growth. Consequently, an intense loyalty has grown over time, the magnitude of which is illustrated by numerous instances of MML staff going the extra mile for their client. "On one occasion a part-time merchandiser broke her leg and instead of letting the team down engaged her husband to drive her around to the stores and supervised while *he* completed the merchandising! While SFX didn't create this attitude, it has definitely enhanced it through the provision of training and formal procedures which make it easier for field staff to do their jobs", explains Mr Narraway.

MML provides permanent staff with annual and bi-annual performance reviews, records of which are maintained on each employee's registration card. Feedback is also obtained from supervisors and account handlers on every short term campaign to which an employee contributes and this is recorded on their registration card.

Lisa Hopcraft, Staffing and Quality Director of MML, is responsible for taking a brief from the account team and selecting and appointing the appropriate field staff for the duration of each programme.

SFX assists with the management of the field-based staff indirectly. "They do not have to know all about SFX but everything they do is influenced by SFX in terms of the procedures and standards to which they adhere. Everything from the briefing to the way they discharge their duties is consistent with the guidelines provided by SFX, the principles of which are printed on the back of each employee's contract", explains Miss Hopcraft.

MML intentionally limited the number of procedures documented in its Quality manual to 15 procedures supported by 26 forms so that head-office employees were not deterred from referring to it. Equally MML has incorporated sufficient flexibility so that procedures can be adapted and modified as required.

"One of our procedures is correcting and updating our procedures. If we find something isn't working as well as we hoped then we change it. For example we use a checklist for initial enquiries to MML so that anybody picking up the phone can respond to a client or prospective client's requirements and ask the right questions to obtain sufficient information to take the appropriate action. We found that the original A4 format was not effective so we modified it, making it a smaller pack that sits by the telephone", explains Areta Breeze, Information Manager who is a member of the SFX committee. "If we do our job correctly and are performing well as a company then we will retain our clients which in turn makes greater return on our time and efficiency. By having SFX we can make every client believe that they are our most important client. Everybody in the company needs to be able to assist a client even if they are not working on that specific client's business because at the end of the day we are all part of the client's team."

"The introduction of formal Quality processes is important but also needs to be fun. I would recommend making the quality system user friendly and make it supportive rather than stifling. Everything has to be structured and ordered. An analogy I use myself is: we are the surgeons and the client is the patient on the operating table. If the team and I cannot reach a scalpel or a blood pack when we need them the patient dies, and that applies to us in a commercial situation. If we can't find a file when a client rings with a problem or a question then we have failed that client in the same way as the surgeon might fail the patient", explains Mr Narraway.

Central to MML's philosophy is the freedom of every employee to strive for excellence within themselves. Mr Narraway continues, "It was very important that SFX supported the creativity and initiative of individuals and gave them the freedom to learn from their mistakes and evolve." For instance through bi-annual reviews the Managing Director discusses with every head office employee how they think they are progressing personally and how their role should be developed to advance the company and stretch their individual capability. Training needs are then modelled on the outcome of this discussion. "We insist that people look forward rather than back. For instance, Sue Murphy, the Financial Director traditionally conducted a historic analysis of our accounts, however, we have changed the role so Sue is now our Commercial Director and is responsible for reviewing future contracts as well rather than just collating historic management information. Sue is involved in the early stages of structuring negotiations and signs off all our proposals", explains Mr Narraway.

MML operates each client contract on what is described as a 'Solus' basis to ensure maximum focus and commitment to individual client objectives. To this end MML emphasises the importance of working with clients as opposed to simply for them. MML has defined the key factors in this process as: work to defined objectives; confidence and understanding through communication; work pro-actively; and add value through strategic input.

"The number one thing is to communicate with the client. We ask them what they want to achieve and then we provide suggestions from our own experience. You need to get specific, measurable objectives and if they can't supply them, you then give them the options", explains Mr Narraway.

The deployment of a field marketing campaign is always reliant on a systematic approach to ensure that the right people are at the right place at the right time with the right resources to fulfil the requirements of a brief.

One situation which particularly tested the effectiveness of MML's processes and people and brought home the relevance of procedural discipline was a product launch it facilitated for Coca-Cola Great Britain and Ireland. This campaign was facilitated at the time MML was crystallising its SFX policy and procedures. The brief was taken on a Thursday evening to develop the field launch operation for a soft drink to take effect only four days later on the Monday. The programme involved the selection and recruitment of 100 mime artists and dancers across the country, procuring outfits, conducting rehearsals and setting up a central London theatre venue for the press launch.

The next phase of the campaign required that exactly three weeks after the initial briefing, 23 teams of three samplers equipped with vans and sampling equipment were placed in venues around the country presenting the new drink to potential consumers.

"SFX focused us on making this project happen logistically and systematically so that we could record the steps, processes and the information requirements of both the information department and the staffing department", explains Miss Breeze. While many of MML's procedures were in existence, with 75 per cent of the required forms such as staff requisition forms already in use, they required a degree of formalisation and documenting. Ted Jones assumed responsibility for documenting the procedures with the assistance of MML's external Quality consultant in conjunction with the people managing the job.

Certification was received in June 1993 and MML remains one of a few companies in the industry to have attained ISO 9002. The value of certification is recognised as becoming increasingly important to prospective clients. MML can already associate particular business wins to its Quality philosophy and commitment – a fact that is being emphasised in presentations to prospective clients.

"Because we have standardised procedures our presentations become much tighter. We have formalised the approach and communicate this to the prospective client in the knowledge that MML has the procedures to cope with any particular issue. Subsequently we come across as a much tighter organisation. Even if ISO or SFX is not specifically requested it is an important point to raise", explains Miss Breeze.

The most adamant sceptics often make the most loyal supporters once converted. In the union of SFX and MML this is most certainly the case. Mr Narraway emphasises that the company's success has been dependent on a team effort. "We are only as good as the entire group – we have some great strikers but we need fullbacks and goalkeepers too. The staffing department or the information department can't win the match on their own, and to win a match you have to define the goalposts because if you don't know what the goals are, how are you going to score? You have to approach each project with the same passion as a footballer approaches each game. The top people at MML have to drive Quality but they also have to demonstrate Quality."

44

Lessons Learnt

— Mobil Oil Company – Coryton Refinery —

MOBIL'S Coryton Refinery in Essex is the most complex in the organisation's worldwide refining network outside the United States. Coryton is the foundation for Mobil's extensive marketing operations producing products for UK and continental consumption. The plant currently converts approximately 200,000 barrels of crude oil and other inputs for fuels, lubricants and special products per day.

The Coryton Refinery was commissioned in 1953 and while many of the original facilities including the lube plant, power plant and tank farm continue to operate today the refinery continually strives to introduce the latest technologies and processes to meet the ever growing demand for high quality, high energy, clean fuels in a competitive world environment.

It is against this background and with a wealth of experience in integrating environment, health and safety measures into all business activities that the Coryton Refinery introduced its Quality programme.

During 1989 and 1990 the refinery reviewed its customers' requirements, including Government Departments and many multi-national companies, which revealed an increasing focus on special products such as asphalt, bitumen, waxes and special lubricants for which they expected suppliers to operate a Quality system approved to ISO9000.

"In some of the special product areas Quality may be the most important factor considered by a customer when selecting a supplier, however price is still the dominant factor at the pumps for gasoline and diesel for example," explains Martin Hinchliffe, Quality Management Superintendent for the Coryton Refinery.

At this stage the refinery had to make a decision whether to just

Martin Hinchliffe
Quality Management Superintendent
Mobil Oil Company – Coryton Refinery

adhere to customer requirements and gain BS5750 Part 2 (ISO9002) certification for its special products or exceed customer expectations by pursuing certification for the entire refinery.

"Although we had to maintain our cost competitiveness at the pumps we could not let customers equate lowest price with a lack of Quality, even though BS5750 (ISO9000) is not a product standard, we decided to cover the entire refinery," says Mr Hinchliffe.

"I think a lot of people view ISO9000 certification as something that will get them out of trouble or keep business for them, but they don't realise the full benefit from it because they don't link it to their Quality programmes. It can provide a powerful framework for business improvement if organisations look at it as something more than just what their customers want."

While the Coryton Refinery introduced the standard because it needed a basic plan for Quality and to help it operate more effectively, the primary reason for its introduction was to allow it to build better products more economically.

To this end certification to BS5750 Part 2 covering organisations in the business of 'manufactured goods or installation, or offering a service to an agreed specification, whether internal or provided by a customer, but specifically excluding design' was received at the start of 1992. By the close of 1995 the company had received certification to the revised standard ISO9002:1994.

"While many of the procedures were already in place and systems existed at least in part we needed to direct our efforts towards formalising and documenting the system and ensuring that all parts of that system were complementary and resulted in synergy. We looked to ISO9000 to help develop our system. We have to work within environmental, health and safety regulations and of course to product standards so ISO9000 serves as a useful foundation to incorporate all these elements into a holistic system," advises Mr Hinchliffe. "Many companies document their existing processes but don't recognise that they may be formalising something which is inadequate or could be improved upon."

Mr Hinchliffe admits that the Coryton Refinery is still in the 'early days' of its Quality journey, although it has gained and retained its ISO9002 certification. It is currently streamlining the number of procedures within its Quality system from 77 documents to a more manageable 40 to

50 documents which will reduce the number of audits and the level of administration required to maintain the system.

The importance of maintaining momentum for the programme is highlighted through one example of the frustrations which the refinery initially experienced: "Despite being audited after the receipt of ISO9002 in December 1994 we still found people using documents which were not 'controlled' documents. People would keep copies of their Quality procedure in the draw or on a wall even though they were two years out of date, so obviously misunderstandings of the standard's basic requirements did exist," explains Mr Hinchliffe.

ISO9000 certification was considered as the starting point to a Total Quality Management programme which was introduced as the basis of continuous improvement, founded on the Quality guru, Crosby's principles. The Crosby route was selected because of its alignment with manufacturing organisations and also because the refinery had observed it successfully used by other organisations in the industry.

The programme commenced with training at the Crosby College where managers learnt about Quality principles and techniques, but also received 'train the trainer' tuition. In turn this generated in-house training of a large proportion of the refinery's 650 strong work force.

The Coryton Refinery introduced Quality training in both classroom and workplace environments: "We initiated two single days of interactive training in a classroom environment with groups consisting of disparate disciplines which did not share a close working relationship, and then conducted work group type sessions in the workplace with people like operators and craftsmen based on resolving problems using Quality principles. The second method is much more powerful and perhaps in hindsight this should have been the preferred method of training. The beauty of work group activity is that once you resolve one problem people can see the benefit of the process straight away."

The Coryton Refinery found that the adoption of a Quality system prompted recognition of problems which existed within the refinery but went largely undetected because formal systems were not in place to measure their incidence and magnitude. For example, computers link the refinery's stores ordering and issuing systems to all the terminals in the refinery. Subject to the correct authority any employee can enter the system through their computer terminal to order equipment and theoretically it should be processed for collection or delivery. However, multiple problems were associated with this seemingly simple procedure such as the inability to log on; the unavailability, non-listing or misfiling of required equipment; or inaccurate processing and reservation of equipment.

"There was something wrong with the system. It was not until we introduced Quality procedures and tools that people started to measure the incidence and assign a cost to non conformance in terms of wasted time and money. Although it is only a two minute job when you put dollars to it people start to pay attention," admits Mr Hinchliffe.

Similarly, it was soon realised how many different pieces of equipment were used to complete the same or similar jobs and the Quality procedures proved very useful in rationalising the types of equipment retained in stock and in turn this resulted in cost savings of thousands of dollars.

Another issue the refinery has wrestled with is that of ownership of the Quality system. At its inception the process was owned by a Quality department and consequently line managers and staff didn't view Quality as their priority. Quality manuals were originally written by the Quality department in order to expedite the process, however as Mr Hinchliffe describes, "the pain we now have to endue for the gain we received in completing it quickly is trying to ensure that people take ownership and use it properly. We've got it and we are keeping it, however, we still have to use ISO9000 to make the organisation operate more effectively and link the benefit to the bottom line because many people see it as purely a means of keeping customers."

It wasn't until the Quality Improvement Team was disbanded that the refinery started to successfully move ownership and responsibility for Quality assurance to the line departments. "They are the people who should be driving the Quality initiatives and while you have a central department charged with the Quality function people will always look to that department to provide Quality assurance." However, Quality still has the undivided support of the Refinery Manager, Mr Robin Reid and top management which meets monthly to discuss Quality issues.

"My role will become more educational," explains Mr Hinchliffe, "what I would like to occur is for departments to become more proactive and come to me to ask what they should be doing about a particular situation. Until now it has been a case of me or my department going to other departments and saying you need to be doing something about a particular situation."

Three hundred operators are still to receive Quality training which remains a major challenge because of the refinery's exhaustive shift patterns – it operates five shifts 24 hours around the clock every day of the year. However, it intends on tackling this problem by including the principles in a new 'Improvement Through Teamwork' training module.

The training of this group of operators will be a vital piece of Coryton's Quality programme as Mr Hinchliffe explains: "A significant proportion of the benefit will come once the operators who control the process equipment are trained. They will then contribute to making this Quality programme take off because as Crosby counsels, 'Quality is free – it's getting it wrong that costs!'." The Coryton Refinery analysed the cost of non conformance in the late 1980s prior to starting their Quality programme and estimated it to be in the region of $US40 to $US50 million. In the last five years the refinery has reduced this by $US10 to $US15 million through the introduction of Quality improvements, which are expected to continue.

Benchmarking was introduced when Mr Hinchliffe was appointed to the role of Quality Management Superintendent partly to assist him in understanding his role in relation to current practice and also to assist the organisation develop its Quality culture. After attending benchmarking training seminars he developed a benchmarking strategy for the refinery. "If somebody in the refinery wants to improve a process they are working on we recommend benchmarking as a means of looking at what other people are doing and what best practice is. Of course we emphasise that it is important to measure your own performance to provide you with a worthwhile comparison."

The Coryton Refinery has taken heed of words of wisdom obtained on benchmarking visits such as: 'Every member of the organisation is given two jobs - their job as defined and the task of improving that job.'

"We are trying to embrace this thinking within our culture because we realise that we can no longer expect a handful of managers make 500 people change. This type of culture has been evident here and there is a tendency for people to feel that so long as they are following their job descriptions and doing a Quality job there is no need to improve. We now recognise that if we unleash the creativeness of these people and encourage them to come up with ideas for change and improvement implementation will come without resistance."

"People are beginning to realise that managers and employees need to share an open environment and work together to improve the business. We will achieve this by involving all employees and providing them with continuous improvement education and creating a culture where they feel that they are able to contribute openly and without threat. If you don't tap into the knowledge and experience the workforce has got you are going to fall behind your competitors," admits Mr Hinchliffe.

The Standard calls for a system that is 'visible, functions properly and is understood.' To achieve this the Coryton Refinery produced and issued an educational booklet to all employees outlining the requirements of BS5750.

It explains that BS5750 (ISO9000) is a set of requirements contained within a British national standard that provides a basis for the assurance of Quality in an economic manner and by involving everyone in the company.

In order to achieve certification a company must comply with up to 20 clauses of the appropriate standard. For instance, ISO9002 requires conformance to 18 clauses as well as cross referencing between sections and clauses. Complying with all the relevant clauses may be costly, confusing and time consuming so to simplify process for its employees the Coryton Refinery outlined the precise implications of each clause.

"It may seem complicated but if you think about it, it is really commonsense. We ought to be able to control what comes into the company and what we do with it; we should have procedures so that we all know what we have to do; we should have records of what we have done; and use them to take corrective action; our tools, methods and processes should be correct; and we ought to identify things and protect valuable equipment from damage," employees are told in the refinery's Quality handbook which goes on to describe the clauses with which the refinery needs to conform (See excerpt at end of chapter).

The message the refinery is attempting to impart on each and every employee is that, "Our customers want a quality product and if we cannot supply this to them in an effective way others will. By working to BS5750 Part 2 (ISO9002) all our jobs will be a lot easier and safer too."

Requirement 4.1 Management Responsibility

This defines the status of Quality in the organisation. Management is required to publish and support a Quality policy, and to ensure that it is understood by all levels of the organisation. It is also charged with reviewing the operation of the Quality system at appropriate intervals.

"We must have effective management for Quality with all responsibilities clearly defined in writing. We must appoint management with authority and responsibility, and to identify problems and provide effective solutions."

Requirement 4.2 Quality System

Really says that we should have a definite programme for Quality which:

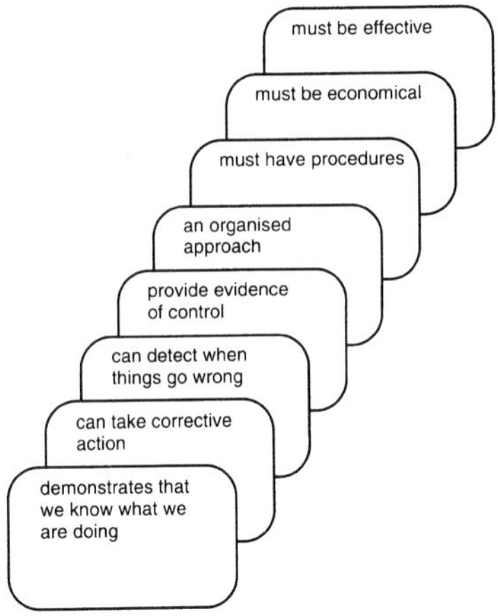

Obvious really.

Requirement 4.3 Contract Review

Review all contracts to ensure that the company has both the knowledge and the time available to fulfil them. The reviews must be recorded.

Requirement 4.4 Document Control

People must know what they are required to do and have the information to do it. We must control change. This is done by:

- *Recording new changes*
- *Destroying old paperwork*
- *Having procedures*
- *Making somebody responsible*

Are we up to date?

Requirement 4.5 Purchasing

This is quite a lengthy requirement which indicates how important it is to be sure that we are only buying good materials and equipment to incorporate into our products. The requirement means that we should only buy from good companies who can control their own quality. We should monitor their facilities and any changes that take place.

We should check on their suppliers to ensure that only good quality material goes into our products. Purchase documents must be clearly written so that a supplier knows what we want and what is expected of him exactly. The aim is to supply good material to production.

Requirement 4.6 Purchaser Supplied Product

Sometimes our customers supply their own equipment for us to include with our products. This equipment must be securely stored and special care taken to prevent deterioration.

Requirement 4.7 Product Identification and Traceability

When it is a part of the contract we must identify the product during processing and be able to trace its history back to the raw materials used.

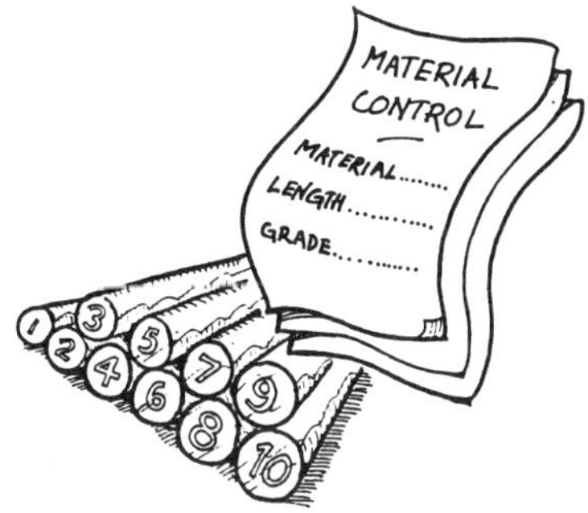

Requirement 4.8 Process Control

We must manufacture our products under controlled conditions.

Personnel must know:

- ***How to perform their tasks***
- ***Have standards of workmanship***

To ensure that only good quality work is carried out. Any special process must be:

- ***Identified***
- ***Qualified***
- ***Continuously Monitored***

Requirement 4.9 Inspection and Testing

We must inspect and test materials:

- ***On receipt***
- ***In process***
- ***Prior to release***

To ensure that when we have completed our product it will meet the specified requirements. We also need to keep records of the inspections and tests carried out.

Requirement 4.10 Inspection, Measuring and Test Equipment

Any piece of equipment used for checking or testing must be demonstrated to be capable of checking and getting a correct result, this is called calibration.

In the company we will:

1. *Identify each piece of equipment used for checking or testing.*
2. *Record how often each piece of equipment will be calibrated.*
3. *Prepare and issue procedures describing how we can calibrate it.*
4. *Ensure that the equipment we use to calibrate against itself is accurate.*
5. *Relate all our calibration activities to National Physical Standards.*

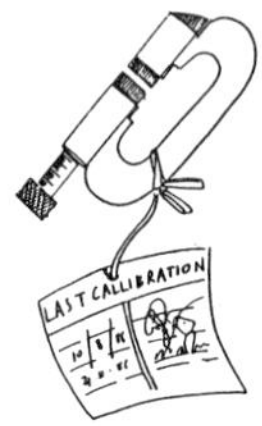

Requirement 4.11 Inspection and Test Status

When any item is on our premises we must be able to determine its status ie awaiting inspection, checked and OK, rejected, non-conforming. We must therefore have marked areas or an identification system to do this.

Requirement 4.12 Control of Non-conforming Product

Even in the best systems things go wrong and scrap occurs. When this happens we must control the situation: identify and segregate the material and establish precise procedures for rework and disposal. Above all we must not allow defective items to become mixed up with acceptable ones in our manufacturing areas. Scrap and rework levels can tell us how good, or bad, we, and our suppliers are.

Requirement 4.13 Corrective Action

We must use our records as a basis for corrective action. They should record when and where we are going wrong. We must then decide why and take the necessary action to correct permanently. Our actions must be positive and effective to prevent recurring problems..

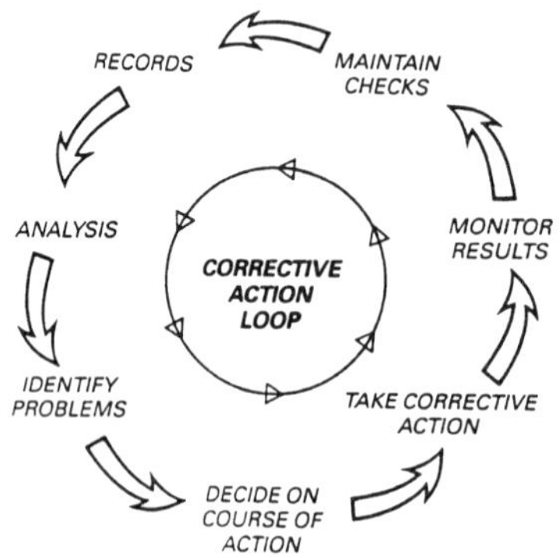

Requirement 4.14 Handling, Storage, Packaging and Delivery

We must control all items through our entire processes. We must protect in storage, we must handle correctly, check on condition and arrange for completed products to be safely delivered to the customer.

Requirement 4.15 Quality Records
We must provide records to demonstrate that our systems are working effectively. They must have sufficient detail to initiate corrective action by other departments such as Technical, Production, and Purchasing. Records must also be stored in areas to minimise the possibility of loss or damage.

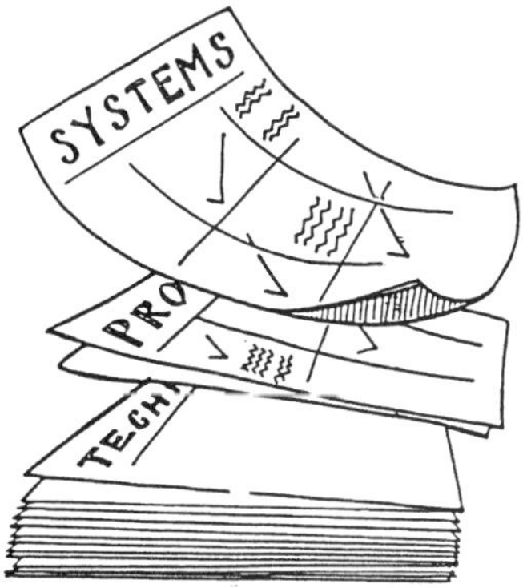

Requirement 4.16 Internal Quality Audits
The systems and procedures that we devise will be meaningless if just install them and leave it at that. We must audit the systems from time to time. Are they still compatible? Pertinent? Do they allow for changes that have occurred? In short are we as good as we think we are?

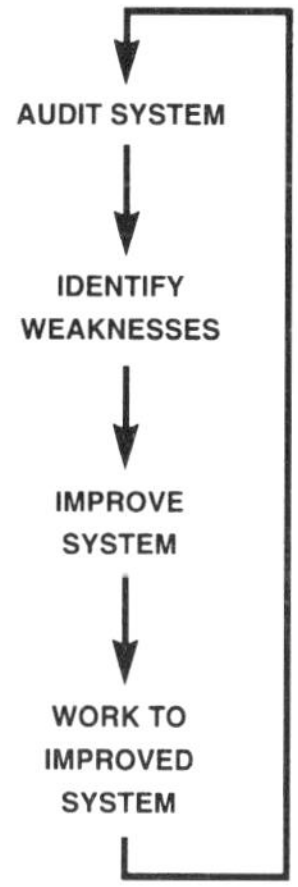

Requirement 4.17 Training
We all need special skills and knowledge to do our jobs effectively and we must have a system to ensure that training needs are identified and that people performing particular jobs have the necessary knowledge, skill or experience.

Requirement 4.18 Statistical Techniques
Where it is appropriate we must establish techniques to verify the capability of our processes and to ensure our products meet the customer's requirements.

Ken Wilkie
Chief Executive
Xyratex

45

A Brand-New Company with a Blue Chip Heritage

—Xyratex—

XYRATEX is a major manufacturer of information storage products, which it markets under its own name and produces under contract for major computer companies. Xyratex also makes networking equipment, test systems for disk drives and provides IT consultancy.

Xyratex was established as an independent company in December 1994 and is headquartered in Havant, England. It also has offices in San Jose and Irvine, California. Customers are further served by a worldwide marketing network covering Europe, USA and the Far East.

Blue-chip heritage

Xyratex, formerly a manufacturing facility of IBM UK, is a compelling example of a new model manufacturing enterprise. Since becoming independent, the company has undergone a fundamental sea-change in Quality focus from product Quality to customer requirements.

As a host of high technology manufacturers have found to their cost, product Quality, while important, is no longer a guarantee of competitive advantage. Customers demand cheaper and better products as a matter of course. Development cycle time is contracting to the point where market leadership is short lived and high product Quality is the rule not the exception. Xyratex was aware that another form of USP was necessary to make an impact on the market. "Our aim is to move as close as possible to the Customer" said Piotr Nahajski, sales and marketing director. "So we start and end from the customer's perspective." This increased customer responsiveness is cited by Ken Wilkie, chief executive, as the company's single most important achievement to date. "During 1995, by extending and enhancing our relationship with customers, we achieved a portfolio of 600 new customers."

Bringing this about required a complete re-working of the company's management processes. For Xyratex, formed in December 1994 following a management buyout from IBM UK, it would entail combining part of its Quality heritage with new processes. The clean slate offered by the creation of a company out of a successful part of one of the world's largest corporations, brought with it unique opportunities. This was noted by industry analyst Dataquest in its assessment of Xyratex as "unique among storage companies... essentially a start up with years of experience in the manufacture of leading edge drives and test equipment".First-year results bear out this optimism. Turnover of £279 million generated pre-tax profits of £11 million, with excellent growth in volumes and revenues in every area of operations. Disk drive manufacture grew by over 20% and Xyratex's newly-established test division enjoyed a four-fold growth. During this year, four new divisions were formed; Test Systems, Warranty Services, IT Consultancy and Storage Solutions. Xyratex also acquired Peer Protocols, a California-based test specialist.

Launching, changing focus, investing and staying above the line like this requires more than textbook management skills. Equally, increasing sales volumes called for more than strong products. Moreover, adding new business streams that generated real products in quick time to market, needed more than a good business plan. Nothing less than a total understanding of every business process was needed, from all the stakeholders in the enterprise.

"At the rarefied level where Xyratex competes, compliance to external Quality standards is taken as a given, and therefore not viewed as a critical issue of competitive advantage. Where we have really made innovative progress is in devolving our Quality processes", says Gary Medlow, Quality and IS manager. "Quality is a company-wide issue practised and understood by every employee, by choice and as a way of working. This determines our key processes and key measures. The pure and simple goal is applied continuous improvement, something that is often spoken about but seldom practised. We are creating a manufacturing environment with a self-sustaining formula to unleash creativity, devolve responsibility and implement improvements. It's about deployment and action, in contrast to other approaches which were long on strategy and short on implementation. Armies of inspectors are a thing of the past because everyone understands their role in Process Quality."

The Change Catalyst

Quality was an established way of doing business at Xyratex within its IBM history – it achieved BS5750 certification (now EN ISO 9001) in the mid-1980s – but after independence, the new company needed to quickly adapt and develop advanced business process models to gear up for rapid expansion and to grow its customer base. Like any new company, Xyratex needed to put in place the infrastructure to carry out specialist functions such as sales and marketing. And customer service issues and relationships are vastly different in the open market than as a dedicated in-house supplier. The need immediately to widen its customer base and add new business streams were themselves powerful and dynamic agents for change.

Xyratex were fortunate in having some significant advantages, not the least being the retention of IBM as a key customer. The volume disk drive market was also in a dynamic growth phase. People were used to working together, most of today's employees are the same as under the previous management. All these factors worked in Xyratex's favour.

The management determined that continuous improvement would be embedded into every process, and it elected to manage by process as well as by objective.

From the outset, Xyratex constructed a dynamic business process blueprint the 'Enterprise Model'. This is the glue which holds the management operation together, and the place where the company's culture is embedded. The model was designed to keep the company on course in line with its key business objectives of

- long term, sustainable growth
- anticipating and reacting to customer demand
- global brand recognition
- synergistic expansion of Xyratex products and services

Buy-in on the part of all employees is accomplished by means of training and education (the company is a recognised 'Investor in People') and cross-functional activities. Feedback as to their efficiency comes from direct customer contact. Xyratex estimates that one in three of its permanent employees now have regular direct customer contact. The company's plant at Havant, Hampshire, was cited by the *Financial Times* as one of Britain's most frequently visited manufacturing locations.

A complete focus on customers, processes and people, managed and served by decision support systems using statistical and quantitative methods is easy to formulate in theory, but desperately difficult to achieve in practice. Management by objectives only, with its linear, task driven activity boundaries, simply does not provide a viable paradigm. Management by process, while demanding, ultimately reaps richer rewards, and was certainly more suited to the company's ambitions and goals.

Recognising that service differentiation is the key to competitive Quality in manufacturing was a great strategic leap forward for Xyratex. Honing each business process through a combination of traditional statistical analysis and measurement has been the springboard for breakthrough continuous improvement. Xyratex processes are designed to be ultimately self-managed, and the Quality team sees its role as facilitating greater devolution and involvement by all employees in the business excellence process. Inspection has largely given way to drilling Quality into every fibre of the plant, focused again on the customer.

The primary focus on customer satisfaction permeates down through the company from the boardroom where accountability in this area is self-evident. An original initiative at the launch of Xyratex was the introduction of a monthly 'self assessment' session at board level. The General Manger of each of the six businesses which make up Xyratex – Contract Manufacturing, Warranty Services, Test Systems, Storage Solutions, IT Consultancy and Contract Network Products – is called on to present an overview of customer satisfaction within his or her area.

Piotr Nahajski explains "A subjective presentation is required from each manager. They outline in some detail what customers are happy or concerned about, to highlight customer concerns and report on how these are being addressed." This forum demonstrates the type of cross-divisional approach to Quality which Xyratex is keen to foster in its bid to serve the customer well. "We are a multi-business company but we have teamwork integration throughout. Market focus is not diminished through passing on lessons learned by one business to the rest of the group. On the contrary, this process benefits all our customers. The barriers are down as far as company structure is concerned."

As a former IBM UK facility, Xyratex began as a player in its own right with the considerable advantage of tried and tested conformance systems, a deeply ingrained knowledge of statistical process control methods and a justifiably high reputation for world class manufacturing capability born out of its IBM legacy. Where the new company differs from the old, however, lies in how Quality is now an integrated exercise rather than an addition. Gary Medlow explains: "While external standards compliance BS5750 (EN ISO 9000) maintenance – is still a function of the Quality group, our key task today is to talk to people about their processes, about the things they do and then place this within our 'Enterprise Model'."

While information technology systems play a crucial strategic role in automating processes, Xyratex determined that management information systems should be a means to an end, not the end itself. This saved the new company from thinking it was making progress by just replacing legacy system activity. Once processes were mapped, tested and understood, the technical challenge of building a state of the art management information system (MIS) was dramatically streamlined. "Developments in information technology are the catalyst for improving processes rather than entities in themselves", said Medlow. "We organise the business around systems, not disciplines. We harness IT to create greater efficiency – but it will be a support tool for our tasks, processes and system, not the driving force."

The Quality team asked each work unit to describe its activities, suggest areas for improvement and contribute to the thinking which would streamline operations and serve customer needs better. Each element was fed back into the Enterprise Model, checked against the core requirements (customer, process, people) and analysed as to how it affected other parts of the operation. The work of building a computerised MIS only took place when the analysis had been rigorously checked, agreed and proven to work on paper. The result is a system which not only satisfies requirements in terms of efficiency and relevance to customers, but one which employees willingly use because they can clearly see its benefits in terms of smoothing and facilitating their own work processes.

Continuous Improvement as a Way of Doing Business

Fundamental to the company's hallmark Quality Programme for all staff is the understanding that good ideas without implementation are not worth the paper they are written on. For this reason, it avoided from the outset a traditional suggestions scheme – which generates many good ideas but often little follow up activity. Instead, the culture created at Xyratex is one in which people bear responsibility for implementing their ideas individually or as part of the team. A continuous improvement (CI) group is on standby to assist with the documentation and development of ideas and solutions.

Graham Salisbury; who heads up the initiative, takes a pragmatic approach: "Quite simply, Continuous Improvement is presented as being part of everyone's job. Everybody has a role to play in the success of the company." Halfway through the company's first year, fresh focus was put on the programme with the introduction of a new suite of CI activities designed to stretch the whole workforce. Careful monitoring of the first few months of the programme rendered impressive results: Over one-third of employees put forward and generated ideas. By the end of Xyratex's first year, more than 40 per cent of the ideas suggested had been fully implemented.

The company consciously avoids any implication that the process is introspective. On the contrary, continuous improvement is a customer driven concept. Customers frequently demand cost reductions as a condition of their agreement with Xyratex. In the face of such demands, CI is a necessity, claims Graham Salisbury. "The best way we can compete is through being smarter. We compete on total cost - productivity, efficiency, flexibility and Quality. Continuous improvement is no longer a choice."

An impressive case study in action is the tangible commitment shown by the Disk Drive Group to the CI concept. Each manufacturing manager within the group dedicates a percentage of their budget to continuous improvement activities. Three manufacturing employees were given the full-time roles of CI facilitators. A central area of the manufacturing floor is designated as CI space and used for feedback meetings after the implementation of an improvement project and for imparting general CI information and project status news.

Facilitators work with manufacturing staff to brainstorm, elicit grass roots ideas and work toward improvements and solutions. Ideas are outlined on a simple form which encourages the instigator not only to highlight the area of opportunity for improvement which they have picked up on, but to define potential benefits and develop a solution. The endgame is to continuously improve products, processes and the working environment in order to reduce costs and improve customer satisfaction.

People putting forward improvement suggestions are involved at every stage - from presentation of the initial idea through to implementation. Feedback is provided at each stage with each suggestion carefully considered by a panel comprising the CI team, a manufacturing manager and an engineer meeting in open session. The panel deliberates on pursuing or rejecting the idea, supporting its decision with a rationale. Alternatively, suggestions may be put on hold pending resource allocation.

The Xyratex brand is stamped on its CI programme by means of an improvement map, specially tailored for the company. Effective problem solving flows in a natural progression through the four quadrants - problem definition, solution development and test, implementation and maintenance of the improvement. But for Graham Salisbury, the proof of the programme's worth is not merely in successful problem solving:

"'The true value of continuous improvement activity lies in the development and refinement of methods which can be applied across all processes," he said. "We are conscious of the need to underline the direct link between suggestions made on the shop floor and the contribution they make to process improvement. A number of the opportunities which arise from continuous improvement are fixing problems created by inadequate processes. We need to fix these."

Business Improvement Awards

Xyratex's fresh focus on Continuous Improvement convinced Gary Medlow's Quality group that the time was right to launch a new team incentive to recognise excellence in the workplace. Xyratex launched the 'Business Improvement Award' designed to take a more holistic view of improvement initiatives as they impacted on the business.

A format was drawn up to reflect the type of culture which Xyratex is keen to establish. Award submissions must not exceed three A4-sized pages and are judged on set criteria;

- customer satisfaction
- contribution to company goals
- impact on business processes
- the approach adopted
- results

An informal discussion between each team and Xyratex directors follows before the winners are announced at a recognition lunch.

As with every other facet of the CI programme, care is taken to ensure that the ultimate focus is on the customer says Medlow.

"We have developed effective processes using statistical techniques and we have exceptional people in our workforce. Thanks to their enthusiasm and commitment, the customer is central to everything we do. Our aim is to continue to move ever closer to our customers."

It is a stance which has the firm support of the Chief Executive, Ken Wilkie. He reinforces the link between responsiveness to customers and employee involvement: "Attaining customer responsiveness requires employees who are empowered to make things happen. We are driving the decision points further into our organisation and closer to the customer. The pace at which our business operates is increasing. People are working with greater responsibility and, I believe, they are enjoying the challenges that this brings."

46

Harnessing Potential

— Pirelli Cables —

PIRELLI Cables Limited UK, which is part of the world famous Italian conglomerate, employs around 1,800 people at six sites in Southern England and South Wales. Its products include supertension cables for the world's electricity supply companies, copper and fibre optic cables for carrying both power and information under the sea. The company is divided into three business groups, namely Energy Cables, Communication Cables and Fibre Products.

Energy Cables employ around 1000 people based on 3 sites in Hampshire and at Aberdare in South Wales. It is a world leader in power cable technology and has been at the forefront of high voltage cable and accessories developments for several decades. All types of medium to high voltage systems have been supplied throughout the world to meet the exacting requirements of the local Utilities organisations. Products range from low voltage building wires (240V) through medium voltage mains cables (1000V to 33kV) to high voltage supertension cables (60kV to 400kV) for use in electricity transmission systems. Examples of recent contracts undertaken include the £10 million supply of 600km of 33kV and 11kV power cables to the Mass Transit Railway Corporation in Hong Kong for the Lantau and Airport Railway project. 12Km of 400kV supertension cables for the Public Utilities Board in Singapore worth £25 million, and 400km of mainly 22kV and 11kV cables and accessories for the London Underground contracts (primarily the Jubilee Line Extension) worth £6 million.

Communications Cables and Fibre Products employ some 700 people based in Newport (Gwent), Harlow (Essex) and Eastleigh

Bryan Davies
Managing Director
Pirelli Cables

David Wilson
Quality Manager
Pirelli Cables

(Hampshire). It is a world leader in fibre optic technology and the leading supplier of optical cable in the UK, with over 50% of the market and clients including British Telecom, Mercury Communications, Cable TV companies, and British Rail. Continental European clients include Sprint Poland, Hungarian PTT and Slovakian PTT. But Pirelli Cables now not only successfully competes in the UK and wider European market, but increasingly on the international stage, particularly the capital-intensive Far East, with non-domestic sales growing from 5 to 20% in the last four years. Recent contracts that it has won following highly competitive tendering include a £4.5 million contact in Sarawak, Malaysia to supply 900km of aerial optical fibre cable suitable for installation on existing power lines and a £5.6 million contract to supply optical cable for the world's longest synchronous digital hierarchy link in Wuhan Province, China.

It was only as recently as 1989 that Communication Cables, then STC Communication Cables, was a company without any guarantee of an immediate future that was struggling in an increasingly competitive marketplace. The turnaround, says Pirelli Cable's Managing Director Bryan Davies, was almost entirely due to the adoption of TQM in April 1989. Since then, the Company has been a textbook case in achievement and success: within a year of the adoption of TQM, STC Communication Cables was again a profitable asset; in 1991 it was sold on the open market to Pirelli who wanted, among other things, to utilize the innovative ideas and business culture that STC Communication Cables had developed.

Bryan Davies' introduction to TQM came when he attended a quality training course as a manager at ICL. He admits he was initially cynical about the new religion of Quality, partially because his employer was paying consultants to do what seemed at the time common sense, and also because it was a top-down management directive. Yet despite this reluctance, there were he says, a few concepts that 'struck home' as being valuable, if one was prepared to ignore the hype. Not knowing yet whether he was a believer, he decided to actually be one of the Quality teachers at ICL, believing that the best way to understand a subject was to actually teach it to others.

It was not until Bryan Davies was Managing Director at STC Communication Cables where in conjunction with the Quality Manager, David Wilson, they had the opportunity to introduce firsthand the fundamentals of TQM. From a financial perspective, this was probably not so much an opportunity as an essential for the survival of the Company. It was primarily for this reason that Bryan, David and the management team were able to turn around the culture of the Company and its profitability within a very short period of time.

When Bryan Davies was appointed Managing Director of Pirelli Cables UK in 1991, he continued to vigorously apply TQM principles in the day to day operations of the company. In essence, this implied unambiguous goals of total customer satisfaction and world class performance in all aspects of the business. Far from being an esoteric business school axiom, this is nothing more than pure Bryan Davies pragmatism: "without the customer there is no business, and if we deliver the wrong products then there are no customers!" In fact, one of the distinguishing aspects of Pirelli Cable's attitude and perspective on TQM is more than a healthy dose of scepticism for the quality 'industry', and an emphasis on simplicity and 'doing' for the difficulty with TQM is not working out what it is , says Bryan Davies, but actually having the resolve to implement the concept in its totality. And 'implementation' from the management's point of view is not delegation and supervision, but the opposite:

"If you, as the Managing Director, are not prepared to undergo the big change yourself, forget it. There's no use saying that you're going to put TQM in this company now who's going to do it...no. The guy who implements TQM is the guy who sits in the chair – the MD. One thing you cannot do is delegate TQM. You've got to have integrity and sincerity if you are to do it. Because what people forget is that you can't play act, because we are talking about 24 hours a day, 7 days a week, 52 weeks a year and if the managers don't believe in it, the people who work for them will see straight through them."

Needless to say then, the management commitment is Pirelli Cable's first critical factor for a successful TQM operating philosophy. This commitment is by necessity all-embracing so that any barrier which prevents the manager from implementing quality has to be removed. This has resulted in the creation at Pirelli Cables of an egalitarian culture, spanning everything from removing parking privileges and separate eating arrangements for managers, genuine rapport and first-name familiarity between all employees and the manager being a familiar figure on the factory floor. Pirelli Cables of course is like every other organisation that has attempted to introduce some form of Quality programme, in so far as it encountered its share of worker resistance and hostility. But the last 5 or 10% of those who resist change and refuse to cross the worker-boss chasm are worth going after says Bryan Davies, because "if you work on them and get them, you have a disciple".

The second pillar of Pirelli Cable's formula for success is communication, being the oil of the culture of Quality. In order for the oil to flow smoothly, Pirelli Cables have adopted a number of measures such as an open-door policy, the publication of an in-house magazine *CableTalk*, formal monthly team briefings for everyone in the organisation, and attitude and knowledge surveys to ascertain how much of the TQM procedures employees understand.

A successful communication tool created by Energy Cables has been the PICA Board, which has been increasingly used by quality-conscious organisations throughout the UK and Europe. The idea of the PICA Board arose as a result of the difficulties in conducting effective Quality Improvement Groups within the constraints of shift patterns. Instead of conducting the Improvement Groups at one particular time, the PICA Board enables a form of on-going and continuous discussions between managers and process operators. In this sense the PICA Board literally demonstrates the realities of continuous improvement.

As its name suggests, the Process Improvement Cause Analysis Board is a medium for focusing the improvement activities for a given process or area of operation, which entails problems and suggested solutions being highlighted, and then the progress of implemented solutions being monitored. The PICA Board is organised on the fishbone analysis principle into three categories of methods, machinery and materials. When a problem is identified, the process operator notes the problem on a blue label and attaches it under the appropriate category. Any suggested solution to the problem (or the actual solution employed) is noted on a yellow label and attached below the blue label. The PICA Board administrator is required to acknowledge the problem and/or solution within 24 hours of the blue label being attached to the Board, using one of the following 'status indicators': suggestion under consideration, suggestion under trial, trial successful – now part of standard procedure or trial unsuccessful. All successful suggestions are incorporated into Company procedures and documentation and a record is kept of all unsuccessful trials.

The success of this simple tool is remarkable, providing over 2,000 improvements to procedures within Pirelli Cables since its introduction in 1993. Just as important has been the greater involvement of employees in the manufacturing processes and their resulting 'ownership' of the process, which is fundamental in order to bring about the cultural change required to successfully implement TQM.

The third critical success factor is training, reflecting the obvious, yet often neglected, fact that people cannot be expected to give their best if they are not adequately trained. The training material is also designed to change the attitude of all employees towards the importance of Quality and emphasises four particular principles of quality improvement, namely meeting the customer's requirements, preventing failure and mistakes, attaining the defect free performance standard, and calculating the costs of failure and waste. Pirelli Cable's own uniquely crafted training package also includes one day courses on the operating methods of Quality Improvement Groups (QIGs) and the development of cause and effect diagrams. An integral part of the Quality training strategy has been the development of effective internal courses and Pirelli Cables was recognised in 1993 for the high standard of its training programs when it won a UK National Training Award.

The last critical success factor is having the appropriate organisational structure to support TQM. A Total Quality Management Team (TQMT) leads and drives the Quality improvement process, consisting of the Managing Director, Bryan Davies and his first line management reports. The 'nuts and bolts' Quality issues are discussed in the QIGs, which are forums for workers to address issues pertinent to their own area of work. Cross functional Corrective Action Teams (CATs) are set up as problem solving teams to address issues which require a number of functional experts to investigate and resolve. Lastly, Process Teams are established to address the key business processes, monitor ongoing performance and to manage improvement activities. The QIGs, CATs and Process Teams are facilitated on a day-to-day basis by the line management.

Another feature of the 'systems' approach to TQM at Pirelli Cables is Quality Decision Management (QDM), a powerful tool for improving processes through data analysis and statistical process control. QDM, which is used throughout Communication Cables and Fibre Products, collects numerical and attribute data such as fibre geometry and selected electrical and optical parameters, and defects and non-conformities controlled using a specifically developed Pirelli Cables programme. With QDM terminals installed at each manufacturing stage, it allows the operator to detect problems as they occur and initiate remedial action immediately. The QDM software, like every other aspect of Pirelli Cable's approach to TQM, is continually being improved and updated to better support the factory operators in their tasks.

Pirelli Cable's training methods have not only been recognised within the UK, but also in Europe. In 1991, Pirelli Cables was awarded funding from the European Union's FORCE Programme for a two year project to develop a multi-media training programme for use in a wide range of organisations and companies. The programme deals with the basic concepts of TQM and was produced with the assistance of several partners within the European Union. The finished product has been translated into French, German, Dutch, Portuguese and Italian and is being distributed by the McGraw-Hill Book Company Europe. Pirelli Cables offers copies of the product to its customers and suppliers.

The involvement of every employee in the process of continuous improvement is not only expected but is seen as an essential requirement in order to harness the latent potential within the company's workforce. Hundreds of awards have been made to individuals and to teams who have demonstrated exceptional improvements in their work place. An example from the Fibre Products plant relates to the method used to treat effluent at the fibre making process in Eastleigh. The effluent treatment plant uses a flocculant to enhance the separation of solids from clean water before disposal to the drain. The material used was specified by the consultants who designed the original plant in 1985. The composition of the material has always been a closely protected secret and therefore the development of an alternative has been difficult. An engineer at the plant investigated the material used, found an alternative and carried out experiments to prove that this replacement was just as effective as the original material at treating the effluent. The outcome was a staggering 97% reduction in costs - a saving of £16,000 per annum.

Another example from the Energy Cables business involved a team of seven process engineers and shop floor personnel who reduced the amount of scrap copper arising during the manufacture of supertension cables by over 50%. For many years the scrap level was around 7.5% but after six months work using the TQM improvement tools and techniques this had been amazingly reduced to less than 3% with a saving of GPB200,000 per annum. This was achieved by changing the machine set up to improve routeing procedures, by utilising all the copper on production bobbins by means of improved jointing techniques, and by minimising process setting up waste.

A further example from the Communication Cables plant concerned the manufacture of quad cables which have notoriously had a high failure rate for capacity imbalance for many years. A team of eight engineers and shop floor staff examined the long established production methods and procedures being used and compared these with basic physical and electrical principles. As a result the manufacturing process was modified and improvements thought impossible were achieved, the failure rate was reduced by a factor of 50 with savings in excess of £160k per annum being achieved. The attitude that 'we have always done things this way' was successfully overcome – despite the doubters – with outstanding results.

The change that has taken place at Pirelli Cables has been truly remarkable. Over the last three years, failure rates in many of the manufacturing processes have halved, delivery date compliance has dramatically improved, and lead times have fallen. For example, the lead time has reduced from an average of six weeks to four days for a standard communication cables product, from 5 weeks to 5 days for a standard LV mains cable and from 16 days to 3 days for a fire performance cable. Another notable success story is the manufacture of supertension cables where the in-process failure rate has been reduced by a factor of 85 and a final test pass rate of over 99% is now achieved right first time. The market share for the main product lines has not only been maintained but in some cases actually increased enabling the business to steadily grow in an increasingly competitive market. These operating achievements have enabled Pirelli Cables in the UK to face the future with some considerable confidence.

Despite this increased confidence, both Bryan Davies and David Wilson realise that with the speed of change in the market place accelerating, today's successful companies cannot afford to bask in past glories. The emphasis then, is now on developing an in-built culture within the organisation that regards Quality and continuous improvement as norms of operation. Quality then will become not only one feature of the business but how business is done. For as Bryan Davies says, "change brings risk and challenges. It's the attitude that greets change that determines whether the outcome is successful". At Pirelli Cables, the 'methodology of cultural change' is designed as a virtual loop, where indicators of change are regularly monitored and results are reported back and prominently displayed to all employees and customers, to either encourage 'more of the same' where results are positive or highlight the need for specific action where results are negative.

An important management tool being used to help focus on the challenges of the future and to assess progress towards world class performance is the British Quality Foundation (BQF) business excellence model (this is equivalent to the European Foundation of Quality Management (EFQM) excellence model). An assessment has been carried out across all Pirelli Cables UK sites using this model and a score has been established for each of the excellence criteria. This has enabled benchmarking to be introduced both across the company and externally with other companies and organisations. This evaluation has highlighted both strengths and weaknesses and has enabled the continuous improvement process to be more focused towards achieving business excellence in all activities in all parts of the organisation.

"We have demonstrated that a TQ approach is just as effective in the public sector in raising standards and securing value for money..."
Robert Howie (District Manager) and Annette Cook (Deputy District Manager)

John McLaughlin and Allan McMahon, the District IT specialists, sharing their expertise with colleagues at a staff Opportunities Fair

47

Agency Of Change

—Springburn & Cumbernauld District Benefits Agency—

FIVE years ago, the social security benefits offices in Springburn and Cumbernauld were organised along traditional Civil Service lines to meet administrative objectives. When the government moved clients to the top of the agenda it sparked a fundamental upheaval that the amalgamated Scottish offices have met head on with Quality techniques.

Springburn & Cumbernauld District Benefits Agency was formed in 1991 by the amalgamation of two discrete local management units as part of the establishment of the Benefits Agency within the Department of Social Security. It was one of 159 field business units, 20 of them in Scotland, that make up the operational network of the parent Agency, itself the largest of the executive agencies created under the government's 'Next Steps' programme. It pursues its objective to deliver social security benefits to its local customers from main sites in Springburn, Glasgow, and Cumbernauld. Its 232 staff posts, 30 fewer than in 1991, serve an area that encompasses inner city, rural and new town environments. Last year they handled 120,000 personal calls, 300,000 letters and 420,000 telephone calls.

The District was among the first to achieve a Charter Mark (1993) and Investor in People (1995) status; it was one of only three districts to gain the inaugural BA Quality Award (in March 1994) against the Agency's own Quality framework. In efficiency savings and other performance areas it regularly sets and achieves above-national-average targets.

Springburn & Cumbernauld District Benefits Agency was not so much thrown in at the deep end of organisational change as made to walk the plank in the middle of the ocean. Created in the wake of the government's establishment of the Benefits Agency on April 2, 1991, as an executive body within the Department of Social Security, the District did not exist in name until it hit the water.

The 262 civil servants who on April 1 had been working in the two discrete management units of Springburn and Cumbernauld must have thought that Rip van Winkle had been tampering with their Ovaltine. Overnight, their organisational model had changed as the government sought to jump start an improvement in the standards of public service in the delivery of social security benefits. But, while reorganisation gave a mighty impetus to cultural change, the culture did not change overnight. Responsibility for leading that part of the process was devolved to the 159 newly minted district business units, which included the Springburn & Cumbernauld organisation.

The one certainty in such a situation is that without a clear set of priorities people will be swamped by the enormity of the task. Under the leadership of the district manager, Robert Howie, the new unit steered itself by the Agency core values, the main being customer service, which for the first time was identified as a key objective. (Historically, the service had tended to organise in classic bureaucratic fashion around its administrative needs rather than those of its customers.) A new post, customer service manager, was created and a major service planning exercise undertaken to identify who the District's customers were and what they wanted of the service. Best site practice from the old Glasgow Springburn and Cumbernauld units was adopted as District standard.

In hindsight, the way the District integrated its very different parts – the one, Glasgow Springburn, a typical inner city area with the attendant social problems that implies, and the other, Cumbernauld, an active new town – was crucial to its later progress. Where many new districts retained the discrete unit model, Springburn & Cumbernauld at the outset reorganised its management structure on functional lines and cross-site responsibility.

It was not the easiest option and many staff in Cumbernauld felt threatened by the loss of a dedicated site manager. But the aim behind the strategy was to head off site rivalry before it could gain a foothold, and four years later the initial pain is seen to have been worth enduring. "If we hadn't done it this way we couldn't have got to where we are today", says Annette

Cook, deputy district manager. "We crossed the pain barrier in the first year to 18 months and then it made the interchange of staff much easier."

The first year's theme of bringing the District together was reinforced by setting new District targets and efficiency goals. Customer care training was centralised and everyone was involved. Telephone, face-to-face and related skills training were targeted to begin to roll out the tools and techniques needed to back up the brave new words.

'Quick hit' results were important in fuelling the momentum and reinforcing the primacy of core values. Within a year the public reception area in the Springburn office had been raised to the standard of that in Cumbernauld – a clear message that all customers should and could expect the same treatment. Cumbernauld's one-stop service for retired people was taken up in Springburn; in turn, its work organisation good practiccs were introduced in Cumbernauld.

Low morale, a long-term problem in the public sector pre-dating the recent spate of reforms, was not helped by the radical nature of the changes sweeping through the Benefits Agency and its new district units. Measures such as market testing and central efficiency drives reinforce a general feeling that more is being asked for no more money or recognition. The response within Springburn & Cumbernauld has been to concentrate on things it can influence, such as training and management style, to reinforce the high levels of commitment staff have to doing a good job however trying the circumstances. "We made a commitment in the early days that there would be no compulsory transfer of staff to other sites", Mrs Cook says. "That helped, and when we had to implement centrally directed initiatives, such as extended opening hours, we consulted on the best way to introduce them locally for customers and staff."

From an initially "disappointing" low level, the response rate to staff surveys suggests a progressive winning of commitment, but managers were slow to realise the need to chart the progress. "We didn't record improvement in the early years and that was a mistake, As improvements quickly become the norm it is important that you recognise them and plot progress", explained Mrs Cook.

A key change in management style – and one of the hardest for some Civil Service-reared managers to make – has been devolving decision-making down to operational level and becoming facilitators and supporters rather than always directors.

This really took off in the wake of the Action for Quality programme launched in 1993 to head up the District's commitment to Total Quality. Quality improvement teams are now formed to take forward improvement ideas. "Unless the proposal has security, resource or health and safety implications we will accept the recommendation of staff themselves", Mrs Cook says. "It may not be the way we would do it but if they think that is how it will work best, they have ownership of it. The parameters are clear and people know what level of accountability and responsibility are operative.... You can only empower people if there are clear lines of responsibility and accountability. But if you don't give staff ownership and custody, how can you deliver a Quality service?"

Although the pace and scale of change in 1991 meant empowerment issues had to take a back seat, she believes with the benefit of experience that staff involvement could have been harnessed earlier rather than waiting until 1993. "One lesson we learned is that you have got to get staff involved at the earliest opportunity", she says.

Given the time again, the District would also have worked towards the Investor in People (IiP) standard ahead of Charter Mark, though both have brought valuable insights and tools to the District's Quality agenda. Charter Mark, achieved in October 1993, provided an external audit of standards in customer service areas and highlighted areas where performance could be further improved; IiP, gained in April 1995, gave a framework for staff development and a sharper business objective focus to training. "In hindsight, perhaps we should have adopted IiP as part of staff involvement and pursued it before Charter Mark", Mrs Cook says. "In Charter Mark we had a standard for customer service but we hadn't taken all of our people along with it."

While Citizen's Charter and IiP standards have given useful steers to the District's Quality approach, the main vehicle for translating core goals and values into policy and strategy has been the Benefits Agency (BA) Quality Framework. The framework is a 12-point self-assessment model developed by the Agency to drive continuous improvement and is grouped around four main elements covering 'customer service', 'caring for staff', 'bias for action' and 'value for money'. However, its deployment mirrors the cascading of responsibility within the District; it sets the parameters but allows for freedom of deployment within them.

"The BA framework is made available but is not wholly prescriptive.

It gives ideas", Mrs Cook says. "It feeds in best practice, but it's how you do it locally that counts. We were one of the first districts to reach the award-winning stage of the framework and we are pleased to give help and advice to Agency colleagues on using the framework to raise their standards. But we are careful to stress that what suited our circumstances may not be appropriate for them. There is no magic wand or quick fix to guarantee improvement."

The BA Quality Framework was the first self-assessment tool the District had used and it differs from the nine-element business excellence model used for the UK Quality Award in two major respects: there are currently no separate leadership criteria and no weighting of the different elements in the overall scoring. The UK award model also provides a means of assessing the District against a wider community beyond the Agency. "It is important as a district for us to go outside and see what is being done there", Mrs Cook says. "It gives us good ideas but also lets us appreciate that we are doing things better, that we have made changes."

Reproduced with kind permission from *UK Quality,* Nov 1995, UK Quality Award edition.

Standing: Colin Davies (Chief Executive)
Seated: Mark Bevan (Group Managing Director)
Forms UK

48

From Information To Intelligence

—Forms UK—

FORMS UK plc can source or produce almost any type of printed form or documentation on request. However, to describe Forms UK as a company which supplies continuous forms, self adhesive labels, tickets and tags would significantly undersell the scope of this company's activity and indeed its responsiveness to the changing business and technological environment.

Forms UK has moved into the realm of value adding to assist customers to design forms and information systems around their management needs to improve administration, processing, handling efficiency and subsequently cost effectiveness. Forms UK has progressed substantially from its days as a business forms broker. Formerly Standard Continuous the company was established in 1970 by Colin Davies, the current Chief Executive and has since become a leader in the business printed products industry which can be attributed to its proactive approach in meeting the needs of both customers and the changing market place.

It now has an annual turnover of £17 million and is the UK's largest independent distributor of business forms and continuous stationery providing a range of services including forms design, cost engineering, orientation, maintenance of corporate image, printing plate/negative maintenance, forms requisition, procurement, stock control and management.

Information systems have changed dramatically in the last 25 years and Forms UK has adapted to meet the demands of information management recognising that the strategic use of information systems can make the difference in keeping a business cost effective.

Standard Continuous was originally a business forms broker, sourcing products from a variety of suppliers on behalf of its customers. The next significant stage of the company's progression occurred in 1985 when the company introduced internal manufacturing capability and purchased Listing Paper Presses, a decision justified by the increasing volumes of business generated in this area.

After this early diversion into manufacturing the company was forced to re-evaluate its entire market position in the early 1990s in response to the rapidly changing technological environment. "Technology came to greet us and the advent of computerisation in industry resulted in a number of swift and aggressive changes in the print and business forms market. Many functions which had previously been facilitated through paper transactions were now handled electronically and subsequently we experienced a sharp decline in the usage of multi-part stationery", explains Mark Bevan, Group Managing Director.

In fact the advent of computer networks and EDI linkages between branches or remote company locations for example not only reduced but in some instances eliminated the need for paper communications such as facsimiles, letters and memos.

Coupled with the impact of computers on the industry was a 50 per cent decline in the price of wood pulp which had a dramatic effect on returns which were based on a cost plus principle, resulting in the percentage margin being calculated on a falling base figure.

"In the early 1990s we looked at how the market was moving and made the decision as a Board that unless we dramatically re-engineered our organisation it was unlikely that we would still be in business in a decade. We decided the way forward was to develop a value added mentality and embrace technology", says Mr Bevan. "The vision was to provide a single source service to our customers which could accommodate a customer's total print requirement encompassing computer capability and origination, factory, and a pick and pack warehouse."

The strengths of the company at the time of this revelation were primarily two fold: a highly skilled sales force with expertise in a number of niche areas in the print and business forms industry; and an internally developed computer software system with a history spanning the company's existence. The software provides a highly sophisticated real time system which can, for example, calculate the company's gross profit for any period or track product, stock and sales. Forms UK then adapted this technology to provide its customers with management information they previously did not have access to in relation to their usage of print and business form products.

Forms UK employs 90 staff, 60 of whom are based at the Solihull headquarters in sales and administration, 20 in the factory and 10 in its pick and pack warehouse.

As the life blood of the company a motivated sales force is crucial to the longevity of the company. "Their sole purpose is to go out and get the business. We structure their remuneration package so that they are paid a basic salary and then depending on the sales level they achieve a commission is paid as a percentage of those sales. We pay 10 per cent on up to £145,000, 15 per cent up to £250,000, and above that we pay 20 per cent. The practical maximum is 25 per cent, but it encourages sales people to work up through the bands", explains Mr Bevan.

The second element is that the process is front end cash loaded so that commissions are not paid unless the salesperson delivers the customer payment – raising a customer invoice is not sufficient.

While the sales force's incentive is largely financial, another prime motivation is the knowledge that the company they are representing has a reputation in the industry as a leader as Mr Bevan explains: "Sales are becoming easier although the market is not expanding, so we are taking market share from our competitors which in turn gives the sales people greater confidence. They know that it doesn't matter quite so much if a customer says no because there will be another 10 around the corner who will say yes."

Guiding pearls of wisdom provided by Forms UK to its sales force are outlined in an information sheet describing how to become the greatest salesman in the world and includes advice such as:

"I will persist until I succeed; I will never consider defeat; I will ignore the obstacles; always will I take another step; I will try, try and try again; if I persist long enough I will win."

"Today I will be master of my emotions; unless my mood is right the day will be a failure – weak is he who permits his thoughts to control his actions; strong is he who forces his actions to control his thoughts –

if I feel depressed I will sing;

if I feel sad I will laugh;

if I feel ill I will double my labour;
if I feel fear I will plunge ahead;
if I feel inferior I will wear new garments;
if I feel uncertain I will raise my voice;
if I feel poverty I will think of the wealth to come;
if I feel incompetent I will remember past successes;
if I feel insignificant I will remember my goals;

I will also understand and recognise the moods of he whom I call: no longer will I fail to call again tomorrow on he who meets me with hate today; from this moment I am prepared to control whatever personality awakes in me each day; I will master my moods through positive action and when I master my moods I will control my destiny; I will become master of myself."

The Customer Service Department processes all the orders and ensures that deliveries are made on time. The salespeople undertake only minor responsibility for activities such as the completion of forms. 'Meeting the Customer's Requirements' is a credo shared by everybody in the company from the Chairman to the most newly hired employee.

"We don't regard the fact that we do not have the business of a particular customer as a permanent situation. We think of everybody out there as a customer past, present or future. Whether we are dealing with them on a direct issue in a formal contracted way or not they all have the right to the same degree of service. If we can help, we will", explains Mr Bevan. For example, Forms UK had a small local grocer shop as a customer to whom it supplied till rolls, but when the grocer decided to source all his paper requirements from the one supplier to achieve economies of scale and the company lost the contract. Two months after this occurred the chief executive received a call on a Saturday morning from the grocer saying he had run out of till rolls. Instead of ignoring his request for assistance Forms UK called a sales representative, Peter Clark, who knew where he could obtain stock and he drove the till rolls to the company.

Forms UK has a strong customer service ethic which is evidenced by examples like the one above. As Mr Davies explains: "People think that customer service was devised only a few years ago. The reality is that customer service has always existed, but it has only recently become fashionable to talk about it. If you have a successful company, you have to have happy customers otherwise they will go elsewhere."

Typically Forms UK's customer relationships are contractual agreements over a period of time comprising a large element of trust. Forms UK is ever conscious of what margins the market will tolerate and provides customers with a relationship based on open book accounting so that they are aware of Forms UK's margins and can discuss concerns where they exist.

"Progressing from the open book concept we developed a software system which we could provide externally to suppliers for example through an innovative interface requiring a comparatively small investment on their behalf to update their existing systems. In a typical situation from the supplier's point of view we bring them on line to eliminate paperwork between us. Electronically you can not distinguish the join between the two operations so the order and production schedules are transmitted electronically, the invoice is then generated by Forms UK and transmitted again electronically to the supplier. It requires some education because many suppliers prefer the security of raising an invoice and putting it in an envelope so we had to convince them that it will save them money and time and that the systems are secure", explains Mr Bevan. This is a situation which can also be applied to customer relationships.

The vision for the company's progression from business forms broker to provider of business intelligence is attributed to the foresight of the company's founder and Chief Executive, Colin Davies. In 1992 the company changed its name from Standard Continuous which was perceived to be too narrow in definition of the company's business activity and so the name Forms UK plc was christened. "I realised in the early days that I was an information worker and if I was to survive and prosper I would have to turn information into intelligence faster than my competition. The 75 per cent of the western world who go to work and merely shift information will become obsolete in the next decade", says Mr Davies.

Forms UK is fundamentally an entrepreneurial company which is dominated by the influence of Mr Davies, who admits to running the company like 'almost a tyrant'. This is in part because he knows every facet of the business first hand from opening the mail to driving a forklift truck to working the printing press.

Line management and reference to management is preserved by the introduction of systems which elevate information and communication to a higher priority as Mr Bevan explains: "The only reason that anything ever goes wrong or misunderstandings arise, whether its in a marriage or between countries is because of a lack of effective communication. Given that the communication aspect is just as important in a commercial environment, by introducing better systems of communication potential problems can be averted."

Forms UK takes internal communication and involvement beyond a theoretical level for the same reasons that telling customers what a company can do for them is no substitute for demonstrating the product and the benefit.

This has been addressed in part by introducing an appraisal procedure which is not tied to salary review. It is purely a mechanism where employees meet with the managing director to discuss their role, problems, concerns, ambitions within the company and training requirements. As Mr Bevan says, "I don't mind how trivial their grievance may seem, if somebody is upset because the canteen isn't clean, I'll clean it because when employees are satisfied they are more productive."

Another element crucial to improving communication within the company was the establishment of a management meeting structure to allow all management to receive and disseminate information relevant to the company as a whole and the operation of their respective departments.

Each department has a departmental head some of whom are Board members who provide a regular departmental report. However, those departments which are not directly represented on the Board take it in turns to provide a personal presentation.

Three years ago Forms UK introduced a suggestion scheme, the 'bright ideas scheme' which provided every employee with the opportunity to suggest to the Board, through a manager, a mechanism for reducing costs or improving efficiency which was rewarded financially so long as the benefit could be quantified. While the programme has not been utilised to its full potential Mr Bevan believes: "Jobs are becoming increasingly pressured and in many instances there is physically not enough time to sit down and come up with ideas to save the company money. If you come across something in the normal course of business, fine, but these tend to be micro issues which are part of doing the job. The important issue is to provide as many positive opportunities to the staff and make them aware of these."

During the turbulent early 1990s there was an awakening in the industry that if companies did not possess BS5750 certification they would jeopardise their tender list status. Forms, which already conducted many of its business processes within the parameters of the standard made the decision that it was more of an advantage than a negative to pursue certification. Despite the company's rapid growth during this period it expedited the certification process without the use of consultants.

"I am not entirely convinced that BS5750 had a big influence on our ability to provide a better quality service because the way we functioned prior to certification was largely consistent with the standard's requirements. The benefit it did provide was that it enabled us to demonstrate to the outside world that we were a company committed to Quality. At the end of the day however, if you are providing a price product you still need to provide value for money at the service level and the fact that you have attained ISO certification is neither here nor there", emphasises Mr Bevan who acknowledges that utilised correctly certification does provide a degree of efficiency improvement.

Forms UK's Statement of Quality Policy conforms to BS/EN/ISO9001 which it received in 1992 and recognises that:

Implementation of Quality Management Systems will, by rigorous planning and execution, limit quality problems through identification of responsibilities and documented procedures.

Ultimate responsibility for ensuring that the Quality Management Systems function correctly within Forms UK plc lies with the Board of Directors who delegate this responsibility through Departmental Managers and hence, to each individual staff member.

The Board of Directors recognise that the most efficient method of achieving the necessary levels of quality is through committed personnel, suitably trained and qualified, working within proved and documented procedures with the finest available equipment.

The overall success of our enterprise is dependent upon everyone working, in a co-ordinated manner, to predetermined objectives and being suitably monitored by those charged with the day to day responsibility for the corporate Quality Policy.

On entering the premises of Forms UK you are greeted by a barrage of plaques pledging the company's commitment to customer service, Quality, health and safety, and environmental protection. These principles are observed and undertaken by every employee engaged by Forms UK who signs off against the company's code of ethics, which is framed in the entrance in the same fashion. The importance of these documents is that they define the spirit with which the company operates.

Its mission statement promises that Forms UK takes customer satisfaction personally and is committed to being a leader in providing customers with quality products and cost efficient services. It sees its responsibility as being to add value both to its customers and its suppliers by introducing innovative and cost effective ideas while providing reliable performance.

As Mr Davies says, "Customers are the most important thing in the business and the way you meet their needs is through enthusiasm, caring and propriety, all the things that school can't teach you."

Forms is run today with the same enthusiasm and ambition with which it commenced trading in 1970. Mr Davies attributes success in part to a long term view, "For years and have minimised our returns so that we could invest to build the business. I feel as though the last 25 years have just been a dress rehearsal and we are only now starting business. Now we have everything in place our competitors can't compete."

49

An Open Plan To Innovation

— Co-Cam Computer Services UK Ltd —

CO-CAM UK specialises in the design, supply and support of sales and marketing software and automated call centres. It is incorporated as an independent company within the Co-Cam Computer Group, Australia's largest software and services company. In turn the Co-Cam Computer Group is part of Australian life and pensions group, Colonial Mutual which has a total of $A32 billion under management. Co-Cam UK is the third most profitable company in the group and much of this success can be attributed to its management culture.

The prime motivation to perform well at Co-Cam comes from pressure exerted within the peer group rather than from senior management. "Because we recruit professional people who are well motivated and then equip them to maximise their ability there is no need to be dictatorial", explains Mike Friday, Director of Development and Support, who has assumed primary responsibility for facilitating Co-Cam's Quality activity and the attainment of Tick It certification, a 'superset' of ISO9000 designed specifically for the software industry.

Co-Cam readily admits that it is small, flexible and doesn't follow fashion. This it has done with astounding success. The company can boast that it is the world's biggest and most successful Brock software distributor. It has installed comprehensive systems in over 40 Blue Chip companies in six countries. In fact it is the only Call Centre supplier in Europe with a 10 year track record of successful delivery.

Co-Cam has expanded rapidly since January 1994. In this time the company has quadrupled in size, expanding its workforce from six to over

David Parcell
Managing Director
Co-Cam Computer Services

40. Such rapid growth may potentially sabotage an organisation's culture. However, this danger has been avoided through constant and open communication of organisational changes throughout the company.

Co-Cam recognised the need for a Quality system in 1993 partly in response to market pressure for telephony based system suppliers to have ISO certification, but primarily to help the company keep control of its rapid growth and formalise its communication processes. "Initially the entire team consisted of less than six people so when an order came in, for example, everybody jumped up and down including the accountant who invoiced the client accordingly. However, as the group has grown to over 40 people we recognised that we lacked formal procedures and information was not reaching the relevant departments", explains Mr Friday.

Initially Co-Cam applied for assistance from the Department of Trade and Industry and engaged a consultant who worked with the senior management to produce an overall policy document specifying activity on a functional basis which was then broken down into high level procedures for each department.

"The first thing that became obvious was that we had concentrated on overall procedures and lost sight of what the Quality system was established to achieve. The second layer of procedures was not tangible because we had neglected the implementation mechanism, the physical thing to say that we had done it. We then concentrated on reviewing the procedures with an aim to producing the relevant forms", explains Mr Friday. Using cross-departmental meetings involving both staff and management, Co-Cam ensured that the procedures provided all the necessary information and delivered what was intended. From this understanding the company created the standard forms and the procedures to facilitate their movement within the organisation.

Co-Cam is a growing organisation attempting to maintain the small company mentality. In line with Co-Cam's open management style Mr Friday emphasises the importance of implementing a Quality system as a collaborative process involving everybody in the organisation to avoid rejection of the process. "When you have a small company people tend to share objectives, ideals and ideas and this shows in your customer service. By keeping things like the open plan environment and not distinguishing between management and non management groups we hope we will preserve those small company ideals and encourage team spirit."

Co-Cam experienced a few minor problems when defining its procedures, which arose primarily because of the open environment the company encourages in which employees are free to speak their minds. Typically problems can be traced back to semantics. On one occasion involving two departments that conceptually designed and built the same systems it was decided that they should adopt the same procedures and then tailor them to suit their own environments. "The problem was that they would not understand one another because they couldn't see past their own terminology", explains Mr Friday.

"In the end we produced procedures and said this is the standard we will adopt but we will hold regular review meetings of the procedures at all levels to ensure they are meeting your requirements. Although you need to allow everybody to have their input there comes a point where you have to stop debate. Once the groups have had the opportunity to run with the procedure to determine whether it works they will have the chance to decide whether there is a need to change it."

The selection and training of internal auditors was viewed as a critical factor in maintaining the process. "Co-Cam chose not to use department managers in these positions because of existing pressures on their time. However, we needed to appoint people with sufficient authority to get things done so we trained all the deputy managers, and also all the department administrators. We selected administrators not so they could actively conduct internal audits but on the premise that they are the people responsible for the paperwork. If they know what to look for and what the internal auditors are expecting they are more likely to buy into it and ensure that it is there", advises Mr Friday.

In order to obtain acceptance for a Quality programme Mr Friday asserts that a company has to "show the workforce that it is improving what they are doing and how they are doing it. You need a thorough understanding of why you are doing it and what the company is going to achieve from ISO certification."

Co-Cam is very results conscious and has commenced quantifying the business benefit it will derive from the system on a basic level. A review of the invoicing system, for example, indicated that the company was losing £30 thousand per year on maintenance payments because customers were not being invoiced at the appropriate time following a system up-grade. Mr Friday describes these as only immediate measures: "The next stage after implementing all the procedures is to establish success criteria for each and determine appropriate measures. While it will be more bureaucratic I think it will be morale boosting for people to find out that they have been doing better than they thought."

Co-Cam operates in a £2 billion market place, of which it transacts £5 million and predicts future growth. More than ten million telemarketing calls are made in the UK each week and it is predicted that the industry will continue to grow at a rate of at least 20% a year. Within the next five years the market will be valued at between £5.5 - £7 billion. "With a market place as large as this which has the potential to grow there is enough business for everybody. It is therefore better to form alliances with other people who want to play in that market place so we can at least have some influence on them and all succeed", comments Mr Friday.

Automatic Call Distribution Systems (ACDs) were introduced to the UK 20 years ago and have undergone significant changes in this time. As the needs of the market have become more sophisticated systems have evolved anticipating future requirements. The emphasis is no longer on simply answering a customer's call but accurately and rapidly routeing incoming calls to the right point within an organisation.

Co-Cam sells its product both directly to the customer and through a reseller channel consisting of six outlets throughout Europe. Co-Cam concentrates its sales efforts in several key markets: financial services; retail and distribution; telecommunications; and selling telemarketing products in a cross-industry environment.

The financial services market is the largest and includes organisations and institutions dealing with products such as insurance, mortgages, pensions and loans. However, as this market becomes increasingly mature Co-Cam is turning its attention to growth areas such as retail and distribution where it has the opportunity to earn higher margins and become involved in the education process.

Since 1988 Co-Cam has specialised in helping customers automate their sales and marketing functions. The products and services provided by Co-Cam enable their clients to automate the complete sales cycle, seamlessly closing the loop from lead generation to after-sales support.

Solutions range from database marketing systems through to complete Call Centres, across a wide range of industries. The strength of the product and service is illustrated in Co-Cam's impressive client list including household names such as Abbey National Direct, Marks and Spencer Financial Services, Eagle Star, Nationwide Building Society, Prudential Direct, Mercury Communications, Energis Communications, BT Syntegra, Amersham International, Guinness Brewing (UK) Ltd and Touchline.

Co-Cam is selling a concept – the concept of what an organisation can achieve by implementing a direct sales strategy. Before a potential client witnesses the software and systems in action Co-Cam discusses the potential business benefits of installation and then leads the client through a practical example, such as the sale of insurance over the telephone and illustrates how the system operates. In a specially designed two room presentation facility the client first experiences the service received by the customer and is only then shown how the system functions from the operator's perspective.

Co-Cam has three distinct product areas: sales automation software; telemarketing and telesales systems; and at the top end call centres which may cost in excess of £2 million to install depending on the number of users. However, central to each Co-Cam installation is the standard Brock module which is customised by Co-Cam consultants in collaboration with the client organisation to produce a system matching their business needs.

The strength of Co-Cam's client relationships is not solely reliant on the superiority of the product but also on the depth and consistency of service offered to clients in both the developmental and operational stages of system installation.

"Years of experience have taught us that the most effective installations are those where our customers have an in-depth understanding of their application. All the way through development, our consultants work with the client's in-house IT function and the end users to transfer our knowledge. Following installation we have the facilities to provide comprehensive training courses either on-site or at our offices and we provide hot-line telephone support", explains Mr Friday. Mike Friday joined Co-Cam in November 1993 from a background of UNIX support and has maintained a proactive view that support shouldn't just involve a hotline service but rather endeavour to inform, train and educate people.

Lifestyle changes in today's society and advances in technology have paved the way for an increasing incidence of people preferring to make financial transactions, for example, via the telephone rather than face to face. Accordingly organisations are having to respond to the changing needs of their customers by improving the efficiency of their operations.

An example of how Co-Cam has contributed to this process is its work with Abbey National Direct which needed to expand its telemarketing operation in-house and improve the interface it provided between their advisers and the customer.

The results of this transformation tell their own story – the £1.6 million investment made by Abbey National Direct in its call centre was returned within seven months; a twofold increase in close rate for acceptances was achieved; and an increase in direct mail response from one per cent to nine per cent resulted. The 60 agent call centre was re-equipped and personnel trained to handle in excess of 6,000 calls per day – every day.

Co-Cam's software has enabled the company to maximise the sales opportunities which resulted from a 300 per cent increase in call traffic since the software was installed in 1992 and allows advisers to focus on their customers' financial needs while increasing their productivity by 20-30 per cent.

Working closely with Co-Cam, Abbey National Direct implemented and developed the Brock Activity Manager, a complete sales and marketing software package which was later integrated with Co-Cam's Softcall software ACD which gives full control over a high volume and multi user telemarketing operation.

Flexibility was a key requirement and the new system allows advisers to focus on the customer's inquiry rather than on administration as the system completes any which is required. The software can recognise the telephone number of, for example, a specific mortgage customer and can route the caller to the mortgage adviser dealt with in a previous call. This assists customer service by increasing professionalism through greater familiarity and focus with the customer. Not only is the cost of the sale reduced but the opportunity for cross-selling is enhanced because of the high level of customer information that is readily available.

Software tailored by Co-Cam to meet the client's needs can provide valuable management information including productivity measures and analysis. Advisers can receive updates on their productivity compared with colleagues in the same department which is a key motivational tool and supervisors also have complete access to all call progress information and can intervene in any call giving them a high degree of control.

This is just one example of how Co-Cam's innovation is creating business benefits for its clients at a startling rate when you take into account that every day Co-Cam's systems enable its clients to accept and process thousands of customer contacts. It is an example of success creating success.

50

Rank Xerox Self Assessment

—Rank Xerox—

IT has been documented that Rank Xerox's greatest achievement was to become the first western company in an industry targeted by the Japanese to regain market share – but this view undersells the accomplishments of this global company. It has become a paragon not only in its core business, the design and production of document copiers, but as a source of innovation, inspiration and referral as organisations worldwide bid to become world class and first in class by integrating Quality principles and processes within their daily operations.

As the inaugural European Quality Award winners in 1992 much has been written and documented on the Rank Xerox experience – its dethroning in the face of Japanese competitors entering the low end of the market, a segment previously ignored by Rank Xerox because it did not produce the profits achieved from mid-range and high end products, and engulfing the entire market. More spectacular however was Rank Xerox's return to market dominance.

In order to set the scene against which Rank Xerox introduced its Self Assessment Quality Programme in 1991 we need to revisit the past briefly. "The 1960s to mid 1970s were our golden years. The 914, the first plain paper copier, launched Rank Xerox into an era of feverish growth and success. Not only had we created a product, we had created, and thought we owned, an industry. Competition was virtually non existent, and Xerox was the fastest corporation to reach $1 billion in revenues", Graham Pearson, Quality Manager with Rank Xerox explains. "As a result, we developed a kind of internal arrogance that stopped us from focusing on

Graham Pearson
Quality Manager
Rank Xerox

what our customers really wanted. This short sighted attitude opened a window of opportunity for competition."

The beginning of the new era commenced with a competitive benchmarking process of organisations regarded as best in class. The findings of which ended a period of denial by forcing senior management to acknowledge both the extent of Rank Xerox's problem and the degree of change needed to return the business to health again. As acknowledged by Mr Pearson: "Benchmarking makes improvement issues easier to sell internally. You are not asking for what appear to be arbitrary cost cuts or impossible sales hikes. You are asking for support to achieve across-the-board performance that at least equals your best competitor which is an acceptable goal for your people to shoot at and very difficult to argue against."

In 1983 Rank Xerox commenced a complete cultural change based on a worldwide commitment to Total Quality. It was shaped by a basic Quality policy:

Rank Xerox is a quality company. Quality is the basic business principle for Rank Xerox. Quality means providing our external and internal customers with innovative products and services that fully satisfy their requirements. Quality improvement is the job of every Rank Xerox employee.

The introduction of the Self Assessment Quality Programme in 1991, in itself a major milestone, was prompted by the realisation that Rank Xerox was driving ahead with numerous Quality initiatives in the absence of a cohesive framework outlining how the business should be run. Self assessment consolidated an established stable of Quality tools including the Quality policy and competitive benchmarking. Everyone at Rank Xerox speaks a common language and has a common set of tools to utilise such as the benchmarking process as illustrated in Figure 1.

The Self Assessment Quality Programme complements Rank Xerox's management structure which is characterised by a cross-functional integrated team approach where team orientation and self managed work groups are commonplace. Effectively and significantly the organisational structure has been inverted so that the customer is at the top.

The role of the manager is one of coach, facilitator and inspector of the process. Every employee is empowered to take authority over day-to-day work decisions. "We expect individuals to take the initiative in

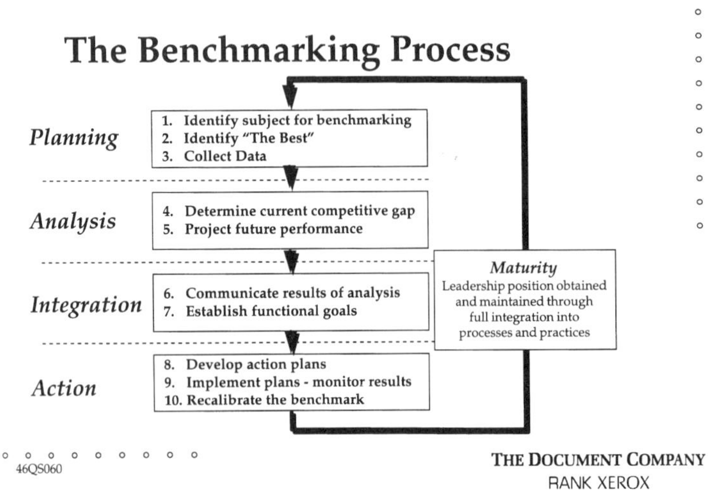

identifying and correcting problems that affect the Quality of our products or services. A production worker has the power to stop the line and pinpoint the problem to management. A customer service engineer has the power to abort a machine install if conditions are not satisfactory. A customer service engineer can decide to replace any customer's machine that is not performing to standard", explains Mr Pearson.

With a background in operations research and commercial computing in the paper and banking industries Mr Pearson joined Rank Xerox in 1987 in the technical support area and progressed to Quality Manager of the UK company in May 1991 and of Rank Xerox Limited in November 1994.

Rank Xerox has seen the benefits of taking a more holistic view of its business and has recognised how to achieve common goals through a greater inter-functional realisation of how functions have to integrate in order to exceed customer expectations.

The cross functionality of organisational structure which the company has retained since the early 1990s, as illustrated in Figure 2, provides a competitive edge by allowing the company to retain the benefits of economies of scale and specialisation gained from having functions, while eroding the issues of functional protectionism to ensure that all company resources focus on processes which meet or exceed customer requirements.

By 1991, when Self Assessment was introduced Rank Xerox was

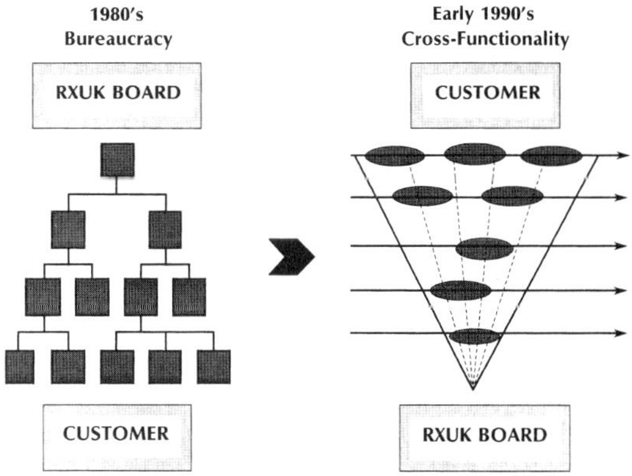

CREATING A MORE PRODUCTIVE,
FASTER RESPONDING ORGANISATION

producing world class products in every reprographic speed category; its customer satisfaction target was set at 100 per cent; and the customer loss rate which it views as the ultimate measure of customer satisfaction had declined to 13 per cent from a previous high of 45 per cent. Rank Xerox however continued to navigate the company to a more desirable state of being the fastest responding, most productive organisation in the industry.

Quality was further embedded into the way Rank Xerox conducted its business by acknowledging that business excellence would require more than continuous improvement. The Business Excellence Model adopted by Rank Xerox in 1991 as the management model, and then world wide as the Xerox management model, provides the vision of Rank Xerox as a Total Quality Company. The model is intentionally simplistic and consists of six basic blocks as illustrated in Figure 3. The primary advantage this model has over the European Quality Model is that visually the customer is at the heart of the model, which is critical to the company's philosophy. This is something that cannot be achieved with the European Quality Model.

"Basically management sets the leadership, the strategy, the direction, the values and the overall aim of the business. But management can only work through people stretching resources because the only real asset we have at the end of the day is the brain power of our employees. That whole employee force must then be focused on the customer in the market place", Mr Pearson explains.

"Historically, we've been product led and believe that we have the best products in the market. However, this is no reason for complacency – in the past it almost put us out of business because we took what the customer actually wanted for granted. The key to this model is that it retains the customer and market focus at the heart of it – the message is that the customer has to be the centre of our world. Customer focus is achieved through process management defining how our people work and in turn process improvement is achieved through the effective utilisation of Quality support, tools and information."

Rank Xerox aims to achieve future improvements through a combination of continuous and discontinuous improvement based on a three level approach.

1. **Business as Usual**

The day-to-day application of tools such as the Quality improvement process, problem solving process and the use of statistic tools. Its application is part of the job of all Rank Xerox people with any number of these initiatives in progress at any time.

2. **Process Simplification**

A specific team is formed to deliver a defined and scoped project, usually of up to six month's duration. Each project addresses process simplification and cycle time reduction and expects to achieve improvements

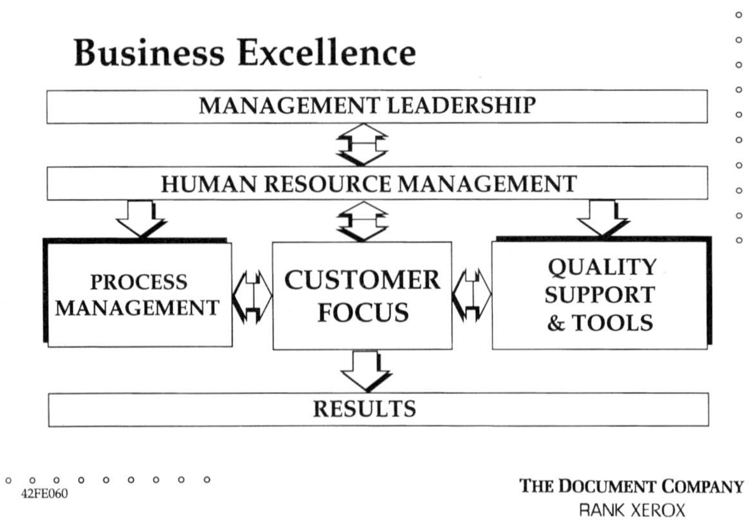

in efficiency and effectiveness of the order of 100 per cent. The scope is broader and the programme more visible than 'Business as Usual', but is still regarded as continuous improvement, with 10 to 20 projects in progress concurrently.

3. Process Re-engineering

This is vision-led fundamental re-design. By definition, the approach looks for the optimum combination of People, Process, Information and Technology to create a re-engineered business process. The scope is broad, each project addressing major 'cradle-to-grave' business processes such as the processing of customer orders from sales prospecting to equipment delivery to debt collection. With each project scheduled over at least a two year period expecting improvements in efficiency and effectiveness of the order of 1000 per cent a maximum of two are undertaken at any one time.

"Through continuous and discontinuous tools, processes and methodologies with the common purpose of delivering value and satisfying customer expectations the Business Excellence Delivery Process provides the overall strategic and operational process with which Rank Xerox is managing its future", explains Mr Pearson.

The Business Excellence Model is also used as an investment model. It illustrates that remedying poor business results by merely cutting costs is not effective in the long term. Mr Pearson explains: "This model leads you to analyse any situation resulting in poor or unexpected results from the perspective of its focus on the customer. It compels the company to return to the tool kit and review the different tools and how they are being used – has the company got the right people doing the right things, in the right places at the right time with the right skills. The end result may be that people are removed from the process or reallocated within it, but these changes have been made from a position of knowledge and understanding of the implications to the entire organisation thus allowing it to maximise business results."

In this context the business results of the company are not only financial. In addition to the bottom line Rank Xerox has adopted four key priorities which are (in sequence):

1. Customer satisfaction
2. Employee motivation
3. Market share
4. Return on assets

To support these priorities the company works to four common corporate goals which shape everybody's roles, responsibilities and objectives.

1. Our CUSTOMER GOAL is to become an organisation with whom Customers are eager to do business.
2. Our EMPLOYEE GOAL is to create an environment where everyone can take pride in the organisation and feel responsible for its success.
3. Our MARKET SHARE GOAL is to establish ourselves as The Document Company, with a leadership position in our market place.
4. Our RETURN ON ASSETS GOAL is to achieve and improve on the Corporate Goal.

The common goals are shared by every employee at every level, and are based on six key principles:

1. Customers define our business;
2. Success depends upon the involvement and empowerment of trained and highly motivated people;
3. Quality is "in the line by the line". Line management must lead quality improvement;
4. Management develops, articulates and deploys clear direction and objectives;
5. Strategic quality challenges are identified and met; and
6. Business is managed and improved by using facts.

The most recent major progression in Rank Xerox's pursuit of excellence was the introduction of its Self Assessment Quality Programme. The first cycle was completed in 1992 in Western Europe after which time it was extended to the remainder of the Rank Xerox world. To facilitate the self assessment process the company was divided into geographical divisions clearly recognisable to customers as 'customer business units' consisting of between 300 and 500 people. For instance the UK was divided into seven customer business units, London being one. Consistent with its departure from a functional organisational structure the company conducts audits at a business operation level as perceived by customers.

Mr Pearson is quick to caution that: "The description 'self assessment' introduces a misleading element of simplicity to the process intimating that staff assess themselves against the model thus introducing subjectivity and a deceiving lack of consistency to the process." To counter this perception Rank Xerox has divided each business operation into a number of very definite and specific 'topics'. For each 'topic' it has conducted benchmark studies to define how the best companies work and subsequently specified the desired state which Rank Xerox aims to achieve in each. There are 42 topics in the full model and therefore 42 desired states which the company strives to achieve.

For example: "Within human resources – we define that it involves: selection and recruitment, development of people, development of managers, working environment, recognition and reward system, and pay and rations system...a number of very definite and specific topics. Breaking that down further, selection and recruitment specifies that the desired state for all our external hiring processes and our internal selection processes should be based on the knowledge, the skills and the leadership attributes as defined by the most complicated in the organisation and the job required. It is basically saying if you want to recruit somebody rather than just scan the market then you must have an accurate job analysis which defines the characteristics of the job and skills required. By doing this we develop relevant criteria for the interviews and in turn can prove that the people recruited have been assessed against those criteria", Mr Pearson explains the desired state approach.

Each unit is then required to rate its performance against a scale ranging from one to seven based on their results, their approach and the level of pervasiveness.

A level one rating is defined as providing results which are anecdotal, generalisations or a guess; an approach which is anecdotal, based on no evident system documented or otherwise; and pervasiveness which is anecdotal, isolated or inconsistent.

At the top end of the scale a level seven rating suggests that the benchmark has been attained. The results are of a world class nature in major areas, good to excellent in support areas, sustained over 2 – 5 years and clearly caused by the approach. The approach is then sound and developed on a systematic prevention basis refined through evaluation and improvement cycles providing excellent integration. In terms of pervasiveness there has been an infusion into core and support areas, full deployment and management; and employees and customers contribute to the resolution of problems.

Any claims made regarding the nature of results must be supported by hard metrics. Rank Xerox makes recommendations on the nature and standardisation of measurements. In areas such as selection and recruitment standard measures exist which everybody is expected to use. However, there are occasions when individual units may use different criteria which are more relevant. For instance, factors in a manufacturing plant may not be relevant in a cells operation and vice versa. The units are looking for absolute results, trends and comparisons against national and international norms and each must be able to prove that their results were derived from the use of the process and not a random incident.

In general the rating process requires that *everybody* within a unit contributes to the process and the results. However, particular criteria may only be relevant to some employees. For instance: "You would not expect every employee to contribute to strategic planning which is a management function. However, if you're looking at equal treatment as an issue then you would expect every employee to be involved in the programme. Accordingly the process has to be matched with the unit you're looking at and the elements which are relative to that unit", explains Mr Pearson.

To finalise this process the groups complete what Rank Xerox has labelled a 'Quadrant Sheet'. The quadrant sheet is a simple one-page summary describing the desired state and the unit's progress towards it.

The information obtained during this exercise includes: definition of the desired state; the performance matrix which demonstrates a trend over the years; listing of the contributing factors which are either helping or hindering achievement up to date; and strengths, weaknesses or improvement areas. These findings are used to design an appropriate course of action to provide improved future ratings.

The Self Assessment programme was introduced in four primary stages:

1. Initial self assessment conducted by management
2. Justification of results through benchmarking and employee involvement
3. Publication of results within the company to promote learning
4. Examination to ensure consistency of results

The initial stage of self assessment prompted many people to review activity on a cross-functional basis for the first time and provided the company with a valuable learning and understanding experience of what was occurring within business units.

The publication of results within units prompted the reaction that management did not have an accurate perception of the nature of activity at a grass roots level – employees did not recognise the descriptions provided by management of their businesses. To remedy this all employees were involved in the process. "When we introduced this exercise for the first time we suspected that the management frequently viewed the world through rose-tinted spectacles so after they had completed the scoring stage and they had to substantiate their claims the ratings started to drop. For example they said we select wonderful people, but then after comparing our standards with other organisations they had to really ask 'Do we have better or worse selection?' and people said we don't know, we have never asked the question. If you've never asked the question how do you know how good you really are?" explains Mr Pearson.

All information was shared worldwide so that units identified as requiring improvement could refer to other units within Rank Xerox which had scored highly in the relevant areas for advice to avoid 'reinventing the wheel'.

Results are illustrated on a Certification Bar Chart as shown in Figure 4, which provides each unit's progressive scores as well as comparison against other units. The bar chart which is published on a single piece of

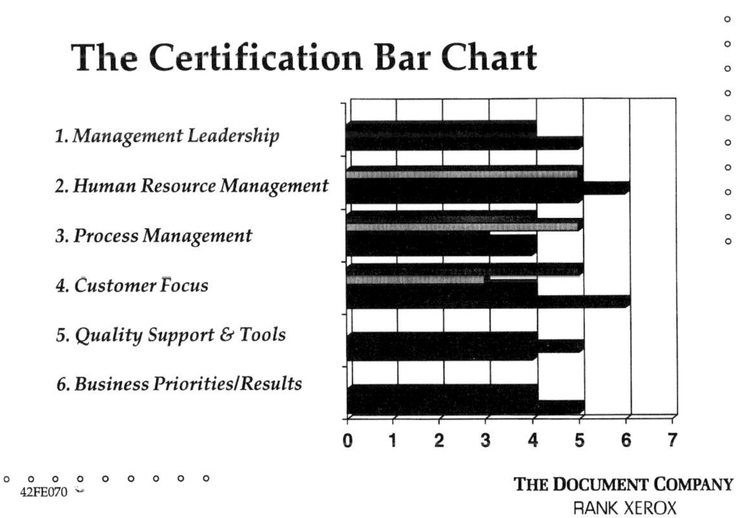

paper provides a corporate health check, and at a glance indicates where a unit is strong or weak and where it should concentrate its effort. The charts are intended to distinguish significant improvement issues crucial for business effectiveness from a multitude of more trivial matters. By doing this the self-assessment migrates from merely being an interesting exercise into a major part of the planning and assessment cycles, by providing the fundamental analysis required for strategic planning to produce dramatic improvements.

"The whole philosophy is one of really understanding your business, knowing where you are trying to get to, establishing the vital few improvement issues, and of course giving you worldwide comparisons so individual units can benefit from shared practices – we are saying don't reinvent the wheel, don't solve other people's problems but do steal ideas", says Mr Pearson.

Up until that point systems checks had not been introduced to the process so in order to introduce objectivity and consistency to the assessment process Rank Xerox introduced a certification phase. Senior line managers from throughout the worldwide organisation were trained to conduct examinations, and provide improvement coaching and counselling.

"Each examiner has to have a thorough understanding of what is occurring throughout the worldwide organisation, and be able to sit down with the management teams of individual units and determine whether they can justify all their claims. They test pervasiveness by going out into the organisation to witness senior management claims – the emphasis is not on catching people out but gauging whether management has an accurate understanding of the issues", emphasises Mr Pearson. "The real value is the learning gained from doing an exercise like this – we often use the example of a glass of water – is it half full or half empty. When you are trying to pass an exam you're demonstrating how full it is. But what this is saying is not how full is the glass, but how big is the gap and what do we need to do to fill it."

Mr Pearson believes that: "There is a tendency for people to make changes to their part of the process without realising the implications on the total process. It is therefore important to challenge why they are making the changes, are they needed, or is the function redundant. Consequently, we invest a lot of effort in distinguishing between employment security and job security. If you are a valued employee your employment is safe even if your job isn't. We will have hit a major milestone when people are recommending that jobs can be closed down because they are irrelevant."

Improvements generated by the new approach to self-assessment have saved millions of pounds. A typical example was the revision to special billing procedures for clients who re-negotiated the standard terms and conditions:

Rank Xerox UK found that on average it was taking 112 days to produce a special billing invoice which accounted for at least 40 per cent of business. This increasing trend signalled that what started as a special practice would soon become the norm and 112 days for a normal billing procedure was not viable.

After analysing the basic procedure the company established that the amount of work required to process these invoices was insignificant and delays were experienced primarily because of the approval process. It found that somebody created the paperwork in one office which was then transferred to another for approval often experiencing delays because of the mailing system and the time restrictions of the various parties. After passing through various layers of checking it was not unusual for one document to accumulate a dozen signatures before being processed.

The revised practice now assumes that the original person has correctly processed the invoice and in so doing has reduced the process from 112 days to two days which alone saves the company £3 million in interest charges. The accuracy of the process also increased because if the original person made a mistake it was him or her who had to explain it to the customer.

While this is a simple example it powerfully illustrates how trusting people, empowering them and simplifying the process can result in huge savings. Mr Pearson encourages: "It's all simple. The whole Quality initiative and everything we are doing is what you could label **codified common sense** – there is nothing magic about it."

Directory of Companies

Ardmac Group, Dundalk, Co Louth Tel: 00353 423 6711
Benefits Agency, Springburn, Glasgow Tel: 0141 5574000
Bentley Chemicals, Kidderminster Tel: 01562 515121
Bio Products Laboratory, Elstree, Herts Tel: 0181 905 1818
Birmingham Midshires Building Society, Wolverhampton Tel: 01902 710710
Blue Circle Cement, Dunbar, East Lothian Tel: 01368 863371
Claremont Business Environments, Warrington, Cheshire Tel: 01925 827388
Co-Cam, Hampton Tel: 0181 941 9997
Color Steels, Crosskeys, Gwent Tel: 01495 270706
Davy International, Stockton-on-Tees Tel: 01642 602221
Domino Printing Sciences, Cambridge Tel: 01954 782551
Eastern Electricity, Wherstead, Ipswich, Suffolk Tel: 01473 88688
Employment Service, London Tel: 0171 389 1371
European Air Catering Services, London Tel: 0181 562 9560
Forms UK, Shirley, Solihull Tel: 0121 733 3131
Hegarty & Co, Peterborough Tel: 01733 346333
Hogg Robinson Business International, Woking, Surrey Tel: 01252 372000
Honeywell, Bracknell Tel: 01344 826000
ICI Paints, Slough Tel: 01753 550000
ICL High Performance Technology, Manchester Tel: 0161 223 1301
Independent Insurance Company, London Tel: 0171 397 6364
J.Walter Thompson, London Tel: 0171 499 4040
London Borough of Bromley, Bromley Tel: 0181 464 3333
Macro Group, Slough Tel: 01628 604383
MML Field Marketing, London Tel: 0171 611 6804
Mobil Oil, Stanford-Le-Hope Tel: 01375 646660
National Vulcan Engineering Insurance Group, Manchester Tel: 0161 834 8124
Nortel, Maidenhead Tel: 01628 813000
NSK Bearings, Peterlee, County Durham Tel: 0191 586 6111
P&P Corporate Systems, Rosserdyle Tel: 01706 217744
PAC International, Stockport Tel: 0161 494 1332
Pirelli Cables, Eastleigh, Hampshire Tel: 01703 644522
RAC, London Tel: 0171 389 8900
Rank Xerox, Marlow, Berks Tel: 01628 890000
Redland Roof Tiles, Westerham, Kent Tel: 01959 563087
Rover Group, Solihull Tel: 0121 781 7250
Royal Mail Anglia, Chelmsford Tel: 01245 243013
Securicor Custodial Services, Sutton, Surrey Tel: 0181 770 7000
ServisPak, Wallingford Tel: 01491 834000
Severn Trent Water, Birmingham Tel: 0121 722 4000
Southern Water Services, Brighton Tel: 01273 606766
Stalbridge Linen Services, Shaftesbury, Dorset Tel: 01747 851585
Stoves, Prescot, Merseyside Tel: 0151 426 6551
Texas Instruments Europe, Northampton Tel: 01604 663045
Thorn Lighting, Boreham Wood, Herts Tel: 0181 967 6331

TNT Express, Atherstone, Warwickshire Tel: 01827 303030
Trinity Motors, Hinckley Tel: 01455 614848
Vickers, London Tel: 0171 828 7777
Willis Corroon, Maidstone Tel: 0181 787 6000
Xyratex, Havant Tel: 01705 486363

Contributors

The British Quality Foundation, Tel: 0171 963 8000
Barry A. Holland, SGS Yarsley International Certification Services Limited, Tel: 01342 410088
Bryan Geraghty, British Standards Institution, Tel: 0181 996 9000
Lloyd's Register Quality Assurance, Tel: 0181 688 6882
Ross Dunn, Blue Circle Cement, Tel: 01368 863 371
Investors In People, Tel: 0171 636 2386
Terry Twine & Graham Salisbury, Xyratex, Tel:: 01705 486 363
Hayden J. Magill, I.A.S Management Services, Tel: 01873 850 460

Further Assistance

The British Quality Foundation, Tel: 0171 963 8000
DTI Innovation Enquiry Line, Tel: 08004422001
Managing in the 90s, Tel: 01443 821877
Inside UK Enterprise, Tel: 01234 840 322
Competitiveness Forum, Tel: 0171 379 7400
Business Links, Tel: 01142 597507
Business Development Support in Wales, Tel: 01222 823497
Business Development Support in Scotland, Tel: 0141 248 4774
Investors in People, Tel: 0171 636 2386
See also your local Training and Enterprise Councils.

Contributing Research Writers

Mark Sumich was brought up and educated in Perth, Western Australia, graduating from Aquinas College in 1984. He studied law at the University of Western Australia, graduated with honours in 1990, and during this time was the full time elected President of the University Student Union in 1989. After graduation he practiced as a corporate and natural resource solicitor with the large Australian commercial firm Robinson Cox/Clayton Utz for three and a half years and is now studying an MBA at London Business School, which will be completed in July 1996.

Samantha Bush graduated from the Faculty of Arts at Exeter University with a Honours degree in Classics in 1991. Having travelled throughout South East Asia, she worked on a wide range of Business and Trade magazines for Reed International publishing. Samantha accepted a position on the Graduate Management scheme with Moss Bros plc and continues writing on a freelance basis specialising in business management issues.

Marjorie Syddall studied English and History at the University of Western Australia. Following this, she completed a Postgraduate Diploma in Journalism at Murdoch University. Marjorie has since been pursuing work as a freelance writer in Perth and is now planning to relocate to London where she intends to continue her writing career.

Born in 1966, **James McNabb** attended Marlborough college before continuing his studies at Oxford Polytechnic. Travelling extensively through Europe, America and Australia, he worked for an Australian business magazine. On his return to the UK he has specialised in the Property, Finance and Marketing sectors.